SPECIAL ACTIVITIES

MARK A. HEWITT

Black Rose Writing | Texas

First printing

ISBN: 978-1-68433-699-9
PUBLISHED BY BLACK ROSE WRITING
www.blackrosewriting.com

Printed in the United States of America
Suggested Retail Price (SRP) $25.95

Special Activities is printed in Book Antiqua

*As a planet-friendly publisher, Black Rose Writing does its best to eliminate unnecessary waste to reduce paper usage and energy costs, while never compromising the reading experience. As a result, the final word count vs. page count may not meet common expectations.

According to open sources, the Special Activities Division (SAD) is a division of the United States Central Intelligence Agency responsible for covert operations known as "special activities." Within SAD there are two separate groups: Special Operations Group (SAD/SOG) for tactical paramilitary operations and Political Action Group (SAD/PAG) for covert political action.

Special Activities are activities conducted in support of national foreign policy objectives that are planned and executed so that the role of the U.S. Government isn't apparent or acknowledged publicly. Special Activities aren't intended to influence U.S. political processes, public opinion, policies, or media and do not include diplomatic activities or the collection and production of intelligence or related support functions.

The *Disposition Matrix*: List of known terrorist leaders identified by the CIA and considered enemy combatants to be removed from the field of battle. The President of the United States authorizes whatever special activities are necessary to remove the terrorist leader from the battlefield.

Also by
MARK A. HEWITT

Special Access
Shoot Down
No Need To Know
Blown Cover
Wet Work
and
Airshow!

Special Activities

Politics is combat by other means.
–Carl von Clausewitz

PROLOGUE

May 6, 1937

Major General Smedley D. Butler, United States Marine Corps, Retired hurried into the Oval Office with a sense of urgency and announced, "Mr. President, there are rich and powerful forces who wish me to remove you from the Office of the President. There is a coalition of the wealthy that has raised millions of dollars to pay for a half-a million man army to facilitate your removal and halt your policies. Under their plan, I am to institute fascism in America."

FDR raised an eyebrow. His cigarette flipped straight up. *This man is full of surprises and could get to the heart of the matter.* After realizing General Butler was only delivering a message and not an ultimatum, President Franklin Delano Roosevelt said, "General Butler that is most distressing. As it was just this forenoon, James and I were discussing the recent rumormongering of you becoming the dictator of Washington. I sense you are *not* here to relieve me of my duties; you believe there is some substance to these vile rumors?" The President motioned for the general to sit across from him.

"Mr. President, they are not rumors. I've been in contact with these people. There is a rising chorus of hatred for President Roosevelt and the President's policies by a multitude of business leaders across our nation. There is an anti-Roosevelt slant in both news and editorials in the business-oriented press. Business leaders and the newspaper editors are terrified. They believe the New Deal is 'creeping socialism.' These industrialists and bankers view President Roosevelt to be—if not an actual or closet Communist—then dedicated to the destruction of our capitalistic society."

FDR had never been talked to in such a manner, even in the third person, but there was a certain elegance in the general's brevity and precision. No braggadocio, no threats, but above all, no *coup d'état.* Simply an observation. Butler's message was information, not blackmail or usurpation. A warning from a career military man who still believed in his oath of office to the Constitution and to the President of the United States.

With a wave of his hand, FDR beckoned General Butler to continue.

"These men are afraid we are traveling down the same road the Russians traveled. Their fear accelerated into immediate action when you formally recognized the Soviet Union. They saw you took the side of the Communists...."

FDR wouldn't allow the general to drag him into such a discussion. The industrialists and bankers General Butler so reviled were the President's most ardent and august supporters. He returned their support with government contracts. President Roosevelt changed the subject, "Are you still involved with speaking for the Bonus Army?"

"Yes, Mr. President. Veterans who returned to America after fighting Germany in the Great War expect their government to uphold their promises and pay them the wages they earned and are owed. It is as if the government planned on them perishing on distant battlefields and is punishing them for surviving the war. The industrialists and the bankers got paid for inferior equipment, but America's surviving troops did not get paid. This is an evil situation and proves that war increases the fortunes of the industrialists. The U.S. Congress has no interest in taking care of its veterans. But this is the same army the industrialists wish to use against you and they will pay the Bonus Army what they are owed as leverage to remove you from this office."

FDR said, "We count ourselves to be liberal, I suppose. Are we liberal enough to have the fascist government these men desire?"

"Mr. President that is a question for others. I am a military man sworn to uphold and protect the U.S. Constitution against all enemies, foreign and domestic, and to obey the orders of the President of the United States. These men have been aggressively recruiting me to overthrow a duly elected president and install a fascist government simply to protect their companies and increase their wealth. We may have political differences, but you are my President. I have no political power and want no part of this. I've come only to warn you of the forces marshaling against you. They may ultimately find a leader. I am not that person."

"General Butler, if not you then who'll lead such an effort?"

"Mr. President, they will find someone. They are looking for a man of stature and accomplishment. I believe they will try to recruit a socialist or a fascist, someone like Charles Lindbergh. Possibly Douglas MacArthur. Someone who'll put politics ahead of the needs of their country. I have told these men repeatedly that I am not their man and I will not do their bidding. They are relentless, nearly pathological in their search for a leader."

"Lindbergh?"

"Mr. President, I don't know him personally, but I understand Mr. Lindbergh has German sympathies."

"Charles Lindbergh has German sympathies. I expect he'll fly to Germany soon to judge the state of Luftwaffe aircraft."

Butler raised an eyebrow. *That's a form of official intelligence collecting, if Lindbergh is on the side of America. If he is not....* The old Marine frowned at the alternative.

FDR continued, "We are not at war with Herr Hitler. One of his airships is expected to land here today. Another example of Germanic engineering and accomplishment. America has nothing like it."

"Socialist propaganda, Mr. President." *It is a flying bomb.*

"Are you aware Lindbergh will be inducted into the Order of the German Eagle by Hermann Goering?"

"Mr. President, I know that is the highest Nazi honor available to a foreigner. While I know a few things about medals and awards, I choose to focus on America's ability to grow and defend her borders. And if need be, her allies."

"I understand you've been evaluating the creations from the Boeing Company. Is that correct?"

"Yes, Mr. President. The Nazi's use of hydrogen instead of helium for their airships chills me. It is a conflagration just waiting to happen. Next year Boeing will have a much faster, safer, and more practical design; a *Flying Boat*. It's being assembled at Boeing's Plant on the Duwamish River in Seattle. It's massive. As a favor to the Commandant of the Marine Corps, Lieutenant General Holcomb, I agreed to determine its utility to transport Marines quickly, from one 'hot spot' or island to another. The ability to fly long distances, land near a beach, and assault the enemy has put Boeing in the category of being a critical national asset."

"General Butler, we see the same thing. Unimaginable potential, but those '*flying boats*' will go to Pan American Airlines for paying passengers. We'll buy a few examples, probably for maritime rescue. In the meantime, the British Short Brothers are building a fleet of flying boats as patrol bombers. I directed the Secretary of the Navy to monitor both programs for potential acquisition. The Commandant could not have chosen a finer officer to evaluate the Boeing." FDR nodded as if his mind had wandered off to another topic, but one that he didn't want to share.

"Thank you, Mr. President." General Butler reflected that the two men had known each other for a very long time. When he was the Assistant Secretary of the Navy, Roosevelt recommended the Marine hero, Major Smedley Darlington Butler, for his second Congressional Medal of Honor and had the honor of awarding the medal in his office.

President Roosevelt nodded several more times when his cigarette holder shot straight up. He said, "Speaking of aircraft and flying boats, you are no doubt aware that the Soviets and the Nazis are in a race to fly a woman around the globe. I believe this to be the last of the grand heroic air races. Amelia Earhart will do it. I wanted to see a Boeing *Flying Boat* trail her, especially while she is flying over the Pacific Ocean. If she has any mechanical malfunction, the Boeing could set down and rescue her. But Boeing said their new aircraft will not be ready in time, so we will have to rely on our glorious Navy to assist her in her crossing, for provisioning and navigation and, if necessary, for rescue. The Soviets and the Nazis have no infrastructure to support such a very special activity, so America will beat them, as long as they are unable to take surreptitious actions to stop her."

"Mr. President, I don't think either one of those socialist countries has the wherewithal to try to interrupt her flight. As long as they try nothing underhanded, she may be successful. She will be first. And if she is successful, women across the country will want to be like her. Want to become pilots."

FDR considered the solicitation. *If we are sucked into a war we will need every abled body to help, even women pilots. Amelia would make recruiting women much easier…. There will be jobs for women pilots.* He returned to the general's issue. "General Butler, back to the issue at hand, is it your contention that these conspirators believe a fascist regime would allow them to still grow their wealth?"

Smedley D. Butler let the question go with a stern look. "Mr. President, my belief is that American presidents should never allow the United States of America to become one of the atheist scourges of Marxism. We are a Christian nation; we are a capitalist country."

FDR sat quietly with his hands in his lap. "General Butler, what is your recommendation?"

"Mr. President, the country and the economy are still very fragile; so soon after the Depression, maybe one or both are at a tipping point. Stalin, Hitler, and Mussolini will claim capitalism was tried and their atheistic form of government is the better way. We know those are false premises. They know they cannot defeat us militarily but must infiltrate our government and organize communities to persuade Americans that theirs is a better way."

FDR asserted, "This is the Lenin model, the prerequisites for revolution, riots are rehearsals for revolution."

"Yes, Mr. President. I contend we are a nation at risk. The Democrats in the House say they can't pay the monies owed to the veterans of the Bonus Army. That must be rectified immediately. It is a national embarrassment and a danger. And once they are paid, the industrialists and bankers will see their scheme to overthrow our government fade away. The Bonus Army will dissolve and no longer be a threat. The Soviets and the Nazis are trying to get their people into our government to affect public policy and steal the nation's secrets. I believe there is more to this cabal of wealthy men who wish to overturn the election of the people. Mr. President, I believe there needs to be a formal investigation to stop this unholy tangent; the perpetrators need to be exposed and punished. We are equipped and manned to repel foreign invaders, but we are woefully unprepared to protect the homeland from domestic enemies."

"I'll speak with the Speaker of the House and the Director of the FBI. They will investigate. It would be best if you can testify in secret. Are you armed? Of course you are. I say that with concern, for I would expect an attempt on your life, your family's well-being. Please take the appropriate precautions. Yes, desperate men do desperate things."

"Yes, Mr. President."

"General Butler, when they find out what you've done…exposed their ridiculous plan; will they retaliate?"

"Mr. President, I've had people shooting at me for thirty years. Those piss-ant traitors do not know with whom they're dealing. I cannot be deterred." Sensing their meeting was over, the general checked his watch, gripped the arms of his chair, and began to stand. The alligator-strapped Breitling chronograph had been battle-tested; the once polished case and crystal were scuffed with deep scratches. Butler knew his time was up.

FDR glanced at his waistcoat watch with the name "Tiffany & Co." on the dial. He had several minutes to spare and the little general was an experienced, thoughtful, and serious fellow. He had seen much of the world. He waved Butler back to his seat. "This is a little off the beaten path, General Butler. What do you know of the legend of burying Mohammedans with dead pigs? As a deterrence?"

Butler relaxed into his chair and furrowed his brows. "Mr. President, it's not a legend; it's history. The practice discouraged fanatical Mohammedans who carried out suicide attacks against Christians while shouting *Allahu Akbar; God is great.* The Spaniards began publically burying the corpses of suicidal Islamic cult members with the blood of slaughtered pigs to deter further suicide attacks."

"Sounds positively barbarian. Did this strategy succeed?"

"Mr. President, if I may? I believe this requires more explanation. The *juramentados* carried out suicide attacks against American forces in the Philippines. *Juramentados* is an old Spanish term for suicide attackers. Officers in the field must protect their men when they come under attack, lest they all shall perish. American officers knew about the Spanish success and found the practice of using swine offal and blood an effective deterrence. The Mohammedan is to have no contact with swine and especially not with its blood. When American soldiers killed these religiously motivated suicide attackers, the commander of the American soldiers held a very public funeral for them. They threw the *juramentados* into a grave, and a pig's blood was splashed over the dead from head to toe. Then the dead pig was thrown in the grave, and the burial was completed."

President Roosevelt was fascinated with the discussion and showed his prodigious memory. He checked his watch again. "I read in the Chicago Daily Tribune several years ago that General Pershing sprinkled prisoners with pig's blood and set them free to warn others. I remember his exact words, 'Those drops of porcine blood proved more powerful than bullets.'"

"Yes, Mr. President. I shared my concerns with General Pershing on the topic, he recounted that burials with pigs were 'a good plan' to discourage 'unbalanced fanatics.' General Pershing sought to stop the suicide attacks, and soldiers continued the practice. The Chicago Tribune article you cited suggested there was every sign that the method 'had the desired effect,' and the attacks stopped, as you say."

FDR nodded and wrenched his lips tight against the cigarette holder. He had more questions for the Great War general before his next visitor arrived. He wanted quick answers. FDR asked, "General Butler, what is your assessment of Herr Hitler?"

"Mr. President, he is a man who cannot be deterred. He'll rearm Germany and look to dominate Europe. Lenin eliminated the Romanovs, got access to the Russian treasury, and started little forest fires of revolution all over Europe in order to upset the balance of power and dominate those countries. Hitler will use *mass*, the concentration of combat power, and the strength of his army to do the same. Stalin will destabilize Europe through propaganda. But Hitler will do it with speed. Advances in technology will allow Hitler to develop the fastest aircraft, ships, and tanks. Nazi equipment will not be the lowest cost, technically acceptable option to conduct warfare. They will build the equipment of war to win and not line the pockets of industrialists and bankers."

"How would you stop him?"

General Butler gave FDR a wry look, the kind you flash before sharing a secret with a friend. "Mr. President, cut off his supply of oil.

Starve the beast. Germany has no oil of their own to speak of. I believe no single country will deter Hitler's ambitions, but his weapons of destruction require massive quantities of oil. I expect the Nazis to make incursions into oil-rich North Africa and Persia."

FDR nodded as he replaced a fresh cigarette in its holder. "What is your assessment of Mohammedanism?" Another glance of the Tiffany.

"Mr. President, religions have their fanatics, but there is no other religion that has *juramentados* engaging in suicide attacks under the guise of *divine killing*. It's the extreme fanatic, the *juramentado* who creates the dilemma. The vast majority of Mohammedans are peaceful human beings with no desire for the *jihad*."

"Do you see them ever becoming a threat? Is there something we can do to deter their aggression?"

"Mr. President, I think Mr. Churchill has been studying that religion for some time. He said something to the effect that 'individual Mohammedans may show splendid qualities, but the influence of the religion paralyzes the social development of some who follow it. No stronger retrograde force exists in the world.' If I understand Mr. Churchill's analysis, Mohammedans won't renounce their religion and embrace Christianity unless they can be educated into the Western world. Educate the Mohammedans; show them the glory of Westernization, turn them from their destructive tribalism through education. Regardless of religion, fanatics need to be defeated."

"Their radicals need to be destroyed utterly."

General Butler said, "Yes, Mr. President. They must be killed. There are always new Mohammedan uprisings hell-bent on killing Christians. Unless there is a fundamental transformation of Mohammedanism toward Westernization, we'll continue to see that."

"Westernization, you say? What do you think of Amin al-Husseini? Don't you think he can bring peace among the Arabs? He is considered an important ally by the British Mandatory authorities."

"Mr. President, the Grand Mufti of Jerusalem, al-Husseini is an anti-Semite, an opportunistic tribalist, and an anti-Westernizationalist. If there is war he will defect and become an ally of the Nazis."

FDR considered the general's comments as Butler continued, "But to answer your earlier question, how do we deter them strategically?

Ideally, we would insert spies, fifth column work, but infiltrating the Mohammedans and expecting success is unreasonable. We do not have a structure in government dedicated for those...special activities. I submit the United States needs more aggressive intelligence gathering and possibly a centralized offensive intelligence gathering organization; strategic services."

FDR formed his fingers into a teepee. *A centralized... intelligence... organization? Hmmm. That is probably a bridge too far. Congress would have a fit! Maybe something smaller, not as threatening. Strategic services.... Maybe an office...of strategic....*

FDR checked the Tiffany one final time. His lack of an expression signaled that the meeting was finally over. "You've done your duty, General Butler. I appreciate your candor. Thank you for the discussion and thank you for your service to our nation."

General Butler knew better than to have the last word, even to express gratitude for the president's time. As he left the Oval Office he ran into the next presidential visitor, a Congressional Medal of Honor winner, General William Donovan. Butler did not know Donovan well, but knew he had returned to the practice of law after his time in uniform. Donovan's family had connections and old money, and it was reflected in the man's timepiece with the alligator leather strap, one of the earliest Rolex watches from Switzerland.

The men shook hands warmly, said a few words of mutual admiration, and departed. Donovan was ushered into the Oval Office as Butler left the White House grounds, recalling that in 1932 Donovan was the overwhelming favorite to succeed Franklin D. Roosevelt as Governor of New York but had failed in his run as a Republican by a few hundred votes. General Butler shrugged his shoulders and wondered for a moment what it was the President and Donovan could talk about. *Certainly not attempted coups, Mohammedans, or juramentados? Hitler, Stalin...Lindbergh? C'est la vie!*

The weather was conducive for walking, and General Butler rarely signaled for a taxicab unless he was running late for an appointment. For a man who's always on tireless feet, he casually perambulated to Union Station via Pennsylvania, Constitution, and Louisiana Avenues. He wasn't worried about being ambushed and killed in those days, not in the openness of the Mall of Washington, D.C. But if the Congress ever took up the issue of a *coup d'état*, organized and funded by fascists, General Butler considered that his family would be at extreme risk for retaliation, much like they had been by the crime bosses and mobsters he threw in jail for widespread voter fraud when he was the Philadelphia police commissioner. It would be prudent to move them to a place where not even the Democrat Party crime bosses could find them. *I have a little ranch outside Del Rio, Texas.*

• • •

President Roosevelt thanked General Donovan for coming to see him. He was the right man for the project he had in mind. FDR rang for his son as he wanted any and all references of the visits with Butler and Donovan erased from the official calendar record. FDR wanted no more interruptions. He wanted time to think.

James Roosevelt said he would comply, but first told his father that the Nazi's giant airship, the *Hindenburg*, had caught fire when it tried to land at the Lakehurst Naval Air Station in New Jersey.

The President's cigarette holder shot straight up. He shuddered at the notion, *Is this the opening salvo of war? This is no-doubt Stalin's doing! What else could it be? An accident? Impossible in today's political environment.*

Book One

CHAPTER 1

December 21, 1988

The Naval Air Station Miramar Air Traffic Control cleared two McDonnell Douglas F-4S *Phantom IIs* to "taxi to runway 24L and hold." The ceiling and visibility were "unlimited," the windsock was filled with winds running mostly down the runway. With canopies raised, the jets departed their position in front of base operations and slowly trundled to the runway, straddling the centerline on the taxiway and not exceeding the groundspeed limits for open canopies. Once at the Hold Short line, the lead pilot aligned the jet at an angle to perform the Before Takeoff Checklist. The wingman followed the actions of the lead aircraft.

Pocket Checklists were held tight on the kneeboards of the two pilots, *Cheese* and *Maverick*. The four canopies were lowered simultaneously, as if the action was choreographed, but it was simply the lead Radar Intercept Officer (RIO) command over the squadron common frequency. When the ground checks were done and the checklist items were complete, the lead pilot fastened his O2 mask to his helmet and turned his head to look for a "thumbs up" from his wingman, indicating he was ready to go.

The RIO of the lead aircraft transmitted, "Sierra Hotel Seven Seven, two Fox Fours for takeoff, 24Lima."

Miramar Tower transmitted, "Sierra Hotel Seven Seven, standby, landing traffic." Two F-14 *Tomcats* were in the landing pattern. Four helmets in two cockpits turned to watch the Navy's big fighters with extended wings make their approach to the runway.

Cheese, the squadron commanding officer (CO) of an F-4 squadron at the Marine Corps Air Station Yuma, Arizona was one of the best dogfighters in the air wing and would lead his wingman to one of the restricted supersonic ranges over the Pacific Ocean, taking the newest pilot in his squadron, Captain Duncan Hunter call sign *Maverick*, for a little friendly aerial arm wrestling competition to see who in the squadron was really the best dogfighter.

The F-4 squadron CO was a rock star in Marine Corps aviation. Most lieutenant colonels considered themselves extremely fortunate to command a single squadron; *Cheese* was commanding squadron number three. For reasons usually attributed to a "lack of leadership," a very few squadron COs became "problem children," suffering a string of "mishaps," where aircraft were damaged or lost, and aircrew were injured or killed. *Cheese* had fixed two squadrons in distress, and he had his hands full with his new one.

The squadron had several "headwork" mishaps before the previous CO was ignominiously relieved of command. A wingman had collided with his lead aircraft during a running rendezvous, damaging both aircraft although no one was forced to eject. A senior pilot had landed with his feet on the brakes—both main landing gear tires blew out on touchdown and the jet skidded down the runway, laying down two lines of aluminum and sparks. It had departed the concrete and come to rest between dual runways. Miraculously, the jet didn't flip onto its back. There had also been an aerial refueling mishap and a takeoff incident which killed the RIO and injured the pilot.

The Wing Commanding General (CG) relieved the previous squadron CO and several officers for a "loss of confidence" and directed the transfer of several high performing officers with stellar reputations—essentially new fresh blood—into the squadron. *Cheese* and *Maverick* were the first of several "*Phyxers*," *Phantom* pilots who were hand-picked and reassigned "by-name" to turn underperforming fighter squadrons around.

Captain Drue Duncan Hunter had come to the squadron with a first-rate reputation and what senior officers called *superlative paper*—outstanding "fitness reports" (FITREPs). *Maverick* had been ranked as the number one captain in his previous squadron. He had been the "Top Hook" pilot during the cruise of the Carrier Air Wing on his last deployment, even besting the Navy's best, most-experienced carrier pilots flying the newest jets in America's arsenal. *Maverick* consistently scored a perfect 300 on his physical fitness tests (PFTs). Hunter had been on the Marine Corps Pistol Team and captain of the Marine Corps

Racquetball Team. He was the finest Marine Corps racquetball champion in the service's history, and he was consistently on the Inter-Service Racquetball Team at the annual National Singles Racquetball Championships.

As the F-14s landed and cleared the runway using the high-speed taxiway, an air traffic controller in the Miramar Tower updated the wind direction and speed and cleared the Marine F-4s for takeoff. Before taking the right side of the runway, the lead checked the position of the windsock and affirmed the slight crossing winds would slightly impact his wingman on takeoff. *Maverick* stopped and executed the Takeoff Checklist: Controls—CHECKED.

Against the positive pressure from the aviator's breathing oxygen (ABO), *Maverick* cycled through the flight controls again and professed he had a safety of flight issue. He engaged the interphone switch. "*Geek*, I got a problem. The ailerons chatter in roll. When I shut off the AFCS, it's gone."

Radar Intercept Officer Captain George Elek, call sign *Geek*, engaged the radio and told lead to go to button one, the squadron common frequency. Hunter told the CO what deviation from normal operations he had experienced. The CO and RIO of the lead aircraft turned in their seats to watch as *Maverick* engaged the Automatic Flight Control System, and moved the control stick to the right and left. The jet's ailerons visibly vibrated when the stick was moved. When he deselected the AFCS, the hydraulically assisted flight controls moved as they were designed to do, be as silky smooth as the power-assisted steering on Jaguar's legendary XKE.

The CO had thousands of hours in the F-4 and assured *Maverick* that it was most likely some air in the system, but it was his call whether to abort. *Cheese* reminded *Maverick* that if he was going to take the aircraft, the AFCS switch had to be engaged for takeoff. "You can shut it off once you're airborne."

While the CO's voice came through his helmet speakers, *Maverick* reflected on the fact that was he was sitting in a jet with a control problem, however minor it appeared. He promised himself his whole flying career never to take a jet he wasn't happy with. Now he had one, and he had the *Cheese*, the *Skipper*, on the runway waiting for an answer. He agonized over the decision. *Cheese said it's not that bad. I can shut off the AFCS once I'm airborne. I'll be ok.* Against his better judgment, *Maverick* said he would take the aircraft.

The air traffic controller in the Miramar Tower was going ballistic and scolding the lead aircraft for switching frequencies on the duty runway without permission. *Maverick* completed the takeoff checklist: "Trim—SET, Flaps—1/2, Hook—UP, Harness—LOCKED & LAP BELT SECURE, Warning lights—OUT, Seat pins—OUT, Lower ejection handle—pin is out, Command selector valve...."

Geek responded to the challenge that the ejection set command selector valve was in BOTH. *Maverick* didn't challenge the selector valve position. For as long as he had been flying the F-4, the RIO had always controlled the ejection sequence.

Both RIOs switched frequencies to Departure Control; the lead RIO made the radio calls for the flight. After receiving clearance to take off, *Cheese* released his brakes and rammed the throttles to the forward stops to MAXIMUM power. The twin J-79's afterburners (AB) lit off together, transforming the interior of the exhaust nozzles from black shadows to red hot blowtorches. *Maverick* quickly counted to ten, released his brakes, and pushed the throttles to AB.

Geek called out the airspeeds as the big jet roared down the runway. "Off the peg, 50... 80... 100... 120...."

As positive-pressure gaseous oxygen was forced into his mask, *Maverick* said, "We're going flying...." Takeoff "trim" had been set and normal rotation technique required gently pulling back on the stick as the jet accelerated through 150 knots; the nose wheel fully extended under his feet with a *thunk*. The main landing gear struts had fully extended when the jet left the runway and became airborne.

"...180...."

Maverick called out, "Gear!" and flipped the landing gear handle. He checked his takeoff angle at eight degrees. Not too shallow, but less than the book takeoff attitude of ten degrees.

"...200.... 250—coming out of blower...."

Before *Maverick* could retard the throttle out of AB, the jet began an uncommanded roll to the left. Hunter applied right pressure to the control stick to stop the roll, but the stick chattered as the jet kept on rolling. Instead of being "wings level," the aircraft continued to accelerate and passed through 300 knots and 45° angle of bank. The F-4 didn't slow down its rotation as it approached 80° angle of bank.

Geek screamed into the radio, *"What're you doing?!"* He was terrified and had no control over the stick or the flight, but he had control over saving his life. *Geek* grabbed the lower ejection handle between his legs.

The aircraft wouldn't stop rolling even with the control stick fully deflected to the right and vibrating like a paint shaker. *It's not wake turbulence. It's the AFCS!* Hunter had practiced the automatic flight control system emergency in the simulator hundreds of times. At 90° angle of bank, *Maverick* reached for the AFCS DISCONNECT switch at the base of the control stick just as *Geek* pulled the lower ejection seat handle.

• • •

Captain Duncan Hunter woke up in a hospital bed. His eyesight was fuzzy, his memory dim, and he was groggy from being sedated. Everything hurt like hell. It took an inordinate amount of effort to move his head. When he breathed, his sides hurt. Everything hurt. *Maverick* took inventory through fuzzy eyes. *Two legs…two sets of toes…two arms…two sets of fingers. All present and accounted for….* Both arms and legs were casted and in traction.

I'm in a scene from a bad movie…. Apparently…I'm alive. Hunter micro-nodded to himself. *I guess I'll live a little longer.* He closed his eyes and went back to sleep.

Sometime later, *Maverick* awoke and had an *Oh shit* moment, and realized *Geek* was probably dead. He cried himself to sleep.

Once *Maverick* could talk, the CO and the mishap investigators were notified. The *Cheese* visited after an obnoxious investigating officer beat him up during a day of questions. When the CO arrived, he pulled up a chair and sat next to *Maverick*. First, he apologized.

Hunter interrupted him through a damaged mouth and an oxygen mask that also covered his nose. "Not your fault, *Skipper*. I took the jet. I had promised myself to never take a jet I wasn't happy with. I went against my better judgment, and it killed *Geek*. The investigation officers are not happy with me." Hunter looked into the CO's eyes and confirmed the death of his flying partner. He turned his head in shame and became very emotional. It took several minutes for him to regain his composure. "I… I… I practiced that emergency, I don't know how many times. Uncommanded roll on takeoff; the one that killed *Disco*. I think *Geek* freaked out. I was so focused on handling the emergency…. I said nothing to him. But we were climbing. I reached for the AFCS disconnect. *Geek* had to have pulled the handle. He did what he had to do. I wasn't in a good…I wasn't in the right position. *I'm so sorry….*" Hunter couldn't talk anymore as tears streamed over bruised cheeks.

The old CO patted the captain's leg cast. There had always been an introspective and emotional quality to the junior officer, even though in uniform, Hunter had looked every inch the academic athlete, sans the glasses. Now he was a loose formation of bandages and casts, bruises and tears. He had been hand-picked to help fix a problem squadron and in an instant he would forever be blamed with screwing up an in-flight emergency.

Cheese waited for *Maverick* to collect himself. *He is more bunged up than a barrelhouse vag and is incredibly lucky to be alive. He knows Geek is dead.* The CO was also there to notify *Maverick* that his parents had been killed by a terrorist's bomb on the day of his accident. Emergency personnel in Lockerbie, Scotland, were still putting bodies into body bags and combing through the wreckage. *Some people have all the luck. He's lucid and rational, and the only good news is that he's not going to be stacking Cheerios in the stroke center anytime soon.*

Hunter strained to talk. "Sir, they must have me on some powerful shit. The first time I woke up everything hurt, and now I can't really feel a thing. I just want to sleep. My brain is completely unhinged and nothing makes sense. I'm in that state of being *Comfortably Numb*, if you know what I mean."

The CO picked up on the Pink Floyd reference. The first step to recovery is humor. "*Maverick,* I have some bad news to convey. I don't know how to say it, but there is more bad news. Your parents were killed a few days ago."

Captain Hunter was stunned. He became emotional again, and the *Cheese* was there with a box of tissue. Several minutes passed before Hunter was composed enough to ask questions. *Cheese* answered as best he could. Terrorism was suspected; no one had taken responsibility for placing a bomb on the Pan American jumbo jet. The U.S. intelligence community was on it.

The CO tried to shift the subject, but death was everywhere. Hunter was in intensive care. *Geek was dead, and so were Hunter's parents. Had anyone ever had this much bad luck all at once? Some Greek tragedy, maybe?* Once Hunter looked like he could be receptive to some positive conversation, *Cheese* said, "The doctor can't explain why you didn't die. I said you were a hard ass. The closest thing the Marines have to an Olympic-quality athlete. Best pilot in the squadron. Must be something to do with where you were born."

"I tell friends my mother had me at Ft. Leavenworth. At the very least, in a little house across from the Big House."

Cheese expected Hunter to lose it again when he mentioned his mother. He had thought it was an innocuous topic, but still Hunter's parents were thrust to the forefront of the conversation. The CO attempted a tactful retreat with, "I think some of most important aviators were born in Kanas."

After several minutes *Maverick* said, "Oscar Wilde said, 'We are all born in the gutter, but some of us are looking at the stars.' Amelia Earhart, was born up the road in Atchison; the best known aviatrix. Lieutenant General Frank Peterson, Topeka—first black aviator, first black Marine general; Silver Hawk, Gray Eagle…played a mean game of racquetball for a general. I know there are some astronauts, too. But *Skippers* are the best pilots and best officers in the squadron. Everybody knows that." Hunter closed his leaking eyes and *Cheese* let the tears flow.

He rarely takes a compliment well. Very odd. "Once upon a time that may have been true, but we don't get the hours to maintain our proficiency like captains do—and I know you live…*have lived* in the simulator or in a classroom while the rest of us are screwing off at happy hour. I'm sure we were all convinced we could've been astronauts, but at some point after flight school, after all the F-4 training, and screwing off in a squadron, reality sets in. Most of us were just grateful to win our wings. You knew *you* would." The *Cheese* could see Hunter was still struggling to talk. He would talk for both of them. "I knew I could never beat you on the racquetball court, but in the air I knew I could use all the tricks I acquired over a lifetime of flying the F-4 to put you in your place. That you would learn from it; not resent it. The best officers set the example."

"Everyone in the squadron knows that while they spend their time at the O-Club or at home with their families, you're the Philomath working on a doctorate or trying to become a better pilot in the simulator. They stopped their education; you blasted ahead. So we know who's the real lead dog, *Maverick*. What is *your* SAT word? *Supererogation?* Going the extra mile? False modesty will get you nowhere. When you have the reputation, when you are renowned as an officer and a pilot who can keep his mouth shut, and I suppose an athlete *nonpareil*, you are not fooling anyone. The CG and Assistant Commandant send their regards. Apparently you know quite a few flag officers who send their regards. I've never had so many P-4s come through my office. They're all from probably lesser aviators, certainly lesser racquetball players."

Cheese went through the list of senior officers who sent Hunter, "Personal For" messages. He tried not to miss anyone. When the Comm Center delivered the P-4s, *Cheese* rationalized, *I'm sure Hunter pulled most of them off barstools when they were too drunk to drive. Hmmm. There are few Mountain Dew-drinking junior officers who could be trusted for such, uh, sensitive work.*

Hunter offered another poor excuse for an appropriate expression at the compliment. His eyes were closed, but the tears had stopped. "I played racquetball with them. Some wanted to get a beer. I just made sure they got home ok. Sir, please tell them 'thank you. I'll be back.'" *Maverick* found exhaling with a bruised chest considerably exhaustive.

"I made sure they got home ok." Well, there you go. I was probably right. Maverick was more than just a racquetball player. "*Maverick*, we also tried to contact your next of kin. We don't have good phone numbers for your brothers." *He has lost his parents and all that remains of his family are his brothers. Someone is going to have to plan a double funeral, and Maverick*

is in no shape to leave this bed. He can't even go to his parent's funeral. I'll have to go. The duties of the CO.

"Sir, I don't know where they are. One may be local, in Chula Vista. But I don't know. They got caught up with the whole drug scene long ago, and we haven't talked in ages."

He looked like he was struggling to stay awake. *Maverick* closed his eyes and shifted gears, "Sir, do you know where my watch is?"

That boy lost his folks and Geek and asked about that watch. Every pilot in the squadron asked about that watch. It's about as subtle as a brick through a window. "I have it. Your wallet, truck keys too. My wife didn't know if you had a dog so she went to your apartment. She only said, 'Why can't all men pick up after themselves like *Maverick*' and 'you have the best collection of colorful Polo shirts and more old movies than some Blockbusters.' The XO locked up anything that's yours in the squadron. The first thing he snagged was your flight jacket."

Maverick opened his eyes in appreciation. A spurious thought came from somewhere that he should check his teeth. He ran his tongue across the front of incisors and canines to see if any had broken or had been knocked out. *All present and accounted for....* Hunter could be heard through the oxygen mask, "Things go missing when you...."

Cheese nodded. "...when you least expect it. Marines sometimes steal and do stupid shit. As for your Rolex, it's pretty well busted up. The bezel is scratched and so is the crystal; but you didn't hurt the band or damage the case. I couldn't help but check the back for an inscription. Now I know why that watch is so special. I'll get it fixed so when you're out of this cast you can actually wear it. I have to tell you, we may have to get the pilots to wash cars or have the wives make cookies for a fund raiser, or maybe I can take out a second mortgage on my house."

It hurt to laugh but it energized him, too. *Maverick* said, "That solid rose gold Rolex with the black dial and black bezel and red DAYTONA lettering is an antique, a 1969 *Daytona* Cosmograph. It isn't just a regular Rolex. There's a reason they call it a '*cosmo*graph.' You saw the inscription."

"I did. That's unbelievable."

He closed his eyes as if he were resting but his voice was becoming stronger. "And it's real. People call it the *Paul Newman Daytona* because he wore a steel one in his racing days. It was always on his wrist when he was racing cars. I bought mine the year I was stationed in Okinawa. I couldn't believe it when I saw it that day. I didn't think it was real, but it had papers. Provenance. I got the serial number and wrote to Rolex. It's real, and it's spectacular."

That Daytona complicates matters.

"I find them—*rare watches*—incredibly interesting. Before she attempted her round the world adventure Amelia Earhart wore a very rare 1937 Longines with the oversized-dial that was made expressly for pilots. I have one, not Amelia's, of course. History and exploration and Rolex are aligned. Winston Churchill received the 100,000th chronometer produced by Rolex. Sir Edmund Hillary and Tenzing Norgay wore a Rolex when they scaled Mt. Everest. Jacques Cousteau wore a *Submariner* to the bottom of the ocean. Chuck Yeager wore one when he became the first person to break the speed of sound. Dr. Martin Luther King wore a gold Rolex."

"The *Daytona* wiped out my savings. I needed my mom and a Navy Federal Credit Union loan to buy it. During my last cruise, I picked up a two-tone *Submariner* Chronometer when we had a port call in Hong Kong. That's also in my apartment. The others are in a safe deposit box. In town."

The *Cheese* was confused. *Others?* "How many do you have?"

Hunter struggled to speak and sighed against the oxygen in the mask. He took deep breaths and said, "Ten. Ian Fleming never specified which model 007 wore. The reference 6538 on Sean Connery's wrist during *Dr. No,* the very first James Bond film, is probably the most famous movie watch of all time. You can see it in various scenes in *From Russia with Love* and *Goldfinger*."

Watch collectors have their own lexicon, like pilots and Brits. "You have...."

"I do. The big-crown 'James Bond *Submariner*' is the most desirable vintage Rolex *Submariner* Chronometer model in existence. Steve McQueen wore one and I have that one too. Classic stainless steel, no-date, *Submariner,* reference 5512. He was driving a Jag XKSS and wanted to race."

Hunter took several breaths before continuing, "You can see his watch in *The Towering Inferno* and *The Hunter.* In twenty years the 'Steve McQueen' will be worth a quarter of a million dollars. The *Daytona* is priceless."

Cheese was momentarily speechless then burst out with, "How the hell did you do that?" He ignored that *Maverick* was in intensive care.

Through closed eyes Hunter sighed, "I made them an offer they couldn't refuse."

"Which was?" The *Cheese* couldn't believe what he was hearing.

"I told them I wanted their watch and would buy them another one plus arrange for a ride in an F-4."

"What?"

"I played racquetball with the generals at El Toro. I said I needed a favor. A good deal for everyone. Connery and McQueen were invited to the air station by the CG, got familiarization rides.... They signed autographs for Marines.... I got their Rolexes in the mail and sent them new ones."

Cheese laughed so hard he thought he would bust his gut. "*Wow!* I heard about those guys visiting—*that was you?* Of course, that was you. *Maverick* you are incredible." *So I'm dealing with a busted-up pilot, a watch collector, probably the greatest negotiator on the planet, and that Daytona is special. My God. Got it. I had no idea!* "*Maverick,* I'll see that it's repaired properly, even though repairing the *Newman* will not be cheap." *Hunter's watch shouldn't even be called....the Newman.*

Hunter replied, "I shouldn't have been wearing it. It belongs in a museum. One of these days I'll get it there...."

"I have to tell you *Maverick,* I didn't want to keep that secret from the family. All the pilots and RIOs in the squadron now know about that watch. They don't want to call it a *Newman* now that they know how special it is."

Hunter thought for a moment. *No they don't.... Not really.*

The *Cheese* looked at *Maverick* in the mechanical contraption and sighed. *Maverick had been on the fast-track to becoming an astronaut candidate with orders to test pilot school, and now all that work had vaporized. A watch we can fix, but that career path to being an astronaut just got trashed. What's really incomprehensible is that he is alive.*

Maverick did his best to nod and thanked the CO.

Cheese asked if there was anything else he could do.

"I have a clock radio in my bedroom. My shaving kit. I need someone to put some water on my plants. I would feel better if I had the two-tone in my possession, even if I can't wear it right now. It's in my safe." *Maverick* gave *Cheese* the location and the combination to the safe in his apartment. He said, "Please use the American Express Card in my wallet to pay for the repairs on the *Daytona*."

"I'll take care of it."

The nurse came in and squirted happy juice into his IV. She lowered Hunter's head, fixed his blanket, checked the fit of his oxygen mask, and turned off the television. *Maverick* tried to turn his head to his Skipper. "Do you think the insurance company will pay for the damage to my Rolex since I ejected from a jet?"

The *Cheese* said, "I don't see where there'll be any controversy."

I was an idiot for wearing it. It should've been in the safe deposit box and not on my wrist.

Cheese patted *Maverick's* shoulder and squeezed the swollen fingers sticking out of the cast.

The sleeping aid worked. Hunter yawned and gently slurred his words. "Thanks for coming, Skipper. I would salute, but I'm a bit indisposed."

The commanding officer waited at the side of the bed until *Maverick* was asleep. He pulled a red rectangular presentation case from his backpack and opened it. A gold medal rested inside. Captain Duncan Hunter had also been recognized as the Military Male Athlete of the Year. Seeing Hunter in such a state was depressing and awarding an athletic medal to someone who might not ever walk again would be a cruel joke. The CO slipped the medal back into his bag, gently patted *Maverick's* bed, and left.

He found Hunter's attending physician who told him, "From what I see, he'll never be cleared to fly again. He'll never get an 'up chit.'"

Cheese said, "He's the luckiest guy I know, but you need more than luck in aviation and whatever that intangible is, Captain Hunter's got it in buckets."

The investigating officer had said Hunter was unconscious immediately after he was ejected. "He got one swing in his parachute before slamming into the ground. To eject like that and to survive is beyond comprehension; it's like... pulling a rabbit out of a hat or sawing a woman in half."

The physician said, "Being limp when he hit the ground probably saved his life. If he had seen the impact coming, he would have braced for it which would have shattered him like a glass jar hitting a marble floor. Had he not landed on his side, his spine probably would've snapped like a twig. As it was, the ejection compressed his spine to where he's probably lost a couple of inches in height. He'll have back problems for a while. We think he hit his head leaving the cockpit or on the ground. There's probably some brain damage, although he exhibits some curious responses to my questions, as if he gained some level of savant syndrome because of the head injury."

"I know he's worried about his watch. But savant syndrome?"

"Yes. It happens sometimes where there is a brain injury. Some people who didn't know which end of a paint brush to use find themselves able to paint as well as Rembrandt. That kind of thing."

"What's Captain Hunter's super power?"

The doctor half-chuckled at the analogy. "Well, in the short time I've been able to observe him, I would say he sees things differently, as if he can predict outcomes or see the simplicity of the complex. Not like Nostradamus or Sherlock Holmes, but sort of like a chess grandmaster who can play blindfolded and see dozens of steps ahead of multiple opponents. It may be temporary. I asked him if he played chess and he said words to the effect that 'chess is as elaborate a waste of human intelligence as you can find outside the Democrat Party. I am so glad my guy won.' I didn't know he was *political*...?"

The CO said, "The book on Captain Hunter is that he has a prodigious memory; his mother was informed that he was a child prodigy, but not one of those turbocharged nine-year-old Harvard PhDs who flames out at 36 and becomes a hermit in the mountains of Idaho. What you're describing is normal for Hunter. He's just in a category of his own—athletic, brilliant, driven. What junior officer do you know owns several patents?" *And he has James Bond's and Steve McQueen's watch?* "He's at the far end of the Bell Curve rubbing elbows with the Einsteins, Teslas, and Newtons. But instead of doing math or secret squirrel shit—because even the CIA wanted him before he went off to flight school—he wanted to fly and he wanted to fly F-4s. It's kind of a cruel joke, but he received his orders for test pilot school the day after he got hurt. I think he's always had NASA in his pipper." He and the surgeon talked for another ten minutes. Hunter would be moved from intensive care to long-term care in a month or so. He had several more surgeries before then.

The doctor asked the CO if he knew what had happened to Hunter in the final seconds of flight.

"The head of the mishap board surmised it was an uncommanded roll on takeoff. The automatic flight control system experienced a fault which continuously signaled a servomotor, called a *'hard over.'* The investigation officer proved his thesis in the F-4 simulator. A freakish coincidence had occurred between the time Hunter had disconnected the erroneous input into the automatic flight control system and the instant his ejection seat had fired off. The moment the AFCS was disconnected, the aircraft jerked hard right to begin its return to wings-level flight. There is a slight delay when both aircrew eject and Captain Hunter was the second person out of the cockpit. He was flung into space as the jet lurched to an 89-degree angle-of-bank turn—one degree above the horizon—the critical angle for survival. His RIO went out first and slammed into the ground. Hunter survived because of that tiny delay in ejecting."

The physician shook his head. "With the injuries he has, I don't know how he is alive. We heard that there was an ambulance on scene within seconds of him hitting the ground. I guess he's the luckiest guy I know, too."

The CO nodded. "I'm just glad the EMTs didn't steal his watch."

The doctor found the statement curious. *Cheese* stood up and shook the MD's hand. "We have a saying in the flying world when something like this happens. 'It wasn't his time to die.' God has plans for him."

"Amen."

CHAPTER 2

May 23, 1989

Captain Duncan Hunter had lived in the Balboa Naval Medical Center for five months moving from ward to ward, but he spent most of his time in Physical Therapy. He listened to a lot of music and read everything he could get his hands on. He spent a few seconds at daybreak shining the gold links of his Rolex *Submariner*. His brain was always "in gear," and he looked for answers to amorphous questions. *What am I going to do now?* When the squadron XO first visited he brought Hunter a box of things, a radio, aviation magazines, his watch, and his textbooks and notebooks for Hunter to continue his PhD program. He had lost so much weight the *Submariner* Chronometer spun on his wrist. It was well past the time to adjust the band.

What am I going to do? He knew without being told he wouldn't be allowed to return to flying jets. He was unaware of anyone getting back in a high-performance aircraft after ejecting from a jet and sustaining significant injuries. Fixed-wing, non-ejection seat aircraft, like C-130s, maybe. Some depression was setting in. He told his doctor what he was experiencing and what he thought. "I've learned that we're tested not to highlight our weaknesses but to discover our strengths. When I feel like quitting, I remember why I started, what it took to get here. I remember my journey in this world. I'm still here for a reason and I have no idea what that may be." *There's a part of me that says I have to go after those who were responsible for killing my parents and everyone aboard that jet. How do you do that from here? With a broken body? I suppose you have to let the government do its work; if they are even interested in finding out who did it. I think it was in Romans, "...never avenge yourselves, but leave it to the wrath of God, for it is written, 'Vengeance is mine, I will repay, says the Lord.'" What if I didn't avenge myself but was the instrument of vengeance for others? That might make me feel better about what happened to my folks. How do you hunt down a terrorist? There are things I can do. That starts with having a better outlook. And a plan.*

His doctor said, "You're healing quickly, but you know that your trajectory to a full recovery may take several years."

It was strange that all his excitement for flying the *Phantom* was gone. Maybe it was because *Geek* was dead. All his endurance, muscle mass and tone was gone. He was a shell of his former self. *Maybe the hole in my heart was a factor in the mishap. Grief is a wound that sometimes never heals. I almost joined Kimberly, but it wasn't my day to die. Kim….*

It had been a chance encounter; flight instructor First Lieutenant Hunter was flying cross country with a student pilot when greater than forecast headwinds forced them to seek shelter at the closest military base, Williams Air Force Base east of Phoenix. The tired Marines stopped at the student pilot club for a drink. An Air Force student pilot with a head of wild red hair mischievously raced across the club to within millimeters of his nose to ask Hunter, "Are you Navy?" Hunter didn't look her up or down, just into her eyes and replied, "No, Marine." He was instantly smitten.

The girl with bright eyes devilishly responded with, "Too bad, I have a thing for…*Sailors*." She turned and laughed all the way back to her table of giggling friends.

Hunter had just met a goddess, and she had rejected him. Stopping in Arizona was going to leave a bad taste in his mouth. He was left with the residue of her Midwest accent ringing in his ears and the image of her walk that effused the poise and confidence of a Miss America contestant. *She probably has a callipygian ass and marvelous legs in that bag. Bag* meaning the shapeless unflattering flight suit she wore. She had the kind of beauty that naturally intimidated undeveloped and immature men who lacked self-confidence, but he had won several games off of touring racquetball pros and didn't lack self-confidence. They were both lieutenants, so she was "legal" in the eyes of the Marine Corps' fraternization policy.

He didn't think he was being shutout, but she had all the points. A minute later, Hunter sidled over to the DJ and requested a song, stuffing a twenty-dollar bill into the hand of the disk jockey spinning old 45s on a sophisticated dual turntable. Eye contact can be more intimate than words, and after exchanging glances with one another over a couple of belly-rubbing songs designed for slow dancing, Duncan Hunter left his student pilot, approached Second Lieutenant Kimberly Horne, and asked her to dance.

She broke a hundred hearts when she stood up and walked off with the Marine. He led her gracefully to the middle of the dance floor. As contracted, the DJ immediately played the Everly Brothers' version of *Unchained Melody©*.

He asked her what she was doing in the Air Force; she replied the Marine Corps didn't have female pilots, and she had wanted to fly ever since her father had taken her to an airshow. "The Marine 'officer selection officer' said 'no,' the Navy said 'no to jets,' but the Air Force said 'yes' to anything and everything in their inventory."

The two pilots talked over the music, about the challenges of officers from different services dating. They talked of the Marine Corps' fraternization rules and the Air Force's lack of enforcing them. She had her arms around his neck, he had his arms around her waist. They laughed. *Dancing cheek-to-cheek is really a form of floor play.*

They talked of love at first sight. Her baggy flight suit was the most unflattering garment in the flight equipment inventory; she could've been hiding the eight arms of a *Durga* and no one would've known. She could have even been wearing a burlap bag—it wouldn't have mattered. To Hunter she was the most naturally glamourous thing he had ever seen or held in his arms.

She beamed like a movie star with perfect teeth and asked, "Do you believe in miracles?" Hunter returned fire and said, "I thought the same thing. I was going to divert to Luke or Yuma, but something made me stop here. I'm thinking divine intervention kicked up those headwinds." When the music played and when the music stopped, they slow-danced in circles. His eyes never left hers. She was convinced she had found Mr. Right. His head was spinning. The DJ spun *Unchained Melody©* again when they were the last couple on the dance floor.

Whoa, my love
My darling

I've hungered, hungered for your touch....

They were the last to leave the club. He took her to his room. A first for him, a first for her.

She was the first person, outside of unrequited loves in high school, who truly excited him; Kimberly Horne said he was her lost soulmate. Her heart physically ached when he left. They called frequently and generated a hot income stream for the long-distance telephone company. They wrote letters, exchanged intimate gifts, and sent romantic cards. When she made first lieutenant, he sent to her enough flowers to fill a Boeing. They traveled to Ireland, her family's native land and walked along the coast holding hands.

When Hunter made captain and deployed aboard an aircraft carrier, she sent a box of candy that was consumed in seconds—Hunter only got a single piece; a mint.

He wrote her every day. During mail calls he was chided, teased by the other pilots in the Ready Room because he received mail on USAF stationary and *Giorgio*-scented cards from an Air Force chick.

When she wrote that she had made captain, he sent congratulatory cards and flowers; during a Hong Kong port call he bought her a woman's Rolex *President* and a ring with three transcendental sparkling diamonds. Hunter mailed the watch but kept the ring until he could get home and get down on his knee to ask her to marry him. He never heard from Kimberly Horne again.

After returning to the United States, he tried to find answers to the sudden termination of her love letters. He drove to Phoenix only to discover from her squadron commander that she had died. The grandparents who had raised her would only say Kimberly had a terminal disease that took her quickly.

He visited her grave; he wept on her gravestone.

He couldn't believe she hadn't told him. What else did she hide from him? After he returned to Yuma, he wondered if there was something the grandparents had hidden from him.

Thinking of Kim and *Geek* and the end of his plans for test pilot school and the astronaut corps depressed him; he kept a full-blown depression outbreak at bay by reading complex philosophical books and looking forward to the weekends when someone from the squadron would visit.

• • •

He had been nothing close to a lothario, although time and age and seasoning gave him the look of a ladies man of the Steve McQueen-class of leading men. Single girls didn't visit him. It was the squadron pilots, their wives, and their children who brought laughter, mirth, and good cheer, the latest thrillers, aviation magazines, brownies and cookies, banana bread, and sometimes, pumpkin bread. They would stop and visit before heading to Sea World or the zoo.

Hunter treated the wives as sisters, and he prized reading to their children. Their favorite book was *AIRSHOW!* and the kids begged Hunter to read the book again and again. Many a wife or husband said that while Hunter may have had some malady relating to women, he had no inhibitions relating to future pilots. He was in a hospital bed and taught the kids how to count to ten on one hand, like a pilot. The girls and boys wanted to be a pilot like him.

The boys who visited were fascinated with his shiny two-tone watch so Hunter would remove the *Submariner* from his wrist and place it on the wrists of the tykes who beamed like kids opening Christmas presents. Every few weeks, Hunter's fastidious next-door neighbor, Tim Watters, a Navy dentist in Yuma, and his family would drop in to see him. Tim would check on his dental health, and they would talk. Hunter admitted, "I didn't really learn about the Christian part of my heritage until my early teens when I was in the Boy Scouts and went to a parochial school—St. James. My mother got me a bracelet for my birthday. It was inscribed with Proverbs 3:6. *Seek God's will in all you do, and He will show you the path.* Boy Scouts and boys going to a parochial school like shiny things too."

When the families left, he asked them to close the door. Being alone had its own rewards. Hunter was fascinated with a couple of his graduate school reference books, *Exile and the Kingdom* and a tome about the Barbary Wars, a tattered library copy of *To the Shores of Tripoli: The Birth of the U.S. Navy and Marines*. Each book had dozens of sticky notes as placeholders between pages. With no girlfriend to ask, he made deals with the squadron wives to pay them "better than scale" if they could decipher his scratchings, ramblings, and ruminations and type up his term papers for his doctoral program. He remained on flight status and continued to receive flight pay; who knew when that would end. When that day came, he would know he was officially "done."

One day Hunter told the visiting executive officer, "XO, you know we have the highest general classification test scores in the squadron. I think I know why."

"*Maverick*, you have the highest score anyone has ever seen. It's like you aced the test. You're probably the smartest guy any of us have ever met."

"Thanks XO. But I think that occurred because I was in Boy Scouts, working to be an Eagle Scout. I learned so much from those wonderful Merit Badge workbooks. The funny thing is I now realize that many of the military entrance exam test questions looked like they came straight out of those workbooks; information like astronomy and rocketry and forestry that isn't taught in school but was available in scouting. I think I got great scores, not because I was smart, but because scouting taught me so much more than what you would get in school. I studied those merit badge workbooks."

It was like a cathedral's bells had just gone off in the XO's head. Once there had been a smidgeon of jealousy. He smiled at the junior officer's insight and agreed; the XO had been a Life Scout and earned dozens of merit badges.

Hunter continued, "The strange thing, my friends from the neighborhood who weren't in Scouts and didn't go to the Catholic school were jealous of everything I did; schoolwork, afterschool jobs, and that bracelet—is that nutty?" Soon after the conversation, the small sons of visiting pilots began showing up in Cub Scout uniforms wearing bracelets for Duncan to gush over.

Pilots, RIOs, and their wives knew how to entertain and help heal the damaged body and mind of a squadron pilot who had ejected from a crippled jet and escaped the dark arms of Death. Hunter wrote letters; *Geek's* wife never answered his letters or visited.

On the day Hunter was scheduled to be discharged from the Naval Hospital in Balboa, San Diego and rehabilitate his injuries at the clinic in Yuma, Arizona he received a "P-4," in the parlance of official communications, a "Personal For" message from the newest

Commandant of the Marine Corps (CMC), one of his oldest racquetball doubles partners. The doctor who delivered the sealed envelope dismissed the message as just a courtesy, like a "welcome back from hell and now get back to work" missive. A Marine patient didn't have to be anyone special for the Commandant to send a P-4. In his ten years in the Navy he had observed how the Marines were treated and said to Hunter, "Marines take care of their own better than any of the services."

Captain Duncan Hunter read the P-4 and remembered how he had met the future CMC on a racquetball court in Okinawa when the colonel was the Group CO of a composite group of helicopters, and C-130s, and a handful of OV-10s. Hunter was an enlisted man, a helicopter electronics technician on the other side of the airfield. They made an odd pair, an older gentleman and the exuberant athletic racquetball star, but they dominated the "doubles" matches and island tournaments. Hunter admired the older officer and modeled himself after him to some extent. Duncan and the colonel collected trophies by the score, and Hunter made a friend for life. The colonel learned how to play racquetball at a higher level than he had ever believed possible, and Hunter was mentored by a senior officer who encouraged him to double up on the college classes and recommended him for officer candidate school and for flight school. It wasn't long after they started playing together that the colonel—a helicopter pilot—received a bombshell of an announcement—he had been selected for Brigadier General. After Hunter had received his commission and pilot wings, Lieutenant Hunter had standing orders to notify the general officer of his arrival when he passed though Quantico or Headquarters Marine Corps in Washington, D.C.

As he was promoted from one-star to four, the general would alter his schedule whenever he could to accommodate a couple of hours with Duncan Hunter on Quantico's or the Pentagon's racquetball courts. Winning doubles matches was like old times and pissed off the old guard at the Pentagon who had long "owned the courts." They accused the general of "bringing in a ringer," which was exactly what Hunter was. Best in the Marine Corps.

Hunter hobbled on the edge of agony after being discharged from the hospital, using a *shillelagh* for a cane. His formerly strong hurried gait had been usurped by fragility and tentativeness, replaced with a reliance on the sturdiness of the stout knotty blackthorn stick from Ireland. The naval hospital had offered him a government-issued aluminum cane, but he favored the souvenir he had picked up when he and Kimberly visited Dublin and Scotland. If someone complained, what were they going to do to him? Pull his test pilot school orders? Pull his wings? Steel-toe boot him out of the Corps?

The squadron officers in Yuma volunteered to get him in San Diego. Over the telephone, he told the *Cheese* he had been summoned to Headquarters Marine Corps.

Military flights were brutally efficient but not necessarily conducive for comfort, and he barely survived the C-9 flight from Navy North Island to Naval Air Station Patuxent River, Maryland.

The office of the Commandant of the Marine Corps was in one of the inner rings of the Pentagon. It took Hunter thirty minutes to get through security and hobble across the courtyard to the opposite side of the largest office building in the world. There were plenty of stairs in the building but few elevators, especially when you needed one and Hunter needed several. Walking and shuffling to the CMC's office was the most effort he had expended in months, and it made him break out into a sweat. He chuffed like an old man with COPD. The effort reminded him that *...all of my conditioning is gone!*

He couldn't discern if it was the polished floor or the wood-paneled walls that smelled of furniture oil. Hunter's senses were assaulted again when he presented himself to the CMC's secretary. The office smelled like old carpet and Brasso. Anything that had brass-work shined like the gold links on his watch. The secretary was a charming middle-aged lady who looked like Roseanne Barr; no possible candidate for executive hanky-panky. She told him when to enter and he entered.

"Captain Hunter reporting as ordered, Sir!" The CMC came around his desk and greeted Hunter warmly with a strong handshake that ended with a very un-Marine-like hug, the kind of hugs reserved for old teammates celebrating a hard fought victory. The

Commandant was "The Gray Eagle," the oldest aviator in the Marine Corps and the Navy. He wasn't as lean as the ground generals who went through a case of running shoes a year but was still reasonably slim and trim. He wouldn't have to worry about squeezing into a flight suit if a ride were offered. He asked how Hunter's convalescing was going. "No racquetball this trip, sir." The CMC admitted he didn't have time as he was too busy learning the job. After scaling three flights of stairs, Hunter could barely walk and was grateful to be offered a seat.

They talked about the talented Navy surgeons who fixed his broken bones with screws and plates and spliced torn ligaments back together with who knows what. Sardonically, Hunter said, "...probably with cat gut. Now I have cravings for fish but I'm allergic to seafood." The general laughed and remembered the time after a couple of hours of racquetball that they had stopped at a Japanese restaurant in Okinawa. Hunter had gotten acutely ill from the octopus in some concoction that looked like sewer water from a live animal market that the locals called "soup."

"Are you interested in flying C-130s? I can make it happen."

"Thank you for the offer sir, but I respectfully decline. Once you have flown fighters...." The CMC said, "I understand. No factor."

Hunter related how his Marine family at the squadron had supported him; wives baked him fudge and breads and his favorite chocolate-chip cookies, and the pilots brought him aviation-related reading material and their kids. He said some squadron wives were terrific; they typed his graduate school term papers and wouldn't even let him pay them for their labor.

The Commandant said, "I kept track of you. *Cheese* wrote me often and kept me appraised of your recovery."

"He's a good man, sir. He attended my parent's funeral when I couldn't."

"The jobs of a CO. He said you're in a PhD program."

"Yes, sir." *That's an unusual statement. Only a handful of people know what I am doing. The information was probably included in one of Cheese's letters to the general or in a promotion brief sheet.*

"When you finish, I know a guy who takes dissertations, Masters' theses, some war college papers and has them published. You would be a published author. I don't know if you'll become the next Alistair MacLean or that Tom Clancy guy, but it would be an accomplishment. I would be impressed if I saw that on a FITREP or promotion brief sheet." The CMC stood, went to his desk, found a business card, and handed it to Hunter.

What I have in mind would never be considered worthy of a publisher's time and effort. Do I tell him I changed the focus of my research? No more Test Pilot School, no more PhD in aero engineering. Now I'm chasing a PhD in economics and researching the dynamics of aviation terrorism on the industry. It sucks starting over. But I think it is important.

Hunter continued his story, "When I could move around the hospital in a wheelchair, I had someone push me to the florist and gift shop so I could send the wives of the squadron dozens of yellow roses and thank you cards. Texas yellow roses. I have a soft spot for the kids, so I read to them. I called the boys and girls *future pilots*."

The Commandant wistfully said, "Girls as pilots." He sighed.

Hunter remembered the first time he had met the Group CO on the racquetball courts; he had a face as stiff as a frozen fish. As soon as the Commandant mentioned, "Girls as pilots," the fish face returned. Hunter laughingly offered, "Sir, it's going to happen to us one day. The other services have women pilots; they're not combat capable but combat ready. I'm sure the old excuses will not fly anymore when you get called up to Congress and get thrashed by a brace of Democrat female senators. I expect the pressure on you will be immense. The Navy and the Air Force saw the writing on the wall and capitulated, and soon they'll have girls flying nearly everything in the inventory. And they're absolutely wonderful." *My Kimberly was wonderful....*

Wow, where did that come from? The CMC probed, "What would you do? I've only seen a few women with wings in this place; none in a cockpit." The CMC was curious. *Was that the acquired savant-thing talking?* He didn't expect the answer Hunter gave him.

Hunter asked the CMC if he knew how the Navy brought "the girls" into the world of Naval Aviation. A rock of the head meant *No, not really*. "I would do what the Navy did. I'm sure you at least heard the Navy hired experienced competent women pilots. Their fathers were airline pilots who owned airplanes. Some of those women had pilot jobs at regional air carriers. They all carried themselves with confidence in their abilities. The Navy brass had to ensure if they were going to have women aviators, the girls had to be hard, confident, and able to get a fair chance at flight school, because the low-impact boys who were guarding the ramparts would not let some high-powered chicks in the door to take their jobs without some serious chicanery."

Hunter realized he was in deep water without a lifeboat. But he couldn't stop. "I know there's the official policy and the official narrative, sir, but I don't see how opening flying to women impacts effectiveness. Women have been flying for the War Department since the last big one. Flying doesn't require the same level of physicality you would expect of the finely tuned and fighting fit Navy SEALs and RECON Rangers. They require the speed, strength, and stamina that nature has gifted to men. The Navy's unspoken truth was that their female pilots shamed the boys around the carrier. As you know, flying requires 'touch and finesse,' and women have that in buckets. It's only a logistics exercise, a separate bathroom, a private locker room." He remembered the male flight suits given to female pilots and Kimberly. "Maybe *custom* flight suits. Girls have *girls*."

The CMC smiled. "You've given this a lot of thought."

"Yes sir. I dated an Air Force pilot for a while. But when women show up at Pensacola in bright shiny new uniforms with a couple of thousand hours of flight time, and their flight instructors only have a couple hundred, it will be hard to bounce them out of the program for being a bad pilot. These are the girls at the same dance as the boys, but they can dance backwards and in heels. It's not that the girls can't do it, you have to reengineer the attitude of the male aviators. That will not be easy, but it's a little like the fraternization policy, the CMC won't tolerate the abuse of its female pilots by whatever means. The Navy sussed it out, showed a little leadership, and got ahead of the curve before some *congresscritter* took the CNO to the woodshed and beat him like a rented mule in a hailstorm."

The CMC pursed his lips, got up, limped to his desk, and jotted down a few notes. While the CMC was writing, Hunter scoped out his surroundings. There were plaques of varying size and craftsmanship and photographs of former Commandants and Marines in combat on all the walls in the office. An American Flag and the Marine Corps Flag with a thick bouquet of battle streamers stood ramrod tall behind the CMC's desk. *Aren't there about fifty of those streamers? I know the Army has about ninety, but some of theirs are for knowing which bathroom to puke in when they're drunk.* Hunter saw the office as a tribute to the few men who had the privilege of leading the nation's Marine Corps. Unlike when he was a colonel, the CMC wasn't a man of quick movements, and he took his time as he returned to his seat.

Captain Hunter appreciated the concern from the Marine Corps' newest chief executive. He told the Commandant, "Sir, I'm so grateful that you are the Commandant. I had actually worried one of the other generals would be named CMC. I know there are generals who are more political, who lean to the left and think only of themselves. We are so blessed to have you as our Commandant." *I'll bet he had a Republican as a sponsor.* Hunter asked how he could help the four-star.

The CMC thanked Hunter for the kind words. He rambled on the politics of the job before coming to the point. "I need someone I could trust for a very difficult special assignment. It will be an ugly assignment, full of danger and intrigue, and it requires the utmost in secrecy. What you've done in your short time in the Marines is nothing short of remarkable. I need some of that. I need someone I trust, someone who has continually demonstrated the highest level of trust and confidence. We go back a long way, Duncan. We have friends that we can count on, like the guy who runs into the sound of battle or the cry of *fire*. We also have friends that we can't count on, but they're interesting to have around, like the guy who's watching TV and hears *fire* but he may call the fire department as he goes to get another beer. You've always impressed me as a person who runs to confront the enemy and you had a plan to kill everyone you encountered. On or off the court. You're very special."

"Thank you, sir, I remember asking you how you got promoted to general, and you said you had a *sponsor*. That's what it really takes. Someone to vouch for you, to let you into the club. And, sir. Let's be real. I couldn't let some Army or Air Force assholes beat us when you got selected. I was sure that it would've reflected poorly on my FITREP if my Group CO had chosen poorly and got on some losing team. I tried to do my part and always appreciated you for getting me out of the weekly field days at the barracks just so we could beat up the Army and the Air Force on their courts. Marine Corps priorities." The CMC matched Hunter's laughing. They enjoyed the old times.

The four-star continued through laughter, "And I always appreciated being on a winning team. You were an incredible player. You played a game of which I was unfamiliar, and you overcame and covered my deficiencies without a thought or comment. You killed the competition; I was just a decoy." Then the CMC got serious. His lips were as tight as the strings on a racquet.

Hunter had a spurious thought that the CMC was going to let him go. Discharge him, on the spot. He couldn't fly and there's no use for a fighter pilot who cannot fly fighters in the Marine Corps. Take all of his flight pay back. Then the CMC's demeanor vacillated, and Hunter realized that he had been summoned for some other purpose.

"Duncan, this is different, more a favor than a request. It's extremely sensitive, completely voluntary, and I think you can do this while you recuperate. You'll work at your own pace."

Hunter was relieved; he wasn't being disposed of like last week's trash. He was honored, but he knew it would be a long time before he could do any real work. He was grateful to be useful. "Sir, I will do anything for my Commandant! You may not know it sir, but you are a hero to many guys like me. What can I possibly do for you?"

"I want you to hunt down the sexual predators we have in uniform."

CHAPTER 3

May 23, 1989

Duncan Hunter froze like he had been caught naked in a girls' locker room. He was unsure that he had heard accurately. He naturally reverted to his fighter pilot lingo, "*Say again?*"

The Commandant of the Marine Corps repeated, "I want you to hunt down sexual predators in uniform."

Senior officers; colonels and generals. Oh crap, oh my. That's way out of my lane. Will there be any I played ball with? "I'm sorry, sir. Of course, whatever I can do for you, sir, you know I will."

With the ugly duckling out of the water, the CMC gave Hunter some time to run the task around in his head; he asked to see the two-tone shellacked *shillelagh* with a rubber foot on the dirty end. Hunter handed the cane to the general for inspection. The CMC said, "Not very Marine-like, Duncan. They gave me a cane when I broke an ankle; it was aluminum and I hated it. But…this…, this I could like."

Hunter was intrigued by the CMC's blue security access card suspended from a red MARINES lanyard. *Probably can go anywhere with that thing.* "You could always whack someone over the head with this one. I hear in Washington, D.C. you need a weapon just to buy gas. No one will bother me with that in my hand; you know, sir, I'm sure those aluminum things fold up like an empty Coke can."

"That's for sure." The Commandant returned the *shillelagh,* pointed to Hunter's wrist and asked, "Didn't you also have a Rolex *Daytona*? I remember thinking I couldn't afford that watch as a colonel and here was this Marine sergeant with one. I swear when I first saw it on your wrist, what was it, *rose gold,* I was ready to accuse you of wearing a counterfeit."

Hunter nodded and said he had been wearing the *Daytona* when he ejected from the F-4, and it was in Geneva being repaired at the factory. Hunter told him the story of what made the rare Rolex so valuable. The CMC was floored. Hunter said, "Sir, I've learned that some things are worth spending the money on. Some guys rob banks—I got loans. And I shine the gold links of the band whenever I shine the brass on my belt."

That Daytona was…. My God! The general grinned uncomfortably and said, "I do the same thing."

They compared their matching stainless and gold Rolex *Submariners*. The watches looked as good as the day they were made.

Boys and our shiny toys…. Hunter asked the CMC if he went to a parochial school. The Commandant said, "Christ the Redeemer. Regis High School. Naval Academy." Hunter asked him if he ever wore a bracelet and was in the scouts. "We all did. My father was stationed in Washington and my scoutmaster was an officer here at the Pentagon."

A few seconds passed in silence when the Commandant erupted into a coughing fit. Hunter wanted to help, but the general waved him away. "Duncan, I'm ok. I just wanted to say I'm very privileged to have highly regarded and outstanding Marines like you on my side."

My side? Of course I'm on your side….We're not talking politics, are we? He let the curious comment pass.

The CMC focused on Hunter's visitor's badge for a moment before returning to face the captain. "Elite organizations do not accept mediocrity, and they do not look the other way when teammates come up short of expectations. We must hold each other accountable. These Marines I want you to investigate have violated the trust and authority granted them as COs and commanding generals. They abuse the power of their office for personal gratification. And they think they can get away with it." He asked for the *shillelagh* again. As he spoke he waved it as if it were a cudgel, as if he wanted to smack a general or two in the head and holler at them, *What were you thinking?!*

"They have violated their oath of office. I need someone to help me build a case against them so I can fire them. I need proof. Their position in the Marine Corps insulates them from scrutiny. I don't need shitbirds or criminals of any rank leading my Marines." He returned the Irish walking stick to Hunter without comment.

As the CMC laid out his concept of operations, Hunter came to grips with the business before him. He would conduct clandestine investigations of career Marines, rapacious men who couldn't resist the challenge of bedding the good-looking wife of another Marine or engaging in an illegal relationship with an enlisted woman or a junior officer. He learned there were dozens of cases that came in via the Marine Corps Hotline. Little brushfires in virtually every corner of the Corps. The Commandant had turned him into a detective. Hunter would use his camera with a motor drive and telephoto lenses to shoot pictures. He would take statements from cuckolded husbands or adulterous wives so the CMC could build prosecutable cases.

In less than a year, Hunter had gone from being the ultimate phallic symbol—slim, trim Marine fighter pilot—to being what he now considered himself, just a dick. A bedroom dick.

The CMC said, "In the big scheme of things, a single photograph of the officer entering or leaving a motel or other rendezvous place will induce most generals and colonels to resign. It'll be important that those who are photographed be recognizable with discriminating features. A picture of a general's ass between some woman's legs will not cut it as evidence." He held up his wrist. "You're not a general if you're not wearing an expensive watch. Most generals have one of these; expensive, rare. You know we may not wear jewelry, but these watches are exactly that, expensive functional jewelry. If you had to identify me from a photo, you would know me from *this*. I know you know watches; most of the generals also have a thing for them."

"Sir, you're saying they might have a *blind spot....*"

"Your knowledge and affinity for them is a little...." *Over the top....maybe? But for a PhD candidate who is wired differently, maybe not.*

Hunter nodded at the compliment and said, "Yes, sir." *Makes absolute sense.* He had the right lenses for those types of photographs in his apartment. *I can barely lift this cane. How am I going to lift my camera with a motor drive and telephoto lens? I'll break my arms! I hurt everywhere. I'm in horrible shape.*

The Commandant explained he had inherited the headache from the former CMC who had been weak and uninterested in punishing the bad behavior of his general officers. As long as they hadn't been caught or brought discredit to the Marine Corps, the former CMC's policy had been "hands off." The CMC lamented that many of the colonels and generals suspected of wrongdoing chased the wives of Marines they had sent on deployment. "They are, thankfully, few in number, but those assholes just piss me off," the CMC hissed.

Hunter was shocked at what the CMC said next. "There was the death of an enlisted woman Marine who served as a driver for a major general, a ground officer. I think he had been fooling around with her, and one night she was found dead in her apartment. No one wanted to interview the general. He had an ironclad alibi—he had been at an all-day official function when the WM was found. The authorities wanted to close the case. He wasn't a suspect because he was a general. They botched that investigation because another of his drivers, another WM, had died earlier and he had an ironclad alibi for that one too. My advantage is that I know these guys; I know who is a solid citizen and rock-solid patriot, and I know who has a personality disorder." *Maybe even a sexual disorder....*

He couldn't utter the words, "I could see a Marine general killing an enlisted Marine for sex." Hunter raised a sickly finger. "The Marine Corps has done a good job of keeping those guys out of uniform, the personality disorders, sexual identity disorders, but I know a few have been able to sneak in here and there. They can disrupt the good order and discipline of the Corps. If Congress ever changes the law, DOD will be in for more *bat guano*, more unnecessary distractions than it could ever imagine. And we'll see an increase in suicides. Personality and sexual disorders have the highest rates of suicide on the planet, and that rate is about forty percent. If they are allowed to enlist, the Marine Corps will experience forever increasing numbers of suicides and there will be nothing the CMC can do about it."

What a curious and stunning observation. The CMC took a moment to process the brilliance of what Captain Hunter had said. After a full minute of reflection, he said, "I will be on the lookout for that. Back to my COs and generals; they have demonstrated that they're not trustworthy. They're more interested in committing adultery or fraternization than taking care of Marines. When they bed a subordinate, the relationship is exploitive by definition; it violates common sense, Marine Corps policy, and the Uniform Code of Military Justice. A sleazy politician might use the 'consenting adult' defense, but that excuse will not pass muster with me."

"It sickens me to think we could also have a possible murderer in our ranks; that he has used the inherent power of his rank and position to commit a crime and be absolved of it." The CMC clasped his hands and leaned forward. "Just as I know you, Duncan, I know these guys. I wasn't involved in the decision of promoting them, but I'm now in the position of removing them from our Corps. We have an incomparable reputation...." *And they have tarnished every scrap of cloth, from their uniforms to their fender flags. They must have slept through ethics classes at Annapolis.* Unconsciously, the CMC rapped his USNA ring on the arm of his chair.

Hunter glanced at the ring knocker's gold ring and offered, "Fifty battle streamers...."

The comment made the CMC grin. *He knows his history.* He continued, "...and I would like us to keep that reputation. These are not special *operations* with a cast of dozens or hundreds, but special...*activities*. A one-man show. And you've always been more effective as a one-man show."

Hunter nodded; the general was all transmit, he was all receive. And then the meeting was over. As they said their goodbyes and shook hands, the CMC pressed a blood-red enameled Commandant of the Marine Corps challenge coin into Hunter's hand. *That's new!*

As directed, he stopped at the Office of the Inspector General for additional instructions. The one-star general greeted Hunter warmly and commanded, "You must check the Comm Center daily for any 'Personal For' messages. You'll be given a special coded address for message traffic, and a letter signed by the Commandant. Only you and the CMC have that special address. I won't know your identity for P-4 purposes; it will be known only to the Commandant. You'll present the CMC's letter at the Comm Center to get your P-4. Expect coded language; I will provide a key you must memorize. You need to remain at the Comm Center until they shred your P-4. TAD orders will come through official channels within a batch of other orders from Headquarters Marine Corps. To inform you of the subject Marine,

Federal Express or UPS envelopes will come from anonymous addresses." Hunter nodded, formally thanked the IG with a handshake, no salute, and left the office with another challenge coin—beautiful Marine Corps emblem on one side, five-sided, gold and black—from the Office of the IG—on the other.

The IG hadn't mentioned their previous relationship, that Hunter had played racquetball with him before he was the IG, although always on opposite sides. *Well, that's how I remember him; directive, no-nonsense, get-in, get-the-hell out of my office kind of guy. I'm sure he remembers getting his ass whacked. Glad I never hit him with a ball. I could still beat his ass on a racquetball court. Oh, how I wish….*

On the way out of the Pentagon, Hunter let his mind wander. *Why did some generals and colonels perform their responsibilities perfectly while others abused the power of their office in various ways? Could it indicate their political leanings?* Hunter was reminded of what the CMC had said: "…they may have a personality disorder." Maybe there would be answers in one of his reference books, the *Diagnostic and Statistics Manual for Mental Disorders*, the "DSM," the definitive publication for the classification of mental disorders published by the American Psychiatric Association (APA). Then again, maybe not. *General officers are political animals. Was there a connection between one's political views and a position in one category of the DSM? Is there a link between undesirable political behaviors and those sexual rapacious behaviors associated with some mental illnesses? Good God, Hunter get a grip on yourself! There will be time for this later!*

Learning new or complex information never threatened Hunter as he studied psychology and the DSM and its many categories of personality and sexual disorders researching who commits aviation terrorism and why. Islamic hijackers, bombers, and other evil men hell-bent on destroying aircraft in the name of a religion obviously had mental disorders; the trick was to determine which one. And Islamists had a counterview to established politics. He had been in the Marine Corps sixteen years and had only recently learned of the terms "personality and sexual identity disorders" in a graduate school class he had taken while flat on his back in the hospital. It opened his eyes to other classifications of human behaviors, men who were preoccupied with the conquest of women, wealth, sports, ...murder.

He had seen that specific nature—being preoccupied with the conquest—in some senior officers he played racquetball with, some of the many he always beat. Hunter didn't live and breathe racquetball, but *they* did. After one encounter with a dynamic Navy commander, another USNA ring knocker, the commander's secretary had called him and asked in a whisper, "What did you do to him? He went into his office, closed the door, and cried." He chuckled, "He just had a bad day at his *other* office. In his heyday, he was unstoppable. But now there's a new kid on the block. I found out what it takes to beat him, and now he knows he'll never win another game from me."

Finding an elevator to the ground floor, he wondered if the men involved with mass shootings could also be classified with diagnosed or undiagnosed personality disorders or both. *Might that explain why they do it? Would explain much. I'll have my hands full dealing with sexual predators. Trying to figure out why mass murderers commit mass murder is a subject for another day....* His earlier question, *"What am I going to do"* had been answered.

After turning in his visitor's badge, the Commandant's driver, a male Marine sergeant, took him to Washington National Airport. On the way traffic was diverted for a group of protesters. Hunter leaned forward to see what all the commotion was about. The driver apologized. "Sir, I'm so sorry—I thought these protesters would be out of the area by now."

Hunter asked, "Who are they, and what are they protesting?"

The driver didn't respond as a police officer vigorously directed the military staff car to go around the block to avoid the protesting group. Hunter saw the signs as they turned and had his answer. They were protesting the American Psychiatric Association, who were apparently hiding inside the Crystal City Marriott Hotel. *I was just thinking about the APA!* Virtually every protester held the same red signs with white letters: DOWN WITH APA! DSM IS UNFAIR! HOMOSEXUALITY IS NOT A DISORDER! Hunter wondered if he was imagining things; he thought he saw a small white fist with

CPUSA painted in a lower corner. Three minutes later the CMC's driver had Hunter at the National Airport Departure Terminal.

Hunter was in such pain that he refused to take the military flight back to the west coast and paid for a first class ticket to Arizona. He convinced himself that he needed the hip-room and legroom the expensive seat at the front of the jet afforded. His seat mate was a professional woman in a dark business suit. She could have been a lawyer or a politician. Shortly after taking off, she introduced herself as a federal judge and asked, "Are you a conservative?" Hunter struggled to answer the question. He wasn't political. At least he didn't think he was political, and before he could utter a response, she said, "Conservative lawyers, senators, and congressmen wear that type of Rolex almost exclusively."

Hunter acknowledged her observation, and they discussed politics, working their way backward through the years. Didn't the Democrat president blow the Iranian situation? America should've never deserted the Shah or let the Ayatollah Khomeini into the country of Iran. Wasn't his foreign policy an unmitigated disaster; it was as if it had been torn from the pages of the *Communist Manifesto*? "Like what Lenin did to Europe, Khomeini said he was going to 'fundamentally transform Iran, Islam, and the Middle East.' He was going to return Islam to its roots. He raided the Iranian treasury and funded anti-Westernization, terrorism, and unrest in the Middle East. Iran is the number one sponsor of terrorism in the world." He listened to the sound of his voice and wondered, *Where did that come from?*

He had paid little attention to politics but held some strong views culled from his readings. "...so not making excuses for a Democrat president, I guess that makes me a conservative." He removed the *Submariner* from his wrist and gave it to the judge. She appeared to be impressed. She said it was heavier than she thought, and it was *pretty*. Hunter didn't think his Rolex was pretty; it was *manly*. *What would she have said if I had worn the Daytona?*

When he arrived in Phoenix, he rented a car. Hunter would take his time checking back into the squadron at Marine Corps Air Station Yuma. He had annual leave to burn.

Near the conclusion of his month-long leave, Captain Hunter received a phone call at his apartment. An admin clerk asked him if he was aware of the message traffic notifying the squadron that Captain Hunter had been assigned a temporary additional duty, TAD, to California. When Hunter hung up the telephone, the doorbell rang. A Federal Express courier handed him a distinctly purple and orange envelope and a dark brown and white DHL box. He put the envelope and the box on the table and still using the *shillelagh* for a cane, went out to collect his mail and newspaper. He checked the newspaper; the headlines read, *Marine Leader Orders Women to Flight School.* Hunter laughed all the way back to his apartment.

Inside, the Federal Express envelope beckoned, but he opened the box first. His Rolex *Daytona* had been repaired and it looked as perfect as the day it had been presented to a special man in a group of patriots in Florida. The Rolex factory had included a new cherry wood presentation box and a green outer box for the watch, with letters, certifications, and photographs attesting its special provenance. Hunter was relieved to have his watch back, but it gave him new concerns. *It's a dazzling watch....and it's not just any watch. I can't wear this. It is too rare to wear. It has to go into my safe deposit box*. He set the *Daytona* aside and ripped the tab off the envelope. He extracted two sheets of paper. After decrypting the contents, he held a general's biography and a copy of the original HQMC Hotline complaint. The general was stationed at Camp Pendleton.

Captain Duncan Hunter sighed heavily and shook his head. He had his first assignment. He had worked hard and received the ultimate gift in being able to fly the F-4 Phantom, the aircraft of his childhood dreams. He knew he would have to pay for all that joy one day. Playing Sam Spade, apparently, would be the payback.

CHAPTER 4

November 3, 1992

The Operations Duty Officer (ODO) confirmed to the former Squadron Executive Officer (XO) that there would be a new president come January. The Democrat Party candidate for president had defeated the incumbent Republican and won the election. The ODO turned off the television in the corner of the Weather Shop, turned to make a comment on the election only to find the outgoing XO had disappeared without a word.

The door of the S-1, the squadron Administration Office, was open and the inside was lit up like it was open for business. It was, but it wasn't, as the time on deck was 2000 hours, about four hours before night operations ceased for the evening. The well-built man in black nylon shorts walked in with a backpack, an armload of books, and a towel draped over his shoulder. Several of the Admin troops greeted the former XO warmly; he returned the courtesy with a wave. Their eyes dropped to the scars on his legs, especially the long jagged Achilles repair, the album tracks of surgeries that had been necessary to save life and limbs.

The opening riff of a ZZ Top song filled the room; an unseen hand turned down the volume of the unseen radio. An officer was "on deck."

She's got legs, she knows how to use them....

Captain Drue Duncan Hunter appreciated the music. *She's probably here. If she is, she'll show up soon enough – she's got my stuff! And I need a distraction. A new president means they have fatally wounded the Boy Scouts, gays in the military, and some vets will lose their Second Amendment rights. The Republicans were supposed to win, meaning the Democrats probably cheated, but those things are outside my purview.* Hunter wasn't happy, how could the Republican lose, but he did. Hunter knew that once he got to work he would quickly forget the political ramifications of the election. He turned his back to the troops, sloughed off the towel, and dumped it on the secretary's chair in a heap; the rest of his load was dropped on the desk. Hunter fired up her word processor and printer.

This had been his evening ritual for a couple of weeks and tonight was the last time Captain Duncan Hunter, the doctoral candidate, hours from military retirement, would use the commanding officer's secretary's government-furnished antique computer system. He would make final corrections to his dissertation, print a turn-in copy using one of the first Xerox laser printers he had ever seen, and save a copy on an 8-inch floppy disk. *The technology is moving so fast, but not us, everyone else is on 3½-inch floppies! Typical Marine Corps. We are still in the Stone Age.*

After wiping his face with his towel, he withdrew the two-inch thick final draft with a hundred colorful Post-it notes from the backpack. He looked at the title one last time. *Terrorists Will Target United States Airports and Aircraft, and We Are Not Prepared.*

For aviation aficionados and policy wonks, Hunter's treatise wasn't a good news story. He argued that near the turn of the century, Islamic fundamentalists would infiltrate airports, specifically airport security. Within a few years they would help other radical Muslims bomb or smuggle weapons into airports in order to highjack commercial airliners and fly them into government or major financial buildings or crash them into the ocean. His main solution was to federalize airport security and to polygraph all airport security workers. And to help finance the increased cost of securing the nation's aviation transportation system, a passenger fee should be imposed on every ticket.

The university review committee believed Hunter's paper to be more offensive than the capstone of his academic education; he looked at his paper as a warning that no one would take seriously, but one review committee member indicated it should become a classified document. The review committee looked at it as controversial and politically incorrect but still approved it by the slimmest of margins, one vote. He wanted to scream, *When are the law, the facts, and the truth considered controversial? They are only controversial to criminals!*

Academia might think his concepts and designs were controversial but how could the airlines and the airport security firms? The American Association of Airport Executives? The FBI? It had become more apparent that his dissertation was an exercise in futility.

Besides polygraphing airport security workers, Hunter had designed some schemes to detect and stop explosives and biological hazards in luggage and prevent them from going onto an airliner. A patent attorney took Hunter's money, the applications, and a dozen more concepts. Patents were awarded. Some were pending. Some money flowed into his bank account. The letter to the patent attorney just needed to be printed, signed, and sent with his latest prototype patent drawings and applications.

Whatever his research found, it would never get into the hands of the "right people." Not the FAA or the FBI or the CIA. Those who sighted UFOs or had a close encounter of the third kind or those who questioned the government's mythical weather modification research—what the clinically paranoid called *chemtrails*—had a better chance of having their papers critically reviewed by the authorities. The media listened to freak shows. Hunter had resigned himself to look at his opus as just the final requirement, the last stop on the road to say he was a "doctor." The school got their money, and he received a fantastic education. Would he make anything off his degree? Only time would tell.

He would still graduate, be a doctor of philosophy, and go off and do unexciting things like teach, if he was lucky. The economy sucked and would get worse under the new Democrat president.

Hunter was fresh off the air station's racquetball courts and still dripping sweat. He had played more racquetball than he should've on his last day in the Corps, but visiting colonels and a general from the Third Marine Aircraft Wing at the El Toro Marine Corps Air Station requested to see him on the court after hours. One last time. It was more an order than a request. Captain Hunter was somewhat notorious after all, in high demand, and when the most demanding men in the Marine Corps wanted some of his time, Hunter always found time to play "some ball." He sighed. Four years ago, before his accident, he was in such peak physical condition that he wouldn't have even broken a sweat. Now the towel soaked up the perspiration that ran from his head, and his shirt absorbed the rivulets that ran down his chest and back before they pooled in his shorts. The chilled air in the room tightened his nipples. Cliff Richard's *Devil Woman©* cranked up somewhere behind him. *She's just a Devil Woman with evil on her mind....* He knew he would miss one of the best radio stations in America when he left Yuma, and one of the prettiest girls he had ever seen. He would never forget her name.

Captain Hunter had half-hoped the office would be abandoned tonight so he could work without company, but it was not to be. Did it look bad for the former XO to be using government equipment for personal business? Definitely. He had asked his squadron CO for permission and had offered to compensate the government for the use of the equipment. He brought paper, ink cartridges, and floppy disks; whatever he didn't use would be left for the secretary or another graduate student to use. And Hunter had ensured a florist would deliver two dozen yellow roses to the secretary. She was from Texas. She would understand; yellow roses were a "Texas thing."

The CO had rebuffed Hunter's offer, terms and conditions; he said that he owed Captain Hunter much more than a favor. As Executive Officer (XO), Captain Hunter had rewritten the CO's and several other senior officer's official biographies and résumés. The CO approved his request to use the word processor and told Hunter to, "Go ahead. I think it's good for the troops to see you working on your education. It will inspire them to do the same. It wouldn't hurt me to see the Admin Office become a study hall in the evening." That was exactly what happened. The S-1 troops were in college.

The ground shook, but the insulation in the walls kept most of the triple-digit decibels from the fighters in AB blasting into the near triple-digit night air from reaching the Marines inside. Hunter ran to the outside door and opened it. Arizona heat and the sound of two F/A-18s in afterburner assaulted him as he stood and admired the pilots zorching off to one of the restricted areas for night bombing or radar intercept work. The new jets reminded him that his old beloved *Phantoms* were being sent to the "boneyard."

Hunter stood there, arms akimbo, in the flimsy black nylon shorts which once accentuated massive chiseled thighs from fifteen years of tournament racquetball. A ratty, wet, and virtually transparent racquetball shirt from a U.S. Open tournament a decade past stuck to his still wet chest as if it had been spray-painted on. Loose on his wrist, he wore a five-year-old stainless steel and gold Rolex *Submariner* Chronometer. The gold links and bezel shined to a mirror-like finish.

The female Marines in the office watched the Captain Hunter show with all of his affectations and expensive baubles. In the time he had been in the office more than one female Marine bit her bottom lip and curled her toes every time he stood up or sat down. The thick scars on his arms and legs made him appear more rugged than the Marlboro man. The Marines in the office knew he would return inside after the jet noise could no longer be heard or soon after the afterburners were extinguished, no longer needed for takeoff.

As Hunter stood in the doorway he lamented, *Airshows shouldn't be over until the kids got to see the fighters take off at night, so they could admire American engineering and airpower, and the cones of fire from the powerful afterburners that make the ground tremble, and car alarms go off and stop all conversation on the flight line. The stuff that drives the military-hating Democrats insane.* He had once been part of that life. Now all he could do was stare and be grateful to still be alive and living in the greatest country.

The S-1 shop buzzed with the activity of a dozen Marines working late preparing for an inspection by the Wing Inspector General. One Marine corporal had a special task besides her normal duties—to complete the retirement paperwork of one Captain Hunter. From her office mates, she had a nickname: *Legs*. To her officer-in-charge, *Legs* knew how to use them.

While Hunter was an exceptional athlete and one of the smartest officers in the Corps, senior Marine Corps leaders at Headquarters also considered him one of the Corps' most trustworthy and accomplished Marines. A letter from the Commandant of the Marine Corps had been affixed to the front cover of his Officer Qualification record (OQR): "Captain Hunter can be assigned to the most sensitive or difficult of assignments requiring special trust and confidence, at the highest level of discretion and diplomacy. Any questions, contact this office. This letter can only be removed by direction of the Office of the Commandant of the Marine Corps."

The letter's genesis was somewhat of a mystery, but those in the know believed a Marine Corps officer on the National Security Council (NSC) had heard of the racquetball prowess of the fighter pilot and deemed him the perfect candidate to solve a very special problem. Hunter was sent to Washington, the city of monuments, and was ushered into a room in a high-rise in Crystal City where he was asked would he do some work for his country. *They drag me to the other side of the planet to ask me this?* It will be in Cuba. *That's good to know*. The work was voluntary. *Now they tell me.* The Central Intelligence Agency and the Drug Enforcement Agency needed someone unknown to the drug lords to coax a very special target out of hiding. *Now this might be interesting.* Someone at the Agency would equip him with the latest in disguises. He was given a battery of polygraphs. *Now I know what all the secret squirrel stuff is all about.... Oh, who am I kidding, I will know no more than what they tell me.*

The Agencies' concept of operations focused on Hunter eventually playing racquetball with the head of the Medellin Cartel who was expected to visit Havana, Cuba. Over a period of days during the Pan American Games, disguised as a Puerto Rican racquetball champion, Captain Hunter met, played with, and beat the drug lord, and good-naturedly gave him some lessons to improve his shot selection.

As the Pan Am Games were wrapping up, Hunter informed Pablo Escobar that he would soon return to Puerto Rico. Escobar, always surrounded by a dozen men with heavy weapons, insisted on buying all of Hunter's racquetball equipment—racquets, balls, gloves, goggles, shoes. Less than a thousand dollars' worth of equipment traded hands for ten thousand dollars, cash. A homing transmitter had been fitted into the handle of one racquet by the CIA, allowing the Agency, the DEA, and the Colombian National Police to locate the cartel chieftain in Colombia.

At the consummation of the assignment and with a new ribbon for his uniform, a Meritorious Service Medal (MSM), Hunter returned to the aircraft carrier and finished his deployment with his squadron. He would check the newspapers daily to see if the Agency's bait and switch operation ever worked.

CHAPTER 5

November 3, 1992

In the early days of his new assignment, Hunter had been assigned to investigate a two-star and one of the commanding generals on the East Coast. He was the most widely read of the general officers and had a personal library of thousands of books. Before he could begin that investigation, he had been reassigned to investigate a Marine colonel, an extremely difficult case, a high-profile NASA astronaut. Hunter's photos ensured the astronaut would not return to space because the colonel couldn't say no to a pretty young captain.

A year before his accident, Hunter distinctly remembered meeting Major General Bogdan Chernovich. It was during one of his best seasons in competitive racquetball when Hunter won the All Marine Racquetball Championship. Major General Chernovich had been the Commanding General of the Second Marine Division at Camp Lejeune where the tournament was held.

The general had presented Hunter with a trophy and a medal, and then the two-star had asked him about his Rolex *Daytona*. He accused Captain Hunter of wearing a fake, saying, "That is a fine counterfeit." Hunter remembered the general's watch; it wasn't a Rolex. *Maybe it's a TAG or a Breitling GMT. Is the general jealous of my watch? Is the general...did the general...? It's very possible the rumors were true.* The encounter upset Hunter, but he did not respond. He did, however, notice the general's hardened, different colored eyes. He had played racquetball with many general officers and could see that Major General Chernovich was different on hard to define levels. It was inconceivable to think a Marine general could be gay. There must have been another reason Hunter was so affected by the encounter.

What should have been a joyful occasion, was actually perplexing. Hunter recalled several thoughts about the six-foot eight-inch tall general. They mostly had to do with the man being too tall to fit in an ejection seat aircraft which excluded him from pilot training. It was a well-known fact that men who would otherwise have qualified for flight training but were too tall or too short or had bad eyes, always seemed to carry a chip the size of Mt. Rushmore on their shoulders. They quietly hated the men whose average height was a natural advantage. And several Marine ground officers carried their petty jealousies around with them like a voodoo doll and treated aviators with disgust and disdain, ready to jab a needle into a surrogate effigy at any opportunity. Hunter recalled thinking the general could be the tallest person in the Marine Corps and maybe the only one with eyes of different colors.

As he waited for his completed dissertation to print, Hunter let his mind wander to his incomplete investigation of General Chernovich. Hunter knew the law, the Uniform Code of Military Justice, better than most of the regular officers. The Commandant of the Marine Corps trusted him to conduct sensitive investigations into corruption, abuse of power, and fraternization. The assignments had honed not only Hunter's legal skills but his powers of observation. A captain conducting a low-level investigation didn't alert the base leadership like a colonel conducting a high-level investigation. The CMC needed someone who could escape scrutiny and provide photographic evidence. Captains were everywhere on a Marine base; colonels were always surrounded by a brigade of subordinates. Some of them misused the concept of "commander's intent," instead of expressing the desired outcome of a military operation, they expressed the desired outcome of a personal liaison.

A long-time pescatarian and marathoner, the three-star general was the senior Marine in Hawaii. He was a Congressional Medal of Honor winner who was suspected of being a sexual predator. Over several years, many of the general's former drivers had been found dead in their apartments. Hunter had copies of the police reports; the general had airtight alibis. One of his drivers in North Carolina had accidentally taken a fatal dose of tetrahydrozoline, a vasoconstrictor commonly found in over-the-counter eye drops that, when ingested, rendered a person unconscious or to stop the heart. In Hawaii, two of the general's drivers had been attacked by an unknown assailant.

Apparently, only Hunter noticed in the reports that all three had been sodomized.

The lieutenant general's current driver was an alarmingly angelic and leggy married Woman Marine from the administration office of a helicopter squadron at MCAS Kaneohe Bay. Shortly after her new assignment, the woman's husband suspected his wife had been compromised by the lecherous senior officer. He notified the Marine Corps Inspector General.

The IG briefed the CMC on the Hotline complaint, and Hunter was detailed to Hawaii. Hunter interviewed the husband who informed him that he had followed his wife and the general several times. He knew all the motels they used. Hunter took pictures of them together as they entered a secluded motel near Oahu. He tried to photograph of the general's different colored eyes, but the general was too crafty for that. So he took several photographs of what Hunter recognized to be a TAG Heuer *Autavia* GMT on the general's wrist. *Just as briefed. Just as I remembered. A Jochen Rindt Autavia. Named after another race car driver, only Jochen Rindt was killed.*

Duncan Hunter knew a few things about fine watches, and in the viewfinder of his Canon F-1, he recognized the *Autavia* as an original. Hunter would have the photos of the watch and the man's USNA gold ring enlarged, evidence that an academy grad and general officer known to own one of the rarest watches in watchmaking was fraternizing with his driver. It was unlikely anyone else in the Marine Corps had that *Autavia.*

The general obscured his face when entering and leaving the motel, but the combination of photographs of the government vehicle in the hotel parking lot, pictures of the general and his driver entering the vehicle, the general wearing the *Autavia* on his wrist, his USNA ring, and the three silver stars on his Marine Corps shirt collars were damning evidence.

Hunter suspected that the general would poison the driver when he was through with her. But Hunter couldn't determine the mechanics or the logistics of how the general could kill her, sodomize her, and then distance himself from the act. *Killing a person wasn't easy, but it was infinitely easier if you had help. Did he have help? Who could that possibly be?* Hunter didn't like the trajectory of that line of reasoning. *If he had help, who would the general trust enough?*

Hunter recalled that he had been a commanding general's aide-de-camp for about six months and had formed a bond with "his general." He saw "his" two-star as a rock star in Marine Aviation; as the man's aide, there wasn't much Hunter wouldn't do for him. And that was the dilemma. *I wouldn't commit murder for him, but are there others who would have? For what reason? Crap! A personality disorder? Someone loyal, someone with rank? Could a three-star have someone so loyal and dedicated to him that his word could direct a loyal follower to kill someone? Did Lieutenant General Bogdan Chernovich hate women? Was he really gay or was that just a bad vibe on my part? Why would that matter? It matters to a good number of people. I'm sure if the APA hadn't had security that day in Washington, the sexual activists protesting on the ground could have been motivated to get even with a psychiatrist or two by killing them. Crazy people do crazy things sometimes. Why would a gay man have sex with a woman?*

The following day, Hunter followed the general's driver when she left her apartment and drove to work. While General Chernovich was in a series of meetings, she traveled to the Base Exchange. Hunter watched her pick up the general's dry cleaning and some sundries. He followed her into the pharmaceutical aisle, pulled her aside, read her, her rights, and offered her a statement to sign. She was embarrassed, stunned. While she wept, Hunter looked at her shopping basket; at the bottom was a large bottle of Visine. He confiscated the bottle of eye drops and shook it at her, "If asked, say they were out of Visine and all the eyes drops. A *factory recall* or something. Do you understand me, Sergeant? This stuff will kill you if you ingest it. And be assiduous…uh, be very careful of what the general gives you to drink. Accept nothing from him! Your life depends on it. *Do you understand?"* The woman was now scared beyond belief. She nodded her assent.

As an investigating officer, Hunter didn't provide recommendations or interfere with the investigation, he was to provide only findings. Photographs were "findings." But he had just interjected himself into the case. If the general didn't have murder on his mind, nothing would happen. However, if the general had designs on eliminating her, maybe Hunter could save her life. He believed it was a risk worth taking.

It was the purview of the four-stars to punish or relieve the three-star general of command. In his room, Captain Hunter reviewed the Hawaiian police reports of the Woman Marine drivers who had died on the island. The cases were of the open-and-closed variety—the women were strangled and there were plenty of marks on the women's necks, and the medical examiner checked to see if the women had been sexually violated. Hunter couldn't shake what was becoming more obvious to him. *That general is creepy and strange as in I wouldn't ever let him walk my dog. He has rock-solid alibis for the women in Hawaii and North Carolina; but he is the guy. He must have had help. Murder by proxy? That's been going on since the beginning of time. But who and why?*

Before sunup, Captain Hunter's jet lag prompted him to present himself to the Communications Center to see if any messages had come in for him. There was one message—a "Personal For" from HQMC, CMC, transmitted before the sun had risen on the east coast. The line was like others he had seen, but the string of acronyms in the body of the message this time were unlike any others that he had read: CANX ACTS TNFA RTB AFI. He deciphered the message in his head: *CANCEL ACTIVITIES, TAKE NO FURTHER ACTION, RETURN TO BASE, AWAIT FURTHER INSTRUCTIONS.*

He returned the message flimsy and asked the communications clerk to shred the "P-4." The Comm clerk tossed the paper into a shedder and said, "You may not be aware of this, sir, the President announced this morning that the Fleet Marine Force Pacific Commanding General (FMFPAC CG), our Lieutenant General Bogdan Chernovich, will become the new Commandant of the Marine Corps." He proudly held up a copy of the announcement as if it were a trophy. "You know, sir he has a personal library that is as big as a city library."

Hunter remained at the counter, now fully understanding the terseness and directive of the "full-stop" P-4 from HQMC. The Commandant's health had worsened and he could no longer perform his duties. It wouldn't look good if the current CMC relieved his Congressional Medal of Honor-winning replacement for conduct unbecoming a general officer, or for fraternization, or suspected murder. Hunter was stunned and his thoughts ran together. *Marine Corps politics has interfered with my mission. Chernovich graduated number one at the U.S. Naval Academy with an engineering degree in chemistry, a minor in biology; and was selected for a follow-on year at The Harvard Academy for International and Area Studies before being sent to Vietnam, where he would win the nation's highest honor. He's famous for his pithy sayings and how many books he has read and owns. But…but he is as slippery as an eel…. Untouchable, and now the beetle-browed gangster was about to become the next Commandant of the Marine Corps. This is not good, but I cannot do anything about it because I've been told to "stand down."*

Hunter departed the Comm Office in a fog and hobbled to the Travel Office to arrange his return trip to the states. The Travel Office was a hubbub of activity. The FMFPAC CG had just departed for Washington, D.C. Although the general had solid alibis, Hunter felt the general definitely had something to do with the deaths of three women. Three sodomized women. *He's the guy!* The question that needed an immediate answer: was his driver alive? A call from a phone booth to the husband confirmed the wife was alive and well. And talking. Hunter asked to speak to her. He had one question. He told her to answer yes or no—he didn't want her husband to overhear his question. After asking the single simple question, there was a significant pause before she said, "Yes." Hunter was crushed. *Just as I thought. He's the guy!*

The travel office clerk easily secured a seat for Captain Duncan Hunter on an Air Force C-141 *Starlifter* departing Hickam Air Force Base in a few hours. He had one of a dozen unattractive, overly worn, mothball-smelling, reclinable gray seats mounted on a standard 463L pallet in which to park his keister and rest his legs. All passengers' bags were stacked on another pallet under a taut cargo net. Like all C-141s, the inside of the jet had the faint smell of jet fuel and jet exhaust.

Once airborne, Hunter reasoned the FMFPAC CG's former driver and her husband would probably be reassigned stateside, both with promotions and choice assignments to keep them quiet, to keep them from blabbing about the peccadilloes of the Marine Corps' newest four star. He removed the documents he had collected and reviewed them more thoroughly.

Hunter re-read the Oahu police department's reports on the two women. The official cause of death was attributed to criminal activity. They were strangled in their apartments. Hunter had asked if there was an "Oahu Strangler" on the loose; had there been any other murders by strangulation? He banged hundreds of questions around in his head. *Why weren't they living in the barracks? How was it possible for two duty drivers, working for the same guy, to die in the same way? It was assumed the first one was poisoned but there had been no toxicology report. Who sucks on a bottle of eye drops? Was I assuming that the others were also poisoned? Something just isn't making sense. All of his drivers had been sodomized. He had to have had help? Who? Who? The FMFPAC CG's last driver had escaped; she confirmed what I suspected; the general only engaged in anal sex.* After several minutes of pondering the obvious, he reached back into time and discovered something ominous. *There are cults; Charles Manson, Jim Jones. Destructive cults? Where you have charismatic leaders corrupted by power? Some people would do anything for their master. Even kill.*

Hunter stepped away from the topic and chose another direction, something he was going to have to face. He knew that he wouldn't be conducting any more investigations of general officers. *What am I going to do now? I guess it is time to quit. Maybe there is still hope. Maybe if I won the lottery and could buy an old fighter…like that's going to happen.*

He had made a lot of money on his patents and quickly dismissed buying and flying general aviation airplanes. Once you've flown a jet faster than a bullet or been shot off the pointy-end of an aircraft carrier, Hunter knew it would be impossible for him to enjoy flying slower than dirt in a general aviation aircraft. *General aviation aircraft are the cars of the sky and are never offensive weapons. That is the purview of the military…and maybe the intelligence community. Isn't Air America dead? Killed off by the left?*

Upon landing at Norton Air Force Base, a place he knew well, he found lodging at the visiting officers' quarters. At first light, he walked to the Base Exchange and had a roll of film processed in one hour. Two sets of 8 x 10 glossies took nearly all of his cash. There was a copy machine inside the AAFES and he made ten-cent copies of all the documents he had accumulated on General Chernovich.

As he milled about the Exchange waiting for his film to develop, immediately behind him were two large book and magazine racks, overstuffed with hundreds of magazines and paperbacks; his eyes locked on the one magazine with Lieutenant General Chernovich's picture on the cover. He had heard of *The Eastern*, an American version of the British *Socialist Review*, with a white-on-red banner like *The Economist*, but Hunter rarely got past the inside the cover before returning it to the rack. Both magazines had a pronounced editorial stance for socialism and claimed to have little reporting bias, but the reporting was anything but fair and balanced.

Hunter was struck by the incongruity. *Why was General Chernovich on the cover of* The Eastern*? Why was* The Eastern *even available in a Base Exchange? Do they really sell enough of these here? Must be some of that Air Force stuff that I will never understand.*

Out of cash, Hunter used a credit card to buy the new editions of *The Economist, The Eastern*, and the *Socialist Review*. He rarely looked at the socialist rags. He would try to read them, but they were awful magazines. As for research materials, they were destined for the bottom of a wastebasket.

After securing a rental car, he stopped at a UPS outlet on his way out of town. To complete the mission required sending the Chernovich package to HQMC IG. *But the P-4 said to take no further action. Await further instructions.* Hunter was conflicted as he stood in the middle of the shipping establishment.

Take no further action. Await further instructions. Wilco! Hunter left the UPS store without sending the documents. Hunter would safeguard them. *If the new CMC....* Hunter felt strangely radical. He would deposit the documents in a bank vault when he returned to Yuma. *And await further instructions. I'll read about General Chernovich, and maybe I'll learn something more than my assumptions. Some things have a way of resolving themselves.*

• • •

Captain Hunter knew better than to look up at the comings and goings of the pretty twenty-somethings in PT shorts, and especially the twenty-two-year-old administration clerk with the funny first name, shocking violet eyes, the face of a young Liz Taylor, and the loveliest legs in the universe. Tiny ankles, muscular calves, and *length,* there was a reason she was called "Legs" by the other Marines in the Admin Office. The nickname absolutely fit.

Hunter had seen thousands of lovely legs; strong, long, shapely, smooth and curvy women's legs on basketball, tennis, and racquetball courts. Mention "Legs" and the men and women of the air station knew of the leggy corporal with probably the most hypnotic legs on the base. Nylons were required with the uniform, but she often went without pantyhose, much to the delight of her admirers.

Other than the aluminum wings of an F-4 Phantom under a high August sun, nothing on Marine Corps Air Station Yuma was hotter than the corporal in the Admin Office with the unusual name. Corporal Saoirse (SIR-sha) Nobley, in her form-fitted uniform, with splashes of *Giorgio* perfume strategically placed behind her ears and the cleft of her breasts, inflamed the desires of most of the male Marines on the base and drew approving and heaving sighs of admiration from some of the women. The smoky-voiced blonde always overshadowed the other Women Marines with her cool demeanor and statuesque beauty. Her winsome looks had furrowed the brows and dropped the jaws of men and women beginning when she turned thirteen.

• • •

At an Iowa Pizza Hut a brood of prepubescent sisters of increasing height excused themselves as they tried to sidle past a heavyset man waiting to pick up an order. They herded to a side room with a dozen different pay-to-play electronic games because their mother had given them each a quarter. The family frequented the establishment, and the female servers gushed over the two redheaded girls, one with green eyes, and one with iceberg blue eyes.

But the girl with the curly Irish blonde hair and eyebrows that seemed to melt into her skin had vibrant violet irises of the likes of Elizabeth Taylor and had stopped the waitresses and the man in their tracks as if she was some new species of beauty. The reaction was always the same wherever the mother took her girls, but that day the man at the counter was stunned by the girl's resemblance to the popular film actress. The mother waited behind him as he stumbled through gratuitous compliments and an introduction. He could not take his eyes off the oldest of the girls, that was until he spun around and fell knee-deep in the scintillating eyes of the mother, Siobhan Nobley. The mother was polite yet proud of her daughters' beauty and Irish names. The man was thrown off balance; his ears weren't working. In a seductively husky voice Siobhan Nobley explained, *Saoirse,* meant "liberty," *Caoimhe,* meant "beautiful," and *Niamh,* meant "bright."

He withdrew a business card from a shirt pocket. "Those are *divine* names, especially when spoken with an Irish accent." The man had never seen bright green eyes like hers, the color of a mamba. He wondered if the woman's green eyes could be from colored contact lenses. The look mother Siobhan Nobley gave him after the New York talent scout gave her his card and made his pitch was nearly as lethal as a bite from the deadly snake. His eyes kept darting to the oldest, Saoirse. A blonde Elizabeth Taylor. Mother Nobley wasn't interested in the man's card or in any of her children being taken from her for the bright lights and fancy Hasselblads of New York City or Hollywood. She told the man, "Your world is the antithesis of what childhood in our society should be; a child being exposed to a world she isn't yet equipped to deal with solely to serve the desires of the men who scheme to be around her. She is too young to know she would lose her liberty and lose her soul. No thank you."

The man had been spanked pretty hard and left with his order without another comment. Siobhan Nobley paid for her pizzas and ushered her girls out of the restaurant.

A mother can tell if her children are handsome or average, and she now faced the fact that her daughters were developing into attractive women. It had happened much too quickly for her desires. Their looks would attract unwanted affection from boys and men. Especially the men. In Ireland when she was growing up, no one could ignore Siobhan for she was also a phenomenal looker. She had fought off the advances of rapacious possessive men for years until she met and married an American Marine Corps helicopter pilot who was on an exchange tour attending the Irish Defence Force Command and Staff School.

After the encounter at the pizzeria, Siobhan Nobley admonished her oldest, "I understand, boys will be boys and girls will be girls, but Saoirse, please understand it will be the men who'll hurt you the most. You have to be very careful and very selective. And we have to get you a better bra."

There is one in every school; a girl that drives the boys and the male faculty wild. The energetic ballet dancer and high school cheerleader from Ottumwa, Iowa, wasn't only eye-candy for males because of her exotic looks and natural athleticism, but also for a quirk in genetics. Store-bought brassieres were insufficient for Saoirse Nobley's "girls," she required multiple spandex-type "sports bras" when she was competing or cheerleading. While Saoirse effortlessly did front and back handsprings, aerial cartwheels, split leaps, and shook her short hair as vigorously as she did her pompoms the men appreciated her legs, but it was her chest that they watched like a jaguar stalking its prey.

Saoirse heeded most of her mother's advice; she told her mother that she would know the right man for her when she saw him, and that he would be a fine man like her father. The farm boys throwing hay bales and driving tractors or working at the co-op weren't on her radar. She kept secret that she was interested in Marine Corps pilots, like her father. Mother Nobley nearly suffered a stroke when Saoirse announced that she had enlisted in the Marine Corps. She was deferring college and was leaving for Parris Island after graduation.

CHAPTER 6

November 3, 1992

As the printer slowly spooled off perfectly printed pages, Hunter stood, stretched, and turned around. He asked if anyone had today's edition of the *Yuma Daily Sun* newspaper. One of the male Marines did and brought it to Hunter. The front-page headline below the fold read *Former Marine Corps Commandant Dies.* The short article detailed how the CMC, General Bogdan Chernovich, had tried to save the life of his predecessor, giving him cardiopulmonary resuscitation. Hunter had heard of the former CMC's untimely demise and found it suspicious, simply because it happened in proximity to General Chernovich. He returned the newspaper to its owner.

At the secretary's station, he retrieved his backpack from the floor and removed a copy of *The Eastern* magazine with General Chernovich's picture on the front celebrating his rise to the Marines' top job. Looking at the cover of *The Eastern*, it was hard not to see evil in the face of the stoic, hardscrabble, Marine general. *What could have happened to the CMC? I knew he had been sick. I may never know.*

He returned *The Eastern* to his bag and plopped in his seat wondering, *How did the CMC actually die? I would love to see the toxicology report. Did he have tetrahydrozoline hydrochloride in his system? It's a vasoconstrictor and the former CMC had health issues.*

Images of living and dead commandants were pushed aside as Hunter's eyes swept the room and for a fleeting second, locked on the wide-eyed purple pools of passion of Corporal Nobley. His feelings for her were way out of line but he needed a distraction from thinking how the former Commandant had died. She was definitely a distraction.

Was he obsessed? No; he was too old for that, but everything about Nobley thrilled him. Her legs, her eyes, her "girls" under a PT shirt that was insufficiently covering her assets.

If anyone had gotten past first base with her, that news would've been all over the air station, and Hunter would have known it. Sifting through and assimilating salacious news bouncing around base was one of his fortes. Locker rooms where the men talked and the Base Exchange cafeterias where women shared coffee with confidants were goldmines of information. In his investigations of sexual predators Hunter found it essential to discover the predator's habits. The classic predator leveraged intrinsic power, the significant difference in their ranks, to compromise their targets. Businessmen and men of power had been doing it for centuries. Like the frequent "love interests" of Captain Louis Renault, the Prefect of Police in the movie *Casablanca,* these victims had never encountered such brazenness and power.

Those commanding officers who relished the thrill, those that chased wives or subordinates, were so preoccupied with the conquest that they ignored how clumsy and ignorant they had become in leaving clues to their actions all over the base. Evidence of such lasciviousness was grounds for termination, and Hunter had become an expert on documenting such evidence.

Sometimes even the most disciplined commander let his guard down for an especially attractive Woman Marine. Hunter wasn't surprised when the Base Commanding Officer in Yuma—the only officer on base to warrant a duty driver—had tried subtle ways to get Corporal Nobley to be his official driver. The temporary additional duty would likely have meant a promotion for her. But with knowledge of how some senior officers set or baited the trap, Hunter knew the high-visibility, special-assignment was a very bad idea, and he said so in a closed-door meeting with Nobley's officer-in-charge.

There was more to Saoirse Nobley than a shocking resemblance to the sixteen-year-old actress from the movie thriller, *Conspirator!* Like Liz Taylor, Nobley was shockingly enthralling and glamourous, with her eyes on an older man in uniform. She was *something*; wonderful to look at but to be entirely avoided.

Hunter acknowledged that after he retired, there would probably be some colonel in the rotation who would find ways of reassigning the leggy Nobley, make her a driver, promote her, find ways of making her wear a skirt for the Uniform of the Day. But the Air Station COs wouldn't kill their leggy female drivers. Chernovich was unique and Hunter didn't want Nobley anywhere near him. For the moment, she was safe from a rapacious colonel in Yuma.

Some day there would be someone of sufficient stature or power to turn Nobley's head, a pilot or other officer. He had seen it before. Someone somewhere would relish the sexual joys and intimate explorations of youth. But not him. Getting close to her would be like approaching the edge of a volcano. He had lived through an ejection and that was enough. Pilots were not issued nine lives.

He reminded himself that while Saoirse Nobley was an eyeful, it was best to remember her as *Just the perfect girl…the girl everyone wants but no one can have. If only I was fifteen years younger; but if I were fifteen years younger, and not wearing pilot wings she would have ignored me, just like she ignores all the boys in the Admin Shop*. Introspection forced him to consider the men he had effectively forced out of the Corps, two score over three years he investigated senior male Marines who couldn't control their passions when they encountered their local version of Corporal Nobley.

As the printer slowly spit pages, he lowered his head and glanced at her under his brows like the pasty-white creep from *A Clockwork Orange*. She wouldn't break his heart now, nor when he retired. He was getting old, as if 39 could be considered "old." Besides, his heart had long been broken by an Air Force pilot and that shattered heart hadn't ever fully mended. With the printer tray slowly filling up, he closed his eyes and remembered the one who made his heart beat out of his chest like a cartoon character in love.

Some of the admin troops stopped on their way out of the office and shook Hunter's hand one last time, wished him good luck on his new life. Hunter said, "It's a good time to leave. I think this new president will not be good for the Marine Corps. I think you have to ask *why* he is so hell bent on having gays in the military. I do not trust his motives." There was vigorous agreement from the troops. One lance corporal asked why there would be a problem.

Now you stepped in it. Hunter frowned at himself and said, "You may not know that all of you were screened for a personality disorder during your entrance physical. You are here because you don't have a personality or a sexual disorder. We have a thing called the *Diagnostic and Statistics Manual for Mental Disorders.* We call it the DSM. So what is this DSM, really? You are healthy males and females; you are probably naturally preoccupied with members of the opposite sex if you are not thinking about work. But the people of the DSM are likely to be *clinically preoccupied* with members of the same sex, they question their own sex, they want to be another sex, or have sex with animals or children or car parts. There are some *personality* disorders, like aggressive or destructive behaviors. The interesting thing about the people in the DSM is their documented suicide rate is off the charts crazy." Hunter pointed at the group, "You guys *are* normal. You do not give suicide a thought, and *most* of those in the DSM are obsessed with it. They are *not* normal."

"So the Marine Corps and DOD, and places like the CIA, our leaders use the DSM and medical interviews to identify personality or sexual disorders from entering the military. I don't think you want someone who is preoccupied with killing himself or is confused about which head to use to be your airline pilot. Reasonable people don't want *them* driving jets or submarines or aircraft carriers; you wouldn't want them in our intelligence communities. They have a history of stealing secrets for the Soviet Union. Those kinds of things."

Vigorous head nodding interrupted the rapt attention of the troops in the office. Hunter continued. "So now we are going to have a president who doesn't see any problem with gays, with their super high suicide rate, in the military. The Democrat Party will change the definition of 'protected classes,' like Native Americans or African Americans, to include something like 'sexual orientation.' Then they will redefine 'discrimination,' attack the Boy Scouts and force them, through the courts, to hire homosexual men as scoutmasters. This will be like putting pedophiles in charge of day care centers. It is a cultural time bomb and lawsuits will follow. The Christian Boy Scouts will go bankrupt, and the political left will turn to their next targets, women and veterans. All vets will be designated to have post-traumatic stress disorder (PTSD) and cannot be trusted with weapons. The girls will have boys who may or may not want to be girls but demand access to women's locker rooms and dressing rooms."

It was so quiet in the Admin shop, all anyone could hear was the air handling unit pushing cold air into the room. One by one, the Admin Marines shook Hunter's hand and were out the door. Hunter returned to his seat.

As the clock approached 2200, the last of the admin troops working late had gone home for the evening, with one exception.

Every few seconds Corporal Nobley would gaze at the back of the captain sitting in front of the monitor of the secretary's word processor. Her heart raced like a thoroughbred at the starting gate. She was forever being lost in a string of ever-increasing explicit fantasies with Captain Hunter.

She remembered the first time she had seen him, how he had captured her heart. Newly assigned Captain Hunter had stopped in front of her desk to begin the check-in procedure. Then Private First Class Nobley looked up and found the most sensational man she had ever seen standing in front of her. And he wore the gold wings of an aviator. She instinctively pushed from her desk, tilting her chair and began to fall backwards. Years of honing lightning-quick reflexes and anticipating the location of fast-moving objects, Hunter reacted instantly, dove across the desk, and caught Nobley's flaying arms before she toppled backwards and cracked her head on the floor.

Every eye in the S-1 was transfixed at the sight of a Marine captain sprawled across the desk of one of the most remarkably fetching admin clerks the Marine Corps ever had in uniform. He held her arms in a death grip. They weren't sure how, but everyone in the Admin Office knew that the captain had saved Private First Class Nobley from harm. Captain Hunter slowly pulled her to him, which righted her chair. When the chair's four legs returned to *terra firma,* the two Marines were almost *beak-to-beak,* another old briefing descriptor from the obsolete fighter pilot.

His skin tingled, maybe from the adrenaline spike or maybe from reinjuring surgically repaired muscles, or maybe from the sudden proximity of the girl with the familiar perfume. Maybe it was his common sense leaving his body. Except for handshakes, he hadn't touched a woman since the last time he and his Air Force love had spent a long weekend at a castle in Ireland.

It had happened so fast that Nobley couldn't speak; she was mortified. But after a few seconds she smiled and flashed her dimples. Her scent filled his heaving lungs. *Kimberly's perfume!* Hunter grinned like an old fool who might had just slipped a disc as he slowly backed away from the dangerous lips and inviting violaceous eyes of the PFC and slowly climbed off the desk.

As Captain Hunter's toes touched the floor, he glanced at her nametag and her rank on her shoulder and said, "Well, PFC *Nobley*, this is another fine mess you've gotten us into." She hadn't expected that deep bass voice. His words snapped the tension like a number two pencil under pressure, and the office broke up in laughter and applause. The commanding officer poked his head out of his office to see what all the commotion was about—it was just the incoming XO standing in front of one his admin clerk's desk. The CO's secretary returned to pounding on her IBM Selectric.

Hunter was acutely aware he had likely traumatized his old injuries, but looking into the girl's face and her atypical eyes made him momentarily dismiss the pain. An hour on the massage table, a couple of thousand milligrams of aspirin, and a good book would help him achieve much needed relief and ataraxy.

For days on end, PFC Nobley and her friends in the S-1 shop talked about the good-looking captain with the supreme reflexes. She had also seen the stack of ribbons on his uniform. Under Naval Aviator wings of gold, the one on top that stuck out, the pink and white-trimmed Meritorious Service Medal (MSM) had a gold star and the number 4. She looked at his OQR and saw multiple MSM awards with dates and signatures and the following entry for each: Citation classified, contact CMC Code 1A in writing for details.

Nobley mentioned to her friends the card stapled to the face of his OQR. It was most unusual and a source of bewilderment and some questions. Did the Commandant of the Marine Corps really write and sign that? Why was the good looking XO always going on temporary additional duty (TAD)? Basically, if he wasn't on TAD, Captain Hunter hung out at the gym, the library, and education center. Word around the base was he didn't have a girlfriend; no one had ever seen him in town on a date. He was a good looking man and there were the stirrings of rumors. But he had a Rolex, one of the expensive strange colored ones. No one had really gotten a good look at it but the consensus was that it wasn't a watch worn by gay men.

Corporal Nobley typed up Captain Hunter's TAD orders virtually every month, orders that came directly from Headquarters Marine Corps. Multiple MSMs, classified citations, and TADs by direction of the CMC got the squadron CO's attention. He asked the Admin Officer to run the last three years of Captain Hunter's official travel from the Unit Diary. The commanding officer scanned copies of the Navy Times to see if there was a correlation between actions which were approved by the public affairs office and Hunter's travel, but that proved to be too broad a search.

On a hunch, the CO looked at the last set of orders from HQMC that had taken Captain Hunter to Hawaii for about two weeks. After Captain Hunter completed the TAD he immediately submitted his retirement papers. Seeking some answers the CO flipped through more copies of the *Navy Times* until he found what he was looking for. He went through the stack of *Navy Times* on his desk. He annotated the date of the articles when a general or a senior officer had been relieved and from what duty station. He compared the list to a readout of Hunter's TADs and realized what Captain Hunter had been doing for the old CMC. The word on the street months ago was that the former Commandant could no longer manage his health issues and would step down from his office as soon as a new Commandant could be named.

Maverick was no mere former fighter pilot, he was a real live private investigator, a Phillip Marlowe in Service Charlies. Every time Hunter had returned from TAD, with one recent exception, a Marine colonel or general retired, was removed from command, or relinquished command earlier than scheduled. The exception was

Hunter's last temporary assigned duty. The day the FMFPAC CG in Hawaii was named the new Commandant was the same day Hunter terminated his TAD and departed Hawaii. And when Hunter returned to Yuma, he submitted his papers to retire. There had been no more CMC-directed TAD orders. There would be no more TADs.

These are no mere coincidences. Maybe that's why the generals are so nice to him! But the only general officer movement in Hawaii while Hunter was there was General Chernovich.... He checked and double-checked the dates. He looked up at a blank spot on the office wall. *That cannot be possible! Was there an underground war between the former CMC and his generals? And...and...like a sleeper inside agent, was Hunter used to collect...detrimental information in order to flush COs and generals from the Marines? What could they have done? Oh, yeah. I know. Fraternization. I heard rumors some colonels and generals could not keep their hands off the young wives of Marines on deployment.*

What to do about it? Probably the best thing is to let Hunter get out of the Marines as quick as possible. If the new Commandant knows he was the subject of an investigation, it makes me wonder if he plans some revenge. It makes me wonder if Hunter has something on Chernovich; to keep him from getting killed. That lad is playing with fire.

CHAPTER 7

November 3, 1992

Captain Hunter leaned back in the chair and gazed at the light-green walls with perfectly framed lithographs of 200 years of Marine Corps uniforms. It was sinking in. He was going to miss the Marine Corps. The star over his head had flamed out, not in supernova fashion but as if someone had cut the gas to a pilot light. A new Commandant had been installed in Washington, D.C. One general had escaped him and that general was now the guy in charge. Hunter was no longer wanted or needed, and after considering the possibilities, it was not a good idea to stick around. Immediately after the new CMC assumed office, the letter on the cover of Captain Hunter's OQR had been removed, and another officer was now captain the Marine Corps' racquetball team, per Headquarters Marine Corps directives.

At 2300, Corporal Nobley entered the office with a burger and a drink. Hunter wondered how she could've gotten food at such a late hour and then remembered, *night flying*. All the eat joints on the air station remained opened until the squadrons ceased night flight ops. *Maybe Godfather's Pizza was still delivering*. He called; they were so he ordered his favorite.

She announced that she had finished his retirement paperwork, as promised, and that his discharge had been signed, he was on terminal leave, and technically, he was no longer on active duty. She promised Hunter that she would deliver his "package" as soon as she made copies. He wouldn't have to come by the office at the crack of dawn to check out. He thanked her for the update.

Corporal Nobley had heard through the Admin grapevine that there had been no "hail and farewell" for Captain Hunter; a directive had come from Headquarters. No end of tour award; no presentation plaque for his time in the squadron. The troops in the office figured that was by choice; one more piece of wood would probably get tossed into the trash. Nobley assumed that after he finished printing, he would leave Yuma, and she would never see him again.

She returned to her desk and shuffled through papers as her half-eaten burger got cold. Nobley was convinced that he should have received something for all of his time in the Marines when it finally dawned on her. *He had four when he arrived and now has twelve MSMs! One more won't matter.*

As Nobley returned from making a head call, Hunter stole a quick glance at her legs and noticed how her girls poked against the taught shirt in the chilled air of the building. He wasn't embarrassed for looking, but returned to focus on his work. The newest printer on the market was spitting out pages at a blistering three pages per minute. His little passing daydreams couldn't harm either one of them, as long as he kept them to himself. *She's 22! She's off limits! And you'll be gone before you know it. It is just not safe. Don't be stupid.* A glance at the clock overhead indicated it was near midnight. He was so close to the finish line he could scarcely believe it. *I would be gone but for the printer.*

The stillness of the S-1 was broken as the pizza delivery guy crashed through the door with Hunter's pizza.

After every other admin clerk had left, the pride of Ottumwa slowly approached the secretary's desk. She held Hunter's retirement package, a thick manila folder filled with documents and certificates tight across her chest. It was midnight, flight operations had been terminated, and the operations building would have been shuttered if not for the two Marines still working in the S-1.

She stared at the back of his head, willing him to turn around and look at her. Make her smile. Make her tingle. Nobley's heart was about to jump out of her chest. She was 22 and in love. Duncan Hunter was 39 and hadn't a clue. It could've been a Bogie and Bacall moment only in reverse; Nobley was the pursuer of the older man, the most impressive man she had ever met, the man of her dreams. But he had rebuffed her gentle advances, and now he was leaving. Forever. There wasn't a thing she could do about it short of shredding his paperwork. She believed he was interested in her; he was just too much of a professional to pursue her.

Caught up in his reverie, checking printed page after printed page, Captain Hunter didn't see her in his periphery. He didn't hear Corporal Nobley pick up a chair and move to sit down next to him. Suddenly he inhaled and his lungs filled with *Giorgio*. He closed his eyes for a moment before he became fully cognizant of her presence; could he feel her body radiating heat? Hunter didn't overreact.

The Cars' *You Might Think I'm Crazy©* played on the radio station:

I don't mind you comin' here
And wastin' all my time
'Cause when you're standin' oh so near
I kinda lose my mind.

Hunter exhaled at the song's timing as the last pages of his year-long work fell noiselessly into the printer tray; Hunter turned innocently and smiled at her as a polite reflex. He didn't recognize the trouble that had slithered next to him, like a cobra coiling behind the protective aegis of paper. Being so close, Hunter was grateful she was covering "her girls" behind the manila envelope stuffed with his documents, his military history. He was so distracted, he didn't see what was coming.

His eyes followed Corporal Nobley actions as she placed the thick manila envelope on the corner of the secretary's desk. Then she clutched her hands to her chest; she couldn't get the whispered words out fast enough, although she had practiced what she would say if the moment ever presented itself. "Captain Hunter, you're the most *incredible* man I have ever met!"

It took a second before he fully comprehended what he had heard. *Say again? NO – don't say again!!!* One part of his brain told him to act like he misunderstood what she had said. Another part of his mind said to ignore her. But he had been conditioned to analyze and respond to immediate threats to his environment, and warning bells went off in his head. After flying a jet for years, nothing scared him, but now he was terrified. This wasn't just a dilemma; this was a disaster. He couldn't move. A falling Nobley would've crashed and burned; no superhuman reflexes to save her this time.

The adorable corporal with doe eyes continued. "Every minute of every day, I think of you." Her tremulous sultry resonant voice oozed, *"I want to kiss you before you leave."*

Duncan Hunter made a half-hearted effort to retreat. His eyes darted from hers to the windows and doors. *I'm behind closed doors, in a compromising position, with a creature that's spraying sexuality from a fire hose. They'll take my papers and send me to jail. I'm going to get booted out of the Marine Corps! I'm so totally screwed!*

Hunter put one hand on the envelope on the desk and held up his other hand. Corporal Nobley stopped talking in mid-sentence. He outranked her and she complied with the visual command. Hunter finally regained his composure as he waved his free arm like a coach calling for time-out. As his mind raced, he whispered words that were barely audible but purposeful, "Corporal Nobley…both of us…could be in *serious jeopardy*…if *we* allowed that…. I don't want that happening…to you or me." He pleaded with his eyes, *"Understand?"*

Resignation and failure registered on her face. Nobley dropped her clasped hands into her lap; she was crushed and on the verge of tears. She didn't want to understand. She wanted to kiss him. No, she *wanted* him. She wanted him to take her into his arms and kiss her. They both sat still for a minute, afraid to move.

Hunter suppressed a natural response to take her hand; even that was too dangerous. He lowered his head an inch, his voice an octave, and said in a deep whispering rumble, "Saoirse, I'm sorry. Please understand…I'm not… *rejecting* you…." His mind was back in a jet, life was a blur racing ten feet over the ground at ten miles a minute. "It's just that…*this isn't the time…or the place.*" An uncomfortable silence stretched between them for several seconds until the radio blared the refrain from The Talking Heads' *Life in Wartime*©:

This ain't no party, this ain't no disco
This ain't no fooling around
I'd love to hold you, I'd like to kiss you
But I ain't got no time for that….

They both heard those timely words. A smile emerged from her; a dimple appeared and faded. The music trailed off to a commercial. His words came more quickly. "There is a bank of windows behind me; there could be a hundred people looking into this office at this very moment just waiting for the opportunity to catch us alone; an officer and a beautiful girl, alone. They would all be witnesses at our courts martial." *At least at my court martial!*

He's not saying no.... Her bright violet eyes darted to the string of double panes. When her eyes met his again, she softly beamed the smile of a woman who suddenly did understand their predicament. Her brows rose perceptibly.

He patted his retirement paperwork. It was after midnight. *39 years old and I'm retired! Technically, I'm official.... I'm done! Now can I get out of here?*

Hunter added quietly, her first name rolling off his tongue like a gumball into fresh whipped cream, "*Saoirse*, it's not that I'm *not interested....* It's just that I'm more interested...at the moment...in keeping *you...and me...out of the brig*. I think I know how you feel, and I'm flattered. Every guy on this base wishes they could be where I am at this moment. Please know we have... *reciprocity. Capiche?*" He winked and smiled. Her dimples appeared. She nodded, not knowing what *reciprocity* and *capiche* meant, but she read his face and was relieved. There was another pause as their hearts recovered from the pounding in their chests.

He remembered the time he had seen her enter the Blue Parrot Mexican Restaurant with her friends from the S-1 shop; she wore bangles and rings and a flowing cobalt sundress which highlighted her figure. Her legs were things of beauty and at that moment, Mitch Ryder's *Devil With The Blue Dress©* popped into his head:

She's the devil with the blue dress, blue dress, blue dress,
Devil with the blue dress on!

She had bounded over to him at his table, dragging her officemates. He stood and greeted the troops appropriately with handshakes. There was no room for them at the tiny bistro table; no time for small talk. He had to grab a bite to eat before class. It was a challenge to keep his eyes above her chin.

This time Hunter found comfort in looking deep into those dark violet eyes as he whispered, "I propose...*another time...and another place.* Not here and not tonight, but in another location, very soon. When it is safe. Where no one can get hurt. *Do you think you can do that? Do you want to do that?"*

Please say yes, I don't want to go to jail on my last day in the Marines!

Saoirse's outlook brightened noticeably. She flashed her megawatt smile and nodded quickly. She whispered, *"I will do anything for you."* She was vibrating in her seat. This man who excited her so had a much better plan.

Hunter kept his distance, as if they were discussing the weather or his retirement package, and whispered what he had in mind. Saoirse nearly fell out of her chair. She was agog, her mouth agape as she nodded in vigorous agreement. She could barely hear him as he breathed, "You need to get out of here, go home, get a shower and some sleep, and I will call you when I'm settled. That's a promise. Our secret."

Saoirse Nobley nodded and mouthed, *our secret.* She wanted to lunge at him to kiss him *thank you,* but Hunter anticipated the spontaneous outburst—a well-timed admonishing finger kept the little vixen at bay. Patting his paperwork, he said, "Thank you again, *Corporal* Nobley."

She slid out of her chair, turned and walked out of the office more like a zombie than a tired overworked admin clerk. Her running shoes squeaked on the waxed tile floor until she left the building.

Adrenaline had shocked his body every bit as much as if an emergency room nurse had administered it directly into his heart. Hunter jumped up, returned the chair in which she was sitting to its proper place. He checked to see that she had actually departed the premises. He turned and walked to the flight line-side door. As he stepped outside his face and arms were assaulted by the incinerator-like desert air. No jets rolling down the runway. Even Crash Crew had secured for the night.

Hunter's heartbeat started to return to normal. He didn't see anyone walking along the flight line and no one was peering into the windows of the Admin shop. *No people, no cameras, no witnesses. It's after midnight. I have my retirement package. I may just get out of here alive!* He exhaled a trapped lungful of the dry oven-like air. He might've just flown too close to the sun and not had his wings burned off by a classic fraternization trap. If fraternization were graded on the Saffir-Simpson Hurricane Wind Scale, Hunter had been blown onto the beach and had slammed face-first into a palm, but he had found a way to survive the Cat 5 storm.

He staggered into the building and right before he shut off the radio, Creedence Clearwater Revival started singing *Bad Moon Rising*©. A few words passed through the speaker before he shut off the radio.

I see a bad moon a rising, I see trouble on the way….

Hunter returned to the secretary's seat in a daze. A few molecules of her perfume remained in the air. He gripped the arms of the chair, panned his eyes to the open door, *Did I really do that? She's friggin' 22! Maverick, you can't do that! You may avoid jail and a bad conduct discharge, but you're going to hell! You've got to get the hell out of here!*

Hunter had always understood why some pilots and generals succumbed to the smiles and wiles of pretty girls who were *off limits*. They were probably like him, a no-name nobody the high school girls ignored. But when guys like him conquered and achieved something so monstrously complex and difficult, like flight school and were awarded wings of gold and flight suits, and landed *Phantoms* on carriers, then those same girls saw in them the same things they had seen in the football jocks with the oversized jerseys. Boys who turned into men, men who were "late to light" with women late to the fight. The plumage of flight suits and helmets and pilot wings could now entice the amazing female Birds of Paradise, but Marine Corps Orders put those same delectable and provocative uniformed women "out of bounds." They were something that could be admired from a distance but not ever touched. He never considered that he would allow his discipline to lapse, to put himself in that position. But he did.

Newly retired *civilian* Duncan Hunter collected the pages of his essay and his bundle of retirement papers. He shut down the secretary's workstation and left it as he had found it. He pulled the Admin door closed, walked through the operations complex one last time and went out to his truck—the only vehicle in the lot. He threw his "trash" in the passenger's seat, but before he started the big black Chevy Silverado, he paused and looked up into the stars and wondered if he would go through "with it." Would he keep the promise to the beautiful little corporal? He didn't know. He had plenty of time to decide. But first he had to escape from the scene of the crime. Depart the premises. Get out of the state before the military police rounded up the chief suspect and hauled him off in cuffs to the hoosegow.

In less than twenty minutes Hunter had returned to the bachelor officer's quarters parking lot, hooked his truck up to the trailer with his Corvette race car already packed and strapped down tight, and drove off of the Marine Corps Air Station and into the big little city of Yuma, Arizona—population 30,000 during the summer and 100,000 during the winter. The patent letters and application packages were in a Federal Express envelope. His monograph filled a Federal Express box the size of a Denver suburb telephone book. In front of the tallest building in town, he found the Federal Express drop-off box.

He got out of the truck and deposited the envelope and box in the container. When Hunter returned to the Silverado, he caught a glimpse of one of the old UPS envelopes peeking out from under his well-worn G-1 flight jacket. For the second time that night, something shook him. Stupidly sitting out in the open was the contents of his safe deposit box; a green Rolex box with his *Daytona* inside, a dozen presentation boxes containing the watches of former aviators and manly movie stars, and bags of old silver coins. He inhaled the hot air. *I have to stop taking my security for granted. I'll be on the outside where there are people who will steal the shoes you are wearing.* He checked to see if anything had been disturbed. He fingered the UPS envelopes containing General Chernovich's documents, originals, and copies. He exhaled the desert air. *Time's up! I waited for further instructions, but they never came.*

It was the moment he had looked forward to. The final walk around check before he departed Yuma. In the truck bed was the seven-tube carbon-fiber racing bike he hadn't been able to ride since his accident. He wasn't about to give up on the notion that one day he would ride it again. The bike was old and passé, like him, technology had raced ahead with lighter and faster designs but he treasured the beauty and elegance of the polished aluminum and the dark carbon fiber. The bike was now an expensive collectable.

He had always taken for granted the security of his "trash," as Marines were apt to say about their "stuff." For over twenty years, Hunter had had nothing stolen from his locker, his desk, his home, or his vehicles. He realized he had been living in a perfect world for over twenty years where crime outside the fence of the base or air station didn't touch him, and now he would drive home to Texas to the house where his parents used to live.

The Marine Corps had borrowed him for two decades and now he was going to an empty home. His family had been torn apart by drugs and terrorists. He reminded himself that he had invested a sizable amount of time and money in his possessions, and that they needed to be protected, especially when he was traveling.

There is often something you overlook when you're in a hurry; he was grateful he couldn't think of any unfinished business he was leaving behind. He stood with his hand on the truck handle and closed his eyes. If he had kissed her like he wanted, he would've never have been able to let her go. *Such is the power of love. We are of two generations. She deserves her life and I've got to get on with mine*. As he mounted the black beast and fired up the engine, his pulse rate returned to normal.

The Chevy truck's engine struggled a bit to pull the heavy trailer through the steep mountain pass on Interstate 8, where behind him the night lights of Yuma were fast becoming a memory. Hunter pounded on the steering wheel in frustration. An anti-military dope-smoking Democrat had been elected president, the former Commandant of the Marine Corps died unexpectedly. *And the guy who gave him mouth-to-mouth is probably a serial killer. Maybe he even killed my old racquetball partner. I have the file that would have booted him out of the Corps. I waited for further instructions, but they never came.*

And that girl from Iowa.... What am I going to do about her?

Blowing through Tacna, Hunter's tummy rumbled, and he realized he had left his Godfather's Pizza in the Admin Office. *Godfather's is good, but not good enough to go back.*

Hunter also realized he had been lost in unrequited fantasies and a future undefined. *That's how I found her and I did whatever it took to avoid her.* He finally turned on the radio to find Pink Floyd's *Learning to Fly©* wrapping up. It was one of his favorite songs, it always lit a feeling of duende in him like a blowtorch, and it summed up his life in the Marine Corps thoroughly. He cranked up the volume and belted out the final refrain with Dave Gilmore on vocals.

There's no sensation to compare with this
Suspended animation, a state of bliss
Can't keep my mind from the circling skies
Tongue-tied and twisted just an earth-bound misfit, I....

CHAPTER 8

November 30, 1992

Several weeks after Senate approval, a "Hail and Farewell" event, where those coming to and departing from Headquarters Marine Corps were celebrated, there had been a promotion ceremony, the running of the Marine Corps Marathon, the pomp and circumstance of a Marine Corps change of command ceremony, the installation as one of the Joint Chiefs of Staff and the new Marine Corps Commandant, General Bogdan Chernovich had the privilege of leading the caisson for the interment of his predecessor at Arlington National Cemetery. He had also presided over the Marine Corps Birthday Ball in Washington, D.C. and extolled the virtues and reflected on the remarkable career of his predecessor.

His new life was largely ceremonial. When some free time opened up on his calendar, the CMC walked into the Office of the Inspector General. General Chernovich had questions and wanted some answers. The IG, a brigadier general not as tall as the Commandant, warmly greeted the new CMC.

General Chernovich had closed the door of the IG's office and asked point-blank had there been an operation to find and report general officer misconduct in the Marine Corps. The IG was taken aback by the CMC's laser-like directness; he said, "Sir, upon announcing your new assignment, the former CMC terminated all pending investigations into senior officers. He stated that the new Commandant could deal with any Hot Line difficulties involving general officers and commanding officers in his own way."

"Have we any new reports of general officer misconduct on the Hot Line?"

"No sir, we haven't."

"Have we any outstanding cases of senior officers accused of fraternization?"

"No sir, we haven't. We always have a couple of cases of company and field grade officers which are investigated and adjudicated at the local level. We get a copy of those cases for trend analysis. But no; no generals, no colonels. It is usually fairly quiet in November and December."

CMC Chernovich nodded casually, and said, "The pilots, the fast movers with the mirrored Ray Bans, flat stomachs, and Rolexes are the worst. They can't keep their hands off our WMs."

The IG couldn't help but glance at the Commandant's TAG Heuer *Autavia* GMT and grinned. "That they do, sir. That they do."

Chernovich didn't pursue the issue with the IG again. To do so could have brought unwanted scrutiny on himself. He would have to let his former driver slip away quietly in the night. *Who would believe her?* He would send a P-4 to all the colonels and generals, and outline his expectations of executive-level leadership, trustworthiness, and honesty. Fraternization at any level will not be tolerated.

It was during the "Hail and Farewell" that General Chernovich had become reacquainted with a colonel who had worked for him before, someone who hadn't pissed him off or let him down. Someone that he knew and trusted. General Chernovich had asked him to come to the CMC's spit and polished office after all the ceremonies had been completed. He gave the colonel an assignment.

The following morning, the bald colonel from the Manpower Management Officer Assignments (MMOA) office was waiting in the Commandant's office. He told the CMC that he had found the requested information. "Sir, your predecessor commissioned investigations on several general officers, but, there are no copies or official records of any investigation on the Commandant, there are no appointing investigative officer documents, and there hadn't been a Hot Line complaint with the Commandant's name."

"How can you be so sure?"

"The Marine I replaced did not leave on good terms. He was removed for fraternization with an Air Force officer. He did not have any kind words to say about your predecessor."

General Chernovich dismissed the colonel with a simple "thank you." He rested in his thickly padded black chair and ruminated about the possibilities. He strummed his fingers in a teepee for several minutes, then engaged the intercom and asked his secretary to bring all of her calendars to him.

By the end of the day General Chernovich found what he was looking for. Someone who wouldn't normally visit the CMC in his private office. A name, devoid of subject information. A name the former CMC would have said to the secretary in passing, "Put this Marine on the calendar." Marine generals were not used to having their directions questioned.

The following morning the CMC's secretary left a message for the old colonel at MMOA to come to the CMC's office. General Chernovich gave the colonel a script and asked for information on the Marine whose name was on the piece of paper. An hour later, the colonel hand-delivered to the Commandant a manila file folder with several pages. It was an officer's brief sheet from the officer selection board. A captain who had been selected for promotion but requested immediate retirement. An F-4 pilot. Injured, DNIF, duties not involving flying. Retrained as an aircraft maintenance officer. Assigned duties as a squadron executive officer. Current assignment, Retired to the Fleet Marine Force.

General Chernovich dismissed the colonel and scanned the computer readout. He looked up from the document and wanted to shout, *What captain, what XO goes on a dozen TADs a year?* He continued reading, Personal awards: 12 Meritorious Service Medals. *No one has twelve MSMs! Not Smedley D. Butler, not Chesty Puller, not even God.* Citations classified, contact CMC Code 1A for details. *Code 1A? That's this office! But there are no citations in my office safe!*

Then he knew, *So, my predecessor ran a special activity from this office. He thought he had me. He destroyed all traces of the investigations and covered their asses pretty good, but not good enough.*

General Chernovich recalled the last few days he was in Hawaii. He remembered sending his driver for his laundry, some supplies, some Visine. *But she returned without the eye drops. She acted differently. I couldn't make it work. Then the P-4. I was the new CMC and had to leave immediately. She and her worthless husband went into hiding and received transfer orders after I left…. That unfinished business nearly waylaid me.*

The name on the officer brief sheet: *Captain Drue Duncan Hunter.*

I stopped you, asshole! You were saved by a timely retirement. You're out of my Marine Corps forever. No one will ever take your word over mine, a captain over a general. You wouldn't dare. You got close, asshole. I won't be seeing your sorry ass ever again! Chernovich broke out in a vicious sneer and a laugh that would've made Vincent Price proud.

The Commandant's secretary heard the strange laughter and wondered if a nutcase was now occupying the office.

CHAPTER 9

April 2, 1993

He had never sat in the upper deck of the 747 where the first class passengers were separated from the other classes of passengers. First class on a jumbo jet was unlike first class on a domestic flight with personalized service from a dedicated flight attendant, limitless drinks, and food fit for a visiting prince. The two-abreast seats were significantly wider with greater legroom, and the seats could almost fully recline; all at the touch of a button.

Hunter was lost in thought. Airport security in Honolulu hadn't changed thirty-five days after the bombing attempt on the World Trade Center in New York City. Al-Qaeda had attacked America again but it was like it never even happened. Hunter stared out the jet's window in reflection until someone plopped into the seat beside him. He introduced himself and found that he was among friendlies; another Marine.

The retired Marine colonel relayed how he found his position. Hunter listened intently. After months of looking for work the colonel said he walked into an airport and saw a help wanted sign; he applied for and got a job as a "pre-board screener." His job was to operate the X-ray machine at the airport security checkpoint, to screen passengers and their baggage. A month later he was a Concourse Security Supervisor, and two months after that an Executive Vice President (EVP) of Trans-Atlantic Support Services. He said, "My rags-to-riches story was even featured in my parent company's magazine, *The Eastern*."

The Eastern? What the hell? Duncan Hunter was accustomed to senior officers leveraging the power of their position and taking credit for the work of subordinates. He sat there knowing he was probably talking to another one. *But The Eastern? Was that a product of the Trans-*

Atlantic Security Corporation? He looked at his seat partner with a different light. *That is a socialist rag; are the Trans-Atlantic Support Services and the Trans-Atlantic Security Corporation socialist companies? I can only live off of my retirement and savings for so long. If he offers me a job, I'll take it. I'll try to be more productive than Winston Smith in Orwell's 1984.*

He enjoyed the comfort of the first class accommodations and said he didn't mind starting from the bottom, anything to find work. He told the colonel about his PhD program and the title of his treatise. A year before leaving the Marine Corps, Hunter had said he looked for employment without success. Aviation jobs for future or newly minted PhDs were virtually nonexistent; the degree wasn't a badge of honor but a disqualifier. The airlines wanted pilots, the aircraft manufacturers wanted engineers, and the airports wanted *American Association of Airport Executives* accreditation. The airport security jobs needed minimum wage screeners and skycaps who worked for a fraction of minimum wage but got great tips. He was overqualified for virtually every position in the world of aviation, but no one would give him the time of day. Hunter still needed work. Few things were more pitiful than a broken fighter pilot who could no longer pull loads of Gs; an unemployed retired Marine officer with a doctorate ran a close second.

The old colonel said, "You have too much of that 'education stuff,' but with employment at an airport, you could apply academic theory with hands-on practical experience. What I have in mind would be a perfect match for you."

Before they landed in Los Angeles, the colonel offered Hunter the job of General Manager. As soon as they landed, the colonel called his corporate office and asked which GM positions were open in the company. He asked Hunter if he would be interested in working at the Cleveland Hopkins International Airport.

"They always have challenges finding a suitable manager for the corporate's 'crown jewel,' the airport where the company's latest airport security products are tested and put on display. The contract consistently runs in the red and no one knows why."

He immediately replied, "I'll take it! Some of the finest racquetball ball players in the nation live in Cleveland, such as Bobby Sanders, a five-time National Champion. I love to play racquetball. It will be like seeing old friends."

Hunter moved to Ohio and found an apartment in one of the most desirable zip codes in the country, Shaker Heights. He was ready to assume the GM's position at the airport. He worked all day in the scrum that is airport security. At night Hunter worked out in the gym and played racquetball with Bobby Sanders and his talented friends. He couldn't play at the level from before his accident, but he was a marvelous addition to the group of "racquetball elders," at the Shaker Heights Racquet Club, all former National Singles Champions in their age groups. Hunter thought he was getting stronger.

Duncan Hunter's official title was the Total Aviation Security Services (TASSER) General Manager. TASSER, the "airport security services" line of business, was a wholly owned subsidiary of Trans-Atlantic Support Services, which was an arm of the Trans-Atlantic Security Corporation (TASCO) conglomerate. Hunter managed the airport security contract. A coalition of all the airlines, led by Cleveland Hopkins' dominate airline, Continental, negotiated a lowest-cost, technically acceptable contract and the airport security employees were the lowest paid workers at the airport. They received the minimum wage plus a nickel, and they got free parking. Turnover was horrific. The contract ran in the red.

He looked over the company's books and noticed some discrepancies. Hunter walked through the airport and "counted heads." He determined that there were more employees "on the books" than there were on the floor. One of his first official acts was to invite all the airport security employees to come to his office for pizza and drinks, to meet the new general manager, and to get their paychecks directly from him. A couple of dozen screeners and skycaps offered to pick up checks for their friends who they claimed "couldn't come in because they worked the night shift." Hunter determined that there were about fifty "phantom employees" who were all drawing full-time wages. As the GM of Total Aviation Security Services, he fired the crooked employees and posted new vacancy announcements for replacement screeners and skycaps. It was the first time the contract had been in the black.

A few days later, Hunter's supervisor briefed him about the special, once-a week flight of a Trans World Airlines Boeing 747 from Cleveland to Tel Aviv. The outbound flight required special handling, the same level of enhanced security demanded of all airlines that flew into or out of Israel. TWA ticket agents interviewed all Israel-bound passengers before they received their boarding passes. All passenger bags were X-rayed and bomb-sniffing dogs went over all passengers' checked luggage. The departure was at night so the jet would land in Tel Aviv in time for businessmen and women to go to work in the morning. Hunter supervised the process; passengers would pass through magnetometers set to the most sensitive setting, there were two X-ray machine operators to ensure nothing dangerous was carried on the aircraft, and he monitored the bomb dog handlers to ensure the dogs fully checked every bag destined to go aboard the jumbo jet. Hunter walked out onto the ramp with an airport police officer to admire the Boeing 747 with *The Spirit of St. Louis* painted on its nose.

Several hours after the TWA requirements brief, Hunter spent a few hours in the racquetball club's hot tub thinking about his parents' last moments together before a terrorist's bomb had blown them and 257 other passengers and crew out of the sky. The CIA claimed Gaddafi's spies had planted the bomb. Hunter vowed to never allow a lapse in security that would let a terrorist plant a bomb on any jet. He was in "airport security" and he would do whatever was necessary to keep explosives and weapons off of the aircraft leaving Cleveland Hopkins International Airport. It pleased him to see screening equipment with his patented explosive and biological hazard detection technology in use at the airport.

A few days later after a security meeting with the airlines, Hunter returned to his office and learned that twenty Muslim men and women in traditional garb had applied for open security positions. The event should have set off alarm bells with the secretary and duty managers. He asked his subordinate managers for their opinions. One said, "The company can't discriminate; if they pass the background check, we have to hire them."

The other manager nodded and repeated as if she was a parrot. "Can't discriminate! Can't discriminate!"

Hunter was flabbergasted and stated, "Don't conflate discrimination with requirements. It has nothing to do with who they are or what they believe but do they meet or exceed the requirements. I don't think they can pass the background check. A background check is not only a requirement it is a qualification, and can they pass a five-year FAA background check? There's no friggin' way!" After a week of trying to verify employment and references, the duty manager reported back to Hunter, "I was wrong. They all failed the background check. It wasn't even close." Hunter sighed with relief. "They do not meet the requirements for the job." He had escaped what he viewed as a terrorism problem of the Trojan Horse variety.

Hunter grinned at the victory but frowned at the larger problem. *They are so conditioned not to discriminate, but we discriminate all the time. To fly a jet – there are requirements, you have to meet anthropomorphic standards – you have to fit in a jet. Military jets are built on the Goldilocks principle; you can't be too tall or too short to safely eject from a jet. There is no religious test. And SEALs have to be strong and able to kill a man with bare hands. Yeah, we discriminate because there are physical and mental requirements. There's that DSM again. You don't hire a diagnosed personality disorder to be an airline pilot. You would think these things are obvious. But it seems the human resources people don't even know what the word means and just want to fill openings with warm bodies, regardless of their mental capacity. Yet there are groups of individuals – Muslims predominate for the moment – who come to the U.S. under the auspices of simply seeking employment, but many of them seek government jobs for subversive purposes. Our leaders do not seem to recognize that we are on the front lines in airport security, and the likes of al-Qaeda are continually looking for ways to get past airport security to blow up an airliner or hijack one. What is HR going to say when that happens; '…our diversity is our strength?' That is what got my parents killed.*

Hunter's thoughts chilled him, or it could have been the cheap wall unit pouring frigid air down his neck. He said to an empty office, "I punched fifty phantom employees out of the program and just saved $75 a pop on a piss test on those Muslim applicants. We're in the black for the first time on this contract." Before heading to one of the concourses, Hunter asked his secretary, "Could you give the failed applicants a courtesy call telling them they won't be hired and repost that vacancy announcement?"

Half of the twenty Muslims applicants stormed into the company office the following morning and threatened the secretary, demanding they be hired. Hunter's radio went off; he and the duty manager ran through the airport concourse to Hunter's office and took control of the situation. The Muslim men were incensed, which was a "tell" that not everything was as it seemed.

Hunter explained, "Your applications were declined because you didn't have the required five-years of verifiable employment per Federal Aviation Regulations. If you want to work at the airport, Burger King is hiring, so is McDonald's, and they will pay you more than I can." Hunter monitored the men's faces. *And we have a grooming standard—no beards! Are you really going to shave your beard for a minimum wage job? I don't think so. So what the hell are you really up to? My money is on "access to a jumbo jet filled with Israelis."*

The leader among the Arab men became more livid as Hunter talked. His warning was explicit, "I will sue TASSER."

Hunter told him, "That's your prerogative. But my business with you is over. Total Aviation Security Services wishes you much success in your future endeavors. Thank you for your time and consideration. Good day." Hunter opened the office door and showed them out.

He called the colonel who had hired him. A couple of hours later, the TASSER Executive Vice President returned his call and asked what was going on. Hunter told him, "They couldn't pass the background check, so there really wasn't an issue. The one dude threatened us with a lawsuit—for a minimum wage job—I'm inclined to believe we're dealing with something more than a simple case of denial of employment. I called the other GMs at our airports. The ones who have direct flights to and from Israel had experienced the same thing. But the company mandated we hire them against FAA regs."

The old Marine colonel asked, "What are you trying to articulate? Human Resources will want you fired. I may not be able to stop it. Tell me the whole story, Duncan. No bullshit."

"Sir, I told you my paper was about aviation and airport security and that criminal Muslims will attempt to infiltrate it. Here in Cleveland, we have a weekly TWA 747 that goes to Tel Aviv. I will not hire some Muslims with no verifiable history for corporate's politically correct accounting purposes. To do so violates the Federal Aviation Regulations. We could lose our contract. These guys don't really care about employment. They could be on a mission from Allah regarding that jet scheduled for Israel. If so, then it's clear they want to gain an insider's knowledge of the internal workings of an airport's security network. They want to know how to bypass the security protocols and put a bomb on board a jet. Or we'll find out the hard way that pre-board screeners in a *hijab* ignored weapons that roll through the X-ray machine. Once those weapons find their way on board a jet, these folks will walk off the job, never to be seen or heard from again, because their mission is done."

The old Marine colonel was furious. *"Are you serious?* Duncan, return your badge, your radio, clear out your desk, and get the hell out of my building. You're fired."

Well, that was fast.

The Total Aviation Security Services secretary was mortified as she watched her boss remove the pictures of jets from his office walls. The pretty redheaded mother of four daubed at the tears that streamed down high cheekbones and told him, "You're the best thing that's ever happened to us. Corporate doesn't know what they're doing."

"It's apparent to them that I don't know what I'm doing."

She radioed the duty managers to come to the office. Hunter briefed them, a man and a woman who had been with the company for years, on what had transpired.

After they helped him move all of his things out of his office, Hunter hugged the women and shook hands with the man. They promised to stay in touch, but Hunter knew they wouldn't. They would return to their work at the bustling airport. The man without a degree would get the promotion to general manager that he always craved and the woman with a degree would be promoted to the senior duty manager. And somehow, HR would find a way to break the rules so the Muslim men and women would get hired for the airport security jobs, even though they couldn't pass the background check.

And I'm the problem? Duncan Hunter said he would return to Texas hoping to never ever read about an Israeli-bound jet exploding over the Atlantic Ocean.

As the TASSER GM, every day had been an adventure for Duncan, seeing fashion models and rock stars who passed though Cleveland Hopkins. He had seen how pro athletes and cinema figures worked their way through the airport and the airport lounges, being adored by people who would tell them how great they were.

Duncan's last night at the racquet club was bittersweet. The wise Bobby Sanders told Hunter he was simply in the wrong job. "You're educated, a smart guy. I'm a bus driver. Maybe you can't fly any more, but you can teach. You should be a teacher, a professor. There is a special place for you. You just have to keep at it. Someone will eventually figure out you're a superstar. I fit in here, in this world, but you don't. I will miss you, my friend. Go home to Texas, and I'll look for you at the National Singles. You can buy me lunch at Whataburger."

The men shook hands; Bobby returned to the courts waiting for someone to beat up. Hunter drove out of Cleveland headed south and west for Texas.

CHAPTER 10

October 10, 1996

The U.S. Border Patrol's Director of Aircraft Maintenance shielded his eyes from the morning sun in another cloudless sky. Technically it was fall and the weather gods on the cable news network promised another day in the nineties. They promised that it would cool off into the seventies in a month. If there was something positive to report it was the winds. No winds meant there would be no dust kicked up from the Chihuahuan Desert, and when there was no dust and haze, then his Border Patrol pilots rejoiced with CAVU weather, where the ceiling and visibility were unlimited, and they didn't get bounced around the sky in a Super Cub like an old Kansas farm house in a tornado.

Hunter walked from the Border Patrol hangar, the largest building on the property, to the opposite end of the Del Rio International Airport. The windsock in the middle of the field was limp for the first time in a year; there was no breeze to move or fill the bag. He reread a letter that included a photograph while he waited for a very special airplane to park. He put the letter from Saoirse Nobley into a suit pocket as the former CIA Chief Air Branch, Greg Lynche, landed, taxied, shutdown, and stepped from a camouflaged Schweizer SA-37 motorized glider.

He greeted Duncan Hunter warmly. Lynche was a distinguished-looking man with spindly legs and a full head of perfectly coiffed "executive hair." He had the rugged face of a leading-man, a Hollywood swashbuckler-type of leading man like Errol Flynn on the set of Captain Blood. Central casting could not have found a better actor for a retired Agency executive.

Another man—big and broad shouldered—crawled out of the other side of the Schweizer. Greg Lynche and the other gentleman exchanged glances, as if sharing a private joke. The men from Washington wore white, long sleeve, button-down shirts with modest Brooks Brothers emblems embroidered into the material, dark gray slacks, insipid ties, and high-end black oxfords. Hunter considered their attire, which was a little out of place in the heat of Texas, the uniform of East Coast executives. But more than that, he recognized the tall man. Lynche tried to make introductions. "This is…."

"Art Yoder, I presume." Hunter looked up at the man. "Army colonel and All-Army racquetball champion? It has been a very long time, sir."

Lynche was speechless. He crossed his arms across his chest; a solid gold Rolex *Yacht Master* poked out from under French cuffs with gold CIA emblem cufflinks.

"Army Special Forces," responded the older gentleman, like Army Special Forces was a separate service, and maybe to the Vietnam veteran it was. The hardened warrior eased up a little. "Have we played? I don't recall, if we did." Yoder and Lynche continued to exchange glances.

"Sir, we played a couple of times at the POAC (Pentagon Officers Athletic Club). I played with Bobby Sanders when I was in Cleveland. He said you two had some real battles at Nationals."

"For a while there it was whoever had the better day who got the win. We passed the trophy around with Bobby getting—what, five, I think."

Hunter concurred, "Yes sir. Bobby Sanders—five-time National Champion."

Lynche redirected the conversation. "So you're the guy trying to bring Border Patrol aviation into the 20th century or to keep it from becoming a glorified flying club?"

"That's me, good sir."

Lynche said, "I read the Government Accountability Office report— the Border Patrol needed an experienced aviation manager to fix their air program or it should be shut down. So you're the adult leadership they hired. You have your work cut out for you. I know you want to see this, so let me show you what I brought, although you may have trouble selling it to your pilots."

"These guys have lost their work ethic. They have stopped being border cops."

Hunter, a retired Marine, had been a dark-horse candidate for the Border Patrol's Director of Aircraft Maintenance. He told Lynche what that was like. "Within my first hour on my first day, I met the Chief Pilot. Instead of congratulating me, he jabbed a finger in my chest and yelled at me like a Marine Corps drill instructor, *"Who the hell do you know in the Border Patrol?"*

"I told Art you're the right guy for the job. But for the *hoi polloi*, the line guys, you're an inimical threat. I bet you wanted to break his finger."

Hunter laughed, "I told him that if he tried it again, I would do more than break his finger. I would club him like a baby harp seal with his own damned weapon. He had a 9mm Beretta in a shoulder holster, and I would've broken him like a twig. When you see him, you'll agree that he's an empty bag of bones and should have retired long ago. But he got lucky because of HR's 'new guys rules' that said, 'Thou shan't break the heads of assholes on thy first day of work,' or something like that. Just for clarification, I didn't know anyone in the Border Patrol until the day I got here."

The retired CIA officer and former Green Beret howled with laughter. Hunter had proven again that he was a smooth operator with a strong sense of humor. Lynche had seen Hunter's Agency file, in fact he had actually created it some fifteen years earlier. He had tried to recruit Hunter but the new Marine Corps officer hadn't been interested. After helping the Agency and the DEA find Pablo Escobar, he just wanted to return to the Marines and fly jets.

"Greg, I haven't seen one of these planes except on the internet."

"Well, Duncan, let me show you what we brought for today's demonstration. This is your basic Schweizer SA2-37B two-seat, single-engine, low-noise profile airplane. It's optimized for low altitude surveillance and reconnaissance. This one has a suite of infrared and electro-optical sensors to monitor activities on land and sea. Endurance about fourteen hours."

Hunter showed his knowledge of the Schweizer and other special purpose airplanes. "She's beautiful—sleek, conformal antennae. The propeller and muffler system are unlike that on the YO-3A. Our pilots will munity if they hear 'fourteen hours'—they're old with prostate problems and have to piss every few hours." Duncan grinned broadly at Lynche, hoping for and receiving reciprocation. Then he turned and pointed to the Mexican side of the border. "You can see that we are less than a mile from the Rio Grande—that is Ciudad Acuña, Acuña City, population a quarter million, and you can see dozens of *maquiladoras* in the distance. U.S. factories. They make everything from seat belts to Sunbeam blenders. There are watchers over there with telescopes. Heads exploded when you landed." Hunter patted the aircraft and said, "You can bet they have seen nothing like this."

The comment got Yoder's attention. He crossed his arms and furrowed his brows. A vintage Rolex emerged from a sleeve. "*Watchers?*"

"Yes, sir. I learned shortly after taking this job that we can't do anything without someone watching us. If you assume no one in the Border Patrol is corrupt or working for the other side, then the only possible explanations for knowing our operations beforehand is that they're watching from across the border. If an airplane departs to the north, our Agents come back empty handed. If a helicopter departs to the south, same thing. We would be more effective in apprehensions and seizures if we were to mask our operations better. I would move the air operations out to the Air Force base east of town if I could and operate it like—well, like I expect the CIA would conduct air operations. You shouldn't telegraph your adversaries when you're off on a mission."

Lynche beamed broadly. "You're a smart man, Duncan. That's exactly what I would do."

Art Yoder asked who would be at the meeting.

"All the Chief Patrol Agents and Sector Chief Pilots on the Southwest Border, and maybe a congressional staffer. Our Congressman's a Republican who was just elected, I guess last go-round. This district had been in Democrat Party hands for fifty years," said Hunter. "He is something of a Republican rock star and the Democrats hate him."

• • •

The Del Rio Sector Chief Patrol Agent began his introductions with, "I would like to thank Mr. Lopez from Congressman Hernandez's office for making the trip from San Antonio." He recognized the Chief of Air Operations from El Paso and the other Sector Chief Patrol Agents from San Diego to McAllen, Texas. He stressed, "The security folks wanted to make sure I announced this brief is at the TS/SCI level; this requires special access, and clearances have been verified. Is that correct? Ok, for background I asked our Aviation Maintenance Director to get information on different aircraft which may improve our ability to secure the southwest border, and today we have Mr. Greg Lynche from the Schweizer Aircraft Company. Mr. Lynche retired from the CIA after a 35-year career and was a member of the Senior Intelligence Service. He served in leadership positions across the globe as Chief of Station, Chief of Counterterrorism, Chief Air Branch, and was the Director of Operations. Ladies and gentlemen, Greg Lynche."

Lynche acknowledged all dignitaries and added Duncan Hunter to the list, which earned Duncan a gentle round of applause from the Chiefs as the pilots sat on their hands. Lynche quickly compared the challenges facing Border Patrol Agents to those from "his old place," finding narco- terrorists and drug labs. He suggested the aircraft here today was developed to solve most of those challenges. "One of the most overwhelming liabilities of aircraft in the field is that once narco-terrorists or drug smugglers, for illegal aliens or *coyotes* or contraband smugglers, hear the aircraft, they scatter."

Lynche said *coyotes* with a Spanish accent to distinguish the difference between the animal and the name Border Patrol Agents had given to alien smugglers. He related the Arab proverb, "The eagle that chases two rabbits catches neither. With a low noise aircraft you control the aural environment, and because you operate silently you can identify targets, coordinate an interception, and control the apprehension or drug seizure from the acoustically silent platform. I understand this is what you attempt to do at night with your Super Cubs and night vision goggles, looking for campfires, but you are several thousand feet high with your lights off to mask your presence and prevent your adversaries from seeing and hearing you. If the illegal aliens or drug smugglers don't start a fire, you will not find them. Not with NVGs. But if you had a thermal sensor, that would improve your odds, but you still have the problem of aircraft noise. Our airplane changes the game."

Hunter thought, *Another incredible aircraft from the minds of Air Branch; the guys who conceived and developed the U-2 and the A-12.*

"With a Schweizer, you can be effective in your job at whatever altitude you choose to fly. It also allows you to look over the border to see who or what may be coming."

Most of the audience nodded, waiting eagerly for Lynche's next bullet point when the Del Rio Sector Chief Pilot spoke up: "No disrespect Chief, but we have tried these technologies before and they don't work in this environment." The Chief Pilot seemed proud of his outburst. Some agents in flight suits nodded in the affirmative or rolled their eyes in disgust.

Lynche nodded to Hunter and said, "Art, the video?"

Duncan moved quickly to a cart with a biggest cathode-ray-type television money could buy and a VCR player on the lower shelf. He rolled the stack of electronics in front of the assembly of Chief Patrol Agents. Art Yoder waited for Hunter to turn the two devices on before inserting a tape and pressing the PLAY button. The Chiefs leaned forward for a better view. The Chief Pilot hadn't expected Lynche to ignore him; he wasn't pleased.

As an image popped up on the screen, Lynche began, "I don't know who made the comment about this technology not working here, but let me tell you what we did last night on our way to *delightful* Del Rio, Texas. We took pictures; we made movies. We flew from Elmira, New York, took on gas at Corpus Christi, flew southwesterly along the coast and then up the Rio Grande from Brownsville to Del Rio. This is what we recorded; these were the *activities* we found along your border."

For the next hour, Lynche and Yoder relayed where they were and what they saw and highlighted the location and movement of hundreds of illegal aliens, some in columns of a 120 or more, and drug smugglers, some in columns of ten to forty human mules carrying huge bales on their backs. Lynche said, "Here we are south of Laredo; a dozen horses are carrying immense bales of contraband across the river where the Rio Grande is shallow—you can see here, there are men in the river and the water doesn't reach their knees. Further up river, in four instances, snakes of 70 to 120 illegal aliens and smugglers passed within twenty feet of Border Patrol vehicles with agents inside. We know exactly how many were in a row because Art counted them."

"We know these were Border Patrol vehicles—we used an Infrared Night Vision Laser Spotlight to verify the big Border Patrol emblem on the side of the truck and the "J-tags" license plates of the trucks. I wrote down the numbers of the plates just to highlight the technology that you do not have but need. Men and women of the Border Patrol, you are being overrun. The United States is being invaded. I wished we had your radio frequencies; we could've helped." Lynche and Yoder's seven-hour flight documented over 2,000 illegal aliens entering the U.S. without being detected and over 200 drug smugglers with countless pounds of contraband that evaded detection and apprehension. The FLIR captured an invasion of illegal activity, long suspected but never caught on film. The audience was in shock.

Lynche wrapped up his presentation as he fast forwarded the video. "I think you'll like this. This was extraordinary. It was just before sunrise and there had been no activity for about ten minutes when I saw something flash in the FLIR scope that didn't look like a rabbit or a *javelina*. I asked my sensor operator, 'Art, was that a foot?' You can see from this aspect—we are turning—that there is no thermal image, but when I came around 180°, there is a guy, laying down and maybe sleeping. You get on the other side of his makeshift lean-to and he disappears. I hadn't seen that before, but it's obvious he's hiding under a thermal blanket that blocks his heat signature. Now let me fast forward a bit......here we go. This is a Border Patrol helicopter on a southerly heading that flew right over the guy in the lean-to. We were northbound and had the helicopter at ten miles in the FLIR. We zoomed to 1,500 feet above ground level (AGL) at that point, and I think when the helo passed under us he was at 500 feet AGL or so. Our lights were out, and it looks like he never saw us. That helicopter also had a FLIR ball on the nose—but if we didn't pop up on his FLIR, it must have been off or inoperative. Our engine heat should have been obvious, just like our FLIR picked up your guys at ten miles."

"Anyway, our sense is the guy on the ground had to have heard the helo coming—we know anecdotally helicopters can be heard in this environment, at night, at ten miles or more—and the helicopter was making such a racket these illegals had time to employ countermeasures, throw up the aluminum blanket to mask heat signatures. We stayed on station for ten minutes. Once your helicopter was well out of aural range, well, watch what happens. For those in the back, the guy crawls out from under the blanket, stands up, snatches the thermal blanket, and runs off to the east. Then watch this—there he goes—he's waving 'bye bye' to the Border Patrol helicopter."

"These guys know all the tricks. They use basic countermeasures," said Colonel Art Yoder. "We see the same thing when dealing with narcoterrorists and drug smugglers. When they are comfortable they haven't been detected at night, they go about their business as if nothing is wrong and that is when they make mistakes that can be caught in a FLIR."

The crowd murmured as heads slowly shook in disbelief.

"Mr. Hunter thinks if you had one of these aircraft, flying this corridor, the sensor operator could talk to ground agents and vector them into position to capture, I'm sorry, 'apprehend' people like you see on the tape. Please note the high level of clarity of the video—this high quality is only possible with a low-level quiet aircraft and a top-notch new-generation FLIR flying above the targets. The high definition, almost photographic quality is essential for the government to try these cases in a court of law, for you can plainly see who you are apprehending."

"What altitude is that?" The chief pilot was suddenly interested in the aircraft's performance specifications.

"The altitude at which a human can detect an overhead quiet aircraft is classified. In the 'need to know' category. Millions of dollars were spent at MIT to silence all the noisemakers on a similar aircraft…."

Hunter thought, *Like the YO-3A….*

"…and some of those 'quiet' technologies are on the aircraft outside. But I will tell you that when we weren't flying as low as practicable to capture the perfect image of Juan Valdez and his donkey full of dope, *we* flew between 500 to 2,000 feet, basically north, VFR, no lights, to prove the point. I didn't want to run into power lines or an antenna without its lights."

The Del Rio Chief Patrol Agent said, "That's an unconventional capability and a game changer. We could really use those airplanes." Mr. Lopez from Congressman Hernandez's office suddenly stood and approached Lynche, Yoder, and Hunter; then the ten Sector Chiefs and the Air Ops Chief joined the group in the middle of the hangar, ignoring the other attendees. The Del Rio Chief broke out of the pack, threw up a hand as big as a catcher's mitt, and waved, "That's all folks. Thank you for coming."

The Chief boomed to the impromptu meeting, "Let's go into Duncan's conference room."

Hunter dashed to open the double doors of his makeshift lunch and conference room and held open the door for the Congressional aide, the Border Patrol Chiefs, and Lynche.

Art Yoder wasn't needed for what would be a business meeting of "heavies." He had been watching the chief pilots' reactions. Hunter closed the conference room door, and with nothing else to do for the moment, he made an impromptu guard outside the conference room. Yoder walked over to Hunter and said, "I think you made an enemy for life but I am at a loss for why they are so afraid of you."

Hunter crushed his lips and nodded. "It's been like that from day one, actually." He didn't need to look to know what was happening behind him. He jumped out of the way as the door flew open and a smiling Chief Patrol Agent motioned for Hunter to "Get in here!" Yoder followed him in. No one in the meeting missed the Chief Pilots.

An hour long meeting with the Chief Patrol Agents, Mr. Lopez, Lynche, Yoder, and Hunter resulted in a commitment from the Congressional aide to have the Congressman meet with Lynche and Yoder when they returned to Washington, D.C. Hunter had commandeered a classroom-sized white board. He took notes and action items, and sketched out a pilot program and a concept of operations that Yoder kept referring to as a "CONOP."

The plan entailed a handful of quiet aircraft being used at night, with contract pilots and Border Patrol Agents as sensor operators. Operations would be based at semi-distant airfields away from the prying eyes of border watchers in Mexico. When the issue of funding came up, the aide indicated the Congressman would work to get crucial funding for three aircraft for a pilot program. The Del Rio Chief cautioned him that with a Democrat in the White House, it had been his experience that the Border Patrol couldn't count on receiving the earmark or any monies. "We don't even get O&M when a Democrat is in office. (Operations and Maintenance). The funding would likely be siphoned off by the Democratic I&NS Commissioner and reprogrammed for something other than quiet airplanes."

Hunter blurted out, "What about using drug forfeiture funds?"

There are things a non-agent can do or say that doesn't reflect adversely on Border Patrol Chiefs and won't come back around to haunt them for the rest of their careers. Mr. Lopez asked Hunter directly, "The Chief is correct about receiving funding. Congressional earmarks are difficult to acquire under the current administration. What're the chances you can get drug forfeiture funds?"

Hunter was surprised to be a focal part of the discussion. "For quiet airplanes? I don't know if that's permitted. At my level, I've asked the DEA to transfer a couple of out-of-service, seized, or confiscated aircraft for us to overhaul and integrate into our fleet. And I got a hundred grand to build an FAA Repair Station so we could repair Border Patrol, Customs, and DEA aircraft components. I haven't thought to ask for specific funds for quiet aircraft. That would be in the millions of dollars."

The Del Rio Chief chimed in, "They have gotten every bit of their money back in the support Duncan gives them. I should have invited the DEA Chief to this—probably the U.S. Customs Chief too. I'll talk to them."

No one noticed Lynche and Yoder silently exchanging raised eyebrows and tiny head nods.

As the meeting broke up, the senior Border Patrol Agents departed out the back door of the hangar while the Del Rio Chief and his Deputy escorted the congressional aide out to his vehicle. Lynche and Yoder promised to stay in touch with the Chief and the Deputy. After the Del Rio Sector Chief and the Deputy departed, Hunter turned toward the hangar doors which looked toward Mexico. He led Lynche and Yoder back through the hangar and out to the Schweizer.

"I think that went well." Hunter was beaming like a lighthouse on a dark night.

Lynche patted Hunter's back. "You're a master of understatement and a factotum of the first order. For starters, you just sold three aircraft to a group of ground agents who know Border Patrol aviation should be more than a flying club. You know how to leverage a spinning mass; Duncan, you know how to apply pressure at the right spot to get things done." Lynche raised a heavy gray eyebrow at Yoder, and Yoder nodded in return.

Hunter knew it was time to get the spook and the old colonel off on their way. "I can't thank you enough for coming out to our little patch of *caliche*. I figured you might've been able to sell a few airplanes to the Chiefs; the line pilots cannot be interested because the Chief Pilots aren't interested. These are the Chief's programs, and they have to see what will work for them. I hate to say it, you can't trust a bunch of guys who have been here since rocks were new. They have long lost their motivation." He placed his hand on the sunbaked cowling of the quiet airplane for a moment, appreciating its lines and beauty and thinking it would be very cool to fly. *I think you could consider this to be an offensive weapon.* Hunter also had a question the old CIA man might have some insight on. "Greg, I got a question—you're a senior guy working within the beltway."

Intrigued, Lynche said, "If it's not classified."

"I don't think so. What do you think happened to Flight 800? The TWA jet that exploded....recently...off of Long Island, New York. I'm teaching the aircraft accident investigations course...."

Yoder interrupted, "What do you think happened?"

Lynche continued, "I'm a little familiar. I know my old place was brought in. They did some modeling for the FBI—which is very unusual—but everyone assigned to the investigation has been very tight-lipped. Normally, my friends who are still there would tell me. But regarding that 'incident,' I would say, something isn't right about the way they handled it. And I would be disinclined to believe the official narrative."

Yoder interjected, "I believe at least one of your patents has stopped explosives from being loaded aboard some two dozen European or Israeli-bound aircraft."

Hunter was struck mute.

Lynche added, "And the FAA and the FBI opened investigations into the hiring practices of Total Aviation Security Services."

Hunter was a little shocked and said nothing.

Lynche asked, "Didn't they let you go after you raised the alarm on hiring Muslims for security jobs? Didn't you talk to the airport police?"

Hunter nodded and said, "I did, and you've done your homework."

Yoder offered, "If you want answers, look for the *brick agents*, those FBI special agents who got fired from the investigation. They'll be pissed off at the government and their bosses, and they might tell you what really happened, at least from their point of view. They will write books, but in the eyes of the FBI they have been officially discredited, and they are on an NDA, a non-disclosure agreement, so no one will listen to them."

The observation confused Hunter.

Lynche asked, "What do you think happened?"

"If it wasn't al-Qaeda who compromised airport security and got a bomb on board, I think it was shot down on purpose. By al-Qaeda with *Stingers* from the Afghan war with the Soviets. If not *Stingers*, then there are other MANPADS. *Strellas* or *Blowpipes*. I know from the information I acquired from teaching my class out at Laughlin Air Force Base. I have an article citing two Congressmen telling a *Washington Times* reporter…."

Lynche asked, "Not the *Washington Post*?"

Hunter shook his head. "You cannot get a straight story from the *Washington Post* or the *New York Times*; maybe the *New York Post* but only the *Washington Times* carried it. You can't trust anything leftist media puts out. At least I can't. It is Goebbelsesque misinformation. And I try to be as accurate as I can in my classrooms. Anyway, the Congressmen acknowledged they were in a closed-door meeting on the proliferation of shoulder-launched, surface-to-air, anti-aircraft missiles. MANPADS. And they said they 'were going to make sure another Flight 800 never occurred again.'"

Yoder rolled his bottom lip and Lynche was noncommittal. Yoder said, "What little I know of Greg's old place is that there was a very tight investigation. And the more there is to the issue, the tighter they control the narrative."

Lynche said, "I wasn't aware of the *Times* reporting."

Yoder turned to his friend and said, "That is because you only read the *New York Times* and the *Washington Post*." Lynche grinned as Yoder winked at Hunter.

Hunter offered, "The official version from the government, is an impossibility. The *Washington Times* article is the only thing that resembles the truth. Truth from the investigation wasn't a process of collective discovery. It was an election year, al-Qaeda had declared war on the America's aviation industry, and the president and the newspapers reported a political orthodoxy already known to an enlightened few. The only difference between the *New York Times* and the old Soviet Pravda is that Pravda readers knew they were being lied to. I've seen this playbook before, and they have already made it look like it was an accident, a bad wire, or some such folderol. Which brings us back to the situation I had in Cleveland."

"The president is in a bad position," offered Yoder. He crossed his arms and the Rolex made another appearance. An ancient gold *GMT Master* with a lizard strap. Root beer bezel.

That is a beautiful watch. Hunter's eyes popped as he had only seen a watch like that once before; on his father's wrist. *And the bastards who put my parents into body bags stole it. If I had it, I would wear my father's watch.*

Lynche hugged himself. "If you're right and airport security has been compromised in Cleveland, and that contracted service provider did nothing, the FBI will run it down and see if Cleveland is a one-off or if there is more to the story. If there are Muslims in airport security throughout the country...."

Yoder spat, "They've infiltrated the contracted airport security—I can see it. My question is, what is the FBI doing about it? The complete seventh floor at 935 Pennsylvania Avenue needs new occupants. And if the Attorney General ever went through that airport with her FBI bodyguards, sometimes all it takes is a mention from the airport police to the FBI to get an investigation started."

Lynche asked, "So you think al-Qaeda is at war with international and American aviation?"

Hunter said, "Yes; at my level and lack of access, it is obviously an undeclared war. I lost my parents in the Lockerbie bombing in 1988. No one has been held accountable. I've paid attention to what our government has done, which isn't much, but I could be wrong. I hold a few patents for explosives detection devices in X-ray scanners at airports and mail rooms. The concept is taking off. I make a little money. In January, I believe your old place and the FBI helped stop what we know as the *Bojinka* Plot to blow airliners out of the sky. I don't know if it was my stuff which prevented explosives from getting on a plane, or if it was intel from your old place that stopped the *Bojinka* Plot. I don't know if it was equipment, or if someone who blew the whistle on the mastermind behind something like that."

You're not supposed to know it was Ramzi Yousef and Khalid Sheikh Mohammed. You don't have the clearances or the need to know any of that information at this point while the FBI and the CIA are conducting their investigation. Lynche wiped the thoughts from his mind and nodded. *He is on point—I had considered none of this, yet he was well ahead of me and I thought I knew everything there is to know on aviation terrorism. We found our guy.* Lynche and Yoder offered condolences on Hunter's parents. Lynche said, "I've followed the reporters who covered that story, and some of my friends at my old place said the *New York Times* was all over it, and the FBI channeled any new information through the *Times*. Did we answer your question?"

I shouldn't have said anything. The FBI took over jurisdiction of the investigation because witnesses reported an explosion, that there might have been another bomb that went off on another jetliner. Then my folks and PanAm and now TWA. Then some fool at the Times introduced the possibility of a missile strike? Was that reporter laziness and conjecture, or did someone have evidence of a terrorist's missile strike? What they say in public differs from what they say in private. The Washington Times reported the FBI "missile team" had interviewed 144 "excellent" witnesses immediately after the crash and found the evidence for a missile strike "overwhelming." But in August The New York Times flipped for the bomb explanation and ran a front-page headline that was eerily reminiscent, almost verbatim of the PanAm 103 crash, "Prime Evidence Found that Device Exploded in Cabin of TWA 800." None of the rafter of turkeys at the Times ever spoke to the official FBI witnesses about a likely missile strike. It was worth the shot! But they're not going to add anything to the discussion, so it is time to move on.

Hunter capitulated and said, "Close enough for government work. Again, I want to thank...."

Yoder had been looking into Mexico when he turned around and interrupted Hunter, "Did you know your PhD dissertation was published?"

Hunter cocked his head as if he had heard wrong. He made funny little movements with his hands. Caught completely unawares, the turn of topic was a total reversal of where his mind was going. He said, "That's just beyond my feeble powers of comprehension. I only submitted it to the university...to complete the requirements for my doctorate. *I* didn't have it published."

Lynche chose his words carefully and said, "There's a company in D.C. run by former Agency-types. TASC, the think tank, the Trans-Atlantic Security *Council*. They are part of TASCO who pays the rent and keeps the lights on. TASC takes documents that are in the public domain—dissertations, theses, treatises, war college papers, university research—slap a cover on them and have them published as 'pamphlets.' Your paper is published as a pamphlet, albeit it is the size of an Omaha phone directory. You can probably find it on that new company that sells books over the internet." *And my old place used them to ensure the outcome of elections in the Middle East.*

Hunter was incredulous on two counts. He tried the latter thought to give him some time to think about the other. "Amazon? I didn't know, but isn't that illegal?"

Yoder offered, "Only if they're caught and are taken to court. No one takes them to court, because there is no real money in these pamphlets."

"So why do they do it?"

Lynche expressed his admiration at the most senior person in the Border Patrol who wasn't an agent. He and Yoder exchanged looks. They knew. The tall solid, Boris Karloff-looking Yoder said, "If an aviation terrorism paper is in the public domain, the Trans-Atlantic Security Council is interested in it. And so are the Russians and Osama bin Laden and the al-Qaeda—I can just about guarantee that every mosque in the Middle East *and the U.S.* has your exposition on aviation terrorism...." After a pause, Lynche said, "...and they are copying it and are using it."

"*That's crazy!* It pisses me off someone is using my research...."

Lynche expounded on his statement and said, "They are heavy into the aviation security industry and the intelligence security field. TASC—the council—is sponsoring this year's annual OSS Awards Dinner. Art and I have to be back to attend—one of your guys is getting the Office of Strategic Services' William J. Donovan Award—you might know him. General Bogdan Chernovich?"

All thoughts of asking Yoder where he got his watch evaporated like smoke. Hunter hadn't heard that name in a couple of years. He purposefully hadn't been following the man's career and his face registered abject disappointment. Hunter mashed his lips together, kicked an imaginary rock, looked away momentarily towards Mexico, and said with obvious disgust, "Yeah, I know him." *He's a bloody murderer.*

Lynche and Yoder knew they had struck a negative chord but had little time to unwrap it. Yoder was blunt, "Duncan, who are you voting for?"

"Not Democrat. They've been horrible for the Border Patrol and America."

Lynche was nonplussed and didn't change his expression. Then he asked, "Are you medically cleared to fly?"

"I have my tickets. But no more fast movers like the F-4 for me."

Yoder asked, "Duncan, you have a security clearance?"

Hunter suddenly considered giving Lynche a call-sign. He was still smoldering from the mention of Chernovich's name. "TS/SCI from DOJ."

Colonel Art Yoder became introspective and said, "There is one thing about security clearances—if you desire, you can go places to see the real evil in the world."

Like awarding the really evil Chernovich with the top OSS prize? I used to think he was just a flaming ass, but now after looking at satellite photos you can tell he was just gay criminal. A sex murderer. Hunter found Yoder's comment odd. The look on Hunter's face said he was confused and conflicted. Suddenly he wasn't sure about the two men from D.C.

Yoder said, "There are some guys who are not afraid of the real evil in the world. Like Escobar."

Hunter was shocked still.

Lynche said, "Duncan, you were the guy who got us close to Pablo Escobar. Before you, we couldn't get anyone close to him and we had no idea where to find him. It took a couple of years to get him. My old place never forgot what you did."

Hunter didn't know what to say. *That was such a long time ago.... I was the bait to a trap. It took a couple of years to find him. But I didn't know if the homing devices worked. I had heard nothing and thought we failed until the papers announced Pablo was killed.*

Lynche asked, "Would you be interested in a job?"

Hunter's emotions were being whipsawed back and forth. He was surprised and his demeanor changed as drastically as the Texas weather. He wiped the sweat from his brow with the cuff of his shirt; he slowly cocked his head again; his brows narrowed in wonder. *What interesting men. What an interesting question; what an interesting day.*

Yoder put his hands in his pockets and the Rolex disappeared.

Lynche's thin smile suggested he wasn't kidding.

Hunter looked at Yoder and then at Lynche. Their faces etched with sly smirks. He patted the spyplane gently, as if to calm a nervous thoroughbred colt. *Why would anyone want a washed up fighter pilot for anything?* He broke the silence with a question, "What do you gentlemen have in mind?"

Book Two

Chapter 11

December 24, 2017

Twelve years later it still smelled of fresh paint. It wasn't a new building but it had new carpet and a robust fire suppression system. The old 7 World Trade Center was the first and only steel skyscraper known to have collapsed due to uncontrolled fires. The fires resulted from a wave of flaming debris as the North Tower of the World Trade Center collapsed. The replacement building was the first commercial office building in New York City to receive the U.S. Green Building Council's Leadership in Energy and Environmental Design. It was the perfect location to hide a politically right-leaning business.

Three people knew who worked at the business office, the Manhattan suite on the 26th floor of 7 World Trade Center. One of them, the building manager, placed a notification card on the door that a container had been received in the building's mail room. The second person who knew about the business office received mail at the office only when his benefactor, the third person who knew about the office, told him to expect a box. He would have to borrow the mailroom's hand-truck to bring it to the quiet, obscure, and anonymous corner office. Like before. Times three.

It was becoming an annual event. This time, like the last time, a text message to the correspondent's smart phone provided no clues what might be in the "box." Like the previous times, there were multiple shipping, FRAGILE, and FedEx labels on the fiberglass shipping crate designed to ship precision or delicate instruments. The first time he hadn't known what to expect; this time he did. The sender wasn't entirely predictable. The receiver moved the gray box to his office, and like the previous times, it barely fit through the office door.

It was Christmas Eve, and he knew what was in the box. He unlatched the fasteners like an excited child at Christmas, and he was taken aback. It was another antique and rare typewriter in pristine condition, and a large tin of chocolate-covered toffee. It didn't take a genius to see that the typewriter had been subject to a comprehensive restoration.

A sheet of paper was perfectly aligned between the paper table and platen. Unlike before, it wasn't a proposal for another political article but a proposal for an activity. His benefactor had typed, "As you well know, to circumvent the Soviet media juggernaut, dissidents created what they called the '*samizdat*,' their word for the clandestine copying and distribution of literature banned by the state. America's media are similarly corrupt and in order to circumvent the propaganda arm of the Democrat Party, America's dissidents—Republicans and Conservatives have been forced to create their own *samizdat*. They are an unorganized network of blogs, news-aggregators, talk radio shows, and legal monitors."

"Our fellow Marine, the late great Captain Peter Ortiz of the OSS, led French Resistance movements that fought against the Nazi German occupation of France and the collaborationist Vichy régime. I'm enlisting members for a similar resistance movement. You have become our nation's premier citizen-journalist. Your country needs you. You have the special skills we require to thwart the Democrat's communist agenda. Is this something you would consider while remaining thoroughly anonymous? This expertly restored 1907 Williams No 6 'Grasshopper' typewriter is another shameless incentive to engage your support. Please keep me appraised of your whereabouts so I may arrange a meeting to confabulate on this proposal. Semper Fi."

Demetrius Eastwood was almost giddy, and for a man over seventy, giddy was not a good look. He checked the dictionary for the meaning of *confabulate*, opened the tin of toffee, broke off a piece of the chocolate-covered confectionary, and popped it in his mouth. Savoring the candy, Eastwood got on the internet, found the outrageously expensive signed copy of a novel by an obscure author on the world's largest on-line auction, and selected the option to "Ask the seller a question."

His response wasn't a question. "Merry Christmas! And thank you for the presents. There's a reason they call this candy 'Dangerous Stuff!' I'm acquiring quite a collection of machines. Of course, my friend. I would do anything for you to help protect our country. I await your directions, good sir."

Chapter 12

January 28, 2018

After takeoff with the landing gear firmly retracted, Duncan Hunter flipped the switch to pipe music into his headphones.

It was twenty years ago today,
Sgt. Pepper taught the band to play.

It had been over twenty years since the former CIA executive, Greg Lynche, first brought Duncan Hunter into the fold at the Central Intelligence Agency. Paperwork, polygraphs, accesses, and restricted special access programs, all to become an approved Agency asset, primarily a contract pilot. Through Lynche's sponsorship and mentoring, Hunter became the Agency's contracted subject matter expert on aviation terrorism, domestically and internationally. They made an incongruous pair, the old lanky liberal rarely talked politics and the younger muscular conservative always did. When the time came for more kinetic work of the airborne variety, Lynche checked Hunter out in the Lockheed YO-3A and taught him how to use the aircraft's suite of sensors, thermal and night vision, to find the terrorists who didn't want to be found. When the YO-3A was outfitted with a gun, the Democrat Greg Lynche, now called *Grinch* by *Maverick*, walked away from the program. The *Grinch* said, "I've created a monster. It's *Maverick*'s baby, now."

Hunter wasn't a Francis Gary Powers clone, a pilot who flew a ballistic path over the Soviet Union or China taking high altitude photographs of the enemy's facilities. Hunter flew the U.S. Army prototype, first-generation YO-3A low-level, nearly in the weeds, and was much more active in the cockpit than the high-altitude and highly automated spyplane pilots of yesteryear. He didn't take pictures; he used the latest counter-surveillance and sensor technologies to peek into the hiding places of those who thought they were undetectable. He observed the enemy in real-time. A video recorder coupled to the sensors captured every image of the activities on the ground. And the aircraft had a gun.

When his counternarcotics missions were completed, Hunter would sometimes overfly the Chinese embassies. At low altitudes and critical angles, the YO-3A's night vision, FLIR, and synthetic-aperture radar (SAR) systems could image vehicles and people under awnings designed to thwart camera-carrying satellites and unmanned aerial vehicles (UAVs). CIA analysts and modelers built computer models of the communist compounds from the thermal and SAR imagery.

The YO-3A had received upgrades in the electronics and in the airframe during much of its history as a secret asset. The 57-foot wingspan had grown to almost 84-feet, and its propeller, originally designed by MIT's acoustical labs to achieve virtually silent flight, was improved and hand-polished by an old propeller maker. The aircraft, the prop, and its wings were specially modified to fit into a commercial 8X8X40-foot shipping container. All the structural and avionics modifications made to the basic YO-3A allowed it to be removed from its container and reassembled in seconds. Six of the original eleven 1969 aircraft had been re-engineered and extensively modified by one of Hunter's aviation companies; two had been destroyed while conducting operational missions, and four were airworthy, flying missions for the CIA. Four aircraft were in museums and looked nothing like the modified versions.

On his first mission, Hunter had found the location of fourteen hostages on a Colombian mountain top. He had used the quiet airplane's aural stealth capabilities as a weapon of sort. In the silent mode the propeller turned at a few hundred revolutions per minute—just enough RPMs to keep some wind flowing over the airplane's glider like wings. But on that night, Hunter had pushed the throttle to takeoff power for a few seconds. Supersonic shock waves spilled off the propeller tips and created a two-second roar, a deep guttural sound that discombobulated the men holding the hostages on the mountaintop. The thermal sensor captured how the kidnappers turned their faces toward the sound, doused their cooking fire, ran down a path, threw their cigarettes into the jungle, and took up defensive positions around a makeshift hut. The hut where the hostages were being held.

It wasn't shocking to Hunter that the FARC of twenty years ago was back on the same mountaintop holding another group of hostages. This time there was a guard outside who appeared to be taking a siesta. Hunter threw the switches to activate some of the newest capabilities of the FLIR technology. He overflew the hut and turned up the gain of the sensor to "look through" the thatch roof to find the thermal signatures of humans leaning against the walls. He recorded the thermal imagery and the GPS coordinates of the hostages' location, turned, and silently glided back to the coast. His job was to assess the situation, find the hostages, and determine the capability of the FARC. Hunter would not engage the narcoterrorists in gun battle unless he was sure he could eliminate all terrorists on the mountain. He could not fully incapacitate all of them; there were too many FARC hidden in the jungle. If a single terrorist were to get away he could reveal the means and methods of the Americans: *gunfire came from the sky…and I never saw an aircraft*. The local military would use the detailed photographic information from the U.S. Intelligence Community to design plans to rescue the hostages.

After completing surveillance on the mountain, Hunter engaged the artificial intelligence (AI) system which turned the YO-3A into a robot. The AI program enabled the aircraft to patrol the edges of the known fields of *Boliviana negra*, the *supercoca*, and search for the thermal signatures that would signal drug lab activity under the jungle canopy. With nothing in the FLIR scope to investigate, he reflected how the YO-3A and the Agency's drug eradication program had revolutionized the dynamics of the drug war.

Previous annual multimillion-dollar aerial eradication campaigns had killed a fraction of the millions of coca plants using the herbicide *glyphosate* but they became impossible to spray because narcoterrorists forced children to sleep in the fields, and Americans would not spray herbicide with children in the fields. When Hunter's YO-3A and his precision crop-killing laser system, *Weedbusters*, began eradicating millions of *Erythroxylum coca* plants, even with children sleeping in the fields, the drug lords surmised they needed to change tactics. A network of coca farmers began using selective breeding techniques to create a strain of the plant that was resistant to the glyphosate and unwittingly, virtually resistant to *Weedbusters* UV laser.

The CIA found they could still be an effective deterrent and used a FLIR to locate drug labs and positively identify the locations of jungle-covered streams where submersibles were manufactured. As quickly as the YO-3A recorded their locations, the Colombian National Army were sent in to destroy the labs and submersibles. This "passive" approach of locating the labs and subs was intermittently more productive than glyphosate or UV lasers could ever be. After several significant battles in the rainforest, the strategy became "let them make cocaine; we'll derail their logistics train."

The U.S. Coast Guard stopped many of the fast boats and engine-powered submersibles. The Drug Enforcement Agency stopped cocaine-laden aircraft flying under the radars. Success of the interdiction program was attributed to the half a dozen times a year Hunter flew into a military airfield near Bogotá, found drug labs, and marked them for disposition by the Colombia National Police, which basked in the glory of winning a chapter of the drug wars.

For narcoterrorists, the key to smuggling success was to reduce the thermal signature of their submersibles. Hunter found the cocaine-laden subs in open water by using the YO-3A's FLIR's sensitivity to discern the engine's nearly indistinguishable exhaust signature in the surrounding air and cold water or find the different thermal signatures of underwater trails left by a spinning propeller. He could find submersibles at great distances from a "bloom," a significantly different temperature gradient in the open water as plankton fluoresced when disturbed by the bow of the underwater boat. When Hunter found them and verified they were cocaine subs, he lowered the YO-3A's gun and shot holes into the sides of the submersibles.

Hunter could find a well-hidden drug lab under the jungle canopy or deep in the rainforest using the FLIR manually, but the AI system, even after multiple passes couldn't differentiate between the tiny heat signatures of a drug lab worker and a monkey. And the AI couldn't find any cocaine-carrying submersibles in open water. Frustrated with the lack of progress, Hunter disengaged the AI and the autopilot, and flew lazily along the coast investigating rivers and streams to find traces of makeshift boatyards that could build submersibles or where labs had been found. He was about to bypass one riverine system when he spied something unusual in the FLIR. Three equally spaced humps in the overgrowth. Mother Nature doesn't create "equally spaced" anything; even Alnilham wasn't equidistant from Altniak and Mintaka in Orion's Belt. Hunter had never encountered symmetrical "structural anomalies" in the thermal sensor before. The last time he had been over the area he had noticed nothing out of the ordinary.

He flew around the "anomaly" twice trying to see if miniscule variations in heat reflections captured in the thermal sensor could help "shape" and better define the unknown object. If it even was a man-made object, it was just off the river between Mangle and Estambul, Colombia. He flipped between the various modes of thermal imagery to night vison and back and then lowered the synthetic-aperture radar system to collect more information. He supposed the "anomaly" could be a string of oddly shaped, vine-covered cypress trees in the mangrove swamps protected by caiman, crocodiles, snakes, and sharks. But they were just too perfect.

He didn't think he was projecting, hoping what he was seeing was the vestiges of a lost aircraft. In the FLIR Hunter could only make out the faint outline of the three-tails and tail section of what might have been a 60s-era Lockheed Constellation. *Maybe it's a crashed Connie, but it's so close to the water, which makes no sense. I can see finding a lost airframe in the mountains or in the jungle but along the coast?* Hunter didn't have time for more exploration but "tagged" the center of the "anomaly" with GPS coordinates for the aircraft's video recorder. Maybe if government troops ever went into the area looking for drug smugglers they could also see if there was anything under the layers of vegetation. Maybe a group of aviation enthusiasts who recovered missing aircraft would be interested. The FLIR image wasn't definitive, and the SAR data would require analysis. Maybe the "anomaly" was just trees. He set a course for the Chinese embassy.

Just then, an airplane flew into the thermal sensor's field of view. It was running in the dark: no heat signature came from any of the aircraft's position lights, but the engine compartment and exhaust were as bright as a magnesium flare. He looked out into the inky night but couldn't pick up the aircraft with his Mark II eyeballs. Hunter powered up the YO-3A's Continental and maneuvered the FLIR to recapture the airplane in its field of view. Was it a drug smuggler's airplane or a private aircraft with an electrical malfunction? It had been over 25 years since he had flown radar intercepts in a fighter; this time he would make the turns necessary to do an intercept with none of the spine-cracking Gs. He had never even heard of anyone using a FLIR like a radar, but the principle was the same. Hunter shut off the music in his helmet.

Within a few minutes, he matched the speed and was within a wing length from the Piper 350. The other pilot was mimicking the slow flight characteristics of a small general aviation aircraft; his flaps were partially deployed as he was trying to avoid any attention from any surveillance radar in the area. A Cessna 150-class of aircraft had little cargo carrying capacity and would normally be overlooked as a smuggler's aircraft whereas the Piper 350 could easily carry tens of million dollars' worth of cocaine. The pilot didn't realize Hunter was flying formation on him. Hunter was mindful of the YO-3A's long wings and lowered one in order to look down into the Piper's rear seating area. *Those aren't bundles of rags, those are packages of cocaine; and that boy is full.* Hunter retarded the throttle then turned for some lateral separation. As he paralleled the path of the low-flying Piper, Hunter lowered the YO-3A's gun, the TS2 *Terminator Sniper System*, into the airstream and engaged the targeting system. All tracking and targeting symbology was overlaid on the FLIR image. Flying at co-airspeeds it was easier to track the aircraft with the laser designator (LD) than tracking speeding vehicles on the ground. Through a hand controller on the right side of the cockpit, Hunter put the LD on the white hot imagery of the engine, waited for the TS2 gun's system to indicate that it had locked onto the laser-designated target, and pulled the trigger. A white-hot streak of a laser-designated rocket-propelled bullet dominated the FLIR image.

Hunter watched the fire coming from the streaking bullet until it struck the aircraft's engine compartment. *AI is not programmed to engage airborne targets. The night isn't a complete bust.*

With its engine on fire and the Piper going down, Hunter retracted the FLIR, gained another twenty knots in airspeed, and pointed his black airplane toward the coordinates of the Chinese embassy in downtown Bogotá. After a low-slow flight over the embassy with the SAR imaging and the FLIR recording the activities in the compound, Hunter saw platoons of troops training in hand-to-hand combat and assault-style vehicles being maintained under wide and broad awnings. He sucked the two sensor systems into the fuselage and made a turn to the military airport.

He selected the artificial intelligence system again to engage the autonomous flight feature; the computer correctly determined the aircraft was near the military base and selected the YO-3A's automatic takeoff and landing system. Hunter was along for the ride, thinking that the pilots who had flown the aircraft in Vietnam would never believe what their quiet airplane could do now. The YO-3A flew a perfect hands-off, autonomous landing profile, landing perfectly astride the runway centerline. Before the aircraft shutdown automatically as programmed, Hunter disengaged the AI, bumped the throttle to taxi the aircraft quickly to the Hercules, and spun the aircraft 90° near the tail of the LM-100J.

From start to finish, the *Yo-Yo* performed almost flawlessly, except for the issues that would give the AI software engineers a conniption. The YO-3A wasn't ready for primetime as an unmanned platform to locate hostages, or engage submersibles and flying targets. *Director McGee will not be happy*. Bob and Bob deconstructed the airplane and placed the wings and fuselage into the *Yo-Yo's* container in the cabin of the Quiet Aero Systems LM-100J for the ride back to the U.S.

Flying drugs is dangerous business. You never knew when holes would appear in the hull or your engine turned into a can of worms. Sinking in the gulf or crashing into the jungle at night were some of the hazards of working for the drug cartels.

Chapter 13

January 28, 2018

On a new bulletin board on the *dark web*, a new player jumped into the political fray.

Greetings to the truth seekers who find today's media corrupted by special interests. It is Sunday, January 28th, 2018, and Maxim Mohammad Mazibuike was the most corrupt president in U.S. history. He was the only U.S. President who can recall the opening lines of the "Call to prayer," reciting them with a first-rate accent, and he was the only U.S. President who couldn't recite the Pledge of Allegiance or the words of the Star Spangled Banner. America deserves a president who knows the words to "O' Come All Ye Faithful."

I have a few questions that deserve to be answered accurately and not politically. I hope you find these posts thought provoking and illuminating.

Do you believe in coincidences?

Is it a coincidence that the FBI and the CIA – which are rarely involved in domestic aircraft accidents – investigated the case of Flight 800, the TWA jet that exploded off the coast of Long Island in 1996?

Is it a coincidence that when some FBI investigators concluded that a streak of light consistent with a surface-to-air missile launch, brought down the 747, these agents were removed from the investigation?

Is it a coincidence that in 1996, one of the most active periods of international aviation terrorism conducted by al-Qaeda affiliates, the CIA stopped the Bojinka plot – the name of the plan to blow up ten 747s over the Pacific – but their domestic counterterrorism partners, the FBI, couldn't find a trace of aviation terrorism even with a divining rod and a miner's helmet?

Is it a coincidence that the official report on Flight 800 stated that it was an accident and not shot down, even though Congress curiously mandated the DOD to look at putting anti-missile technology on commercial aircraft?

Is it a coincidence that in order to, and I quote, "prevent another Flight 800," closed quote, the shoot down of commercial aircraft, the CEO of the air cargo conglomerate, Federal Express, offered to have the military's anti-missile system designed to protect aircraft from infrared homing missiles installed on their cargo jets?

Is it a coincidence that since that fateful day, almost 200 of the world's worst terrorist masterminds – those that hit the FBI's Most Wanted Terrorist List – have died in the Middle East or Africa under mysterious conditions and the media hasn't said a word? The Muslim Brotherhood has their strategic plan to overthrow the U.S. government. It seems to me the U.S. government has their own secret strategic plan to find and decimate the Muslim Brotherhood's friends wherever they try to hide.

And is it a coincidence that since President Mazibuike was elected, not a single democratic candidate in dozens of countries has prevailed in national elections over their socialist or communist opponents? I think it would be the job of the FBI Voter Fraud Division to investigate the analog and electronic ballots, and the software and computer companies that provide voting machines for countries across the planet, but today the FBI are little more than the Keystone Kops in thobes. America and her allies need help.

This is the Omega.

CHAPTER 14

March 19, 2018

The cockpit was awash with lights that could not be viewed by anyone on the ground, even at night. Far below him, the pilot observed the comings and goings of the Somali pirates in a thermal sensor. He monitored the activities of those who stayed to guard their latest batch of hostage acquisitions and those pirates who filled marginally seaworthy skiffs to capture one of the commercial fishing vessels in the waters of the Indian Ocean.

After waiting for the small fleet of boats to make their way downriver and into the open waters of the ocean, Duncan Hunter easily located the hostages' and their captors' thermal signatures in the forward-looking infrared. He assessed the level of security within the collection of huts in the Somali jungle. Confident the pirates on the water with roaring outboard motors would not hear his weapon's report, Hunter lowered the aircraft's gun into the airstream. He checked that the aiming system worked and targeting information was displayed as an overlay in the FLIR scope. He located and removed six kidnappers from the battlefield in a few minutes. The last man was the most difficult to kill. He had his wits about him and seemed to have a sixth sense from which direction the bullets were coming.

Hunter barely got the IR laser on him when he moved again, in random directions and doubling back until the pirate stopped behind a tree, thinking he had found safety. Hiding behind a tree didn't disrupt the targeting system's tracking feature. Hunter placed the laser designator in the middle of the obstructing tree and pulled the TS2 gun's trigger. He followed the white-hot bullet to impact. Within seconds, the hostage-taking pirate hiding behind the tree collapsed in a dead heap. The FLIR recorded the man's fatal chest wound.

Isolating kidnappers from the kidnapped had been simple: who had an AK-47 with bandoliers slung across their chest and who was tied up. The men with bullets got a very big one right above the point where the bandoliers crossed. When all the apparent kidnappers were neutralized in the camp hideout, Hunter retracted the TS2 into the fuselage and typed a message into one of his multi-function panels. A separate red laser designator used electronically as a "laser pointer" spelled out the message on the ground, inscribing words which flashed like a laser show at halftime at a professional basketball game. Red letters transformed into a red arrow which converted to a bright pulsating red line to show the way to safety. Hunter checked the surrounding area for other thermal images while leading the group of hostages through the jungle to the beach with the laser designator. His last message flashed in red: WAIT HERE. Several hostages raised their thumbs to the sky.

After Hunter got the hostages safely to the pickup area, he used the FLIR to locate the heat signatures of the rest of the Somali kidnappers out on the waters of the Indian Ocean. By their direction of travel, he could see which of the slow-moving commercial fishing vessels the pirates planned to attack. In the distance, a U.S. submarine surfaced right on time, and Hunter made radio contact, provided a status report, and requested a few minutes for some "housekeeping." He swept behind the Somalis to put himself between the kidnappers and the submarine. If there were ricochets, he wanted them to be away from the hostages and the submarine.

Hunter didn't want to take a chance that the Somalis might puncture a SEAL team's Zodiac rubber boat with a lucky shot, so he shot their boats out from under them. Three bullets obliterated the motors and three bullets shattered the sterns of the three skiffs. The skiffs quickly foundered and the fifteen or so pirates found it very difficult to swim with weapons and bandoliers weighing them down. And if the men couldn't swim, it wasn't his fault that they became well-armed shark bait. Such were the hazards of pirating at night.

Hunter orbited overhead as Navy SEALs loaded the hostages aboard their Zodiacs and returned to their submarine, then he headed north to the rendezvous point.

CHAPTER 15

March 21, 2018

For those who were wearing headsets, the LM-100J pilot announced they had entered Afghan's airspace. They were level at 10,000-feet mean sea level (MSL) and descending into Kandahar Air Base at 1,000-feet MSL. There wasn't the usual angst among the aircrew for the descent into the Afghan city. Taliban and al-Qaeda fighters would leave the white airplanes alone. If any of them shot at a landing airplane, the Kandahar Air Base's gunfire detection system, using acoustic, optical, or other types of sensors, would detect and convey, virtually instantly, the location of gunfire or other weapons fire, such as a rocket-propelled grenade. Patrolling American attack helicopters would respond in seconds and destroy the shooters. It was a form of Pavlovian response; shoot at white airplanes and you would be killed instantly. The rules for dark aircraft, combatants, were different.

In the late 1980s, the CIA had issued hundreds of *Stinger* anti-aircraft missiles to the Taliban to run the Soviet aircraft out of Afghanistan. *Stingers'* battery packs had a shelf life of only a few months and new batteries were not available, even in the black markets of Islamabad where they had everything a terrorist could want. When the Russians left the country, an Iranian colonel showed the Taliban and al-Qaeda cultists how to harvest the explosives in the *Stingers'* warheads and turn them into improvised explosives devices that could kill the invaders from America.

With the pilot's announcement that they were over the Afghan border, the LM-100J aircrew, Hunter, and his support crew donned oxygen masks and opened the regulators to fill their lungs with pure O2 from portable bottles of Aviation Breathing Oxygen, ABO.

Maverick always wore an oxygen mask in Afghanistan, not because he would fly at higher altitudes, but to keep his lungs full of *clean* ABO. The odor of the air in Kabul and Kandahar was a hundred times worse than a Dalhart, Texas feedlot in July. It was also gritty, vile, and disgusting. He avoided breathing the miasma of suspended abrasive, caustic fecal particulates that left a lumpy and dusty residue over everything, including the back of your mouth.

Once a year, Duncan Hunter and his quiet airplane with a state-of-the-art laser system deployed to Afghanistan for a one-night stand performing aerial eradication of the country's most notorious cash crop, the opium poppy. The specially built laser was now so advanced there wasn't anything like it anywhere. The latest generation of the *Weedbusters* system had been perfected; this mission to Afghanistan would show that the state of artificial intelligence technology no longer required a pilot or a sensor operator to be "in-the-loop."

Once airborne in the YO-3A, *Maverick* would sweep the area with the thermal sensor looking for clues of human activity near the poppy fields or worse, men hiding in the hills with AK-47s hoping for a chance to shoot down an aerial eradication aircraft from *Âmirikâ*. The snows had retreated from the fields and the new poppy crop was emerging from the ground.

Hunter anticipated the lightshow when the chemical processes were activated as the unseen scanning beam of the ultra-violet laser irradiated a swath of the infant opium poppies. It was a natural reaction that once made him a bit uneasy; the plants under attack would fluoresce; soft, green, and hazy, much the way plankton fluoresces in the nighttime surf. Before the YO-3A's airframe and wings were coated with the light-killing nanotechnology, the underside of the YO-3A would be exposed by reflection, illuminated by thousands of fluorescing plants. Now, the belly of the YO-3A remained unseen.

The intense application of ultraviolet radiation set into motion the plant's ultimate demise. Even as tiny plants, their naturally occurring and protective photochemicals leeched back into the plant's stalk after sunset. When blasted with the UV light, the plants immediately flooded their leaves with photosensitive compounds that had evolved over the eons to protect plants against excessive radiation from the sun. Hitting plants with a laser during daylight hours was akin to a slow-speed crash between dump trucks; not much happened.

However, hitting plants with a laser at midnight when the protective photochemicals had returned to their stalks to rest and recharge was akin to a speeding dump truck running over a child's tricycle. It wasn't a fair fight.

Killing plants with UV was a sophisticated science. An article on how an ever-expanding ozone hole over Antarctica was decimating the plant life in Patagonia on the tip of South America had led Greg Lynche and Duncan Hunter to consider mechanical means of eradication. Could specifically tuned lasers destroy illegal plants? What kind of lasers? Visible, infrared or ultra-violet? What were the technical secrets to killing opium poppies and coca—even cannabis? Was it in the wavelength or dwell times—times on target—or the power of the laser? Or was it a precise combination of all three vectors?

Hunter had approached the head of the Photonics Laboratory at the University of Arizona with a proposal. The professor slipped into his building on a weekend and irradiated the opium poppy's closest and legal-to-possess biological equivalent—*Eschscholzia californica*—and was astounded at the result. The California poppy shriveled into a ball of death; its once vibrant green leaves turned brown over a period of seconds. He had witnessed the first plant to be killed by a laser. The professor told Hunter that he had validated the concept, but there would be tremendous technological challenges to take the process from the laboratory to the field.

The CIA's Science & Technology Directorate had jumped onto the complex engineering question; they divided the challenge into several R&D (Research and Development) contracts that went to companies with the best scientists in America, and the rest was history. The first generation of *Weedbusters* had been born.

For centuries, killing opium poppies had been a losing battle for countries with eradication programs—there were always political entanglements until the CIA developed the ultra-violet laser which could be deployed from the belly of a very low-flying, special-purpose airplane. In the first year, a five-night aerial eradication operation with a single aircraft resulted in a 25% reduction in opium production in Afghanistan alone. After twenty additional years of R&D and continuous improvement the laser system, now essentially a UV

LIDAR, had achieved a "probability of kill," a P_k that approached 100% for plants just emerging from the ground. No longer did they kill thousands of mature plants over several days. Now they could kill half-million hectares of baby plants in a single night from a low-flying airplane. Significantly damaged baby plants were just as good as a dead plant, as it would not put up an opium poppy seed pod.

In theory, the process no longer required a pilot at the controls; an autonomous UAV could do the work. CIA contract pilot Duncan Hunter acted as "a safety pilot" as the artificial intelligence-driven aircraft did all the work. He was just along for the ride. Hunter sat back and took notes for the software engineers about any issues encountered during the proof-of-concept flight. He loved pissing off the drug cartels by infecting their crop with an "unknown virus" that annihilated their drug crop and destroyed their opium production.

At the beginning of the growing season the drug lords celebrated the record number of hectares under cultivation. Then days later the inconceivable occurred; 99.99 percent of the tiny poppy plants were dead and brown like tiny scraps of Kraft paper. A record bounty became a record failure overnight. Some slow-to-emerge plants survived but none of those would produce the bulb from which the opium latex would be harvested.

The conclusion of *The William Tell Overture* played through his headphones as Hunter monitored the aircraft instruments and performance as the autonomous *Weedbusters* software set up its antepenultimate run over the remaining plot of opium poppy. The music contributed to the euphoria of the closure of another mission. He would chronicle, via an after action report, that the *Weedbusters* and AI software performed flawlessly.

CHAPTER 16

April 10, 2018

An overnight, short-duration ice storm and heavy fog covered every branch and twig with lucent crystalline ice. When the occasional rays of sunlight poked through the "sucker holes," those openings that naturally occurred in a broken sky, the landscape turned into a sparkling sea of glass, a forest of diamonds. Every blade of ice-covered grass shimmered as scintillating shards of crystal, the branches of leafless trees coruscated in familiar rainbow colors as the sun emerged from behind the clouds.

Overhead a soundless drone flew with a camera taking video of the ice-covered scenery and monitoring the boss, his wife, and the surrounding area for any hint of danger.

Duncan Hunter and Nazy Cunningham wore deer leather jackets as they rode a pair of Silver Dapple Sooty Buckskins through the backwoods of white ice, in awe of what Mother Nature had provided them that forenoon. Once she turned up the heat and the ice-covered branches and twigs warmed in the sun, the melting ice would fall like gentle hail into a ground fog.

After their ride they returned the horses to the stable and handed them off to Carlos Yazzie.

Breakfast was served on the veranda. Hunter opted for a new topic, one that had to be addressed before they returned to Washington, D.C. It was work related, and the married lovers often talked about work. He said, "I'm thinking I'm about done. The *Yo-Yo* is nearly fully autonomous, meaning the Agency can manufacture others to replicate its capabilities for their program. In very many ways, I'm no longer needed." Duncan sat with his wife at a little bistro table on the massive deck overlooking the Grand Tetons to the west. A dozen low-profile radiant heaters on the veranda kept the chill at bay. A hundred plants of varying height and rarity in colored individual Mexican pots, mostly unusual succulents from across the planet, were scattered about the deck and against the railing.

The home appeared to first-time visitors as something of a science project deep from the mind of a drug-addled Denver architect. Some considered it a weird wooden tribute to Frank Lloyd Wright. The finished structure had once been described as a "hideous accident," as if Wright's iconic *Fallingwater* had a collision with the Yellowstone Lodge. The designer called his 6,000 square-foot "masterpiece" *Timber Rock.* He had used mammoth cedar logs from Canada as main supports and cantilevers for terraces and decks. The boulders and stonework throughout the residence were considered as good as the stonemasonry found in Edgar Kaufmann's summer home on Bear Run, but some people found the odd red granite a turnoff.

Builders had rerouted a creek and hauled in huge stones from a local quarry to create a declivity and a waterfall and had cantilevered the residence over the creek and waterfall to face the Grand Tetons. The dozen fireplaces throughout *Timber Rock* played upon the theme of ledge and cantilever. Critics from the big cities hated the design of *Timber Rock;* its enormous stone fireplaces were outlandish and its water features bizarre. But the millionaire architect who meticulously oversaw every aspect of the residence and surrounding buildings considered the six-year project a labor of love.

Duncan Hunter had toured the home after it had been vacant for over a decade. With Grand Tetons in the backyard, a majestic backdrop for any residence, he had immediately submitted an offer to buy. Carlos Yazzie, Hunter's longtime friend and foreman, oversaw the remodeling of the lodge, the construction of a multi-car garage, and installation of a comprehensive security system with multiple fixed cameras, cameras on drones, night vision and thermal cameras, and hundreds of microwave and seismic sensors. Much of the additional expense was in the construction of a considerable underground network of safe rooms, thousand-gallon propane tanks, and emergency backup generators. Hunter wanted the elaborate entrance gate replaced with something less ostentatious and said the property needed a perimeter fence. An intelligence community-level security system and safe rooms were a must; they were the priority.

On multiple occasions in Texas, impenetrable safe rooms had saved Duncan Hunter and the Yazzies from Islamic terrorists.

She turned from the Grand Teton view and blithesomely looked at her husband of fifteen years. "Well, I *still* need you." Nazy Cunningham oozed naughtiness and sincerity. Her words brought a smile to Duncan's face. She always knew what to say, unless she was trying to respond to one of Duncan's aviation idioms, then silence was golden. "But Duncan, darling, I know you can do things in the airplane that a computer, even with AI cannot do." She picked up a folded copy of the *Denver Post* and shook it at him while pointing to an article with a lacquered nail. "This is you! From Bamako—'Al-Qaeda terrorists lose in surprise firefight with Mali Army!' And Mogadishu; 'Hostages freed and rescued by coastal patrol.' That's all you. AI cannot do that."

"I know. A week ago the AI couldn't categorize the difference between a hostage and a pirate. I have to take care of the situation when the computer does nothing. Just when I think the software guys are making progress, the system hangs up like an old rotary-dial telephone that had its wires yanked from the wall. I took care of the pirates when the software wouldn't and led the hostages through the jungle until they were rescued by SEALs off of a submarine. But it kills poppy like a champ."

Nazy said, "Oh, here's something I know you're interested in. Originally from *The New York Times;* Hungarian-born Rho Schwartz Scorpii, *the Black Scorpion....*"

Duncan protested, "They call that evil little old commie who lives under a bridge the *Black Scorpion*? Since when?"

Nazy continued, "...is an East European energy billionaire who founded the Red Star Aggregate in Romania. He supports progressive and liberal political causes, to which he dispenses donations through his German foundation, the *Befreie die Nationens Stiftung*, the 'Free the Nations Foundation.' Free the Nations has donated more than $100 billion worldwide to various philanthropic causes 'to reduce poverty, increase scholarships, ensure free and safe elections, and promote better governance around the world.'"

"That's putting lipstick on a pig." Hunter was interested in more.

Nazy put the paper down; her face said she was confused.

"They are trying to paint Scorpii as someone better than he is. The only problem is there can never be enough lipstick to make that commie look good."

Nazy now understood, nodded, and read the editorial. "It says, 'Well done good and faithful servant: Scorpii appoints TASCO's Bogdan Chernovich to chair the huge *Befreie Nationens Stiftung*, the 'Free Nations Foundation' is Scorpii's flagship, the socialist billionaire's principle vehicle, the *apparat* he uses beyond the electoral system to create chaos under the phony rubric of 'openness' and 'democracy.'"

"Doesn't his foundation provide voting machines across the continents...?" Hunter knew a little of the *Black Scorpion's* dealings from an occasional reading of *The Eastern*. If it wasn't Chernovich's face on the cover of the magazine then it was Scorpii's.

Without looking up, Nazy nodded and continued, "It says here that he served as the TASCO chairman, the company whose 'Free and Open' voting technology merged with *Democracy Innovations'* voting machines used throughout the world. The rest is about Scorpii's financed revolutions in Eastern Europe and he warned the western world that he will bring chaos to America. 'Rho Schwartz Scorpii loathes the American people and would now be in a position to push the Scorpii chaos button to create more trouble.'"

Hunter narrowed his brows. *Commies cannot change their spots.*

She didn't look up and casually mentioned the special access program, *Liberty Machine*. "It was developed in the late 1980s to ensure free elections in the third world. Now private foundations have taken over that responsibility." Then Nazy collapsed the newspaper and looked at her husband. He had that hard look in his eye that told her he was thinking. She continued, "What are you thinking, darling?"

He didn't say what was on his mind; he would need more time. He pulled a coin from a pocket. "*Catch!*" He flipped the coin to her; she caught it after releasing the newspaper. "Everyone has these now so I had one made."

Nazy looked at it carefully for an instant, shrugged her shoulders, and handed it back to Duncan. As she resumed reading he said, "It's identical to the Air America patch but instead of 'Air America' spelled out in the shield, it reads 'Air Branch.'"

"I saw that. Very clever." She wasn't impressed in the least. The coin craze in DOD and the Agency had gotten out of hand. Everyone had them or were having some made. The most desirable of the coins came from the Special Activities Division. They had the most creative designs and the CIA bookstore couldn't keep them in stock. The Agency's executives displayed racks of coins in their private offices as if they were silver dollar-sized trophies.

She returned to the article. "Well, I know this is new. Apparently when he was a general in Europe, Chernovich actually lived with Rho Schwartz Scorpii." Nazy quoted, "Some look at this appointment of Bogdan Chernovich to the top of the Scorpii empire, brimming with bottomless cash derived from Scorpii's huge fortune, is just a return to the mothership for old General Chernovich."

He pocketed the coin. His thoughts were aligning into something coherent. Hunter said, "The media said the President would lose."

"But he didn't. I think I know what you're thinking but the *Liberty Machines* were only used overseas, they were all destroyed, and that was many years ago. That SAP has been long dead."

Hunter frowned. "What were the difference between your *Liberty Machines* and Scorpii's *Democracy Innovations*?" He tapped his finger in random thoughts.

"How would I know that?" Sometimes Duncan could be irritating.

Hunter said, "The media virtually guaranteed he would lose because President Hernandez got on their shit list when he openly questioned Mazibuike's *bona fides* when 3M was a senator. He asked, 'How is it possible that the son of a foreign national is a legitimate candidate for president when he isn't a natural born citizen?' Simple question with a simple answer. American kids were taught 'children born of U.S. citizens—*citizens* plural—are natural born citizens regardless of where they are born.' Children born of foreign parents are not eligible to be president."

"Even I know that." She smiled.

"And that should have been the answer, that 3M could not run and wasn't eligible. But the totally corrupt media and the DNC convinced enough people—*classic disinformation campaign*—that he was eligible and rammed him through the system. And when the Republicans never challenged him, that was the green light he needed. Then when 3M ran away and Hernandez was appointed president, the DNC, the liberals, the left, and the media went nuts and accused President Hernandez of orchestrating 3M's downfall. I never understood why Mazibuike's Republican opponent didn't take him to court. He would have won that election easily but.... It wasn't possible unless...."

"Unless what, Duncan?"

"It's an issue of mechanics. I was going to say they would have to control the outcome of the election. I don't think they could do that in America, so I'm left wondering how it happened. You say the Agency's old *Liberty Machines* were used overseas to stop terrorists and then you say the *Black Scorpion's* foundation's voting machines are used all across the globe to ensure fair elections and I say, not so fast G.I. Dog. What about here? Could some have been brought to the U.S.? Was there any cross-pollination? But I'm on the outside and it seems to me we could be talking about the same machines." *If the Liberty Machines are obsolete and were replaced with Democracy Innovations machines, what really changed? The cover? The label?*

"But the president won this time. I mean, it was close but he won."

Hunter sighed heavily, as if he had given up on a very difficult calculus problem. She avoided the question too. It was too silly to conceive. "I haven't figured that out yet, but the media was doing everything it could so Eleanor Tussy could win and the DNC Chairman killed himself. Who kills himself for losing an election?"

As an afterthought, Nazy said, "Maybe he failed his master. Oh, there's more. The left has increased their complaints that 'American conservatives' have promoted 'false claims' that characterize the eighty-year-old Scorpii as a singularly dangerous 'puppet master' behind many of the elections won by socialists."

Hunter repositioned himself in his seat and edged closer. "Is *he* the *Puppet Master*?" *The Puppet Master?* Hunter thought the old commie had failed the Kremlin. Now he wasn't sure. Sometimes Nazy's insights could be brutally and breathtakingly illuminating. Hunter pondered the possibilities, slightly shifted gears, and asked, "Does it say anything about Scorpii's funding socialists, Marxists, communists, and anarchists in America and Europe?"

"No. But I've seen the intel and it is true he does and openly pines for America to be overthrown by a foreign power."

"He wants Russia." Hunter frowned. *Maybe he wants America....*

"We think he orchestrated the outcome of the socialists winning in Venezuela and Grenada; but not the Muslim Brotherhood winning the presidencies across North Africa. The Middle East. I'm sure that is our purview. We have guys controlling those machines. Through a third party, a dummy corporation."

There it was again. Is the CIA and Scorpii collaborating in some way? Hunter continued his line of thought. "We expect the Democrats to cheat here. And it all came down to Philadelphia; President Hernandez won Philly and won Pennsylvania and won the election."

"It didn't seem possible. We were lucky."

The election confused the professional pollsters. They had seen nothing like it, that it was puzzling. Impossible. He let the issue drop. Hunter frowned, bit a lip for a moment, and said, "Darling Nazy, you can say that again. Any word on global petroleum-related tragedies?"

Nazy returned to her paper. "Only that Republicans claim that when the Red Star Aggregate attempted the hostile acquisition of Blue Star Fuels, the CEO of Blue Star was killed and Blue Star Fuels main oil refinery was destroyed in a catastrophic explosion."

"Nothing about Scorpii funding Islamic terrorists in North Africa or the Middle East?"

"No. Should there be? Funding terrorists is the sole purview of Iran and sympathetic wealthy Muslims in the Middle East."

Hunter nodded. "It's easy to blame Iran for all the terror. But from what little I know, Scorpii wants to control oil. Everyone's oil. Russian oil. Venezuelan oil, Libyan oil, Iraqi oil—if he could get to it, Iranian oil. He'll do whatever it takes. I assume he was behind the Blue Star Fuels CEO getting knocked off. He's on my shit list for buying up all the collectible watches." Hunter reflected momentarily that no one really knew where to find Scorpii. He could hide in a European castle or a *dacha* in Russia. Money had a way of insulating the politically active from danger.

Nazy moved on and returned to the articles where Duncan's exploits were reported. She asked, "Do you care about who gets the credit for the rescues?"

Hunter said he never even considered it. "I'm just a very paltry piece in a very portly puzzle. Your guys do all the hard work and heavy lifting. They make the contacts, surveil the area, and live in trailers or hotels for years. They chase down terrorism leads in Africa and the Middle East looking for al-Qaeda and their derivatives. They find the hard targets; they get me into the right grid square so I don't have to spend all my time looking for a heat source. Your guys are unmatched—top-drawer. *Nonpareil*. I'm just glad to be there, proud to serve. All that stuff. And I know you reward them for their work."

Rescuing oil workers captured by an al-Qaeda splinter group or rescuing sailors from Somali pirates who hijacked a container ship and tried to hold the seamen for millions in ransom was routine for Duncan, and he didn't need to be celebrated. His issue was the airplane. It was about worn out.

"These validation-verification flights are exposing a lot of gaps in capability. I don't see how software can overcome these gaps, regardless of who the programmers are."

Nazy turned the newspaper pages, looking for something more but finding nothing. She offered, "The real issue is some people think you're very expensive. The Chief Financial Officer nearly *had a cow*—is that how you say it?" Hunter nodded. She continued, "...nearly had a cow when you submitted your after action report and fee for services. I was in the office with Bill, and I just knew that woman's head was going to burst when he said to 'pay it,' that 'our contractor is the only capability in town.' He told her, '*Noble Savage*, like other sole-sourced restricted special access programs is actually a bargain at any price. The ten-year $500 million contract is fully funded to the end of the year and may be extended another ten years.' Bill also told her, 'Before *Noble Savage*, the Agency had squandered billions on unmanned technologies that went nowhere, and we used to spend hundreds of millions of dollars trying to find and kill the worst of the worst terrorists with little to nothing to show for it. I've probably told you too much, but now you know.' She wanted more details before she would approve the invoice, but Bill wouldn't give her anything. He asked me if she was cleared for the program, and I reiterated to Miss Deng that she wasn't. Then he dismissed her because Yassmin made his head hurt."

Hunter laughed his guttural *ha-ha. I'm sure she made his head hurt.* "What is her beef?" He thought he was being clever maintaining the bovine references, but it silently passed through the conversation like silage through a bull.

"I'm pretty sure you would call her a liberal. She's one of the few women who came in during the time of Mazibuike's edict who remain."

"Is she African-American? Muslim? Are you uneasy about her? Do you suspect her, like the others?"

Nazy shook her head. "Yes, no, no and not really. Unlike the others that came in off of the street, she had been the Chief Financial Officer of the Defense Intelligence Agency, and she's career, been employed by the government for many years—well before Mazibuike came onto the scene. Army War School graduate. She's not new, nor is she a blackmail target. She has history; she's passed the polygraph over there. It was a promotion for her."

"So she can pass the polygraph, and she's still working. Doesn't that suggest she's in the clear? Hadn't all the aggravations you had with the people 3M forced into the Agency been terminated? Gone? Weren't most of them Muslim? They came in during a specific window of hiring, but they couldn't pass the poly?"

"We think we've...."

Hunter interrupted, "Mucked out the stables?"

Nazy liked that. "*Scrubbed* is more like it. We used Clorox® and a fire hose, as you say." She laughed. "We have done some major *housecleaning* and reorganization, but as for the CFO, I don't think she is even tested any longer. The leadership isn't. Bill isn't; I'm not. You're not."

Hunter grimaced, "I'm executive leadership? Who knew?" He allowed Nazy to glower at him. He said, "I don't think Miss Deng would like me."

"I don't think she likes anyone. You're definitely the wrong color. She is short and abrupt with men, especially white men, and thinks Bill is an ally only because he's black. As if they are in some special club for 'people of color,' that they all think alike, and the rules are different for them. I think they say."

"Bill will not put up with that BS for long. He'll give her a verbal thrashing she will never forget. You never want a pissed off SEAL (Sea, Air, Land) on your ass."

Nazy said, "She ripped into the Deputy when he said he needed to hit 'the little boy's room' before a meeting. She dressed him down and told him he couldn't say 'little boy's room,' that it was racist. You can imagine when Bill got involved and told Miss Deng that saying 'little boy's room' isn't racist, that her response to an innocuous remark was stupid and juvenile, and the Deputy deserved an apology; but most of all, Bill said he would not tolerate any hint of the left's Critical Race Theory at the Agency. I was in the office when he counseled her. You have to have another women in the office if you go behind closed doors."

"Even you?"

"I'm not demented. We have some stupid personnel rules. Some women think every man is out to get her; some men think every woman he meets wants to hop into bed with him. When those two collide, the personnel office has problems. She's a little better now, but she sees things differently."

And you and Bill have history. "Sounds like she has all the charms of a North Korean prison guard. Are you trying to say she's probably a lesbian?"

Her husband could sometimes be abrupt but on target. Nazy had avoided mentioned the woman's sexual preferences; she nodded and said, "See, this is why she would hate you. You're perceptive and don't buy in to the narrative. But back to Bill, it isn't a factor of paying you, I think he doesn't want his job—he doesn't want to be there if it means losing you. Once the *Yo-Yo* is autonomous he's convinced you're gone. I think Air Branch is demanding more aggressive unmanned capability, and he is not convinced spending money on them is a worthwhile venture. They have spent billions; literally hundreds of millions. You are doing what they cannot. That, and I believe he had so much fun flying with you—you even arranged for him and Greg to ride in a *Blue Angel* jet; he said the Navy wouldn't have done that for him, with all of his awards—that he regrets taking the Director's job. He wants to get out more. He still wants to be a part of the action. Not behind a desk. In my humble opinion."

He once said he always wanted to be a pilot. It is not for everyone. Hunter refrained from saying what he was thinking: *We made a bang-up team when the solution called for two dudes. He was always saving my ass when I got too far over my skis. And I would let him fly. He loves flying about as much as his extraordinary father.* Nazy was more than insightful.

She returned to the view beyond. The overcast had opened up and the sky was now brilliant blue dotted with "puffies," as Duncan called minor clouds when he was giving an impromptu technical weather report. The sun was warming the landscape and slivers of ice had begun falling from the tree branches. She lovingly smiled at the lifelong aviator who had his own monosyllabic vocabulary for polysyllabic things. She gently shook her head in wonder and nodded toward the Tetons. "You don't find '*hills*' like that in the Middle East, except maybe the *Hi..MAL..yas* in Afghanistan and Pakistan."

Duncan loved her British pronunciation of *Himalayas.* "I don't know, baby. I've been all over this planet and the Grand Tetons, *them thar hills,* are in a class by themselves." He took a moment to admire her profile and reflect on their relationship—he tried to work as hard as she did in Washington, D.C. Had the right person found her she might have been a supermodel walking a runway in Paris in her skivvies, but Duncan had found her first, and twenty years of working for the CIA had taken its toll on both of them. Below the waterline of Nazy's beauty was the residue, the backwash of twenty years of fighting the radicals of Islam. Wrinkles, gray hair, scars. She would say, "A little gray hair is a trifling price to pay for all the worldly wisdom I've gained since coming to the Agency."

Nazy wore a billowy white cotton top which hid pendulous breasts; her jeans were from a specialty shop in Jackson Hole, and the brown caiman boots came from the Lucchese store in San Antonio. A gold ribbon cross from James Avery hung from her neck; a testament of her defection from Islam and acceptance of Christ. A gemstone store in a mall in Colombia provided a silver belt buckle with a thick irregular polished emerald that matched the color of her eyes. These weren't mere tokens of places they would run off to for dinner or shopping to get Nazy away from the cesspool that was Washington, D.C. She choose her clothes carefully to hide the scars from surviving the violent and near-lethal encounters of radical Muslim men.

Nazy's floor-length hair and scalp had nearly been removed from her head by a psychopath with a knife. Now her hair was wrapped tightly atop her head and held in place by long silver hair pins the size of crochet needles. Tinted frames with opulently round lenses rested on the tip of her nose.

Duncan was the perfect uxorious husband—he was completely devoted to her and excessively affectionate and complimentary. She wasn't just supermodel eye candy on his arm at a state dinner; Nazy was accomplished in her own right, leading intelligence professionals in finding the hideouts of the world's worst terrorists. Hunter, the husband, was comfortable being in a subservient role; he would go where the analysts expected to find a specific terrorist or terrorist group. And when Hunter found them, he dispatched them with extreme prejudice. Nazy's analysts got the credit, because the pilot of *Noble Savage* didn't officially exist.

At home or in the cockpit, Duncan usually wore a plain-Jane denim shirt and jeans, black crocodile boots, and a silver buckle; clothes and a two-tone Rolex that also hid the scars of violent Muslim radicals and many American and Jordanian surgeries.

The key to their collective success was that Hunter used his powers of observation to discern the clues that told him if there were terrorists in the area; like a chess grandmaster Nazy used her powers of understanding Muslim men and their weaknesses to determine their next move. When she could predict their movements she and her team could predict an intercept window. And they had, over 200 times in twenty years.

The man who had saved both of their lives was now their boss, installed in the corner office of the top floor of CIA Headquarters. In gratitude for rescuing Nazy from the hands of troglodytes, Duncan

Hunter had made the retired SEAL and former Naval War College classmate, Bill McGee, a very wealthy man. Like many of the former special operations warriors, he had been a contract security specialist for a few years after retiring from the Navy. After saving Nazy's life, Hunter gave McGee a new life as the owner-operator of a law enforcement and special operations training facility near Hondo, Texas. If Bill McGee asked for something, it was unlikely that Nazy or Duncan would ever refuse his request. And vice versa.

He asked, "What else in in the paper?"

"Let's see what you would be interested in. Oh, in forty-eight of the fifty largest cities—all Democrat Party strongholds—there are riots and protests against the Republican president who they claim stole the election."

"Well, she was supposed to win despite having the greatest voter fraud operation ever devised by man. Her words, not mine."

"Yes, darling. And we have Republicans and Conservatives fleeing Democrat-controlled states. U-Haul can't keep up with the demand. More articles on electric cars that cost too much, and California is determined to kill the combustion engine, have more electric cars, and they have rolling blackouts...."

"Who expected California becoming a third world country?"

Nazy didn't reflect on the joke she didn't get. "Um, let's see. What else." She turned the page, found an article, and said, "The Mossad told the FBI that al-Qaeda infiltrated airport security...."

"When?"

"Early 1990s."

"In other words, old news. That was a time under a Democrat president which led to September 11th; not Benghazi, of course."

Nazy momentarily looked over the top of the page and then resumed scanning the paper. "We knew that. You knew that. You called Greg. But apparently no one at the FBI took the Israelis seriously. It may have been because an agent with ties to the Muslim Brotherhood deep *sixtieth* the information." She stopped, knowing that something didn't come out right.

"*Deep six*—it's a reference to being buried six-feet deep."

"And *check six* means to always look behind you. They use that in the surveillance course."

Hunter nodded without any malice or ridicule in the usage error. Nazy was still learning American idioms and Hunter was learning British sayings and terms.

The person responsible at the FBI had converted to Islam and has retired and nothing has changed over there. Nazy nodded. "Then there is California; they have a measure on the ballot to break up the state to get more senators and electoral voters. Democrats want to give fifty million illegal aliens amnesty and the right to vote."

Hunter said, "They think they are going to make President Hernandez the last Republican president."

"I think they plan to turn the U.S. into a one-party country. What do you think?"

"If you listen to media.... I know things are not looking good, but I don't think we are anywhere close to that. But what do I know? I don't get the brief."

Nazy collapsed the newspaper. "I don't brief domestic issues with the President. That's the FBI's purview, and they have been struggling of late. I hope the President does something with them soon. They need new leaders."

Hunter always gave his wife his undivided attention and nodded in agreement with her statements. "I'll talk to Dory and get his take. There's nothing I can do but.... You know we've been a team for a long time, you, me, and Bill. I've been thinking Eastwood is an oddball fourth. Eastwood walks the walk of honest journalism and has the scars to prove it. He unleashes on the mainstream media, he's an honest broker, and guys like that are as scarce as hen's teeth, as my mama would say. I trust him more than anyone else outside of our little group. He's becoming the face of accurate and truthful media."

Nazy said, "I've listened to him. There are few independent journalists who put fact over opinion, and he is one of those."

Hunter said, "I've been working with Eastwood on a project, and I have plans for him. I wouldn't have brought him aboard without an ok from you and Bill."

Nazy flashed a "thumbs up" with her smile reaffirming the previous approval.

The war correspondent, retired Marine Lieutenant Colonel Demetrius Eastwood, had been with Bill McGee the night the two men raced against time to save Nazy's life. Eastwood was a good man in Hunter's and Nazy's eyes.

Hunter said, "He helped to ensure I didn't get shot after I took out the little Agency imposter you replaced at the NCS." Hunter didn't have to mention the name of the former head of the National Clandestine Service who had tried in vain to assassinate the President on Election Day; she knew. "I can see where Bill wouldn't like losing me, like I was abandoning him. I don't think I could do it anyway. I'm to blame that he has that job, but it's not like I threw him out of the cockpit. Some jobs are two-man special… activities. There were times I just needed a little help, and he helped. Lord, that man helped."

"Like Turkmenistan?"

"Yeah, like Turkmenistan. He and I have been in the middle of some of the craziest events, like stealing suitcase nukes from Soviet colonels who stole them when the Kremlin fell."

"President Hernandez asked you to do the work. He approves these special activities. You share his world view and understanding of the Middle East. He trusts you above all others," Nazy said.

"We go way back. Before you and me and a YO-3. But you say, the finance folks are in Bill's chili to reduce the cost of killing terrorists? So let the Air Force take them out with a three-million dollar missile from a ten-million dollar unmanned system. I do it for a-quarter of that, and I don't leave a stinking mess of dead women and children as collateral damage, and they rarely know I've even been there. And everyone knows when the Air Force is *in the house*." Nazy looked at him curiously. He said, "…when the Air Force is on a base."

"You *are* very surgical, Duncan darling." He knew just how to make her squeal with the tip of his tongue, but he also knew what she meant and grinned at her.

After a yawn and a stretch, he became more serious, "Air Branch…the Special Activities Division (SAD) have always wanted to make any aviation program unmanned. They've spent the equivalent of the national budget of Angola to make unmanned aircraft work. Here we are almost sixty years later, and they're no closer to making anything they have into the perfect robot than Elon Musk or BMW is to making an electric car that doesn't catch on fire." He rolled his eyes; *Even Boeing tried to support the communist green energy initiatives by putting batteries in the tail of their 787 until the jets started catching on fire. And some place in Alaska they celebrate twenty minutes of flight from an electric airplane – when it catches fire they better be in the touch and go pattern. I just don't see any utility in a twenty-minute airplane. Liberal morons promising greater battery life have no business being in the computer battery business. Or windmills. Or solar panels. And definitely not politics.*

"Bill's expecting you to complete the trials to make sure the airplane will do what the engineers say it will do."

"Completing the trials I can do, easy. The conundrum is the sensor can only pick up a heat signature, and the AI is only as smart as a three-year-old; it can't tell the difference between a Chihuahua and a pan of blueberry muffins. It's not smart enough to hunt for the bad guys. It's like cutting sign at the Border Patrol. A robot can fly over a patch of desert, but you have to know how to look for specific clues. In the Border Patrol it is *footprints* that can't be discerned from looking at them straight down but can easily be seen at a critical angle. You have to look at where the sun is in the sky and then look for the indications where scrubby cavities of footprints in the sand make shadows. I can give them the answers; I don't think the software guys can make the artificial intelligence smart enough. At least, not yet."

"You said animal trackers do the same thing."

He nodded. "Yes. It's also how golfers read a putting green. But to develop that kind of 'eye' it's kind of *proprietary*, like learning a trade secret. Trade secrets are complex and specific and take years of experimentation and experience to perfect. The Russians and the Chinese are always trying to steal them. AI software engineers who haven't left their parents' basement in twenty years have no concept of the operational environment. They think they know what the world is like from a search engine, but they're actually clueless. They'll never figure it out." Hunter moved to another topic. "Break, break. New subject. I think when he took the job he figured we would be partners until President Hernandez got tired of him or me or something."

"What about me?"

"Oh, baby, no one could ever get tired of you! Do you really think the President of the United States is going to have someone that looks like Steve Buscemi in a dress deliver the President's Daily Brief? I mean seriously. If that ever happens, you'll know you are on the outs. If your choice was tall glamour girl with long *sezy* legs and a British accent or anyone else with your credentials, like the former Attorney General Eleanor Tussy, who wasn't smart enough to put on her own makeup and who looked like Michael Jackson's driver's license photo, I ask you, who would you choose? Baby, as soon as you walk into that place I know the men and women of the NSC crash into the walls and bang into each other with all the grace and aplomb of a Texas longhorn in a china shop. You're like a *chaos bomb,* because when you enter the room or the building, boom! People run around like cartoon characters, crashing into walls.... Maybe it's just the *Obsession,* your perfume that turns people into blubbering fools. I was a blubbering fool from that first time I laid eyes on you and flipped over on my back in the racquetball court. I was shamefaced, but I knew I was in love." He playfully pointed at her.

Nazy laughed, nearly uncontrollably, when Duncan got into one of his comedic rolls. "I was quite the *muggle* when it came to any sport. I was so fascinated how you chased that little ball."

"I crashed and burned right at your feet, and you applauded. I said this is a women who could love me for the idiot I am. I knew I was in love." *And after my little tumble, I needed painkillers and a massage. Oh, yes, what a night!* At that moment, Hunter had an insight, a flash of inspiration and jotted on a 3X5 card he carried in a pocket, *chaos bomb, UV bomb, firestarter, anti-jammer.* He pursed his lips for a moment and added, *NBC PPE.*

Nazy noticed he was always making notes for one concept or another. One wall of his office was full of metallic plaques awarded for his patents. She giggled at him throughout his comments and scribblings; she threw him an air-kiss and took his hand. He always made her feel like a million dollars. She said, "Whatever you decide will be fine. We'll be fine. I'm nearly at the mandatory retirement age.... Maybe the right thing to do is go when President Hernandez no longer needs us."

"Us? You mean, you, me, *and* Bill?"

She nodded. "And your airplanes. Absolutely. We're a team."

He said, "It's not like we need the money."

"No, that's not it; it's just so hard to leave that place. We've done some out-of-this-world things there. But the country is being split apart by radicals and criminals...."

"Not to mention criminal Democrats...."

"...I fear for America, and the FBI will not do its job."

"It can't; it's been infiltrated. But I submit, Miss Cunningham, you've been a marvelous citizen and intelligence officer. I would vote for you for president, if you were only eligible."

"Thank you, baby. I'm not, and that is not for me anyway. I'll stick to intel, delivering the PDB. But I'll miss the State Dinners at the White House.... the most."

If there was one event on the earth that left Nazy in awe, it was the pomp and circumstance of being the guest of President Hernandez at a State Dinner. Hunter said, "But you go there every day!"

"Not in an evening gown!" She half-smiled, half-frowned.

Hunter howled. If he had worn dentures, they would've fallen out of his mouth. "That's true. Because when you're in a gown, I get to say 'You're lovely, you're exquisite, you give me vertigo...."

Nazy finished the line from the movie she couldn't remember the title of but had seen with him a few times, "I adore you. Duncan darling, I never get tired of hearing that, even if you plagiarized it from an old movie."

"When I'm near you, whatever original thought I may have goes out the window."

Nazy giggled.

Hunter asked, "Are you going to be invited this year?"

"We should. President Hernandez looks for an opportunity to thank you for all you do for him and the country."

"I'll only go with you on my arm. We would have to sit at Director McGee's table. I'll go, but I don't think I can wear a disguise that long.

They always run long and the President always wants to talk privately."

"We could leave early. Go across the street to the, ah, JW Marriott…."

He pointed another finger and tossed a smile her way.

She was thinking naughtiness could soon be afoot in the Presidential Suite of the hotel, if only they had an invitation to the White House. Or the time. There was never enough time.

CHAPTER 17

April 10, 2018

Nazy continued, "You can do anything. Eradicate poppies and terrorists and assassins. Free hostages. President Hernandez loves you. I bet if he had the chance he would bring you out of the dark. Maybe work for him. No more disguises for you."

"I'm already working for him; I just don't report to him unless he calls me to the Oval Office. But you. You're the finder of master terrorists, interrogator of Osama bin Laden and other ridiculous clowns of the Islamic Underground; the discoverer of Iran and Iraq's WMD trifecta—their NBC, their nuclear, biological, and chemical weapons programs, and, of course, the *pièce de résistance*, the prime exposer of a bogus president. And you're the first woman to be the Director of the National Counter Terrorism Center (NCTC) and so many more things that drive the other Agency executives wacky, like all of your successes, promotions, and visibility."

Nazy beamed from the praise.

"How did you find him?"

"Who?"

"...bin Laden. You never really told me the details."

"Oh Duncan, that was a long time ago."

"I know."

"Well, I hadn't been at the Agency long when I started asking questions. The older intel officers ignored me, I think, because I'm a little darker and have an accent. Maybe they even hated me for I said things that should not have been spoken. It took me a long time to understand the politics and the complexity of these situations, where they were actually protecting bin Laden as a way of protecting the people we had in his camp. I wasn't cleared and obviously, it was very sensitive."

"Sounds to me that bin Laden knew he had Agency guys around him and used them as human shields. What did you do?"

"There had to be a way to get bin Laden away from his people in camp and with his family when he was home. I used what I knew. My father knew of bin Laden from falconry hunting. He was the Chief Justice on the Jordanian Supreme Court, and he and the king would travel to Riyadh or Dubai or Tehran or Islamabad for hunting. Bin Laden was a professional falconer, and like all Islamic elites, he traveled to Saudi Arabia or the UAE or Iran for extended stays in which he and others and their families would vacation and take part in top-level falconry hunting."

Hunter hadn't heard of the story and was fascinated with the topic.

"The main difference was my father could only travel to these competitions for a week or two each year, while I heard the others like bin Laden and sheikhs and emirs, traveled to Iran and Pakistan, all across the Middle East, for several months each year."

"That's incredible. The American public never knew."

"The IC ignored or dismissed the importance of the hunts. They had their way of doing things. I was a young girl and remember my father speaking directly with those people in the palace who organized the hunts. I had heard of the name bin Laden at home, in the context of those falconry hunts. I tried to find out more about those men-only trips. My family was not invited. All I ever learned was that there were few special places in these countries, and my father sometimes offered vague details about what they were and where they were, but rarely who was there. That gave me a hint that the people who were at these competitions might not be good people."

"So you can imagine, after September 11 when we heard that Osama bin Laden was responsible for the attack on America, I could not believe it. I was convinced it was a mistake. Media propaganda. I didn't want to believe that my father knowingly consorted with a mass murderer. The media in the Middle East ridiculed the American press. They said they were bad conspiracy theories."

"In one of the last conversations I overheard between my father and another judge, the judge mentioned that they used temporary hostages, family members, to ensure bin Laden's safe travel between

Muslim cities, specifically to get to the hunts. I didn't know it at the time, but the CIA would have forced airliners to land—or worse—in order to take him into custody, but I quickly learned that there was a presidential edict that directed we could not do that. At the time I was convinced the Near East Division chief knew much more sensitive information about the terrorist leader, but he also had his orders."

"It was five years before I was brought into the fold and was granted access into the special access program. I didn't want to believe there had been a deal made between the last two presidential administrations that allowed bin Laden to remain free and in charge of al-Qaeda on the condition that he did not attack the United States in its own territories. I know Bill supposedly chased him in Afghanistan, but that was really for optics. Bin Laden was in Iran."

"What about the hostages?"

"Once bin Laden was safe in the country his family would be released and would join him."

"That is simply incredible."

"I told you the raid nearly didn't happen. The day I walked into the Operations Center and announced I knew where bin Laden was, of course the men didn't want to believe me. It was all men. Some knew of the Mazibuike executive order, but I forced them to take action. I said bin Laden has not missed the Islamabad Falconer's Club Championship for twenty years. It is a live prey event and is one of the most keenly anticipated falconry competitions. Veteran falconers regard it as the fiercest and most important of all falconry contests. He will not miss it; he will be there. And we will know he is moving when his family leaves their hotel in Saudi Arabia."

"I briefed everyone so they knew when and where the meet would be held. Bin Laden had a house specially constructed near the military base where the championship was held. I held fast that we should not negotiate with terrorists, and we should remove them from the battlefield when we find them. There was a countervailing view. We had men in the al-Qaeda camp; in-place defectors, and they couldn't be harmed. I said they have to get out; the others said it was impossible, they must maintain the *status quo*. It became a matter of will. Then one of my guys made a positive ID that bin Laden was hunting with falcons."

"So, you could say falconry was the *Rosetta Stone* for understanding the operation of the Islamic Underground."

Nazy smiled. "Not just the Islamic Underground. The old KGB and the new FSB, as were MI-5 and MI-6—all were dedicated—what do you say—oh yes, *diehard* falconers. The sport of the elites. In our archives we have photographs of bin Laden, Victor Bout…."

"*The Merchant of Death….*"

"…in falconry camps in Iran, the UAE—multiple locations. Of course, the photos were all taken before the attack on September 11th. And we had photographic evidence after *nine-eleven*."

"In Jordan?"

"No. There was too much U.S. presence in and around Amman."

"Nazy darling, *you* were the *Rosetta Stone*, the essential clue to crack the code on the elite terrorists, like bin Laden."

"Follow the falcons and hawks, and the heads of the foreign intelligence community and terror groups will be close by."

"That's what I mean. No mere analyst understands the business of terrorism. No mere analyst has done what you have done. And no mere slouch in a skirt with amazing legs and a Level 1 Yankee White clearance delivers the President's Daily Brief." *Mine is a simple job, I just pop the bad guys your guys find.*

He is so funny! Nazy loved getting her ego stroked and added, "Break, Break, my turn. New subject. Iraqi's biological laboratories may be gone, but the Iranian's National Biosafety Laboratory housed at the Ayatollah Khomeini Institute of Virology is the latest attempt to hide an Islamic biological weapons program. It has been on line for a few years and has been making news, and some sources have it that Rho Scorpii's fingerprints are on it. First, we had a hunch; then it became a suspicion that they were up to no good. Then that evolved into a likelihood, which has now become a strong probability. The world isn't prepared to deal with what they're researching. Last year a Chinese researcher from the facility defected and said they were weaponizing viruses in Iran. Reportedly, Iran's supreme leader took a billion Euros to construct the institute and the laboratories near the border of Turkmenistan. Satellite photographs suggest much of it is underground and apparently we can't use cruise missiles on it."

Nazy's last comment made Hunter frown. "In the movies, those labs are always pint-sized things. Seems to me they would be huge, like Y-12. And complex, like Y-12. And if the Iranians had a clandestine facility, it would just about have to be underground. Specially constructed facilities. And they would need a lot of help." *Of course! Chinese! Communist Chinese.* Hunter removed the 3X5 card from a pocket, circled NBC PPE with a Vertex pen made of rare curly Koa and returned it to his pocket. After a moment of reflection, he returned to the card and added more questions.

Nazy watched him write with the exquisite handmade pen and marveled at how her man's mind worked. "Well, in real life, from the overheads, they're not really *mammoth.* The compound is fully self-contained. They are like flattened bunkers that, supposedly, are built at such an angle that if a cruise missile were to hit it, the blast would be deflected. They even have a water treatment plant, backup generators like you would find at an airport or a hospital, and an incinerator. It's only recently that we learned President Mazibuike secretly transferred some thirty billion dollars in cash and gold to Iran—and that money wasn't only for the ayatollahs. He was supposed to get 'a pinch.'"

Hunter smiled and nodded; he removed the 3X5 from his pocket and circled his last entry and commented, "That's how they launder U.S. foreign aid to enrich themselves."

Nazy continued, "We've tried to get a defector in place for some time to tell us what was going on at the institute. We've had some success, but Iran keeps executing people who are not working for us; they do it as a deterrent to prevent defectors. Since its creation, their bio-weapons program has been very difficult to penetrate, and the area is basically 'outer limits' to outsiders." She knew immediately that the term she used wasn't right.

"I think that's '*off limits,*' baby." Hunter welcomed the new topic and direction. "And that's the perfect name for an institute of virology since Khomeini unleashed more death than any pathogen ever could."

"You extracted the mother of a nuclear scientist who had copies of Iran's nuclear weapons program files. It has been a very high priority for us to have an Iranian defector from Khomeini's labs, and now we might have one. Bill wants him out of there before they find him and kill him, but the deputy wants to milk him for all the information he can give us. Mostly to prove that he's legitimate."

"I could extract one, and for Bill, I would do it again. But the last couple never showed. So Iran has an active…."

"Yes, now, near Bājirān, yes, they announced a couple of years ago that they have the first ever lab in a Muslim country. It's supposedly designed to meet biosafety-level 4 (BSL-4) standards, the highest biohazard level. 3M lifted all Iranian sanctions as soon as he entered office; the analysis was so a foreign company in Europe could build it, and it became active with the help of the Chinese."

3M; derogatory code speak for the dead former president, Maxim Mohammad Mazibuike. 3M was disastrous for the Middle East; he undermined Israel; he abandoned our allies in North Africa and supported the Muslim Brotherhood – the granddaddy of al-Qaeda and ISIS and all the rest – return to power in that region. He watched ISIS grow from a minivan in Aleppo to controlling a region the size of Great Britain. What a communist piece of shit. Hunter said, "I don't know all that much about bugs – especially the electronic type, but I do know that a level-4 facility means they can handle the most dangerous pathogens. My estimations of a bug. And just because they have one doesn't mean these clowns have mastered the concept of safety. Anytime the Iranians say they are doing something 'peaceful,' they are lying. Only our media have more prolific liars."

Nazy nodded. "It was constructed and set up after the SARS virus leaked from Chinese labs. China has long been home and incubator to many of the world's most deadly viruses, pestilences, and diseases, and they have been the source of the three most deadly plagues on our planet in the last 2,000 years. We used to believe these diseases were from their wet markets where they sell live animals. Fleas from bats, rats, pangolins. Everything you can think of."

Hunter said, "Saddam Hussein sent his weapons of mass destruction programs out of the country; Syria got the nuclear and chemical programs while Iran got their Russian-made jets and the bio-weapons technology, which I am convinced they got from the French. I used to think maybe the Germans were involved, but it was probably the French; their politicians are so corrupt."

Nazy added, "…and the money 3M sent to Iran funded part—maybe all of its construction. Iran tried to say they funded it, but it really was the U.S. taxpayers. We suspect a foreign contractor owned by a U.S. firm did the work." She didn't specify which U.S. firm, and Hunter didn't ask. His focus had been on the Middle East, Africa, and South America; not Europe.

"3M was so not on our side." Hunter rolled his eyes at the news.

Nazy nodded. "According to the *chicken feed* from the in-place defector and European media, with the lab up and running with European, Chinese, and Iranian scientists, they are studying 300 coronaviruses from bats and rats, with maybe 4,000 viruses being researched. Those numbers are so off-base that we don't know if it's low grade information that's been fed through a double agent, or if it is direct intel; accurate."

Hunter asked, "Under the auspices of doing humanitarian research on the world's most dangerous viruses, are we to believe the Muslim Brotherhood doesn't have other objectives? Remember these are the same class of *jihadis* who said they just wanted to learn how to fly an aircraft but not land so they could fly them into buildings. They don't want to research bugs; they want to get inside the wire and steal them and use them."

Nazy said, "I know that if the opportunity ever presents itself, Bill would like you to get the in-place defector out of there. He said, you're the only one who can do something like that. He's also afraid that al-Qaeda or the Islamic Underground will try to penetrate the facility soon, if they haven't already. Maybe before the institute makes an announcement that's supposed to shock the world…."

Hunter added, "But they've been promising the moon for the last three years. Integrity is not their bag, baby."

Nazy said, "You know these things are all about money, and I don't think the Islamic Revolutionary Guard Corps will let them disrupt their good deal unless the money borders on the unrealistic."

"Aren't they in deep *kimchee*? Is al-Qaeda really broke?"

Nazy nodded. "If he's forced into action Bill wanted to know if there is anything you'll need, or think you'll need."

"Baby, I don't think so. I just need a place and a time to pull your guy out of there. I submitted an after action report on the rescue mission into ISIS-controlled Syria. There is nothing else I need."

Nazy lamented, "I remember." *Duncan's daughter hadn't done well when he opened fire on the group of ISIS. Duncan found out the hard way that the former Director Greg Lynche sometimes made decisions with his heart and not his head. Greg shouldn't have insisted Duncan put Kelly in harm's way. It should've killed them all, but Duncan found a way to save our troops and Kelly and himself, and kill ISIS. But absolutely no more kinetic special activities for the daughter.*

Hunter said, "*Weedbusters* disabled them. I hit them with the aircraft's UV laser and blinded all the armed-for-death ISIS on the ground and rendered them unable to mount a defense." *And I don't think any AI would figure out how to set up the battlefield to kill almost fifty ISIS. I reloaded the weapon, changed the magazine four times; how could a robot do that? What if there was a jam? A robot can't clear a jam.* "It would be nice to have a similar capability to toss into a building and blind everyone. I'm thinking about the size of a *Growler*, the size of a baseball or a softball. It would need something like a few red diode lasers to draw the human eye. Explosives like hand grenades create too much noise and too much damage. Sometimes you need explosives, but a one-man breeching party needs a different weapon. Stealth weapons, silent weapons. If you can disable a man without firing a shot, you can save a lot of weight in ammo. Weight is the bane of the special operations warrior. My lab guys are the wrong group to do something like that."

"Ok, I got that. Anything else?"

"A couple more. Have you seen the video of the Tesla in a parking garage spontaneously combusting?"

Nazy asked, "Which one? I think there are dozens." *If you've seen one car fire you've seen them all.*

Hunter continued, "Electric vehicle, battery tray between the tires. Puncture that battery tray and it releases two chemicals, essentially a binary weapon. It makes a strange and wild chemical fire that can't be contained by usual means. I would love to have that capability—I would call it *Firestarter*. Grenade-sized, something the size of a large pill bottle. I would want a bunch of them to start a fire that can't be extinguished through conventional means. Maybe a similar capability would be a magnesium hand grenade. I could even drop them on a drug lab from the air. When magnesium is on fire it burns hotter than you can believe. We lost too many Marines in Vietnam to magnesium fires when their helicopters crashed. And you need PPE."

"PPE?"

For the CIA's strategic planners to be having discussions on al-Qaeda's ability to penetrate a bioweapons laboratory means they or a surrogate will attack some facility soon. A job for SAD, not for me. Al-Qaeda and the Islamic Underground have had plenty of time to infiltrate the lab. Only the most clueless researcher would think they're safe. I would want out of that place before I even got in. "Yes ma'am. Personal protection equipment."

Nazy asked, "Like what?"

"Well, I know DOD has been developing PPE for the NBC crowd for years. (Nuclear, Biological, Chemical.) It's difficult to protect troops against infection from the biologicals, and there have been efforts to replace the cumbersome protections the military uses to work in nuclear and chemical environments. I know a little but not enough; way out of my lane and I don't know anyone in the field. There was a study accomplished by Battelle and Lawrence Livermore, briefed to the JPEO…."

She interrupted, "JPEO?"

"I'm sorry. That's the Joint Program Executive Office for Chemical, Biological, Radiological and Nuclear Defense; they manage the nation's chemical, biological, radiological, and nuclear defense equipment. Anyway, 3M ensured the JPEO funding shriveled up and died on the vine. The state of technology just wasn't there yet. Still might not be. I don't know."

"Not so. You know everything." He squeezed her hand.

"But there is a side of me that just wonders why the former president killed that program. The cynic in me says it was decidedly for a purpose." Hunter sighed as she finished making notes to carry back to McGee. He was madly in love with Nazy and wanted to glare at her a bit, but he couldn't, not even playfully, she was just carrying the message. *Islamists and viruses were the biological equivalent of binary chemical weapons, where firing the munition requires removing a barrier between two precursors. Pull the lid off the petri dish, expose it to the atmosphere, and release all seven levels of Hell. If those crazies ever weaponize the worst viruses, they'll have martyr-wannabees lined up by the hundreds to infect the world. And if the infected ever get into an international airport, past airport security, to scatter their seeds of death.... God, I hate bugs!*

Carlos Yazzie's stacked heel boots thundered across the deck of the lodge and interrupted the conversation as Hunter concluded his ramblings. The ranch's foreman and half of the caretaker team announced, "I have taken some indescribable video of the ice storm with the drone and have kept the horses saddled in case Miss Nazy wants to ride before you have to leave." Carlos' wife, Therese, followed him without speaking and cleared off the colorful Fiesta breakfast plates. Hunter complimented Therese on another stupendous *huevos rancheros* plate with Julio's salsa. Whenever he could, Hunter brought back fresh Julio's from Texas.

Carlos and Therese, both Apache Indians, had looked out for Hunter and his homes since both men retired from the Marine Corps. Hunter looked after the Yazzies, and now they looked after him.

When Hunter and Yazzie were sergeants returning to Okinawa from a deployment in Korea, Yazzie had received an exorbitant reenlistment check. Hunter demanded Yazzie give him the check for safe keeping if he was going out to the bars of Iwakuni, Japan. Hunter told him, "Carlos, I will not let you buy booze for every dumbass in town and then find out in the morning when you wake up, that boom, you have nothing. That check will be gone, *off like a prom dress*—give me that check!" Therese loved Hunter for that. At the culmination of their Marine Corps careers, Yazzie had obtained the rank of Gunnery Sergeant and Hunter retired as a Captain. For almost 25 years she and Carlos had done everything the Captain asked of them, and he paid them very well. They were millionaires in their own right.

Nazy Cunningham said, "Thank you, Carlos, I would love to ride before I have to go back, but I don't think there's enough time. Even if

I could, I would be in a *hailstorm*; the ice from the trees is falling. I'm grateful you captured some video. I'll look at it the next time I'm home. I think we really must go *anon*. Thank you so much."

"Carlos, I should have a new car or two to be delivered in the next few days," said Hunter. *Two? Three!* "Maybe even four. I'll send you the information."

Two cars or four? Two days or four? I'm confused. "Captain, I will supervise the offloading and have them placed in the hangar with the others. Sir, if you get any more cars I'll have to rent another hangar and hire a full-time mechanic to keep them running."

Another car? Cars? Nazy squished up her face asked, "Are you ever going to stop collecting cars?"

Hunter laughed, "My mama didn't raise no quitter!"

Nazy rolled her eyes.

"Carlos, I don't know how they will be shipped. Yellow, black. Together or in singles. You can look under the hood of the Grand Sport and see the ultimate in *man jewelry*—eight single chrome fuel injectors. 700 horses; no hot rodding up and down the runway!" Hunter admonished his longtime friend with a menacing wagging finger which meant *No racing*! More conversations of Iranian bio labs and misfits from the Islamic Underground would wait until he and Nazy were airborne. He would also tell her about the anomaly he found in Colombia. The potential of finding a lost aircraft made him pleasantly reflective for a second.

When Carlos Yazzie departed, Nazy said, "He is so thoughtful."

"I don't know about all that. I'm sure I'm not the only one who would love to see your girls bounce out of your shirt when you get your horse to canter!" She playfully threw her napkin at him and said, "*You're incorrigible!*" Nazy unconsciously covered herself as Duncan's eyes followed her protective hand.

"You can call me anything you like, my darling Nazy, but just don't call me late for Therese's *huevos rancheros*."

It was an easy and maybe a natural thing for any set of eyes to fall into the woman's abundant cleavage, and her breasts had been things of beauty. However, since the attack on the Embassy almost killed her, Nazy was sensitive about her breasts. While she was unconscious and being raped, a troglodyte from hell had fancied at least one breast as a trophy and attempted to remove it with a knife. The barbarian's butchery was interrupted by a bullet to the forehead from the person who was now "the Boss," the Director of the CIA.

Hunter couldn't keep his eyes off of his wife and her *girls*, and took the opportunity to give Nazy a small purse. He explained, "I know you're wearing scarves now to protect your girls, but I remember an old clip of how Princess Diana's used small clutch bags to protect her royal cleavage. I have one from Coach—if you like it and want to use it." He showed how Lady Di had done it, moving a small purse to hide the exposed cleft when she stood up or bent over.

Nazy was pleased at the gift and Duncan's solution to one of Nazy's dilemmas: wearing dresses with an exposed bodice while getting into and out of vehicles or chairs. She practiced the movement.

"…you make it look natural, baby, but does it feel natural?"

She eagerly agreed, "It does. It does. *How avant-garde*. Thank you, baby. You are always so thoughtful."

Hunter collected the purse and set it on the table. He stood and took Nazy's delicate hands and brought her to her feet. He embraced her, Hunter could feel her heart pounding against his chest. They moved inside to the living room, what Nazy called the "snuggery," one of those British terms that sent Hunter and the Yazzies scrambling for a British-to-American dictionary. He thought he had done something good, but he could tell something was bothering her.

She whispered, "If something were to happen to you…."

"Oh, Nazy…." Hunter kissed her passionately before she could say anything else.

When she came up for air, Nazy said, "I don't know if I can do many more of these separations. Bill has me locked up at HQ or at the conference center. Kelly isn't at home much; she's attending graduate school, and I rarely see her."

"You're a senior executive. She's just starting out. My folks didn't see me when I starting working at Shakey's Pizza Parlor."

"I know, but there hasn't been another credible attempt on me in a couple of years, by the Brothers or the Underground, and although I feel safe enough to drive to and from work, Bill won't have any of it. I travel with a protective staff."

"I suppose you go to *Victoria's Secret* with a protective staff. Hopefully they're all girls. And you get nice pretty things…to show me. And I appreciate it. You get the full security treatment because you're the CIA's MVP—most valuable professional. Bill is right to protect you. Greg was right to protect you. But if you don't want to do this anymore, we'll tell Bill. We'll go riding into the sunset. Then we can ride at sunrise, or whenever you want."

She pressed her breasts against his chest until he noticed. "Thank you, baby. But you…now that I think they're probably no longer after me, I worry about you. I can't help but think they have been quiet, trying to find you, and when they do, they will take you from me. If I didn't have you, I truly wouldn't know what I would do. You're the most wonderful man I have ever met."

He wanted her boobs to erupt right out of her shirt as he held her tighter and kissed her again.

"Promise me you won't jump out of any more airplanes."

Hunter tried to hide his emotions. He had been spending time at McGee's Full Spectrum Training Center (FSTC) in Texas making dozens of night jumps above flight level 250. High Altitude, Low Opening jumps. He didn't want Nazy to worry since he had jumped out of two YO-3As: to save Kelly in Liberia and President Hernandez in Washington. The last night jump from a *Yo-Yo* nearly killed him and required hip and knee replacements and time in the hospital. But since then, he had been making multiple HALO jumps perfectly. He fudged the truth, "I haven't *needed* to jump in a while." He wanted to run from discussions of parachute jumps. The little stirring in his groin could be enough to bail him out. He pressed into her again, but she wasn't through talking.

"Greg, and now Bill, have you landing and doing…unimaginable things that just scare me. You are being *overexposed*. I am terrified that they will find you and you'll be caught…."

"In Bill's ideal world we'll be all unmanned aircraft going forward. I won't need to jump out of an airplane. Bill will have me flying a desk or I'll tinker with the cars. When you are ready, we'll dynamite you out of Washington. These separations are brutal, I agree." He pressed his groin into hers. "I miss you so much."

"I miss you too, baby."

She's worried about me jumping out of an airplane because she can see the future. Does she think Bill will send me to attack a bio-lab? That's Ground Branch stuff. I don't do ground work and God, I hate bugs! But that's not going to happen; DOD will send Tomahawks to destroy any bio-weapons facility, wherever it's at, whenever they need to. I can't imagine any situation where they'll need me. One-man shows attacking large facilities are only in the minds of espionage novelists who know nothing of that work.

After they looked at each other and rubbed noses like youthful lovers, Nazy said, "I know we don't have time for horseback riding…but I do think there's time…." They gently bumped foreheads. Hunter took Nazy by the hand and led her to the master suite.

Therese Yazzie was in the kitchen, drying plates as she watched the lovers walk from the *snuggery* to the *boudoir.* She said, emphatically, "*She loves him very much. He would die for her!*" Carlos nodded but was slow in spitting out the correct response, "I would die for you too, Therese!" *What the hell was that man thinking?* Suddenly her tongue was like barbed wire dipped in acid. She barked at him, "Move the truck to the front door, unsaddle the horses, leave the drone in the garage, and to come right back." She had lots of things for him to do before the Captain and Miss Nazy had to leave.

Instead of carrying the four-rotor drone to the garage Carlos flew it. Yazzie had mastered the handling characteristics of the aircraft. One of Hunter's companies produced very unusual flying machines, everything from a long-endurance jet pack for a human to the quiet drone. Six battery-powered, silent drones with cameras and lasers were built for a contract that the government did not buy. The engineers had built in sensors and software that continually monitored the amplitude of the frequency of the tiny rotor blades and adjusted the rotor speeds to send noise-canceling, frequency-modulated signals to cancel out the noise of the four rotors and audible harmonics. The result was a flying machine that could operate a few feet from someone without them being able to hear it. Yazzie was fascinated with the noise-canceling technology. The drones were configured with night vision systems, surveillance cameras, and laser designators and had been transferred to Wyoming when the contract award went to another vendor. They became Carlos Yazzie's playthings until Therese had more chores for him.

• • •

At the Manassas Regional Airport, Duncan Hunter handed control of his wife over to the Agency's security women. Having to go back to work meant a broken heart. She would miss Duncan terribly until they were reunited. Nazy told him to, "Keep well," as she entered the black limousine followed by women in black suits with black guns. Once the Suburban had driven off, a fuel truck pulled alongside the Gulfstream. Hunter entered the airport terminal, paid for the fuel and fees, and hit the men's room before returning to the jet. He walked around it, looking for any evidence the aircraft couldn't safely fly to its next destination.

To avoid the possible tracking prowess of *Tailwatchers*, Hunter rocketed the G-550 direct to the tiny airport in Hondo, Texas. He parked the jet in front of an oversized aircraft hangar which had only one airplane inside; a Chance Vought F-4U *Corsair* with the name *Samuel Carlton* painted under the canopy. His twin-engine radial, Howard 500 taildragger was already positioned on the ramp and ready for flight. Both the *Corsair* and the Howard 500 were powered by Pratt & Whitney's R-2800, 18-cylinder, air-cooled radial engines. Several spare motors sat in shipping containers or on engine stands awaiting QECs, quick engine change harnesses. The propeller-driven aircraft were extremely desirable to collectors, but they were incredibly difficult and expensive to operate and maintain. They required old, dedicated master aircraft mechanics and an airplane load of money to keep them flying.

Hunter always wanted to take the *Corsair* back to Jackson Hole and show it off, but it didn't have the "legs." The Howard 500's range of 3,600 miles was achieved by an auxiliary fuel cell which allowed it to carry enough of the 115/145 leaded aviation gasoline to make the trip to Jackson Hole and back. The Hondo airport featured 10,000-gallon aviation gasoline storage tanks just for Hunter's old aircraft with the big loud radials.

At the time Duncan Hunter was considering purchasing his first warbird, the *Corsair,* he didn't know buying a warbird would put him into the oil business and in Federal Court. After acquiring the *Corsair,* Hunter found he couldn't get the proper fuel for it. He could *buy* a warbird, he just couldn't *fly* a warbird—at least not at performance power. Oil refineries needed to produce the high-octane fuels not only for his growing number of operational warbirds but for all restored warbirds and supercharged radials used in vintage aircraft. Proper octane numbers were necessary to obtain rated power in vintage aircraft engines. Using low-octane fuel in multi-engine aircraft was a safety issue, for without the proper fuel some aircraft couldn't reach takeoff power or speeds.

He had run into a roadblock at the Mazibuike Administration's Environmental Protection Agency. It had championed regulations which had killed off high-octane aviation gasolines.

One of Hunter's companies, Quiet Aero Systems (QAS), took the EPA to court over the issue of high-octane fuels and won. With the win, QAS immediately contracted with the Valero Three Rivers Refinery near Hondo to reintroduce 115/145 leaded aviation gasoline into the market. The 115/145 Avgas wouldn't be available to the public and was formulated only by special order, but it was no longer illegal to own, manufacture, or use. QAS became one of several national distributors of the purple fuel. Owners of warbirds came to Hondo, Texas for fuel and stopped to eat at Hondo's downtown hole-in-the wall, the *El Restaurante Azteca.* Silver Belly Resistol John Wayne War Wagons were optional wear. The best beaver fur cowboy hats had the best names.

By getting the politically motivated law expunged, QAS facilities and aircraft were terrorized by environmental groups for contributing to the nonsensical "global warming" problem, that is until QAS lawyers slapped a $500 million lawsuit against the Democratic National Committee for threatening and terroristic activities. As the lawsuit wound its way through the courts, Hunter and his mechanics worked with the local FAA Flight Standards District Office (FSDO) to conceal from view legal QAS assets. Once approved, QAS aircraft no longer had to display the aircraft's registration number prominently on the aircraft. This meant Russian *Tailwatchers* could not track the movement of plain-wrapper white paint QAS aircraft, as there were no obvious registration numbers on either side of the aircraft. The numbers were there but out of sight when viewed from a distance. They were only visible if one took the time to look underneath the engine cowlings where the undersized yet visible "N number" were found. And the Howard 500 was virtually invisible to *Tailwatchers* who were more interested in tracking the comings and goings of business jets than a flying museum piece.

CHAPTER 18

April 13, 2018

Carlos Yazzie wanted to argue with the delivery man. He had expected a yellow Corvette delivery, however, the man had three 1957 300 SLs and paperwork. Two black, one blue; a Gullwing and two roadsters. Carlos knew there had been a temporary suspension in the restoration of the Mercedes'. Being delivered early was a complete surprise. He looked them over. *They are engineering perfection and are as sensational today as they were the day they rolled out of the factory.* Yazzie shook his head. *If these cars don't do it for you, you probably should just collect stamps.* Carlos beseeched the gods above and asked the sky, "Where am I going to put these?"

The delivery man moved million-dollar cars daily and said, "Not my problem. I just deliver them. And I'm early, so I get a bonus per my contract. Please sign for them and note that they arrived before the 'must deliver date' and without any damage."

Technically Yazzie had room, he just didn't have room for three more two-seaters *and a jet. The Captain will be abroad for a few more days, and he just wants me to take care of them. So I will.*

Three sparkling rare Mercedes' in the springtime sun of Jackson, Wyoming brought onlookers. He convinced the delivery man to help him drive the two black Mercedes' into the aircraft hangar on the other side of the airfield. Yazzie drove the robin-blue car safely inside the hangar then disconnected the cars' batteries and covered each of them with their own custom-fit car cover. After closing the door and locking up the hangar Yazzie marched to the other end of the airport to leave when his cellphone went off. He didn't recognize the number but took the call anyway.

After several minutes of back-and-forth discussions, Carlos leaned against the doorframe outside the airport manager's office. He was at a complete loss. *Where am I going to put another car?! I need another aircraft hangar!* The Corvette had arrived.

CHAPTER 19

April 19, 2018

The White House called for a press conference. Hostages held by a Somali warlord had been rescued by unnamed special operations forces. The President of the United States made laudatory comments extolling the virtues of the U.S. military and Special Operations Command. After taking dozens of questions President Hernandez announced he would take two more. He called on a reporter from one of the cable news networks who asked, "Isn't murdering destitute Africans a clear sign that America is a racist country to its core?"

Demetrius Eastwood weighed the obvious, *There's nothing like a former Oberlin women's studies professor uttering angry communist screeds on camera....*

President Hernandez didn't take the bait. He disagreed with the reporter's statement and remarked, "When another nation is used as a staging base for non-state actors like pirates, and when other non-uniformed terrorists attack the United States or her allies on the seas or in the air, they're essentially attacking all Americans. These non-state actors do not care for the rule of law or nations. Pirates are criminals, not destitute law-abiding people. Let me be clear, if international criminal elements choose a life of crime of intimidating, threatening, or capturing Americans to hold them hostage, in an effort to extort monies from Americans or American companies, they will be annihilated in a place and manner of our choosing. And when someone attacks Americans, whoever they are and wherever they are, they will be held accountable and the country from which they operate will be held accountable. Next question. Colonel Eastwood?"

Of all the reporters in the White House Press Conference Room, only Demetrius Eastwood of the independent on-line news network, *Unfiltered News,* stood when addressing President Hernandez. A

Tudor *Black Bay* with a black face, red bezel, and a leather strap peeked out from his cuff when he held up his notepad. "Mr. President, kudos to the SEALs of SOCOM for another successful rescue and recovery mission. There was a time when Americans abroad would never have been molested, attacked, or murdered, as tourists or during the lawful performance of their duties, such as embassy duty. This makes ten significant and successful hostage rescues in three years. When do you think the countries from which these criminal organizations operate will learn that if they foster attacks on Americans or put American lives at risk, there will be severe consequences? I understand there were no surviving pirates. Thank you, sir."

President Hernandez smiled as presidents do when conservative correspondents inject levity into the air. As he walked from the lectern he replied, "Dory, I suppose when these criminal organizations and their state sponsors run out of pirates they may figure it out. I've directed American ships to have armed forces aboard to repel pirates and other criminals. They will not be firing warning shots." President Hernandez stopped in the doorway and continued, "Wasn't it John Wayne who said, 'Life is hard; it's harder when you're stupid.' I would add, you have to be incredibly stupid to threaten Americans abroad. In America we have to put them in jail and give them a trial. But overseas I have no qualms in using the full force of America's military might to destroy the criminally stupid when they menace our citizens. When they take up a weapon for criminal behaviors, they become armed combatants in the eyes of the law. Thank you for the question. Colonel Eastwood, did you want a follow-up?"

Eastwood put his hand down. "Yes, thank you Mr. President. I'm getting some mail that the executive leadership at the Sandia National Laboratory and Y-12, the National Security Complex, are forcing 'critical race theory,' race-segregated training, and white male reeducation on their employees—where any dissent will be severely punished. Progressive employees are rewarded; conservative employees are being purged. I must admit I had heard nothing like this until a friend of mine said that was exactly how the FBI was infiltrated and compromised. Is this something your administration could look into? Thank you, Mr. President."

President Hernandez took a few seconds to assimilate the question. "Dory, we'll look into it. Thank you for bringing this to my attention." President Hernandez and his advisors walked toward the Oval Office for the President's next meeting. The White House correspondents went to their network's cameras to report on the lawlessness, inhumanity, and arrogance of the Hernandez Administration.

Eastwood was in the middle of it all, watching reporters react with vituperation for the president. Within seconds their faces were square-on in front of a camera "reporting from the White House." One reporter announced, "It's a knee on the neck of democracy!" while another called the president's views "impeachable offenses." Eastwood crossed his arms in disgust; he heard all the lies and distortions. *The usual stuff from these mental cases. They are like a paranoid populace. Would the American people really fall for it? The press corps represents all the newsrooms and networks across America and some international networks and papers. In seconds, this tripe will be international news; spread across the United Kingdom, Europe, Australia – and it couldn't be more ridiculous, more partisan, more wrong. Just another batch of processed left wing fantasies…wretched, paranoid, sad. They are pathetic people who have no backbone and no moral character and no courage – and really no brains to speak of. The usual stuff from these mental cases. How does President Hernandez do it?*

• • •

When directed, the Executive Vice President of the American Federalist Society (AFS) and a White House adviser on judicial nominations entered the Oval Office. Burnt Winchester's hands were full; he was carrying a hatbox and two three-inch binders. He placed his load on the edge of a sofa, withdrew a white Stetson from the hatbox, and presented the personalized cowboy hat to President Hernandez.

President Javier Hernandez broke out in a Texas-wide smile as he accepted the gift; he spun the hat with the tips of his fingers and placed it on his head. As the men shook hands vigorously, the atmosphere in the Oval Office transitioned from staid, learned, and polished to ebullient.

Laughter rippled across the room when President Hernandez said, "All I need now is a white horse."

"I wanted to bring the world record longhorn out to the Rose Garden, but the Secret Service threatened to toss me out onto Constitution Avenue like yesterday's *New York Times*. Next time, Mr. President." The men laughed again and sat on opposite sofas. The friends motioned to each other that they were wearing matching black crocodile Lucchese boots.

President Hernandez explained to the people in the room, "Burnt Winchester and I had gone to the San Antonio bootmaker's store to celebrate my election to the 23rd Congressional District in the House of Representatives and his appointment as a U.S. Attorney for the Western District of Texas. I bought the boots; the new U.S. Attorney was on the hook for the more expensive Stetson if lightning ever struck and I became President."

"That was the day I told the President that he was 'on his way' and one day he would become President. He is an uncommon man for uncommon times. I have kept our bargain and there you see his Stetson." Winchester said exaggeratedly, "An *El Presidente* for *El Presidente*." The room erupted in laughter and applause.

The President tried to hold back his emotions. The times when a president can laugh and rejoice with friends were few and far between. As the Chief of Staff spoke for a few seconds, President Hernandez regained his composure. "Burnt, what else do you have today?"

Winchester held up two dark blue binders and said, "As requested, Mr. President, the American Federalist Society has delivered a slate of judicial nominees. Contained herein are fully vetted, experienced, credentialed, and accomplished jurists ready for positions of greater responsibility in the service of our nation. Your team can review these candidates. They are the best constitutional scholars and legal minds in the country."

Immediately after his inauguration newly elected President Javier Hernandez and the White House had issued a "Request for Judicial Nominees" to the AFS. The Democrat Party, the party out of power, and the media had expressed outrage that the new president would stack the courts with conservative judges, a clear affront to the norms of civilization.

The newspapers ran a cacophony of lengthy anti-Hernandez and anti-Republican articles which could've been summed up with three words: *Elections have consequences.* The Republicans had bitterly accused the previous Democrat administration of President Mazibuike of outsourcing the nomination process for cabinet members, political appointees, attorneys general, jurists, and generals and admirals to radical and anti-American special interest groups.

President Hernandez faced replacing thousands of Mazibuike-approved civil servants and flag officers or create a system to determine who could stay in his administration. Mazibuike had been a disingenuous president and installed like-minded people into his government. Time after time, those that remained after President Mazibuike left power had proven to be unreliable, bordering on treasonous as they spread perverse and damaging false stories to the media. People who were apolitical and would actually do the work of government without imposing their politics could stay on the job.

The political parties were at opposite ends of the special trust and confidence spectrum. The Democrat bureaucrats couldn't be trusted to faithfully or dutifully serve a Republican president. They had taunted the Republicans and predicted that a Republican would never again hold the Office of the President. The Democratic National Committee (DNC) had effectively declared war during the previous election. They were convinced their candidate would win, but something went wrong.

Dozens of special interest groups functioning as personnel placement organizations had raced to the White House to advocate their candidates be placed in "the top jobs" in the Hernandez Administration. The White House had multiple proposals to consider and chose the American Federalist Society's slate of conservative candidates. The political left was blinded by rage.

After Winchester completed his recommendations President Hernandez asked, "Is there was anything else the White House can do for the AFS?"

He listened closely as the AFS EVP replied, "Well, Mr. President, since you've asked there is something. The American Federalist Society would like to see the reversal of the U.S. political colors; flip the not-so-longstanding convention of the political colors of the past. Red symbols, such as the Red Flag or Red Star, have always been associated with left-wing intimidation politics, and right-wing movements often were left with no option but blue as a contrasting color. Up until the 2000 election, Democrats had always been represented by red and Republicans by blue. Comrade Democrats should return to their past socialist and communist glories and be represented by red; then Republicans can return to being 'true blue,' the color of freedom. The Democrats should replace the background color of their logos with Soviet or Chinese Communist red, which I believe is between the chaos of fire engine red and blood red on the color charts."

President Hernandez howled with laughter along with everyone else in the Oval Office. The President said, "Chief of Staff! I think Mr. Winchester's comments have merit; please take those for action."

The Chief of Staff offered, "Changing the political colors might be a declaration of war. Political war, of course."

"We're at war, and we've always been at war with them. The Republican Party just hasn't acknowledged it. The Democrats should rename themselves to the Fifth Communist Union or the Progressive International. They are constantly trying to hide their countervailing subversive communist positions. A Republican could cure cancer, and they would scream that millions died as we slow-walked the cure." Even though he knew the reversal would never happen, he said, "Let's draft a letter asserting our new colors and see what they say."

President Hernandez then pointed at the Chief of Staff. "Find out what the hell is going on at Sandia and Y-12. If Colonel Eastwood is right, I want someone fired and heads rolled. I have had enough of the bullshit and their political correctness. The brainwashing of America is coming to an end."

• • •

After walking off of the White House grounds, Eastwood extracted an olive Tilley's *Wanderer* from his computer bag, snapped on a pair of dark Oakley sunglasses, and stopped at a Starbucks Coffee shop for a *grande coffee frapuccino*. He looked more like a tourist than a longstanding member of the press as he waded around the latest assembly of protesters who were still furious that President Hernandez had won the election. Eastwood guided toward a police officer. He stopped, identified himself as a member of the press, and asked the cop who recognized him, "What is going on this time?"

Eastwood got the lowdown. "There has been gunplay—murder—near Union Station. Don't quote me, but we have chaos in this city, on our streets—anarchy; Democrats are running this city into the ground. This is a horrible and a perfectly predictable occurrence. It is obvious. The sometimes 'peaceful protesters' mask what the others are doing; burning, looting up and down the streets. They are rioting all across the country; these are rehearsals for revolution. These violent criminals in the street are organized by Democrats."

Eastwood inquired, "Are these Tussy voters?"

"Belligerent leftist mobs still pissed about the last election." Another exhausted-looking policeman in riot gear gave Eastwood directions how to get to Union Station without being accosted or molested, beaten, or killed. He said, "I don't know. Sometimes I think they are more basement dwelling Mazibuike holdovers than Tussy's sissies. In the last election I remember there were more cars in the McDonald's drive through than there were at the Tussy parade, but she was supposed to win. The Democrats were cheating and thought they had the election in the bag...."

"...but something happened. Philly and the state went for Hernandez. No one saw that coming."

"Well, yeah. Now she's dead and they are still howling at the moon mad." The cop nodded. "It only proves you cannot listen to the BS machine that the Democrat Party owns and operates or their polling companies."

"Why are they protesting?"

"From what I see, I think they protest because they suck at life, or their dad is now their mom, or their winners are supreme losers. I am not to be quoted."

Eastwood told the tired cop, "It's all off the record." He found another policeman in the rear being tended by emergency medical technicians and asked what had happened. "I got hit by a bottle filled with concrete. This is not hijinks. Others are throwing bags of urine or feces, like animals in a zoo playing in their own waste. They hate President Hernandez. I don't understand it, but they've been doing the same thing for years, only this year these people are *Looney Tunes.* They convinced themselves that Tussy was supposed to win, and when she didn't, they accuse the other side of cheating and go crazy on the streets."

"That *is* crazy." Eastwood was sympathetic.

"Some finite minority are peaceful in the technical sense but they are only cover so the criminals can loot the businesses, and the others.... They cannot get over the fact their girl didn't win the election. Their side cheated and they still lost."

"I've heard that twice today."

"They are anything but peaceful, and their idea of 'rock and roll' is to throw rocks at us and fight us in the streets."

There's an element to the policemen's words that were very true. The media studiously avoids reporting any of this, because it wouldn't be good for the Democrat Party. Eastwood followed the cop's instructions to avoid the BLMs and found his way to Union Station for the Acela to New York City. The cop had triggered a memory. He hummed a little Led Zeppelin: *It's been a long time since I rock and rolled....*

Once settled on the train he began to pull out his laptop but stopped, and quietly reflected in frustration: *Their girl Tussy lost two years ago, and they are still howling at the moon crazy. Their pollsters had her winning Philadelphia bigly but the votes weren't there and that was the difference. The Democrats have gone off the rails. The President's a regular guy, a straight guy – and they hate that. He is a sturdy, traditional, American male, a man who isn't confused about his gender or sexual preference. They really hate that in a man. They like men who are more like women and women who are more like men. Is it drugs? Is it brainwashing?*

The Democrats in the streets have become paranoid, generally speaking, universally fearful, generally psychotic, and very often dangerously, violently, criminally psychotic. There was much of that; I saw so many more attacks, more violence, more lunacy. Could it be the DNC is actually funding the riots? Is that even possible? Last night I heard there had been some haymakers, some real donnybrooks with the psychos in the street, with fireworks and explosives and rocks thrown at the police.

Eastwood looked outside as his thoughts came into sharp focus. He had seen some of the old black and white documentaries. *If I didn't know any better, I would say these are the Democrats' "Nazi shock troops," the brown shirts in the streets attacking people, beating people, the violence against the police. It's extraordinary. And everywhere there are protester's signs with a little red fist and a little red flag of the old Soviet Union in the lower corner. Incredible.*

They are lefties; they have destructive lefty values, not American values. They're not honest or trustworthy; they are not Boy Scouts. They are not truth people. They are criminals. Leftist mobs of mental cases.

I believe the Democrats have organized and unionized the mentally ill.

Something is going on, and damn if I can put my finger on it. Or maybe I just did.

CHAPTER 20

April 19, 2018

Greetings to the truth seekers who find today's media corrupted by special interests. It's Thursday, April 19th, 2018, and Maxim Mohammad Mazibuike was the most corrupt president in U.S. history. Under the banner of "How the Red Flag of Communism was Inspired by Anarchists," this week's cover of the Anarchists Black Flag magazine features a caricature of President Mazibuike in the style of a famous image of Argentine Marxist revolutionary Ernest "Che" Guevara, over the headline "The Anarchist's Greatest Friend." President Mazibuike's friends are all Red and dead, and they should not rest in peace.

Is it a coincidence that the three main sponsors of terrorism – Iraq, Libya, and Iran – all engaged in developing nuclear, chemical, and biological weapons and hid their programs from the international watchdogs under the guise of programs of peace? These programs require massive amounts of funds in R&D and construction, funds derived from the sale of oil, and they weren't easily hidden. They were some of the most poorly kept secrets in the Middle East. Only Iran remains engaged in the secret development of weapons of mass destruction.

Is it a coincidence that after the September 11, 2001 attacks on the U.S., two of the three main sponsors of terrorism ultimately witnessed their demise with the destruction of the Gaddafi and Saddam Hussein regimes? As American policy proscribed Iran's WMD programs, Iran, a country awash in oil, stubbornly held on to the fiction that their nuclear facilities were solely for peaceful purposes: generating electrical power for the Iranian people. Chemical plants produced fertilizer for Iranian crops, and the Khomeini Institute of Virology was solely constructed to research and develop vaccines to counter Middle Eastern Respiratory Syndrome and other respiratory diseases. Like SARS.

Is it any coincidence that contrary to U.S. policy, the former president, the charlatan Christian, the Muslim Maxim Mazibuike, whose closest advisors were from Iran, secretly engaged in talks to approve Iran's WMD and approved and funded European companies to construct Iran's biological facilities?

Is it any coincidence that the most corrupt presidential administration in American history was engaged in supporting the most corrupt and evil country in the Middle East, and that the most corrupt news media on the planet kissed their feet and covered their collective asses with creeping phlox? I think not.

Is it any coincidence when Indonesian Sky Link Flight 7070 disappeared without a trace and Qantas Airlines Boeing 747-400, The Spirit of Australia, Flight 1144 experienced a catastrophic electrical malfunction where half of the passengers and crew lost their lives, that the source of those aircraft accidents was tied to former President Maxim Mazibuike? He was behind those catastrophes, for they were the first, the trial runs, and he was behind the plot to bring down a thousand jets all at once. His punishment for being the quisling and criminal that he was. That he was. Was, as in past tense, for I have it on good authority that Mazibuike's assault on aviation was met with a fatal blow. DNA analysis reports from the dark web confirm what we have long suspected, the former president was decapitated in Dubai. His death is a marker to those aviation terrorists still out there planning attacks on aircraft and airports. You will be found and disposed of in the manner in which the juramentados were eliminated. You had better take the hint. There is a fresh breeze coming from the White House. The war on aviation is over. Politics may be combat by other means, but America has a new field general and he not intimidated in using the military might of America for righteous purposes.

This is the Omega.

• • •

Readers of *Omega* were beside themselves, scrambling for the definition of *juramentados*. Their research turned up a few random hits but nothing like the August 11th, 1927 *Chicago Daily Tribune* article. If it were true, that Mazibuike—who had run away and hid—had, in fact, been removed from whatever hole he had crawled into, that wasn't enough. He had met his demise by the sword, apparently. If the former president had been punished in such a way, then Islamists across the globe might need to think long and hard if they wanted to be an aviation terrorist and die an ignominious death at the hands of the unnamed madman infidel, the killer of a false president.

CHAPTER 21

April 19, 2018

In the shadow of the National Reconnaissance Office complex, in the largest industrial park in Chantilly sat a nondescript high-rise building without a trace of the expected large external signage that would define or announce the name of the corporation or its activities. The six-lane two-way access road that ran in front of the structure had a single cutout for a tiny parking lot for visitors to access through a single door. Near the visitor's parking was an obligatory flagpole. All the action was at the rear of the facility, an above-ground and underground parking garage; access to a cafeteria, and a massive security office that rivaled those found in the intelligence community's facilities. On the doors were six-inch white block letters: TASCO.

The senior intelligence analyst hurried to her seat and waited for the Trans-Atlantic Security Corporation Chief Executive Officer (CEO) to join her at the conference table. Linda Miller placed a copy of her brief at his position at the head of the table. From his desk he told her to start, and she began with an overview.

"It looks as if the CIA did everything possible to hide him, even stage a full-blown fake funeral at Arlington. In the pouring rain. It is unprecedented."

Arlington National Cemetery he corrected her in his mind. *She's just a civilian* he reasoned. His interest was piqued, and he encouraged the woman to continue without interruption. He held the phone to his ear waiting for an international call to connect and fiddled with a book.

She watched him; it was hard not to. He was reputedly mercurial, supercilious. He was also the busiest man she had ever met; his fast walking could've qualified him for the Olympics. He was also the only one who didn't look at her suggestively. A woman can tell when a man is interested in her, in women, in all women. And she can tell when a man only tolerates women; those are the men who are only interested in men. Her partner who worked at one of the networks and discussed the dichotomy all the time said, "Men are pigs."

Linda Miller continued, "Mr. Chernovich, the bottom line is the CIA did their best to hide him, but I think *I found him*. I don't have photographic evidence, but the documents indicate he's likely in Wyoming. Jackson Hole. He's very wealthy, but he doesn't flash it."

The CEO replaced the phone receiver on its cradle and hurried to the table. She referred to an Excel spreadsheet in the briefing materials and thanked Chernovich for the opportunity to research the man. Finding people who did not want to be found had been her forte at the CIA. The CEO had given her the name and said, "I need the 'right people' to look into this gent."

Linda Miller walked him through her processes, how she had determined his assignments with the Border Patrol and the Air Force and the Naval War College. "He holds at least eighteen patents, and I believe owns a former CIA front company full of scientists and engineers; they have many significant Agency contracts."

"I couldn't get anyone to tell me what went on in that building. We have some old hands here at TASCO who knew of the company when it was CIA, but it was just one of a hundred. I believe he has several businesses, from building armored vehicles to restoring aircraft, police cars, and race cars. He has no disgruntled employees." She explained that she had interviewed the people who worked with him and those who were his students in grad school. Then he all but disappeared from public view en route to Sydney, Australia. He had been declared legally dead after an international aircraft experienced a severe malfunction. Over half of the passengers and crew had died.

A new page from the PowerPoint presentation detailed a unique special access program which was run by the CIA Director without the Deputy's or the Director of Operations' knowledge. "The former Deputy and the DO are now working for TASC; I interviewed them for this project. All they could tell me was that the SAP began well before Greg Lynche became the Director, and now Director McGee continues it with the approval of the President. The SAP apparently included a range of special activities, none of which were reported to congress. It could be a twenty-year-old program hidden from congressional oversight." She paused for the CEO to read the slides.

Director McGee was the first African-American to become the head of the CIA, and it was a nomination that shocked the body politic in Washington, D.C. It was a nomination that was totally unorthodox. The newly elected President had done it again; he had made a nomination without any input of the Trans-Atlantic Security Council.

Chernovich motioned for her to continue.

"The CIA Director ran interference for this unknown SAP asset. I found that the Agency had approved the SAP, initially conceived to have little outside help. If they couldn't use agency assets to put the players into the field, then the Air Force Chief of Staff would provide help. They eliminated virtually all traces of their contractor. The record of success was spotty. There is some evidence and reporting by conservative radio stations that President Mazibuike didn't allow the CIA to go after certain terrorists, although the headlines went wherever Mazibuike directed them. The record, open and closed-sourced, was that during President Mazibuike's term of office there were no major terrorist figures killed by unknown means in Africa or the Middle East. There were several times where this *Maverick* may have been discovered, by the Muslim Brotherhood and the Islamic Underground. There were several one million-dollar bounties on his head, and *Maverick* has the dubious distinction of being the only person to ever have a ten million dollar bounty put on his decapitated head. It was offered by al-Qaeda. All are official *fatwās* published on the *dark web*. He had hidden his external activities and his internal whereabouts."

"Hunter is a pilot. I know he's the missing man, the person responsible for eliminating some 200 narcoterrorists in South America and radical *jihadis* in Africa and the Middle East," said the CEO. *The Party needs those men to foment unrest across the globe.*

"Yes, sir. Those are consistent with my findings." Linda Miller finished her brief with discussions on Hunter's friends, residences, and businesses.

Chernovich touched his fingertips together before speaking. He used the language of businessmen. "I think there are several downsides with your analysis. From what aircraft can a pilot shoot a target—these men were all killed at night, if I'm correct, with a gun? Pilots at night are as helpless as a sleeping rattlesnake." *Clark Gable in Night Flight proved that. They might have sensors to get them from A to B, but shooting a gun from a moving platform at night; impossible! The high fire rate of Gatling guns are necessary, but they are massive and require heavy aircraft to haul them around. And they are not precise. Each man who died in Africa and the Middle East have a single fatal entry wound.*

"There is no perfect answer, but there are two aircraft, both out of production, which were specifically built to operate at night. A motorized sailplane the CIA used to conduct surveillance on narcoterrorists in Colombia—every one of that type can be accounted for—and the other is Lockheed's other spyplane, the YO-3A that was built solely for the Army. Eleven prototypes were built in 1969 and delivered to Vietnam."

Chernovich shook his wrist to move his watch to a better position. Miller wasn't impressed, although it was probably a rare and expensive watch. He pointed at the photo of the YO-3A and said, "This is the one."

"Yes, sir. Of the eleven built, one was destroyed in an accident, one aircraft was transferred directly to NASA after the war and was sold two years ago to a Vietnam Helicopter Museum in California. Five copies are in museums, and the others, of which four are remaining, are in private hands. Ownership of them is so private I couldn't determine who owns them, whether there are separate owners or one. They are not registered in the FAA's database."

A secret aircraft would not be registered. There's only one owner and it is Duncan Hunter. Chernovich gritted his teeth for a moment. He felt he was getting closer to destroying that pilot.

Miller said, "No recent photographs exist of him, but there are some from when he was in the Marine Corps. They're in the brief."

I vaguely remember what he looked like back in the day. Typical poster-board Marine. Straight as an arrow. Made the girls squeal, I'll bet. Chernovich returned to the beginning of her brief and flipped through the pages. She watched him closely and tried to keep up with him.

She provided a summation without being asked. "These are the men who logged time on the FBI's Most Wanted list and unexpectedly died in their home countries. Every victim had one thing in common; a massive bullet hit the sternum, obliterated the heart, and removed several inches of the spinal column. Formal investigations in these countries do not exist, but some believe the fatal injuries were from a *Terminator* round."

Chernovich turned his head to her. He remembered the Agency issuing a contract for experimental ammunition, something about laser-guided bullets, but the award went to an obscure laboratory in Texas. *Was that one of his companies?* He stopped and re-read the entries in the briefing materials. *A Nigerian woman sang the praises of "Maverick" after a white man and a black man boarded a hijacked jet in Liberia and killed the hostage takers – the same night dozens of Boko Haram were killed in Northern Nigeria.*

He shot up the Boko Haram in Nigeria and flew to Liberia and boarded a jet that had been hijacked? What aircraft would allow him to do that? What person could even consider doing something like that? He asked for clarification, "The people who were interviewed were singing the praises of *Maverick*? Someone on the jet called him *Maverick*. I don't suppose anyone had an answer how he and his partner got on that jet?" Linda Miller shook her head.

Another page detailed his personal history. *There was only one fighter pilot in the Marine Corps who went by the call sign "Maverick." The name on the headstone at Arlington was Captain Drue Duncan Hunter. It's the same asshole. And he is still alive.*

Chernovich had determined that the Commandant he had replaced and a Captain Duncan Hunter had investigated him. *I'm sure "Maverick" sent those detectives to investigate me. But why? That had been such a long time ago. What happened, what changed? What was he after? What am I missing?*

The file was comprehensive yet missing some material. She said, "The source of his wealth appears to be patents active in countering aviation terrorism."

He asked, "Is there a woman in *Maverick's* life?"

Linda Miller shook her head. "Not that we are aware of."

No women? There is no way he is one of us.

"Addresses?"

"Page 12 of the report has his former addresses. I suspect he's living in Wyoming in a house purportedly owned by his long-time foreman. A man named Yazzie."

Chernovich turned to the page of addresses. "Yazzie?"

"He's an Indian. Apache. A millionaire, according to the IRS, and no one knows how he came into his money. But he pays his taxes."

He read "Del Rio" and "Fredericksburg, Texas." And there it was, a homestead under the name of Yazzie in Jackson. He stared while tapping his finger on the back cover of the book.

Miller put her hands in her lap. She knew she had done a masterful job. He called her a "goddess" without meaning it and thanked her profusely. He said that no one else had done what she had accomplished, that he was grateful, and she would be rewarded for her diligence. Chernovich said to expect a bonus; Miller said it really was nothing.

He insisted on celebrating her accomplishments with champagne and by giving her a book.

She looked at the title and didn't make a face. She had heard of it before. *The Flowers of Evil*, by Charles Baudelaire, was a body of love poems of lesbian love and the seamy side of urban life. It was old and rare and for a lesbian woman, was greatly appreciated. Then to Linda Miller's utter amazement, Bogdan Chernovich fixed them drinks. He made idle chatter about where she had come from; he showed her the champagne bottle. He popped the cork. She didn't see him remove a bottle of eye drops from a shirt pocket and squirt the liquid into her glass. He brought the drinks and the bottle to the table. They chatted informally; she reveled in telling him how she had made leaps in logic to find the man and what he had done across the globe, leaving hundreds of dead terrorists in his wake. "*Dead men leave footprints,*" she said. "Every time he killed a terrorist, he left a little clue. Like a puzzle piece. Collect enough pieces and soon you have a picture," she said. "They never knew they were being targeted by an aerial assassin because there hasn't ever been an aerial assassin."

True, he surmised. *You didn't find them all, but I have enough to find him and finish him.*

He watched Miller struggle against the tetrahydrozoline but quickly lose the battle. Any other time he would've sodomized her, like a conquering Viking who had vanquished a foe, but this wasn't the time to be greedy. He tossed *The Flowers of Evil* onto his desk and buzzed his secretary to "clean the room."

The CEO's male secretary, bruising retired Marine Corps Sergeant Major Jimmy Slaughter, had a bashed-in nose like a New Jersey prize fighter and a post-Marine Corps physique of a bulldog. He stopped what he was doing, went to a file cabinet drawer, and removed an aluminum foil-covered bag. After donning a N100 respirator, Slaughter cut open the hermetically sealed bag and slipped into Tyvek® coveralls and gloves. The former Marine and former weightlifter looked like he was part of a paint crew. He carried the unconscious woman to the CEO's private elevator. He recovered Linda Miller's purse and verified that her house and office keys and Tesla fob were inside.

On the ride to the basement, Slaughter dumped the remaining bottle of champagne down the woman's throat. Once the elevator doors closed behind him, he waddled around in the white plastic head-to-toe covering until he located the woman's car in the electric car aisle by pressing the emergency button on the woman's car fob. It was hooked up to a charging unit. He disconnected the plug from the charging unit and drove her car closer to the private elevator. When he had determined there was no one else in the garage, he unlocked the private elevator, retrieved the inert body of Linda Miller, and placed her in her car. He threw the empty bottle of champagne in the back seat.

Slaughter removed an old rubber-handle screwdriver from a sleeve, got on his knees, and strategically poked a hole in the electric car's battery tray. It took only a few seconds to slip out of the coveralls, toss them into the lap of the dead woman, and close the door. By the time he returned to the elevator, the Tesla was smoking and spitting orange jets of fire from the underside of the car like an industrial-sized Fourth of July sparkler.

He stood in the elevator and watched the woman burn. He would never forget it was Captain Chernovich who had pulled him and several other Marines from a helicopter that had been shot down and caught fire. The magnesium fire burns singed only his leg and arm. A week later it was Slaughter's turn to return the favor when a Vietcong with an AK-47stepped out of the bamboo and tried to waste the tall lanky officer whose back was turned. Slaughter blasted the diminutive dark-skinned man; he and his captain had escaped death together. They were awarded medals for their valor. There wasn't anything Slaughter wouldn't do for him.

When adjacent vehicles were engulfed in flames, he activated a nearby fire alarm and sent the lift to the CEO's office using the tip of his screwdriver. He took the stairs and with every step, lamented that the disposal of Linda Miller had been easier than finding and shooting the straight whistleblower, Stephanie Bartholomew, in Maryland.

TASCO employees emptied the building quickly. When the Fire Department arrived, eight vehicles near the electric car were totally consumed in flames. Fire trucks couldn't enter the basement parking area because they were too high. It took several minutes for the first of several firefighters with hoses to descend the parking lot entrance ramp and worked furiously to put out the fire.

The Fire Chief arrived and stood well away from the fire.

The CEO walked over to the man with "Fire Chief" stenciled on his helmet and offered his assistance. The Fire Chief asked for the security tapes of the basement parking area. Bogdan Chernovich was courteous and helpful, "Chief, the system has been shut down for a week, and we've had the repairmen out here for days—they're still trying to fix a massive wiring problem. I understand a wire bundle was cut out of the system...."

Those things don't happen in Virginia. The Fire Chief said, "I've heard of those things happening in Africa; destitute people cut wires from establishments for the copper and sell it to a metal recycler." Thick white smoke roiled out of the garage.

Chernovich was ramrod straight. "I know my facility manager filed a police report when it happened a few days ago. Please feel free to talk to him and the repairmen; they can help you more than I. I'll have my secretary provide you with copies of the police report for your records." *It wasn't like the system had conveniently gone down. Some events require planning and direction, and some imagination.*

The Fire Chief asked if anyone was missing. The CEO showed that a preliminary accounting found only one person was missing, an analyst had just had a meeting in his office. "My secretary informed me that she hasn't been accounted for. We had a good meeting, and then she left my office. I gave her the rest of the day off and expected she would return to her office to tell her manager, but her manager said Ms. Miller hadn't returned. For whatever it is worth, her co-workers said she drove a Tesla—she was very proud of that car and its impact on the environment. Her office mates have seen videos of electric car fires on YouTube and seem to think that the car on fire in the garage had to be her Tesla. I'm thinking I should have prohibited them from parking in the underground garage."

The Fire Chief looked up at the taller Chernovich and informed him that many businesses were moving the charging stations for electric vehicles well-away from their buildings. "That seems to be the best place for a charging station. The safest parking area for the fire-prone electric vehicles is along the outer edge of the parking lot." He harrumphed. "I'm actually tiring of responding to these; we have seen so many electric car fires just in the last couple of months; they are straining our resources."

Chernovich was surprised, "*Really?*"

The Fire Chief continued, "When dealing with a *Tesla* we have two options, try to drown it or let it burn. He spat the word *Tesla* as if it was an Egyptian mummy curse, *For all who dare drive the catastrophic chemical combustible contraptions are condemned to die in a conflagration of apocalyptic proportions.* "When these things go off, the ion-lithium batteries explode all over the place which sets more fires. They are like grenades—no, they are like mortars going off. Individual flaming batteries that are launched everywhere. Yesterday, we responded to one on I-95. It shut the road down for six hours; after 45 minutes of knocking down the fire with as much water as we could pour on it, we thought we could move it—got it up on the transporter and the battery re-ignited. They can spontaneously re-combust and need to be separated from other cars."

Chernovich said, "You try to be environmentally friendly, do the right thing and reduce carbon footprints, and reward those who are concerned with vehicles polluting the air with parking close to the entrances, and then... something like this happens." Both men crossed their arms in disgust.

The Fire Chief continued, "If she was inside an electric car, then her body has probably been totally consumed by the chemical fire. She could've been overcome by the noxious fumes—it doesn't take but a whiff when those things decide to go off. On-line videos don't show the cars when people can't get out, and the electric car manufacturers won't talk about it. They burn so much hotter than other fires. We might not retrieve her teeth or dental work."

"It takes nothing to poke a hole in their batteries and set them off. We hate them. You will not find a policeman, a firefighter, or a wrecker driver in the country driving one of those things. The Los Angeles PD bought 300 of them and no one would drive them." *They are vehicles for morons.* The Fire Chief leaned closer to Chernovich and said, "Some have used the vehicle's peculiar habit of spontaneous combustion to cover up a murder. Those cars have such a bad reputation. That should tell you they're bad business."

"Apparently you can't tell millennials anything. They aren't going to be this nation's greatest generation."

The Fire Chief said, "Just wait until one of these things go off at a massive airport parking lot. The parking garage at the Baltimore-Washington airport is constructed so if a Tesla went off there it could burn down the whole damned parking lot. It will happen, and all you can do is watch it burn. We try to drown them, but you really need chemicals to put out a chemical fire."

Bogdan Chernovich wasn't interested in the man's ramblings but remained helpful, polite, and concerned. *There's nothing like standing by an open fire and watching the evidence burn.* Chernovich shook the Fire Chief's hand and bid him farewell. He walked around the building to the entrance. He stopped to talk with his secretary and give him a slip of paper as he said, "Take care of this." Jimmy Slaughter said, "Wilco." The CEO told everyone to go home.

The limousine driver opened the door for Chernovich, who gave him instructions to take him to the Capitol Grill, Washington's premiere steakhouse. He had a dinner-date with a chief financial officer. His eye had been on her for quite some time.

CHAPTER 22

May 3, 2018

The Boko Haram's mission was to drive the white man, his religion, and his God out of the country; a total war on Christianity. The intermediate goal was to decimate the Nigerian military sufficiently to prevent them from conducting counterterrorism operations in northern Nigeria. It hadn't always been that way. When Boko Haram was first formed in 2002 their actions were nonviolent; their main goal had been to purify Islam in northern Nigeria. When Abubakar Shekau took over in 2009 radical elements within Boko Haram forced him to align with al-Qaeda for the funds and weapons to drive the Christians out of the country. Boko Haram rampaged across northern Nigeria, killing tens of thousands and displacing over two million Nigerians. Then during raiding parties Boko Haram leaders died in the field under mysterious circumstances. Thirty, forty, and sometimes fifty terrorists would be killed on the field of battle with no apparent explanation, and the Nigerian military were adamant that they didn't engage the Boko Haram on the field.

For fifteen years, Boko Haram's reputation for bloody vicious butchery kept the Nigerian military in their barracks in Abuja and Lagos. But after losing one hundred of their top leaders, al-Qaeda believed the Boko Haram was on the way out and ceased providing terrorist funding. The Boko Haram needed funds to survive, so the group realigned with the vicious Islamic State of Iraq and Syria, ISIS. Abubakar Shekau believed the Boko Haram had weathered the storm of American aggression. With ISIS backing and funding the Boko Haram was back in the lucrative terrorism and sex trade business.

The Muslim government had essentially turned a blind eye, and Boko Haram had *carte blanche* to carry out nighttime raids of villages spreading an intensifying war on Christians in Nigeria and other parts of Sub-Saharan Africa. The former Nigerian president had been behind what several international observers called a "genocide" of Christians. He had turned his back on the plight of all Nigerians and especially the Christian majority in the north. The American President Mazibuike had played a major role in the country's first Muslim president's rise to power. Voting machines from a European human rights foundation ensured a fair and honest election although the Christian majority suspected the election had been stolen from them.

When twenty Nigerians and six Christians had been burned alive in an attack in the central part of the country carried out by thirty armed terrorists, the government was pressured into asking for much needed help. Nigerian Christians and their advocates in the United States, including religious freedom organizations and Republican members of Congress, beseeched the President of the United States for help. American assistance was badly needed to help the Nigerians stop the Muslim Boko Haram from stealing children, raping women, and stealing oil from pipelines. They needed help to stop them from dragging pastors and priests from their churches and unceremoniously beheading them for Al Jazeera to post on the internet. Many Christians felt that regardless of what criminal Muslims in Nigeria defined as justification for honor killing in the name of Mohammad, it was still murder, and murderers should be brought to justice for their crimes, even religious crimes.

• • •

Months of intelligence work looked like it had finally paid off for the Boko Haram Counter Task Force. American and Nigerian intelligence officials huddled in a conference room in the U.S. Embassy in the capital city of Abuja. They had reached the most critical stage of the trap they had set and hoped it wouldn't be compromised.

Intelligence officials regularly required massive amounts of intel; counterterrorism operations required planning and direction to the nth degree, and getting a trustworthy agent into the Boko Haram area to conduct surveillance, monitor movements, and report their activities had bordered on the impossible—the average Nigerian was so corrupt they didn't know the meaning of the word corrupt. It was imperative they find an incorruptible man with a cell phone and a motor scooter for the deadly work. Members of the National Clandestine Service had scoured their sources until they found a candidate. It took a long time before the American intelligence apparatus had found a man that they could trust to report "contact" on the ISIS affiliate. Once he was in place monitoring the Boko Haram and infiltrating their operation, the informer learned the date and place of their next raiding party and could transmit the data. The quality of the intelligence from the shopkeeper was trending positive. A radio call to the task force group announced, "Visitors inbound."

The two Nigerian intelligence officers were insulted that they hadn't been given full access to the intelligence. They were convinced the white Americans were keeping secrets from them, and they were right. But there wasn't anything they could do. It was disgraceful to be a Nigerian intelligence officer and not be fully trusted; allies were supposed to share intelligence. However, the Boko Haram had great success infiltrating the army's ranks so it was understood that the Nigerian army could not be counted on to keep their plans secret. That left a handful of Americans in the U.S. Embassy to do the dirty work of stopping another Boko Haram raid on another village.

The CIA's Chief of Station (COS) believed he was managing the operation adequately, given the limitations of his knowledge. He didn't need to know the specifics of the Agency's special access program. The only hint that another American might be in the area of the Boko Haram was a single two-word radio transmission from someone with deep voice and a hint of Texas accent.

The Nigerian intelligence officers didn't bother asking who they were trusting to interdict the ISIS affiliate; the American spies didn't seem to know either. The CIA Director in Washington had been emphatic when he told the Chief of Station, "I'll have an asset in place at the designated time and place. You'll be notified when the targets are identified and when the area has been cleared."

The Chief of Station, a veteran of many counterterrorism operations in Africa and South America, wasn't impressed with the new CIA Director's succinctness and pragmatism. *Nothing goes as planned at first contact! How can you be so sure? This has screw-up written all over it. Now I'm going to look like a boob in front of the Nigerians.* He was convinced the interdiction operation was doomed to fail. He would be demeaned. It was impossible to know the location of two hundred Christian children and that a raid on their school and village would occur on a certain date. The information had to be inaccurate. *Does the Director have instantaneous satellite intel? Why can't he tell me?*

As midnight approached in the northern savannah of Nigeria, an Agency contract pilot quietly arrived over the target school with time to spare. The Moody Blues' *The Other Side of Life* filled his headphones. He sat in the rear seat, the original pilot's position in the aircraft, and set up an orbit that would allow him to observe the Boko Haram leadership in action. Piloting from the back seat allowed him to reload the onboard weapon system. This wasn't his first rodeo. He would kill terrorists if the intel was correct. He got to visit the Boko Haram's hunting grounds once or twice a year. He would fly in to ambush and kill as many of the murderous marauders as possible. The thermal sensor aboard allowed him to record the precision surveillance.

From a few hundred feet in altitude he monitored the thermal imagery of a line of vehicles bumping along an unpaved road. The image of military-style assault vehicles that filled his FLIR scope was clear and crisp. He scrutinized the imagery for details. He noticed the men wore military-style uniforms and carried AK-47s, but their unkempt uniforms were inconsistent with the standards of military forces. *What we have here is Boko Haram rolling in on the Christian village. How many times in the last fifteen years have I seen this movie? Don't they know how predictable they are following the same MO? No they don't! They are lazy. They are unprofessional. Their brains are cooked.*

He interrupted the Moody Blues, moved the control stick to alter his direction of flight, and flew out to meet the advancing party.

The train of trucks were a mile from the village as Hunter continued to monitor the men's activities and decided when to engage. *These aren't the cowardly, gutless, neatly dressed soldiers of the Nigerian army; these guys are jumping around like they're on speed, anticipating when they will attack the sleeping village, kill the men, and drag terrified women from their beds. They probably have a hard on in anticipation of demoniac sex. Fight's on!*

He had no sympathy for the terrorists. He threw the switches to lower the YO-3A aircraft's gun and the infrared laser designator (LD) from their stowed positions in the airplane's belly. The Terminator Sniper System's ammunition was second-generation, experimental, laser-guided, rocket-propelled bullets. Like laser-guided missiles the *Terminator* bullets hit the laser-designated spot with pinpoint precision; the system's effectiveness and probability of kill approached 100%. It also had a hybrid silencer device developed by an independent gunsmith to make guns quieter.

After both systems locked into place in the airstream, gun targeting information and symbology were overlaid onto the FLIR image. Whatever the CIA pilot aimed at would be stilled in seconds, and the two-liter bottle-sized hybrid muzzle brake-silencer would "quiet" the rounds fired which would confuse the enemy's sense of direction of the attack. The muzzle's flash could still be visible but was greatly reduced.

Weedbusters was then lowered into the airstream. An incapacitated enemy can be manipulated.

Not one man in the trucks looked up; their eyes were focused forward. They had no conception that they could be attacked from the air. It wouldn't have mattered if they had; the airplane was as black as a raven's wing at midnight and was perfectly invisible in the cloudless night sky. The YO-3A couldn't be seen, and it couldn't be heard at the altitude the pilot had selected. As long as the on-ground background noise was enough to mask the susurrus of the attacking low-level aircraft, the predators would never know they had become the prey.

As the trucks halted at the edge of the village Duncan Hunter surveilled the area with the FLIR, looking for opportunities. Men ran from the vehicles and spread out in the manner of a tactical raiding party. He knew their reputation for murder and rape and pillaging; they always brought brawny military vehicles to carry their booty—prepubescent girls—to their hideouts in northern Nigeria and Cameroon. Those they didn't "make wives," rape on the spot, or want to keep, would be sold to Islamic slave traffickers.

There was a computed altitude and critical angle to engage the Boko Haram. If he flew too low, innocent Nigerians in the village could permanently lose their eyesight to the UV weapon. Hunter would fly higher to blind the Boko Haram for the short period of assault and if any villagers were caught looking outside, their vision would only be temporarily affected.

When the men stopped moving, Hunter jammed the throttle to the firewall for a full two seconds; when the Boko Haram turned to find of the source of the unusual noise, Hunter engaged the *Weedbusters'* ultraviolet laser for several seconds. The men stopped to shield their eyes. Some dropped their weapons. Some tried to find the safety of vehicles or buildings, but blinded, some crashed into one another. The assaulters had been assaulted.

Hunter placed a laser dot on the chest of the obvious leader. The first shot from the airborne TS2 passed through that terrorist and killed the man standing directly behind him. The supersonic crack of a high-velocity bullet sent the blinded Boko Harem scurrying in rage and fear. Men jammed themselves into doorways to make themselves a smaller target or they stumbled out of the buildings. One Boko Haram seemed to have his wits about him and tried to engage what he believed to be the Nigerian military. His Kalashnikov erupted into the only place he had remembered that could have provided adequate cover for an ambush, the tree line of the forest. Hunter had the aircraft on autopilot, on altitude hold, allowing him to target and kill a stationary or moving terrorist with the laser-guided ammunition every six seconds.

Men screamed and in 200 seconds, all the AK-47s were quieted. Minutes passed before an intrepid child wandered into the killing zone, looked up to the sky where the flashes had come from, and thanked God for delivering him and his family from evil.

As the bright glow of Abuja appeared on the horizon, Hunter radioed the Chief of Station that the mission was complete. The U.S. Embassy erupted in celebration, but the Nigerian intelligence men were unconvinced. They wanted proof before joining the jubilation. The Chief of Station told the bewildered Nigerian intelligence officers, "Proof of their destruction will come soon. You now know they can be found and defeated with superior training and firepower. But more importantly, your soldiers and the soldiers of neighboring countries need to know they're not dealing with demons. They are just terrorists, mass murderers, and marauders. And with additional training and leadership, the Boko Haram's days are numbered."

After a low-level orbit of the Chinese embassy, recording SAR scans and FLIR imagery, Hunter returned to the Abuja airport still under the cover of darkness and landed within the width of the runway. He taxied to the rear of an LM-100J, the civilian version of Lockheed Martin's cargo workhorse, the C-130J, spun the tailwheel around, and shut the engine down. The propeller hadn't fully stopped before the old CIA men began disassembling the YO-3A and the LM-100J pilot started the number two engine. Bob and Bob moved with the efficiency and choreography of a NASCAR pit crew, taking seconds to remove speed tape from panel joints, unfasten quick-disconnects, remove tiny clevis pins for control cables and oversized ones from the wing attachment mounts. When the three main structures of the aircraft were safely aboard and secured inside the *Hercules,* the aircrew closed the aircraft ramp and upper door. By then all four LM-100J's engines were "turning and burning."

From Hunter's landing to the LM-100J's takeoff was only a few minutes. Hunter and his exhausted support crew settled down for the flight as the LM-100J proceeded to Djibouti, specifically Camp Lemonnier, the U.S. Naval Expeditionary Base and only permanent U.S. military base in Africa. It was also the only combat-capable American military base on the continent. The base which formerly belonged to France was home to several thousand American troops whose primary role was carrying out counterterrorism operations in the terrorist-rich failed-state of Somalia.

The *Hercules* landed at the Ambouli International Airport for fuel. Hunter, the Bobs, and the rest of the aircrew crashed for the night in a high-security, high-rise hotel just outside of the base.

• • •

Christian churches had been attacked and the events went unreported or underreported by the media. Nigerian Christians from surrounding villages had marched on Abuja to protest government inaction and lack of protection from the murderous and evil Boko Haram terrorists. Then killing suddenly stopped. In one village after another religious men rejoiced that their prayers had been answered. They thought the

Boko Haram's murderous rampage had been stopped because of divine intervention. The village women and children huddled together in doorways and blessed themselves with the Sign of the Cross.

Against the entreaties of their Christian priests, the village men dragged the bodies of the terrorists off into the jungle and dumped them unceremoniously into a mass grave. There was a warlike quality to their movements as they punished the dead by stabbing and spearing them before they kicked them into the pit. They butchered a male and a female wild boar over the dead Boko Haram invaders. The priests stood aside and watched the village men sprinkle the blood of the boar throughout the grave until blood covered the faces of the Muslim men. When the forest pigs were totally drained of their life's blood, their entrails were thrown into the pit. Finally, four men with gold crosses around their necks threw the wild boar carcasses atop the Boko Haram men. The villagers covered the bodies with dirt so that lions wouldn't find them and make a meal of the men and the boar.

Word got around about the impure burial of the fanatics of Boko Haram. Other village leaders in the northern third of the country copied the strategy and the blasphemous burial of the Nigerian criminal Muslims had the desired effect. From then on, the Boko Haram avoided the places where boars had been slaughtered after they had been defeated, humiliated, and demeaned. The attacks on Christians stopped in those areas.

• • •

Finding and killing the men of the al-Qaeda affiliate in Nigeria had been a relatively simple matter and had provided the United States an economic benefit. After years of civil and internecine war and with the successful destruction of the Boko Haram leaders in the north, the Chief of Staff of the Nigerian Air Force announced they would award $500 million in contracts to U.S. firms. Instead of having to program money to fight the Boko Haram, the government could rehabilitate their Lockheed C-130s that had been parked on the military side of the Lagos airport and left to rot during years of civil war.

The newly elected Nigerian president, a Christian, had run on a platform of Westernization, establishment of better relations with the United States, and making the Nigerian Air Force the dominate humanitarian assistance capability in the region. President Hernandez, the newly elected American President offered to help Nigeria eliminate their terrorism plague, develop a more robust counterterrorism capability, and return to the good old days when Nigerian Air Force officers attended U.S. Air Force flight schools and America's military war colleges. It wouldn't be long before American companies began to work with the local air force personnel to make the Nigerian Air Force C-130s airworthy again. As Nigerian forces shucked old Soviet-era Kalashnikovs and vehicles and transitioned to U.S. manufactured equipment and arms, they would train with U.S. Special Forces to confront the remnants of the Boko Haram in the northern part of the country.

Chapter 23

May 3, 2018

Thousands of people across America, the United Kingdom, and Australia were glued to their computer monitors in anticipation of the latest message from *Omega*. They each had a powerful VPN, a virtual private network that allowed access to the *dark web* and the *Tor* browser developed by the National Security Agency to protect U.S. intelligence communications online and to maintain their anonymity. Once they successfully negotiated the many traps and pitfalls of the *dark web*, they could enter a message board on the anonymous online forum, *The Cross of Laraine Day*, and get their monthly dose of intelligence from *Omega*. *Omega's* posts were usually on the anniversary of some terrorist event of historical significance, but not always. Sometimes *Omega* would provide bits of information, a nugget or two of secret intel, that had never before been revealed to the public. *Omega* had to have top secret credentials and a desire to share information that was not designed to be shared. The authorities called him an "outlaw." To those who knew the inner workings of the *dark web*, the quality of *Omega's* intelligence was as solid as stone, and his tiny resistance was becoming something of a movement.

Omega's post began with a statement: *It's May the third, 2018 and the recluse Rho Schwartz Scorpii is one of the most corrupt people in the world. Today marks the day that radical Islamists have carried out 30,000 terrorist attacks since September 11, 2001. We are very close to the date, 238 years ago, the great Carl von Clausewitz was born. He noticed in his epic, On War, that "Politics is combat by other means." It is a tragedy to know the left is at war with us, and we don't even know it. We will talk about the shift in the news, from the media's focus when they reported the facts to what they have become, pushing a commie narrative on the American people, which is just another way to say for twenty years we have been subject to KGB-inspired brainwashing. It pains me greatly to see how little people are fighting to defend freedom.*

It is not enough.

Do you believe in coincidences? 19 al-Qaeda hijacked four jets and the response was to federalize airport security? Is it just a coincidence that there were no surveillance cameras at the checkpoints of the three departure airports; at two airports surveillance cameras weren't installed and at the other it was out of service? There are photos of Mohammad Atta and Abdulaziz al-Omari passing through the Portland International Jetport in Portland, Maine but none at the departure airport, Boston Logan.

Is it just a coincidence that after the 19 AQ passed through security, the Muslim men and women who worked at the checkpoints left their positions on the x-ray machines and magnetometers and were never seen again?

Is it just a coincidence that their airport security uniforms were found in trash cans, abandoned in the restrooms?

Was it just a coincidence that Federal action was necessary to prevent a repeat of radical Islamists who infiltrated airport security and facilitated the 9/11 attacks on the U.S.?

Is it just a coincidence that European countries discovered radical Islamists had also infiltrated airport security across European international airports and have quietly prohibited Muslim men and women from serving in airport security positions?

This is the Omega.

It was understood that *Omega* was taking a tremendous risk by informing the public on what he knew. In chatrooms across the globe people wondered who he could be and what his motivation was. Several names were bandied about, but the candidates, mostly college professors, were either dead or too old to be knowledgeable of the *dark web*. The DNC, the networks, and newspapers had hired detectives to find the *Omega*.

At midnight eastern time, *Omega* was typing: *Do you believe in coincidences? Revisit the OKC bombing. Who helped the OKC bombers – the media did everything in their power to avoid identifying the co-conspirators, the Islamic Underground. These are the same people proven to be masterminds of aviation terrorism. There was a reporter in Oklahoma who found out that the OKC bombers had significant Islamic Underground help.*

Was it just a coincidence that the newspapers would not run that reporter's story, or that the corrupt networks would not report on her research? One of the greatest powers of the media is their power to ignore. All too often the press averts its eyes, like Victorians confronting a public display of affection, and refuses to investigate some subjects. In fact, leftist corporations like TASCO have hired investigators by the dozen to find Omega's trail on the dark web. Good luck, assholes.

Was it just a coincidence that the OKC bombing occurred during an unprecedented outbreak of international aviation terrorism? Was OKC actually "a dry run" to see what it would take to collapse an airport-sized building? Recall al-Qaeda and the Islamic Underground failed to bring down the World Trade Center in 1993. They monitored the explosion in OKC and learned what it took to destroy an airport. Their goal is to shut down all aviation. One jet and one airport at a time until they can shut it all down.

Beware of socialist Greeks bearing gifts of electric cars, windmills, solar panels, and voting machines. A corrupt government can pull the plug anytime; they can change your vote; they can shut it all down. They can and do change your vote to ensure their candidate always wins. The Democrat Party is not your friend.

This is the Omega.

• • •

With the emergence of the Unabomber, Ted Kaczynski, who killed three people and injured twenty-three others in an attempt to start a revolution, explosives in the mail had become a concern, but bioterrorism had never been on anyone's radar until after September 11, 2001. After receiving suspected anthrax-tainted mail in its main mail processing facility, the main office of the New York City U.S. Postal Service announced to the international newspapers and television networks that they were stopping and destroying any suspect mail destined for newspaper companies and networks. While it was clear there were risks of encountering additional tainted mail and packages, postal employees sought a way to deliver documents and packages instead of having them incinerated for safety reasons.

Overnight, newspaper and network mailrooms were significantly remodeled to counter the threats. Contractors claimed the mailrooms now reflected the same high level of detection and remediation technologies as those installed at the intelligence agencies. The scientific community had determined the quickest way to detect deadly viruses was with military-grade biosensors, and the optimum process to eliminate biological contaminants from the mail was through high technology—ion beam sterilization—that killed anthrax and other spores and viruses as they traveled through the mail pipeline.

High-energy gamma rays, electron beams, or X-rays penetrated the mail and rapidly stripped electrons from molecules inside the bacteria, a process known as ionization. Once the DNA and other crucial molecules in the bacteria and viruses were ionized, the organisms couldn't survive long enough to cause deadly infections. Soon mail coming into the newspapers and networks was routed to devices that used powerful beams of high-energy electrons to kill anthrax or other deadly organisms, like coronaviruses.

Post-9/11, airport security assessments envisioned terrorists introducing anthrax and other deadly viruses into aircraft and airports. Aircraft were outfitted with HEPA filters (High Efficiency Particulate Air). Airport x-ray machine manufacturers were flooded with orders for new equipment with detection and sterilization capabilities. The new x-ray machines were fitted with scanning ultra-violet lasers operating at a specific wavelength, a technology military units relied on to detect terrorist-planted improvised explosive devices (IED) imbedded into roadbeds. The machines could now detect trace elements of explosives at the parts-per-billion level, and the UV-C laser system also instantly destroyed viruses, bacteria, and spores. A patent had been issued for those processes years before, and there were over a million machines in use with the technology.

The holder of the patent for the high-speed detection of explosives and the eradication of biological hazards became a very rich person. Few knew or cared who that person was. The special machines were installed in every major international and domestic airport, newsroom, and network and all the mailrooms in DOD and the U.S. Intelligence Community. They were also in hotels throughout the Middle East.

Every day a bag of cleaned mail was delivered to part-time correspondent Demetrius Eastwood's office where three journalism interns in personal protective equipment opened, stapled the envelope to the letter, and read the letters.

Once a week, the inboxes labeled *Grieving Relatives* and *Whistleblowers* were emptied into a FedEx carton and forwarded to the mail room at 7 World Trade Center.

CHAPTER 24

May 5, 2018

Duncan Hunter awoke when the Quiet Aero Systems pilot dropped the LM-100J's landing gear announcing their arrival in the opium producing capital of the world, Afghanistan, and his next mission. For the second time in as many months, the pilot landed the LM-100J expertly at Kandahar Air Base. Hunter and his support crew were already sucking Aviation Breathing Oxygen from portable green bottles. The Taliban didn't fire on the white cargo airplane. When the engines and auxiliary power unit (APU) shut down, Hunter noticed the unusual quiet on the base. He did his best not to rub his eyes and embed the suspended fecal matter from the air into them.

The two superannuated mechanics, Bob and Bob, worked at their "assembly speed," to roll out and assemble the YO-3A and ensure it was safe for flight. With an oxygen bottle stuffed into his shirt, Hunter walked around the *Yo-Yo* and covered several exposed joints with "speed tape." Less than five minutes after hooking up the battery, Hunter started the engine and went airborne. Once above the haze layer, he switched from his O2 bottle to the aircraft's oxygen system and breathed through an oxygen mask.

His mission was to recover an Iranian biologist in Iran near the border of Turkmenistan. Hours later he was over the rendezvous point at the designated time, but Hunter couldn't find the heat signature of the biologist. He picked up the thermal imagery of a meager herd of ibex, but no human.

Hunter usually gave a defector fifteen minutes to show up. When thirty minutes elapsed and there was nothing in the FLIR for many miles, he headed back.

CHAPTER 25

May 5, 2018

The radio crackled in the ear of the CIA woman, "One is on the move!" General Mostafa Javad Roustaie, the leader of the Islamic Revolutionary Guard Corps (IRGC), stepped out of the German Ministry of Defence headquarters building in Hardhöhe, Bohn and hurried into an awaiting Mercedes limousine. The Iranian general with white hair and beard could've easily been mistaken for a Hollywood icon like Omar Sharif and Maximilian Schell in their later years. Whenever Roustaie boarded commercial jets and took his seat in first class, the flight attendants would coo about him and wonder where they had seen him before, what movie. They hadn't seen him in a movie or on the top of a most wanted list from the American Federal Bureau of Investigation, FBI, or Interpol, the International Criminal Police Organization. But if they wandered the marketplaces of Tehran, they would see his visage on posters exhorting service for the Islamic Revolutionary Guard Corps.

The CIA agent who spotted their target was excited that the *Lion of Iran*, effectively the number two person in the Iranian government, was on the move. Ostensibly, he had completed his business for the Islamic Republic of Iran, procuring proscribed military hardware that the Iranians were prohibited from purchasing directly. The former U.S. president had lifted sanctions for a few years which allowed Iran to buy billions of dollars of Boeing airliners and the best American-made missile defense systems. When American President Hernandez was elected, one of his first official acts was to reinstate the punishing sanctions on Iran.

There were many ways to get around American, United Nations, and NATO sanctions. The Germans were often willing to ignore the sanctions, so were the French. Socialist politicians were never suspects in the illegal transactions. It was the system.

The American intelligence officer was aware of the German Federal Intelligence Service, the *Bundesnachrichtendienst* (BND), ability to capture, monitor, and locate cellphone transmissions. German electronic intelligence gathering equipment was top-notch. But the American encryption for voice and data were virtually unbreakable. If the Germans wanted to crack the coded American transmission, it would take a warehouse full of Cray computers and six months of processing time. German intelligence knew it wasn't worth their time. It was the Americans being Americans.

The U.S. Intelligence Community had an ace in the hole for identifying terrorists: the Occult Terrorist Identification System, OTIS. Used in conjunction with a passport or travel document-reading device, OTIS' hidden pressure-sensitive pads at Customs' kiosks captured fingerprints of bored passengers and anxious terrorists, then matched those fingerprints with people on the international terrorism watch lists, the FBI's Most Wanted Fugitive List, and the no-fly lists.

When the task force had been created to track down and intercept General Mostafa Roustaie, the CIA Chief of Station at Bonn announced, "Ever since the travel ban was reinstated on him, General Roustaie's been arrogant and is still traveling in the open like he did when Mazibuike was president. He's a high value target and is the Director's top priority, even before the Libyan intel officer who planted the bomb on that PanAm jet that went down over Lockerbie. Roustaie runs the ayatollah's spies, guns, and assassins and car bombing and IED schools. He is disguised as a middle-aged economist from Kassel traveling on a genuine German passport. Roustaie will eventually slip up; these guys always do."

The U.S. intelligence officer nearly missed Roustaie when he got on the train to Frankfurt. It was logical for General Roustaie to be heading for the Frankfurt am Main Airport if his work in Germany was done. But the target had bypassed OTIS, and now intelligence officers had to rely on facial recognition systems to keep track of him. One task force officer ran down the hall of the U.S. Embassy and tasked one of their computer hackers for help. He handed the man a photograph of the general who began the complex process of cracking into the German Customs Service to see if he could find the passport the Iranian general was using by getting a photographic match. Two other intel officers raced out of the embassy and headed for the airport.

When the bullet train from Bonn stopped at the airport departure terminal, General Roustaie disembarked with his two-person security detail. The three men entered the first class line at the security checkpoint. General Roustaie didn't see a single Muslim working airport security. His eyes drifted to the different work stations. No Muslims at customs, no Muslims at passport control, no Muslims at the magnetometer, no Muslims at the X-ray machine, and no Muslims in uniform on the concourse. *There are probably no Muslims working in the passport office.*

No Muslims anywhere in airport security could only mean one thing. The airports had finally awakened to the threat, the Islamic Underground's treachery had been discovered, and their infiltration had been stopped. He palmed his passport. He always made sure not to touch anything unless he wore gloves, but during the summer months the use of gloves indicated someone trying to hide their fingerprints. The uniformed soldiers who were ubiquitous and carried weapons would notice the gloves. They were the airport's first line of defense, an actual deterrent to any ideations of terroristic acts or destructive intrigues.

Roustaie passed through the security checkpoint and waited for his flight in the airline lounge. *Airports are now fortresses; no Islamists anywhere except those traveling.* It hadn't always been that way. There were times where a *jihadi* could wreck airplanes and airports with impunity, but that was no longer the case. He couldn't remember where or when he had received a copy of an obscure American university research paper which had presaged the structured plan for Islamic terrorist organizations, such as the Islamic Underground and their masters the Islamic Revolutionary Guard Corps, to infiltrate international airport security and aircraft maintenance organizations.

The American author of the paper spelled out how radical Islamists were infatuated with Western aircraft, spectacular monuments to air travel, engineering marvels, the most impressive aircraft ever conceived. Infidels had built them and the preposterous international airports that serviced them. General Roustaie remembered being incensed; he remembered what he said to the elders of the Revolution, of the Islamic Underground, "*We will raise a warrior of our own to destroy the infidels from within.*"

Not only were terrorists fascinated with aircraft, they found the commercial air carrier or cargo jet to be the perfect flying bomb or carrier of bombs. Exploding airplanes and airport bombings were "spectacular" events, facilitated by Islamists who had infiltrated contract airport security firms. It was a simple process; get hired, get trained, and then ignore weapons and bombs as they passed through X-ray machines. *Allahu Akbar! God is great!*

Americans worshipped freedom, unrestricted and inexpensive air travel, and the jets that took them wherever they wanted to go at a breathtaking groundspeed of ten miles a minute. Americans worshipped the military pilots who flew higher than the sky and faster than a speeding bullet. General Roustaie not only found blasphemy in worshipping the aluminum icons, but he also found a captive audience. People who willingly entered the planes. Roustaie knew that once the door was closed, commercial airliners were the perfect traps; one long tubular prison cell from which there was no escape.

He crossed his legs and nursed an alcoholic drink. Roustaie mused about the game of cat and mouse. As the leader of the Islamic Revolutionary Guard Corps, he became aware almost immediately when American intelligence agencies informed their European counterparts of the threats outlined in a college student's paper. *So the paper was not to be believed initially by the German and French governments and was ignored by the rest of the European Union as they believed it portrayed Muslims in unfavorable light. Once translated, the document was the perfect training manual on how to reverse-engineer special activities such as hijack aircraft, infiltrate airport security, and spread a biological weapon across the planet. Mosques all across America and Europe received flimsy copies of the document. One day they would be called upon to infiltrate the American's airports and assault their aircraft. When you shut down American aviation, you shut down the world.*

Mostafa Roustaie's most celebrated aviation success had been in early 2000 when an aircraft maintenance man from one of the local mosques run by a firebrand imam had planted a bomb on an Air France *Concorde.* A communiqué from an anonymous terror group claimed credit for the *spectacular,* the inconceivable and sensational crash. French aviation authorities disallowed the terrorist group's claims; the fiery crash was officially blamed on an American jet which had preceded the *Concorde.* A piece of metal had allegedly fallen from the American jet and had magically penetrated the wing's fuel cell with the precision of an Olympic javelin thrower.

The investigation that followed the Islamic Underground's bombing of France's most acclaimed aeronautical achievement had put the Muslim community on notice, not by French politicians whose conscious were becoming more elastic with every passing day as they scoffed at the existence of the Islamic Underground, but by the French intelligence and law enforcement communities who had security clearances and access to surveillance programs.

In 1995, the United States Intelligence Community had warned European governments and Moscow that the security at all of their international airports had likely been infiltrated by radical and criminal Islamists. Airport security offices ignored the American warning. They wouldn't shame their Muslim population with surveillance or investigation or dismissal, nor would they allocate the money to harden their security infrastructure. The intelligence community knew that many Muslims were employed at airports throughout Europe and were over-represented in airport security. No one had ever questioned "why?"

European politicians hoped their gentle handling of Muslim employees would keep them from becoming Islamic radicals. Few politicians could see that *Dark Islam,* the Islamic Underground, and the Muslim Brotherhood had totally infiltrated airport security worldwide. The intelligence and law enforcement communities also knew the realities. Longstanding leftist policies stopped any meaningful corrective action.

A lackadaisical attitude toward aviation security was exploited several times a year at Europe's international airports. Two suicide bombers, former airport security employees, detonated explosives at the Brussels airport. In Italy, an individual was arrested who helped make false documents for the terrorist network in Brussels. A suicide bombing occurred in Moscow's Domodedovo International.

Learning from mistakes infiltrating American airports and the airports in Brussels and Moscow, the Islamic Underground increased the funding, logistical coordination, and support to attack the Paris Orly International Airport. The execution phase of the attack had been progressing well until a radical Muslim who couldn't wait for martyrdom attempted to seize a weapon from a soldier patrolling Orly International while shouting that he wanted to kill and die in the name of Allah. He got his wish and was shot dead by security forces.

American airport security was overhauled and federalized. Governments across Europe quietly federalized airport security, nixed new Muslim applicants, and deployed heavily armed soldiers to protect their international airports against attacks. Muslim airport security employees who refused to take a polygraph were dismissed.

General Roustaie marveled at how quickly and effectively the Americans and Europeans fortified their airports against his *jihadis*. Those active in the aviation terrorism food chain were becoming frustrated at their inability to create more *spectaculars*. They tried many options before settling on the only option available to them, flying drones into the intakes of departing jets to crash them. It was apparent to Roustaie that the airports were using countermeasures against drone attacks, even if he couldn't see the lasers or transmitters. It was just as well; he wanted to fly terror-free from Europe to Iran.

He looked around the airline lounge, expecting the boarding call for his flight to Jordan, first class on a Royal Jordanian Airlines' Airbus A340. Once he arrived in Amman, General Roustaie and his security men would take another Royal Jordanian Airbus to Baghdad. There he looked forward to being separated from the *hoi polloi* and escorted by limousine to the separate executive terminal on the Baghdad International Airport (BIAP), once the personal lounge of Iraq's president, Saddam Hussein. General Roustaie had been in and out of Baghdad some fifty times; sometimes dressed in the Western attire of a German, French, or American businessman, sometimes as an Iranian pilgrim. In Europe and Africa, he traveled on legitimate passports, German, French, or a U.S. passport issued courtesy of the previous Mazibuike Administration.

General Roustaie couldn't wait to be back in the lands of the Prophet. The cradle of civilization. The valley between "the rivers," the Tigris and Euphrates. Once he set foot in Iraq, he would be less than a couple of hours from home. And once he was firmly on Iranian soil, he and his adoring crowds would celebrate another completed mission under the nose of the "almighty-in-name-only" Central Intelligence Agency.

CHAPTER 26

May 5, 2018

The conclusion of *The William Tell Overture* was playing in his helmet as Hunter monitored the aircraft's instruments, performance, and still-empty FLIR scope. *No heat signature, no defector, no more time; I gotta go.* He disengaged the autopilot and pointed the aircraft back to Afghanistan for the long slog back to Kabul and then Kandahar. He unplugged the memory stick; there was no appropriate music to ameliorate a failed mission.

The UHF radio came to life and the voice at the other end asked, "Number ten?" He rarely received a radio transmission while on a radio silent mission. Hunter pushed the transmit key. "Go."

He recognized the grandfatherly voice of Bob Jones. "RTB."

Hunter double clicked the transmit key to indicate he would return to base. He bypassed the overflight of the Chinese embassy and flew directly to Kandahar. As soon as he landed, Hunter met the CIA Chief of Station from Kabul who briefed him on revised plans from Headquarters. While Bob and Bob disassembled the *Yo-Yo* and secured it in its custom shipping container in the belly of the Lockheed-Martin *Hercules,* Hunter received new orders: *Proceed to Talil.* Prince Ali Base in southern Iraq. *Something's up.*

He thanked and shook hands with the head spook in country, who slipped him one of his personal challenge coins. After the *Yo-Yo* had been loaded, Hunter followed Bob Jones and Bob Smith onto the cargo airplane. The three men inspected the intricate and enameled coin from the Kabul COS.

The aircrew of the LM-100J expedited their takeoff. Hunter switched to a fresh O2 bottle, wiped his face with disinfecting wipes, donned an eye mask, inserted ear plugs, and snapped noise-canceling headphones over his ears before spreading out along the troop seats.

He was asleep in minutes, as were the septuagenarians Smith and Jones.

• • •

The *Hercules* taxied toward base operations at Prince Ali Base and into a parking spot adjacent a Cessna Caravan with Iraqi Air Force Markings.

After the LM-100J aircrew left to seek food, drinks, and toilets, a man in jeans, a dark Tommy Bahama shirt, and wraparound Oakley sunglasses dismounted the Caravan and was welcomed aboard the *Herc.* Duncan Hunter shook his hand and introduced himself as *Maverick.* The Baghdad Chief of Station wordlessly handed Hunter a double-wrapped package. He stood by quietly as Hunter cut the strapping tape and withdrew a single sheet of paper and a memory stick. He asked if there was anything more he could do for him.

I wonder what the mighty Bullfrog has in store for us? Hunter read the information on the impromptu mission. *It's virtually impossible to execute a pop-up; in Iraq it's impossible to organize a one-car funeral…without help from the locals. But the air is breathable.* He checked his watch. *Well, this has the trajectory of a plane crash. Still…. Technically, it's doable, but I'll need some help.* He leaned into the CIA man and whispered into his ear. Mr. CIA responded with an expression of conspiracy and nodded. "Maybe. No promises. I'll see what I can do."

Hunter grinned and said, "Hey, if you can make that happen, you're a great American."

The Chief of Station replied, "In Baghdad they can't control the parking spot of the general's airliner. Jordan is friendly, and we can do some things there; Baghdad is still Injun' Country. Iranian infiltration of BIAP is complete; ideological subversion is ongoing. There are too many Iranians everywhere, but here, we're okay."

If he knows of this activity, would he know of the activity in Iran? Worth a shot to ask. Hunter asked the Chief of Station if he knew what the general had been doing. The COS took a moment to formulate an answer to the provocative question. He said, "While he was making arms deals with the German government, Iran publically executed one of their top biologists this morning on claims he worked for CIA." Hunter thanked the man and shook his hand.

As the CIA men had done on every stop of their circuitous journey, the Chief of Station pressed a coin into Hunter's and the Bobs' palms before leaving.

Hunter directed Bob and Bob to prepare the *Yo-Yo* for immediate flight and to load the YO-3A's gun with ammo and the "cans," with flares and chaff countermeasures. Hunter planned for the nighttime impromptu mission while there was still daylight left. He read that General Mostafa Roustaie, the Islamic Revolutionary Guard Corps general who helped orchestrate the 1983 Hezbollah operation that killed 241 Marines in Beirut was scheduled to fly into Baghdad International. Hunter understood that the general could take extraordinary countermeasures, but he was free to engage the general if he could positively identify him, and the general was clear of innocents, aircraft, and buildings. *McGee thinking outside the box again.*

Hunter unholstered a matte-black Colt Python .357 magnum and squeezed the grip to check the strength of the green laser pointer. He replaced the Python in his shoulder holster and strapped a Bowie knife and a sheath to his calf. Hunter was ready for flight or for fight, if he had to leave his airplane. Nazy would just have to understand.

If the winds cooperated Hunter was certain he could be at the designated location at the specific time. The winds in Baghdad could become calmer as the evening progressed, or they could remain fickle, and he didn't have services of a combat meteorologist. But there was a possibility to gather some weather information. Hunter withdrew his Blackberry and assumed he had international service. He texted the pilot of their LM-100J: *Baghdad forecast WX?* Hunter had flown into and out of the Prince Ali Base for missions into Iran and knew receiving forecast weather from the anemic weather office was a hit-or-miss proposition. Sometimes you just had to eyeball the skies and hope for good weather and favorable winds like Amelia Earhart did on her round-the-world attempt. *I don't need no stinking forecaster!*

When the *Hercules'* pilot arrived, the weather brief was barely adequate, but the essentials were there and they were favorable; the weather outside the LM-100J seemed to validate that it should be clear and calm for the next few hours.

Hunter would fly directly over the airport when Roustaie's jet landed at night. Making a positive ID would be a very tricky and dangerous procedure. Hunter wasn't concerned about being picked up on the airport's surveillance radar; the YO-3A's stealthy nanotube technology paint would preclude an air traffic controller from detecting him. He downloaded the photograph of the Iranian general into the YO-3A's mission computer. The face recognition software would help verify the identification of the general and track the target through night vision and thermal systems.

Bob Jones and Bob Smith rolled the *Yo-Yo,* hidden under bedsheets, out of the back of the *Hercules* and pushed the YO-3A into the cold unlit concrete bay of the nearest hardened shelter. Using LED lamps strapped to their heads, they assembled the black airplane in minutes and loaded the countermeasures buckets with flares and chaff. The men exchanged glances. If Duncan needed countermeasures, he was likely flying into a nightmare.

Bob and Bob watched the nighttime takeoff of the quiet aircraft and wondered if this was the last time they would see their friend and boss. It was like the other takeoffs: uneventful, quiet, and strange. They heard the low frequency of the airplane at takeoff, but once Hunter retarded the throttle, the YO-3A disappeared into the night, aurally and visually.

• • •

Roustaie's nerves were shot. He had never been delayed twice during a single trip. He couldn't help but think he was being set up. For the first time, he considered himself a hostage in a tubular prison. The airliner into Amman had been postponed for over an hour, and the connecting flight for Baghdad had been delayed another thirty minutes for a maintenance issue. A sixth sense that had for years kept him from being captured or killed was ringing in his ears like the bells of Notre Dame at Christmas. But was it self-induced paranoia? No one else on the jet seemed to be bothered by the delay; international flights in the Middle East rarely ran on time. But he was sweating like a cow in a slaughterhouse. The flight attendants were well aware of his nervousness and paid him more attention in order to calm him.

Roustaie assured himself he shouldn't worry, but he did anyway. You don't survive in this business without being able to anticipate what your enemy has planned for you. *Does anyone know I'm on this jet? The Mukhabarat? Impossible! I'm on a German passport – someone would've stopped me in Germany if they had the slightest whiff that I was traveling on a forged or stolen passport. The CIA or German intelligence could've snatched me off the street. No…no…no, they don't know I'm on a jet. I'm simply a German traveler on business on my way to Baghdad.*

When the airliner finally departed Amman, Roustaie relaxed. After landing at Baghdad International what Roustaie saw out of his window comforted him immeasurably. One of his men was leading the security detail. He had worried for nothing.

Ten vehicles were parked in an arc on the BIAP tarmac, as armed airport security personnel ensured disembarking passengers recovered their bags which had been removed from the belly of the jet and spread out neatly on the ramp. Owners of luggage were directed to find and stand next their bags. The leader of airport security directed traffic. He sent Roustaie and his men under the joint of the fuselage and the wing. In order to defeat any armed, high-flying, unmanned aerial aircraft, General Roustaie kept his head down as he descended the stairs and scurried under the Royal Jordanian Airlines jet. Roustaie and his security men had checked no bags. The general cautiously looked up into the clear sky searching for any hint of a missile-carrying drone observing the ramp operation.

After a drug-sniffing canine cleared the baggage, rude airline security agents rumbustiously frisked and herded the other passengers off to the concourse, marching with their luggage. General Roustaie and his security detail comingled with the dozen airport security men near the airliner. Then as before, Roustaie and his men kept their heads down as they entered separate airport vehicles for the trip to the exclusive executive terminal, Saddam's old place at a secluded part of the airport.

• • •

Missile shooters at the command and control center at Creech Air Force Base in Nevada were frustrated. Their target had executed missile countermeasures perfectly. Again. Agency lawyers wouldn't give permission to launch a *Hellfire* that could blow up an ally's commercial jet or kill innocents. The collateral damage would be too significant and the terrorists knew this. The number one terrorist on the FBI's Most Wanted List was a high-value target, but his death wasn't worth the collateral damage.

The long-range cameras had videoed the shell game of musical airport security Suburbans, but no one in a bunker in Nevada had the clarity to know who was in which of the vehicles, or if their target had avoided the *Reaper's* cameras entirely. A space camera could take a detailed picture of the Horsehead Nebulae billions of miles away, but their camera couldn't find the master terrorist from Iran on the ramp at BIAP. Roustaie had outwitted the Americans again. The unmanned aerial systems remote pilot was about to "stand down."

The duty CIA program management officer directing the acquisition and tracking operation snapped his fingers loudly. He told the CIA remote pilot and lawyers, "Continue monitoring the situation, look for an LD. If there is an LD spot on one vehicle, I'm the authorizing official for you to engage that vehicle."

This directive from the CIA PMO snapped the heads and energized the pilots. The Agency lawyers were caught unawares. The implication was clear: there were other Agency options, other Agency assets in the area. There was no other possible conclusion.

• • •

The Chief Air Branch had understood the Director's guidance clearly. If normal time-sensitive targeting operations and other available legal options couldn't be used due to conditions beyond their capabilities, the Agency might still accomplish the mission. "You call me, I may be able to help."

Director Bill McGee apparently had an ace in the hole. The Chief Air Branch discerned that there was an unknown and secret capability buried in a special access program somewhere. It pissed him off to no end not to be aware of the obvious airborne capability. It was probably the sole purview of the President of the United States to approve the use of that capability, and it was the CIA Director's prerogative to use that asset. This was one of those "need to know" capabilities and CIA Director McGee would be totally responsible for the consequences of releasing the secret capabilities for the direct action.

The Air Branch Chief blinked wildly. Secret capabilities buried within secret programs buried within secret operations like Russian nesting dolls were the things from the old days of CIA aviation, of U-2s and A-12s. He was aware immediately that this was a very special activity. Members of Congress wouldn't be advised of the special capability for fear of Democrat Party members would leak specifics, means, and methods of the special access program. *It was about time the Agency had a patriot in charge. It's time to get a bit more medieval on these people.*

• • •

Director McGee was called as the situation quickly developed—General Roustaie was on the move in Germany and would likely fly into Amman then to Baghdad. Director McGee had another option, but it required close coordination with another asset in another country. Could that asset get into Iraq in time for an intercept? Could he make a positive ID? Could he eliminate the target? Could he remain undetected and escape?

The special access program's primary capability was designating and tracking high-value targets who were adept in satellite and UAV-detection and tracking countermeasures. The asset would need to maintain positive identification of the target, even if multiple vehicles played leapfrog, and then use a laser designator for a depressed-angle shot from a high-altitude, long range, missile-carrying drone. It sounded simple, but the intelligence required to get all the players "to that spot" in the decision tree was predicated on delaying the en route airliners, one from Europe and one from Jordan. The attack "window" had to be managed for a precision intercept.

• • •

Before daybreak, Hunter brought the YO-3A back to Talil. The old mechanics removed the wings and put the aircraft to bed in its container. Bob Jones unloaded the weapon and noted it hadn't been fired. He then offloaded the flares and chaff; they too were unused.

Once they were airborne, Hunter's other mechanic, Bob Smith, shot a silent interrogative to Hunter with inquisitive eyes and gyrating eyebrows. Duncan Hunter nodded slightly in acknowledgement; he removed the Colt Python from under his arm, squeezed the grips, and shot a two-second brilliantly bright green beam to the aft part of the LM-100J. He gave the old guy a look of confidence, holstered the weapon, and winked. Bob Smith understood: *Mission accomplished by other means. The YO-3A carried a powerful and precise infrared laser designator.*

Bob Smith would watch for an article about the death of a terrorist, likely in Baghdad, maybe on the airport who had probably been killed by a *Hellfire* missile launched from an Agency *Reaper*. He would know for sure his boss had been successful when bonus funds were added to his bank account.

Duncan Hunter wasn't as ebullient as Bob Smith. There had been more to the operation than being an airborne target designator. Hunter had activated an artificial intelligence program that functioned as a fusion center: all the aircraft systems, sensors, and weapon were under the control of the AI computer. Hunter's only input to the process was to engage the AI and monitor the aircraft's ability to operate as an autonomous unmanned platform. Search, acquire, and verify a target through face recognition technologies. Positively track the target through obstacles or to a vehicle without error. Record all functions for analysis, then fire the YO-3A's gun or activate the laser designator for another unmanned system with missiles.

Hunter was hands-off except for retracting the Terminator Sniper System for noise abatement and a lower altitude. After the successful weapons strike, the AI retracted all other sensors into the fuselage and set a course for return to its departure airport. The AI was fully in control of the YO-3A. Hunter hadn't touched a thing in the cockpit. He had listened to the *Best of the Doors* and patted his knees for the major drum and bass parts of *Roadhouse Blues*.

The final test was to ensure the automatic takeoff and landing system functioned under the authority of the AI computer. The airplane landed perfectly astride the runway's centerline at Talil, taxied to the programmed GPS location, and shut down the engine. Not only had the AI and facial recognition system performed flawlessly when loaded with the photograph of the Iranian general, the Yo-Yo could now do just about anything Air Branch wanted in the Middle East. The twenty-year CIA pilot told himself he was out of a job. Human replaced by technology. Retired again.

CHAPTER 27

May 10, 2018

The faint but unmistakable sound of a dog barking wildly somewhere in the compound indicated that the *Âmirikîs* had discovered their hiding place. When black uniformed men behind black *shemaghs*, carrying black assault weapons burst into their room, the five women in *hijabs* didn't shriek or react with fear or anger. They huddled where they stood as if their response had been drilled into them. The women expected to hear an explosion; evidence that their husband had detonated a suicide vest he always wore for just such an occasion.

From under her floor-length garment, one woman raised an AK-47 and aimed it, not at the attackers in black but at a lone woman in a black *burka* sleeping in a corner across the room. Trained to neutralize threats before advancing, the first soldier to enter the room saw the weapon rising and placed the aiming laser mounted on his silenced Colt M-4 carbine on the woman's temple. In one sweeping motion devoid of any extraneous movements he shot the woman with the *Kalashnikov* twice. His body was filled with adrenaline; he was prepared to kill anyone else who raised a weapon.

In the corner the woman under the *burka* awakened at the sudden splattering sound of metal tearing through soft flesh, bone, and gray matter. She turned to the sound, unable to comprehend what had happened. She was unaware that she had escaped assassination from one of her own. Within seconds she realized her situation as other soldiers, men in black uniforms and helmets and M-4s, entered the women's inner sanctum.

With one woman dead in a heap on the ground as if she were roadkill mixed with black laundry, the target of the dead armed assassin raised her hands slowly in a nonthreatening manner as if she was surrendering. The other women in the room defiantly hissed at the interlopers. The woman with her arms over her head saw the red light of a sighting laser emanating from the front of the soldier's weapon. The M-4 was aimed at her, but she was not afraid. She knew if there was a red laser pointed at her then there was a red dot on her forehead. She blinked calmly, knowing she was probably milliseconds away from being terminated. Seconds passed, and she hadn't been shot. The soldier was perplexed by the woman's lack of actions. With the lethal end of the M-4, he leaned forward and lifted the bottom edge of the woman's *burka. A woman's legs and tiny feet in worn out sandals. No man trying to hide under a burka.*

Even through layers of the body armor's ceramic plates and uniform parts, she read his body language as he withdrew from his position. She took a deep breath. The gun was nearly the same weapon she had fired annually in a life that was now just a distant memory. She recalled the M-16 derivative's lethality. She could probably still field strip the weapon. She knew the entry wound would be a bit bigger than a Daisy BB or a Crosman pellet; the exit wound would be the size of a baseball or an orange, depending on the entry angle of the bullet; although the dead woman on the floor would need a bag of grapefruit to plug the hole in the side of her skull.

The woman in the *burka* exhaled forcefully. She had no control over the situation. *Make a decision! Are you going to kill me or save me? Decide!* In the normal trajectory of events, the man behind the black *shemagh* would likely shoot her and release her from the hell she had lived in for over twenty years. She had tried to kill herself several times. After her first failed attempt, the other wives had been scolded and punished. They learned to watch her continually and thwart any further damage she might try to do to herself.

Blonde women in the Middle East always commanded a high price if they were unmarked and had all their teeth. She had come so far just trying to survive, to live another rape-free, pain-free day; hoping for a miracle, hoping one day to be rescued. But she had long given up on that fantasy, just as she had given up on escaping. They always caught her—where did she think she could go? They always dragged her back and took harsh pleasure as they beat her and destroyed her once beautiful face.

During the last few days before the attack on the compound, she had drifted deeper into despair. She had given up physically and mentally. She had stopped eating. She could do no more. The one who had rescued her before couldn't help her now or ever. One way or another it would soon be over for her. She would be traded again to an ancient man without teeth who would use her like a prized sex slave, or worse, she would be sold to a group of drunken men who would abuse her like a Girl Scout at a Taliban picnic. She wouldn't let those things happen to her again. She was tired of existing. Only death could release her from the torture of being handled and sold like a bag of rice. The once robust and appealing woman was nearly unrecognizable: malnourished, too weak to walk and barely strong enough to hold her trembling arms over her head.

The red laser remained illuminated; its brightness constricted her pupils. She didn't dare try to shield them with her arms raised in submission. More seconds passed. She still hadn't been shot. *Maybe this is what a rescue looks like....* She squinted at the man behind the scarf and knew it would be a shame if she gave up now. She found the voice she hadn't used in months. Tears gushed from violet eyes. She trembled and cried out with a sense of urgency; her words garbled and losing volume with every syllable. *"I'm an American. I'm an American. Please help me. Please help me."*

CHAPTER 28

May 11, 2018

There had been something resembling a pattern to the postings of *Omega*. With his latest post, some followers were gleeful and some were disappointed.

It's Friday, May 11th, 2018, and Maxim Mohammad Mazibuike was the most corrupt president in U.S. history. In the Islamic world, today marks the beginning of the weekend, the "Gathering," the weekly day off.

Do you believe in coincidences? The CIA Director will give testimony at a Senate Intelligence Committee hearing which will undoubtedly result in the eccentric questionings of the left, the Senate Democrats, on a topic that is near and dear to their hearts. Let's revisit the actions of the media and Congressional Democrats.

Was it just a coincidence that the media used the opinions of the ladies of 'The View' and others on network daytime shows to adjudicate the questionable eligibility of the former senator to be president, while never once interviewing an immigration attorney on the topic? Remarkably important things can be learned, not from what's presented, but from what's purposely omitted. This is exactly how the KGB brainwashes the masses.

Was it just a coincidence that a law student from Yale, who's no longer with us, could cite the law and the facts surrounding the eligibility of Senator Mazibuike, while the media and the Democrats, who didn't have the law or the facts on their side, ignored the law and the facts and presented a distorted view, some would say a 'disinformation campaign,' of the truth. I've stated before that one of the most insidious powers of an abusive media is the power to ignore. And they ignored the evidence just as the Democrats ignored the evidence room when a Democrat president was impeached.

Is it a just a coincidence that during the presidential election where pollsters guaranteed Attorney General Tussy would win in a landslide but she lost because she didn't carry the Democrat Party stronghold city of Philadelphia? The election was close and was turned because of one city. Is it just a coincidence or a conundrum that there were no calls for an investigation into Philadelphia? The Democrats scream and protest everything that does not go their way but there wasn't a peep about Philadelphia?

Will it be just a coincidence that during the CIA Director's testimony he'll present the law and the facts, while the Democrats will throw a fit akin to upending the pieces on a chessboard or rail at him about why Gary Powers didn't kill himself or engage the self-destruct switch almost 58 years ago? Will there be a disruption of untold lunacy that will force the hearing to be canceled? Pay attention; the actions of the lunatic fringe speak volumes. Their goal is to shut down Director McGee using whatever pretext they can. You must ask yourself "why?"

This is the Omega.

CHAPTER 29

May 11, 2018

The Central Intelligence Agency Director, William "Bill" McGee greeted several of the Republican senators and exchanged a few business cards with hearty salutations. The CIA Director was a rock star in the U.S. Intelligence Community. Once the senators were called to take their positions, McGee took his seat and quietly waited to deliver his opening statement to the Senate Intelligence Committee.

A disproportionate number of reporters and independent journalists watched the pre-hearing interactions with aplomb and amusement. The colorful raconteur Lt. Colonel Demetrius Eastwood, long since retired from the Marine Corps, didn't make eye contact with the CIA Director or the NCTC Director. He was certain they knew he was in the room. Sitting alone in the back row he was hard to miss. The other reporters thought it was odd to see him without his trademark post-Marine Corps hat, a crushable Tilley's *Wanderer*.

The Seal of the United States of America was centered on the high oak paneled wall behind the senators. McGee commanded the witness table. Behind him an anonymous woman sitting with a briefcase at her feet commanded the attention of nearly every eye in the room. She didn't get out of the Central Intelligence Agency much. She was a bit overwhelmed to be sitting in one of the imposing and majestic congressional hearing rooms for the first time, but she didn't let it show. She took in her surroundings with critical purpose and noticed the profile of Colonel Eastwood. She acknowledged him with eye contact. Her focus returned to her boss. The CIA Director had much more experience in dangerous locations than she, and he appeared to be at ease behind the big long table facing the curved dark wooden dais that protected the senators high atop their thrones.

Nazy Cunningham would not want to be seated in the single chair at the witness table; it was a formidable and terrifying position. It was the center of focus, like the keystone—the acoustical center of the Roman open-air amphitheater she had visited as a child in Jerash. She remembered standing on the gravestone-shaped "keystone" and being told to shout toward the amphitheater seating. The act of shouting reflected an unseen hand of concentrated sound energy back at her; the precisely focused soundwaves nearly knocked her over. If she stepped one foot away from the keystone, the concentrated acoustical effect was lost. Nazy realized that the room was designed to be acoustically efficient before there were electronic means to amplify a witness' voice. The witness effectively sat on the room's keystone.

Senators and their staffers milled about as if they were unsure why they were there. The members of both political parties had their agendas, but agendas were not their focus. The men and women on the committee could barely keep their eyes off the exotic, statuesque, and Rapunzel-like, dark-haired woman behind the CIA Director, although no one seemed to take notice of the black aluminum Halliburton Zero case at her feet. *Who is that?* reverberated among the senators and the staffers via text message. Some thought she looked like Sophia Loren.

The committee chairman pounded a gavel and commissioned the hearing. He thanked McGee for taking time out of his schedule to answer the committee's questions.

Demetrius Eastwood stole glances at Nazy as he took copious notes. It surprised him that she now looked more like Loren's less-celebrated body double. *Watching old movies would do that to you sometimes. Maybe it was age. We're all getting older, gravity works in strange ways on a body, and this business sucks the life from you.*

McGee nodded politely as the Intelligence Committee Chairman droned on about the president's brilliant choice for CIA Director. He mentioned McGee's record in uniform. The comments were all favorable. He was a Republican giving accolades and honors to another Republican.

However, when the ranking member from the Democrat Party, an African American from the Communist State of Virginia, got her turn at the microphone, she ripped McGee to shreds. The woman's coldness could be felt; the atmosphere had reversed in seconds. The mood in the room shifted from congenial to adversarial. It was like blinking one's eyes; one second there was courtesy and professionalism, the next it was as if McGee had been dragged before Torquemada, the Grand Inquisitor, to explain what had happened to the former president.

Bill McGee was dismissed as an African American ignoramus who wasn't a graduate of an Ivy League university and hadn't been thoroughly vetted by the nation's most prestigious think tanks, such as the supremely reputable Trans-Atlantic Security Council. And he had only attained the rank of captain and was therefore unqualified to hold the office of CIA Director. She said, "More than 1,000 ex-CIA officials have written letters demanding that you, Director McGee, resign. As you're well aware, these patriots have called for current CIA officials to rise up, report your abuses of power, and withdraw from any cases that involve allegations of 'misconduct of Muslim employees.' You're a disgrace to the African American community and this nation, and I will seek your immediate impeachment."

There is it again, as big as a house; the racism, the prejudice, the denigration, all because of race. And she's a black woman. Her accusations of racism have nothing to do with the color of my skin, but with which political party I support. Good God, these people are insane. McGee didn't respond to the woman's diatribe. Nothing could be gained by attacking an adversary who was mentally deficient.

As he had done in previous appearances before other intelligence committees in both chambers of Congress, McGee expected ridiculous and asinine statements and questions from the Democrats, insightful remarks, and penetrating interrogatives from the Republicans. As a man who didn't suffer fools well, it was a challenge to be respectful to the blockheads that American citizens sent to Congress, especially those who were convinced they were the smartest people in the room and were infatuated with the sound of their own voices. It was difficult to be respectful to members of Congress who had attended some of the nation's most prestigious schools but still didn't understand simple science, basic geology, or astronomy. Some politicians made up their own set of assumptions and called them "facts."

After the first time McGee testified before Congress, he had lamented to Nazy in the privacy of his seventh-floor office, "I had no idea Uncle Fester had so many children. American taxpayers haven't sent their best to Congress."

The NCTC Director didn't know who "Uncle Fester" could be but countered with, "Maybe that's the best they could find at the time." McGee harrumphed. He knew Nazy was only being charitable.

After salutations and greetings, the CIA Director spoke from prepared remarks. He adjusted the microphone in front of him. "During my 35-year career in the Navy I was too busy to think of anything but my mission, which was to protect this country from its enemies just as my U.S. Air Force father had during World War II, Korea, and Vietnam. I was blessed and honored to have led the finest counterterrorism unit organized to confront America's enemies on the field of battle. In the field or out, I didn't think of politics. I obeyed the orders of the president. I had a job to do; my men and I went about the work of protecting America from its unseen and lethal enemies, which I may add is an inherently apolitical activity."

"That was a lifetime ago. Today I'm more understanding of the needs, demands, and goals of our politicians. Had I paid more attention to politics I might had become an admiral." The Republican senators nodded their agreement. Democrat senators turned up their noses in disgust or ignored him altogether.

"A few years before my appointment as the Director of the Central Intelligence Agency, I paid more attention to the politics of this country, especially Washington politics. I noticed the shift of the political narrative of the parties, but as the CIA Director I'm required to be nonpartisan. I believe I'm fair, balanced, and judicious in my judgments. I'm fiercely loyal to this country because of the untold opportunities given to me and my family. I'm also loyal to the Agency and the Intelligence Community I represent. I have taken an oath to obey the orders of the President of the United States, and that is regardless of my president's political affiliation."

"Coming here today, I knew I would get the same questions as my predecessors. I would be asked about the events and circumstances at the Central Intelligence Agency which precipitated the resignation of President Mazibuike."

"But the Democrat Party's senators and congressmen want to know how the CIA could create and maintain a file on an American when that specific action is not in the CIA's purview. By law the CIA may not collect intelligence on U.S. citizens, wittingly or unwittingly. If a subject under our jurisdiction, such as an international terrorist, becomes an American citizen through, for example, the naturalization laws those files are transferred to the FBI for disposition. The record is clear; this is what happened with President Mazibuike. He was a British subject under the surveillance of multiple international intelligence services. Officially, when he became an American citizen, our interest in him vaporized."

"His meager file at the Agency was delivered to a former CIA Director who handled it as required by law. Several FBI investigations of the CIA concluded that the original file on President Mazibuike was neither copied nor held in Agency archives. That's the record of the FBI investigation."

Eastwood hid his scribbles and notes like an artist threatened with violence for drawing the Islamic prophet Mohammad.

"The resignation of a president is an earthshaking event. Even more earthshaking was discovering evidence that President Mazibuike was a Communist and a Muslim, and Washington Democrats knew of President Mazibuike's past. Leaving his office and the United States in the dead of night for locations unknown corroborated that the material within the suspected purloined CIA file was accurate and legitimate. President Mazibuike was ineligible for the office, and he used his administration to hide his history and nefarious agenda."

"Was there more to this improbable event? Was President Mazibuike afraid for his life? As a former leader of a SEAL Team, I have received unthinkable orders, but I know I would've drawn the line at any set of orders that called for the elimination of a sitting or a former president. No one in the DOD would ever conceive such an action, regardless of presidential malfeasance. We take an oath to obey the orders of the president; we do not conspire or make plans to murder them. And if it was not DOD, then who terrified President Mazibuike so much that he was never heard from again? It wasn't the CIA or Special Operations Command. We do not conspire or make plans to murder presidents like the U.S. Intelligence Community was accused of doing to President Kennedy. Please recall, President Kennedy warned America about the secretive and disciplined Marxist attempt to take over the world. He chided the media for misinforming the public, which helped the enemies of America. I submit, the press must find the right balance in reporting properly to the American people while not advancing the cause of Marxists. The role of a free media is to inform and not to brainwash Americans."

"President Kennedy was prescient when he made reference of Americans' distrust of secret societies. In the released Mazibuike papers you see a secret society at work. It installed him in the White House, and when the treachery was exposed, it drove him from the Oval Office. I will refer to that secret society, the communist members of the Democrat Party, the media, and some members of the U.S. Intelligence Community, which includes the FBI, as the *Dark State*." Gasps reverberated around the room.

"I took an in-depth look at the evidence in the file. I will repeat the assertions of former CIA Director Lynche who said, 'The CIA doesn't engage in assassination.' He and I categorically assert that the CIA does not know and cares little of the whereabouts of former President Mazibuike; Director Lynche and I categorically assert that the CIA has not retaliated against him and that the CIA has not gone after him or assassinated him. I am on the record, we have no interest in him. However, for this hearing, I expanded my probe to include other sources for corroboration or exculpation."

Eastwood stared at the back of McGee's head. The Democrat senate staffers who had been chewing gum and eyeballing the woman behind McGee, suddenly froze and looked at each other; *Did he say what I think he just said?* Democrat senators glared at Director McGee with venom and vituperation, and tried to interrupt the Director only to have the Chairman tell them, "You are not recognized. You must be 'recognized' in order to speak."

After some minutes of aggressive and spirited conversation between the Democrat senators and the Republican Chairman, Director McGee was encouraged to continue. Eastwood was having a field day. He had pages of notes. Throughout the committee members' discussions, Director McGee had quietly allowed the congressional shenanigans to play out.

Upon the invitation of the Chairman, McGee continued, "I perused the taped testimony of previous CIA Directors. Congressmen and Senators argued that the Mazibuike documents were improperly collected and maintained and therefore should be expunged from any discussion or record. Congressmen and Senators argued that the documents used against President Mazibuike were counterfeit; they were the product of Russian intelligence agencies or the CIA."

"This wasn't some Shakespearian tragedy. Abetted by the media, the Communists and Islamists penetrated the U.S. government and installed an ineligible president, and when his actual history was exposed, President Mazibuike ran from his post and his past. The Mazibuike Administration wasn't a presidency, it was a crime spree abetted by the Democratic National Committee and a horrendously corrupt media."

"When faced with overwhelming evidence of his treachery, Congressional Democrats did everything they could to protect President Mazibuike. There had to be much more to the story than just arguments over documents in a stolen CIA file; there had to be *entanglements*. President Mazibuike didn't rise to power on his own volition. He had help. I gave the Inspector General of the Intelligence Community thirty days to investigate. Agency whistleblowers passed through my office with incredible tales of malfeasance."

McGee poured some water and took a drink. He continued. "The fact is several levels of supporting documentation do exist; the former president had help. The IG ignored the law and the facts and instead told me what he thought had happened. I wasn't interested in what he thought; I was interested in what he found. I wanted the documents. Last evening I fired the Intelligence Community's Inspector General for insubordination and dereliction of duty."

Eastwood thought, *Well yeah, he had help! The Democrats are a cult.*

Democrat members of the panel roared their disapproval. The committee chair pounded his gavel so hard Eastwood though it would shatter.

McGee continued, "These documents show the nature and the extent of the help Senator Mazibuike received along the way to inauguration. They have been revealed in part thanks to *Whistleblowers*, which has acquired secret internal documents from the DNC's archives and provided them to the public. Some Washington Democrats and the media not only knew the extent of the political perplexities of President Mazibuike but were active participants in the conspiracy. It is as if they—Washington Democrats and the media—were the orchestra leaders of a band of domestic terrorists."

"*Whistleblowers* provided emails from President Mazibuike to his campaign manager which directed him to, quote, 'Hire Muslims for the top jobs. You can get candidates from the bros,' and 'You tell the CEOs that they will enact Muslim Outreach and diversity training and diversity hiring programs immediately, or they won't get any government contracts.'"

Suddenly every Democrat donor, lobbyist, and politician in Washington, D.C. was terrified his or her name would ooze from the mud and be released by *Whistleblowers*. It was apparent that *Whistleblowers* probably possessed the DNC's missing archives and a comprehensive and illegal file on every Democrat senator and congressman, lobbyist and donor.

Several senators' shoulders slumped. An audible groan came from the Democrat senators. Republican senators sat back in their chairs and reveled in the CIA Director's words. Colonel Eastwood took notes on how the individual senators responded to Director McGee's charges. *One thing is certain, Director McGee is fearless.*

"It's not yet known exactly how *Whistleblowers* acquired the late DNC Chairman's personal papers and diary, but selective releases reveal the scope of the media and DNC conspiracy to manipulate public discourse and the elections. Some of our allies have contributed to the case and provided substantiation. Everything suspected by the American people but conveniently ignored by the media, the Democratic National Committee, and President Mazibuike regarding his treachery and treason has been validated. He was not the man he claimed to be. Today we live in a world of disinformation. The intelligence communities must be eternally vigilant in seeking or discerning the truth. The truth must be told. The brainwashing of America must stop."

Several senators leaned forward as if they knew where the CIA man was going next. Eastwood stopped taking notes and simply watched the proceedings. *He's going to talk…about…me?*

"Last night U.S. Federal Marshals raided a computer company in Germany, *Democracy Innovations,* whose voting machines and software have been manipulating the outcomes of elections around the world. Funded through third party corporations by the billionaire socialist, Rho Schwartz Scorpii, the DNC Chairman's personal records confirm the DNC's most top secret program was called *Democracy Innovations*. The voting machines of *Democracy Innovations* were first developed in Venezuela with a $100 million grant from the late socialist dictator Hugo Chavez. Long suspected for being able to flip votes and possibly even determine the identity of voters, which is what apparently happened in Venezuela, 90% of Venezuelans boycotted the election once word got out."

"To steal elections has been the agenda of the left for decades. The voting machines from *Democracy Innovations* were fully programmable and would flip sufficient votes from the winning opposition party to the socialist party. Most noteworthy, the DNC's archive prove the *Democracy Innovations* software and voting machines were used to great effect during the fraudulent election of President Mazibuike but failed during our most recent election."

Bill McGee added, "We have also looked at some comments from the *Omega,* a person or persons who imply that they have top-clearance knowledge of past and future events. This *Omega* posts on the anonymous online forum *The Cross of Laraine Day*. Many of *Omega's* cryptic posts deal with the Mazibuike presidency and his election, and the voting machines and software."

Eastwood stifled a grin. *How about that? How did Hunter know that?*

"For the record, the entity *Omega* appears to be an off-the-grid intelligence operation that lays a trail of intelligence bread crumbs designed to expose the media and DNC lies."

"Today *Whistleblowers* downloaded tranches of information specifying that Democrat members in Congress, some of whom are in this hearing room today, had full knowledge of the Mazibuike files and the compromised voting machines from *Democracy Innovations*. Once this body receives the latest release from the DNC archives courtesy of *Whistleblowers*, we will know how members, especially Democrat members of the Senate Intelligence Committee, were rewarded for their support."

Nazy strained to contain her composure. Eastwood was speechless.

"I understand partisan politics, and I understand that the parties must protect their leaders. But now I know the depressing truth. My fellow Americans, Congress has demanded answers regarding the life and times of President Mazibuike, and I'm here today to deliver them and the documents that prove President Mazibuike and the Democrat Party were more interested in stealing elections than securing them. *Foreign and domestic elections*." Nazy Cunningham stood up with her briefcase and passed it to the CIA Director. McGee opened the black metal attaché and extracted a stack of papers as thick as a ream of paper and let it fall onto the table.

Eastwood was stunned. *Wow! He's prepared to tell it all!*

Nazy could sense the hearing was coming to a close, like in the final scenes of a movie when the music begins to play and increases in volume until the final scene announces "The End." But this time it was the screeching of imperious Democrat senators on the panel who erupted into outrageous protests. One screamed, *"We'll impeach you!"* Republican senators looked at one another and erupted into chuckles or commented, "Over my dead body," and many shouted over the mayhem to their friends sitting beside them, "I have heard the U.S. Intelligence Community can screw you six ways to Sunday." The Senate Intelligence Committee Chairman pounded his gavel for several minutes, but he could not control the riotous Democrats and was forced to close the hearing and dismiss the CIA Director.

Over the cacophony in the room, Director McGee said, "Mister Chairman, you have the rest of my prepared remarks and the documentation requested by the Democrat senators. I will deliver an official copy to the media via our Public Affairs Office."

McGee turned and gave an imperceptible nod and subtle wink to Eastwood. As Nazy arose her hair unbundled and cascaded down her back. For the briefest of moments she and Demetrius Eastwood shared an unspoken communication. *Hello Nazy! You look like you're doing okay. Dory, I am doing ok – thank you, again.*

Eastwood was out the hearing door before McGee and Nazy could extricate themselves from a horde of reporters. As the CIA executives were ushered to an Agency limo, Eastwood turned to watch the commotion behind him.

The Senate Minority Leader on the panel raced to the first camera she saw. She ripped into the CIA Director's opening remarks, "They were nothing more than a lecture on disinformation and obfuscation. The CIA Director's restructuring of the U.S. Intelligence Community is a 'virtual decapitation.' Congress didn't approve of the CIA's recent reductions in staffing nor did it approve of the harassment of diversity-hired employees with superfluous, arbitrary, and capricious polygraphs. This committee is reviewing the illegal dismissal of thousands of career intelligence officers."

A reporter from the right wing cable news network asked, "What about *Democracy Innovations'* voting machines stealing elections?"

"*Russian disinformation!* Unmitigated Russian disinformation! Director McGee's latest acts of reprisals against the hard-working and patriotic members of the U.S. Intelligence Community threaten to have a chilling effect on all those willing to speak truth to power. He must cease these attacks on those who sacrifice so much to keep America safe and must immediately resign his position. If he fails to resign, I will draft articles of impeachment to have Bill McGee forcibly removed from office. In the middle of a national emergency, it's unconscionable that Director McGee is undermining the integrity of the USIC by firing yet another senior intelligence official simply for doing his job. The Inspector General of the Intelligence Community is a man of integrity who has served our nation for almost three decades.

Being fired for having the courage to speak truth to power makes him a patriot. If anyone should be fired, it is Director McGee!"

Eastwood left the Senate Minority Leader's impromptu presser and walked to the Union Station for the Acela Express back to New York City.

While resting in a first class seat he didn't think about McGee's explosive testimony or the Washington Democrats' mobster tactics. He was teleported back to Algeria and the evening he and McGee had saved Nazy's life. He rarely recalled that night, but the imagery was so powerful, especially when Nazy had been present to remind him of his and McGee's heroism. *She's back at work and is still as beautiful as that first day I met her. She knows how to wear her clothes and hair to hide her freakish wounds. They tried to filet her and rape her after she had been blown unconscious by a bomb blast. The side of her body looked as if it had been shot at with a shotgun filled with gravel. When we got her in the truck, Bill tried to sew her back together again. It looked like a dog had ripped a child's favorite rag doll to shreds, and McGee was the mother with the challenge of sewing up the damage. She leaked blood from a hundred shrapnel wounds on her arms and legs, and I used every bandage from our first aid kits. Several times I was sure she was going to die on that makeshift operating table, McGee's lap. That she is alive is a testament to Bill McGee's fearlessness and bravery and skills in combat first aid. He is dauntless, truly a man of action. We are blessed to have him as the CIA Director.*

Eastwood allowed a few more indelicate reflections to penetrate his mind. *I wonder if McGee is the first CIA Director to have actually killed a person. In Nazy's defense, eight in one night. 35 years as a SEAL. He's likely to have killed many in the course of a career. Eight could be a drop in the bucket. Questions Congress would never ask; a truthful answer would give them a case of the vapors.*

The Muslim Brotherhood called him the Black Shadow. Yeah, the list of America's enemies he has probably killed would give those Democrats on the panel a heart attack. And that minority leader…if she only knew, if she dared to ask….she would soil herself.

CHAPTER 30

May 11, 2018

"Bismillah al-Rahman al-Rahim," In the name of Allah, the merciful, the compassionate chanted the men. They raised both hands to recite the *Takbīr* in prayer. Ceremonial tea was served; the ritual was completed once the tea service had been cleared. *Allahu Akbar!* They all tried to speak at once. The leader attempted to signal for one brother to speak, but the men were outraged and would not listen.

"Why didn't his martyr vest save him? Why didn't his martyr vest save him?" The al-Qaeda leaders demanded answers to questions that could not be answered. Their confidence had been shattered; they were in complete disarray. *How could the Âmirikîs find and kidnap their chief intelligence officer so easily? Why hadn't his suicide vest killed him? How did the Âmirikîs disarm the guards protecting him? The Âmirikîs had never taken a woman prisoner, but this time they did? Was the Âmirikî woman valuable? What did we miss?*

On the top floor of the Amman Marriott in one of the most elegant and expansive suites, the al-Qaeda's leaders worried that their chief intelligence officer would be turned over to the *Mukhabarat,* the Jordanian secret police for interrogation before he was processed by the *Cee âh ā* for transfer to Guantanamo Bay, Cuba. He couldn't be rescued from the Jordanians.

As an organization being decimated by the *Âmirikîs,* the al-Qaeda elders all knew but dared not say that they had experienced their worst possible strategic defeat since losing the Sheikh Osama bin Laden to a similar raid in Pakistan. The same secret stealthy helicopters were used; the same secret dogs were used; and the same secret debilitating devices were used that instantly incapacitated the security guards and allowed the raiding party unfettered access to the compound. *Âmirikîs and their aircrafts! Âmirikîs and their toys!*

All their planning would be for naught when the *Âmirikîs,* specifically the evil *Cee âh ā* subjected Toraluddin Haqqani to what the media defined as "torture" and known as "waterboarding" in the Muslim world.

"We must move our timetable up," said the number two man in the hierarchy.

From behind a hooded *thobe* the beardless man said, "We should have been protecting Brother Haqqani and the *Âmirikî*; this tragedy should not have happened. The *Âmirikîs* always find ways. We study their operations, their methods, their clever devices. You need us, you need us more than ever, for if you do not engage us, you will be next. The *Cee âh ā* are working their way up the ladder in order to destroy our glorious movement. The *Qur'an* calls on Muslims to seek global governance: 'Fight them until religion is all for Allah.'"

Sheikh Saleem Ali al-Qasimi was the leader of al-Qaeda's most elite special operations forces unit and one of al-Qaeda's most aggressive and successful affiliates. *Jabhat Fatah al-Sham,* also known as the *Front for the Conquest of the Levant,* was al-Qaeda's last line of defense. Unlike other members of al-Qaeda, the men of *Jabhat Fatah al-Sham* were clean shaven. They were in another hotel torturing and gang raping a teen.

"At the very least, my men wouldn't have allowed *Brother* Haqqani to be captured…*alive.* The *Âmirikî,* I can assure you, they may have found a way to stop a martyr vest from detonating, but they haven't found a way to stop a bullet. Haqqani would've been more grateful for the bullets I would've put into his skull. He wouldn't have to betray the *Brothers* and speak to the *Cee âh ā* torturers." He shook his head in disgust, "And they allowed the woman to be taken. She should've been killed long ago; she has been with him from the beginning. She can't be allowed to live. She may know nothing, or she may know too much."

One of the al-Qaeda elders barked a dismissal. "As a woman, she knows nothing of our plans. She knows not the language."

The androgynous Ali al-Qasimi countered, "It is too late for that. The fact that the *Âmirikî* infidels took her suggests she was *Cee âh ā,* and Toraluddin Haqqani could no longer use her as a human shield. Didn't Brother Haqqani ever suspect her?"

In a voice that could barely be heard, one elder of al-Qaeda waved off the question with an enfeebled arthritic hand and offered, "The *Âmirikî* needs to be punished. Our plan will unleash hell onto them."

The head of the al-Qaeda said, "The Pakistani politician and Islamic scholar Maulana Maududi wrote in his commentary on another verse calling for the conquest of non-Muslims, *Qur'an* 9:29: 'The purpose for which Muslims are required to fight isn't, as one might think, to compel the unbelievers into embracing Islam. Rather, its purpose is to put an end to the suzerainty of the unbelievers so that the latter are unable to rule over people. The authority to rule should only be vested in those who follow the True Faith; unbelievers who do not follow this True Faith should live in a state of subordination. Anybody who becomes convinced of the Truth of Islam may accept the faith of his or her own volition. The unbelievers are required to pay *jizyah* (poll tax) in return for the security provided to them as the *dhimmis* (protected people) of an Islamic state. *Jizyah* symbolizes the submission of the unbelievers to the suzerainty of Islam.'"

"The invisible weapon the Iranians have developed is part of a global war in the name of the 'New World Order.' The Jews want to rule the world, and we have spies who say that they have developed a weapon that kills only Muslims. We cannot allow that. They will soon launch a 'virus war' to rule the world."

"Ali Al-Qasimi, what do you know of the enemy's virus?"

"Beyond its religious aspect? The enemy's efforts are conducted in secret in *Âmirikî*; impossible for our Brothers to find or do anything about it. What do you intend to do, my master?"

"There must be disease across infidel lands. *Allahu Akbar!* This requires the disease to take the form of epidemic. It is necessary to undertake the remedies that are taught by the *shari'a*. The *shari'a* has ordered that it is not correct to go to a place where epidemic spreads, nor is it right to leave from there. *Allahu Akbar!*"

Another said, "Recall your history! When the Apostle raided a people, he waited until the morning. If he heard a call to prayer, he held back; if he did not hear it, he attacked. We came to Khaybar by night, and the Apostle passed the night there; and when morning came, he did not hear the call to prayer, so he rode and we rode with him, and I rode behind Abii Talba with my foot touching the Apostle's foot. We met the workers of Khaybar coming out in the morning with their spades and baskets. When they saw the apostle and the army they cried, 'Mohammad with his force,' and turned and fled. The Apostle shouted, '*Allahu akbar*!' When we arrive in a people's square, it is a bad morning for those who have been warned."

"We have been warning them for centuries!" shouted another.

"We see that Israel is using *Âmirikî* as a front to weaken Muslim powers through militancy. It will try to subdue other big powers which stand, in non-militancy form, as obstacles in its path, with China at the top, through the virus war. Therefore, no one should have any doubt why *Âmirikî* and the Jews must be first to be affected by this virus. *Inshallah!*"

Another man spoke in a harsh, guttural staccato. "I say kill them in their beds. Their tributes to their false god, the aircraft, kill them. Their economy will collapse; the rich will fight the poor for bread. There will be chaos and the world's economy will collapse. We have the means to do this now. *Allahu Akbar!*"

The al-Qaeda men mumbled, "*Inshallah! Inshallah! Inshallah!*" The leader said, "I vote to allow Sheikh Ali al-Qasimi to proceed."

Another elder wasn't finished. There is always one who believes he's the Supreme Leader or should be and has to get in the last word. "The *Âmirikî* will not know what to do. We must ensure they will blame their president. We must have their media ask why didn't the *Cee âh ā* see this coming? We must strike back! We must be bold and we must act now. Before they can act. *Inshallah*!"

Ali al-Qasimi said, "I will need additional passports for myself and my men. We have passports from the *Âmirikîs,* but to travel internationally we will need additional assets." One of the newest elders asked how Sheikh Ali al-Qasimi acquired passports from the *Âmirikîs*. The answer didn't disturb anyone except the person asking the question. "It was before your time, my Brother. The *Âmirikî* president, Brother Mazibuike *facilitated*. His was a terrible loss. We look for the day when we have another one like him in *Âmirikî,*

Inshallah!" The old man delicately waved his hand to suggest the former American president had Muslims who could be counted on to continue to do his bidding.

Ali al-Qasimi said he would also need much cash and credit cards issued from European and American banks for the operation. "I know that takes time. I appreciate your indulgence and your blessings on our success. *Inshallah!"*

The plan was a simple one; the Khomeini Institute was provisioned every week by a food distributor in Ashgabat in Turkmenistan. Ali al-Qasimi and his men would commandeer the convoy of foodstuffs and consumables from Ashgabat going to the laboratories outside the mining town of Bājirān.

For the next hour they discussed from which capitals they could buy government-issued passports and visas; which *cobbler* would be best suited to create false identity papers on an as-needed basis. Each man of the team would need a separate *legend,* a background supported by manufactured documents whose details would have to be committed to memory. This was one of those times. Ali al-Qasimi was directed to take his men to one of the passport picture kiosks outside the various embassies and bring the photographs back to the group. A messenger would take the photographs and visa applications to the embassies. The process to buy legitimate passports was very expensive and involved bribing senior officials. It was also very time consuming and would take a few days for "processing."

Ali al-Qasimi raged inside. He knew Islamic history and was driven to repeat it. *"So he got off his horse and came at him and 'Ali advanced with his shield. Amr aimed a blow which cut deeply into the shield so that the sword stuck in it and struck his head. But 'Ali gave him a blow on the vein at the base of the neck and he fell to the ground. The dust rose and the apostle heard the cry, 'Allahu Akbar' and knew that 'Ali had killed him." And I will kill them. I will kill them all. But there is much to do to ensure the success of this blessed event.*

He bowed deferentially and said, "*Inshallah!*" He felt the waiting was interminable, the product of weak men who flaunt their meager unearned power given to them by friends or family. If he had his way, he would beat the perfumed government officials to the point of crippling them for life and then rape and murder their wives while the husbands were forced to watch. Violent activities that send a signal: do not trifle with him lest you are prepared for an obvious outcome you will not like.

The old men found themselves bewildered by the *jihadi* who shunned the accepted traditions. But what choice did they have? Six head nods from the leaders signaled that they hoped for blessed success and the mission was approved. *"Inshallah! Inshallah!"*

The leader of *Jabhat Fatah al-Sham* couldn't wait to depart. The old men were tired of war; he still had a taste for it. Was it what he lived for? Was he to be the next martyr? Would he wear the martyr vest? He would not. *Never!* Martyrs are fools who die because they want to. He would destroy the infidels and take their belongings.

Ali al-Qasimi ensured the sleeves of his tunic didn't reveal what was on his wrist; he sat in the ornate overstuffed chair and wondered. *Destroy the infidels! This is their plan? The mighty Russians have learned to not compete with them for they fail. I will mind my manners. My day will come. One day I'll be the ultimate decision maker in the image of the Jerusalem Mufti Haj Amin al-Husseini.* Before turning and departing the assembly of the ancients, Sheikh Ali al-Qasimi said deferentially, *"La illaha illallah." There is no god but Allah.*

His was not the customary departure prayer or acknowledgement of Allah's blessings. He would return. The old men weren't amused at Ali al-Qasimi's insolence and only uttered, *"Allahu Akbar! Fī amān Allāh." In God's protection.*

CHAPTER 31

May 12, 2018

There had been a paradigm shift in the world of journalism. The viewership at the big three major broadcasting companies, the cable news networks, and the readership at the major newspapers, such as the *New York Times*, the *Washington Post*, the *Los Angeles Times*, and the *Chicago Tribune* had plummeted to levels not seen since the 1940s when Americans were nervous about getting into another world war. Almost eighty years later, Americans were turning their backs on the established news media. Newspaper classified ads, obituaries, and advertising were being replaced by computer-based websites and application programs—apps. More than any other reporter, the retired Marine Corps lieutenant colonel and former war correspondent had suddenly become the nation's preferred alternative news journalist. His hard-hitting and factual articles and on-line news specials had captivated the soul of America.

Escape from The Devil's Hole chronicled how almost three hundred women and girls had been kidnapped—some off the streets in Middle America—held in an underground prison and forced into the centuries-old trans-Atlantic sex slave trade headquartered in the United Arab Emirates. Eastwood profiled a minor from Abilene, Texas who had been taken from her local skating rink and survived in a shipping container for weeks before landing in an Abu Dhabi harem. The show did not mention the man in black who had rescued the women and guided them to safety.

Eastwood's television special, *Is Your Neighborhood Mosque a Sleeper Cell?* provided a forensic case with many examples of circumstantial evidence which suggested that neighborhood mosques might not be places of worship, but actual fortresses to stage men and equipment, and possibly even extremist training centers for wannabes *jihadis*. Called "Islamic Cultural Centers" many were actually training compounds. Eastwood had interviewed former imams who had defected from Islam and converted to Christianity. They told him what really went on inside their mosques and their so-called cultural centers. The former members of the Islamic Underground were adamant that there is no such thing as a "rehabilitated jihadist." These defectors from Islam were often killed in gruesome fashion; their murders were to send a message and were posted on the Arabic network, Al Jazeera.

The television special, *Was it Espionage*, focused on the grotesque email practices of the Democrat Party's bint for president, Eleanor Tussy. The former Attorney General insisted that she "had broken no rules" in conducting government business through the use of a private email server, even though leaked documents suggested highly classified material was being spirited out of the Justice Department and dumped onto her unsecure, hackable, homebrew server. Some spied and passed the nation's secrets for free because of shared communist ideology, however it was widely believed the new generation of spies conducted espionage for the money. Every classified document was worth something to America's enemies, and it was a bidders war.

Everything Eastwood had said on radio or television or had written down over the past twenty-plus years was now taken as gospel. His articles were meticulously researched and footnoted. His predictions were coming true. The old Marine was the new "Disciple of Democracy" and the "Doctor of Truth" for his investigative reporting. While his radio show openly operated on the internet, his specialized blog operated discretely on the *dark web* and couldn't be traced back to him. His blog handle was *Omega,* as in **Ω**, the symbol of resistance of Georg Ohm's Law. He posted his messages on the anonymous online forum called *The Cross of Laraine Day.*

After leftist editorials in the *New York Times* admitted they wanted to abolish the Constitution, *Omega* quickly gained a following with a growing band of anti-Communist patriots, conservative attorneys and congressmen who also waged war against the existential threat to the United States—the corrupt Fourth Estate and America's Fifth Column—the enemies of the U.S. Constitution. The undeclared war movement on the media and the communist collaborators that made up the Democrat Party in Washington, D.C. was having a profound effect when *Omega* began typing *Do you believe in coincidences?*

A collaboration with Duncan Hunter had started it all. *Hunter had asked, "In the curious case of Flight 800, the TWA jet that exploded off the coast of Long island…."*

"Wasn't that in 1996?"

Hunter nodded and continued, "The president lied to keep the traveling public and the airlines flying. He had to keep the airlines solvent. The truth would kill the airlines. The government's position was an electrical malfunction created the accident when the truth was, the TWA jet was shot down. The government's response was to protect commercial airliners from terrorists' surface-to-air missiles, not from 'broken wires,' which was the official cause of the incident.

His earliest posts dealt with the stolen CIA documents that brought down the Mazibuike presidency. *Omega's* view was that the Democratic Party was a criminal organization masquerading as a political party, and the Muslim Brotherhood was a criminal organization masquerading as a religion. People were listening, and his following was growing.

He had founded a right-wing syndicated American news, opinion, and commentary website. After years of part-time gigs on television networks he took advantage of Duncan Hunter's sagacious counsel and his largesse to create the *Unmasked & Unspun Network*, providing unfiltered and unspun news the left-wing media would never touch. Eastwood had secured a White House, DOD, DOJ, and a CIA press pass that Director McGee approved.

Ensconced and protected in the corner office of his Manhattan suite on the 26th floor of 7 World Trade Center, Demetrius Eastwood was sprawled out in a 1957 Herman Miller Eames lounge chair editing a new post-election article. The décor was a mix of minimalist and bohemia; one wall featured the recovered lumber from the floors of railroad boxcars. The furnishings included a nine-foot black leather sofa, an imposing 1960 Leopold office desk of tiger oak, a black judge's chair, a glass chair mat, and a double extendable dining table made of teak. Antique lamps and fans from a 1929 failed bank mixed with a butcher-block computer desktop, a five-foot Sony high-definition television, and a recording studio where Eastwood recorded his broadcasts. There was also a covered buffet table with three antique typewriters under plastic. Strategically placed freestanding partitions prevented anyone in adjacent buildings from seeing into the office.

He got up from his Eames chair and crossed the room to the soundproof recording studio. He energized transmitters, cameras, and microphones and got to work.

"Thank you for tuning into this episode of *Unfiltered News* and welcome to the only American news network where you will hear that there is no difference between the communist message and the media's talking points. Demetrius Eastwood here and reporting that the sewage of the Washington, D.C. septic tank flows on. As we do every time, we'll review the newsworthy events of the past week that you likely heard nothing in the legacy news media. *Unfiltered News* will report things you already knew, like ninety-five percent of the media is overtly anti-President Hernandez. It is the most absurd, partisan imbalance I have ever seen. The total collapse of media fairness prompted by a seething hatred of Republicans is a harbinger of an enduring one-party state. We will comment on anniversaries, good and bad, and newsworthy events." Eastwood acknowledged a long line of sponsors who made his on-line telecast possible and then dove into the news of the week.

Eastwood began, "I'm going to start today on a positive note, as in the good guys win. Last week, a police officer from Turkmenistan interrupted a suspected burglar trying to sexually assault a preteenage girl. The criminal ran and in a near-suicidal move, jumped out of a 10th story window with the policeman hot on his trail. The cop landed on top of the *pedo* who had crashed onto a terrace just two floors below. The cop fractured his foot, but he still caught the criminal pedophile. The part of this story that I want to emphasize is that even Muslim countries have criminals and law enforcement heroes. Not all Muslims are terrorists. The Democrats accuse the Right of believing that all Muslims are terrorists. Once again, the Dems are lying. It is as obvious to us as the nose on Eleanor Tussy's face."

"And speaking of Eleanor Tussy, this is as good a time as any to share with you why we are doing *Unfiltered News*. It is primarily because no one reported on the Muslim adviser for former Attorney General Eleanor Tussy who tweeted immediately after the last election *'Inshallah' Hernandez dies, and when he dies, we thank Allah.* This doesn't make me an Islamophobe, but it pisses me off. Two noteworthy things occurred on election night; Tussy was supposed to win but lost Philadelphia, and there was an attempt on the president's life—which apparently the Democrats knew about and probably orchestrated. But our FBI was out to lunch and are so corrupt they wouldn't investigate."

"Another item the news media failed to report because they are a godless, baby-sacrificing, atheistic, Satan-worshipping arm of the Democrat Party: last night several churches were attacked with 'Molotov cocktails.' We now know who is re-popularizing Molotov's cocktails, of course they originated with the Soviet revolutionary Molotov who created the incendiary device for the Bolshevik Revolution. One church was broken into and surveillance video showed the anti-Christian Democrats smashing the statue of the Virgin Mary. So the Mazibuike supporters who attack churches and throw Molotovs now want you to come out and vote Democrat."

"Isn't it the left who wants to ban gasoline—how are they going to construct Molotovs without gas—what are they going to do, throw solar cells or cell phone or laptop batteries at the police? These people are crazy."

"At the other end of the spectrum, it saddens me to report that Stephanie Bartholomew, a Department of Homeland Security whistleblower, was shot dead while getting into her vehicle at a Maryland Safeway parking lot. You won't be shocked to hear that the story of her death still hasn't been reported by the mainstream media."

"You may not have heard about Stephanie Bartholomew, a DHS counterterrorism specialist, because for over a month the news media has placed a blackout on her and her story. She was the DHS whistleblower who dropped the hammer on the Mazibuike Administration by recognizing and calling out *Dark Islam*, the Muslim Brotherhood and ISIS, and the DHS's reluctance to investigate domestic Islamic terrorism. We thought only the FBI had been compromised, infiltrated, but apparently the DHS has its own problem with infiltration by the Muslim Brotherhood."

"I had interviewed her a couple of months ago and I played snippets of that interview. She told me she was very concerned that someone from the former Mazibuike Administration would find her and kill her."

"Miss Bartholomew's story is a heartbreaker. She said that her manager was a devout practicing Muslim who had a prayer mat and a finding compass in his continually smoked-filled office. He was a political appointee of the Mazibuike Administration and wasn't interested in conducting investigations into radical Islamic terrorism in the United States. Miss Bartholomew said she had been investigating instances of domestic Islamic terrorism for several years until her new supervisor put a stop to her investigations."

"Let me play parts of my interview for you. If this doesn't blow your mind, then you must be a Democrat."

A woman's voice: "We were connecting the dots. Focusing on individuals and organizations, networks across the United States and affiliations in foreign countries."

Eastwood: "You were ordered to scrub the records of radical and criminal Muslims with terror ties? By our government? Who told you to do that?"

A woman's voice: "Six years ago, I was directed by the new administrator at DHS Headquarters to delete those records. It's important to keep in mind that this was after the Holy Land Foundation Trial, the most monumental terror trial in U.S. history that irrefutably proved these individuals from the Muslim Brotherhood front groups and Islamic Underground network were receiving direct financial support from Hamas, which of course received direct funding from Iran. All were members of what the U.S. Intelligence Community called *Dark Islam*."

"That was the first 'great purge.' Six years ago. The second database I was directed to erase, delete, whatever you want to call it, contained information on a number of mosques in the United States that sheltered and trained *jihadis*. The evidence showed there was an entire network of mosques hostile to the United States. There were networks of radical mosques led by radical imams, like the Islamic Society and the Haqqani Network."

Eastwood asked her to clarify the targets of her research.

She said, "Of course. These men are different from regular criminals who commit petty crimes—primarily theft. The difference is that these men are motivated to atrocity and murder and rape in the name of Islam. Muslims call their criminals 'criminals' but they distinguish these religious psychopaths in *Dark Islam* as 'Islamists.'"

Eastwood: "Please continue."

"We had their names. We knew where many of them lived, where they worked, and the mosque where they prayed. We could've stopped many of the attacks on Americans by putting these people on the terrorism watch lists, the FBI's Most Wanted Fugitive List, the no-fly lists. If they had plausible ties to terrorism, then law enforcement could arrest them, remove them, and deport them. The shocking thing was that many of these people were on student visas. Their visas could've been pulled; they could've been deported back to their home countries. But there was a lack of leadership within the DHS."

"A lack of leadership?"

"Remember why DHS and the TSA were created. Before 9/11, al-Qaeda had infiltrated the airport security establishments. This is not widely known. They infiltrated the contract security companies at the major airports. Once he was elected, President Mazibuike put political appointments in key aviation security oversight positions."

"Thank you for the clarification."

A woman's voice: "The DHS and the FBI leadership had ordered their agents to disengage from any ongoing Islamic Underground investigations. Our investigators and the FBI's Special Agents—any federal agency tasked with conducting surveillance on suspected Muslim Brotherhood activities—were directed to stop investigating anti-American mosques and collecting data."

Eastwood said, "You and your counterterrorism experts did your job. In comes the Mazibuike Administration, and they wiped out all information that identified radical Islamist imams and their networks, information that could have potentially saved the lives of Americans attacked and killed by Islamic terrorists. Is that a fair statement?"

A woman's voice: "That's a fair statement. My records were all tagged. I got the email when it happened, when all 600 files on mosques and Islamic cultural centers were entirely deleted from the official record. Years' worth of work wiped out by a keystroke. They also destroyed all of my backup files."

Eastwood said, "President Mazibuike stopped your work."

"Yes, President Mazibuike stopped it all. Through his surrogates like my Muslim supervisor. And we were to maintain the narrative that the U.S. was not at war with Islam. We were told to make Muslims feel good about themselves, feel wanted; we were to articulate the surveillance had all been a mistake. And they had an additional narrative that the Republican Party drew no distinction between the radicals of *Dark Islam* and Islam."

Eastwood stopped the recording to add, "She claimed her supervisor ordered her to cease all investigations and instead, scrub—no, *erase*—the records of radical or criminal Muslims in the United States with terrorist ties. All the work she had done over the years to identify radical Islamic terrorists was purged immediately. She contacted the DHS Inspector General and lodged a complaint." Eastwood's voice lowered an octave. "She was about to name names but ended up with a bullet in her head."

"Miss Bartholomew said political correctness during the Mazibuike years killed hundreds of investigations into the activities of *Dark Islam*, the Muslim Brotherhood, ISIS, and the clandestine Islamic Underground that might've stopped mass murders committed by radical Islamic terrorists."

Eastwood continued to speak as he held up a letter with a stapled envelope in front of one of the cameras.

"You know I receive many letters from around the country. I also received a letter from Miss Bartholomew outlining her concerns. She warned me that if she was ever found dead, not to believe official reports that she had committed suicide."

"In her final words, Miss Bartholomew denounced the Democrat Party and the media, calling both a 'cult' that pretended to be interested in the common people, the workers. She said, 'I used to be a proud Democrat. I was raised to be a Democrat; my parents and grandparents always voted for Democrats.' She explained that she had been an activist in her youth for the Democrat Party."

"Miss Bartholomew said Republicans were painted as the bad guys, and she had assumed they were a cult of fancy suits, expensive watches, and Italian ties. The Democrats were the good guys."

A woman's voice: "But now I realize the Democrats and the media are the true cults, the real Kool Aid drinkers, lining up for that magical elixir. I was a fool."

Eastwood offered, "I received information from the Sheriff's Department that Stephanie Bartholomew was murdered. Not a suicide, but murder. Law enforcement verified that there is a murder investigation underway. This isn't just a crying shame, it's validation that the bad guys who did this are still out there. And it's hard not to suspect that someone in the DHS did this. I believe Stephanie; I believe someone from the Mazibuike mafia found her and killed her."

"And the FBI was nowhere to be found; it's still stewing in its own corruption as anti-Hernandez, pro-Mazibuike supporters. A handful of FBI Special Agents who are reportedly not Muslim by birth were caught on camera kneeling with Special Agents who are Muslim and applauding groups like the Muslim Brotherhood and Islamic Underground. I believe it can now be said that there are a significant number of Special Agents who have endorsed the political views of those organizations. Although each of those episodes can be attributed to only a relative 'handful' of people among an FBI workforce of 15,000 Special Agents, the combined effect is to tell roughly half the country that the FBI has become a 'political opponent' of the American people and the president. We can no longer trust the FBI."

"The skidmarks on the FBI left by Mazibuike will not be scrubbed away anytime soon. President Hernandez needs to get some adult leadership in that place immediately. That will infuriate the left, the media, and those afflicted with various brain maladies—Washington Democrats—but I repeat myself. I believe that all men are created equal; the ridiculous special interest groups of the Marxist left demand they are more equal than others based on their—fill in the blank."

"And isn't it interesting, we have many government employees like the late Stephanie Bartholomew who took the oath of office and promised 'to defend the Constitution and laws of the United States of America against all enemies, foreign and domestic; and bear true faith and allegiance to the same,' who fear for their lives to this day? They know there are people within the U.S. Intelligence Community who'll hunt them down and kill them for the treachery of being an honest American. A patriot. I think this is all related to the dark side of the U.S. Intelligence Community and their unholy alliance with the Democrat Party. I have been calling the communist part of the USIC the *Dark State*. This is clearly our domestic enemy."

"Isn't this the very definition of a domestic enemy? A secret police force to keep people in line or kill them if they get out of line? Some of you know that for one of my specials I interviewed imams who defected from Islam, and they said the same thing, that they feared for their lives from within. I find it incredible that some of our guys act like their guys. Just today we learned Iran executed a former defense ministry employee they accused of being a CIA spy. That's ten Iranian government employees this year who were murdered under the auspices of being an agent provocateur for the CIA."

"Many in the right-wing media believe that the CIA, under 3M's orders, plotted to kill the head of *Whistleblowers* in Europe and make it look like an accident. Their actions resemble what the Corleones did in the *Godfather*. Only this is real. This is the ugly part of the business of intelligence, what the IC calls '*wet work!*'"

"No one will even say 'off-the-record' that the U.S. Intelligence Community has an internal enforcement arm that hunts down and punishes whistleblowers, some secret organization that resembles the old Soviet Union's KGB, the Thirteenth Directorate, colorfully known as the 'Directorate of Wet Affairs.' Is it the CIA or is it the FBI that has a version of a Directorate of Wet Affairs? Or is it some other rogue organization? I've asked but haven't gotten a straight answer. Maybe the answer is that in a free society where you pledge allegiance to God, the Constitution, and the Flag, there is a counter group committed to another supreme being or no supreme being, someone who is actively attacking the Constitution and trampling the Flag. How is this not a domestic enemy? And if they work in the Intelligence Community, then they are double agents, clandestine operatives."

"I know that some of you have read the recent libidinous eulogy for General Roustaie in the *New York Times*. It reads like something from a bad romance novel, so I wondered who could write such clueless tripe. I discovered that it was authored by some pathetic, defenseless, and sensitive female journalist who apparently has the hots for brutal Islamic strongmen. Her résumé may show that she is the *Times'* eminent expert on Iran, but her version of Iran is a fantasy. There is nothing erotic about sadistic tyrants in rape rooms. Is she part of the clandestine enemy network, the 'fifth column,' working 'behind the lines?' If I uttered these observations at a gathering of Democrats they would collapse like a flea market lawn chair or drag me off for a re-education camp—if they didn't just shoot me and put me out of my misery. I'm as serious as four heart attacks and a stroke."

"I'm on the docket to interview CIA Director Bill McGee tomorrow. If I get the chance I'll ask him about the death of Roustaie and who is really doing *wet work*. Wet work of the first kind, the second kind, the third kind."

"I hope to ask Director McGee about Mazibuike commuting the sentences and pardoning terrorists and radicals who bombed places in the U.S. One guy had bombed 130 buildings in America and 3M commuted his sentence."

Eastwood's sighs and anguish could be heard over the airways. After he composed himself, he continued, "In other news that you won't find in the American media, Afghanistan's dominance of the opium poppy market has collapsed. All the poppy fields have been wiped out by some unknown disease. There's not enough opium coming from Afghanistan now to keep a single opium den in business in Islamabad."

Eastwood shifted topics. "In part of my 'Eyeballs on Iran' segment, I would like to know what happened to Sheldon Marsh and Christine Simbach, two hikers who had reportedly been trekking along the Turkmenistan-Iran border. They were part of a tour group and were last seen leaving the capital city of Ashgabat three weeks ago. I ask every time I'm at the State Department. They don't know. No one knows, officially. However, the word on the Muslim street is that they were captured by Iranian border guards and are being held by Iran. No one will acknowledge that they're in Iran. If I'm able, I'll ask Director McGee."

"Saudi Arabia claimed on Tuesday it has received secret documentation that Muslim Brotherhood founder Hassan al-Bana had worked for the Nazis in the past. Not 'with' but 'for.' The documents have come from newly discovered Nazi archives that had been hidden behind a wall at the Tempelhof Airport in Berlin—which may have been Hitler's escape tunnel. A copy of a report entitled, "The Nazi Brotherhood," outlined the relationship and the discussions between the founder of the Muslim Brotherhood movement, the Jerusalem Mufti Haj Amin al-Husseini, and Adolph Hitler."

"Intelligence officers had long suspected that al-Bana and al-Husseini served as spies for the Third Reich and recruited hundreds of Arabs to fight under the flag of the Nazi army. The secret report was provided by the Hungarian-based, international non-profit organization, *Whistleblowers*, and it delineated the extent of Muslim Brotherhood founder Hassan al-Bana's reach and power, his secret ties with several foreign intelligence apparatuses, and his attempt to infiltrate Nazi forces with Arab Muslims loyal to him."

"Adolph Hitler promised his full support for al-Bana's political agendas by using the Nazi's *Afrika Korps* to expedite Muslim Brotherhood infiltration of the Egyptian government so Hassan al-Bana could take power in Egypt. So think about that. The Muslim Brotherhood has been trying to overthrow the Egyptian government through radical religious subversion since World War Two. I have to say that was news to me, but it also makes me better understand that these terrorist groups, however they are organized, never give up until they achieve their goal of total domination."

"Al-Bana increased his influence in Egypt and Libya, and established the Muslim Brotherhood and the Islamic Underground as the Islamic Leadership of the World. Another related translated document was titled, *An Explanatory Memorandum;* it was the Muslim Brotherhood's strategic plan to rule North Africa and Palestine. A copy of a similar document with the same title was discovered in a basement in Virginia—the Muslim Brotherhood's strategic plan to infiltrate the U.S. government and rule America."

"My favorite news clip of the day comes from *The City Paper*, Bogotá's most widely read English-language newspaper for consequential news. The feel-good headline reads, *What Happened to their Subs*? It is reportedly from sources within the drug cartels. It seems the cartel leaders have been spending millions of dollars building colossal submersibles—not submarines that can travel under the water, but boats that can travel just below the ocean surface—only to lose many of them before they could offload tons of cocaine in Panama, Costa Rica, San Salvador, Guatemala, Honduras, and even Europe. No one in the U.S. government has claimed credit for stopping these subs, and no one in the cartels will assume responsibility for losing hundreds of millions of dollars of cocaine by building subs that can't cross the gulf or the ocean."

Eastwood held up another letter for the cameras. "This week marks the twentieth anniversary of the death of Jack Dickerson and the attack on the airport in Casablanca, Morocco. Mr. Dickerson was a renowned airport manager, an engineer who specialized in turning African airports around after years of civil war or tribal unrest. Jack Dickerson's family in Del Rio, Texas sent a letter to remind us that he and his crew were captured and killed by Mostafa Roustaie, an Islamic Revolutionary Guard Corps colonel who helped orchestrate the 1983 Hezbollah operation that killed 241 Marines in Beirut. The detestable colonel-now General Roustaie singled out Jack Dickerson because he wouldn't submit to Islam; the monster Roustaie didn't even give the condemned man a blindfold when he decapitated Jack in front of Al Jazeera cameras. Al Jazeera also aired Roustaie as he chopped off Dickerson's hand to get to the man's watch. Al Jazeera ensured the horrific scene went viral, as they say. Rest in peace Jack Dickerson, one day your despicable murderer will be brought to justice."

"Al Jazeera's reporters can be found in places where the strongmen of the Revolutionary Iranian Guard are at the forefront of fomenting unrest. Americans should be reminded that although our former Democrat vice president is on the board of directors of Al Jazeera, Al Jazeera was created to advance Islamist foreign policy objectives, anti-Americanism, while providing major support to Iran and promote Hamas. Al Jazeera supports the entire Palestinian terrorist enterprise and their efforts to delegitimize and destroy Israel. This is where you find the highest levels of Iranian leadership openly supporting leaders of terrorist and extremist groups."

"Now, I'm not particularly religious myself, but I'm sufficiently moved by Christianity's noble plight for survival in the face of the unrelenting evil that is radical and *Dark Islam*. All across the Middle East you will find that Muslims are pleasant hosts. The dirty secret the left keeps from you is that these nice and peaceful Muslims are also at war with the radical and dark side of Islam, and they knowingly call them *Islamists*. The Islamic countries' secret police are brutal to the *Islamists* and the radical Islamic terrorists they arrest. Remember, these are not regular criminals doing regular crimes. These religious criminals are mass murderers."

"And speaking of radical Muslims, German intelligence is now reporting that they have discovered the Muslim Brotherhood plans to undermine Germany. The Muslim Brotherhood in Germany seeks to establish a comprehensive system of government which doesn't guarantee the sovereignty of the people, the principles of freedom, or equality. In other words, they're trying to transform German society in order to overthrow the government. Where have we seen this picture show?"

"Some of you may know that CIA Director Bill McGee is known as '*Bullfrog*' to his friends in the Special Ops community. He had a field day at a Senate Intelligence Committee briefing yesterday. Things that we—you and I—knew to be true but wouldn't dare say were said by Director McGee. It has been a bad couple of years for the Democrat Party; it's been especially bad for them the last few months. The CIA Director has been exposing what I call *activities of the Dark State*, and he stabbed the Democrats in their chests with the pointy edge of truth and facts. All the Democrat senators on the committee could do was spit blood and foam at the mouth."

"Let me say, President Hernandez showed brilliance in appointing Director McGee to his position; he is the right person at the right time, exactly what this country needs to lead the U.S. Intelligence

Community. I have the utmost confidence Director McGee will drain the *Dark State* of its swamp-like creatures."

"That's it for today. We'll be back in a couple of days for another episode of *Unfiltered News*. Semper Fi to all of my Marine Corps brothers and sisters. I close this as I always do by saluting the men and women of the military, first responders, law enforcement, the farmers and the factory workers, and all the law-abiding citizens across the fruited plain who make this country work. Good night. Eastwood out."

• • •

As he usually did when he had time, Hunter listened to Eastwood's radio show on his computer. Like his other live shows and podcasts, it was a good show. If it had been a bad show, Hunter would've let Eastwood know.

Chapter 32

May 13, 2018

The men, both former officers of the Department of the Navy, greeted each other warmly. A crew had set up their cameras and microphones on the grounds of the CIA in the shadow of the Agency's A-12 *OXCART*. Director McGee suggested an outside venue; Eastwood suggested under the spyplane. Director McGee commented that it felt good to be outside. Dozens of onlookers formed a half-circle to watch the interview, including Nazy Cunningham and Yassmin Deng, the Agency's CFO.

Under the watchful eye of the Agency Public Affairs Officer, Eastwood asked the CIA Director for an official comment on the President's announcement, that General Mostafa Javad Roustaie, the head of the IRGC, had been removed from the battlefield. McGee said he didn't have any additional information.

Eastwood wasn't happy with the Director's response and wondered if the rest of the day was going to go the way of "no comment." He tried again with a question, "Director McGee, what happened when you testified in front of Congress? Your statement seemed to set off the Democrat members of the Senate."

"Dory, you and I are old military men. We're given a mission, and we complete that mission to the best of our ability. When you testify at one of the congressional subcommittees, the two political parties also have a mission. One party wants to hear what you have to say. The other political party wants you to substantiate their view of things, 'their narrative.' Their mission is an all-out effort to destroy a member of the administration in order to discredit, delegitimize, and destroy the president."

"I don't play that game. I truly believe most Americans would weep if they knew what has happened to our country. The comrade

Democrats on the committee ripped former Director Lynche to shreds and browbeat him every time he came before them. That was their agenda; they wanted to hide the fact that a Democrat Senator, who wasn't constitutionally eligible, had been elected president. And they wanted to prove someone in the CIA had exposed Mazibuike for the fraud he was. All the rioting in the country and the hostilities in Congress can be traced back to when President Mazibuike left office. They are determined to punish the Agency for not stopping the release of those documents and for not maintaining the narrative that Mazibuike was the second coming. They worshipped him and maybe believed he was the twelfth imam or something."

"Their political activism continues to this day. They're not interested in the threats to America, only the threats to their political party. We think in terms of what's necessary to protect America; they think of what they must do to advance the Democrat Party agenda. It hasn't always been like this, but it's the system we have today. We used to think the Democrat Party had been taken over by radicals. But that isn't exactly the case. They've been taken over by a consortium of the *protective classes who have become radicalized.* The Democrat Party leadership in Congress are members of one of the minority groups, one of the *protective classes*—they can be black, women, Latino, gay, Muslim—there are others. But they are to their soul Marxists, communists, and leftists."

"So the Agency is focused on their mission overseas, while at home the Democrats attack you."

McGee nodded. "Like a Yorkie with a bad temper nipping at your heels. Doesn't it feel like they have help, that they are receiving help from overseas? Take the case of the driver of the senior senator from California; he was arrested by the FBI for being an undercover agent for the Chinese the last twenty years. This case shows just how corrupt the Democrat members of Congress have become, and it demonstrates how lackluster and emasculated the FBI has become because they knew he was bad from day one and chose not to arrest him. The corruption is obvious if you look for it."

McGee said, "We have a mutual friend who tells a story of when he visited the Monrovia, Liberia airport, specifically their customs office and found three small desks with chairs and two signs that showed, 'NO BRIBES TAKEN AT THIS DESK.' Of course there wasn't a customs officer at the two desks with signs but there was an official at the desk without a sign. Corruption can be endemic."

Eastwood said, "The left, especially the Democrat Party in Congress, is focused on protecting themselves; their *protective classes.*"

McGee agreed, "Or with President Mazibuike, forcing the Agency, and the FBI, to hire unqualified and uncleared people in the name of *diversity*. It was all a subterfuge to place radicals and communists in government by other means."

"I can see where it impacts the CIA."

Director McGee said, "They attack the Agency through congressional surrogates. We're supposed to be apolitical and mostly we are. But the Washington left has an agenda, and that agenda is their mandate. They seek to control the CIA through extra-legislative means. Government oversight is fine and warranted, however, any *attack* on the CIA warrants an appropriate response, whether the attack is domestic or international. The laws are written in such a way that we have little recourse on scurrilous attacks. We have hired several new lawyers to work these cases."

Eastwood offered, "How is the Agency supposed to ignore the malfeasance and treachery of the Democrat Party that seeks to undermine you and your people? With the release of the Mazibuike file, Americans saw how the Democrats had hidden President Mazibuike's past with the help of a compliant media, Democrat judges, an aggressive Democrat National Committee, which we find out was being led by a Russian agent of the Yuri Bezmenov school of ideological subversion and the systematic coercive psychiatry that the KGB inflicted on Vladimir Bukovsky."

Citing Bezmenov and Bukovsky? Dory has done his homework. "As I stated in my recent testimony, recent disclosures from the organization that receives purloined documents—ah, *Whistleblowers*—dropped a few bombshells. Washington Democrats were quick to refute those documents as counterfeit. Reasonable people will see that the Democrats' assertions were disingenuous. Portions of the DNC's archives that have been released so far point to one undeniable fact, the former Soviet Union's efforts to infiltrate the Democrat Party and the DNC and orchestrate the installation a communist president came to fruition with the election of President Mazibuike."

Eastwood chimed in, "So, to get this straight, there were two document drops—one a few years ago from an unknown patriot which proved President Mazibuike was not the man he claimed to be. The other document drop, we believe, came from the former head of the DNC's Office of Opposition Research. The evidence is sketchy, but it seems Mr. Tommy Bonneville had discovered he was working for an illegal or corrupt organization and had enough of the DNC's shenanigans. The evidence suggests he copied and transmitted the DNC's archives to our favorite website which we are supposed to hate, and I mean *Whistleblowers*. For his treachery, Tommy Bonneville was assassinated, apparently the victim of a DNC-paid contract murderer whose identity is still unknown."

Director McGee picked up the conversation, "Both release-of-documents events have long been denounced by the DNC, the media, and Democrat Party members in Washington who declared them to be forgeries generated by the Republican National Committee or the Russians. Thanks to *Whistleblowers*, we now have copies of the original documents, and our allies have provided substantiation. It's like a businessman who claims the kiddie porn on his computer isn't his, that his computer must've been hacked. Only an imbecile would believe such a gallinaceous and bovine narrative. But when you have the originals, you also know you've been lied to." Eastwood chuckled at the cock and bull story.

"What we have long suspected, we now know emphatically. It has been the Russians, the media, *and the DNC*. What's that old line? What do you see when you turn on Al Jazeera television? The Islamic Underground's spokesperson, the contemptible androgynous Muslim rage boy, shouting, 'Death to America,' and on the Russian Television Network, the Russians shouting, 'Death to America,' and on the communist news network at home it's the main-stream media and the Democrats, a man in woman's clothing at the DNC screaming, 'How can we help?'"

"It's very much like having the *Venona Papers* declassified so we could see the documented treachery that the spies of the old Soviet Union had actually held some of the top jobs in the Roosevelt Administration," said Eastwood.

McGee offered, "For those who may not know, the *Venona Papers* was a top secret World War II U.S. Army Signal Intelligence Service counter-intelligence program which decrypted the intercepted messages of the intelligence agencies of the Soviet Union. At the time the *Venona Papers* were released and declassified they were poo-pooed by the national media and Washington Democrats as fake. Now you can see facsimiles of those original declassified intercepts at the National Cryptologic Museum at the National Security Agency at Fort Meade. There's a lesson to be learned here: even when members of the media or Washington Democrats are forced into a discussion on the *Venona Papers*, or the DNC archives, or the Mazibuike file, they insist they are 'fake without any substantiation' even when there is a dump truck load of substantiating documentation. Which only proves you can't see anything when your eyes are closed."

"From intercepted Soviet messages in the *Venona Papers* we see that the U.S. discovered the *Cambridge Five* espionage ring in the United Kingdom and uncovered the extent of Soviet espionage of the *Manhattan Project* in the U.S., and my favorite, Whitaker Chambers. He defected from the atheist Soviet Union and found God, and unmasked the man he ran for them, the highest placed Soviet mole in the U.S. government—Alger Hiss. The political Left and the Democrat Party have always screamed that the *Venona Papers* were *horsehockey*, a bag of flaming *guano* left on a porch, the product of the CIA's S&T or a Soviet disinformation program. The news media should ask, 'Why is it that highly placed Democrats are always the subject of these disclosures?'. You would think the law of averages would capture some Republicans engaging in espionage and subterfuge. Maybe, just maybe, it's all leftist or communist ideology, all Washington Democrats—the vomit licking dogs that they are—who engage in these activities. The same could be said of who actually commits mass murder in this country. It's not ever a member of the NRA; it is always someone with a diagnosed or an undiagnosed personality disorder who votes Democrat. 'Social justice warrior' should be its own category in the DSM, right between 'oppositional defiant disorder' and 'schizophrenia.' Many Americans are unaware that there is a war going on within the APA to keep 'liberalism' out of the pages of the *Diagnostic and Statistics Manual for Mental Disorders*."

Eastwood was impressed with the insight. "Most Americans know that when the unknown CIA file on the former senator was released to the public and Congress, and President Mazibuike was exposed to be an unmitigated charlatan, he resigned in disgrace and left the country before he could be impeached. Some on the left claim he was sure he was going to be assassinated, so he got out of the country before DOD special operations forces arrived at the White House to take him out." *And when Whitaker Chambers realized the truth, he grabbed his family and ran for cover for years.... Escaped the murderous bastards of the Communist and Democrat Party. I remember....*

"Does the Agency have something like the KGB's Thirteenth Directorate, colorfully known as the 'Directorate of Wet Affairs?'"

McGee said, "Let me say, we do not engage in domestic affairs or such illegal offensive tactics. Militaries and special operations forces the world over and in the U.S. train in these techniques. If a member of a Special Forces team gets captured and has the opportunity to escape, but that requires killing the enemy, the kill is permissible under the Geneva Convention. But your real question is, did someone at the CIA collect intelligence on Mazibuike when he was a civilian, when he was on a British passport, and did someone within the Agency release his file? There have been dozens of investigations by the FBI, the Inspector General, and others, and they found nothing. Anyone who brings up the issue at a Congressional hearing is ignorant, pursuing an agenda, or mentally defective. I assert, Mazibuike would've been an excellent defendant at a trial, but the political left and the Democrat Party couldn't allow that or any investigation which would have led up to that. While I believe in my heart that special operations warriors wouldn't have given him the time of day, the left would have marked Mazibuike for elimination for his epic failure. Much like how the DNC Chairman, Dr. Zhavrazhinov, took the defeat of his candidate, Eleanor Tussy."

"For failing to get Tussy elected, he jumped off of the 23rd floor of the Marriott Marquis on Times Square."

"It was the 22nd floor."

"You are right. I stand corrected, Director McGee."

"I believe they would've used someone like the person contracted to silence Tommy Bonneville when he sent the DNC's archives to *Whistleblowers*. The American people deserve to know that these people, only the Democrats, have mob ties or mob-like ties. These aren't nice people. And let me say, the FBI used to investigate these people. Hopefully, one day soon, they will again."

McGee turned his face into the wind; he appreciated the breeze and the discussion. He took a drink of water from a plastic bottle.

Eastwood said, "Director McGee, during your open-door testimony you offered some *Whistleblowers* materials to add color to President Mazibuike's treachery when he met with high level spokesmen from the Muslim Brotherhood and Islamic Underground in the Oval Office. *Whistleblowers* provided pictures—pictures we didn't know existed, pictures we hadn't seen until recently—leading some to believe the CIA may be working with *Whistleblowers*."

"We are not. But like any intelligence agency that uses open source materials, we would be derelict in our duties not to analyze their documents."

"Yes, sir. You would think that after Agency spies stole government documents, like that wretched excuse for a human, Edward Snowden, the CIA would be loath to work with someone like *Whistleblowers*."

"As you know, Colonel Eastwood, we do not deal with domestic intelligence issues; that's the purview of the FBI."

"Now, Snowden wasn't a whistleblower. That's a false narrative manufactured by the corrupt media. The facts of the matter are that he was a contracted employee who was given a job with the highest level of trust and confidence. He misused his position, he stole the nation's secrets, and he gave them to the Russians. If you have issues with someone in the chain of command or with some program manager, you go to the IG and voice your concerns—only a criminal spy runs to the embracing arms of the Kremlin. 99.9 percent of legitimate whistleblower cases reveal a misunderstanding. However, if you look at the point-one percent who get caught *stealing* secrets, trying to remove classified documents, I am at a loss to explain their reasoning for committing espionage. We have some at Leavenworth right this minute. When given the opportunity, these people rush to a microphone and assert they're a different gender, they have a different sexual identity, or they have a personality disorder. They have a *disturbance* of their own creation that in their mind only money and espionage can correct," said McGee.

Eastwood said, "You're correct, sir. It screws up the process. Prosecutors have discovered that these criminals who commit espionage have what was once defined as a mental disability under the DSM and therefore would've been deemed *non compos mentis*, not mentally capable and unfit to stand trial. Now they assert that since they're not on the DSM anymore, they're considered normal human beings and demand sex change operations and demand to be sent to the jail that corresponds to their chosen sexual identity."

McGee added, "Those aren't the activities of a whistleblower; those are the illegal activities of someone with a significant mental disorder. Most Americans are unaware that intel agencies across the globe do not have this problem. The American taxpayer should insist their intelligence community be staffed with the best and the brightest and not people with mental disorders of any kind. The IC is not a socialist science project. This situation is solely a product manifested by President Mazibuike's Administration."

"It sounds like they dropped a turd in the proverbial punch bowl."

Director McGee had no comment.

"Director McGee, regarding the DNC's archives, does the CIA have them or are they interested in them?"

"If *Whistleblowers* put that information into the public domain, we will look at it."

Eastwood's time was nearly up. He asked one more question, "Washington never expected you for CIA Director. Any regrets?"

McGee said, "I'll answer that this way, a friend of mine said you're able to do the most fascinating work in federal service. And I agree, if you are interested in working." The friends shook hands.

Once free of his interview obligation, McGee and Nazy Cunningham started toward the main entrance of the New Office Building but were intercepted by the Agency's CFO, Yassmin Deng. McGee stopped; he towered over her. She asked if she could get on the director's calendar. McGee didn't want to hear any more complaints regarding the expenses on the *Noble Savage* SAP or what white member of the senior intelligence service had uttered a presumably racist *double entendre,* but she said the request was personal. He and Nazy exchanged glances and shared a telepathic: *Can you wait?* Nazy's eyes said, *I can wait,* and she walked away, giving the Director and Deng some distance.

McGee asked Miss Deng, "Can we talk about your issue right here? When I get back into the office I'll be up to my eyeballs in work." The opportunity to deal with personal matters sometimes took minutes. He could give her a couple of them.

She was slightly intimidated but nodded and said, "I have received a job offer to work in the private sector."

McGee stopped walking. He had expected a shotgun blast of complaints. "So, what do you want to talk about?"

Yassmin Deng crossed her arms. "TASCO; the CEO offered to hire me as their CFO at ten times what I make here."

McGee didn't overreact. There was no adverse response. It wasn't all that uncommon for senior members of the USIC to be wooed by the companies that specialized in contracts for the intelligence community. He was giving the TASCO CEO the benefit of doubt that he wasn't some *nightcrawler* who prowled the bars looking for government employees who could be compromised using alcohol or sex. McGee had met Chernovich and over the years had seen him on several covers of newspapers and *The Eastern* magazine. He knew the man's sexual proclivities and couldn't imagine a situation where Chernovich would try to seduce a lesbian woman. Director McGee said, "That's a very generous offer. Few of those come around every day. Congratulations Yassmin....unless there's a problem?"

She whispered, "I am a lesbian and TASCO is a gay-driven organization from the top-down."

McGee stifled exasperation and said, "We know that."

Ms. Deng continued, "I would likely become the most powerful African-American woman in American business, maybe even the most powerful gay woman in American business."

Like I didn't know that too, but, yeah, so? He leaned in to her and quietly responded, "Yassmin, I really don't care about your sexual preferences. They are immaterial to me; that's your private business. There's no reason for a honey trap; you aren't in an operational chain where you can be blackmailed. I'm someone who wants a job to be done. Is there more? Do you have concerns?"

She nodded the nod of a petite woman, which was barely noticeable. "I think that…the CEO wants to use me as a way to get information…." She swept her arm to indicate Headquarters and the complex. "…on this place."

This is our place…. It was McGee's turn to cross his mighty arms. "Info—in what way? TASCO is our biggest contractor. They already receive more work and more money from us than any other company—and you know that. They have more people with green badges than any other contractor—and you know that, too. They have raided the CIA, actually the whole IC, as I understand, even for people we have let go as being undesirable or retired. And now they have made a go at you. You've been doing this a long time without the spotlight of the corporate world shining on you, and the money can be a substantial difference. But I gather…that…there's something else? What am I missing?"

"Bogdan Chernovich offered me *ludicrous* money if I accepted his CFO position, and if I didn't, he still wanted to put me on a retainer. He was interested in you and the Agency's leaders…and our special access programs."

McGee registered the natural curiosity of a leader who had just been told a subordinate had been approached by a foreign entity who wanted her to spy for them. That Chernovich wanted to use her race and sexual preference and the CFO's position to turn her wasn't entirely unpredictable; McGee considered the pitch *untimely*. "What did you tell him?"

"I tried to refuse, but he told me to think about it. He said that either way, he would reward me for my efforts and that by coming to work for him, I could punish the Agency and the government for their past social and racial injustices in not promoting high-performing African American women."

CIA Director McGee, the highest-placed highest-performing African American in government, rolled his eyes. *Espionage riding on Critical Race Theory. What bullshit.*

Nazy overheard the woman's soliloquy but did not express any emotion. She turned to look at the black jet on display.

McGee glanced at Nazy and unfolded his arms. *Well, that was probably music to her ears.* "You know what this means, right?"

Deng was flustered and shook her head.

McGee tore into her. "Yassmin, your problem isn't with white men or how the government has abused you or black people. It is more than just politics; it's your *mind*. You believe those who say you're oppressed, you have listened to those seeking the complete overthrow of the existing rational system; they argue what is required is a complete deconstruction of anything that legitimizes or upholds systemic power in any regard whatsoever. You've been led to believe that whiteness itself, in all of its various manifestations for example, must be unmade to end systemic racism. That is what you get when postmodernism, post-Marxism, and neo-Marxism are fused into Critical Social Justice Theory. It's the product of systemic brainwashing, it's destructive; it's the ideology of the left and sponsored by the Kremlin for the sole purpose of throwing this country into chaos, and it is absolutely wrong."

"To be having this conversation is a sign of a sick and damaged—*not diseased*—mind, and if you cannot fix your outlook at this very minute, you should go to TASCO as fast as your little feet can carry you. Take the money, for you will not work here. I cannot have mental cases in charge of the nation's most sensitive programs. I don't give a shit that you like girls—that's your friggin' business. But let me be perfectly clear—I have major issues with people who cannot see that this Agency and the United States are under assault by fascist organizations like the Democrat Party, the Muslim Brotherhood, TASCO, and the Islamic Underground, and the communist clowns in Russia and China, not to mention that Mazibuike leveraged his office and his melanin level to destroy this institution and this country. I cannot have someone with eyes wide open who ignores what they see and believes the bullshit on the left and thinks they are a friggin' genius when they cannot see or understand that they are actually an idiot who can be led around by a nose ring. This is your opportunity to get your head out of your ass and see that you've been lied to and have been manipulated, or you can pack your trash and leave."

No one had ever talked to her in such a way. Yassmin Deng was speechless for a full half-minute, staring at the big black monster she had considered an icon. He was black and he was the Director, and like the former president, a tremendous source of pride for African Americans. McGee's politics were opposite of hers, yet he had been honest with her. She trembled from the ultimatum and said, "Director McGee, you are the most impressive man I have ever met, and I admire you greatly. Please do not mistake my poor choice of words to be something they are not. I do not want to leave here. I will do whatever you think is necessary to...."

"Work for America? Work to protect this Agency?" mouthed Nazy.

McGee was shocked. He would have bet the deed to the training center that she would have caved. "There is an antidote to the brainwashing. First, stop listening to that drivel on the left and get better friends. Find a better cable channel to watch. If you can see that they targeted you because you can be manipulated, I think we can save you. Like a starfish that had been washed up on shore after a storm. I can't save them all, but I can save some. I'm not wasting my time on damaged starfish. Critical Social Justice Theory is bullshit and it is poison."

Yassmin Deng nodded.

"Can you see you've been pitched by a hostile entity? You should be livid that they assumed you were a mental case like they are. Do you still want to stay? Are you willing to try?"

"I am. Maybe I can talk to Nazy."

"You do that. But if you are going to stay, then you know what's next."

"I do—polygraphs. I know. I know. I love this place despite your absurdly expensive SAPs. You know more than anyone that they are worth the money, because we do not have whatever capabilities those contractors provide." She sighed and scanned her surroundings. She didn't want to leave. Yassmin Deng said, "But I wanted you to know."

"Thank you. We must talk more on the subject when your body can repel the poison the left has been feeding you. That garbage is mind control. In this place we are smarter than that. Now, to get you back into your office.... We have much to do to counter the influence of the left. Nazy understands the nature of these men and the left and their agenda. You girls should talk. But if you are going to stay, you know the rules."

McGee was fired up and gestured wildly. "Part of the polygraphs are designed to find the personality disorder and sexual identity disorder that could make you a blackmail target. You've been pitched because you're a lesbian, pissed off at men and maybe the Agency makes you a prime candidate for being turned. It isn't so much that Chernovich wants you to work for him, he wants what you can get for him. Information."

"Why does that matter? Isn't it a form of discrimination?"

"*Of course it is! The CIA is not a socialism project!* You don't know the game they play! They don't give a shit about you; they only give a shit about what's in this agency, what's in your head, and they will do anything up to and including murder to find your weakness and exploit that weakness for their side. They claim we're the bad guys while they exploit you—your sexuality is the oldest blackmail leverage on the books. It's all to try to turn you against the agency and America. They will take whatever they can get and then walk over your rotten corpse thinking nothing of it. You do not know these people, but you can find out what they are up to or you can leave."

"Yes, Director McGee, I know the rules."

"Good. You can't go back to the office. Report to the off-site testing facility. You'll have to pass the polys just for this situation. Nazy can set it up." He turned to Miss Cunningham who nodded her assent.

"I suppose you have to let others know."

"It could be worse. This is serious business. I have to inform the IG and the USIC that TASCO has gone rogue."

McGee re-crossed his arms and thought, *Noble Savage. They have a gap in their intel, a SAP that the people they have hired know nothing about.* He didn't raise his voice. It was a teachable moment. "The charter members of the *Dark State* and *Dark Islam* know we have to polygraph anyone they pitch. It's an inexpensive form of detection. Our guys get pitched, our guys report it, and then they are pulled off the program for a while. That's one way the bad guys know we're making inroads on them. And when our guys get pulled from a program for a 'contact poly,' we can't let them back in until they are cleared."

"If you are freed and cleared, it's more of an imposition on your time than a termination for suspected illegal activity or espionage. I thank you for being upfront with me. Quit watching the crap from the networks and suspect everything you read from New York or Washington. Critical Race or Social Justice Theory is unmitigated bullshit. There are other sources of news. Our own *Early Bird*. These aren't easy times. But it's your choice."

Director McGee walked with Yassmin Deng to the awning. Nazy was on her BlackBerry setting up an impromptu contact polygraph. Without word or finale, Yassmin walked to her car. McGee and Nazy walked back inside for their next meeting. McGee slowed his pace for the high-heeled NCTC Director. He asked, "Did you hear?"

"I did. All of it. That's a first."

"I don't know if she can be saved. I'm afraid she's another one of the Kool-Aid drinkers who is late to the party and is probably a lost cause. As for TASCO, I'm not messing around with them. I need the IG to look at their contracts. By approaching Deng, they must be desperate. Your recommendation?"

Nazy said, "Cancel their contracts. They want intel, most likely *Noble Savage*. But there may be other SAPs. They…TASCO are everywhere in the IC. But there are others; former company people with their own companies. We can always bring back some retirees."

"I was thinking of the same thing. This is what happened to this place when Snowden cross-decked. It has to be *Noble Savage*. Suddenly everyone and their brother wants to know about that SAP. Cancel their contracts. Get legal to kill them. 'Convenience of the Government' is the best escape clause on the planet. There might be more to them than meets the eye, but I don't think so." *Why would Chernovich do that? Intel on Noble Savage is making more sense. That is simply bizarre.... Is someone trying to find out what the program is all about?* Then an epiphany, *Is Chernovich trying to find Duncan? Duncan investigated Chernovich when they were Marines. Is he trying to confirm Maverick is on the program?*

Nazy said, "We have probable cause. It will hurt us for a while until we can get others to take over the work they are doing, but this is not as bad as when Snowden defected. I'll second any vote if you get pushback from the principals."

McGee nodded at Nazy. *We have work to do.*

CHAPTER 33

May 13, 2018

Duncan Hunter sat in the cockpit of the Supermarine *Spitfire* and grinned at the old man who had just sold the seventy-five-year-old warbird to him. Of the 20,000 World War II *Spitfires* manufactured, only a handful were still in existence, survivors of the carnage that befell so many of the others. There wasn't another *Spitfire* anywhere that looked as good as the one Hunter was in. The attention to detail of the four-year restoration was eye watering; the aircraft was in better condition than the day it rolled off the production floor in 1943. The *Spitfire* was perfect, as good as anything Hunter's warbird restoration mechanics could've done in Texas. Authenticity was perfect down to the serial number "7A" emblazoned on the aft fuselage.

Hunter was becoming the *de facto* expert on acquiring, restoring, and flying WWII fighter aircraft and some post-war multi-engine airplanes, like the uber-rare Howard 500. The *Spitfire's* design had been ahead of its time with elliptical wings, stressed-skin aluminum body, supercharged Rolls Royce engine, and ultra-thin airfoil. In 1943 the fighter had maneuverability like no one had ever seen before.

The cockpit was a trip back in time. It was primitive by today's standards of glass cockpits and ergonomic control placement. Hunter's eyes dropped to the cockpit as the previous owner went through all the levers, indicators, switches, instruments, handles, knobs, levers, and dials. The next phase of instruction was how to start the Rolls Royce Merlin V12.

Hunter's antiquated cell phone buzzed in his shirt pocket. The numbers on the BlackBerry's tiny screen read 0000. Whatever code was transmitted on the cell carrier, he knew it to be the private office number of the Director of the Central Intelligence Agency. Hunter knitted his brows. *Bill doesn't make social calls*. Hunter exhaled gallons of British air, fished a Bluetooth earpiece out of his shirt pocket, and wedged it into his ear.

He wasn't annoyed at the intrusion, even though when Bill McGee called it wasn't to invite him to a State Dinner or an Office of Strategic Services (OSS) soiree of old spooks to give a medal to an old general from the intelligence community. Hunter excused himself and told the old man he had to take the call. As the old man carefully climbed off the wing, Hunter pressed the connect button and answered, "Captain, my captain. What can I do for you this fine day?"

There was a low-frequency hiss in his ear that suggested encryption technology was working. Bill McGee asked, "Where are you? Number two said you were in London?"

He replied, "At this second, I'm in the cockpit of a Supermarine *Spitfire*. I was just about to get checked out in it and go fly.... Five minutes and I wouldn't have been able to hear my BlackBerry. We're at the London Luton Airport between the university towns of Oxford and Cambridge, home to a few dirty lefty professors and hundreds of far-out leftists of the Karl Marx stripe who don't know how to use a toothbrush or take a shower. I understand big burly Karl is buried not too far from here. Rest assured, good sir, I won't be making a pilgrimage there unless it's to whiz on his grave."

The comments amused the CIA Director. He spoke into the speakerphone, "I know something about wanting to whiz on dead people, and it's not good form at any age. Do me a favor—don't go there." *I need you but things aren't time-sensitive. I can spend a little time with you. But not much.* "So...you bought a Submarine *Spitfire*? Talk to me!" It was the question you could ask of a best friend who lived on the edge of the quicksand of life and sometimes did things that were out of character. McGee knew the former fighter pilot had a thing for historical aircraft that could still snap his spine like a twig and could make him smile like a poor kid finding an old Schwinn *Stingray* in a barn. Now that Hunter had wealth, it was predictable what he would spend it on: watches and sports cars for family and friends, and World War II warbirds for himself. *His fighter pilot career was interrupted too soon, maybe this was his way to return to those glory days.*

Hunter said, "Yes, sir. I'll have you know your dad would love this bird. It'll look fantastic with the F-4U *Corsair* and the two-seat TP-51C *Mustang*. This one's fresh off a restoration. There are fewer than fifty airworthy *Spitfires,* and this one is the best of the lot, and the only one remaining that flew in the Battle of Normandy. As you know because you are a history buff, we're about a month away from the seventy-third anniversary of the Normandy Invasion. Kind of apropos, kind of a big deal in these parts as nostalgia fuels the warbird hobby. I was going flying…but, I have a sneaky feeling you have other plans."

A Submarine Spitfire! McGee sighed heavily. *My father was one of the original Tuskegee Airmen, an Army Air Corps P-51C Mustang pilot. A combat veteran. Dad would understand why Duncan collects warbirds. The old fighters were the sports cars of the air. Even at his age, he would leap at the chance to fly any of those old airplanes.*

Hunter's words brought a smile to the face of the CIA Director for a moment. McGee raised a serious eyebrow. *Old fighter pilots…. Dad killed Nazis by the score and Duncan kills terrorists when we find them.* They're not so different, but McGee wasn't an aviator and he had work to do. He said, "I need a *recovery….*"

Hunter should've known. *Not an extraction but a recovery.* He pursed his lips in a moment of pique. He understood the meaning of the CIA Director's four little words: *Rendition flight. Nasty work. They wouldn't use any of their aircraft, no….no executive travel transport; no Agency Gulfstream. There are too many Tailwatchers that scrutinize every move of Agency aircraft. No, this good deal was reserved for contractors. Mum's the word. No evidence. Hard to track and I'll make a little money. Not enough to begin to pay for the cars I bought on this trip and definitely not the Spitfire….this is more of a favor. I'll find some little way to pay him back.*

This rendition flight would most likely be like several previous ones. Someone on the FBI's Most Wanted Terrorist List had screwed up. Someone's suicide vest hadn't detonated as designed in an emergency, and as a consequence, a terrorist got himself captured by the CIA's National Clandestine Service Special Activities Division or DOD's Special Operations Command. Hunter envisioned that some high-profile terrorist, probably extracted from an al-Qaeda hellhole in the ground, or from an ISIS battlefield, or at the terminus of a Syrian tunnel complex—the latest hotspot on the War on Terror—was in American custody. Whoever it was, they would need a ride to their new home in the tropics.

Name and reputation at this point was immaterial. Someone important—a high value detainee or multiples—who the CIA deemed worthy of interrogating rather than eliminating, needed a ride to the place where U.S. forces would provide clean orange jumpsuits, three culturally sensitive meals a day, their very own *Qur'an*, and a private room at the specially built and isolated Camp Seven for "non-compliant" prisoners: America's terrorist holding complex at Guantanamo Bay, Cuba. GITMO as it was called in the parlance of the special operations warriors, the new residence for the worst of the worst terrorists that American forces captured on the battlefield in the Middle East.

Hunter unbuckled the seat's lap and shoulder straps and crawled out of the *Spitfire's* cockpit with a parachute strapped to his legs and back. "For you, good sir, I'm your guy. I brought the *four* so it's not an issue. I assume this is a rush." The number *four* indicated he had flown an older Gulfstream G-IVSP to England and not the newer G-550 that he had taken from a terrorist he had killed years earlier. The G-IVSP jet was sterile, configured with two seats to accommodate captured terrorists strapped to stretchers. Like a Boy Scout, Hunter was always prepared.

McGee had barked at the CIA underlings who had tossed "a dead monkey" onto his desk, their problem of not being able to acquire immediate transportation for captured prisoners. His solution was this phone call. "That's why I called you." Nazy Cunningham sat in a sideboard chair with legs crossed. As she bounced her black Valentino-clad foot, she knew if she didn't get the chance to talk to Duncan, she would see him in a few days. She sighed in anticipation of their reunion.

Standing on the *Spitfire's* wing, Hunter unbuckled the leg and chest fittings and slipped out of the parachute harness. He handed it to the former owner of the airworthy museum piece.

There was a sense of urgency in McGee's Barry White voice. "When you're airborne, I'll have number two call and give you the details." *Number two* meant his wife, not her position at the CIA where she was technically the number three person.

Hunter tried to calculate how much time he had. Could he take the *Spitfire* for a spin around the English countryside? In reality he knew he would be too distracted, like someone who is heads-down and texting while tumbling into a fountain. McGee continued, "It takes three days for contracting to find a jet, and you're already halfway there. You're quick. And with you, I get a discount. Your *Spitfire* will wait for you. I assume you have sufficient help."

Hunter looked at his baffled daughter and said, "10-4. Number three is here. I took her for the best pizza in Italy. I bought a Ferrari *Daytona* 365 GTS in Vienna and a BMW 507 in Berlin. There are few things better than a good *kaffeeklatsch* with my little girl. She has a thing for fast cars like her old man."

Upon hearing "...my little girl," Kelly Horne now understood with whom her father was talking.

McGee presumed the quixotic Hunter was making up for time lost as a father. *I suppose when he has some down time and can't take Nazy to Europe for dinner or shopping, he takes the daughter? Of course cars and watches are in the mix.* He probed a little. "You collecting cars or watches for your retirement or something? She is with you, but shouldn't she be here working?" McGee then asked, "Is she on annual leave?" McGee allowed an indecorous thought, *Nazy and Kelly were strong women, comfortable being on their own, but Duncan did spoil them. And me, I suppose. We are teammates.*

"Call it mentoring." Hunter looked off into space. A few thousand miles separated him and the CIA Director, who nodded at Nazy Cunningham, who was acting Director of Operations.

Nazy's smile telegraphed, *Of course Duncan will do it. He'll do anything for you, if he can. Was there any doubt, Bill?*

The CIA Director continued, "Of course you're...*mentoring*. I'm always the last to know these things. And just so you know, your boy Eastwood has made me run a little late."

"I'll have a word with him, Director McGee. He's correctable." Hunter grinned at the thought.

I bet you will. "Maverick, something funny also happened that only you can appreciate. You mentioned a *Daytona.* I was up on Capitol Hill, and before I made my remarks, a senator made a crack about my watch." Nazy unconsciously raised her eyebrows and listened to the speakerphone conversation with interest. She recalled the episode with the director at Congress but hadn't been close enough to hear that conversation.

"Your Daytona?" Solid gold, green dial, cool watch. One of Rolex's latest. Hunter had given McGee the watch when he became the Director of the CIA. The Ferrari *Daytona* was named after the race track at Daytona Beach, Florida and the Rolex *Daytona* became synonymous with the actor and race car driver Paul Newman.

"Yeah. When I held it up, all the Republicans around me held up their wrists. Every one of them had Rolexes. *Submariners,* Chronometers; colorful and distinct, like The Hulk Hogan, The Kermit, the *GMT Masters* with the bezels in the black and gray Batman colors, the colors of Pepsi and Coke, and Root Beer. Not as nice as mine but still severe bling for men. The Dems, I thought they would be proud of their rubber watches, those idiot-bit things, Apple-core watches, or some slim effeminate thing you could get at Tiffany's." Nazy held up her hand to reveal an extraordinary three-diamond wedding ring and a gold Rolex Ladies *President* on her wrist. McGee nodded approval of the other proud Rolex owner. His cost more; a lot of gold and extra links were needed to strap the *Daytona* Cosmograph onto the wrist of the big man.

The amusing anecdote inspired chuckles at the childish nonsensical rabbit-hole contest between Rolexes and colorful rubber watches. *I could be flying a Spitfire and you're talking about lefties and liberals and their asinine excuses they call watches? Bill McGee, you have too much time on your hands!* He shook his head before crouching on the wing and sliding off.

Hunter glanced at the antique *Daytona* on his wrist, sparkling in the sunlight, but it wasn't the time or place to be discussing watches. Hunter sucked air, changed subjects, and said, "I'm sorry I missed your speech in Congress and Eastwood's interview. I've been busy."

McGee had his own take on the event at the Senate. "The Democrats left their dress whites and hoods at home."

Hunter understood the coded language. The senators, the party of the Klu Klux Klan, had left their bed sheets in their closet. "Disgusting, huh? Don't they know who you are?"

"They think I'm the one with the mental disorder. They've been that way since rocks were fresh off the shelf."

"And you can't get rid of them, kind of like herpes. You better watch your back, or you'll find yourself rolled up in a rug in Fort Marcy Park."

McGee laughed into the telephone. "Are you really buying a *Spitfire?*"

"Yes, sir. I really was actually within seconds of cranking up a Merlin V12. Supercharged. 2,000 horsepower. I had visions flying low-level over some canals and chasing some English Longhorns, Ayrshires, Galloway Belteds, or if I could find some, harassing an ancient Auroch with horns like football goalposts. Your timing sucks, good sir. But, as you know, work before pleasure. I'm on the way."

"I know you can make up some time with the tailwinds. Thank you, good sir. See you soon. Bullfrog out!"

The hissing in Hunter's ear stopped. He double-checked to see that the line was dead and it was. No sympathy from the boss. No more ridiculous discussions on watches—no, *cosmographs* was the proper term when discussing Rolex *Daytonas. Submariners* were *chronometers;* TAG Heuers and Breitlings were chronographs. He didn't tell McGee of the other cars he had bought on his shopping trip, an old Aston Martin 3000 and a Jaguar XK 150S. All the cars were "red on black," red leather interiors on black paint.

He attended a Sotheby's auction in London for several collectable timepieces; one, the Nazi's Chief of the Abwehr, the head of the military intelligence service, Admiral Wilhelm Canaris' Tudor wristwatch. The others, as expected, Hunter was outbid on a pair of very rare and pristine Minerva chronographs, a 51mm pocketwatch and the other a 50mm mono-pusher wristwatch without the image of the Luftwaffe's ME-109 on the dial. The Minervas were the finest examples of Nazi aviators' timepieces to have survived World War II.

The auctioneer claimed that the Minerva mono-pusher wristwatch—minus the ME-109 image—had been given to Charles Lindbergh in 1936 as a gift by the Nazi Minister of Aviation, Herman Goering. What got Hunter's attention wasn't that the Minerva hadn't been seen since it was presented to Lindbergh, but that it was purchased at *No Reserve* by the private attorney of one of Europe's most eccentric billionaires, the octogenarian Rho Schwartz Scorpii. Hunter learned much from the event primarily that when billionaires started collecting watches of famous aviators, his hobby was probably at an end.

Duncan was disappointed that there had been no comments from his wife; she surely had to be in McGee's office. She usually was when the Director called. *She said she had been outrageously busy and didn't have the time for a little pizza and a romantic nighttime gondola ride. Take Kelly. A little father-daughter trip. That girl is so busy. Nazy called another one; I never saw this coming. I wouldn't have been able to do a rendition with her; I needed Kelly.* As he placed the BlackBerry in his pocket, he contemplated some combinations of the situation, *I'm sure she's getting close to calling it quits too. One of these days when I say let's go get some pizza she'll say "ok" and not "I really am too busy, take Kelly."*

No time for indignation. No recriminations that he didn't get to talk to his wife, but he would see her soon after delivering the "package" to Cuba and *sanitization.* As for not being able to fly the *Spitfire,* Hunter said to his daughter, "I hate it when the boss gets between me and my love life. We have work to do."

The youthful Kelly was awkwardly out of place with antique aircraft and the old men who flew and restored them. And she was puzzled with the one-sided conversation. *Work? From here? What love life – with an airplane?*

Hunter was burning daylight. He whipped out an American Express Card and told his daughter with all seriousness, "I need you to run into town and buy snacks and drinks for a very long road trip. I don't know how long it might be before we can get a real meal. Buy disinfecting wipes, three or four containers, and buy enough food so that we can feed the homeless in Washington for a month with the leftovers. And put everything in separate plastic bags."

After Kelly ran off like an unsupervised nine-year-old with a $100 bill, Duncan found the former owner of the *Spitfire* and asked him to walk with him. The old man agreed to Hunter's business proposition and agreed to move the aircraft to the United States after the anniversary of the Normandy Invasion.

CHAPTER 34

May 13, 2018

Flying to Amman required an anfractuous route. Once they busted out of Great Britain and got above the clouds, "on-top," Hunter flew lower and lower until he had the Gulfstream wings-level, just over the constantly shifting undercast where, at almost 600 mph and with a gentle tailwind, the jet was more like a rocket. Ever mindful of the time they needed to arrive, he negotiated the G-IVSP around, into and out of clouds over the Atlantic. He was playing. Kelly realized her father was acting like a big kid, a big rich kid with enviable manly toys that he rarely had time to enjoy.

When the cloud deck no longer supported his foray of fun, he explained the odd flight route they would be taking; a left sweeping turn that would take them over, technically, "through" the Straits of Gibraltar, then out over the Mediterranean Sea high enough to make no contrails before their approach into Jordan, which required overflying Israel. "For a mission like this, it isn't wise to fly directly over Europe. Every country has their own air traffic control, and we don't want to identify ourselves in every airspace we enter or depart. We don't want anyone knowing where we've been or where we're going. No transmission of N-numbers, and we don't make any spurious radio calls. We want to avoid all *Tailwatchers*. The last I heard, Israel and Jordan deported all the known *Tailwatchers* who set up shop near their airports."

To pass some time, Kelly peppered her father with questions, beginning with, "What's the deal with '*chemtrails*?'"

Hunter said, "They're the fantasy of partisan simpletons who want to think the government is poisoning Americans, that chemicals are clandestinely added to jet fuel so when a jet is conning at altitude, leaving contrails, they think they are *chemtrails*. It's another ridiculous attempt of the left to ban petroleum."

"It's not like adding a date-rape drug to a cocktail to knock a woman out. Now, there are uniquely equipped jets that do release an infinitesimal amount of, say, a radioactive isotope for another very specific jet carrying sensors. All part of nuclear weapons treaties. They want to see if they can detect the specific isotope of a thermonuclear blast at parts per million or billion. The X-ray machines at airports and the mailroom at your place do the same thing using ultraviolet lasers as LIDARs to detect explosives and kill spores like anthrax. The liberal snowflakes who embrace chemtrails have no scientific background and no functioning brain cells. I'm certain their brains have been fried from the marijuana and mushrooms."

"What about global warming? Ed Snowden said that the government doesn't have space aliens in a hangar in Nevada and chemtrails are just contrails for, as you said, liberal snowflakes in overdrive, but that global warming is real."

"Michael Crichton summed global warming up by saying, 'This is not the way science is done, it's the way products are sold.'"

"You'll learn that anything the leftist media put into print or on television is a hoax. For over a hundred years the loony left has been trying to discredit the wealth that naturally occurring petroleum brings to the world. Millions and billions of dollars oozed from the ground while they were too busy gazing at the detritus in their navels to notice. Now they just want to steal it."

"Global warming is a game the left plays to delegitimize the established energy sector, because they were boxed out of what they call 'fossil fuels.' It is as simple as that. They tout manufactured predetermined studies they buy with government funding, studies by unscientific people the leftist media says are reputable experts on the climate. They've predicted Armageddon for a hundred years. They made a few inroads to respectability when the *Concorde* came out, and the American aircraft industry looked to produce their own supersonic transports. People who had liberal arts degrees in unicorn flatulence asserted those jets would destroy the ozone in the atmosphere, and we would all die. These people were 'heard' because of the noise they made. When they got violent, suddenly the rules changed. The left paid attention; crying is only good for nursing babies to get what they want. If you're a liberal and you want something, blow it up or steal it or shout from the rooftop that is it bad for you, and give me your money so I can fix it for you. And there is nothing worse than an indignant loony leftist stomping his or her feet when they're trying to steal your stuff or other people's money."

"It's like when law school professors tell their students, 'If you have the law on your side, pound the law. If you have the facts on your side, pound the facts. If you have neither the law nor the facts on your side, pound the table.' Liberals know they don't have the science on their side—so they make it up. Liberals know they don't have the facts on their side—so they skew them to fit their narrative. But liberals also know how to pound the table to get their way. They protest and threaten and intimidate. If it was real science, people could work on a technical solution, but their solution is for you to give them money. It's a scam and mass hysteria and a form of brainwashing."

Kelly asked, "The *Concorde*?"

"The *Concorde*, that was in the late 1960s. Today, it's just politics. The left has done a good job of convincing uneducated Americans that oil is bad, and they have won some battles in liberal states where they have killed off the oil, coal, and gas industries and fractionally replaced the state's energy needs with highly subsidized windmills and solar panels. Maybe one day they will face reality and sober up, but until that happens.... Look, the left has never been interested in anyone's health, or well-being, or esurient behavior. It has always been about how much they can take from you by taxing your wealth as a means to deprive you of your freedom."

"When they take your money, you become their slave. You can see this at work in liberal states where people pay so much more for gas and energy than people living in, say, Texas. Under the pretext that they're saving the world and the environment, they've been able to enrich themselves with exorbitant government subsidized power-generating equipment, while the rest of the world just pumps it out of the ground at the lowest market price. They are not interested in the environment."

Hunter concluded, "But when you have a clearance, they want to take your life. They want what's in your head. Information has value and secrets are the most valuable information of all. When they have taken your life, they discard you like yesterday's trash. If you could look at the issue strategically and not tactically, you would see that this old engineer with a PhD in economics knows a few more things than the chemtrail crowd or the clowns on television—they should be dressed in Barnum and Bailey and not Brooks Brothers."

• • •

Jordan didn't require the runway lights-off, spiral approach to land in Afghanistan and Iraq. Kelly Horne flew the approach and landed the business jet perfectly at Muwaffaq Salti Air Base. Several dozen Royal Jordanian Air Force (RJAF) F-16s, a dozen U.S. Air Force MQ-9 Reapers, and Air Force Special Operations Command (AFSOC) C-130s were visible in the light of stationary and portable floodlights. Hundreds of men and women from the U.S. Air Force and the RJAF were working on their aircraft in maintenance shops in RJAF hangars.

Ground controllers told Kelly where to turn and where to taxi the Gulfstream. She stopped and shutdown the jet in front of an open hangar. A refueling truck, a panel truck, and a few cars waited outside the structure. Two men attached a tow bar to the Gulfstream's nose wheel and pulled the G-IVSP inside. The panel truck also moved inside the hangar as the hangar doors were closed by electric motor. When the doors were fully closed and the aircraft came to a stop, Duncan Hunter opened the aircraft's cabin door and lowered the airstairs. Kelly left to find a girl's room. Duncan told her to binge eat when she returned because she might not want to eat after the "packages" arrived.

At the bottom of the airstairs Hunter met two CIA men on a spotless white painted floor and shook their hands without introductions. One said, "We'll get them aboard. We'll have two officers who'll accompany you." No other communications were exchanged although a box of "N100" particulate respirators were offered and accepted. According to the carton, the medical-grade, maximum-filtration carbon filters trapped and blocked 99.97 percent of bacteria and viruses. This told Hunter that the detainees were likely a virulent odious bunch who could carry the terrorist's biological trifecta: plague, tuberculosis, smallpox. Or, maybe even a coronavirus.

The names of the captives on stretchers wrapped in plastic like a mail-order mattresses weren't revealed, and it didn't matter. Hunter wasn't interested in the least. He ran to the nearest toilet and when he returned, he donned the N100, walked around the jet with a flashlight, inspecting the aircraft's landing gear, flight controls, and engines for the next flight. Conducting the loading of the prisoners in a closed hangar was to prevent any potential *Tailwatcher* with a telephoto lens from identifying the Gulfstream as a *de facto* rendition aircraft.

As in previous rendition flights Hunter had made for the CIA, the terrorists had been fully "processed," stuffed with laxatives to empty their bowels before flight. It had taken the Agency a couple of years to perfect the transportation of uncooperative captured terrorists who did whatever they could to make it as uncomfortable as possible for the intelligence officers accompanying them for the fourteen hour flight. They were immobilized in black body bags, earplugs were placed in their ear canals, mouth ball gags wouldn't allow them to speak or spit, they wore diapers and were heavily sedated. The terrorists could still breathe easily, even with black masks over their eyes which prevented the detainees from recognizing an American intelligence officer. The Agency men wore respirators throughout the flight to prevent aerosolized tuberculosis bacteria (TB) and other pathogens from being transmitted from a detainee.

Kelly Horne had bought a chuck wagon-load of packaged foods and cases of bottled water for six people. Now with diseased detainees aboard, she wasn't sure if it was safe to break the form-fitted seal of the N100 in order to eat or drink anything. Her father was right about putting everything in bags and she was glad that she had. Rendition flights were nasty work on so many levels.

Hunter monitored the refueling operation with an N100 strapped to his face. As soon as the aircraft was loaded with a maximum fuel load, he buttoned up the refueling panel. He watched the last detainee being loaded aboard. It took four people to manhandle a terrorist shrink-wrapped on a stretcher through the aircraft's cabin door. He shook hands with the men who loaded the Islamists aboard his aircraft. The Agency officer overseeing the operation slipped a coin into Hunter's hand. Global Response Team. *Those boys and their coins!* He thanked the intel officer, adjusted his mask for better comfort, ran up the airstairs, and closed the door behind him.

He glanced at three stretchers and the two men in chairs with their N100s. He gave them a "thumbs up" and a questioning look with raised eyebrows to ask if they were ready to go. Thumbs up were returned. Hunter entered the cockpit and closed the door. He gave Kelly the challenge coin and told her to "…wipe it down."

This cargo of detainees could have represented the handful of terrorists Duncan Hunter hadn't been able to find and kill at night with his quiet airplane. He hadn't been able to get them all, but he had taken as many as possible off the battlefield and sent them to a place other than Paradise. Hunter felt no remorse for the world's top 200 "celebrity" terrorists, the ones who obnoxiously preened in front of an Al Jazeera camera as they chopped off the head of an infidel or a Christian, or burned an enemy Muslim pilot alive.

Kelly was masked and her eyes looked a bit forlorn. The rendition flight was a new experience for her. She wasn't sure if this was the stuff she had signed up for, if she was the right person for this type of job. She had flown jet trainers in the Air Force and had worn a positive pressure oxygen mask that provided life sustaining aviation breathing oxygen (ABO) at 99 and 44/100 percent purity. Now she wore the N100 particulate respirator to prevent airborne diseases from entering her lungs. *I must've missed this part of the brief. But my father brought me along and I trust him implicitly. Nothing bad will happen…to us, to me.*

Hunter showed Kelly how to clean their aircraft O2 masks and transition from N100s to the aircraft's ABO.

The hangar was darkened before the doors were opened. The same crew who pulled the Gulfstream into the hangar pushed the jet outside and turned it 90° so the nose wheels straddled the taxi line. Once the tow bar was uncoupled from the nose wheels, Hunter started the auxiliary power unit and engines.

He flew the published departure over Israel, turning west once they were over the Mediterranean Sea. Hunter set a westerly heading back through the Straits of Gibraltar. Once over the Atlantic, he set a course for Ireland. Hunter mentioned to Kelly, "During the day when you're over the Med you can see all around you except to the south. Winds from the Sahara Desert blow so much dust that it looks like there is a wall of sand that extends from the surface to about 35,000 feet over the northern part of Africa."

Duncan and Kelly took turns sleeping and flying, where "flying" was monitoring the autopilot. Refueling in Ireland was uneventful; Hunter returned to his N100 and supervised the refueling operation outside and ensured their fresh O2 bottles were secure in their mounts and the regulators were opened for use. It wouldn't have been pleasant to find that no oxygen flowed through the O2 masks after they were airborne. Based on the forecasted winds, they waited aboard the jet until Hunter was assured they would make a night landing at Guantanamo Bay, Cuba.

It took longer to refuel the Gulfstream than to offload the Agency's cargo at their destination. It would likely be months before the names of the latest residents of Club GITMO were released to the public.

As Hunter brought the aircraft to a stop in front of an unmarked hangar at the Manassas Regional Airport, Kelly admitted that she was totally exhausted and would probably sleep for two days. Crawling out of the jet after almost a 50-hour operation, the old man was stiff and the athletic, redhead, and freckled daughter was spent, but there was still work to do.

After deplaning they entered separate locker rooms with industrial showers designed for decontamination. Still wearing their N100s they stripped off their clothes and showered with soaps designed to kill any of the superbugs, such as TB and methicillin-resistant staphylococcus, and viruses and bacteria. Their clothes and particulate respirators went into medical waste hazardous materials bags to be burned.

The servicing crew wore Tyvek® HAZMAT suits and were specially trained for sterilizing the interior of the rendition aircraft. They weren't allowed on board until after a pair of four-rotor drones with dozens of C-band UV LEDs mounted above, below, and along the four corners of the square flying machine were flown aboard the jet, switched on, and left to do their work after the crew closed the door. The pancake griddle-shaped drones flew to every corner of the jet. Pulsed xenon ultraviolet light LEDs flooded the cockpit and cabin with enough C-band UV to kill instantly any bacteria and viruses that may have become attached to the most remote or hidden nook or cranny of the interior.

Specifically-designed UV-C lamps which had been strategically mounted in the aircraft ducting were activated to immediately kill viruses and pathogens that entered the aircraft air conditioning system but were not stopped by HEPA filters. When the UV-C system was switched on, high-voltage electricity passed through the LEDs and released a spectrum of UV light that altered the DNA of bacteria, viruses, and microscopic organisms and unlike the UV-B systems, killed them instantly.

Once the flying machines returned to their starting position at the aircraft's door like a robotic home vacuum, a masked technician opened the cockpit door, recovered the inactive flying robots, placed a tracked robot into the aircraft, and closed the aircraft's door again. The tiny autonomous tracked vehicle sensed the center aisle of the aircraft and slowly made its way to the back of the aircraft releasing an aerosol spray to saturate the interior with a gaseous insecticide used to kill any fleas, ticks or mosquitoes that may have hitched a ride on a Navy SEAL or a detainee and burrowed into the carpet or crease in the seat cushions. After a few minutes, an anti-bacterial spray, the same aerosol flight attendants release in aircraft cabins when transiting African countries, filled the cabin and cockpit.

After an hour, a technician opened the Gulfstream's door and removed the robot which had also returned to its starting place at the cabin door. Once the flight crew had left the "sterile" side of the locker room, the technician took the tracked vehicle and the flying machines and turned them loose on the locker rooms, completing the sterilization process.

Several other men went to work servicing the Gulfstream. It was refueled and both engines received an engine oil check via a military-grade, spectrometric oil analysis system. All tire pressures were checked and topped off with nitrogen. Before being towed to a stand-alone corporate jet hangar, the aircraft's exterior was washed, the interior's carpets were shampooed, and the leather seats were treated and wiped down.

The exhausted duo, father and daughter, freshly scrubbed and showered, emerged from their respective locker rooms and waited inside the business office for a ride to the nearest place to sleep.

CHAPTER 35

May 16, 2018

Heavy fog from the coast rolled across the eastern quadrant of the airport in waves, shutting the airport down. It was just as well; the last jet scheduled in was safe on deck and would not depart soon.

Nazy Cunningham met the *knackered* pilots as they stumbled out of the corporate hangar each pulling black commercial pilot roll-aboards. Duncan also lugged a leather flight bag full of maps and international approach plates, his genetically engineered spider-silk body armor, and a Colt Python .357 magnum revolver. An Agency driver helped with their baggage as Nazy ushered Hunter and Kelly into the armored Suburban. Kelly was dropped off at the house in Maryland that she and Nazy shared, while Duncan and Nazy were deposited at the front door of the JW Marriott in downtown Washington, D.C. Kelly got to sleep in her bed; Nazy and Duncan commandeered the Presidential Suite.

Before the sun came up the next morning, Nazy slipped out of bed, showered, and left her sleeping husband in a pile of untucked sheets. An Agency limo picked her up, and she was at her desk before seven. She hadn't been in the office for a few minutes when Director McGee called a meeting of the principals and the deputies. The topic was the three terrorists recently extracted from Jordan, however, McGee had something for her ears only.

When she entered his office, McGee was blunt. "You know Duncan transported Hamsi Fareed al-Amirikiu and Toraluddin Haqqani to Guantanamo last night."

Nazy shook her hair and said, "Two of the four *Beatles* of terrorism. The real prize is the missing brother of the Haqqani terrorist network. The Islamic State's 'intelligence minister.'"

McGee asked, "What else do you know?"

Nazy repeated what she had seen in the President's Daily Brief. "We know a little of al-Amirikiu and his association with President Mazibuike. The Haqqani Network was one of the most favored CIA-funded anti-Soviet guerrilla groups in the 1980s and 90s. They were charter members of *Dark Islam*. We have a few dispatches; basically Toraluddin Haqqani grew up with a mother who carried weapons and ammunition for the Muslim Brotherhood, while his father organized Brotherhood rallies in Egypt and advised Brotherhood leaders."

Nazy filled in the man's history. "In 1995, when Hosni Mubarak escaped an assassination attempt in Ethiopia that was engineered by the Muslim Brotherhood, the Egyptian president cracked down on all known members of the Muslim Brotherhood in Egypt. Some Haqqani family members fled to the United States, some went to college, and the father became an interface between the Agency and the Afghan resistance to the Soviets. The CIA finally got wind of the treachery of the Haqqanis, really more of an undercover offshoot of the Muslim Brotherhood, and terminated their relationship."

McGee added, "I remember Mazibuike wouldn't designate the Haqqani Network as a terrorist organization and thought that was odd back then. One of President Hernandez's first actions was to ban the Haqqanis, and the male members of the family who weren't in the U.S. were placed on the President's *Disposition Matrix*."

Nazy said, "I may be mistaken, but all the Haqqanis in America had been deported for various immigration issues. The Haqqanis supposedly settled in Jordan and-or Syria and were some of the few who escaped the dragnet."

She continued. "The father led the group, but he is dead. That left the mother and the brother and the sons. After they left the U.S. we looked for Toraluddin Haqqani in Afghanistan, but he was in Syria. When he popped up on the grid a few years ago, he vowed to never be taken alive. He always wore a suicide vest."

McGee said, "So, we have two of the four *Beatles*, Toraluddin Haqqani and Hamsi Fareed al-Amirikiu—one of Mazibuike's buddies who had actually been photographed in the Oval Office—and one of Haqqani's wives." McGee paused. "Apparently one of the other wives attempted to kill her before she said that she was an American."

"That's extremely odd." Nazy had never heard of such a thing. *Why would she do that? That makes no sense....*

McGee interrupted her train of thought and unconsciously nodded. "The wife begged not to be killed, *in English,* and thanked the American soldiers who rescued her. *In English.* No one had seen or had heard of one of these situations before." He consulted a paper and said, "Special Forces used a *Growler* on a dog. Toraluddin Haqqani wore a suicide vest, and the *Growler* did its job, killing the signal to detonate the vest while the canine took him down."

Nazy said, "That's fantastic. I'm sure SOCOM is grateful you offered them the technology."

If you only knew! "A *Growler* can stop a lot of signals."

She sighed a bit. Her British upbringing would sometimes get in the way. She was learning the American terms and idioms quickly, but every so often an American word would be uttered whose British counterpart had a different meaning. *They don't know a Growler in England is a vulgar term for female genitals covered in pubic hair.* She told herself she wouldn't say anything.

McGee smiled as if he had a secret, which he did. "So, the rest of the Haqqani story is that the wife said she was grateful and appreciative of being rescued. She has plenty to talk about, but she said she would only talk to...*Duncan Hunter.*"

CHAPTER 36

May 16, 2018

The sound of her husband's name in the utterances of a terrorist's wife made no sense. It had to be a mistake. *It's not possible....* Nazy sat down; her green eyes never left McGee's cold dark eyes as he continued. "Apparently Duncan knew her from the Marine Corps. We don't know how she wound up in Syria married to Toraluddin Haqqani, but we'll know soon enough. She's about twenty years younger than Duncan. And Duncan retired from the Marine Corps about 25 years ago. We've asked for her service record book."

Nazy was suddenly concerned and asked, "What are you going to do?" She smoothed her dress as she crossed her legs.

"First, I don't want to mention this woman's details. We need to establish her bona fides; see if she is really who she says she is. Duncan will know if she's the real deal."

"How is that even possible?" Her British accent was enhanced when she was stressed.

McGee reminded her that in one of Demetrius Eastwood's television specials, "Remember, an unnamed man in black, your Duncan, singlehandedly rescued over 300 women and girls from an underground harem in the United Arab Emirates. Girls who had been missing for years. They were mostly pubescent girls and juveniles, and most of them were blonde."

Nazy remembered that after extracting the women from their underground prison, Duncan had commandeered one of the emir's yachts and transported the women to a U.S. aircraft carrier plying the waters of the Persian Gulf. The President of the United States declared that the UAE's clandestine sex trade was coming to an immediate and ignominious end.

The CIA Director added, "And there was the night where Duncan and I rescued Kelly and a Nigerian airliner full of people. It's what we did during those days." For a moment, McGee relived the moment when Hunter hadn't perfected the nighttime parachuting skills to make the spine of the jumbo airliner and had crashed short of his intended landing target. McGee, the master parachutist, was there to rescue Hunter by snagging his parachute and hand-over-hand, dead-hauling Duncan to the top of the airplane.

Nazy nodded absentmindedly. She was trying to resolve how Duncan could know the wife of an Islamic terrorist. The NCTC Director knew the FBI had created a missing women task force; was this woman one of those? She was reminded that the FBI woman who headed that department also knew Duncan Hunter from his days at the Naval War College. In her best British, Nazy Cunningham said, "My husband has a disconcerting way of knowing women I think he should not know. This is another one." She crossed her legs and her shoe was getting a workout, bouncing around in the air.

Impishly, the CIA Director said, "Well, he *is* your husband. He can't help it that he's a chick magnet. Frankly, I don't know what you see in him. You know the Navy put him back together with all sorts of hardware. I don't think they would even let him on a commercial jet now. I'm certain the magnetometer would explode or go gonzo like a Reno slot machine that had hit the jackpot."

Nazy laughed. She was initially a little disappointed with McGee for impugning Duncan, but then she realized her boss was trying to be funny. Duncan would have laughed as well. When her men—Duncan and McGee—got together they could be brutal to one another. She was about to say something when McGee laughed. Then they both laughed. Humor didn't come easy in the USIC where death and mayhem lurked around every corner. Nazy wiped a tear from her eye; McGee sighed like an overworked fireman at a three-alarm fire. Laughing with a woman was therapeutic.

McGee could tell Duncan was in town. Any other time, Nazy would be all business. To deliver the PDB, she would wear a silk blouse under a black business suit from one of the designer houses, but when Hunter was in town Nazy was ebullient and vivacious and always wore a dress and fashionable heels. She wore an expensive black and white Valentino giraffe-print dress that hid her girls sufficiently. She had always looked mesmerizing, but age, the toil on her from attempted assassinations, and the pressure cooker of being an Agency executive was having an effect. Her formerly unlined face now sported tiny creases at the corners of her eyes, and there were traces of gray in her nearly floor-length hair. McGee asked, "You want to call him?"

She scrunched up a porcelain face. The ace intelligence executive had returned. She said in a natural Newcastle Geordie dialect, "It's not a good thing for a wife to request her husband come to the office to help interrogate one of his old girlfriends."

Suddenly wide-eyed, McGee asked incredulously, "You think she was one of his girlfriends?" He did the mental math in his head. He couldn't believe Hunter would've had a fling with a troop in uniform, especially a woman who was half his age. The Marines were strict about fraternization. But then again, there could be more to the story. McGee acquiesced, "I'll call him."

Nazy said, "I'll arrange for a car to pick him up," and she left the office. Her dress flowed like waves in the wind; her leopard-print Louboutins left crush marks in the office carpeting.

She might be pissed! McGee's eyes stayed glued on shapely legs and delicate ankles for entirely too long. His call went through just as his secretary buzzed and reminded him of his meeting.

• • •

He didn't have to wait long. Hunter had an unimpeded view of Nazy's legs. They were polished sculptures in motion, as if from the mind of Michelangelo and not the rough hands of Rodin. Her hair was pulled behind in a ponytail; it swayed in a sinusoidal wave as she and McGee walked from the Director's elevator toward the cafeteria. Her walk and poise radiated her delicately sensual presence and physical grace. Hunter grinned as he always did when he was treated to watching his wife move with the confidence of a jaguar walking through a rainforest, *Oh baby, you're soooo good looking. How does anyone in this place get any work done?*

Her perfume arrived before she did; *Cinnabar* had its own bow wave and washed over olfactory senses that had been abused and assaulted by aromas from the greasy spoon. Hunter had images of Cinnabons fresh from the oven whenever his wife entered a room. Hunter inhaled every free molecule of *cinnamomum verum* and told Nazy, "Miss Cunningham, I heard you were the most beautiful woman to ever grace the walls of this fine institution, but I now see that that assessment is a gross underestimation. I know that it's entirely inappropriate and worthy of dismissal to make comments on a woman's looks. But I have to say, that's an exquisite dress, and you look like a million dollars!" Then he gentlemanly held the chair for her. She appreciated the attention. As she often did when taking a seat, she automatically bundled her hair into loose knots, smoothed her dress after she sat down, and crossed her ankles under her chair. Nazy repositioned the oversized glasses on her nose; she crossed her hands under her chin and beamed; she was thrilled to have Duncan home. It had been nearly two months; two long months.

When Director McGee sat down with his food Hunter asked, "How's your Muslim problem? It seems like the Muslim Brotherhood destroyed the FBI, and the media think you are next in the rotation." Hunter was rarely politically correct; he refused to play silly liberal games with halfwits.

McGee didn't let the direct question interrupt him. "We missed you while you were dead. But to answer your question, Nazy is on it, and I think we're doing well." *God, I miss the good old days of tromping through the jungles and killing the enemies of America! Meetings and paperwork suck!*

Hunter admired the way the boss delivered a line with *élan*. Thirty-five years of snapping at mouthy arrogant SEALs who relished giving the verbal finger to establishment naval officers had made McGee a master of the retort. He had heard them all; the good, the bad, and the ugly, but those were only shared in impolite company. Hunter knew Bill respected and treasured being the CIA Director, but he had made his reputation in the field, and now that he was confined to a desk he missed operational work. Personnel issues made him grumpy. *But he isn't really grumpy today….*

McGee was jealous of Hunter's work "outside" but couldn't say anything; someone had to be the boss. He said, "But it's coming along. Nazy seems to think we're almost there, that we're probably bad-guy free at headquarters, finally. I'm afraid Greg should have rooted them out, and the Chinese too but I understand why he didn't do it."

It was unusual for McGee to criticize the other member of their quartet, even softly and tangentially, the former CIA Director and Hunter's other long-time business partner, the man who took the obsolete YO-3A from a concept on the back of a napkin to an operational CIA platform, Greg Lynche. The *Grinch.*

Maverick and Miss Cunningham, with *Bullfrog* and *Grinch* had formed one of the closest relationships possible, and close relationships were rare in the intelligence business because one really didn't know who could be trusted. Trust came with limits, qualifiers, background investigations, top secret clearances, access and need to know, and a successful polygraph "as needed" which validated a person's motive for working "in the business." The vast majority of Agency people performed the essential jobs they were assigned. However, there were some very active people who passed through the torpedo nets of single scope background investigations and received security clearances in order to achieve a goal—remove information from the building and give it to someone not authorized to have it. Those fell into three categories: those who stole secrets for ideology, those people who stole secrets for profit, and those who were forced to make a choice—steal secrets or be exposed. 99.999% of the employees of the CIA were patriots. No other organization in the Federal government could boast of such loyalty and dedication.

The Soviets had been masters at identifying potential blackmail targets, primarily dull homosexual men and a few others with modest or restrained sexual identity disorders. Some Agency intelligence officers would rather steal national secrets than risk exposure or lose their position by self-identifying that they had been pitched. The suicide rate for those intelligence agents, ones with personality and sexual identity disorders, those who fell between the covers of the *Diagnostic and Statistics Manual for Mental Disorders,* was astronomical.

The old KGB and the current band of communists didn't care about any American's secret love life or sexual deviancy, they were only interested in using the leverage necessary to get an intelligence officer to commit treason. If that meant exposing a few flaming homosexuals or closet transvestites, then so be it. If they killed themselves, the communists would simply move on to the next blackmail target in the rotation. The Soviets and the Russians who followed them had a primary mission to perform: Infiltrate the U.S. Intelligence Community by *whatever means necessary* and steal America's secrets. *Whatever means necessary* meant there would be a trail of broken hearts, crushed souls, dead bodies. Murder, suicide, whatever was necessary.

Suicides in the IC were a leading indicator that the Russians had discovered the proclivities of a closet homosexual or the hidden sexual identity disorders of an intelligence officer. Preoccupied with maintaining the fiction that they were "normal" on the outside but less-than-normal on the inside, those loyal and patriotic intelligence officers would commit suicide rather than divulge America's secrets or their own. It didn't matter that management would be forced to go through their backgrounds and would discover their secret and their personal failings. No one can hurt you when you're dead.

The people of the intelligence community who lived double lives were regarded as untrustworthy. If they would lie about their sexuality, they would lie about other topics. As a consequence, virtually all employees went through the polygraph process because it was needed to root out the miniscule number of intelligence officers who spontaneously transitioned like a chrysalis from patriotic intelligence officer to an in-house defector. The polygrapher identified the spies, crooks, and the potential blackmail targets before they could do harm to the CIA and national security.

But no one could have prepared the USIC for what President Mazibuike did. He forced the U.S. Intelligence Community to hire people from the dark side of Islam, individuals who were clandestine zealots or radicals who would throw red paint on Christopher

Columbus statues. Tens of thousands of radical and criminal Muslims had been injected into the program by presidential fiat under the guise of Muslim Outreach programs. The vast majority of Muslim applicants couldn't pass the polygraph, but those that passed after multiple attempts found themselves "inside the wire" and began their mission of further infiltrating deeper in the USIC. The secrets they learned didn't require spiriting documents out of the CIA's headquarters building. Simple knowledge of a mission or a special access program that could be detrimental to the Muslim Brotherhood was all it took to develop and implement countermeasures.

• • •

Hunter asked, "Greg wasn't helpful, how so? I know he didn't believe that 3M was pushing Islamic radicals into this place. It's like saying you don't believe there is voter fraud when you know in your heart there is." 3M was delegitimizing shorthand for the former Democrat President, Maxim Mohammed Mazibuike.

Nazy said, "3M didn't push them into the NRO or the NGA. Only CIA and FBI and the NSA where there was personnel involved. It should've set off red bursting bombs...." She knew she hadn't got the phrase quite right and looked at Duncan for clarification.

Hunter reached across the table to pat her hand. "*Red star clusters....*" He and McGee looked at each other when she mangled the military lingo of the distress-call, pyrotechnic signal flare.

Nazy said, "Oh, that's right."

McGee nodded. He knew Hunter's politics and politely ignored him when he "went off the reservation," especially when he complained about the machinations of the former president.

As the CIA Director, Bill McGee had access to the documents, to the programs, to the operations. All of them. Now he knew the depressing truth and the extent of the situation and said, "I know you didn't have access to that intel, but you were right—dare I say it—again. 3M and his friends in the Agency accessed information and intelligence that were beneficial to their friends in al-Qaeda, the Haqqani Network, the Muslim Brotherhood, and the Islamic

Underground." McGee looked up at Nazy, pointed a fork at her, and said, "I'm thinking all the trials and tribulation with the Islamic Underground attacking you and Duncan occurred because we probably had 3M holdovers in this place."

Hunter scowled and said, "*Dark Islam; Dark State.* Same players, different masters."

Nazy nodded perceptibly in agreement, turned to Duncan, and said, "Bill did one of your tricks when he first arrived."

Hunter was curious and his face said so with daggers.

McGee said, "You told me when you took over the airport security company in Cleveland that you announced you wanted to meet every person in the organization, that on payday you would hand them their paychecks. Right?"

He remembered that? A rare compliment! Wow! "I did. Found about fifty phantom employees which explained why the company I worked for couldn't turn a profit. Every month they were paying for fifty people who weren't real."

The Director said, "I announced that any employee hired during the Mazibuike Administration would need to be polygraphed again. And Nazy and I would like to meet them."

Hunter grinned at McGee's cleverness and said, "Good for you. That had to have gone over, as my mama said, 'like a lead balloon.'"

"They were caught in no man's land. If they didn't want to meet us they had problems with the poly. Those who complained that they were being unnecessarily harassed or threatened to sue, they were skylined. And they did not survive the poly."

"I'm sure 3M's buddies went *jihadi* bat-shit crazy."

McGee wasn't amused at Hunter's comments—they were normal for him given the topic of the conversation. But reliving the shocking revelation that the CIA had been infiltrated by members of the Islamic Underground who had dug into the Agency like Alabama ticks on a hound dog didn't make for a happy occasion, and it had all been facilitated by a treasonous president.

Nazy said, "Some of our 'phantom employees' were homosexual men and women. They admitted under polygraph that they had been deceitful and could no longer be trusted."

McGee added, "I signed an executive order. I was channeling my inner Muslim. Submit to the poly or turn in your badge. And I reinstituted the old questions before they were outlawed. If they didn't like it, I said they could try to take me to court. But they didn't."

Hunter asked, "What else can you do when you couldn't trust them any further than my grandmother could throw a Studebaker?"

Nazy and Hunter nodded. *Leadership, at last!* She continued, "The vast majority of our 'phantom employees' were radical or criminal Muslims who were inserted into the Agency by 3M's policies. Our phantom employees weren't stealing money…."

McGee finished her sentence, "…they were stealing secrets. I've pulled about three thousand clearances so far. Two-thirds of the people who were hired during 3M's reign of terror resigned instead of facing a new or expanded polygraph. I have to have cause to fire them. If they refuse or can't pass a polygraph, I pull their tickets and they're gone. If they don't like it—I can send them to jail."

Hunter asked, "Any takers?" McGee shook his head as he looked over and made eye contact with Yassmin Deng, the Chief Financial Officer, as she entered the eat joint. McGee's darting eyes bounced to Duncan and then to Nazy who turned to look at the woman.

Nazy said, "We don't know how many are still in the embassies. 3M did a number on the FBI; it's a massive infiltration problem that has them one foot in the grave. I'm very grateful it wasn't us."

Hunter was fascinated by the lanky extremely dark woman, not in a sexual way, but in the way a cat is interested in a mouse which suddenly appears across the room. He watched her as he interjected, "I assume you have a plan to test them when you can?"

"When they return stateside, a minimum of two polygraphs and interviews…. Like the others, then they get interview questions that root out their hidden proclivities. Remember when that Muslim billionaire wanted to build a mosque near Ground Zero to 'Unite the

City' after 9/11? The U.S. Intelligence Community's analysis was that any mosque or cultural center would actually be a shrine of martyrdom for those nineteen hijackers. A mosque near Ground Zero after 9/11 wouldn't have united the city, it would've been a recruiting poster for al-Qaeda. All that would have been missing was al-Qaeda's black flag on a pole. Employment at the CIA sends the same signal. In the aftermath of 9/11 some people on the left believe America is the greatest cancer in the world...."

Hunter asked, "Who's she?"

McGee answered, "Yassmin Deng, CFO."

Nazy nodded and continued, "...and that peaceful overtures or gestures would demonstrate their sincerity, but the liberals and radicals saw a mosque near Ground Zero as a mechanism for more poison to be injected into the American bloodstream. Same for Muslims in the Agency. It would've been another form of communist, socialist, or radical Islamic agitation to undermine the country. Polygraph machines nearly melted down as these people who thought they could get away with the charade exposed themselves."

McGee said, "Speaking of 'meltdown,' the HR department actually went into meltdown, as you can imagine. I've had to replace virtually the entire human resources department. They were so dysfunctional, loyal to Mazibuike. At first I thought they could not believe he was dirty, so they continued to act as if he were still president and supported his policies, and allowed these people in. It made no sense other than they had lost their collective minds. So I hired troops, uniformed intelligence, admin, and HR types from SOCOM. The SOCOM Commander said I stole them; he trains them and I steal them. I said, 'That is exactly correct. But what's the problem?' They aren't political; never have been; they could easily pass a poly, and I could trust them. They hadn't been exposed to the left's social justice BS. And they are hard workers."

Hunter said, "What you are also saying is that your old HR had been reprogrammed. Brainwashed."

McGee and Nazy exchanged glances. Hunter felt he had struck a nerve and continued, "I'll bet they had 3M's picture up in their offices, as if he were still the president."

They nodded. Nazy asked, "How could you know that?"

"It is how they keep their poodles on a leash. Bill knows. It's really brainwashing. Now it's called Critical Social Justice Theory, and the left is trying to manipulate civil servants to remake the human relations system, reprogram it into focusing on 'critical equity' instead of effective HR. HR becomes a political system, a political act. Muslim outreach, diversity hiring. Critical Race Theory; bullshit rationales to discriminate against whites. Most leaders don't even know these things are being taught in their places. Classic KGB brainwashing dynamic. So that is Yassmin Deng."

They were not shocked by Hunter's analysis and nodded.

"It's nice to finally put a face with the name," said Hunter.

McGee said, "She thinks I pay you way too much."

"What's it to her? Does she complain about anyone else in this place? I think I would polygraph the snot out of her."

McGee said, "You're sounding a little racist my brother."

Hunter chuckled.

"You're sitting with us," offered McGee. "Whatever it's worth, we polygraphed her. She said she had been pitched by TASCO. Their side has been in indoctrination overdrive; that they want her and she can blame white men and the government for her problems. But she stood tall; we ran her through the mill. And she is getting better."

"Bill talked to her," said Nazy in a way that made it clear the Director's discussion was more than a chat. No one on the planet ever wanted to be officially counseled by a pissed off SEAL.

CHAPTER 37

May 16, 2018

Hunter was wide awake and keyed on the acronym TASCO. *The Trans-Atlantic Security Corporation conglomerate. Bogdan Chernovich's place. Why am I not surprised?* He turned to his bride and asked, "How did they find you when you were up on the mountain top? Inside job?" Hunter couldn't immediately remember the name of the remote compound the CIA used to interview defectors. It would come to him.

Nazy gently shook her head and said, "Different vector. The attorneys of the terrorists being held in Cuba—when I interrogated them they always remarked about my eyes—that they weren't Arab eyes, they were Persian. The Shah and his ancestors had green eyes. They told their lawyers who told their contacts in the mosques...."

McGee returned to the conversation. He interrupted and said, "...who told their buddies in the Islamic Underground...."

Hunter said, "Nasty bunch." *Another member of the Dark State.*

Nazy nodded and continued, "...and pretty soon there was correspondence between the U.S. and the Middle East and...."

McGee said, "...and they found the missing green-eyed goddess who had been running from Islam for years working for Uncle Sam and interrogating their shitbirds." He mischievously held up with his hands in supplication.

Hunter turned to look at Nazy critically, "She *is* a green-eyed goddess, isn't she?" He squeezed her hand under the table. He was glad to be back, but he had things he wanted to talk to McGee about. *Those guys have been flying drones into the intakes of airliners and taking pictures over nuclear power plants. CIA headquarters cannot be far behind.*

Nazy blushed. McGee nodded.

Hunter said, "You have to watch Democrats like a hawk eying a field rat, and I'm sure the Islamic Underground votes Democrat, maybe multiple times, whatever they think they can steal."

McGee and Nazy agreed. "They're not on our side." It was one of Hunter's many politically weighted sayings pilfered for the cause.

Hunter wondered, *Democrats or Islamic Underground? Or both?* He asked, "Wasn't Salman Rushdie subject to an eighties' *fatwā* calling for his assassination issued by the Ayatollah..., uh,...Khomeini? Isn't he able to move around freely now?"

Nazy's stern observation said it all, "Rushdie still requires personal security." *Once under a fatwā you're never really free.*

There was a long pause between the friends, as if there was unpleasant news to be shared but no one wanted to go first. Nazy wasn't concerned, she gripped his hand under the table which made Duncan turn toward her. Love flowed between them like an electrical current. She said, "One of the people you picked up in Jordan was a wife of Toraluddin Haqqani. Of the Haqqani Network. She claims her name is Saoirse Nobley."

Until that moment, Hunter had been happy with the trajectory of his life. Nazy's mental state was back to normal, and she was back at work with a vengeance. He was proud of her recovery. No one had tried to kill her in years, which only meant *they* were waiting for a lapse of security. He had finally become serially active in a way that could never had been imagined by his highly regarded and renowned friend, the former CIA Director Greg Lynche. McGee had him hopping all over the world conducting private special activities with the quiet airplane. And he was happily holding hands with his wife.

A blast from his unspoken past. *Saoirse Nobley? That's impossible.* The look on Hunter's face told the story of utter disbelief.

He sat quietly, thinking. He ran his hand through Cary Grant-like perfectly gray Hollywood hair. His eyes moved from wife, to friend, and back to Nazy again. *Are you serious?* He recalled the images and memories of the dainty Corporal as she was then. *Legs! She said the kids in school tormented her and called her legs "toothpicks." Nazy had told me a similar story; Muslim children unmercifully teased her and called her "bird legs." By the time Saoirse came to the Marines her legs were definitely not toothpicks.* He couldn't help but recall the image of Saoirse Nobley the last time he had seen her at the Hawaiian airport. She wore a tight yellow halter-top sundress which highlighted her long legs, the exposed deep cleavage of her poitrine, and the youthful face of a movie star. Modest-heeled sandals put just enough tension on the muscle to accentuate her calves. An orchid in her short blonde hair. Fresh polish on her nails from a manicurist. He could've looked at her all day and never tired of the view. That would always be his vision of her, a flawless example of a twenty-two-year-old who should've been on the cover of a magazine instead of mashed against the shower wall or in his hotel bed without a sheet. She could've made a mint in a bikini on a poster. *And, I haven't seen another one like her since.*

McGee killed the old memory and brought Hunter back to reality. "We would like you to interrogate her."

Hunter stopped breathing. He was mildly shocked and asked the odious question, nodding at Nazy, "Why me; why don't you?"

"She wants to talk to you." Nazy's comments were as dry and indifferent as a harried waiter reciting the specials of the day.

McGee said, "Only you."

Flummoxed, Hunter leaned forward in his chair as if he were in considerable pain from bad Thai food that would require surgery to fix. His eyes darted back and forth between wife and boss. He pushed away from the table, and asked, *"How is that even possible?"*

McGee had no time for the folderol. "Yeah, I know. Doesn't seem possible." He sighed the sorrow of a tired man; it was a time to get serious. He hadn't ever seen his friend this perturbed, like a man who lived with a dirty dark secret, like an escapee from a chain gang who had to face the music when the cops arrived.

Hunter continued, "Can you get her out of there? GITMO? Like, take her to...." He turned and pointed to his wife, "...what's the name of that place they took you...in the...*Shenandoahs*?"

Nazy asked, "You mean *Spindletop*?" She was intrigued at her husband's interest in the woman.

Hunter nodded. He was emphatic. "I don't care what the circumstances were surrounding her in Syria. She needs to be out of *there*. I'll go get her."

Nazy looked at McGee who looked at Hunter incredulously. McGee glanced around at the hundreds of tiny ponytail palms that lined the windows of the dining room to ensure they couldn't be heard or weren't being watched. The CFO had disappeared. A half-a-dozen smokers were making billowing gray clouds in the courtyard on the other side of the glass, but their toes pointed toward each other and not toward the restaurant. *No lip readers.* McGee indicated his need for more information with his fingers. He asked, "What do you know?"

Hunter said, "When I knew her she was a petite twenty-two, exotic, Scandinavian blonde. She had Liz Taylor's deep purple eyes. I got a letter with a picture from her a year or two after I retired. She married some Egyptian she had met in college here in the States. She made a comment that she liked a man with lots of chest hair and as Nazy can attest, I have none to speak of. I had muscles, I have no hair. I assumed he had to have been wealthy and treated her like gold...."

"Apparently, she married Toraluddin Haqqani. He was in university here. The Haqqani's sold intelligence for the Brotherhood, al-Qaeda, and now ISIS. He and his brother and father were very rich." Nazy authenticated the information with a squeeze of his hand.

"And probably a hairy bastard. Anyway, I purposely forgot his name, and I didn't know if he was a citizen or not. That was a long time ago. I was at the Border Patrol on a collateral duty as an inspector, and my time learning citizenship issues at the DOJ's Office of Internal Audit definitely slanted my understanding of marriages of convenience and my views of the men who preyed on young girls with inferiority complexes. Nobley was a very good girl and very picky.... No issues with an inferiority complex; she was one of those inimitable women who could've had anyone...at the air station, and she knew it. I could never understand why she chose an Egyptian...unless...like I said, maybe he was rich."

McGee said, "The Haqqanis all were and he *was*. Now he has an orange jumpsuit."

Nazy's platinum green eyes flashed. "Did she pick you?"

"If you mean, was I pursued?" Hunter calculated a response and nodded, and let his eyes acknowledge his assertion. "She wasn't shy, but twenty-twenty-five years ago I would have told an I&NS evaluator that she's not the kind of girl to go for a marriage of convenience. That's way out of character for her. Democrats, liberals, radicals do it in a microsecond to make some money or if it would help their anarchist causes. She's not one of those; she doesn't have a personality disorder. Belay that. Wasn't one of those. I don't know how or why those two got hooked up, but I will bet the keys to the *Daytona* I bought that he tricked her into marrying him to get American citizenship. An American passport. Do you know who this guy is?"

McGee said, "Toraluddin Haqqani? The missing brother of the Haqqani terrorist network. For the last several years he's been spotted in the Middle East where he's been ISIS' 'intelligence minister' of late. There was an unconfirmed sighting in Iran."

"Ooh. Wasn't he on the *Matrix*? Years ago? One of the few where the Intel was always insufficient to locate him?"

McGee nodded. Nazy nodded with tight lips. Neither Nazy nor any of her analysts had located the missing Haqqani brother in the Middle East. One of the NCTC's very few failures.

"I think that puts a different spin on things. Nazy, you must've known this? Haqqani Network. Muslim Brotherhood. Al-Qaeda affiliate heavy. ISIS Intel Chief. All of his movements and relationships? He had to have had a file." Hunter asked, "Did you know she was his wife?"

With barely a single waggle of her head, Nazy said, "The intel is nonexistent on her. Intel was always insufficient on him. Secondary and tertiary mentions in dispatch. It wasn't for a lack of trying. He was always on the move, and it would be months after-the-fact before we learned where he had been. Anyone on an American passport and not on a watch list could cross countries without molestation."

"What about that *Sunni-Shia* thing? I understood AQ is profoundly *Sunni*, and if he showed up at *Shiite* headquarters in Tehran, there would be a fight to see who would get to lop off his head and use it as a soccer ball. No reciprocity."

McGee said, "That may apply for the rank and file guys, but the leaders play a different game, like Washington Democrats and their coalition of special interest groups. Think of them as leftists of a feather who conspire together. The 'enemy of my enemy is my friend' type of thing. Team terrorism transcends tribalism. They would naturally gang up and go after Republicans."

Nazy said, "Nobley is a complete mystery; no photographs and no mentions of her exist in the files. From the time Bill called you, we received some history....we got her file from the Marine Corps. She attended college during and after the Marine Corps, was married while she was on active duty, and went to Egypt on their honeymoon. They returned from Egypt, graduated from college, had children, and then her mother filed a missing person's report with the FBI. Haqqani and Nobley disappeared after they went through U.S. Customs for places east, but until we get the details from the State Department, that's only a working theory."

Children? There were children, too? Hunter shook his head. An old memory stirred. "Any mention of the State Department and I'm reminded just how compromised that place is. Didn't 3M have the State Department issue hundreds of passports to Iranians and Iraqis?"

McGee said, "Don't stop there. Egypt. Libya. Syria. Lebanon. Jordan. Saudi Arabia. The Middle East countries. Thousands of passports. And of course, Iran. The 9/11 hijackers traveled on their own passports. That's a need to know."

Hunter asked, "What was his major?"

Nazy and McGee looked at each other as if they didn't want to share the secret. Hunter was a master at reading body language and knew immediately, the answer wasn't good. McGee said, "Chemistry and biology."

"What you really mean is he is a *bioterrorist*. Crap. *I hate those guys.* Anthrax, H1N1, bubonic plague, hanta and coronaviruses, viruses that cause diseases in mammals and birds, but the rarer forms such as SARS and MERS which were so potent and lethal to humans when they were first released. The stuff global epidemics, pandemics are made of. Are you kidding me? What was the FBI doing? Oh, that's right, not a frickin' thing except attending sensitivity training and ensure diversity hiring." Hunter turned to Nazy and sighed as if he had finished running a marathon. He continued, "I also remember a headline in the *Old Gray Lady*, the *New York Times*; Iranian 'Prophetic Medicine' Leader: *Camel Urine Cures MERS Coronavirus.* Some stupidity is breathtaking, felony stupid. I really have a hard time believing anyone 'over there' has enough smarts to be a real bioterrorist, but I know, darling Nazy, you're right."

She nudged her husband and rubbed her leg against his. He had moved on to other topics. Nazy had read somewhere that geniuses were like that.

Hunter continued, "The rules of engagement are always to not ask questions or even say anything during flight. I wasn't even curious who was in the back of the jet. That Saoirse Nobley was on my jet is simply a miracle, and her lovey-dovey is probably a bioterrorist—that's just...*incredible.* One side of me wants to say 'Good work guys!' but another side tells me life just got more complicated." He asked McGee and Nazy, "What do you plan to do with her?"

McGee said, "She's being discussed right this minute by a National Foreign Intelligence Council working group. You can bet someone will ask about Haqqani, too. And the other detainee; Hamsi Fareed al-Amirikiu. He was one of 3M's buddies in the Islamic Underground. He had dropped off the grid; no one really cared because he wasn't directly engaged in illegal activities, but now he's in GITMO."

Hunter said, "I just deliver turds....wrapped in plastic."

Nazy said, "He's not doing so well, reportedly."

"Did he get shot?"

McGee shook his head. "Canines with *Growlers* stopped suicide vests from going off. The dogs are not happy with bad guys who try to fire off the detonators."

Hunter allowed that image to cold soak his brain. *Good!* "What about the National Center for Medical Intelligence?"

"That's scheduled on an 'as needed' basis. Sometimes the DIA invites us, and sometimes they don't. I expect something soon since there's a sniff. An implied vector in the initial analysis is that Toraluddin Haqqani's been involved, however tangentially, with Iran's virology lab."

Hunter narrowed his brows in concern. "Iran's virology lab?" He looked at Nazy then at McGee.

McGee said, "But nothing will happen until the CDC Working Group convenes. They don't like to see us in their meetings. Kind of a Hatfield and McCoy thing."

Hunter nodded. *And crooked....*

Nazy said, "And because of that, we have long suspected them of foul play."

Hunter listened.

"We hope she can talk about Haqqani's movements and activities. She might explain contradictions or fill in lacunae in our intel. He has a thick résumé of terror, but our file on her is as thin as aluminum foil. I don't know how the head of their ISIS intelligence network could escape our efforts to find him for this long...."

Hunter was impressed at the way his wife used *lacunae* and placed the wrong emphasis on the wrong syllable when she said *Alu...mini...um.*

McGee said, "Before our guys picked him up, Haqqani was mentioned in dispatch, seen in Teheran, and took a helicopter to the Ayatollah Khomeini Institute of Virology."

The furrowed brows were back. Hunter wasn't impressed, but he was starting to worry. Now the Nobley story was sounding like a mission brief. "You think he was soliciting help."

Nazy nodded and said, "Maybe they wanted to talk with him. We know the Iranians sometimes use proxies when they don't want their fingerprints on something. But we need more information."

The concept muddled Hunter's mind, "*You were serious?* The Iranian Shia would team with al-Qaeda even though they're Sunnis?"

McGee said, "In the terrorism world at the leadership level, everything is possible as long as no one ticks the other side off. Terrorism is a mission; Sunni, Shia are teammates with the same mission if the enemy is the United States or Israel. The Iranian leadership may be the ones soliciting help. I say their fingerprints are all over it, but we don't know. Maybe Miss Nobley knows something."

Nazy said, "She's special. The only woman in GITMO."

Hunter noticed McGee had divorced Nobley from Haqqani and was glad of it. He wanted to be her sponsor now, but he was so deep in a special access program that he didn't officially exist. He wondered who would give a terrorist organization counterintelligence and then realized all intelligence agencies have their spies and their double agents. Hunter shook his head; the belief was too outré to share. *A conspiracy theory!* He had developed another concept and seriously asked, "Bill, can they—did they check her for plague and such?" He swore he saw the big black man turn a dark shade of gray when the blood rushed from his face.

Nazy leaped into the conversation. "You don't think...."

"I don't know. They want to use bugs to kill millions but wind up only killing themselves. The *bioterrorist* Haqqani...may have been... experimenting on her. You don't know with these guys. You never know. That's why you have them check. I'm up-to-date on all my shots; anthrax and plague and yellow fever. And as Nazy knows, since I am always going to equatorial Africa, I'm on an anti-malarial."

McGee was on his feet, on his BlackBerry, and talking rapidly. After a minute he returned to the conversation. "They'll check."

Hunter's deep mellifluous and commanding voice lowered an octave. "Thanks, Bill. If she's clean, will you allow her release? Nazy and I can interrogate her."

Nazy said, "As an American with a sponsor, she'll probably get tossed into the government's defector program, and I'm afraid we'll—this place will lose contact with her. Technically she's not on U.S. soil, but there will be liberal activists screaming for her release once she is known to be a detainee. It's a little strange that they have said nothing about Hamsi al-Amirikiu. They may not care, or they may not know yet. This is fast moving intel—front-of-the-line stuff. Under normal circumstances I would read the debriefings, or the deputy would provide the details needed for the president."

Nazy nodded. She was glad she was being included tangential to the plan, however, she needed no more work, and she didn't want to meet Duncan's old flame. Although she was curious. Duncan was a devoted and doting husband, and he never gave Nazy any concern about his fidelity and trustworthiness. Still, she wondered, *What will he do when she sees her? Lord, what will I do when I see her?*

McGee rubbed his eyes as if he had a sudden headache. Hunter and the discussion were giving him one. "I don't know—this may take a week or two. This is new ground for me. Technically I don't believe she's ours. I don't know what DOD will do. Maybe the FBI has to be involved, and right now they have so many challenges they don't know which way is up. And I'm scheduled to go on a ten-day trip to Europe and Australia. *Five Eyes* and all those guys. I'm going to be gone. My return, TBD."

Oh, that sucks! Ten days – two weeks! Bullfrog! "If ever there was a time when we need competence in an organization, the FBI disappoints. Until they get some new blood over there, they'll never figure out what's needed to turn that sinking ship around." Hunter asked, "Two weeks; really?"

"Two weeks. At least." McGee nodded and continued, "Negotiation stuff. Here, there are committees discussing Haqqani, Nobley, and Iran's virology labs. With her being American there may be laws, which means lawyers of a different stripe, buddies of the former president who do *pro bono* work for anyone captured on the terrorist's battlefield. She's likely DOD's responsibility; possession is nine-tenths of the law, that sort of thing. I'll need a legal opinion. The more people I touch, the more complicated it gets. But I do know this, having an outside contractor do the interrogation will not fly with anyone and leveraging my position to spring her will unnecessarily highlight her. And you. I don't want that. For the AQ who are detained, those lawyers are the most…."

McGee was searching for the right word when Nazy came to his rescue. "…radical leftists in the Democrat Party."

Hunter had moved onto a new subject, one that had been bothering him. He asked, "Why would a terrorist visit a virus research institute? Better yet, why would a *bio*terrorist visit a BL-4 lab? Only one reason. They're interested in playing with bugs in order to start a biological war." *And they would love to open a new front on their war with us.* Hunter frowned as a new thought ravaged his mind. *Could there be other reasons?*

The sudden mention of insects made Nazy's skin feel like they were crawling up her bare leg. She brushed off an imaginary bug and felt foolish.

McGee chose his words carefully, "This Nobley really complicated matters by demanding to talk with you. Now your name is all over that island, and by extension, every one of those asshole, lefty, communist lawyers defending the detainees will hit the *dark web* and their contacts in the Islamic Underground will try to figure out who you are and why she wants to talk with you. These turds uncovered Nazy based on just the color of her eyes. They'll have your name, and I don't want them out hunting for you and finding you again."

"Thanks, *Bullfrog*."

"That's *Director* Bullfrog to you."

CHAPTER 38

May 16, 2018

Nazy agreed. "We killed one *fatwā* on you. After the extraordinary lengths we took to kill you off, with your name out there again, if your cover is blown again, there will be new *fatwās*. It will happen." She shook her head in disappointment.

McGee said, "Maybe we can manage it, but it's going to take a lot of help."

Hunter flushed the viewpoint that he would be targeted again. "That's not her fault." Nazy was supportive; her eyes seemed to beg forgiveness for a woman she didn't know and could dislike intensely when she met her.

McGee said, "I know, I'll think of something. Let's hope she's clean. If she isn't, she could easily wipe out the GITMO population; we never considered they could've infected her with plague and baited us to grab her. The only information we really have on her is that she was an American. But it is early. Like any bride of a terrorist she's suspected of being a willing accomplice, and in virtually all cases, even when they turn themselves in, they'll always be looked at as a conspirator, a defector, a Judas."

Nazy was on her BlackBerry, her thumbs flying over the tiny keyboard, texting something to someone.

Duncan looked at his wife and smiled at her. He offered, "Kelly and I were on N100 masks or the aircraft's positive pressure system the whole time and went through the decon protocol when we returned. We're healthy, our immune system hasn't been compromised. Shots up-to-date. We're ok."

McGee said, "I see that look; there's more to this than just viruses."

Hunter pouted for a second. "These guys are infatuated with aviation for all the wrong reasons. Always looking to attack it. We've seen little bioterrorism spread by aircraft or through airports in twenty-plus years. Much success rests in the aircraft's design, the HVAC units, the heating, venting, and cooling system, and HEPA filters that stop most viruses and bacteria. I've always thought the real issue is that *Islamists* don't do bugs very well."

Nazy said, "That's why we believe it's in Iran. It's protected. Mazibuike made sure of it. The French and the Germans couldn't do all of it for what they envisioned. They needed China's help. Scientists and certification."

Hunter asked McGee, "Doesn't China have huge labs everywhere?"

McGee retorted, "Not really.... They take a centralized approach, like communists are required to do. We take a decentralized approach. The U.S. has several labs scattered around the planet and there are a couple on Muslim bases. Our allies. The U.S. military base in Peru serves as an infectious disease research center, and they work on vaccine testing, infection prevention, diagnostics, and insect control measures. All these centers' primary focus is on viral pathogens common to the region, such as the flu, dengue, and Zika. Then in Egypt we have a U.S. Naval Medical Research Unit. It is DOD's preeminent overseas laboratory. They conduct research and surveillance related to infectious disease to support U.S. military deployed across Africa, the Middle East, and Southwest Asia."

Nazy said, "Since the creation of the Khomeini Institute we have had little success getting anyone close to it...." She glanced at McGee for permission to continue. He nodded and she continued, "...until just recently. Details of Iranian activities were in the PDB."

Hunter's eyes and face said he was impressed.

"It's not a secret that Iranian government deception regarding the remote Khomeini Institute raises new fears about Tehran's biological weapons activities, including population-specific research on germ weapons capable of attacking ethnic groups."

McGee added, "3M set them up nicely with the help of the Chinese. Our in-place defector appears to have some direct knowledge of the Iranian and Chinese programs. He claims they're looking at biological experiments on ethnic minorities."

"You mean Christians. I should probably add, Jews. They're always on their target list." Hunter wasn't liking the trajectory of the conversation. Nazy appeared to be a little concerned.

"Them too," McGee said. "There was a U.N. biological security assessment about three years ago which detailed Tehran's rapid technological advancements in creating population-specific biological weapons and other exotic pathogens capable of attacking DNA-specific ethnic groups. There are no cures or vaccines for manufactured *chimeras*."

"Really? Why not?" asked Hunter.

McGee looked around the cafeteria. "It's a long story, and one we are just starting to understand. And it is not pretty."

Nazy said, "The National Intelligence Analytics office monitors all chemical and biological weapons activities in the United Nations countries using software and that place you so derisively call the *dark web*. They look for evidence that a country is blurring the line between virus research for good and virus research to create bioweapons."

Hunter said, "Okay..."

McGee said, "So keep that thought; there is more to the story. Apparently in the 1990s patents for coronaviruses starting showing up. The work of research labs."

Hunter offered, "I thought they, coronaviruses, were natural. You can't patent a natural process."

McGee said, "You are correct, my friend, holder of many patents. In 2003 the CDC struck gold with a coronavirus outbreak in Hong Kong, a virus they knew could be easily manipulated. The CDC was first in the door and patented the SARS coronavirus."

Nazy said, "That means the CDC controlled the propriety rights to the disease and the detection and the means to measure it."

McGee said, "This is how big money is made. So, we have the CDC taking credit for inventing the coronavirus and as the owner of the patent...."

Hunter said, "...controlled 100% of any monies generated by that patent."

Nazy said, "Not only that, but they controlled the cash flow of a whole clandestine empire built around the industrial complex of manufacturing coronaviruses."

Hunter thought, *Uh oh....*

She continued, "The head of the CDC is famous for his decades-long chimeric coronavirus research. He found that laboratory-made coronaviruses related to SARS can infect human cells. The next year the head of the CDC filed a patent for a coronavirus that was transmitted to humans. Here's where it gets interesting. You know you can't patent a natural process. That's by law. So either the SARS coronavirus was manufactured therefore making a patent on it legal, or it was natural, meaning a patent on it was illegal. If it was manufactured, it could be worth billions, but it would violate the Biological Weapons Convention, international law, and treaties. Are you with me so far?"

"I am, and I don't like where you're driving. You're saying the head of the CDC is a greedy bastard."

Nazy said, "Oh, Duncan, it gets worse."

McGee continued, "So, shortly after Mazibuike arrives on the political scene the CDC asked the U.S. Patent Office to keep their patent secret and confidential, not only on manufacturing the coronavirus but how to detect and how to measure it. Because they had the patent, the CDC was allowed to make inquiries of other research labs that were experimenting with viruses. The patents constrained anyone from using it unless permission was granted, so other researchers weren't able to look at the coronavirus. They couldn't measure it, they couldn't develop a test kit for it, and so on. The CDC, our Center for Disease Control had the means and motive for monetary gain by turning the coronavirus from a pathogen to a profit. Theoretically, the patent could be worth a trillion dollars in the manufacture of vaccines. Easy."

"How is that legal for the CDC to do?" Hunter was confused.

Nazy, the trained lawyer said, "It's legal if the research is for peaceful purposes and any proceeds derived from the activity flow back into the U.S. Treasury. It's illegal if the virus is manufactured or manipulated as a weapon of mass destruction. That violates treaties and such."

McGee jumped in, "He could create a chimeric virus made up of a surface protein from a flea and the backbone of a SARS virus grown in mice to mimic human diseases. Then Mazibuike curtailed U.S. funding. So the head of the CDC gave the Chinese a contract to continue his work, his patented work. The Chinese went to the Iranians with a proposal that was a little crazy; would they be interested in engineering a coronavirus that would attack white people, Jews, and Christians and leave Muslims free of the disease?"

Nazy said, "The FBI has turned a blind eye to all of this. Before Mazibuike fled the country, federal funding for coronavirus research was suspended in the U.S. A classified document we have only recently seen indicated that the CDC breached the Bioweapons Convention by developing a potentially lethal flu-like virus."

The CIA Director said, "That research was offshored to Iran, we believe. You know Mazibuike lifted sanctions and sent them 150 billion dollars. Some of that money was used to build the Khomeini Institute. There's been some noise coming out of European media...."

Over the voice of McGee, Hunter interjected, "Our media is so horrible and corrupt."

"...of an unconfirmed report that researchers out of the Khomeini Institute claimed to have found a coronavirus that attacks DNA-specific ethnic groups. They have to say 'they found' it, because if they created the virus, it would violate international bioweapon proliferation treaties. And oh by the way, there are no cures or vaccines for manufactured *chimeras*."

Nazy said, "Since President Hernandez slapped more sanctions on them, Iran has refused to allow international investigators to examine research work on bat-originated coronaviruses conducted at the Khomeini Institute's laboratories."

McGee added, "It's not fully staffed at this moment—at least we don't think it is. They may have had an accident that they could not contain."

Hunter asked, "But you don't know?"

Nazy shook her head.

McGee said, "The bottom line is we do *not* know. For an intelligence agency, that is a bad place to be. We are supposed to know."

CHAPTER 39

May 16, 2018

Hunter was becoming more interested in bioterrorists than some nutty epidemiologists and said, "I could be wrong, but I'll bet their bioterrorists are like Afghani bomb-makers who blew everybody up when teaching a group of Taliban how to make an IED. If they're trying to develop or exploit viruses, wouldn't they kill more of themselves than us? I know they only have to be successful once, and we have to stop them all. What a place to be in." After the words left his mouth, Hunter considered, *Would they care? Of course not. They're delirious with jihad, and they're maniacal about killing infidels.*

McGee said, "Unless it's a super bug. We have some evidence the Chinese have been helping them experiment with viruses from rare bats by attaching proteins from plague-carrying fleas from rats."

Hunter leaned back in his chair and offered, "I saw an article last year. I think it was sourced from an Italian newspaper...."

McGee nodded, "That was two years ago...."

"Rare bat viruses. Lethal proteins. The biological equivalent of a binary weapon. The article didn't say, but they're probably only found in China.... All you need is a super-bug seeding a super-spreader event."

McGee asked, "You think this could be one of those?"

Nazy asked, "A what?"

Hunter first answered the Director, "Wet Work of the Seventh Kind. Terrorists have wanted to use biologicals for decades, but you have to have the right virus and a human to spread it. But they never had a proper lab to do the research or to maintain the virus—think of it like a SCIF for bugs. You say your inside person says, 'now they do.' So yes, I do think a super-spreader event may be, could be in the planning stages."

He turned to his bride, "A super-spreader event. If the research and the forecasting are to be believed, an average person with a coronavirus only infects about two other people. The CDC suggests these viruses are primarily transmitted by person-to-person contact and by contact with virus-laden droplets expelled through coughing or sneezing. But when these things get exposed to sunlight, the UV has a natural disinfecting effect. That's UV-B. But to leverage a person's infection rate by a factor of five or ten or even a hundred times requires a super-spreader event. Usual super-spreader events are where there is *mucho* air going into and out of multiple lungs, such as when an infected person attends an indoor gathering with bunches of people. But the ultimate super-spreader event is one that leads into a *super-cascading* event like a long-range commercial flight or an ocean cruise. The heating, venting, and cooling system not only carries the airborne virus throughout the airplane or the ship, but HEPA filters in the HVAC are supposed to stop viruses and bacteria, thus preventing the infected from moving into other aircraft or ships and infecting another several hundred passengers. If it wasn't for HEPA filters in the HVAC, one person could infect a 1,000 people a day. Cascading effect."

McGee said, "So the filters stop the coronaviruses?"

Hunter said, "Coronaviruses are generally large diameter bugs that get caught up in the HEPA filter. But if these new coronaviruses are tiny and can easily pass through the HEPA filter without even slowing down...."

"Oh, my stars." Nazy touched her lips with her hand. She didn't want to believe her husband, but she knew him to be accurate and truthful.

"Of course, some of these clowns may have been working on something else."

"What's that?" Nazy was curious, but she was also intrigued at how her husband's mind worked. She thought she was witnessing the rising wave before Hunter just crashed onto everyone's shore.

McGee waited for Hunter to offer another vector.

Duncan mused hypothetically, "I see two paths. One, to get around aircraft HEPA filters require a coronavirus that is smaller than anything we know that can actually pass through the filter. Second, what if you could spread an inactive virus around like an aerosol or a powder and infect everyone and everything, and then with a flick of a switch, activate the virus?"

McGee screwed up his face as if he were in great pain. Nazy too. She asked, "Like how?" Duncan's mind was out of its cage. She was becoming more concerned and frightened by the second.

"Imagine if they found a way to *mass*-manufacture a coronavirus that could not be stopped by a HEPA filter or one that was inert; in an inert stage it wasn't able to replicate itself. The coronavirus' DNA could hide in a powder or an aerosol and then could be activated by having it come into contact with...oh, I don't know, let's say the Chinese 5G technology?"

McGee was quiet for a long time, processing the information. Another dead monkey problem without a solution. He said, "You're talking about a biological time bomb."

Hunter said, "That's not me—the flick the switch virus is the opinion of a couple of researchers who tracked the rise and fall of MERS and SARS which surprisingly coincided with the introduction of 3G and 4G technology. They believed the Chinese have been planning this for many years. Now you tell me the CDC has a patent on those coronaviruses, and I read where the Chinese are trying to race their patented 5G technology to market...."

McGee and Nazy looked at each other. They couldn't believe what they had just heard.

"At the sub-atomic level, when some amino acids are excited at five gigahertz, they *merge* and form tiny *life* forms." Hunter continued, "I give the contrail crazies a lot of crap but they may have stumbled onto to a process that works. Imagine airplane cleaning crews spreading an odor-killing powder in the carpets and seats to freshen up the cabin between flights."

McGee uttered, "Uh oh...."

"You see where I'm going. So many things are made in China. Pharmaceuticals, cleaning supplies...."

Nazy said, "And if they added inert viruses...."

McGee said, "...that were energized by 5G...."

Hunter said, "…an active virus would bypass the HVAC and HEPA and the UV systems. They would have found a way around the safeguards. With every commercial aircraft you could have a true super-spreader event."

Nazy and McGee were left speechless and shook their heads.

"In many ways this is the same tack as al-Qaeda infiltrating airport security for years, waiting for the optimum time to attack America. They wargamed what was necessary to get around the security systems." Hunter nodded. "But we don't know what we don't know. You could have a very complex problem or a simple one. The lefties in the CDC holding patents on manufactured coronaviruses could turn their secret science project on their political enemies. The Chinese may have helped the Iranians manufacture a DNA-specific coronavirus to eliminate infidels, Jews, and Christians that can slip past the security of a HEPA filter while they developed an active pathogen that is flick-of-the-switch programmable. Maybe a Computer Assisted Biologically Augmented Lifeform?"

Nazy said, "That spells…"

Hunter said, "*CABAL*. I suppose theoretically, the Chinese could spread a CABAL virus that would be transparent to their DNA and exclude them, and with the flick of a switch, kill everyone else. And if it is so small that it cannot be stopped by a standard HEPA filter, they could make everyone sick and take over the world; as long as they can bypass UV-C systems."

No one said a word. After a minute, Hunter asked, "Weren't we on bats and super-spreaders events before I drove the truck off into a ditch?"

McGee said, "I want to know what you meant by Wet Work of the Seventh Kind."

Nazy was interested too.

Hunter said, "Wet Work of the First Kind—clandestine assassination. YO-3A work. Wet Work of the Second Kind—an event which results in the death of a target through direct means; face-to-face shooting, push off a building, push a target into a subway train, lethal injection, strangulation, drive by shooting, bombs, suicide vests, and so on. Wet Work of the Third Kind—an event which results in the death of a target through additional or indirect means; mob hit, proxies, force the target to commit suicide, those kinds of things. Wet Work of the Fourth Kind—an event which results in the death of a target through abduction and interrogation; snatch them and hold them for hostage, and they die because of health issues or during rescue. This is the work I do for the Agency—try to interrupt the terrorist wet-work spin-cycle and prevent the Fourth Kind. We've been very successful. Then there's Wet Work of the Fifth Kind—an event which results in the death of a target through torture. I was nearly a fifth kind of victim until *Bullfrog* rescued me. Then there is Wet Work of the Sixth Kind—the Russians have used events which result in the death of a target through artificial scientific methods; nuclear poisoning, radiation sickness, a polonium pellet delivered by air gun or a single grain of sugar in Alexander Litvinenko's tea—single person attacks. This is the real KGB stuff. And finally, there is Wet Work of the Seventh Kind which results in the death of multiple targets leveraged through artificial scientific methods; a super-spreader event precipitated by an infected person or persons targeted to destroy a country or a civilization."

As Hunter finished, an alarm was ringing in his head. *Wet Work by proxy…. I haven't thought about that case in years. Wet Work of the third kind. Of course! Chernovich had help. Isn't he the leader of a cult, like Mazibuike was? Like Damien Thorne's helpers in the Omen! Destructive, murderous, deceitful murderers?*

McGee interrupted Hunter's thoughts, "*Where* did you get that?"

Hunter said, "There are all kinds of screwball and freaky things on the *dark web*. The Russians and Chinese and their surrogates are engaged in every one of these. The *dark web* is the terrorist's playground; where you can even get a copy of the KGB's Thirteenth Directorate handbook for assassins. I'm certain you have Intel Os looking into this stuff."

Nazy's eyes were wide open in surprise.

"Can you write those down for me? Send them to me?"

"Absolutely, good sir."

McGee thanked his friend and returned to the topic at hand saying, "Need to know. We were talking about bats. The bats aren't from

China. They're from Iran. One of the few times the Chinese have sent people into Iran to study, what do you call them...*critters?*"

Hunter said, "Rare critters probably carry rare bugs. Not just viruses but proteins. Different proteins on a coronavirus make them more or less lethal. The whole purpose of the research, supposedly. And if they're being looked at in a discrete lab in Iran...they won't want to share. It would be almost impossible to study in another lab unless it was transported there." *And you have to have humans in order to conduct experiments.*

Nazy said, "The Chinese would agree to any terms and conditions, and then tell their people to steal the research. That's what they do here."

McGee countered with an inflection point, "I agree those guys in Iran are not disciplined or equipped to handle pathogens safely. But the Chinese are experienced and have a decent track record of stealing trade secrets."

Hunter said, "Like the Russians."

Nazy nodded. "But we can't take the chance. On any of it. We are talking about a possible human extinction event that doesn't touch China if it is immune or they have developed a vaccine."

CHAPTER 40

May 16, 2018

McGee nodded and said, "One of the first things I was briefed on when I came to this place was your doctoral work. A copy of your paper was found in the bin Laden compound. An Arabic copy was considered a secret document during the Holy Land Foundation trial. It was used as an anti-aviation training manual for al-Qaeda, the Muslim Brotherhood, and the Islamic Underground. They developed strategies to counter your anti-terrorism recommendations. The bad news is they removed and replaced terms, they swapped aviation for biology, and created a whole new training manual for bioterrorists."

Hunter asked, "Seriously?"

McGee raised his eyebrows to indicate he was deathly serious. "They translated your paper and are still using it today to attack the aviation industry and guide them in bioterrorism. This discussion screams of their ability to spread bioweapons via the airline industry."

Hunter said, "Aviation security programs had shut them down, more or less, so there is little chance for liberals or communists to turn over aeronautical engineering secrets to the Brotherhood or allow al-Qaeda to blow up airplanes or airports. But if they have moved on to bugs; if they are now into biologicals, and we are not prepared for them, we could be in a deep well with no Lassie."

The comment elicited a smile from McGee, confusion in Nazy's face. She let the comment pass. McGee said, "And now that Haqqani has been captured, all the biological proliferation committees and the signatories of the Biological and Toxin Weapons Convention are agitated and in disarray...."

Hunter looked to his wife for help.

"The organizations that monitor or prohibit the development and production of biological agents have called for an emergency meeting.

That's where we are going after lunch." She frowned and looked at him quizzically.

Hunter said, "I'll bet they know something that we don't know."

McGee continued, "They want to know what Haqqani knows; we can't waterboard them anymore."

Hunter said, "We're screwed."

"Maybe he knows something." Nazy said, "Maybe the al-Qaeda remnants need a spectacular event to remain relevant."

Hunter said, "Maybe it really is a biological war to kill infidels...."

"While the Chinese trick them all and instigate an extinction event that leaves them untouched." McGee rolled his eyes and threw up a mighty hand and said, "Don't do it! Don't even think about it. You've given them plenty to think about as it is."

Nazy cleared her throat to get the men's attention back on the topic. She said, "TASCO International did the work through a third party. When Mazibuike came into power, one of the first things he did was drop all the moratoriums and sanctions previous presidents had instituted on Iran."

Hunter shook his head. "A secret bioweapons lab to weaponize a bug to kill infidels, Christians, and Jews. Spread it around like Johnny Appleseed. Muslims could think they are immune but the Chinese at the lab would never allow China to be impacted. And the Chinese could have a *beta* version that they could turn on whenever they wanted to kill everyone. Stop me if we've seen this before. *Black Swan* anyone?"

Nazy shared a quizzical glance with her boss.

McGee asked, "*Black Swan?*"

Hunter explained from in his MBA studies, "A black swan is a major unpredictable event, a situation that goes well beyond normal and has potentially severe consequences. In the business world black swan events are extremely rare, their impact severe. Smart people can see them coming but others don't want to hear negativity. People who don't understand the nature of business and don't do their homework dismiss them as conspiracy theories. Think Kodak and the electronic camera. Kodak was convinced they had a lock on making camera film for the next hundred years. But then someone took Kodak's own inventions, light sensitive chips used to detect faint light in space and the mini-camera-in-the-cellphone revolution began. Filmless cameras killed Kodak's film business. Kodak management was so preoccupied with film that they failed to see technology from their own R&D efforts was going to bankrupt them. Cell phone cameras were *Black Swans.*"

"I say Teslas and other electric cars are communist *Black Swans,* Trojan Horses meant to circumvent the efficiencies and effectiveness of the petroleum industry and force Americans into inefficient and ineffective—and let's not forget, government subsidized—electric vehicles. That's a storybook, but it is also a terrorist's wet dream because it can be killed with a flick of a switch in Washington. That's not accidental. Shut down electric cars and delivery trucks, and you shut down commerce and the economy creating nationwide chaos. That is their goal."

McGee held open his hand to Hunter; Duncan removed a 3X5 card from a suit coat pocket and gave it to him. McGee wrote down *Black Swan, Tesla, Trojan Horse, Wet Work #7,* and *POTUS.* Nazy smiled at how the men complemented each other.

Hunter nodded, "Since we suspect, I say they can be stopped. It will take a lot of political will." He apologized for the interruption and encouraged Nazy to continue.

Nazy said, "I repeat, Toraluddin Haqqani was sighted leaving the Khomeini Institute of Virology in a helicopter. All the heads of the bioterrorism agencies know al-Qaeda or ISIS was in the building."

"I think we have the proverbial long pole in the tent."

Black Swans. Long poles. Shit! McGee said, "I'm beginning to hate you."

Hunter cracked up, but Nazy was mortified. She knew the men in her life weren't serious with each other, were they?

McGee was somber, "I need to talk to the President."

Nazy was still shaking her head as McGee caught Hunter in a private grin. He asked what he was thinking.

Hunter sighed and said, "It's been about fifteen years since I sent the Navy a White Paper on protecting ships and aircraft from the ease of transmissivity of highly contagious viruses throughout ships, aircraft, and buildings that use HVAC, uh, heating, ventilation, and air conditioning ducting. I argued that if vast numbers of personnel, like what you would find on an aircraft carrier were ever infected with something like a coronavirus that could not be stopped by HEPA filters it would dramatically impact mission readiness and combat capability. And it would likely spread across the Navy."

McGee begged for more with his fingers. Nazy was suddenly interested.

"In the scheme of things, all respiratory viruses and bacteria are transmitted through respiratory micro-droplets. These micro-droplets catch a ride on the naturally occurring aerosols in the atmosphere and are spread when others breathe in mists that contains the virus and bacteria. This happens easily in enclosed rooms or when spread through HVAC air handling ducting and are usually stopped by HEPA filters. Because airborne transmission is tricky and the filters do a good job, the CDC knows this and, as I said before, these viruses are primarily transmitted by person-to-person contact. We can dramatically reduce the impact to mission capability and personnel being infected by using nature's disinfectants—ultraviolet light. The UV-C part of the spectrum has been used to sterilize objects and disinfect waste water; industry also uses UV-C lamps to kill viruses and bacteria in high-volume produce packing factories. UV light kills pathogens by damaging their DNA and destroying their ability to reproduce. *Weedbusters* uses the same principle—kill plants with UV-C. Lasers, not lamps or LEDs."

"My paper simply said that UV-C has a long history of use as a disinfectant. I proposed installing UV-C light bulbs or strips of UV-C LEDs, light-emitting diodes, in the air ducting. This would kill viruses and bacteria which pass through the ducting; not to replace HEPA filters but to augment them. The dirty little secret, some viruses never get into the HVAC. That's it. I patented a drone with LEDs to sterilize jet interiors; I already have strips of UV-C LEDs in the Gulfstream's ductwork. That's just two of my UV-C patents."

"And I tell you, they don't know it yet, but the airlines need to think about sterilizing the interiors of their aircraft and cargo holds. Today they don't see the need—I say they need to start doing it now. The day will come when a bug gets out. Every week now, you read about these idiots from China smuggling materials out of a biolab. On an unprotected jet the bug would make its way into the HVAC system and if the HEPA fails for whatever reason everyone gets contaminated. Same thing on a cruise ship. My sterilization devices ensure any bug that rides the air currents in an airplane or a cruise ship gets sterilized. Neutralized. Killed. It's the silver bullet to coronavirus contamination, either the weaponized or programmable type. Simple and relatively inexpensive products that protect people from a biological release."

Nazy asked, "So why don't they do it?"

"It not a priority. You remember Flight 800 and the closed door hearings on the proliferation of MANPADs—the shoulder-launched anti-aircraft missiles?"

"I do."

"The airlines' insisted it was the government's responsibility to protect them; the Navy protects the shipping lanes—all that jazz. But with a biological event, they don't see the need because it hasn't happened yet. Those guys are wired for profit and loss, and high-dollar sterilization equipment is not on their radar. You need an event to jumpstart these things. With a biological event, we could lose hundreds of thousands of people before a government can spool up the resources to fight it. Our strategic reserves are next to nothing. We are toast."

McGee said, "You mean if we have a super-spreader event?"

"I do."

"I'll call SecDef and President Hernandez. The technology is out there and we aren't protected. You're right. What about cargo?"

Hunter said, "I read where active live viruses have a shelf-life of a couple of days. My solution has always been to have air cargo pass through a box, like the X-ray machines in airports that would saturate the outside of the shipping container with UV-C. But cargo is low risk. Passengers are high risk. To infect the world, you need a breathing person who goes around and coughs on and touches everyone."

Nazy said, "That's their plan." *That's their plan.*

"And remember we are the prime target; if America falls, the rest of the world falls. But if we had UV-C technologies in our infrastructure, we would protect everyone. It would take some time to spool up the manufacturing base. The bad guys are expecting we will do nothing."

McGee added, "Your paper. You told them they should protect aviation, and they didn't."

"But they did after September 11. They wouldn't do it unless they were told to or forced to do it."

Nazy and McGee nodded. McGee said, "Well, your name is out there and we have to protect you."

"Bill, officially I'm dead. Buried at Arlington. Full military honors. *Grinch* and President Hernandez were there in the rain with the Marine Corps Band and the Commandant. As for the *fatwā,* Greg killed me off to pull the Islamic Underground off the trail, and it has been working." He recalled the number of times he had been targeted for assassination or had been declared dead. There had been so many failed assassination attempts he stopped counting.

Nazy said, "Baby, if they think you're still active.... That you're alive, that could be...*catastrophic*."

"It isn't Islamophobia if they're really trying to kill you." Hunter smiled at his bride. "We don't know. They might think she's been away so long that she didn't know I was dead."

McGee reflected on the insight. *Maybe....* He capitulated, "I don't see any reason to depart from that cover. You're dead. Let's keep it that way. We can use that information to our advantage. We'll inform her officially that Duncan Hunter is dead. She must talk to someone else." Then McGee snapped his fingers. He had an idea.

Hunter was still focused on Nobley. "What can you use as a pretext to get her out of there? GITMO is the wrong place to hold a non-combatant."

McGee squished up his face for a moment but recognized where Hunter's brain was carrying him. "Maybe we can say she needs better medical care and transfer her to a local prison hospital."

Nazy said, "I understand she's not in good shape."

Nobley's health seemed to depress Hunter. He looked at the floor, the walls; he looked for an answer to a question that wasn't clear.

Nazy nodded, it was contagious as McGee and Hunter all nodded in syncopation. Once Nazy stopped nodding, she cocked her head as if to telegraph that there were some elements with which she was uncomfortable.

Director McGee asked, "What're you thinking?"

Nazy said, "Terrorist wives generally know nothing. She told the men who crashed into the room that she was an American. Their after action report indicated that one of the other women in the room immediately turned a weapon on Nobley instead of the SEAL with a gun. That was the primary reason the soldiers brought her back. Nobley was a threat. She must know something, maybe important, for them to want to take her out at the first sign of a raid. Interrogation may help—we would like to know if she knows anything of Haqqani's movements to Iran or his business."

McGee wasn't confident. "It may be a complete bust."

Understanding that her health wasn't good, Hunter asked, "Have you seen...her?" After twenty years, living with a terrorist in the Middle East there wouldn't be any way possible for her to resemble her old self. He put his head in his hands and remembered what the pretty thirteen-year-old Afghani girl with the formidable green eyes who graced the cover of a 1984 National Geographic had looked like, and what she looked like as a thirty-year-old wife after a hard life under the rule of the Taliban. *It was only seventeen years later, but she looked like she had aged fifty....* Duncan tried to push the visions of the woman from his head.

Nazy and McGee nodded. "Nobley's photos. They're old stock. We have facsimiles of her SRB. More info is inbound. I was afraid of asking for recent photos of her for fear of highlighting her. Handling this as low key as possible is a winning strategy." McGee opened a file folder with no red TOP SECRET headers and footers so commonplace in the Agency. There were a few unclassified documents and a couple of photos. He passed them to Nazy as Hunter flipped through the fax copies of her SRB. Hunter found Nobley's emergency data page and copied her mother's address and telephone number onto a 3X5 card. There wasn't an entry for duty as a driver. Hunter was grateful; he remembered that day when she arrived in Hawaii, a petite slim leggy supermodel on his arm as they walked through the Kawai airport.

Nazy's eyes went straight to the face of the woman in the black and white 8X10 and was stunned by her radiant beauty. "*She's breathtaking. Like a cinema actor.*" She searched for the name that went with the face. The woman's hair confused her. She was sure she had seen that face before in one of Duncan's old movies. Nazy felt a little jealous, and it showed in her face. "I expect that once she went east, maybe after they graduated from college and landed in Egypt, Haqqani hid that face behind a *burka*. Muslim men can be psychotically jealous."

McGee said the photographic record stopped twenty years ago. "One would surmise she had died."

"Or vanished into the sewer of slavery and terrorism." Hunter remembered, *She was "decorative." I think that's the term they would use today. Drove all the men and a few of the women silly, batty, bonkers. She was one of the few women I suspected would keep her beauty to the very end. That was wishful thinking.* He asked, "So the only file you have is from the Marine Corps?" Hunter suddenly remembered Nobley had sent him a picture of her in happier times, taken during their honeymoon. The picture of her and her husband, a handsome dark-skinned fellow, was the only recent picture he had of Saoirse.

McGee and Nazy nodded and picked at the rest of their food. Time was running out, they had work to do, and meetings to attend.

CHAPTER 41

May 16, 2018

Nazy said, "I'm certain that once she was married and introduced into Muslim life in Egypt, her status was altered. He was in his element. She was not and was probably abused. Maybe significantly abused if Toraluddin Haqqani received citizenship and a U.S. passport. A girl like that could be a tradable commodity. We'll know more when we talk to her. We need to see her immigration records. The after action report indicates the house they were in looked as if it had been abandoned for months. The SEAL's initial evaluation was that they might have passed on it, but they believed the intel that it was an al-Qaeda command post. The number of footprints in the sand was like a billboard. If it had been abandoned footprints would have been lost to the winds. They took it down and found her. She wept in the SEAL's arms and thanked him profusely for rescuing her."

McGee said, "The SEAL said she was so frail that she might've been anorexic. She held on to him for life; she wouldn't let the SEAL go even when he frisked her for weapons. She cried as he saved her."

Hunter was shocked. *She had been so full of life; now she was so weak that she was frail? Anorexic? Oh God…. Bill, get her out of there!* He didn't want to overreact.

"I'm just glad he didn't shoot her." He recalled the time he had been sent to extract a defector from Iran and frisked what was supposed to be a male nuclear scientist. He stopped searching for a weapon when he realized his hands were full of a woman's breasts. The woman said her son had been killed and she had taken his place.

Nazy offered, "When we get her out, we'll have a counselor for her at *Spindletop*." She had had plenty of time to consider what her husband would think and feel about Nobley. That the thirty-nine-year-old Hunter had slept with the twenty-two-year-old immediately after his stint in the Marine Corps was inferred. None of that was relative now; that relationship had occurred well before Nazy met Duncan. Nazy would never forget the beginning of her journey to a new life, *Duncan took me to dinner at the Red Parrot in an elegant old Rolls Royce. After that night, our relationship was implied elliptically rather than referenced explicitly. That was so long ago.*

Hunter scribbled a note and passed it to McGee, who passed it to Nazy. *Get all of her school records? Immigration records on him, passports. Bank statements? Credit card records – their travel. When they left the US and reentered. Children's birth certificates? Where are they?* Interagency research was painful and it took forever. Nazy said she would assign a project officer to interact with the FBI and the various agencies.

Nazy thought back again to Newport…. *Rhode…Island…. A lot of water has passed under that bridge.* Nazy had been a woman defecting from Islam, running from a lecherous and abusive imam in a Boston mosque, and from a cruel husband with vitriol in his veins in Amman, Jordan. She remembered losing weight because of the stress. She remembered standing in Duncan's suite at the Naval War College holding his hand. The floodlights on Narragansett Bay Bridge filled his apartment window. She told him that she had left Islam. No more *Shahada,* no more rituals, no more Islamic declarations of faith. She had attended a church and found solace there. *There was a snowstorm, and we were safe on the navy base. The men from the mosque couldn't get to her.* Nazy sighed at the memory of the most critical and happiest event of her life. It was the first time they had made love, and she was thrilled that Duncan had been a tender, considerate, and passionate lover. With bemused eyes that Hunter and McGee totally missed she looked up to her husband and concluded, *Was it odd that Duncan's orbit always seemed to intersect with women in distress? And why do all the women who meet Duncan fall in love with him? I know, he makes them feel special, all the time.* Nazy telegraphed love by squeezing his hand under the table like a high schooler.

Hunter reciprocated the token of love. McGee was waiting. Hunter asked, "Do you want me to get her?"

McGee shook his head and said, "Let me work on it. We might have to consider letting the U.S. Marshal's do it. But there may be a better solution. Maybe DOD. Maybe I can call in a few favors. But…the less you're exposed the better. At the very least I can make sure she's treated well."

"Thanks, *Bullfrog*."

Nazy was suddenly concerned for the woman. She said, "I can't imagine they will let her remove the *hijab*, although I think she'll want to remove it immediately. I know that when I felt safe enough, I did."

Hunter and McGee considered the wisdom of the former Muslima. Both men nodded. McGee continued, "It will take some time to notify all the plank holders in the IC and arrange the transfer. Acquire her records. Nazy, I think we want to kill any notion she's going to be interrogated by Duncan."

Nazy Cunningham turned to Duncan and said. "I think we may want to relook at *Spindletop*. I have another idea." She pointed a long delicate finger with a pretty blood-red enameled nail at him. "It'll cost you. Can't have Bill fund what I have in mind."

Hunter grinned like a drunk at a wet t-shirt contest and waved at her the way he always did when she talked about spending irresponsible amounts of money. *Whatever it takes, darling wife, do what you think is necessary.*

The amount of money was never the object; it was always an issue of what it was being spent on. Nazy scrutinized, *But on another woman? It's not really for her. Duncan has a soft spot for rehabilitation projects, and we had talked about helping them. He wanted to buy the property, but it wasn't for sale at any price. Now it was a monument for all to see and enjoy. Maybe it was better that way.* The more she reflected on it the more she liked her idea.

McGee shrugged his goal-post wide shoulders and said, "You'll find the right solution. You always do. And I'll entertain all plans to extract her out of there." McGee picked up his trash and said, "Duncan, I have another set of missions for you. More *Special Activities*. Craziness is erupting from everywhere—by and with the usual cast of characters. You'll be back well before we can manage Nobley's transfer to *Spindletop*…or wherever Nazy wants to take her." McGee didn't miss a beat. The man who was used to giving directions pointed at Hunter and said, "My office, 1700? Nazy and I have to go. You can hang out here or find something to do."

"Will we need the *Yo-Yo*?"

McGee stood as gloom washed over him. His eyes cleared the room for ears. "Mostly full slate. Somali pirates, hostages. FARC, hostages, labs. The submersibles are getting huge and are almost real subs, and there is some intel that they are using batteries."

"Electric submersibles are nearly as easy to find as gasoline-powered ones."

Nazy said, "Really?"

"The bow crashing into calm water at night causes the plankton to fluoresce and the heat generated by the prop leaves contrail-like traces in the water. FLIR picks them up—several thermal differentials—easily as long as they are submersibles barely under the water. Submarines are undetectable and I'm actually surprised the Russians haven't sold the cartels one of their obsolete diesel boats. That would be a game changer."

McGee listened, concurred, and was back at work. "We need to ID the black-market weapons pipeline and stop Iranian arms bound for Yemen's Houthi fighters. The usual imagery of Chinese embassies. And if we can work out all the details, an extraction. I'll know more as things develop when you're down-range."

Hunter sighed and blew air through his pie hole. *An extraction. Those are the worse. It was terrifying, flying over an Iranian missile battery, hoping the coating on the Yo-Yo was everything the manufacturer said it was.* But this wasn't a time for alarmist actions; mental preparation had always been key to success. All the operations McGee touched upon might just be the tip of a proverbial iceberg. He articulated some concern to his Boss, "Captain, I believe there's ice up ahead." The line was from *Titanic*.

McGee nodded. "Well, batten down the hatches, full speed ahead. We're in for stormy weather. But you can and will handle it." He put his hands in his pockets and continued, "....a couple of weeks, minimum. Maybe a month if there's a disorder with the lift. There's a lot of craziness going on out there, and I'm going to be counting *Black Swans* jumping fences tonight."

Hunter interjected, "And these aren't even lefties or liberal Democrats...."

McGee wasn't amused. "A lot of work."

Hunter said, "Everyone thinks they can do patriot shit until it comes time to do patriot shit. I hope my bride doesn't forget me." He glanced at Nazy.

Nazy exclaimed in her best thick sensual British, "Baby, you're *unforgettable!*"

McGee chided them with a finger, "Stop it. No one is supposed to know you two are a couple." Hunter and Nazy and McGee laughed. Laughter was good, and Nazy had a way of bringing out men's smiles and informal laughter.

"You know boss, for a month, I'm going to need some stuff."

"Get me a list. Anything else?"

"What are the chances of visiting S&T? Get a tour?"

"That shouldn't be a problem. Nazy, can you set that up?" She smiled and nodded.

On the way to the Director's private elevator, Nazy walked between two of the most dangerous men in the world and felt perfectly safe. She nodded her assent. She was pleased with herself, the men in her life were still protecting her. *Without security, it's difficult for a woman to look or feel pretty.*

There had been a time when Nazy drove her old Mercedes two-seater to work, but after several attempts on her life the CIA Director, with the approval of the President, authorized 24/7 government-furnished security. The other vehicle in Nazy's garage was a rolling safe room. In the event her protective staff could no longer protect her, she could drive the armored beast to CIA headquarters. The Hummer2 had been taken apart and modified by Texas Automotive Designs, one of Hunter's companies specializing in transforming high-value, high-profile luxury vehicles into armored-plated rolling bank vaults for government VIPs from the intelligence community, Round Rock executives, Dallas financiers, Austin entrepreneurs, San Antonio celebrities, and company CEOs from around the world.

Hunter's armored vehicles had 800-horsepower supercharged Corvette engines with armor-plating around the engine and fuel tank. They had armored doors and bulletproof windows, and winches, night vision devices, touch screens to activate other capabilities, such as "Gunfire Horn" and "Quiet Running" which silenced the exhaust. They came equipped with positive pressure fresh air systems to keep any debilitating gases from entering the cabin, fire extinguishers, and run-flat tires. Texas Automotive Designs couldn't build enough of their Hummers and Suburbans, so other manufacturing shops across the country started building their own versions of armored vehicles. Agency armored vehicles weren't purchased from Hunter's company but through a lowest-cost, technically acceptable vehicle provider.

McGee said, "That is one strange-ass name. *SIR-sha*. It sounds much different than it's spelled."

Hunter said, "It's Irish for *Liberty*. I haven't thought about it before but it's a great name for a patriot. John Adams said, 'Liberty once lost is lost forever.'"

McGee said, "But now she is found. Do you have anything else you would like me to do for you, Sir Duncan?"

Hunter handed McGee a 3X5 card with data. "GPS coordinates. If one of your guys could just poke their nose into this unusual place, maybe during a riverine patrol, I would be forever grateful. If it's too hard, I'll get around to it." McGee's lips went flat line as he nodded his assent. *Must be an airplane.*

Nazy interjected, "I would like to exclude *Spindletop*. I'm thinking of another location that's 'off the grid,' as you like to say. A location north. I think it will be better." She didn't add, *It'll be pricey if they let us use their facility.* It wasn't the time or place to discuss outrageous proposals.

"Seriously?" Hunter's mind was running through the requisite logistics of the new special activities. He always considered the logistics of things. Hunter added, "And, if Nobley needs a dentist...."

McGee said, "Count on it."

Hunter finished his sentence. "I know someone we can use—if you go north. Not too much north. Pennsylvania north." Nazy nodded as Hunter added. "I'll get you his contact info."

Nazy thought, *Pennsylvania is looking better every second.*

A security guard decked out in a black battle dress uniform and carrying an M-4 summoned the elevator with a key. McGee told the security guard, "Pass this gentleman when he returns at 1700." Hunter showed the guard his badge.

The guard barely looked at the badge. He wasn't impressed. He would remember Hunter.

Nazy entered the elevator first. McGee entered and waited for the door to close, but Hunter blocked it with his back. The security guard, who was almost as tall and wide as Director McGee, was not amused and gave Hunter the evil eye. He scrutinized the color of the man's access badge; blue with gold outline. Executive staff. The same badge color as the Director and the NCTC Director.

McGee agreed. "I'm sure that when I first arrived here, I wouldn't have liked the perception of you being here in the open, but…."

Hunter interjected, "…but because of your eradication efforts…."

"I'm going to have to get used to it. We've cleared this place of 3M's vermin. This is a big place. An unknown face can now get lost easily. Have fun at S&T…. Who are you today?" McGee scrutinized Hunter's badge. *Oh yeah, someone in security had a sense of humor.*

Hunter hunched his shoulders.

McGee pointed a big thick finger the size of a screwdriver handle at him. *Yes! Enjoy that.* He asked Nazy, "I suppose you'll want to go, lead this operation? Keep an eye on prince charming, here? I'm looking forward to Australia. The beach."

Nazy said, "While I would love to see this woman who made Duncan pay for a ten-day…what he called a *vacation* to Hawaii, with a girl half his age, Director McGee, you have me wearing two hats. You're leaving, and we have a ton of work to do before your trip. I'll ensure we'll have plenty of support staff wherever we take her. A polygrapher. A doctor. Security. I don't think I'll be needed while you're gone, unless you think there will be a problem prying her off of my husband when she sees him."

McGee asked, "Will there be a problem? Can we use Kelly?"

Hunter shook his head to the former as he wrestled with the elevator door and avoided the scrutiny of the security guard. "Kelly will work."

"I would like to keep this in the family, if you know what I mean." He chucked like a conspirator who had just been busted.

Behind the back of the security guard, Nazy threw Duncan a pretend kiss.

Hunter rolled his eyes.

Director McGee wanted to poke at his best friend a little more and said, "Are you sure you saw her only *after* you retired?"

Hunter nodded as if there was any doubt.

McGee asked, "Didn't you say you were on assignment hunting the Corps' sexual predators and those generals who fraternized with the distaff? How did you…ever manage *that* and a *Corporal*?" McGee didn't really want an answer and Hunter knew it. He just wanted Hunter to let the door go.

Hunter lowered his eyes. *When I saw her, I didn't think I would look like a fool twenty years later. But after I had seen her, the day I caught her, I was not in my right mind for some time. If I had been in my right mind, I would have let nothing start between us. But from what I know now, maybe I made the correct decision. Maybe in some strange way I motivated her to stay alive. Had I not seen her we wouldn't be having this conversation.* He raised his eyes to look at his wife and friend. *Maybe Bill and Nazy can see that too.*

For the benefit of a concerned security guard, Hunter shook the two spooks' hands as if an unofficial meeting had ended. Hunter leaned into the Director and softly said into his ear, "Bill, I understand the only thing remaining from Roustaie was a watch attached to his wrist. Can you get your hands on that watch?" Nazy didn't hear the request; she was mildly perturbed at her boss for poking at her husband, even if it was good natured and innocent ribbing.

McGee furrowed his brows as if a bolt of lightning hit him from behind. He answered pensively, "I'll see what I can do." His brain had been working on a solution to a new problem. His mind, forever engaged, was racing again and McGee's sudden inspiration could be verbalized. He asked, "Umm, Duncan, how tall is this Nobley? I mean, what size *flight suit* would she wear?"

Hunter was uncomfortably confused for a moment and told McGee, as he recalled, her height and weight, what size dress she wore and her shoe size. "But that was a long time ago."

Nazy asked, "Okay, Mr. Boy Scout; what about her bust?"

Hunter responded with open lips and hand gestures to suggest the woman had been busty. *As big as Nazy, but that is not something a sane man would say.* He bailed out of the flaming jet with, "Do anorexics have busts?" He did not like the game that his wife was playing with him. Some animals can smell danger; vertiginous men just tumble into the trap.

McGee looked at Nazy who wrote down the woman's measurements. He said, "We're also meeting with the Scientific and Technical Intelligence Committee, and then we're unveiling the National Counterintelligence Strategy of the United States. Threat actors are using enhanced capabilities against an expanded set of targets and vulnerabilities."

Hunter asked, "You mean like unprotected Iranian virology institutes and al-Qaeda mercenaries who may have U.S. passports and are on the loose?"

"You know too much." McGee sighed for a moment and said, "We are going to be awhile—may we please go to our meeting?"

Hunter asked McGee to check on the status of the S&T's experimental incendiary ammo.

McGee was curious. "Incendiary?"

"When we find a drug lab, a well-placed, *fire-starting* bullet is sometimes the axiomatic solution." Hunter had envisioned special ammunition that could start a fire in a structure or a vehicle or a drug lab with barrels of flammable chemicals used to make cocaine. Fire had a way of disinfecting an area.

McGee didn't like being an errand boy, but for Hunter he would make an exception. At least he knew what to do with dead monkeys. Nazy looked at her husband and said someone from S&T would come get him. Hunter stepped aside, saluted, and allowed the elevator door to close. The guard frowned at him. He returned to his seat in the Agency's canteen.

Duncan Hunter, aka *Dante Locke* of the National Clandestine Service, according to his badge, had been abandoned in the Belly of the Beast. CIA Headquarters. *Idle hands are the Devil's workshop. I have some time to kill. This is so unusual. In over twenty years, I've never once been turned loose in this place! You can tell when the old SAP is winding down. What can I see that I have missed all these years? It'll be like the first time I was turned loose in a German candy store with a Deutsche Mark!*

Instead of grousing at McGee for ruining his sex life with future work, he looked up at the black aircraft models hanging over the atrium of the New Office Building; the secret jets the CIA made well-known, especially the ignominious U-2, the noteworthy A-12, and the supersonic drone, the D-21. He sighed and doubted that he would ever see a copy of his quiet airplane hanging from the rafters. The black CIA spyplanes weren't only the sexiest aircraft ever built, they were official Agency top secret "special projects." The Army's prototype was brutish and functional, the YO-3A wasn't anything like what had been conceived by the minds of Air Branch.

The Agency's strong bias against suggestions from the outside was very provincial. *Not invented here* meant the YO-3A wasn't ever going to be put up there with the other black birds. Suspending a YO-3A from the ceiling would officially acknowledge that a contractor had done what the civil servants could not. It would also mean getting the creator of the program back into CIA HQ, and former Director Greg Lynche had left for good. He was away on his sailboat in the Caicos or the Turks, and Hunter was certain Greg wouldn't ever come back, even for a dedication ceremony. Not for him, not for anything.

After dumping his trash in a receptacle he wandered over to the CIA's bookstore and museum, flashed his blue and gold security access card, and spent the better part of an hour inside looking for any of the secret Soviet files that Nazy had discovered years earlier. They told how in-place defectors in American aircraft manufacturing plants stole plans for the first generation unmanned or "remote-controlled" airplanes that were used to try to start a war between Germany and America by bringing down the Nazi's 800-foot zeppelin *Hindenburg*.

He looked, but even in the cleared space of the CIA's own museum he couldn't find any reference to classified Soviet Union files that mentioned how a submarine of the Soviet Navy generated a spurious homing signal that pulled Amelia Earhart off course and thwarted her around the world attempt. There were no displays or placards of Soviet subversion where their loyalists in the United States were stopped from stealing schematics and plans of America's naval vessels, frontline fighters and bombers, and even the Space Shuttle. Those stories, he surmised, were still classified, or, he surmised, those were the histories when there wasn't a CIA.

Hunter stopped and read the displays in the Historical Collections. *Aquiline was a small drone, meant to be kept as close to bird-like size as possible – five feet long, 7.5 feet wide, and a takeoff weight of 83 pounds – under the constraints of the technology of the time. The drone, which was supposed to act as a robotic spyplane and courier for secret payloads, was never completed. While Aquiline never became operational, the concept proved invaluable as a forerunner to today's multi-capability UAVs.*

After reading about *Aquiline's* silent 3.5-horsepower, four-cycle engine, Duncan walked away. *Even in the early 1960s they figured out how to quiet an engine and its propeller.* Allen Dulles, one of the first Directors of the CIA, had mandated after losing the Agency's U-2 and Gary Powers, that the CIA would never again put another pilot in a surveillance aircraft over Communist countries, thus starting the quest for practical unmanned surveillance aircraft. Director Dulles would roll over in his grave if he knew what Duncan Hunter had been doing in a manned aircraft.

The black airplanes hanging in the rafters, the U-2 and A-12 had become obsolete, and parts of those programs could be declassified. Hunter chuckled, *the YO-3A is silent and its propeller is still top secret! More reason not to expose it to the masses, even masses with clearances.*

The old flame suddenly interrupted his thoughts. *Nobley! I knew you married a Middle Eastern dude, and there was nothing I could do about it. Other than…I talked to Greg about you, en passant. That was over twenty years ago. Was it relevant? I'll tell Bill of the conversation. He's the boss. He has all the answers. He is the one person who has a need to know.*

He shrugged broad shoulders and poured over the U-2 displays and the U-2's successor, the A-12 *OXCART*. On the way out of the museum he thumbed through a book, *Spyplanes*. Of course, there would be no mention of the YO-3A. It was an Army airplane. He picked up a dozen unclassified calendars of the history of surveillance aircraft, which obviously had much Agency participation and had been artfully produced by the International Spy Museum in Washington, D.C. And he bought dozens of challenge coins that had been made for various Agency departments that even the most seasoned rank and file intelligence officer had never heard of. He remembered the first coin he received from the CMC. Now he had hundreds and his own.

Hunter wandered outside to see the Agency's titanium A-12 on display. *Maybe the Soviets couldn't make a titanium jet. That's probably it. That was always their problem. Many of the aircraft and engine designs that had been stolen from Western and American manufacturers and found their way into the old Soviet Union aviation design bureaus lacked key manufacturing processes. The trade secrets. Something critical to the manufacturing process the Soviets needed and tried to steal if they wanted an aircraft to fly properly.* Hunter remembered the Soviets had received stolen plans for the *Concorde* from French communist workers. Tupelov hurriedly made their own version of the supersonic transport, the TU-144, and flew it at the Paris Air Show to show the superior manufacturing prowess of the communist collective only to have the jet break apart. During the greatest airshow on earth, it snapped into two pieces in flight. The Soviets reacted to the tragedy by racing across the Le Bourget flight line and screaming at the French leaders for allowing them to build the TU-144 with defects.

He walked around the jet and stopped at the A-12's plaque which provided details such as the black bird's serial number and other technical minutiae. Statistics that were meaningless to the masses, but not to Duncan Hunter when he was in professor mode.

Hunter waved his arms wildly like a mental institution resident and complained to himself that the spectacular *OXCART* should've been inside, not outside exposed to the weather. The engineering marvel on display was in a class by itself.

He crossed his arms, unfocused on the jet in front of him, and reflected on how different his life would have been had he been able to join the astronaut corps. He would have traded his Naval Aviator wings for Naval Astronaut Wings. But then he wouldn't have met Nazy and wouldn't have been doing the work he was born to do. Being an astronaut would have meant a possible single shot into space, whereas he had turned his passion for flying and expertise in counterterrorism into a unique capability that influenced the National Defense. Hunter reflected that he had killed more enemies of the U.S. than anyone since Marine Private Dan Daly's exploits during the Boxer Rebellion in China. Private Daly had received his first Medal of Honor for single-handedly defending his position against repeated attacks and inflicting casualties of around 200 attacking Boxers. Daly's deed defending liberty and his fellow Marines took one day; Hunter's took two decades.

Hunter changed course and reflected on the damage the former president had done to NASA and the Space Shuttle program. He couldn't blame President Mazibuike for the retirement of the SR-71, but Hunter couldn't justify the termination of Space Shuttle. Why would any president not support the space program? Only if the president hated America and the things she stood for, and that included its leadership in space. Hunter was convinced the termination of the Space Shuttle was done to disgrace the United States. Put America in its place. Everything 3M did hurt the U.S. and showed that America was just like the other socialist nations with men stripped of their religion chugging to work like from a scene in Orwell's *1984* or underground in the 1927 *Metropolis. The man was not on our side.* With no funding, no follow-on program, and no service life extension for the Shuttle, the effect was the total humiliation for the United States. Mazibuike even directed the NASA Administrator to focus primarily on Muslim Outreach efforts.

While walking back to the main entrance and across the granite Seal of the CIA, Hunter mused, *What's going to happen to Saoirse? What the hell happened to her? I'm probably not going to know anything until I get back.*

A middle-aged boxy woman with a rat's nest for hair and oversized glassed made a beeline to him. "Dante Locke?" Hunter smiled with a nod. She said, "Yeah, right. What's your real name?" She held out her hand, "I'm Roxanne Foggel. Director S&T."

"My friends call me *Maverick*."

"What do your enemies call you?"

"Are you related to Gunner Foggel, Navy SEAL?"

Taken aback, she nodded.

Hunter remembered him. Commander, looked like Lionel Barrymore in his later years. Balding and not muscular like McGee. It was as if Foggel appeared to have no muscle mass, but Hunter recalled the SEAL was just as hard as a brick as McGee. Foggel said he had the worst feet in the Navy from working the swamps of East Africa looking for al-Shabab and pirates. "He was in my seminar class at the Naval War College a few years ago. I guess that was more than a few years ago." He shook her hand and they became instant friends. Hunter felt his problem was now going to be her problem.

She asked, "What did Gunner know you as?"

"*Maverick*. What's he doing these days and how is he?"

Those guys never give out their names. Roxanne Foggel knew she had been outsmarted and said, "He does an occasional odd job for the Director, going on…fifteen years. Shortly after the Naval War College. He couldn't do the things his peers were doing, like going to work for *Blackwater* or one of those personal security companies. He has had a hard life and his feet are still giving him fits. But Bethesda—I'm sorry, Walter Reed is taking care of him. He has better drugs and custom Merrells. What do you want to know?"

Hunter held up his Rolex and asked, "Is it possible to put a homing device on this?"

They repaired to the cafeteria and took opposite chairs. She asked for his watch and scrutinized it. "You know Gunner has the stainless steel *Submariner*."

"I remember."

"So you want a homing device on this." She sighed, "Well, technically, yes we can do it, but the result, I'm afraid, will not be very effective." She went through the possibilities and impossibilities, pointing out on the watch what was in the art of the possible and what was not practical. She said, "Inserting special capacities in a watch like this is really the stuff from the minds of novelists. Fiction." Handing the watch back to him, she said, "Now, if you had the presentation case for this, we could work magic. Range, signal strength. Battery life. The scalability of things. We can hide everything and track it to the moon."

Hunter considered the information. "What if you don't have a case? You might get one at an on-line auction."

Roxanne Foggel smiled and said, "We can replicate any case ever manufactured. When would you need it?"

Hunter smiled and nodded, he withdrew a pair of 3X5 cards and scribbled some letters and numbers on one and his cellphone number on the other. Handing the cards to her he said, "I can't make any promises on when I would need it. It could be a couple of months. My concern is that it needs to withstand the scrutiny of an expert watch collector. If you know what I mean. If you need a charge code, Director McGee will authorize the cost of the project."

She looked at the card and said, "I have not seen one of those; pretty rare?" A man of few words, Hunter nodded and smiled. He had his answer. Hunter said he was glad Gunner was doing ok and asked Roxanne to give her husband his regards. "And if Gunner wants to talk, he can call me anytime."

The Director of Science and Technology Directorate said she would see what she could do and walked away. *And the Director will just pay for it like that? Must be one of those guys on a SAP.*

Hunter remained in the watering hole to await his meeting with the CIA Director. He got a coffee and yawned; he hadn't been able to sleep much. A wry grin presaged that Nazy would make sure he wouldn't get much sleep tonight, either. That was ok. *There are some things you just don't miss.*

CHAPTER 42

May 16, 2018

The postings of *Omega* were becoming more frequent and terse. His followers reveled in the disclosures which were timely and on target. They looked forward to the next *Omega* posting, and they never got tired of the anti-Mazibuike commentary. People were not aware of the depth of 3M's treachery.

It's Tuesday, May 16th, 2018, and Maxim Mohammad Mazibuike was the most corrupt president in U.S. history and his communist buddy, the recluse Rho Schwartz Scorpii, is one of the most corrupt people in Europe.

Do you believe in coincidences? Do you believe we are winning the war on terrorism? Americans will soon learn that the al-Qaeda or Islamic State's intelligence minister was captured and is likely on his way to or maybe already on a sunny Caribbean island receiving three culturally sensitive meals a day, free health care, a private room where he can gaze upon the most modern facilities and artwork he has ever seen – a flushable toilet.

Is it a coincidence that Toraluddin Haqqani, one brother of the Haqqani terrorist network, who'll never make the ten o'clock news on any of the cable news networks by my count, marks the 201st master terrorist taken off the battlefield in the last twenty years? Let me repeat, over 200 terrorist leaders have been killed or captured, and the media are oblivious. The war on the leaders of terrorism is being waged in the dark in the Middle East and Africa.

Is it a coincidence that there hasn't been a single mention of the worst of the worst international terrorists on the FBI's Most Wanted List, those having been killed or removed by U.S. special operations forces? Is silence the only effect of deviant murderers being silenced? You could fill a Prius with the number of honest reporters in the industry. This isn't the fault of that minority of reporters, but it is the modus operandi of the majority.

Is it a coincidence that there hasn't been a single mention of the executives at the Sandia National Laboratory and Y-12, the National Security Complex, who were fired with extreme haste for espousing critical race theory and race-

segregated training – essentially brainwashing white employees that they are Islamophobic and racist, and they must let unqualified people with no clearances have access to the nation's most valuable nuclear secrets? President Hernandez just drove a stake in the heart of the Muslim Brotherhood and Islamic Underground's infiltration programs, and the media will not report a word. Ask yourself, why is that?

Is it a coincidence that the owners and publishers of America's most widely read newspapers and most-watched networks are some of the biggest closet leftists on the planet? Do these relationships hold true at other companies doing business with the U.S. Government? Let's find out.

This is the Omega.

CHAPTER 43

May 17, 2018

Bogdan Chernovich unbuttoned his dark blue suitcoat as he sat in an oversized judge's chair, taking his place at the head of the conference table. An executive session of the Trans-Atlantic Security Corporation was in session, and all board members were in attendance. It was a special collection of leaders. There were several former heads of their respective branches of the military and intelligence agencies, and several were former CEOs of some of the big-box, blue-chip weapons manufacturing companies that the media referred to as the "industrial military complex." All the men wore dark suits, insipid ties, saddle-colored oxfords, and gold timepieces not manufactured in Geneva.

Not a single Rolex could be found on any of their wrists. They were anathema to groups like TASCO. Rolex and their sister watches, Tudor, were viewed as the marks of uneducated fools who were easily sidetracked by shiny pabulum, trinkets of the rich, and the unserious, and the undeserving.

The men of TASCO considered themselves to be more than serious. From an innate sense of self-worth they had carefully managed life's dangers, distractions, disruptions, and disorders to reach the pinnacle of their professions. From a cast of uncredited, underdeveloped extras they had risen to become the mature stars of business, politics, and the military. They *dominated* the battlespace of their professions in the business world embracing a diversity of perspectives. The TASCO board of directors and legal team were all men; they were often featured in their in-house magazine, *The Eastern.*

TASCO employed over 100,000 people in fifty countries. They had a comprehensive medical plan that featured the first policies in America to pay for an employee's sexual reassignment operation. The international branches of TASCO were run by seasoned experienced intelligence executives, primarily unflashy homosexual men and lesbian women who had kept their sexuality secret from military intelligence, Soviet intelligence, Russian intelligence, and on rare occasions, the CIA polygrapher. They knew the tricks of the tradecraft, and they were the ones who had written the books on the USIC and filled CIA and NSA's secret libraries with their papers. It was well known within the government's IC that TASCO had better intelligence collection capabilities than the CIA, MI6, the *Sûreté*, the Mossad, and the rest of the international intelligence community.

TASCO had mature analysts and intel professionals; the USIC spent an inordinate amount of time teaching beginners the tradecraft.

As CEO of TASCO, Chernovich called the meeting to order with an interrogative, "What happened to the DNC's archives? How did *Whistleblowers* get access to them? Is there any way to stop them?"

No one around the dark mahogany table had an answer. A few seconds passed until the former Air Force Chief of Intelligence offered, "Those *Whistleblowers* goons wouldn't accept our offer. I think they plan to release it, *gratis*. Which makes no sense."

The former Chief of Naval Intelligence (CNI) said, "That's hard to believe. Someone had to have beaten us to them. A paying customer. Was our price too low?" Heads nodded in agreement.

The CEO continued, "Does anyone know what happened to Roustaie? That attack was not on our local radar." *Local radar* meant from *domestic sources*. CIA. "It was unremarkable that they were tracking him, they always tracked him and others of the Iranian Guard, but they and the Israelis always pulled back."

The former National Security Agency Director spat, "Not this time. There's been a change and his name is William McGee."

The former CNI said, "Unusual selection for CIA. Not one of ours. He's not even an admiral. But he is the most decorated U.S. military man ever. Goes by *Bullfrog*. I know him. Pinned a Navy Cross on him. He's built like a Wall Street bull. We could use a man like that. He should be on our side, but he is a *family* man." The comment drew looks but no barbs. "I tried several times to bring him over, but he insisted he enjoyed being retired. Able to spend time with the family. Somehow he acquired ownership of a training facility in Texas. Of course, that's all bullshit." Heads nodded in agreement.

Chernovich declared, "You don't need satellite photos to see that killing Roustaie was an Agency op."

The former NSA Director said, "As much as the Israelis wanted Roustaie dead, they didn't have the resources to execute that level of precision at BIAP."

Chernovich's tone was angry. "It's like they have a new capability we are unaware of. And nothing on the IC grapevine hinted at Haqqani or al-Amirikiu's capture, yet they were taken or eradicated by an unknown team on an unknown black program, yes?" There was unanimity without words.

The former U.S. Air Force Chief of Intelligence offered, "Director McGee and the POTUS aren't our men. We no longer have even one of our men in a deputy or VP position. No one on the seventh floor. I think his actions, and the actions of this President are the matters at hand. They are the problem. They're not playing ball; they're doing their own damned thing."

The former Director of the National Reconnaissance Office (NRO) said, "They've taken down the top terrorists in the world without the benefit of overheads—ah, satellites. They've killed 200—*no!* More than 200 with no end in sight. Under McGee and at this rate, they will find and destroy the rest."

Chernovich said, "Not to worry, it's not like we are going to be out of a job if that happens."

"We'll still have government contracts." The former Chief of Intelligence of the Army could be succinct and to the point.

Chernovich said, "You know perfectly well what I mean."

The retired Air Force Chief of Intelligence said, "I hear there have been several MC-130s dispatched from Andrews to Africa and South America, but mostly to the Middle East. And there is a newcomer—a private LM-100J that's not the Agency's."

He spoke with his hands. "These missions are so secret the aircrew aren't allowed to watch what transpires after landing, what gets unloaded. It's clear it's an airplane."

"Unmanned, no doubt," proffered the former Army Chief of Intelligence whose craggy penitentiary face looked as if it came right out of a 1930s James Cagney movie.

Chernovich sighed, "No. Manned, and do not doubt me. We even have a name, or a 'call sign.' *Maverick*. Over 60. Silver hair. Definitely the pilot, but of what we do not know emphatically. I suspect, but let's leave it there. We have enough evidence to put him within 500 miles of ongoing or in-progress counterterrorism work. I have pages of dates that align nicely with *Hercules*' movements into adjacent countries with unexplained terrorists deaths."

"It seems Eastwood is also on top of the deaths of terrorists. Keeps a database....our IT guys haven't been able to locate him."

The dark rumbling voice of Chernovich filled the room. "We were lieutenant colonels together, he and I. After Vietnam he went to the National Security Council and got shit-canned for conducting unauthorized special activities. Eastwood is a case study for abuse of power. He's been trying to redeem his reputation with insipid exposés on the international sex trade and the occasional battlefield story."

The former CNI said, "And politics. He is deep into politics. Don't forget his exposé on the Attorney General Eleanor Tussy destroyed her candidacy. I don't think we should dismiss him as a lightweight."

Chernovich caustically said, "The DNC has been totally compromised as well. She was expected to win and didn't. There was more than one reason the DNC Chairman, Dr. Zhavrazhinov, took a swan dive off of the 22nd floor of the Times Square Marriott. Director McGee announced *Whistleblowers* had the DNC's archives, and he had the old man's diary and papers, which had to have some information on the voting machines." *Those are our voting machines!* "When these documents are released, we will witness the total destruction of the DNC and the Democrat Party in the United States. I think we will be ok; we were far enough away from any direct action. It is still inconceivable that the DNC controlled the election and the voting machines but lost when Hernandez won Philadelphia?"

Without looking up, the retired Air Force Chief of Intelligence said, "Philadelphia has always voted Democrat, but this time it did not. I believe it was voter machine failure. The final compiler. It is the only thing that makes sense to me."

The board of directors were at a loss to explain the outcome of the election and machines do fail. Two years ago no one wanted to investigate. Chernovich returned to the issue of the DNC. "It doesn't matter. It is almost ours now; then it will be totally ours, and we will fill it with our people. Enough politics." First on the docket to be discussed was the status of billion-dollar proposals.

TASCO's various lines of business—Intel, Federal, International—managed several billion-dollar oil exploration, extraction, refinery, and transportation contracts for multiple government-owned oil fields. TASCO also had won a ten-year, ten billion dollar contract with the National Security Agency and the NCTC for database maintenance and analysis. TASCO mined the incomparable database of the NSA which captured virtually all electronic communications–emails and text messages. The NSA trusted TASCO and its hundreds of former NSA intelligence officers working at Fort Meade. TASCO also monitored intercepts between the U.S. and other countries and performed a range of support services from managing the mail room, the gym, and a health clinic to removing snow from sidewalks and parking lots.

TASCO also had contracts with the U.S. State Department which issued contracts for Red Star fuels to be transported via railcars and delivered to Afghanistan and Iraq for Russian helicopters and aircraft. In the turbulence of war-time efforts, TASCO proposals were expedited through the State Department and they became "sole source" vendors. The former communist countries had petroleum products; the U.S. government needed fuel in a war zone. Declare TASCO to be a "sole source" vendor and move to the next contract.

Like moving pieces on a chessboard to capture the opponent's king, TASCO played the State Department like a rookie chess player and orchestrated one of the most egregious money laundering schemes in U.S. history. The State Department would approve billions of dollars of foreign aid to a country, for petroleum exploration, extraction, and transportation. TASCO would siphon off ten percent of that aid to use for other things unrelated to oil exploration, such as funding charitable foundations and banks and dummy corporations around the globe. Keys to their long-term success in laundering billions in foreign aid was to have trusted agents on the board of directors of the oil exploration companies. These trusted agents would keep their mouths closed and collect obscene paychecks. The rest of the purloined funds increased the personal wealth of the TASCO board of directors.

The scheme to launder billions in foreign aid began under the Mazibuike Administration. With the election of the Republican Hernandez, the pipeline of millions was turned off. Eleanor Tussy was supposed to win the election, thus ensuring another four or eight years of an uninterrupted money supply into the coffers of TASCO and the board of directors. When she didn't win, the Democrats made life hell for everybody. Bodies literally littered the political landscape, for failure in politics isn't an honorable option when you're an outcast member of the Democrat Party and the DNC.

Then another tragedy struck. Congress blamed President Hernandez for the death of Eleanor Tussy even though cameras recorded the moment she lost her balance and fell, splitting her head open. If the accident hadn't been captured on a surveillance camera, all of America would've blamed President Hernandez for her death. With her passing, the fortunes of TASCO began to plummet.

Bogdan Chernovich asked, "What are we going to do about Hernandez? The DNC tried and failed to oust him from the White House; the DNC tried and failed to kill him, and we can't emasculate him and his administration—his message is resonating. He's investigating everything and has stopped all foreign aid until the programs can be validated."

The former Lockheed CEO indicated he might have an answer. He held up his hand then scratched his eyebrow. Chernovich recognized the signal for needing some private time and cleared the room with the wave of his hand. He motioned for the former Lockheed CEO to come closer. He shouted, "Last one out, tell the secretary we aren't to be disturbed." Chernovich arose and the men stood toe-to-toe.

"I was going to say we need to be grateful the FBI is broke, otherwise they would investigate how we re-badged the voting machines. Anyway, before I left industry, we were experimenting with some lethal drones....Highly classified, incredibly effective *stuff*. They can't be stopped; they can't be swatted out of the air. They are relentless. And they carry a shaped charge that strikes the forehead of the target and blows their brains out of every orifice. When I saw the surveillance video of Eleanor Tussy losing her balance, I swore I saw one of those tiny deadly drones leaving the area. I'm convinced someone sent one to kill her, but when she tried to get away from it, she slipped and cracked her skull."

Normally a sullen man, Chernovich seemed to brighten with the classified information. "I need some of those." *I have an address. I want everyone at that address taken care of.*

"That I can do, Bobo." The former Lockheed CEO used his pet name for Bogdan Chernovich.

Some would say it was the first time anyone had seen him smile, but not the man from Lockheed. Chernovich unbuckled his belt and trousers and let them fall to the floor. The Lockheed man did the same.

CHAPTER 44

May 21, 2018

Demetrius Eastwood entered the recording studio in his 7 World Trade Center apartment. He flipped switches all around him to energize amplifiers, cameras, and microphones. He donned headphones and checked the output of the microphone. He did not read from a script.

"Thank you for tuning into this episode of *Unfiltered News* and welcome to the only true American on-line news network. Over on the other side of town, where there is no difference between the communist message and the full war machine of the media's talking points, the Democrat Party's propaganda arm is at it again. Every week we review the newsworthy events that you heard nothing about. We'll comment on anniversaries, good and bad, and we'll acknowledge our growing list of sponsors that make this on-line telecast possible. I've got much to discuss. This is Demetrius Eastwood. Let's get this show rolling!"

"President Hernandez announced this afternoon that the Muslim Brotherhood and Islamic Underground are now considered 'terrorist organizations' and therefore, participation in either group is unlawful. I think this may be directly aimed at the FBI and the DHS, the Department of Homeland Security, for they have had many complications and entanglements with the Muslim Brotherhood and the Islamic Underground, the least of which: the FBI has been disturbingly discriminating against Christians since Mazibuike forced radical Muslims into their ranks and into other agencies, and the DHS stopped investigating radical Muslims in the country. And if you are a Muslim member of Congress, you had best beware if you think you can still be a Muslim Brotherhood member in good standing."

"And if you're a Democrat, this is not going to be your day. CIA Director Bill McGee reported to the House Intelligence Subcommittee that he has been declassifying hundreds of documents, and I quote, 'Any Democrat lamenting the loss of President Mazibuike should reconsider their support of him.' Several of the documents provide information that someone we rarely hear anything about, Hamsi Fareed al-Amirikiu, was a habitual guest at the White House. It's not like the secretive al-Amirikiu pretended that he was some guy who just lived in the neighborhood or that he was a significant benefactor to the Democrat Party who went bad on them. No, the major leaders in the Mazibuike Administration knew al-Amirikiu was bad from the git-go—that he was the undisputed leader of the Islamic Underground in the United States."

"How this is not earthshaking to the mainstream media is a mystery. We are seeing newly declassified documents from several sources, including the intelligence services of America's allies, that indicate the Mazibuike Administration knew exactly what they were doing when they welcomed al-Amirikiu in the Oval Office. Recent attacks on some of our embassies appear to be in response to the political attacks on President Hernandez by the DNC, Washington Democrats, the media, and the Kremlin. Maybe they have a theory that their actions could help take down the president."

"The question our counterterrorism analysts have tried to resolve, before President Mazibuike and his clique of Socialists were elected and since he resigned the presidency, is 'Why did President Mazibuike give al-Amirikiu access to the White House?' Was it to create a photo opportunity for the benefit of President Mazibuike's future presidential library? Three photos have recently come to light courtesy of *Whistleblowers.* The first is al-Amirikiu in the Oval Office with 3M. The second is a close-up of the ring President Mazibuike wore for 30 years. It is adorned with some version of the first part of the Islamic Declaration of Faith, the *Shahada*: *There is no God but Allah, and Mohammad is the Prophet of Allah.* Let me just say that I find this an odd choice for a self-declared Christian to wear all of his adult life. And the third photo includes the head of the Islamic National Party and the three leaders in what seems to be raised arms and 'bumping fists' with their rings; rings inscribed with the *Shahada*. Is that photographic evidence of some ritual? Was this photo staged to send a signal that America had been conquered by Islamic forces?"

"Let me remind you that President Mazibuike delivered a very-specific foreign policy speech in Cairo, Egypt shortly after taking office. He said, 'The U.S. would no longer take interventionist actions to maintain stability against Islamists.' I'm certain the media had their reasons for ignoring his speeches and these photographs. I doubt any of them will make it into the presidential library, if and when a library is ever built for Mazibuike. Which I doubt, since he ran from prosecution. Only now is his treachery being fully understood."

"It was very clear when President Mazibuike gave his speech in Egypt that U.S. foreign policy would change to support the Muslim Brotherhood. It was another way of saying the U.S. would abandon our allies in the Middle East who were fighting the Muslim Brotherhood. The only way we know the Muslim Brotherhood, the hyenas of North Africa, were removing the regional strongmen of our allies in Egypt, Tunisia, Algeria, and Libya was to listen to the BBC, because the American media refused to cover the turmoil."

"Political Islam, *writ large*, is represented by the Islamists, the Muslim Brotherhood, and former President Mazibuike saw himself as the modern leader of political Islam using the Muslim Brotherhood and the Islamic Underground to recreate a new Islamic Empire that the 57 Islamic nations would be forced to join."

"Did that photograph of the heads of the Islamic National Party, the Islamic Underground, and the Democrat Party—give al-Amirikiu substantial stature and standing back home in Egypt; did it enable him to draw new terrorist recruits and resources into the Islamic Underground? After all, al-Amirikiu specialized in all forms of terrorism, foreign and domestic. Or was the reason for his presence in the White House something more impactful, more insidious? More sinister? Would he become the new ambassador for the newly created Islamic Empire?"

"It took an Egyptian general to deal with the outcomes of Muslim Brotherhood extremism by forcibly removing the Muslim Brotherhood president from office. That general formed the Arab coalition of North African nations that is now aligned with President Hernandez against the radical elements of the Muslim Brotherhood and the Islamic Underground."

"And thanks to *Whistleblowers'* release of some of the DNC archives, we're able to better understand the relationship between the DNC and international organizations that sponsored terrorists. These documents positively linked al-Amirikiu to attacks on U.S. interests abroad, to include the attack on the Khobar Towers and the U.S. Embassies in Algeria, Tunisia, Libya, and of course, Egypt. He provided critical intelligence to the bomb-making terrorists in Saudi Arabia where nineteen U.S. servicemen were killed by a bomb blast that ripped apart the buildings which housed American military personnel."

"But again, thanks to *Whistleblowers*, we have received an unusual tranche of secret presidential correspondence between al-Amirikiu and President Mazibuike. These are documents not of peace negotiations but of an exchange of 2,000 U.S. passports for family members of the Islamic Revolutionary Guard Corps, al-Qaeda, and the Islamic Underground. One senior member of al-Qaeda returned to America with his U.S. passport and applied for disability for gunshot wounds sustained in a terrorist attack in Yemen. With this tranche of documents we have unmitigated proof that the head of the Democrat Party, President Mazibuike, was a powerful totem, collaborator, and conspirator in the Islamic Underground's strategy to infiltrate the United States. See, there was a reason Mazibuike ran off."

"It also appears that while the media fixated on the shocking election of President Hernandez, they ignored the number of Muslims who won Democrat seats in the House and Senate. In a story that hasn't yet been fully told, it seems former President Mazibuike facilitated the intrusion of the Islamic Underground into the Democrat Party to such an extent that criminal Muslims with terrorism résumés won nearly seventy percent of the Democrat Party primaries, and twenty-five of them won seats in Congress."

"The record will reflect that because of the latest election, we now have twenty-five new Muslim Democrat members of Congress with loyalties not to America but to the newly illegal Muslim Brotherhood, the worldwide Islamic Underground, and possibly the Islamic Revolutionary Guard Corps. These new congressional members of Muslim faith began calling for the impeachment of President Hernandez before they were even sworn in. The word on the Arab street is that the Democrat Party is no more. It will have to reconstitute itself with a new name, a new charter."

"The CIA Director indicated that he half expected to be the subject of an impeachment inquiry simply for swearing to defend the U.S. Constitution. Enemies of the United States, foreign and domestic are now, I know many of you are familiar with the term, 'inside the wire.' President Mazibuike did a number on America and the American people who voted for him. The CIA Director, a former SEAL Team Six leader, said he is fully engaged to do the best he can under the letter of the law to undo the mess Mazibuike created."

Eastwood was pensive. "I do not know how we are to confront 'the enemy within.' The FBI leadership has principally been removed from any domestic counterterrorism activities, for malfeasance and possibly treason, for trying to destroy a duly elected president. Domestic terrorism is the purview of the FBI. As an organization and a key component of the law enforcement community, the FBI was utterly ruined by President Mazibuike's 'Muslim Outreach' programs and by fifty years of Russian work to place moles within the U.S. Intelligence Community."

"Director McGee assured us that despite the efforts of the Mazibuike Administration and the aggressive efforts of the Islamic Underground, the Islamic Revolutionary Guard Corps, or the country formerly known as the Soviet Union, the CIA has not been compromised by infiltration."

"There is a shiny dime in this pile of pony poop the Mazibuike Administration left us. Despite the new law in the early 1990s which did not exempt the Agency, the CIA received special dispensation by way of a Presidential Executive Order after 2000. For eight years we didn't upend our rigorous employee screening process in favor of hiring practicing unqualified Muslims. The *status quo ante* prevented most of the candidates, primarily from the Islamic Underground, to not be considered. Then the Mazibuike Administration, via a new

Director, forced the intelligence community to hire what were essentially spies. We believe about 15,000 slipped between the cracks at the FBI, but only 3,000 could wiggle their way into the CIA. Virtually all the Mazibuike holdovers have been identified and removed."

"There are some seventeen agencies in the IC. Director McGee said he is aggressively identifying and deterging those few remaining closet members who were able to penetrate the Agency through other means. Some would call these people 'moles.' I consider them to be enemies and spies, much like the deeply imbedded Alger Hiss who stole America's secrets for the old Soviet Union."

"I would like to say I would volunteer as a member of a firing squad and shoot them, or if we needed the intel, I would waterboard the snot out of them if I could. I will say, 'It is so good to be a Democrat' for they seem to get away with wholesale murder."

"*Whistleblowers* recently released classified documents that prove what we have long suspected, President Mazibuike was the point man for the Russians and the Communist Manifesto and the Islamic Underground's *An Explanatory Memorandum.* He was the Democrat Party's wet dream—he was a *two-fer*; a communist and an Islamist. But the Russians don't know they have lost and neither does the Democrat Party. When the Communists had their backs turned the Islamists, and I use this term to distinguish the religious criminals from average Muslims, pushed them out of the way. This is how *sharia* has come to America, via the backdoor. Mazibuike was an active participant, the prime facilitator of infiltration, a co-conspirator in the destruction of America. Mazibuike used the power of his office to demand his cabinet members open their doors to 'a suppressed people' and thus began the subversion of our government."

Eastwood continued, "The released Mazibuike files unmasked the man, and as material dribbles out of the halls of *Whistleblowers* the crucial information in the DNC archives are systematically proving the complicity of not only the Islamic Underground and the Islamic Revolutionary Guard Corps, but the combined efforts of the Russian Federation and the Democrat Party to achieve their ultimate goal, the complete destruction of the USA. It shouldn't be a surprise to anyone who has been paying attention that the DNC files also showed

Mazibuike's plan for one-party rule through a corrupted voting system."

"However, I believe the Islamic Underground, Russia, and the Democrat Party will find an America that is now no longer the lamb they believe it had become. The Communist Party in Moscow is in distress, and defectors from all across Russia are engaged to bring down that communist regime—again—and to thwart their invidious efforts in the United States. The defectors are naming names and bringing documents."

"Beginning about twenty-plus years ago, the Islamic Underground began their campaign and conspired to attack the aviation infrastructure in America and Europe. As you know aircraft were hijacked or bombed, airports were bombed, airport security was infiltrated necessitating the creation of the Transportation Security Administration. Under Republican presidents airports have become fortresses hardened against attack, and the perpetrators have been caught and incarcerated. Infiltrators plotting attacks on the United States will be treated as domestic terrorists and hostile spies and will be subject to the highest levels of prosecution."

"The Mazibuike file and the Democrat National Committee archives have exposed the treachery of 3M and the Democrat Party. The release of those documents has exposed the Islamic Underground as domestic enemies of the U.S. Government. Now that they have been exposed, the Islamic Underground is in a panic and is in disarray."

"We are active and we are winning. Last month, the United States proved that our reach and our memories are long with the killing of General Mostafa Roustaie of the Islamic Revolutionary Guard Corps. He helped radicals overrun the U.S. Embassy in Tehran and interrogate Agency personnel. He helped Hezbollah kill 241 Marines who were on a peacekeeping mission in Beirut. He taught Islamists how to build and use IEDs. He taught Libyan intelligence officers how to build a bomb to bring down a jet."

"Under Mazibuike, the United States embraced a strategy of disengagement and refused to hold Tehran accountable or punish Iranian extremism and terrorism. General Roustaie could travel freely across Europe and the Middle East, possibly on a U.S. passport—no doubt courtesy of Mazibuike—to motivate radicals to attack American forces and our allies. Recently he slithered out of Tehran and into Cairo to lead planned attacks on U.S. forces in Egypt. We thwarted his efforts to kidnap the ambassador and other embassy officials who were passing through the airport. We stopped his plans to hold our ambassador hostage for high-value terrorists being detained in the United States. As we saw years ago in Benghazi, Libya, terrorist plans put into action devolve into murderous chaos." '

"When I was on active duty and when I was a correspondent overseas in the Middle East, I saw then Colonel Roustaie's brand of evil first hand. It was far worse than any of you could imagine. Roustaie was the murderous cretin who butchered and chopped off the hand of American contractor Jack Dickerson just to get to the engineer's watch. When there is no deterrence, top terrorists such as General Roustaie can travel anywhere to create chaos."

"President Mazibuike attacked his political enemies every day he was in office, and his priority was 'Muslim engagement, Muslim outreach, and Diversity hiring' which favored criminal immigrant Muslims over law-abiding Americans. President Hernandez attacks the international enemies of America, and his priority is the elimination of Islamic radicals from the battlefield. On his first day in office President Hernandez declared General Mostafa Javad Roustaie to be the top terrorist, at the top of the FBI Most Wanted Terrorist List, and the IRGC to be a terrorist organization. Roustaie ran this network of sleeper cells in the United States and Europe. President Hernandez authorized the airstrike that killed General Roustaie."

"The man who planned to bomb a Washington, D.C. restaurant that the King of Jordan frequented has been stopped forever. The man who killed hundreds of Americans and trained hundreds of Islamic fighters how to make improvised explosive devices that killed hundreds and wounded thousands of American soldiers and contractors has been stopped forever. The man who planned new opium trafficking lanes between Europe and Mexico has been stopped forever. Mr. Dickerson's murderer has been brought to justice."

"The death of Roustaie should transform the dynamic in the global war on terrorism. Some believe removing Roustaie will be like removing oxygen from a water molecule. We will see. The Israelis, the Kingdoms of Jordan and Saudi Arabia, and others have always wanted to remove General Roustaie and his ilk from the battlefield, but could never seal the deal. Thanks to documents released by *Whistleblowers* we have learned why. It was President Mazibuike who always tipped off Iran; it was President Mazibuike who likely provided General Roustaie and other master terrorists American passports and intelligence that allowed them to escape justice. And it is likely that the Mazibuike CIA plotted to kill the head of *Whistleblowers* and make it look like an accident. This is how the left lies to you. This is how the treasonous play politics."

"Roustaie was pronounced dead by Iraqi officials from the only remains left of his body, a portion of his forearm and hand with a watch still around the wrist. There was also a gold ring on a finger which was inscribed with: 'There is no God except Allah.' May he rot in hell."

"He and the radical Islamists have fantasized about overthrowing the U.S., and in fact produced a video with images of the White House exploding, an American Flag on fire, and a turbaned General Roustaie outside the Oval Office holding a walkie-talkie and directing invading forces. I hope the DOD will soon release the video of the airstrike that removed General Roustaie from the battlefield."

"But now it is time to shift into snowflake overdrive. A few final comments that are sure to trigger your favorite liberal and *lefty*. *Whistleblowers* has promised to release all the files the Democratic National Committee kept on all members of Congress and senior Democrat politicians for apparently, the last forty years. This should prove interesting, especially those files that contain pictures and videos from the private island that the cigar-smoking DNC Chairman, Dr. Zhavrazhinov, ran as a reward for Democrat members of Congress, politicians, and donors. That island and its buildings were wired in order to generate blackmail materials for the Kremlin. We expect the documents will show how Russian spies blackmailed Congressmen and Senators to hire staffers sympathetic to the old Soviet Union. It is an element of fortuity that *Whistleblowers* has a complete listing of the DNC-Russian infiltrators. I think I can hear them bolting out the door for the first jet leaving Washington or hurling themselves off the top floor of the Newseum."

"As you well know, after the late Dr. Zhavrazhinov committed suicide for failing to get the Democrat Party's nominee elected president, the FBI raided the DNC's island resort—now known for its ability to photograph sex parties, conduct sex trafficking, and act as a safe haven for pedophiles. The FBI also raided Dr. Zhavrazhinov's home three days after his death looking for files, videos, photographs, and any other documents that the Kremlin could use against members of the Democrat Party. Only time will tell if *Whistleblowers* has those documents, photographs, and videos too. And if not, maybe the patriot who started it all by releasing the Mazibuike file has them and will release them for America."

"Let me say, in closing, it was apparent the CIA Director's remarks floored the members of the House Intelligence Subcommittee. They had no response to CIA Director William McGee whose IQ surely bests that of the combined intelligence of the Democrats on the committee. The chairman thanked McGee for his remarks and his time and dismissed the witness."

"That's all I have for you this evening. Thank you for tuning in. We'll be back in a few days for another episode of *Unfiltered News*. Be careful out there—the Democrats are a violent party threatening to burn down everything. The Party is an open-air lunatic asylum. 'Semper Fi' to all of my Marine Corps brothers and sisters. And as always, I would like to close this broadcast by saluting the men and women of the military, first responders, law enforcement, the farmers and the factory workers, and all the law-abiding citizens across the fruited plain who make this country work. God Bless America. Good night."

"Eastwood out."

CHAPTER 45

May 21, 2018

In an orange jumpsuit that was several sizes too big for her, Saoirse Nobley sat quietly in one of the interrogation rooms. She wore a black *hijab*, not because she wanted to, but because the Muslim men in the detention center rioted when they heard she could be seen without a head covering.

Every day of the last ten days had been the same. It was going to be another useless period of an interrogator doing all the talking and acting as if he cared for her well-being. Every day Nobley repeated her demands; *I'll talk to Captain Duncan Hunter*. The room, like all the interrogation rooms, was well lit, the table and chairs standard GI, government-issue. The walls were slick and white; they looked like giant white boards. She needed markers to write, *Let me out of here! Let me talk to Captain Hunter!*

For this interrogation, a new man, a bald man with a red beard, a blue paper face mask, and rubber nitrile gloves entered the room precisely as if he were stepping on coals. He carried a thin flimsy manila file. He wore a drab suit, one of those subtle windowpane styles you would find on a discontinued rack at Macy's. The dark Merrell *Moabs* with the business suit made for an incongruous look, but they didn't squeak with every step and the prescription shoes didn't hurt his feet. He didn't offer his hand to her; she had already rejected him with her eyes and body language, like the refusal of a child who didn't want to have any dealings with a smelly or overweight grandfather. He knew of the Islamic traditions, Muslim women and those who had converted to Islam were conditioned not to touch a man who isn't their husband. He pulled a chair from under the table; the chair legs screeched across the concrete floor, and the sound made Nobley jump. She glared at him. *Why am I here?*

The man removed a paper from the file and pushed it in front of Nobley. It was the picture of a standard white marble headstone and inscribed with the deceased's name, rank, branch of service, date of birth, and date of death.

As if a switch had been thrown, the color in Saoirse Nobley's lips transitioned from rose to white. She collapsed, fell out of her chair, and crashed onto the floor. No one was there to fly across the table to catch her this time.

It was quiet in the room for several seconds until the bald man sprang into action. He stood and removed a syringe from his suit pocket. He found a vein, slipped the needle into the woman's arm, and shot clear fluid into her. He forgot his feet hurt and retrieved the photograph of the headstone at Arlington National Cemetery and returned it to the file. He didn't look at the woman on the floor with her mouth open and arms and legs askew. He checked his stainless Rolex *Submariner* and monitored her pulse. He had little time.

He oversaw the removal of the woman from the room. She was carried out on a stretcher, a black sheet covered the inert body. She was placed into a metal casket and transported to the airport where a contingent of men waited for the four-engine turboprop cargo aircraft making its approach to the airstrip.

A pair of attorneys in white linen suits and brown oxfords, government-provided lawyers for detainees, deplaned the U.S. Navy C-130 from the front door as the rear cargo ramp was lowered to unload materials and accept outbound cargo. One lawyer walked under the wing and stopped the man shepherding the loading of the aluminum casket onto the cargo airplane; he asked who had died.

"The body of Hamsi Fareed al-Amirikiu is already aboard, and this one, I understand she was the wife of one of the recent detainees. Both U.S. citizens being returned to their families. I don't know the story on al-Amirikiu, but this one wasn't in very good shape when she was brought in."

The civil liberties attorneys' body language suggested they didn't like the man's response, and they pushed him aside, muttering to themselves. The casket was carried to the rear of the C-130, placed in the middle of the Navy cargo aircraft, and lashed down. The bald man in his Merrells shuffled to the *Hercules* and rode in a troop seat directly across from Nobley's casket.

The Navy cargo turboprop departed to the south and flew around the communist island. The flight plan would take the C-130 to the east and then north-northwest, paralleling the Exuma Cays, overflying Nassau, then via direct to Joint Base Andrews. Once the aircraft had taken off and made all the turns, the man opened the lid of the casket, administered an antidote to Nobley's arm, and monitored her condition. He left the oxygen mask on the woman's face and allowed her to awaken on her own.

After several minutes Saoirse Nobley's eyelids fluttered, then opened fully. She trembled for a few seconds as if she was experiencing a *petit mal* seizure. When her body functions returned to normal, she looked up into the bald man's eyes. She stiffened and blinked wildly. She was terrified, *I've been kidnapped again!*

With a soothing voice the man said, "Hello, Miss Nobley. I'm here to help you go home."

Nobley couldn't take the drastic emotional reversal; she broke down and cried in a state of disbelief. As she reached to wipe tears from her eyes, her fingertips touched the edge of the *hijab*. With tears flowing like geysers, she struggled with trembling hands to remove the head cover. Saoirse's hands found purchase and she clawed at the material. When she ripped it from her head, she shook the *hijab* with devilish eyes and threw it as far as her condition would permit.

The cargo aircraft landed at Joint Base Andrews. The U.S. Navy aircraft taxied to the Navy Operations side of the field.

• • •

Tailwatchers at two strategic locations in Maryland were told to be especially watchful for a Navy C-130 that had departed the Naval Air Station Guantanamo Bay, Cuba. One *Tailwatcher* near Joint Base Andrews in Maryland watched a U.S. Navy *Hercules* make an approach to the runway. After the aircraft landed, she trained a telescope and a camera with a telephoto lens on the offloading operations. She zoomed in on the man in the business suit with the odd dark walking shoes and ignored the aircrew in flight suits.

The briefing provided to the *Tailwatcher* said to be especially watchful for a pair of caskets that would be ceremoniously removed from the cargo hold. When no caskets were offloaded from the Navy cargo aircraft, the *Tailwatcher* concluded the information had been faulty. A quick internet search revealed servicemen recoveries were processed in New Jersey, and terrorists deaths were processed in Texas.

CHAPTER 46

May 24, 2018

It was already dark when Demetrius Eastwood took the subway to the Main Branch of the New York City Library. He constantly rubbed his eyes; the suspended grit in the dirty air of the subway seemed to bother him more than the other passengers. Maybe he just had the delicate eyes of a septuagenarian. It sucked growing old. Eastwood moved along to find a seat that hadn't been barfed or pissed on. It was hard to tell, and the subway's clientele wasn't from the Midwest, so he never really knew what he would find if he sat down. There is a reason people sit on the *New York Times*. Eastwood deliberated on the commonality of the subway and a birdcage—*you lined the bottom of each with the liberal rag*. He didn't have a copy, so he would just stand and try not to touch anything.

Eastwood tugged on his *Tilley* and caught a passenger's passing conversation, a partial sentence, just a couple of words, but he knew the gist of the conversation. He heard *Manhattanhenge*; it was coming. *You might be right, in a month or so*. Eastwood had heard of the so-called Manhattan Solstice when the setting or rising sun aligns with the east-west streets of the main street grid of Manhattan. It was astronomically meaningless, unlike the solstice at Stonehenge. It would be in all the papers when the event got close. Subway travel, like the airlines of yesteryear, of Pan Am *Clippers* and TWA *Super Constellations* had once been an elegant adventure. Now both modes of travel had been ruined as cattle car mass transit.

From the Fifth Avenue exit he sauntered toward the massive library, rounded the corner of one of the iconic maned lions, and raced up the marble steps to the main entrance. At this late hour he didn't have to wait for a library computer. He wouldn't be very long; it would take just a few seconds to access the largest on-line auction company in the world. Once he logged in under an alias, selected Messages regarding an egregiously over-priced book of an anonymous author from a tiny independent publishing house in Texas, Eastwood read: *Bogotá Sofitel. Bring a jacket.*

Eastwood leaned back in his seat. He double-checked the date of the proposed rendezvous. He juggled the logistics in his head. *That's the day after tomorrow. The good news is I don't need a visa for Colombia. The only way I can get there though, at this late date, is first class/business class air. Can do easy….* Without making reservations, he typed: *Wilco.*

He bounded out of the marble building with his unsecured, unencrypted smartphone at his ear. He ran his hand over the smooth plinth of the marble lion guarding the architectural treasure and historic New York City landmark behind him. A paperboy was hawking newspapers at the corner of Fifth Avenue and East 41st Street. He bought a paper, folded it, and tucked it under his arm. He didn't have a bird, but now he could sit.

Eastwood called the special number for his network's travel agency and told the nice lady what he needed. As the travel agent researched the available flights and seats, Eastwood unfolded the newspaper and scanned the pages. Three articles deserved more of his attention: *Somali Hostages Rescued, Kidnapped American Tourists Found Safe,* and *Al Qaeda's West African Branch seeks Negotiations.*

He skimmed the first two articles and read the latter. Eastwood couldn't believe he was reading about two terrorist organizations fighting each other. The Islamic State accused al-Qaeda of launching attacks on its fighters who were battling the "Crusader" France and its allies. He saw the fingerprints of his friend's work on both of them, too. When he saw him, he would ask.

The travel agent came on the line to announce she had secured business class seating on American Airlines.

Eastwood descended into the depths of the subway. While his bottom was protected by the utilitarian *Times,* Eastwood made a mental list of the things he needed to do. He had so much to do first that he would have to sleep on the jet. He sighed, *That's why you buy the business class fare.*

CHAPTER 47

May 22, 2018

Hunter met Eastwood as he exited the lobby elevator; they exchanged muted greetings and walked to what seemed to be a new pewter-gray Toyota 4Runner parked alongside the hotel's courtyard.

Dory Eastwood was shocked when Hunter got down on all fours and checked the underside of the truck. *He's only been away from the vehicle for a few minutes and is checking for explosives? That is a good habit to have, I suppose.*

Satisfied the vehicle hadn't been tampered with, Hunter motioned for Eastwood to get in. When he opened the door, it was extraordinarily heavy and thicker than a standard truck door. He couldn't believe how massive it was, yet the door moved easily as if it was precisely balanced on hinges from a dismantled Boeing.

Armored! Must be Level six or seven! He had been in armored vehicles before and even had one of Hunter's specials, but the 4Runner was a thing of beauty with the thick windshield, the laminated polycarbonate window that was fixed in place, and ceramic plates cleverly hidden in the door that could stop a high-powered rifle bullet.

Hunter drove into the heart of town like he knew where he was going. His eyes were constantly moving from mirrors to front and side windows, on the lookout for anything unusual. "It's been made to look like an ordinary Toyota, but it's armored at Level seven. It'll stop a fifty cal or a hand grenade; I'm confident we would survive an RPG head-on. But the real danger in Colombia is that the FARC knows what subtle little differences to look for in armored trucks, and if they get the chance they'll plant a bomb just to see if they can get lucky and take out a *gringo* or two." Hunter hadn't been driving long when he pulled into a tourist trap.

Eastwood slowly looked up; a cable car was necessary to get to the top of the mountain. *Glad I brought a jacket – I know it's not going to be enough at this altitude. I'm still going to freeze my ass off!* Eastwood noticed Hunter's jacket; it looked like an old English Army movie prop. He frowned at himself as he realized he stuck out like a touristy American with his LL Bean canvas jacket. Eastwood snagged a brochure as Hunter paid for the lift.

They entered a bright orange cable car that was half-filled with children who were likely more interested in the summit's souvenir shops and tourist facilities than the church or shrine devoted to *El Señor Caído,* "The Fallen Lord." Eastwood found the view on the trip to the summit of *Monseratte* stunning and dramatic. As the sun set to the west the ever changing view of the city of Bogotá below them was spectacular. "You timed this perfectly, Duncan. The views are, I don't know, pretty incredible."

"Just wait."

It was near dark when they arrived at the top of the mountain. They walked across a piazza to the Casa San Isidro Restaurant, which Eastwood thought was fortuitously empty until Hunter mentioned that he had reserved the whole establishment for the night. Eastwood and Hunter took their time walking around the premises. Hunter pointed to the gorgeous main dining room, "It must've been a chore to build this old restaurant." They walked past a monstrosity of a fireplace, an elegant baby grand piano, and custom light fixtures made by long dead craftsmen from the city. Eastwood commented, "This place is a work of art."

The men took a table on the patio overlooking Bogotá. Colombian beers, a couple of blonde Club Colombia *Doradas,* were served with chips and salsa. Hunter removed a green donut-shaped *Growler* from his jacket pocket and switched it on much to Eastwood's amusement. Eastwood had seen Hunter with the device before and assumed Duncan always carried one with him.

Once they were alone Hunter got to the point. "Dory, what do you know about Bogdan Chernovich? Your favorite general who has all the charm of a creepy porn lawyer."

Wow! That's cutting to the chase. Eastwood rubbed his chin and recalled long forgotten history. "Well, we were at the Naval Academy together. He was number one out of school; I was top twenty-five. He went to Harvard; I went to Vietnam. He went intel; I was infantry. I saw him occasionally during my third tour in Vietnam but never really broke bread with him or shared beers; definitely did not go on liberty with him. He and his guys did their thing, and we did ours. I heard the locals called him 'Captain Devil' because one of his eyes was a different color, and he had a voice like an alarm clock: loud, strident, and obnoxious. He was also tall and used that to intimidate those around him. Especially prisoners. NVA, Viet Cong."

That's what I remember.... Hunter said, "After graduation from the Naval Academy he attended the Harvard Academy for International and Area Studies. And the eye thing is called *heterochromia iridium*; it's caused by a lack of pigmentation in the iris of one eye. Supposedly, Alexander the Great had two different colors of eyes. One as dark as the night, and one as blue as the sky." *He moved too quickly for me to get a camera on his eyes.*

Eastwood reflected on Hunter's encyclopedic knowledge of the arcane. Hunter knew Chernovich, apparently. "That's Chernovich; brown eye, blue eye. I remember now that some wag described him in the Lucky Bag, the Academy yearbook, as the officer most likely to become president or conquer the world like a new Alexander the Great—he had the eyes for it—or some such bullshit. Anyway, we weren't friends or even friendly, but I knew him. Strong personality but not in a good way." Hunter listened; his eyes encouraged more.

"I remember one encounter. He was typical of the intel turds in Saigon—if you asked them what the hell they did, they would go all SS Stormtrooper on your ass, thinking they had secrets that if told, would cause the world to implode or explode, and at the very least they viewed you as a communist infiltrator just for asking a question. The next time I saw him we were lieutenant colonels. He was a fast burner. Medal of Honor winner. I heard that he had a solid tour at the Agency. Career enhancing tour. That was the same time I went to the National Security Council and got the fifteen minutes of fame I never wanted."

Hunter remembered the *Time* magazine cover that rocked the nation. Lt. Col. Demetrius Eastwood in *Alphas*, the olive green Marine officer's uniform with ribbons and badges, being swarmed by dozens of reporters and hammered with the blinding strobe lights from power-winding cameras. Anyone in the Congressional hearing room was blinded from the flash of hundreds of cameras when Eastwood stood, raised his right hand, and swore he would tell the truth, the whole truth, and nothing but the truth. The mental picture was indelibly seared in Hunter's mind, *He had those ruddy, masculine, poster-boy looks but being on the covers of the national magazines – I'm sure that wasn't the part of the career he signed up for. He was a junior NSC staff member accused of an illegal scheme to secure the release of American hostages held by Islamist radicals. One day he's a hero, the next day he's PNG – Persona Non Grata. A classic case of what happens when shit rolls downhill. He was accused of trying to trade weapons for the hostages, but he ignominiously failed. The CIA could do it but not the NSC? He became the Marine every liberal and leftist loved to hate. I don't remember exactly how their plan failed.... Isn't it ironic that the media's despicable and corrupt Colonel Eastwood is now a war correspondent who reports on government's failures and successes to protect the American people and is cherished by the masses?*

Eastwood continued, "I was forced to retire; Chernovich accelerated up the corporate ladder, became CMC and the first Marine to be named SACEUR. In my day, the Marines had only two four-stars, then Chernovich broke the mold, he didn't retire as CMC and became Supreme Allied Commander of European Forces. His photo was in all the papers, but I always found it odd that the socialist *The Eastern* magazine did several complete spreads on him."

Hunter commented, "I remember. One day the Marine Corps had two four-stars, and the next day there were five or six in top positions that had been the purview of Air Force and Army generals, and Navy admirals: Vice Chairman of the Joint Chiefs of Staff, SOCOM Commander, STRATCOM Commander. The STRATCOM Commander was one of my instructor pilots when I was learning to fly F-4s. Mazibuike fired him for women—fraternization troubles. Anyway I don't remember all the new generals, but I remember being surprised the Marine Corps now had a bunch."

Eastwood grinned and nodded. "There were so many Marine generals because of Chernovich. Then I think he was on a couple of corporate boards before he spent a year as President Mazibuike's National Security Advisor."

"How did it happen? Did someone blow the whistle on you and your team at the NSC?"

Eastwood had often tried to reconstruct that day. "I still don't know. That was forty years ago. Old history."

"But you knew Chernovich. Did you know what he did when he was at the Agency?"

Eastwood drew a long swig from his beer. He looked at Hunter long and hard, then shook his head. *Nope. How would I know that? Although, there were days when the supply of curse words needed to describe what I thought of Chernovich was insufficient to meet my demands.*

Hunter looked at his friend and formed an impression, *I don't think Dory's aware of the picayune jealousies at the CIA, that all international work – working with foreign nationals, training foreign nationals, or anything that involved extractions, recoveries, renditions, and especially rescues – was performed by the National Clandestine Service. Exclusively! And they were cutthroat about interlopers. If you parachuted into the group and assumed you were all on the same team, you would be in for a rude awakening when one of them jammed all your romantic assumptions of teamwork up your ass and broke it off like a stick and tossed you to the curb. The only team at the NCS that mattered was the Special Activities Branch, the guys who made it all happen – Anything, Anytime, Anywhere – Professionally. But you had to be in the Agency to know how their Special Activities misfits really worked.*

"There were times I was sure it was the CIA, but I really didn't know anyone over there. And why wouldn't they help us? *They* being the NCS, National Clandestine Service. I think they did some rescues, but only the NCS could get the weapons, then they moved the weapons, and they had all the contacts with the remnants of – ah, what's their name...oh yeah, *Air America* – to bring our people home. I may have started the ball rolling, but it was a team event. I assumed we would all work together. I dealt with the NCS leaders, not some of their more colorful characters who were trying to make a name for themselves. I didn't care who got the credit; I just wanted to bring our hostages home."

"Weren't you also planning to bomb Libya for the Lockerbie bombing? Punishment for blowing PanAm Flight 103 out of the sky?"

"Yes." Eastwood was confused.

The day my parents died. "What if I told you Lt. Col. Chernovich was the weapons and tactics instructor for the NCS? Special Activities Branch. He primarily taught foreign students. The left loves their revolutionaries and the revolutionaries love their instructors."

Eastwood was stunned into silence. He shook his head. *That's unbelievable.* His brain raced with the possibilities. *It just couldn't be!* After several minutes, he said, "Duncan, what're you trying to say?"

"I could be wrong, but I'm not. You aren't aware of how that place works, but I am. I should say, worked. While you were trying to organize a hostage rescue, you were also in talks with the Special Activities players at CIA and Special Operations at DOD to punish Libya, correct?"

Eastwood nodded.

"The Special Activities Branch wanted OPCON, operational control over both operations as did DOD. But the person who would have profited the most was you and the National Security Council. So there were these two huge operations and in the initial discussions, neither side liked their slice of the pie. The idea of both sides was to ensure they did the work and would get all the glory. Not NSC; not you. If you had pulled it off, you would have made general."

Eastwood was speechless.

"'All the glory' in this context means more NSC funding. In a case of 'what really happened' the Agency freaks made a drug deal with DOD. They cut you out of the loop; NCS would do the hostage rescue on their terms, and DOD would bomb Tripoli on their terms, and information was leaked that you were going to trade weapons for hostages."

It makes sense. Oh, that would explain much! Eastwood closed his eyes and begged the memories to go away.

"I think when Chernovich was hidden away with Special Activities Branch at the CIA, he was in a very special place to call the dogs of war on my buddy Dory Eastwood at the NSC, and in my opinion, had Colonel Eastwood's rescue plans tubed. Someone leaked the plan. Because the next thing you know, Jed's a millionaire, and you're splashed all over the covers of magazines and newspapers, taking the Fifth, and wondering just 'what the hell happened?' You and the NCS were exposed and off the program, and the Agency was back in the driver's seat. Isn't that a better summation?"

"For years, I've wondered what happened. I think your scenario is possible, maybe even plausible. But it's hard for me to believe a Marine colonel would be part of ruining another Marine colonel's operation and career. Ring knockers..., er, Naval Academy grads just don't do those things."

"I have reasons to suspect Chernovich isn't all he should be."

"I'm listening. It's been a long time and much water...."

"My theory is based on insufficient intel, but I'm a believer of odd circumstances—like having Chernovich working for the Special Activities Branch when you're working with the NCS to protect Americans overseas—and knowing the boys at Special Activities Branch played a different game, were very protective of their jobs. They screwed you, *they played you*...they leaked your plan. Don't get me wrong, these guys were patriots but they took you out of the equation and squashed you like a bug."

Hunter continued, "How do I know this? The top operational guys at Special Activities had been trying to find me and kill me for years. I was doing the work they should have been doing and getting credit for, and in a very strange way, it pissed them off. The last of their turds tried to kill President Hernandez and I threw his carcass off the top of the MGM Grand Hotel. But you already know that."

"Is that what really happened? Wow! That was a weird night. You were pretty beat up. Bird shit everywhere. You saved President Hernandez. I'm beginning to understand you live in a different world than I do. I didn't know what happened to me; how could I? I was never part of that crowd. Looking back, it's entirely possible that's what they did to me via Chernovich. Now he's the CEO of TASCO and the president of the Trans-Atlantic Security Council."

"He's dirty," said Hunter. "And I know it for a fact."

Eastwood cocked his head like Nipper, the RCA dog that was the model for Francis Barraud's painting, "His Master's Voice." Eastwood asked, "Do you think, or do you know?"

"Dory, my friend, you have to be deprogrammed. That's why we are here having this conversation." Hunter withdrew a ratty, thick UPS envelope from under his jacket and handed the packet to a confounded Eastwood. Hunter stared off into the distance quietly admiring the nighttime splendor of Bogotá. *He's going to need some time to absorb everything in that envelope.*

I have to be deprogrammed? Eastwood withdrew photos, documents, police reports, newspaper articles, and affidavits, and looked them over as Hunter spoke of what he had been doing his last years in the Marine Corps.

"About ten years ago, I hired a detective to look into Chernovich's background, the Marine Corps, the NSC, and TASCO. Things went well for a couple of years until my detective stumbled into the internal secret workings of TASCO. The board of directors—big donor Democrats—had all visited the Democrats' secret sexual retreat, '*Palacio de la Paranza,*' The Hideaway Palace. It was only for Washington Democrat elites, and flight records indicate the TASCO board members visited often. A couple of years ago when it was investigated after the election, it was viewed as a private island in the Caribbean where one's fantasies could come true. A lot of gay sex and sex with children. CEOs of blue chip, military, and intelligence companies. Hollywood liberals with their own jets—some names would knock your socks off. Some of the *grande dames* of the Democrat Party, respected women senators, congresswomen, and former cabinet members, and let's not forget the old dogs in the media who had an insatiable appetite for very young women."

"I remember. The media barely covered it."

"Exactly, the right-wing media covered it, but their bosses wouldn't allow full coverage of the story, afraid of network and newspaper executives being caught on tape with children or...."

"I got it." Eastwood closed his eyes to the horror. *There's a lot of gay men in positions of power in the media and they do not want any lights on them.*

"My guy went undercover and tried to get a job there in security. When he found out that hiring *gay* liberals was almost mandatory, you see things a little more clearly."

"That explains much." Eastwood shook his head. Data and truth had been sitting in front of him for a long time, but it hadn't been analyzed correctly. *Have I really been programmed? Is this what brainwashing looks like?*

"TASCO HR screened the political background and sexual preference of candidates. Of course, the detective didn't get hired. However, by using a Russian service called *Tailwatchers* he found Chernovich's private jet was a frequent visitor to the island and his name popped up repeatedly in the crime database. He has an interesting history with scores of dead women in his background."

"Then my detective was killed, but I had received hundreds of pages of documents from him. I hired another detective. I interviewed probably twenty former homicide detectives and a couple of former FBI special agents before I found one who was wired like me, unprogrammed, and would listen to what I wanted. I told him to be extremely careful because the men and women of TASCO are some of the finest retired and former intelligence officers on the planet. But about a month later, before he could deliver a report or provide me with any documentation, he was also found dead. Burned to a crisp. Officially his death was an accident, but any 'death by Tesla' is suspect and I know better. I felt like I had been an accomplice to murder."

Eastwood was thunderstruck. "Ho…lee…shit, *kemo sabe.* I know a little, the company is filled with former intel officers." *And they are gay…. Should I say that? Why would that matter? It's not relevant. Is it?*

"Regarding Chernovich and scores of dead women, I never really found out much more than what you have in your hands. There were dozens of deaths, almost fifty women over a forty-year career, where he was in the background—never a suspect. Police reports indicated that he was a person of interest, but he always had a solid alibi."

"At some point you realize the focus shouldn't be on the dead women at your feet but on the man hiding in the background. I asked the detectives to investigate why a man of Chernovich's means and prestige was a person of interest in multiple unsolved deaths. These women weren't found dead in his office; they were at home or in their vehicle, but they virtually all died within an hour or two after being with him. Documented. The police reports that you hold in your hands claim no rapes, but in every case the anus had been penetrated. I knew a WM who had been his driver. I asked the hard question, and she confirmed no vaginal penetration; he only wanted anal sex. She was to pretend that she was a boy." *And I stopped her from buying the bottle of Visine. Did I save that woman's life that night?*

"I'm certain Chernovich has had help. He is the leader of a cult, and it's probably a Marine. Or two. Someone who'll do anything for him. I don't know why, but I'm confident in how he does it; he has an anal fixation. He drugs the women, he sodomizes them, makes his escape, establishes an alibi, and somewhere in the shadows his asshole buddy or buddies comes behind him to clean up after him."

Eastwood said, "A Marine general with incredible power...."

"Always gets a pass. Some guys can naturally avoid the Fatty Arbuckle scandals, able to leave dead women all over an apartment like old sweaty gym clothes and nothing happens to them. We see them as people who have done something inconceivable; we assume they approach some exemplary level of perfection, someone with huge responsibilities who can do no wrong. We view them as infallible," said Hunter. Then he added, "It's a form of brainwashing."

Eastwood stopped reading and started listening.

"Chernovich reminds me of Rudolf Höss, the commandant of Auschwitz. Höss' claim to fame was that he introduced hydrogen cyanide for the gas chambers. I'm convinced 'General Devil' spiked alcoholic drinks with eye drops, like Visine, which makes the victim become drowsy and pass out. He didn't use the concoction as a date-rape drug but as a '*I want to get rid of you drug*.' Destroy the evidence drug. I contend both men used their chemistry background and knowledge in poisons to kill their victims from a distance. I think he even killed his predecessor."

"The Commandant? Seriously?"

"Seriously. I wanted to get that police report. That, and murderers like that—*leaders like that* have to have help. Höss had help. He was the leader of a cult—in his case, he was the charismatic leader whose members put to death their *undesirables*. The SS. Jewish girls who survived the ordeal, those who were sent to his office, those who could tell what happened to them told a harrowing story of child rape and *inversion*."

"*Inversion?*" Eastwood was confused. Hunter defined the term as it was used at the turn of the century until the 1930s. Eastwood closed his eyes and hung his head.

"Maybe that's it. Maybe he enjoys killing women. Uses them as synthetic boys and then punishes them. The girls in school never gave him a second look because he was dorky and goofy-looking, and he found a way to pay them back. Guys like that hate women. Did he like men? I did not know him that well."

Hunter nodded, "I keep going to that scenario as well, but that isn't what got them or my detectives killed."

"You're saying it's the cult of Chernovich."

"Chernovich was obsessed with power. What my first detective found out and verified by the old DNC Chairman's papers, thank you *Whistleblowers*, was that they were involved with voting machines and the software that controlled the outcome of voting machines. One of Chernovich's international subsidiaries made the voting machines, probably with Chinese parts, and the software from Silicon Valley was modified. Scorpii's foundation managed the election process for the third world. If you were to do some trend analysis on the elections where those machines were used, they always called the elections 'close' for socialist and communist candidates. I think they had cornered the market on voting machines and many thousands were sold and used in U.S. battleground states every year, especially major Democrat-held cities, but the machines failed in the Democrat stronghold of Philadelphia during the election for Eleanor Tussy, which was enough to give the election to President Hernandez. Isn't that remarkable?"

Eastwood was confused. *It could be a coincidence!*

"Remember there are no coincidences in the IC. The Democrats' polling and the media claiming she will win, that she had an insurmountable lead? I don't know how many times I heard, 'she was supposed to win.'"

"I heard the same thing. Voter fraud, it's like the greatest non-secret secret. And impossible to prove."

"The papers from the DNC Chairman, Dr. Zhavrazhinov, detailed how Mazibuike got the North African Muslim countries to use the voting machines from Germany. Scorpii's foundation was all for free and honest elections. They were all in on it. Tussy was also programmed to win but for some reason she didn't win, and Zhavrazhinov killed himself over it."

"I remember. Now Tussy's dead too."

"Yeah, I know. Dory, you were at the hearing where Bill McGee discussed the fragility and weaknesses of the FBI and the Agency, that the Muslim Brotherhood and the Islamic Underground had infiltrated the highest levels of government thanks to my dead buddy, Mazibuike."

"How do you know he's dead? No one has heard from him in years."

Hunter looked out over the lights of Bogotá. "Because I killed him."

CHAPTER 48

May 25, 2018

There was a very long pause from the old colonel. He had actually suspected Hunter of chasing the former president to the four corners of the earth and killing him, but he never knew why Hunter would want to do something like that. Eastwood had dismissed his suspicions as preposterous conspiracy theories. Now Hunter had just admitted the crime. Eastwood was at a loss for words. After a minute he asked, "You killed Mazibuike?"

"And bin Laden. I taped bin Laden's ass to the pilot's seat of a Yak 40 that still sits in a remote part of a Liberian airport. Check Google maps. It had been the personal jet of the Merchant of Death, Victor Bout; a murder of white-headed crows flew into the intakes and trashed the engines when he was trying to take off. I'm sure if you want to check, maybe get a DNA sample, you can, but you need to know that black mambas love to hide in that jet. They can get pretty nasty this time of year. Now, let me finish my story and you can ask all the questions you want."

Eastwood was stunned. *200 terrorists and Mazibuike? Bin Laden too? The official version.... That was a concocted story? Holy crap! Was he a murderer?* He couldn't believe what he had just heard and asked for clarification. He tried to keep his voice to a whisper, "*Hold it! You killed Mazibuike? And bin Laden? Isn't there a protocol for...aren't there rules?"* Something wasn't making sense. Then he realized who he was talking to. *Now it all made sense.* "You really killed Mazibuike?"

"I really did. The bastard tried to kill me and several hundred other passengers on our way to Australia. He violated the unwritten rule that former presidents don't go around killing people they don't like. When he was responsible for the deaths of hundreds of airline passengers, he became an enemy combatant. He had become an aviation terrorist. With a click of a mouse, he sent two very large planes loaded with passengers to their deaths. You know part of the story; I promised I would tell you the rest. So here it is. Through hacking technology one of 3M's loyal followers took control of a couple of jumbo jets and programmed them to depressurize the aircraft, knock everyone out, then turn off course until they ran out of gas and crashed in the ocean. There are no radars over that part of the ocean, so they would never be found. However on his last attempt, the sole object of his terroristic plan wasn't to kill hundreds or make the airliner disappear; his plan was to kill *me.* I was the target to be eliminated, and he was fain to kill hundreds in order to get to me."

"You?"

"Me specifically. Mazibuike suspected, rightfully so, that I had released his CIA file to the media and Congress. I essentially stopped him from executing his nefarious communist plans as president, which had been going so well. It's not a stretch; Mazibuike wanted revenge. He was preoccupied with revenge. I don't know how he determined it was me, but it might have been from a former CIA Director, the one before Greg Lynche. His hackers found me traveling to Sydney to give a lecture on aviation terrorism...."

You released his file? I knew it!! I knew it!! I knew it!! Eastwood tried to compose himself but mumbled, "That's right, you're the expert...." The colonel was jumping around in his seat like a two-year-old who's done with his food and wants out of his highchair.

As Eastwood's brain tried to catch up, Hunter continued, "...and he had no qualms about killing every passenger on board."

"You stopped their plan. You saved the jet...."

"Yes, they killed half of the passengers and crew, but the bottom line is I got into the cockpit and resuscitated the pilot. When I got off the jet, we found 3M hiding in Dubai. He screamed at me; demanding I tell him who I was and he nearly shit all over himself when I told him. I decapitated his ass and defenestrated his head and body from the top floor of the *Burj Khalifa.*" Hunter effected a kicking motion like he was punting a soccer ball over the café's railing between potted plants for a score.

The chilly night air, the alcohol, the altitude of the Casa San Isidro Restaurant and Hunter's revelations were making Eastwood hyperventilate. "You…killed…Mazibuike. You…."

"And I let the rats eat bin Laden. I dumped a plate of chicken and rice in his lap. Now there's something that should have been carried live on Al Jazeera. I made a deal with that flea-infested rodent that if he would disclose what I suspected, I would put his ass on a jet. I kept my promise after he verified Mazibuike was one of his, one of the Muslim Brotherhood's pet projects. Osama had taken a special interest in 3M. Which proves you can't trust the *Ignoratti*."

Eastwood was staring at Hunter and breathing hard.

"But what we are dealing with are *narcissistic personality disorders*. 3M and Chernovich are classic narcissistic personality disorders. The Democrats are a vindictive political cult in search of a political leader, and Chernovich's members are a vindictive murderous gay cult in search of acceptance."

For the next two hours Hunter talked, and Eastwood listened. Hunter talked of erasing Jama'at Nusrat al-Islam wal-Muslimin's leaders. *I killed anyone with an AK-47. For destroying the village, I killed them all; Allah can sort them out.* He talked of rescuing hostages in Somalia and hostages in Burkino Faso. "I had to wait—orbiting overhead for that door to be opened. Once the dude with the AK-47 did just that I popped him, and I killed bad guys holding AK-47s. Once the hostages realized they were free, I used a red laser pointer to write a message to them on the ground. I gave them directions on how to escape, and I followed them until they were safe."

"The men I find are designated enemy combatants and killing them is a classified special activity. You've heard of the Special Activities Branch. I put the *special* in those activities. I specialize in *aerial eradication*. Plants, pests, poisons, the bane of civilized people."

Eastwood couldn't speak.

Hunter explained what *Dark Islam* was and how Mazibuike had the goal of one day being able to bring down America so he would become ruler for life. A Caliph; maybe he even considered himself to be the twelfth imam. "He controlled the outcome of the elections.

It was a CIA program that was well in place before 3M was elected that was called *Liberty Machine*."

Eastwood's mind shifted into overdrive. *It's so obvious once the puzzle pieces are fitted together. Guys with clearances have better information. They see things the guys without clearances aren't allowed to see. Like voting machines that are touted to be honest and fair like Liberty Machines but only count votes that ensures their candidate gets elected. The whole concept of Dark Islam. The Muslim Brotherhood's "An Explanatory Memorandum" was not only their strategic plan to infiltrate North America, but it was the handbook to overthrow the U.S. government. Americans wouldn't have been aware of that document had it not been for an accidental discovery by a cop. And the media never covered a word of it or the analysis by senior counter-terrorism specialists.*

Hunter highlighted how the Democratic National Committee had their archives exposed and identified the infiltration of tens of thousands of closet communists into the highest level of every government agency, especially the intelligence and law enforcement communities, with the goal of bringing down America so the two-party system would be replaced with a single, Democratic Socialist Party or even the Communist Party of the USA.

Eastwood now understood. *Yes!* It all made perfect sense. *They even controlled the output of voting machines*. He mewled, "Chernovich's been feeding President Hernandez…."

Hunter said, "Yes, …his guys and gals from the U.S. Intelligence Community for the top jobs in government. Remember, we only found out Mazibuike had pushed Muslims for the top jobs in the government because of a leaked email—thank you *Whistleblowers. Appointed positions* and not elected positions. But the real reason Mazibuike wanted Muslims for the top jobs—*top jobs meaning political appointments in the intelligence and law enforcement agencies*—was because political appointments are exempt; they didn't have to take a polygraph which avoided the possibility of having a polygrapher expose them. Them and their personality and sexual disorders."

"3M removed himself by resigning which stopped his efforts to infiltrate the intelligence and law enforcement communities with radical Muslims. You would've reckoned a good charter member of the Islamic Underground would take one for the team, but no, he ran away squealing like a little schoolgirl who saw a garter snake in her yard. He suspected there would be assassins after him and so he ran."

"Same with the repressive DNC—what a house of prostitutes that place is. With a Democrat president and Congress they got very close to totally compromising the FBI, managing the outcome of elections to their benefit, and tearing up the Constitution. But they found that the CIA was a different beast and a harder nut to crack; they were organized differently and wouldn't capitulate as easily as the FBI did."

"The DNC was stopped cold when their archives were delivered to *Whistleblowers*; and those DNC diehards are running from the public as *Whistleblowers* has been releasing tranches, hundreds and thousands of documents a week. The DNC failed to contain the dynamite in their archives—now it is going to explode in their faces."

"Now, Chernovich pushed his people. They all had the same goal, but with Chernovich power politics were being played by a different set of players. I'm sure the narcissistic personality disorder Bogdan Chernovich envisioned the day when he could tell his minions that he was now in charge after he marched into the president's office to tell him he's being replaced. Which is what Smedley D. Butler was supposed to do with Roosevelt."

Eastwood pointed an index finger toward the sky. "Oh, that's right." He was quiet for a moment then said, "I remember. That's what a bunch of rich people, some fascist lovers, wanted General Butler to do to FDR. FDR got the Congress to pay the World War I Bonus Army the monies that were due them, which essentially removed a 500,000-man standing army from the Mall of Washington, D.C. The rich thought they could engage a pissed off army to help remove FDR."

"History has a strange way of repeating itself." Hunter sighed. "Leftists, Communists, and Fascists. Politics and money. Clausewitz said that *Politics is combat by other means*. All led by a narcissistic personality disorder. Combat is still a blood sport even when Republicans aren't interested in playing. For years defectors have been sounding the alarm that is until they were found by the KGB or their friends at the DNC and were terminated."

"Remember that *Whistleblowers* sometimes function as a news-aggregator; you're like a starter set now that you're a radio star and the one-man-band of *Omega*. Soon, you'll be supersized. *Whistleblowers* are being run out of Islamic Underground-free Hungary. The country isn't letting in any immigrants from Africa or the Middle East. The country doesn't use TASCO's or Scorpii's voting machines."

"That's amazing."

Hunter nodded. "They recovered from being brainwashed by the KGB. They figured it out. You run *Omega* out of a secret location like the illegal radio stations during World War II did. And the name of your bulletin board, *The Cross of Laraine Day*, where did you come up with that?"

"From *Casablanca*, when Berger opens the secret compartment in his ring and flashes Victor Lazlo *The Cross of Lorraine* to indicate he is a loyal member of the French Resistance. I always saw *Laraine Day* as the most beautiful woman in Hollywood during those days—she had been a pin-up girl—and it was just enough of a mnemonic for me to think of her and our resistance movement."

Hunter nodded and took it all in. *Laraine Day was a sophisticated beauty as there ever was*. He continued, "I bet you have a picture of her in your studio."

"I do." *Guilty as charged but how could he know that?*

"Remember Marine Captain Peter Ortiz led the French resistance for the OSS, the Office of Strategic Services. That's what we have here today. Tiny little bands of resistance movements against the criminally socialist Washington Democrat lunatic bomb throwers who are in power and ambush cops, topple statues, and try to set the place on fire. Their protests are anything but peaceful."

"The left cannot and does not believe in a country founded on freedom. They were one Agency and one heartbeat away from capturing the country with the election of 3M, and they thought they were going to be back in business with Eleanor Tussy. But something happened; I don't know what happened in Philadelphia. With the election of President Hernandez they've lost their weapons of domination, and they don't like it. They were supposed to be charge. They knew they were going to win because they had the voting machines from Europe, *Democracy Innovations,* to ensure victory, but those things failed them. In Philadelphia of all places." Hunter began seeing things in a different light. *Maybe the question should not be why did it happen that way, but who could have done it, who could have thrown the election to the Republicans and how.* "And as much as I know about the process, it could have come down to one tabulator machine. Apparently, all voting machines dump their numbers into a tabulator for the final results."

"When liberty is lost, America is lost." Eastwood was a bit melancholy.

Hunter continued, "We were supposed to submit to their superiority—*kneel before Zod!* I'm afraid most of our leaders don't see what's happening. We must have better leaders. We must comport ourselves as if we were the French Resistance, singing *La Marseillaise* with Lazlo leading the band to pushback against the National Socialist German Workers' Party, Major Strasser and his boss, Adolph Hitler. Some people have seen the light and help fund the resistance, these pushback efforts, like *Whistleblowers* and *Omega*. Like me."

Eastwood was speechless. *Yes, you're not only Maverick, but you're Rick! You run a little operation and make a little money, and you make things happen. You have been funding the radio show and bankrolling Omega so that it could be a secret and operational counterweight to white-elephant Congressional Democrat-funded studies. Yes, my friend…you have a way of putting things into perspective.*

Hunter asked Eastwood, "Do you remember that scene in *Casablanca* where the Germans sang '*Die Wacht an Rhein*' but are then drowned out by exiled French singing *La Marseillaise*? The song of revolution?"

Eastwood nodded.

Do you know the words to *La Marseillaise*?" Eastwood shook his head.

"I know enough to be dangerous. The words are, if I remember them correctly:

Arise, children of the Fatherland
The day of glory has arrived!

Against us, tyranny's
Bloody standard is raised,
Do you hear, in the countryside,
The roar of those ferocious soldiers?
They're coming right into your arms
To cut the throats of your sons, your women!
To arms, citizens,
Form your battalions,
Let's march, let's march!
Let an impure blood
Water our furrows!"

Eastwood smiled broadly and became emotional. He could hear the words in French as he recalled the dramatic scene in the old movie, the tears running down the cheeks of the women singing. He scolded himself that he hadn't taken the time to find out what those words meant. Now he understood why that scene was so powerful. The desire to throw off the chains of Nazism was strong, but they didn't dare overtly do anything about changing their condition. To cut off the head of the snake, they needed a leader who worked in the shadows. He realized what was happening to him. He stared at Hunter.

"Today's media cannot and will not do their job; they too have been compromised by leftists and radicals. The owners, publishers, and producers are leftist billionaires who just want to maintain their fortunes. They are the weakest link, and they're not on the side of America. And they cheat. *Whistleblowers* and *Unfiltered News* and *Omega* are doing the job the corrupt media won't do," said Hunter. "And we have Chernovich trying to infiltrate government with his people to take over the country."

And voting machines? Trusting Americans trust voting machines. If you can control the voting machines, yes, it is possible. Eastwood nodded at Hunter's comments. "Chernovich is recommending those FBI vacancies be filled with his people…."

Hunter offered, "…filling the vacuum…. I think what you want to say is, 'under the guise of screened and cleared government professionals who are actually socialists, communists, and Marxists.'"

Eastwood was stunned for the tenth time that night. "That's why you wanted to talk to me....here."

Hunter nodded. "I can understand and articulate the situation and the conditions that surround it. However, I'm not able to do anything about it. But you. You have a pen and a microphone *and a blog* and an audience. You can create one of the best diversions in media. You have to fight corrupt media with honest media. Honest media is the antidote to the poisonous left."

Eastwood regained his composure and questioned Hunter's mental faculties. He didn't fully understand Hunter's meaning. *I have a pen and a microphone and a blog and an audience? What the hell are those going to do against a criminal organization?* He asked, "What can I do? I'm just a war correspondent who hasn't been to a war zone in a couple of years."

"Think about it."

So he did. After a moment the words came to him, "It's easy to get drawn in. I always assumed Chernovich was a good guy—he was a Marine general—but you have the goods on him. Now I see he's a crook, the Lenin and Stalin-type of crook. But he is also a dangerous narcissistic personality disorder. You want to believe your leaders know what they're doing and are...sane...."

Hunter nodded. *Now we're getting somewhere.* "Dory, what do you *really* know of him?"

Eastwood told Hunter what he knew.

Hunter reminded Eastwood, "I had been tasked to investigate sexual predators, but I needed definitive proof, photographic proof of fraternization. General Chernovich wore a conspicuous timepiece. I had never seen a Heuer *Autavia* before, but I had seen pictures. Collecting rare watches, studying them, possessing them. It's an arcane hobby."

"My *Daytona* is a 'reverse panda' and named after Paul Newman, the race car driver. Chernovich's Heuer *Autavia* is also a 'reverse panda' and named after Jochen Rindt, an Austrian race car driver. Rock Hudson had one. Some baddie in *Thunderball* had one. Those *Autavias, like the Daytona,* are what's called in the business, a 'reverse panda,' with three white registers on a black dial; they are chronographs because they have three posts to set and control time, specifically elapsed time. The *Autavia* is considered a 'Holy Grail' in the Tag Heuer watch collecting community with fewer than ten of those chronographs still in existence, the last time I checked. In real life, all three of those guys were/are very gay men. I never thought of a watch as some kind of marker for gay Democrats, but McGee told me a story about leftist senators who ridiculed him and the Republican senators for their Rolex watches like they were some kind of cult."

Hunter continued, "Anyway, you were loyal to him. You and many, many others were impressed, even subservient, when you really didn't like him, all because he was a Marine general. We trust those guys. What we don't know is that we have been subjected to what is in many ways communist-perfected mind control techniques. We were taught to obey them, follow their orders; we held parades for them and held them up to the highest standards. Some retired Marine generals went off to business or politics. But the narcissistic personality disorder who achieved some exalted god-like status found himself with this preternatural power to control trusting people. Chernovich.... Classic narcissistic personality disorder. There's nothing those trusting folks wouldn't do for him. And the right guy or two or a hundred, they would even commit murder for him."

"Shit. I really didn't like him, but once he became a general, he did...he became someone to admire. I had bad intel."

"Dory, you did, but now you are educated and aware. Consider yourself deprogrammed." Hunter sighed; his pain killers had worn off. He said, "The left is livid, and they attack the president. President Hernandez received personnel recommendations from one of the most reputable persons in the left's stable, General Chernovich. The left has owned that pipeline of recommending leftist or left-leaning people for government positions for a long time. I'm interested in reversing that trend and having patriots fill those open positions."

"Will the President listen to you?"

"He already has. This is not public knowledge, but the slate of judicial candidates Chernovich delivered to the White House was rejected long ago. President Hernandez will only use the slate from the American Federalist Society."

Chapter 49

May 25, 2018

After steaks Eastwood said, "This is a story without an ending unless you have some solutions on how to stop them."

"Sometimes I feel like the Count of Monte Cristo, Edmond Dantès, scraping marks on the prison walls."

The reference embarrassed and befuddled Eastwood. *I suck as a littérateur and should have paid more attention to the Classics.*

Hunter's smile turned into a devious grin that he held for a very long time. "I do have a hypothesis and it involves you. Dantès needed help to escape when Death was upon him; he believed he had received divine intervention when he came up with the idea of a bait and switch, and replaced himself in a dead man's sack to be thrown into the ocean." He sighed, "What I have in mind I can't do by myself, but you're the divine intervention."

Eastwood pointed to himself. *Me? What the hell can I do? I don't even know what I'm supposed to be doing.*

Hunter responded, "We have been forced to create our own *samizdat*. You can lead America's dissidents."

The color drained from Eastwood's face. He had known Hunter long enough to know he wasn't kidding.

"You're the king of alternative media. Share a few not-so secrets and your audience grows faster than an opium poppy field in the springtime. You have a voice, and Americans are turning you on and turning the leftist media off. You're like Paul Revere. I think telling Americans what is honestly going on is all we can do. They are hungry for the truth. I can't do it; in this area you have much more power than I could ever dream of having. If the president or Congress tries to inform the public, the media will deride it, distort it, or ignore it. This is one reason why I took the unconventional path to release 3M's file the way I did. The right-wing media always suspected 3M's treachery but had no proof, then I provided the proof to them."

Eastwood silently agreed with Hunter.

Hunter and Eastwood spent the remainder of their time on the mountain in conversation about Eastwood's ventures. He invited Hunter to come and see what he had done to Hunter's place in 7 World Trade Center.

Dory Eastwood looked over his shoulder to double-check they were alone. "I may have a whistleblower at TASCO. He or she says TASCO is a criminal enterprise run by gay people. I don't know how you figured it out, but it looks like you're perfectly on target. The whistleblower makes it sound like TASCO is the gay version of the mafia. And if they control elections with voting machines.... In America...."

"The letter said to look at the Red Star Aggregate; they are into complex construction projects, everything from nuclear power plants and oil refineries to BL-3 and BL-4 research laboratories, and even voting machines."

Where have I heard that before? I'll bet McGee knows, besides their operational Agency contracts, TASCO built the Iranian facility and is laundering foreign aid. Hunter laughed. "If we were in a Star Wars movie, this would be the time you would hear, 'There's been a disturbance in the Force.' Something is changing over there, and someone from the other side with a conscience doesn't like where they are going. Like Whitaker Chambers, like Tommy Bonneville." *I'd like to say my buddy the Grinch. Has the Grinch seen the light?* "So, you do have an in-place defector; that's more than I could've hoped for, because to turn the *U.S.S. America* ship around and neutralize her enemies, we will need a lot of help from inside.

"It could be a trap."

"Could be."

Eastwood said, "I think it's worth trying to make contact. When I made contact with Tommy Bonneville, I had no understanding how comprehensive the DNC's archives were. I was expecting the volumes of Shakespeare, but what we really got was the Library of Congress."

Now they're in the possession of Whistleblowers. Hunter asked, "You receive fan mail? Mail from whistleblowers? You're experienced. That's good. Do you get others?"

"I do, but I might see one or two a year; a company receives federal grants and someone finds a way to skim a little cream off the top. But nothing like the DNC's predisposition with sex and power over communist ideology, or TASCO with their billions in contracts who seem to be more preoccupied with sex than money and communist ideology. They have been in this work, manipulating and brainwashing people with sexual disorders a very long time."

"*Preoccupation* is the hallmark of the personality disorder." By reading his expressions Hunter could tell Eastwood was getting closer to understanding. So he stepped into the breech. "Have you ever heard of the D*iagnostic and Statistical Manual of Mental Disorders*? It has an interesting history. It evolved from several systems that collected census and psychiatric hospital statistics and data for a United States Army manual. The DSM is published by the American Psychiatric Association and is used internationally. It was first published in 1952. Smart people started studying crazy people and the less-than crazy people, people on the spectrum, from normal to the disordered to the psychotic. Over the years as more disorders were discovered and diagnosed, more mental disorders were subsequently defined and added to the DSM. As you would expect. Simple program."

"In the beginning, homosexuality, as observed clinically, was classified as a sexual disorder or a sociopathic personality disturbance 'on the spectrum.' You'll see that term variably applied in cases like Down syndrome, where children 'on the spectrum' range from 'high functioning' to 'low functioning.' Over 99.99 percent of the animal and insect world require a male and a female to reproduce, and they naturally select the opposite sex. So, 99.99 percent became the starting point for naturally occurring 'normality.' It was 'ordered,' and anything that deviated from a position 'on the spectrum' was considered a 'disorder' of various flavors and strengths and even multiples."

"Then the sexual activists and other homosexuals teamed up and began an increasingly intensive campaign to transform the approach of psychiatry and the classifications of disorders. They didn't like being in the DSM, and with funding from the Communist Party of the USA they got organized and fought back. Their little 'special activities' were initially face-to-face protests that focused on the APA as an organization. They didn't complain that they had sexual disorders but that they were being unnecessarily and cruelly stigmatized. During the APA's conventions, when the activists didn't see any movement from the APA the activists changed tactics. They physically threatened the APA membership during the APA's annual convention and said that if the APA membership didn't accept homosexuality as normal, a sexual *variant* on the normality spectrum, they would destroy psychiatry, psychiatrists and their families. The Soviets trained the sexual activists to change their tactics and the Communist Party of the USA funded all their skirmishers with the APA, as you can imagine. The Soviets even infiltrated the APA with communist psychiatrists and those who politically agreed with the activists."

Eastwood listened intently.

"During the 1960s, sexual activists raged against the APA and made the lives of the APA's psychiatrists a living hell. Those sexual activists won the first round when the APA waved a white flag and changed the second edition of the DSM. At the APA convention the APA's psychiatrists 'voted' to remove *homosexuality* from the category of sociopathic personality disturbances and placed it, *homosexuality,* under the general category of sexual deviations alongside gender identity disorder, sadism, masochism, voyeurism, exhibitionism, fetishism, incest, transvestitism, necrophilia, rape, pedophilia, zoophilia, and others. In the face of continued unrelenting attacks and intimidation and more infiltration by communist and socialist psychiatrists, the APA voted in 1973 to downgrade homosexuality to a *'sexual orientation disturbance.'* They eventually removed homosexuality as a disorder of any kind."

"What the left learned is that there are ways to affect public policy, and the sexual activists' war on the APA achieved their goal—removal of homosexuality from the DSM. It was no longer an official disorder and could be celebrated as 'normal.' Because if you're not in the pages of the DSM you must be 'normal.' Under Mazibuike's presidency, the activists and the socialist psychiatrists continued their rage against the APA until transvestitism and transgenderism sexual identity disorders were removed. The latest target of the activists and socialist psychiatrists are the pedophiles."

Hunter continued, "The editors of the *New York Times* have argued pedophilia may be a disorder, but it isn't a crime. They argue that child abuse and possessing child pornography are crimes. They took a poll. That's how they do journalism now; they don't cover the news, instead they are activist leftists posing as journalists. Polls aren't news."

Eastwood offered, "I don't know why the *Times isn't dead....*"

Hunter nodded. "Hollywood and big-ticket donors want to make sex with children legal. There is big money in this for reasons that will come clear. Articles are popping up in newspapers saying it isn't a crime. California has reduced the penalty for having sex with a willing minor to a misdemeanor. This is an abuse of power against the powerless. These people are completely nuts; they are a joke. They are a disgrace to Western civilization. And because they are Democrats, they may get their way."

"That's insane!" But now that you explained it, it all makes perfect sense. The words were an assault on his ears. Eastwood was growing more livid by the minute.

"They believe they can do it. If they can just marshal up enough protestors and socialist psychiatrists to have another go at the APA, then they can get pedophilia removed from the DSM."

Eastwood whispered, "...because not being in the DSM means 'you're to be treated as if you are a normal human being.'" He knew what Hunter said was true. The unspoken truth. The media is a Republican's worst enemy and the Democrat's best friend.

Hunter offered, "The media is so awe inspiring as a propaganda machine that even Joseph Goebbels in his dampest fantasy never imagined having the kind of apparatus that the Democrat Party has in the U.S."

"The protesters were chiefly and unsurprisingly Democrats trying to remodel the public policy to their liking by creating chaos. After chaos comes reconciliation. So in the beginning, the Soviet Union—never one to let a good crisis go to waste—funded most, if not all the sexual identity protesters and the socialist psychiatrists in the U.S. Homosexuals, trannies, trans people, and pedophiles. What these groups learned is that if you push the APA hard enough, the old APA standards will fold and fall. The Christian organizations were attacked with a vengeance, and first to fall—civil liberty unions sued for homosexual men—who are no longer in the pages of the DSM—to become scoutmasters, that is how the Boy Scouts were destroyed."

"If they had sufficient numbers of infiltrators, those socialist psychiatrists, and sexual activists could protest long and hard enough, create enough chaos, they could make the APA jump to their demands and replace the standard, the DSM, and make them, the *ipso facto* homosexuals, trannies, trans-people—and now they're hoping *pedophiles*—legal, commonplace, and acceptable. To do so would be to throw the other half of American culture into chaos. Now children would become legal sexual targets. The average American doesn't have the money to take these predators or the government to court. The Politburo probably danced in the streets when their Democrat president signed the repeal to *Don't Ask, Don't Tell,* and they were positively orgasmic when 3M approved transvestites and trans people to serve in DOD."

Eastwood could see where Hunter was going. "If you get enough infiltrators to undermine the system from within, like an *Iago,* and you get enough Democrats and Communists and Socialists to protest long and hard enough, you wear down the people, so that the system gives in to their demands and changes public policy. Protests create a temporary and artificial *majority,* and a majority is needed to create changing public policy. Once they change public policy, they proceed to their real goal. The goal of socialists isn't prosperity, it is socialism. What's to stop the socialists from making communism legal, commonplace, and acceptable when they are racking up a consortium of activists?"

"It's a form of brainwashing. It's all about communism versus capitalism. You get enough motivated activists to engage in politics and you can prevent capitalist Republicans from seeking or holding office. Then activists seek to control the education and election boards. And when you control the election boards, you effectively control the voting machines, and you can control the outcome of an election. Most people on the right never see it coming: one party rule from indifference. One party rule, shred the Constitution, and when the right wakes up, next will be civil war. People with guns versus people outlawing guns. Civil war."

Hunter shrugged his affirmation. "This is the essence, the goal of the *Communist Manifesto*. Their strategy to defeat the United States is to have Americans fight Americans. Let someone else take the hit. But there is a more insidious reason for Moscow to flip the American cultural switch on homosexuals. They don't give a shit about gay people. The gays are pawns in a much weightier game. So, if you want to infiltrate the CIA and the USIC.... Infiltrate the vanguards of freedom...."

Awareness and enlightenment came across Eastwood's face. He started laughing. His eyes got wide. He got it. "Ho...lee...shit, *kemo sabe*."

"The ultimate test of normality...those guys have to pass the polygraph. Counterespionage laws. Full scope, 'lifestyle' polygraph. Before 1994 if you acknowledged you were gay, you were a potential blackmail target and you didn't get hired. If you were to get past the polygrapher and were later discovered, you would get fired. With extreme prejudice. Some could hide their sexual proclivities from the polygrapher and escaped detection. History shows the guys with real sexual disorders can't be trusted. Like the *Cambridge Five*." Hunter peeled off the treasonous names like a seasoned war college professor lecturing on the greatest spies for Moscow of the twentieth century. "Donald Maclean, Guy Burgess, Harold 'Kim' Philby, Anthony Blunt, John Cairncross. For a researcher parachuting into this, it shouldn't be a surprise to find that they were all gay. I know there were other straight, married spies, Alger Hiss, the Rosenbergs, but isn't it interesting that the overwhelming majority of spies, the stealers of government secrets are and were gay men and women who were able to hide their sexual preference? The point zero zero zero one percent of the USIC found a way of cracking the code to get into the 'National' vault to steal America's secrets."

The look on Eastwood's face suggested he might have missed a piece of the puzzle. Hunter asked, "What event occurred in 1994? I'll tell you. A Democrat president signed the *Don't Ask, Don't Tell* law. Until then the DSM had always been a part of the DOD's personnel procurement system. Potential recruits had enlistment physicals; they were evaluated for physical defects and also for any apparent mental, sexual or personality disorder. Are you with me?"

Eastwood's mouth was open as he nodded.

"For over fifty years, anyone with mental, personality, suicidal, and a range of sexual or other behavior disorders were unfit for service. A Democrat Congress who allowed their K Street lawyers to write the law, wrote that law so that whatever applied to the DOD *also applied to the U.S. Intelligence Community*. Moscow rejoiced; now they could get their spies into the IC without them being eliminated for mental or sexual disorders. Throw enough of your guys at a polygrapher and some were bound to get in. That's how the Kremlin infiltrated the CIA. Another way to undermine the U.S."

Hunter was serious for a moment. "Do you think Moscow would allow people with mental or sexual disorders or people who could be potential blackmail candidates into the KGB or FSB or whatever they call themselves this week? No—why not?"

"You can't trust them."

"Exactly. If the job is 'special trust and confidence' how do you trust someone with a mental disorder? This is a case study on the difference between people who do not have a security clearance and those that do. The uncleared activists wanted one thing, and the guys with clearances in the Kremlin wanted something else. Someone who knew how to get complex shit done found a way to do both; it's like a virus, a disease that is fatal. And getting someone to do your bidding like that, I will tell you, that's a talent. The ultimate bait and switch."

"It was brilliant to throw some cash at them, spin them up, and have the activists do all the dirty work to change the DSM and infiltrate the APA to change public policy all for the benefit of the Communist Party. America found herself in a culture war. The Kremlin, through the Communist Party USA, unabashedly funded those sexual activists while some smartass Democrat K Street lawyer helped the Democrat Congress write the proposed legislation that rewrote American public policy and changed the way the U.S. Intelligence Community screened candidates. The most important thing this did to national security was to crack open the door to homosexuals and those with sexual and personality disorders. That category of people who have been demonstrably 'untrustworthy' could gain positions of great trust and confidence. People who have had an axe to grind, people who had a romantic view of Cuba and Moscow could 'legally' infiltrate the USIC."

Eastwood was crushed. "I never knew—I just went along. I thought nothing of it when the gays won their little battles, but in this context, I can see the hands of the Kremlin at work, like Geppetto pulling Pinocchio's strings before he becomes a real boy. It's criminal."

Chapter 50

May 25, 2018

A server approached with a tray of desserts. Hunter and Eastwood chose the key lime pie with coffee. Another waiter cleared off the bottles and replaced the refreshments with water with lemon. They ate in silence and when they spoke, it was about a part of the Colombian economy they could not see directly but indirectly, such as the lights of the Boeing 747 that departed for Miami nightly with a full load of colorful and different flowers from the growers' half-million acres of flowers under cultivation.

When the dessert dishes were cleared, Hunter continued. "And then we have President Mazibuike who encouraged legal challenges to the Don't Ask, Don't Tell law and legislation to repeal DADT which specified that the policy would remain in place until the President, the Secretary of Defense, and the Chairman of the Joint Chiefs of Staff certified that repeal, quote, 'would not harm military readiness.' Unquote. Mazibuike fired at least 300 generals and admirals until he got the leaders in place who would state repealing DADT would not harm military readiness. A ruling from a federal appeals court barred further enforcement of the U.S. military's ban on openly gay service members. This was not a popular decision with the military service members who saw that Mazibuike was intent on destroying the military and the intelligence community. And of course, some special operations guys got fired for articulating what they thought of their commander-in-chief."

Eastwood was dumbfounded. He said, "I know all of that is true, but I never heard it put together like that. Of course, you are right."

Hunter nodded, "The Democrats and the KGB knew exactly what they were doing. They were the masters. They knew that the people in their little gay world would always blame the government and Republicans for their 'troubles.' So encouraged by guys like themselves, they looked for an escape, for ways to punish DOD and the government. That escape was revenge. Unadulterated revenge. For almost 25 years, the U.S. Intelligence Community has had a steady pipeline of gays and lesbians and trannies infiltrating their ranks, and if you look at who has been locked up recently for passing or selling secrets to the Russians and the Chinese or the Iranians...."

"It's been...*them*?"

"Yeah. This was predicted decades ago. When they were caught stealing secrets, Mazibuike pardoned them. They were sentenced to twenty years or life in prison for violating the Espionage Act, and he still pardoned them. Now they work for TASCO, for one of the most secretive gay men in the intelligence business. He hired them and made them feel 'normal.' Accepted. They recruited others like them into the TASCO 'family.' And they would do anything for him."

"In many ways, Chernovich is the gay buffoonish villain right out of the pages of the Sunday comics.... Dick Tracy never encountered a narcissistic personality disorder and a sexual disorder."

Eastwood finally got a word in. "Chernovich. Narcissistic personality disorder. And they *will* do anything for him for he has done everything for them." Eastwood shook his head in disgust. *They will do anything for him just because he is gay; he is their protector. And I was willing to do anything for him just because he was a Marine general. Bait and switch.* He pinched the bridge of his nose and closed his eyes. *I was in a cult. Didn't even see it. Ho-lee shit.*

Hunter nodded and continued, "Same goes for the radical Muslims and implementing *sharia* law. Get enough Democrats and radical Muslims to protest, get enough criminal Muslims in Congress, get the president to implement Muslim Outreach programs, and soon radical criminal Muslims are in the decision tree. What's to stop them from making *sharia* law legal, commonplace, and acceptable? This really is an advanced form of brainwashing. Can you see it? Infiltration is the very essence of *Dark Islam* and the Muslim Brotherhood's agenda in *An Explanatory Memorandum*. They're here to steal our freedom and force us to submit to their rule."

"Is this really what TASC is doing?" Eastwood wanted to make sure he understood the threat from TASC, the think tank subsidiary of

TASCO who supplied high-level employment candidates to the federal government.

"It was another textbook *classic misdirection*—bait and switch. Remind me to tell you how I got a U-2 flyover for a dedication event when the Air Force said 'reprogramming a U-2 was impossible.' Anyway, Chernovich hands President Hernandez a binder full of TASC-approved FBI candidates. What are they doing? *Classic misdirection.* The expectation is those lawyers will uphold and prosecute the law, but their actual goal is to bend and tamper with public policy for their purposes. For TASC. And it's articulated as the same goal, 'it's in the country's best interest to have a viable FBI and here are first-rate and consummate replacement candidates, Mr. President.' But the replacements aren't working for the president or the FBI; they're working for TASC. Chernovich."

"*Narcissistic personality disorder,*" whispered Eastwood.

"Bait and switch." Hunter nodded. "I've seen better rats in storm drains. The grand prize is the White House. The Muslim Brotherhood wanted to raise the black flag of al-Qaeda; the anarchists wanted to raise their black flag over the White House. I assert the Democrat Party lusts for the day when they can replace the American Flag with their rainbow flag. A gay president picks his or her cabinet, the cabinet disburses monies to their pet organizations. Instead of laundering hundreds of millions of dollars through their favorite pet projects that make them money, they'll launder billions to fund their sexual desires and bribe congresscritters to change the laws to favor them while attacking the non-DSM straight people of the U.S."

"I always wondered what really happened at Benghazi. I was there. There were rumors. I saw the Muslim Brotherhood's green flag...."

"The Democrat ambassador was meeting his gay lover in a remote location. The Muslim Brotherhood found out and punished him. Beat him and sodomized him; cut off his genitals and stuffed them into his mouth. They were animals led by the most vicious paramilitary, mercenary group in the Islamic Underground. You know the bloody hand print?"

Eastwood nodded.

"That was the mark of Sheikh Saleem Ali al-Qasimi. The Muslim Merchant of Death. The Assassin of Alexandria. Al-Qaeda brings him out of his hole for special projects…." Hunter just realized what he said. *The worm on top of the Disposition Matrix. Another turd I haven't been able to flush.*

Hunter added, "They need another Democrat president and Congress, and I can see a powerful businessman like Chernovich attempt a coup or running for the office, to make pedophilia and bestiality and who knows what else legal. Like multiple genders. What're they up to now—57 varieties? I'll bet TASCO's personnel application is a multi-page Chinese menu just for genders. When two won't do, you're through."

Eastwood came alive. "What're we going to do?"

Hunter responded, "I said it before. I think you thought I was kidding. We are the resistance; we're the Sixth Column against the left. They provide disinformation; we provide the truth. They sabotage our government; we thwart their plans. We have created our own *samizdat.* You are the face, the leader of America's dissidents."

Again the color drained from Eastwood's face. Now he knew Hunter was dead serious.

Hunter asked, "Are you ready to be a hero? Their side has Bogdan Chernovich who, like Hitler and the other murderous socialists, has a messiah complex. Our side has a billion guns and eight trillion bullets. We're not the ones who are mentally defective and trying to pull off a coup or commit mass murder; they are. Not mom and pop Democrats but Washington Democrats with clearances. And they're doing everything they can to make it appear as if we are the bad guys, and if any lefty is in a relationship with a Republican or a Conservative, they need to be dropped like a bad transmission. Or worse."

Hunter stood. "It's time to leave. I still have work to do this evening. I'll tell you what I have in mind on the way down."

Eastwood looked like a man who had just been defeated in front of thousands at the Olympics. *Just as I expected; Hunter's going to leave me and go off to kill more terrorists for fun and profit. Why do I feel like a fish out of water, flipping and jerking around and hoping someone will just chop my head off and put me out of my misery? I'm a reporter, not a saboteur! How was I supposed to know they are actually attacking the USIC? Destroyed the Boy Scouts? Thinking they have the upper hand in defeating Christianity?*

Halfway down the mountain, still admiring the view, Hunter said, "You and I have traveled the Middle East and have gone through the hotels and airports in Cairo, Amman, Dubai, Abu Dhabi, Kuwait City, Baghdad, and Kabul. The Muslims who work at those airports and hotels treat us with wondrous respect and courtesy. They're the real Islam, and they're at war with *Dark Islam,* the radical, criminal, and ugly part of Islam. Just like we are. And like they do daily, we have commies and socialists and Marxists to fight here at home as politics is combat by other means."

"What this all means is, Dory, welcome to the updated version of the *Great Game*."

"The *Great Game*? I've head of the *Great Game,* but I understood it was just a contest between the Russian and British Empires."

"It's the same as the *Great Game* from the 1850s, 1860s. It was a conflict between *the intelligence agencies* of Imperial Russia and the British Empire. The Russians were winning because, well, they and the Brits had the only intelligence gathering organizations at the time. We only had a small Intelligence Office at the Navy Department. Then we got the CIA. We collapsed the Russian economy, their satellite countries de-orbited and became independents. For the last fifty years atheist China has been flexing the panda's muscles. China is in a cold war with us—spinning up their intelligence gathering organizations, and we are not paying attention. Now Mohammedanism Islam, funded by oil money, has figured out that entities with intelligence gathering organizations succeed, and those without any intelligence gathering structure fail. They are trying to grow their IC as fast as possible in order to get a bite of the apple that is the U.S. There are multiple players in the *Great Game,* and they have achieved what Clausewitz defined as 'mass." They sense blood in the water because Mazibuike weakened us substantially and we're being attacked from every quarter. Intelligence agencies versus intelligence agencies."

Eastwood said, "You're saying they're not attacking the U.S. military head-on but they undermine them with mental disorders and they attack the USIC and Christians and Christian organizations, like the Boy Scouts."

"Exactly correct. Look at the evidence. Ma and Pa Kettle in Cape Flattery, Washington are not their adversaries; the CIA and western intelligence gathering and Christian organizations are. Destroy the culture, create a vacuum, and fill the vacuum with your ideology."

"While I agree with you, but they have been trying to kill me, you *and* me, for a long time. I think you understand my concern."

Hunter said, "I do understand it, and I live it, too. We have to understand the world has changed, but we do not have to accept that the bad guys have won. They are not that bright. Americans are expecting guys like us to protect them from evil, from the people in this world trying to kill us, Americans and America. It's time everyone knew it. When Americans know it, they will rally. It's time to quit avoiding these poisonous people with mental disorders; we are under attack by the crazies. The great Thomas Payne said, 'Like Hell, tyranny is not easily conquered.' Rule by the tyrannical criminally deranged is no way to live. It's time to fight back. We have guns and bullets; they have shit for brains."

Eastwood laughed at Hunter's description. "Duncan, I agree. You're not an easy man to kill. I'm ten years older. I am in the phase of life where senescence has more effect on my wrinkles than gravity."

"Dory, someone has to do it. We have to play with the team we have and not wait for the team we wish we had. While I'm doing my part to kill off an Islamic totalitarianist genocidal movement overseas, and McGee is purging *Dark Islam* from the Agency, America needs someone to expose the domestic, communist, and totalitarianist head of the effort, like Chernovich. Set the stage with *Omega*, drop the first bomb with your radio show—like a broadcast on Radio Free Europe. Like a seed it will spawn a discussion, a movement. I say we give the corrupt flippin' news media a taste of their own nasty medicine."

Eastwood said, "You're not talking about Visine; you want to plant a seed."

"Thomas Jefferson said, 'The tree of liberty must be refreshed from time to time with the blood of patriots and tyrants.' Yes I want to plant a seed and shine a light on them but I want the other son-of-a bitch to die for his beliefs. I believe it is time to fight back." Hunter nodded a bit. "I find it unbelievable how tangled this web of corruption is, and how lazy and dishonest our news media has become. The only thing that is working for them is that the American people have no clue what is going on. They are blissfully ignorant, and that's the way it should be for mom and pops and the kids in school."

Eastwood looked at Hunter. He stuffed his hands into his pockets and nodded.

"Today's media have become political organizations. That's why I released 3M's file. The DNC and the communist corrupt media hid the truth, used lies and propaganda to make Americans think he was eligible. You could do a show on that topic on *Unfiltered News*."

"I'll take that under advisement. But, yes, that's exactly how it's done, how Americans are manipulated. It's easy when you've a willing accomplice." Eastwood nodded. He was liking being a conspirator.

"And you follow-up the *Omega* outburst with an article or your webcast—or both. We are doing to the media what they have been doing to America, only our stuff is factual. Real references. Use the internet to find proof, but go to law reviews on issues of law instead of some lefty websites that have agendas."

Eastwood looked at his uninteresting feet. "I saw the way things were going in America a long time ago, a long time back. I knew who was responsible. The bad guys had won, and it was time to reassess and take cover. But there was no other place on earth to go, and there wasn't anything I could do about it. I said nothing. I'm one guy who could've spoken up and spoken out. The bad guys are in charge; they're out of control; they're guilty of killing us. I'm guilty of doing what I can to keep off their shit list."

"Dory, you're looking like the wreck of the Hesperus. Let's get a few things clear." Hunter emphasized with an index finger. "With that comment, you're upholding that the left and the corrupt media are a murderous bunch. I provided you with an armored vehicle that you don't drive, so you must have felt like you're bulletproof. Don't make excuses and don't think like that. You're not a coward. You're a U.S. Marine Corps Lieutenant Colonel. *You're strong like bull.* You haven't been able to do anything about it because you didn't have the tools to fight back. But now we can fight back; we have the right tools and the right focus. These things are an issue of timing—like getting everyone in the right frame of mind in the room to sign the Declaration of Independence. Our time is now. And we'll be smart; you'll be in the background. It'll be ok. I'll do my part, but we really need you to inform and educate those Americans who love our country. Together we have a chance to break the back of the *Dark State* and their commie buddies; then we break the back of the Muslim Brotherhood." Hunter collapsed the finger into a fist pump and smiled like he was holding a winning raffle ticket.

Eastwood looked up from under his gray eyebrows until the cable car stopped. Hunter said, "I need to put Nazy's number in your telephone in case of an emergency." Eastwood was living a nightmare, *How can I call anyone when the whole world will be out to shoot me?*

As they approached the Toyota, Hunter said, "I've told you things that can't ever be repeated."

"I know. Thank you."

Hunter dropped to the ground to see if the FARC had booby-trapped his vehicle.

As Hunter made his rounds to the vehicles' four wheels, Eastwood said, "You know, you could sell refrigerators to Eskimos."

"I take it that's a yes?"

"I only hope I live to regret it. We really are teammates. Our word is our bond."

"It is. I can provide you with a very visible protective staff, or you can remain anonymous. Hidden in your office. Travel incognito. Act like nothing has changed. No one knows you are on the side of good."

"Well, when you put it that way."

"Dory, I see the evil encroaching every day. Every day they get closer to their objective. I can no longer just look on. I must do more, but I need help."

"I get it; I really do. When there is no more America, when these people are trying to take the only refuge that peace-loving people, freedom-loving people have, I agree. Someone must make a stand. We must make a stand."

"They won't stop until they turn America into something ugly and evil. Something it was never intended to be—defeated. A place that's untenable for you and me, my family and friends. You just have to create a crisis to get things started."

"God help me," said Eastwood.

"Amen," said Hunter.

The men shook hands at the hotel. Hunter bid his leave and told Eastwood he would be in touch.

Hunter drove to the main air force base in Colombia and was airborne in less than an hour. Before embarking on a quest to find submersibles and drug labs, he had an anomaly to revisit.

Demetrius Eastwood took the first flight out of Colombia. He wasn't able to sleep on the jet.

CHAPTER 51

May 25, 2018

It took some persuasion but Nazy Cunningham negotiated a reasonable price for using the buildings and the surrounding area for a month. Had she been dealing with men, the negotiations would've been quick, but the women who had poured their heart and soul into conserving the structure would not let some ridiculously ravishing thing with eccentric long hair dictate terms and conditions, with secrecy being paramount. At the conclusion of negotiations all parties were pleased with the contract, and Nazy promised payment up front. No one in government ever paid for anything up front. You paid for goods and services after delivery, never before.

The cost of admission would be through an interested third party that would fully fund the necessary repairs to *Fallingwater*, Frank Lloyd Wright's masterpiece, to keep it from tumbling into the rushing waters of Bear Run. The residence, like virtually all of Wright's designs, had been officially closed to the public "for maintenance," but in reality it was shut down for a lack of restoration funds. Ticket sales, donations, and corporate funding campaigns had not been sufficient to maintain and repair the internationally recognized weekend home.

The design was revolutionary, cantilevered directly over Bear Run's rushing waterfalls, and unrivaled by contemporary American architects. Few houses were the subject of books, posters, puzzles, and even Lego construction kits. There was simply nothing like *Fallingwater*.

Over the past eighty years the condition of the residence had deteriorated substantially because of its exposure to a range of climate conditions; humidity, sunlight, water infiltration, and the severe freeze-thaw conditions of southwest Pennsylvania that affected the building's 1930s-era structural materials. The failing concrete cantilevers were one of many structural issues. *Fallingwater's* stonework, concrete surfaces and structures, roofs and terraces needed a full restoration to bring the residence back to its former glory.

The Central Intelligence Agency wouldn't be *Fallingwater's* life preserver; there would be an anonymous benefactor, Quiet Aero Systems of Fredericksburg, Texas. All that was required of the *Fallingwater* management organization, the Western Pennsylvania Conservancy, was to allow an inconspicuous group of intelligence officers and staff the exclusive use of the facility for several weeks and for the conservancy to not mention the arrangement. The Agency woman also promised no one would touch the building's many furnishings.

It was an unusual request, but when the restoration funds were immediately transferred into the conservancy's account, the parties established dates for the group's occupancy and departure. There would be photographic inventories before and after occupation.

• • •

A phalanx of security agents from the Operations Tradecraft Course from the CIA's Helms Center were posted along the roads to ensure the temporary residents would be well protected from the curious or those who hadn't seen the announcement of the extended closure for maintenance. Construction vehicles were allowed past the impromptu barricade by armed Agency students who appeared to be unarmed men and women in gray uniforms from a nondescript no-name contracted security firm. The Chief of the Field Activities Training Group was on hand to ensure her students would take full advantage of the restricted training opportunity.

A string of bread trucks and vans with food and health and comfort products filed through the entry control point. Others carried security relief crews. Several shipping containers were delivered and scattered about. It appeared they were filled with restoration materials, but they were comfortable living quarters, complete with beds, showers, and toilets. The *Fallingwater* Café reopened with contracted Agency personnel to feed the security guards and the temporary residents.

This venue was a dramatic change for the dour Agency polygrapher. Her milieu in Virginia was a windowless, sterile, and dark interview office. Now she was in an open corner of the main living area of one of the most impressive landmark structures from Wright's great mind. *And there are windows!* The woman had never seen such wealth and beauty in a working environment. Then she was confronted with the stark reality that after walking the grounds and the different floors of *Fallingwater*, she would spend her evenings in an air conditioned shipping container without windows.

A technician checked the residence for eavesdropping devices just to be sure the building hadn't been bugged with surveillance equipment. He left several of the bright green *Growlers* just in case a hostile power penetrated the security and used laser-based eavesdropping equipment. The *Growlers* would send spurious electrical waves throughout the residence that would interfere with the latest advances in remote acoustics surveillance technology. He reminded the polygrapher not to use the *Growlers* when the polygraph machine was operating.

Technicians from the Science & Technology Directorate installed portable gunfire detection and anti-sniper defensive systems on the top floor of *Fallingwater*. The S&T team spent the better part of a day strategically placing intrusion detection equipment, FLIRs, cameras, motion and seismic sensors around the compound. As they worked, they admired the synergy of nature with the brilliance of *Fallingwater*; images they would never forget.

When Saoirse Nobley rolled into the forest in Southwestern Pennsylvania's Laurel Highlands in the back seat of an armored vehicle and saw the iconic residence for the first time, she knew that Duncan Hunter was alive, that he was involved, and that this was how he was taking care of her. She relaxed, waited, and relived the memories of him that kept her sane.

The least Nazy and Kelly could do was to keep Saoirse Nobley from finding a mirror. The woman was a mess and covered her mouth to hide missing teeth when she spoke. Nazy and Kelly had talked to

Saoirse but for only a few minutes. She had been spirited out of the Walter Reed National Military Medical Center well before sunrise in order to avoid the rush hour traffic on the I-410 Beltway.

Kelly explained, "We consider you a 'walk-in.' A walk-in is someone who, on their own initiative, contacts us, and volunteers intelligence information."

Nobley said, "I have nothing to hide. I'll tell it all if that's what Captain Hunter wants."

The CIA had their protocols. Nazy said, "Ms. Nobley, you're an American citizen, not someone who's requesting political asylum. Someone you've been close to for many years has been an active member of a terrorist organization, and we would like to know as much as possible about what you know. And we'd like to know how Captain Hunter fits into the equation."

Nobley reiterated, "I will tell you anything, I just want to know if Captain Hunter is alive."

Nazy said, "I'm his wife." She didn't say it maliciously or to make a point that Duncan was off limits. The woman needed validation and Nazy unexpectedly provided it. Kelly was so stunned, she almost fell over. *No one except the CIA Director and the President knows of Nazy's and Duncan's marriage.*

The response generated a pause and a comment. "I always wondered, what kind of woman would capture his heart? You're a very lucky woman." The look on Nobley's face telegraphed *Please understand, I am not in any way a rival. I am just grateful.*

"Thank you," said Nazy.

"I thought of Captain Hunter daily. I thought of him to get me through to another day. I'm out of that place now; I think I'm the luckiest woman in the world. And with you here, I know that Captain Hunter has had a hand in all of this. Thank you. Thank you. I will tell you everything I know. Let's get started. I get tired easily."

"We have a physician and a clinical psychiatrist here if you need to talk to someone. And we have a dentist you can see," said Nazy.

"I really need a dentist. I've lost so many teeth."

Kelly didn't volunteer that she was Duncan Hunter's daughter but instructed Saoirse on their agenda and what she could expect. Nobley agreed without conditions.

As the polygrapher prepared Saoirse for her polygraph interview, Kelly asked Nazy how and why she had selected *Fallingwater*. "The short answer is Muslim men have already had a go at *Spindletop*. If they knew that she was alive and mosques were ordered to look for her, one of the first places they would check would be *Spindletop*. However, no one would ever think of going to a place like *Fallingwater*. I came up here with Director McGee's family. It was on the verge of closing, there were no funds for a needed refurbishment, but it suits *our* needs for a period. Here in the woods we are perfectly safe with our officers as security."

Kelly nodded and concurred. She looked at Nazy and said, "Do you mind if I ask a very personal question?"

Nazy was concerned by the request but said, "I'll tell you anything that I can." *There are still things of which you are not cleared.*

"Isn't it strange the woman that my father saw after my mother but before you is sitting right there? What are you feeling?"

Nazy took a few moments to think about the situation. *Duncan had told Greg Lynche his concerns when Nobley married and Director McGee asked me to see if there was a record. And there was!* She turned to Kelly. "Your father loved your mother with all of his heart, and she loved him. He believes you're a gift from God. After your mother passed he didn't think he would ever find that kind of love again."

"Kelly, in my world, where I came from there are women who give their love but once. I was in an arranged marriage in Jordan and was miserable; I had to leave. I have loved only your father, and I love him more each day. Through all that we experienced, I know that grief is a wound that may not ever heal, but it can be bandaged with time and love from another. Your father may think of your mother from time to time, and he may think of Saoirse, but I know Duncan loves me as much as I do him. I believe your mother was much like me; I am and she was one of those women who find and give love only once. I don't think Miss Nobley is one of those women. If your father loved her, he wouldn't have left her. He wasn't in love with her, and she had professed her love for someone else. She got married; lived her own life. Had children. Miss Nobley was special to Duncan but in a different way. It's a little strange for us if we let our imaginations run wild. But you know, maybe more than anyone, your father will move the heavens and the earth for his family and his friends."

Kelly pursed her lips and nodded, *He came for me in Liberia....*

"I think we have to look at her as one of your father's closest friends from a long time ago. Director McGee took care of me when Duncan wasn't able to; it's the least we can do to take care of her while your father is on assignment."

Kelly took a deep breath and nodded.

"Thank you, Nazy. That brings things into perspective. If you don't mind me asking, why do you do it?"

Nazy nodded for Kelly to follow her upstairs and onto the upper terrace. At a corner of the terrace she clasped her hands and looked up to the sky and said, "Why do I do it? Duncan rescued me. He picked me up in—let's see if I can remember—you know how your father is with cars, and I learn all I can about the cars that excite him. On that day in Newport, it was a 1938 Rolls Royce Phantom III; a 'P3.' We went to the Red Parrot. He knew I was acting out of fear. He took my hand and said he wouldn't let anything happen to me. That with him and his friends, I would be safe. Not just from Islam. I said he rescued me, gave me my freedom. That night and for the last seventeen years, I felt beholden to him. You always love the person who rescues you from harm. He said America would give me the freedom I was seeking."

"Duncan is an easy man to love. It was later in our relationship that I learned that your father was engaged in fighting the people who are at war with America. He lives to protect this country, and you and me, as he often says, against enemies, foreign and domestic. That's Duncan. He showed me how our country is being attacked by communists and radicals and the radical element of Islam that is vile and dangerous. I learned that he does not lie; he was correct. We are in the IC; we know that it is true we are in the fight of our lives, although the rest of America is blissfully unaware."

Kelly said, "I heard some officers who had been to war in Iraq and Afghanistan say, 'We're at war so America can be at the mall.'"

Nazy smiled. "I escaped from that evil world, and your father facilitated all of it. I was terrified of leaving, but once he took my hand and extracted me from that circle of hell we call *Dark Islam,* and introduced me into his world, this world, I was so grateful. I was free. I was his, and if he wanted, he would be mine. He helped me to be free, and in some strange way I wanted to help him. Repay him. Help America. I have skills the Agency finds useful. I love America. I would give my life for this country. I would give my life for Duncan. It just works for us."

"I've seen those things only people with a security clearance are allowed to see. The same criminals that have weaponized that part of Islam have taken over parts of our government. I'm part of the group of people who believe the American way of life is righteous and just, that freedom is worth fighting for. I do this work because I know America is continually under attack from the political left, the communists, the radicals of the world, and the dark side of Islam who are at work to destroy Christianity and America. America is a Christian nation, and in the eyes of the atheist left and the Islamists, it must be destroyed."

"Sometimes it takes a person from another place to see how wonderful America is; that there is a reason people will do anything to come here. America needs people who know that she is under assault to engage the domestic enemy, protect religious liberty, and keep our country free."

"I help my husband fight back in the only way I know how. I'm here. I rejected Islam, and I am a Christian." Nazy fingered the cross around her neck. "We are on the front lines, as Duncan would say. This is a phenomenal country. I understand now what it is to be an American and what's meant by 'America is a shining light on a hill.' I want to do my part to keep all Americans free and safe and to keep that light on the hill."

Kelly was moved by Nazy's soliloquy. "I can see why my father and you make such a terrific couple. It explains your relationship. You guys are teammates, always at work. I'm still trying to find my way. I've screwed up here and there but I think I'm getting closer to where you are, that God has put me here to help protect America. That it's under assault isn't clear to people in my age group, but if you zoom out a little, I think it becomes clearer. I don't know if I can help. I see the woman downstairs, and I feel pity for her. But she is like you in many ways. We extracted her from the Middle East and the mere mention of Duncan has her working with us, providing intel that may be useful to protect our country."

Nazy put an arm around Kelly and said, "You don't have to decide tonight. Life is a journey. We need to return downstairs."

She changed topics and continued, "The interview process will take several days, possibly a week. It's fairly well set up. The specialists who interrogate terrorists for a living gave our polygrapher several hundred questions for Nobley. It's a process that can take some time. I know I've forgotten something; I know I'll think of more, and you can help in that regard. If you have anything you think we should ask her, write it down, and give it to the polygrapher. With that said, this is your show until your father arrives."

"Do we know anything yet? Have you heard from him?"

She shrugged. "I anticipate a couple of days more, but you know your father." Nazy playfully rolled her eyes after she said it. If there was one thing Duncan Hunter could be counted on doing, it was the unusual. "One more thing, you could see about calling that dentist." She withdrew a ratty business card from the day planner she frequently carried. "Here is his contact information. Her mouth is a mess and it's imperative to get her in to see him. Duncan said to use him if possible. Tell him you're Duncan's daughter."

"How does Dad know a dentist in Pennsylvania?"

"How does your father know half the people he knows? Greg Lynche once said he has one of the most gifted minds and prodigious memories in the country. Greg wanted to recruit Duncan for our place, but your father had other plans. He was going to be an astronaut. And I'm sure he would have made it. He doesn't give up and forgets nothing, even if we think he does."

Kelly walked Nazy to the kitchen door and gave her a hug goodbye. Nazy did the three-cheek air-kiss goodbye reserved for close family; she would be taken to the airport for a military helicopter flight back to the CIA.

After Nazy departed the premises, Kelly walked back to the terrace where she could observe the polygrapher interviewing Nobley. She crossed her arms and wondered if her father knew what he was paying for.

After the polygrapher established a baseline for Nobley, she directed her to focus on a point over the fireplace. The questioning began and continued for several hours. Every hour, they stopped for breaks and food, with the polygrapher carefully disconnecting her interviewee and then reconnecting her, establishing a fresh baseline, and asking another set of questions.

After the last polygraph of the day, Saoirse Nobley walked out of the living area and onto the terrace. The sun had set but the air was still warm on her face. She filled her lungs and breathed the cleanest air she had ever encountered. The beauty of the forest trees in full bloom bifurcated by the clearest stream she had ever known was the stuff from travel magazines she had seen decades ago.

Kelly asked the polygrapher what she saw. "At first blush I thought she could be as shifty as smoke, but the longer I interviewed her the more I like her. She's not the typical radical or defector I've done in the past who tries to hide every response. I don't know what's she has been through—I'll get into those issues tomorrow. She's very different; it took a little time for her to relax and now she's been unshackled. Her answers are direct and crisp. I believe she's the real deal. Whatever she has seen, she is motivated to tell us. She's willing to help us. Whatever we want."

"You think she's legitimate?"

"I do."

"Thanks."

Kelly joined Saoirse on the terrace; the former detainee said, "I find the house and the setting thoroughly enchanting, and I really want to see Duncan Hunter. His questions would be better, and I wouldn't have to be hooked up to a machine. I have nothing to hide. At the times when I just wanted to die, I would think of him, and that would keep me going. I never met another person who just wanted to do things for me, encourage me, motivate me without demanding something in return. He wasn't the type of person who would lie to you to get something from you. He encouraged me to go to school, and I did. If he had known the predicament I was in, I knew he would've done everything possible to rescue me." *He had saved me several times before....* "Do you know what I mean?"

An old memory jogged Kelly's emotions. She nodded a response. *He saved me and hundreds of others from hijackers. When he knew I was in distress, he was there for me.* She leaned on the edging and stared out across Bear Run and the trees. She sighed and capitulated, *My dad has saved me several times, even when I failed him. But he still believes in me. He says we are all works in progress, and you have to fail to know what to correct. He loves me. Very much.*

While Kelly explored the limitations of the terrace with Saoirse, she gently reminded herself and Nobley that the Wright-designed built-in furniture and furnishings in the living area were to be left untouched. "We probably shouldn't lean on the edging. If there is something you want to read, someone will gladly go into town to get it. When you want to sleep or use the facilities, there's a bed behind a set of panels that will give you a modicum of privacy, and there is a shower. I don't know if the women of the Conservancy use it when the residence is open for tourists. Someone will be on guard in the living area throughout the night."

After the polygrapher had turned in and the facility's protective staff had eaten their fill at the *Fallingwater* Café, Kelly and Saoirse walked back to the residence and onto the main living area terrace. They sat in Adirondack chairs and propped their feet onto matching footstools. Saoirse breathed deep the forest air. Kelly could hear the cry in Saoirse's voice. "The air here is so clean my lungs can't get enough of it. The air in the desert is horrible. It is putrid, dusty, and leaves a gritty residue on every horizontal surface."

The women talked of innocuous things, Nobley was reflective for several seconds, and she struggled to articulate her appreciation. She said, very quietly, "I was at my limit. I...wasn't able...to keep going. I had given up. Captain Hunter had told me.... He told me that some of the training he had received…that the one thing he remembered…that if you were ever captured or taken prisoner…your job was to do…whatever it took…to…stay…alive. You have to believe someone will come for you. Like the POWs in Vietnam. You have to find ways of staying alive. It is a matter of will." She paused to regain her composure. "At…at…at the time…I didn't understand what he meant. I was so young. My mind drifted off to think of nonsensical things."

"He said that there are people who wanted to kill Americans. I thought he was being dramatic. Kind of showing off. I don't know if you know him, but he was badly hurt in the Marines and wasn't able to return to flying. He said something like, 'there's life after flying, and you can't do anything if you're dead.'" She looked at her feet and spoke the words of the condemned, "They took my children from me and threatened to harm them if I didn't do what they said. I chose their lives over mine. I hope my children are ok, that they have done nothing to harm them. Maybe it is best if I don't know."

Children? Not part of the brief. Oh my! Kelly was seeing Saoirse in a different light. She had been lovely, maybe even an alarming beauty, but now she was wan, worn out, and fragile, like shriveled petals about to fall off a rose. *But she has the most fantastic eyes I have ever seen on a woman.* Once she started talking, Nobley talked non-stop. Kelly took copious mental notes. After a couple of hours, Saoirse said she was tired and ready for sleep. The woman looked like she needed a hug, and Kelly obliged. Then Kelly wrote down the woman's revelations. Things a polygrapher would know how to explore.

Kelly Horne wandered back out onto the top floor; she called Nazy and gave her a data dump. Nazy said to hold on, that she wanted to bring the Director on the line. When Bill McGee joined the conversation, he asked questions, and Kelly dutifully responded. Officially, all the polygraphs were positive. Saoirse was not evasive, and said she still wanted to talk to Captain Hunter, but she would tell Kelly whatever she wanted to tell him. She would do anything they asked. She talked of her husband and where he had been and what he had said. There were things she believed were interesting, were worth remembering, and worth sharing with the senior intelligence officers.

It was late. McGee asked the money shot and Kelly replied, "She said he had returned from Iran with ornate prayer rugs for all of his wives but her. She knew then that her days were numbered. She said he was frustrated. He needed help for a special program, and he didn't want to use the team the elders suggested. The Americans were making it impossible for ISIS and al-Qaeda, and the U.S. had pitted them against each other in Africa and Iraq. She said he repeated, 'The complex was too large.' She didn't know what it meant. And his other complaint was, 'Ali wanted too much money. Money they didn't have.' And that was the last time she saw him."

Bill McGee bid the ladies a good evening. He would try to get on the President's calendar tomorrow.

There was something unsettling in Nobley's contributions. Bill McGee's brain wouldn't let him relax as it processed dozens of scenarios despite getting up several times during the night to jot down some notes. He understood what writers of thrillers faced when confronted with mental roadblocks and their brains wouldn't cease operations as if they were on some cerebral equivalent of autopilot. Healthy brains were programed to solve mind-bogglers and they continually ran until they had achieved a solution. It was as if an alarm had gone off, and McGee's eyes flew wide open. *Duncan told me his concerns!* He might've been exhausted from the lack of sleep and a hyperactive brain that had been shoved into overdrive, but knew he had to get up and record what his brain had determined; what he would tell the President. Then he called the CIA Operations Duty Officer who composed an immediate dispatch for a Chief of Station.

Kelly Horne tossed in her bed. Sleep would not come without reliving the failures of youth and to her father.

Saoirse Nobley slept easily; as she relived the most amazing times of her life when she had gone to Hawaii with a man who turned a girl into a woman.

Nazy Cunningham imaged her fingers were holding the fingers of her husband. When he was sleeping curled up behind her, it was safe to sleep.

CHAPTER 52

May 25, 2018

Ten members of the al-Qaeda affiliate arrived in the capital city of Turkmenistan for passage into Iran. At the airport's port of entry, Turkmen Customs Officers denied the men's immediate travel into Iran until the exit visas were acquired or until sufficient "facilitation payments" were made to officials of the Turkmen government. They announced that it could take up to two weeks for visas to process.

The *Jabhat Fatah al-Sham* team leader, Saleem Ali al-Qasimi, was forced to find lodging in Ashgabat until their exit visas and Iranian entry visas were approved. The postponement in their departure was typical. Hardly anything moved quickly in the Middle East, and everything moved slower when there were insufficient monetary incentives for expediency. Besides being prohibitively expensive, expediting visas would bring unwanted scrutiny and government surveillance on the men. The additional time in Ashgabat allowed them to acquire weapons and reconnoiter the food delivery service.

One man from al-Sham took photographs and made movies of their surroundings. The city of Ashgabat, its buildings, monuments, and walkways were made of white marble, an exquisite unstriated and unblemished grade of stone quarried nearby.

Purchasing vehicles and weapons on the black market was simple; finding adequate lodging for ten men at the same location proved impossible.

Ali al-Qasimi sent his men to an open-air *hookah* bar while he taxied to a business that could provide some of his men with the essentials needed to board in cheap hotels. Others would live off the land until their visas were approved. He disbursed the men into groups of two. He demanded they show restraint and discipline and not get into any situation that would jeopardize their mission. He warned them individually to leave the Turkmen women alone.

CHAPTER 53

May 26, 2018

The *Omega* post began: *It's Saturday, May 26th, 2018, and the reclusive billionaire Rho Schwartz Scorpii is one of the most corrupt people in Europe. He has plenty of politicians in his pocket who now want to blackmail Hungary and Romania and other post-Soviet Union countries for access to EU funds.*

Do you believe in coincidences? Is it just a coincidence that the research laboratory of the Ayatollah Khomeini Institute of Virology was designed and built by a consortium of French and German companies, experts in the business of constructing biological safety level 4 labs, and their program management office was one of the wholly owned subsidiaries of the international arm of the Trans-Atlantic Security Corporation?

Is it just a coincidence that these same labs were tangential to the SARS and MERS outbreaks that ravaged the Middle East and the United States, but left China mostly unscathed?

Is it just a coincidence that the Mazibuike campaign received millions of dollars in contributions from Trans-Atlantic Security Corporation while their international subsidiary was awarded contracts in the billions; one of which was to construct the Khomeini Institute of Virology complex?

Is it just a coincidence that the CEO of TASCO has a sordid history, a cadre of dead women, an addendum to his curriculum vitae?

Is it just a coincidence that the police reports of these dead women, some fifty women, have Bogdan Chernovich in the background as a person of interest because he was the last person to see the women alive? Not holding a gun, mind you, but someone with a background in chemistry and biology.

One last thing. Two detainees, American citizens taken off Islamic battlefields, died at GITMO of natural causes, and they were returned to the U.S. for burial.

This is the Omega.

Chapter 54

May 27, 2018

From: *The Turkmen Portal*, an on-line newspaper in Ashgabat.

When the bodies of 24-year-old Ingrid Lund of Germany and 28-year-old Marcel Sarazin from France were found at a camping area in the Koppet Dag Range, authorities first considered it a random act of sick violence that was sexually motivated. The woman was found inside the pair's brightly colored tent. The man had been beheaded. Both had been mutilated, and investigators say they were both sexually assaulted.

Authorities believe the macabre murders were linked to an Islamic extremist group that had moved into the area. A suspect arrested in connection with their deaths was found to have ties to an al-Qaeda affiliate, according to a statement released by the Ashgabat public prosecutor's office. One man reportedly dropped his identity papers when he fled the area which led to his arrest. The Turkmenistan intelligence agency authenticated a video that began circulating online showing the actual murder of Marcel Sarazen while Ingrid Lund let out a blood-curdling scream before she was beaten and raped.

The local Turkmen television station reported that two men were caught on surveillance tape pitching a tent near where the couple had camped out during a trekking adventure about six miles from the Iranian border. The men left the area after just one night.

"What we know is that they were on a month-long, private holiday in Turkmenistan," the public prosecutor's office said in a statement. "Our thoughts and prayers go out to the families."

Two suspects have been named by Turkmen authorities, but only one has been arrested so far. He was picked up in a busy tourist neighborhood in Ashgabat earlier this week. "We are working to bring before justice the other suspect on the run," according to a statement from the public prosecutor's office.

CHAPTER 55

May 27, 2018

The CIA Director didn't have to wait long to be admitted into the Oval Office. He and President Hernandez greeted each other warmly. The President offered the opposing sofa to the CIA Director and the Texans sat down.

The President nodded for McGee to begin.

"Mr. President, we recently met with the CDC Working Group and the Bioterrorism Task Force; a virologist whistleblower from the World Health Organization has detailed how there has been a large-scale organized scientific effort by the Iranian government to create an ethnic-specific bioweapon. The CDC may have some circumstantial biological evidence, and they have done some in-depth analysis that show the Iranians, with Chinese help, may have created a unique product in the Iranian's Biosafety Laboratory at the Khomeini Institute of Virology. They believe a virus was created by using a template-virus, engineered and owned by Chinese military research laboratories, but it is under the control of the Iranian government. Their analysis explained how the virus was manmade and could be mass produced."

"That doesn't give the world much time...."

"Yes, sir. The Iranians said they have officially destroyed the virus in order to hide their viral research from an unsuspecting public. It is unlikely they destroyed anything. You may have heard a Chinese epidemiologist was stopped at Heathrow with biological samples from the university where she is a student. She was arrested by Scotland Yard and claimed she worked in Iran. She noted that they had made a coronavirus that is a terrifying bioweapon, that it is difficult to trace and contain, and it is the perfect bioweapon to cripple and ruin societies. The CDC believes the transmissibility, morbidity, and mortality of this specific virus will significantly panic the global community, disrupt social orders, and decimate the world's economy."

"The range and destructive power of this super coronavirus is unprecedented and surpasses the standards of a traditional bioweapon and should be defined as an Unrestricted Bioweapon."

"Sounds bad."

McGee had more to tell but waited for the chief executive to digest the latest bad news. "Mr. President, it is very bad. We believe this virus is so small that it can pass through all known HEPA filters. We do not have perfect knowledge on what's transpiring at the Khomeini Institute, and not enough intel is trickling in to make a good assessment. My folks have wargamed the situation with the information at hand and determined possible outcomes; the modeling isn't pretty."

The President asked questions, and McGee hit the high points. "Chinese and Iranian researchers have been studying hundreds of coronaviruses from bats and rats for several years. The intel is solid that they have been experimenting with rare proteins that could turn a virus into an extremely contagious supervirus. There was a recent falling out over the goals of the research...."

"Do you know what those were?"

"We believe so, Mr. President. NSA has come through in a big way. In decrypts, the head of the Chinese researchers in Iran complained to Beijing that the Iranians averred that their focus was to conduct research on developing a virus that killed only Jews, infidels, and Christians and left Muslims untouched. It is possible that the Chinese scientists didn't have the stomach to weaponize a virus which would kill them or they realized their Iranian lab mates had bats in their belfries. It was clear the party was over. Some may have tried to leave, and we believe the IRGC guards may have disposed of them in the facility's incinerator."

"There may be another complication."

President Hernandez raised his head an iota.

"There are others; we believe as many as several dozen American and British subjects are being held at the Institute for human trials. We have confirmed the al-Qaeda and ISIS intelligence minister visited the facility, and we captured him after he returned to Syria."

"Has Haqqani talked?" President Hernandez had been briefed via the PDB that Toraluddin Haqqani was a GITMO resident.

"No, Mr. President we received some information from his American wife. She's been truthful and is working with us."

When POTUS nodded for the CIA Director to continue, McGee said, "An al-Qaeda mercenary group is on the ground in Ashgabat. The Chief of Station has informed the president of Turkmenistan of the situation. We asked that they are not to be disturbed in their planning phase."

"That changes the calculus of the equation. With our people being used as human shields, the situation doesn't lend itself to DOD throwing a couple of *Tomahawks* into Khomeini's place."

"Mr. President, we do not have independent confirmation that there are American hostages at that facility. We suspect there may be as many as four dozen; there are men and women who have gone missing from the area."

"Four dozen?"

"Yes, Mr. President. The Iranians aren't above using human shields to augment their deterrence. We're afraid they're using our citizens and some from Britain and Germany—and there may be some Chinese who are used for… experimentation. In other words…."

"Infidels." The President asked for recommendations and said that he would take them up on advisement with the NSC. He asked, "I agree, *Tomahawks* are probably not appropriate. You really think Duncan can do this? Alone? Isn't that asking too much from him?"

McGee sighed and squeezed his lips. "Mr. President, I know he… *and… I…* could… do… it."

One of President Hernandez's eyebrows shot to the ceiling. "You are… you're supposed to be in Europe this week."

"Yes, Mr. President. Suddenly, I have better things to do. I have trained all my life for these situations. This requires an infinitely small and delicate footprint. Duncan cannot do this from the air or by himself. He will need help. On the ground kind of help. My plan is to send Nazy in my place. The Deputy can hold down the fort. And we'll have a suitable replacement to deliver your PDB. I will probably need some presidential assistance with the Israelis. They are focused on destroying Iranian nukes and military installations, and I would like to deconflict any operations they are conducting. It would be better for us if they stood down for a while."

"Done! So, I'm losing you *and Nazy* for several days? You have it all figured out."

"There is one more thing, Mr. President. I need you to 'lean on' the president of Turkmenistan." McGee told the chief executive the reason. "It won't work if we have *interference*. It will work if we get cooperation."

President Hernandez asked what McGee needed specifically, and McGee told him. The President said, "That might not sound like much, but it will be expensive. I may have to invite him to the Oval Office or give him one of my helicopters."

"They would love to export their granite to the U.S., Mr. President. It really is superb. I would give him a Huey. We have many of those."

"The power of intelligence. That's even better." President Hernandez stood and shook hands with McGee. "You're a *hard man*, Bill. God speed, good luck, and don't get caught."

"Yes, Mr. President; that's the other plan."

CHAPTER 56

May 27, 2018

McGee met Hunter as he stepped off the LM-100J and pointed at the U.S. Air Force C-17 *Globemaster III*. He anticipated Hunter's question, "We have to go as soon as they can transfer your *Yo-Yo* to the C-17."

Glad to be back in the U.S. Nice to see you too. What are we doing? What the hell is going on? McGee's statement was odd since one requirement of the program was that the top secret YO-3A was not to be seen by unauthorized personnel and never be exposed to daylight. *If Bill says to transfer the YO-3A…he has a good reason. However, my question hasn't been answered.*

Nazy was on hand for the homecoming, but with the crowd of onlookers, security forces, aircrew, and loadmasters she stayed within the shadow of the CIA's limousine, keeping her distance. Her hair swirled on the tarmac's air currents; she got fed up with it, rolled it into a ball, and pinned it atop her head.

Nazy was wearing another bright intricate Hermès scarf with a navy blue-white polka dot dress. McGee allowed a passing thought—*Maverick will encourage her to buy more scarves when she is in Vienna.*

Hunter wanted to ask his question, but stopped and watched as Nazy fiddled with her hair. There was something erotic in the way she moved her arms over her head. *I swear that girl gets better looking every time I see her; but what's she doing here?* There was an unnatural sense of urgency in the air, and he was in the way as boxes and crates and materials were being loaded on the cargo jet; there are Air Force processes that need to be followed for a safe loading. *If you're going to put an uncovered YO-3A into a C-17, that's an ominous process.*

Air Force crews helped position the Agency's equipment as it was loaded aboard the *Globemaster;* the loadmaster directed the placement and ensured the security of dozens of unmarked boxes on 463L pallets.

She checked that the boxes were strapped down according to the Loadmaster's Handbook.

Hunter was in shock as the YO-3A fuselage had been removed from its container without a covering—Bob and Bob hadn't demanded the longstanding protocol of using bedsheets to cover the airframe and wings. However, the most important secret of all, the propeller, was wrapped in a sheet.

Something wasn't right. Hunter held up a finger as if he were a student wishing to ask a question. McGee cut him off and said he would brief Duncan when they were airborne. "We have to get loaded ASAP." Director McGee motioned for Nazy to come aboard the gigantic aircraft. He would give the husband and wife team a couple of minutes together. When they entered the *Globemaster*, Nazy could barely speak. Duncan was dumbfounded by the sight of two black YO-3A fuselages and their black wings in the massive cargo hold; and white turbans covering the propellers. *This is huge, whatever it is. No more special access program. Goodbye Noble Savage. Where's Kelly? What the Hell happened while I was abroad?* Nazy kissed him passionately like it could be the last time.

When they slowly uncoupled, Nazy told Duncan that she loved him. "I love you too, Baby. If you knew how much I love you, you would faint." He knew better than to ask her his question; it wasn't the right question to ask your wife. Hunter steered her to a couple of troop seats and had her sit down. He held her hands and wondered when someone would tell him what was going on.

"Bill will tell you when you're airborne."

"I swear you get better looking all the time. You look like a covergirl, but I have to say the C-17 is a poor excuse to stage a fashion show. The dress and scarf and shoes are splendid. You are historically sexy." Then he realized, *She can be sweet, sexy, intelligent, and classy and still screw the soul right out of you like an animal. But the scent of fear is with her.* "I love you, baby!"

She kissed him again. *When I kiss you I don't want to stop! I am so afraid it will be our last time!* "Only when I know I'm coming to see you. I missed you very much. It doesn't matter that you won't be staying for a while. Oh, and Bill is going with you. I'll be in Europe for about a week, then the Middle East and Australia. Possibly a few weeks."

Europe? Middle East? Australia? It takes a week; it takes more than a week to just travel to and through Europe, and another few days for Australia. What the hell is going on? Hunter nodded, kissed her, and squeezed her hand. He remembered McGee having to go to Europe and Australia for about ten days...two weeks.... Maybe longer. *Now Nazy is going? In his place? Hey! Bullfrog, you're ruining my sex life!*

Her interpretation of the lack of communication from McGee signaled again that the mission could be suicidal. If it was, the Director would never tell her. Nazy assumed the worst; this might be her last opportunity to tell Duncan that she loved him. She kissed him again with abandon.

That was the moment Hunter knew he could die. He gave up finding answers to personal and operational questions and focused on Nazy. He kissed her again. In his periphery he saw the shadows of two of his black airplanes. He could not fathom what was in store for him.

Duncan escorted Nazy back to the Agency's limo. He walked at her pace, held her hand, and kissed her goodbye. She said, "I'm the Acting Director until I leave. Bill let me use his jet for the trip." She whispered, "*Meet me at Fallingwater when you return.*"

He didn't wave her *adios. Fallingwater? Didn't anyone do anything with Nobley while I was gone? I suppose I'm to assume she is out of Cuba. And what about Chernovich?*

McGee approached Hunter and announced, "I provided your LM-100J crew coins for their work." He and Hunter watched Nazy's black Suburban leave the tarmac. McGee commented, "Nazy is the smartest and most courageous woman I've ever met—by far."

Hunter replied, "I like women for a lot of things and being smart isn't usually one of them. Nazy is the exception. In my youth it was Emma Peel in a leather catsuit. That show was an early indicator I was going to grow up heterosexual, all because of Diana Rigg. There was a strange stirring inside of me that said, 'Hey, wait a minute, that woman is not like my mom! There is something different here. *What is going on?*' If I had questions about my sexuality, Mrs. Peel drove me straight over the heterosexual cliff. And she is a *dame* now; I always thought that was a pejorative term."

The Director gave one of those Barry White laughs that sounded like a bull with a respiratory problem. He concurred with Hunter's comments as they walked back to the C-17. "You know *Maverick*, for all the time I've known you, you're an original to a fault. You have two whopping weaknesses, women and airplanes. No, make that four weaknesses. Women, airplanes, convertibles, and rare watches." McGee smiled at his friend, who was unsure of where the outburst had come from or why. Maybe it was a sign of nerves. He had plenty. McGee finished with, "You have once again demonstrated that while you may enjoy the company of women, collect airplanes, rare cars and Rolexes, you are still the top resource in the Agency when we need the impossible done. *Maverick*, I know I said you should have been a SEAL, but what you really should have been is a colonel. A Marine colonel. Like Pete Ortiz."

"You and he are the last of the *manly* men. Thank you, good sir, for the kind words. And I have said countless times, 'captain is the best rank,' but you should have been an admiral. Our stars were never aligned properly, nor did we have the right sponsor." Hunter laughed at the friendly ribbing. He still could not decipher Nazy's presumably cryptic comments on *Fallingwater*. He noticed McGee was sweating as bad as a drug mule going through customs. For a normally taciturn man this excessive conversation was unusual. Accolades from *Bullfrog*? *What is going on? Does he want something huge? Or is it just women, airplanes, convertibles, and Rolexes? Nerves? Mine are shot!*

Then Hunter realized Bill McGee would be leading this impromptu mission. The head of the CIA would be in his element directing what he envisioned to be a special operation. *Nazy was right, he is going. Where the hell are we going, and what are we going to do that requires two Yo-Yos and McGee's presence? And where is Kelly? She is nowhere to be seen. Captain, my Captain, did you really dig the other YO-3A out of Elmira just to be a back-up? I don't think so. Something stinks.*

Once aloft, while Hunter *valsalvaed* to get his ears to pop, McGee indicated the flight would take about twenty hours, and they would get refueled in-flight. While the flight kitchen at Joint Base Andrews had prepared dozens of boxes of food, McGee had picked up boxes of pizzas from the Papa John's while Duncan and company were inbound. Air Force chow was damned good, but most of the voters on the jet chose still hot-in-the-box pizza.

Hunter began to ask about fuel when he noticed a dog underneath the jump seats on the other side of McGee. "*You brought a dog!?*"

"I did. He could be useful. I was going to bring your jet pack, but your place had some issues with the fuel."

What am I in the middle of? Hunter pushed fingers though his hair. "You brought a dog."

"Here begins the *Great Game.*" McGee explained the Belgian Malinois could be a lifesaver. "Max can find and disarm insurgents, especially in tunnels. I'm expecting tunnels. Max has jumped out of airplanes, fast roped out of helicopters, sniffed out roadside IEDs. He is the top paramilitary canine at SAD." Special Activities Division. "Max is so smart, it's like talking to a five-year-old who will do anything you ask him to do. I'll introduce you to him and tell him he is to obey only you and me for the mission."

"A dog."

"That's right. An extraordinary elite fighting dog. Even with the most advanced technology, humans are no match for canines detecting explosive devices and ferreting out bad guys in hiding. I don't know exactly what to expect when we get to where we're going. We might not use him for this, ah, *special activity*. It's not an Op." McGee called for Max and the dog crawled out from under the troop seats and sat in front of McGee. He offered a paw which McGee shook. "Max, this is Duncan. He will give you commands." Max leaned over and offered Duncan a paw to shake. Duncan's response was to smile and return the shake.

Duncan asked, "Max, may I pet you?" The dog stood up, wagged his tail and stuck his head into Hunter hands. Hunter scratched behind the dog's ears and patted his sides.

Hunter seemed to know what a dog liked. McGee said, "I think you have a new friend."

"Seems so. I was going to ask you about fuel." He scratched behind an ear and found a sensitive spot. Max closed his eyes and leaned heavily into Hunter's fingers. When the dog was about to fall over, Hunter stopped and petted the critter. Max gave Hunter a look which could have been construed as *What the hell are you doing?! I enjoyed that! Why did you stop?* Hunter went after the other ear, and the dog responded as if he were getting a massage at a doggie spa.

McGee offered, "There are two hundred gallons of aviation gasoline in a leak-proof container in the middle of the aircraft. I had the second *Yo-Yo* moved from Elmira to Andrews, if you haven't figured it out yet."

"I noticed." Hunter continued stroking Max's ears. He was nonplussed. His question on Nobley would not be answered anytime soon and now he had other ones running through his head. *We have a dog going with us. Two Yo-Yos. What the hell is going on? Crisis somewhere, obviously if we need a C-17.*

Bob and Bob hadn't been inside a C-17 since the last time they attended an airshow. Before flight and airborne, they ensured the two aircraft were strapped down properly and securely, and once they were at cruising altitude, the men began working on the airplanes. McGee had talked to them about removing the sensors from one of the aircraft and doing any scheduled maintenance on both *Yo-Yo*s, and configuring the aircraft for the upcoming mission. The FLIR, laser designator, and Terminator Sniper System were designed to be removed and replaced easily, but they were two-man jobs. Bob and Bob removed those systems from the YO-3A that was closest to the cargo ramp. Removing the systems resulted in a much lighter aircraft, which would allow the YO-3A to carry a heavier load.

Hunter wondered, *Why would a Yo-Yo need to be stripped of its sensors and weapon?* The answer in his head did not please him.

Bob and Bob then inspected both aircraft. One Bob polished the transparencies, and the other checked the nitrogen in the tires. They didn't rely on their memories, but checked and double-checked all items on the maintenance cards.

Bob Jones and Bob Smith could feel the tension in the air. As Duncan's maintenance crew for twenty years, it was becoming apparent that this operation was going to be "one for the books," that the success of this upcoming mission was likely essential for some national security imperative. It wasn't about finding and killing a terrorist this time, or finding hostages, or killing illegal plants. Hunter surmised that it wasn't so much that lives were on the line but how many lives were on the line.

McGee said, "Iran and al-Qaeda have ramped up their calls that Israel is a 'cancerous tumor' that must be eliminated."

Hunter directed Max to go lie down, and the dog returned to his spot on the other side of McGee. "Are we still the Great Satan?"

"Of course we are. Al-Qaeda and Iran are making noise." Bill McGee brought out overheads, satellite photographs. Hunter was always impressed with the quality of the imagery. Hunter had few needs to use overheads since he found his targets based on ground intelligence and thermal signature. He never needed the polar-orbiting satellites that reportedly could read license plate numbers from space, but the detail in the Iranian virology institute layouts was dramatic. Bunkers and fortifications were camouflaged to blend with the mountainous surroundings. The photographs indicated doors or embrasures were also sufficiently camouflaged. On top of a ridge, a 1,200-foot runway had been carved out of stone and ran adjacent to the compound with one end dropping off into a valley. The facility's bunkers could be missed easily but not the shortest runway in the world. A loading dock, for the dining facility, was indicated by tire marks. A walking path provided an emergency escape route from the main laboratory complex. With the exception of the gated entrance, the facility in the mountains was surrounded by the pockmarks of mines in fields and barbed wire fencing.

The Iranian Institute and lab were looking like a special operations ground attack. For a lifelong pilot, this would be new. McGee ran through what was essentially a five-paragraph order. Hunter remembered *Situation, Mission, Execution, Administration, and Communication* from Boot Camp and his time at The Basic School. Before the CIA Director laid out the situation on the "bang and burn," a demolition and sabotage operation, McGee stopped the brief to share a little pizza with Hunter. He said, "I think you can be a gastronome and still appreciate pepperoni and jalapenos pizza."

"With extra sauce."

"Of course. I have known you a long time. A man of simple tastes."

"Sir, you are a great American." He asked, "Did you get her out?"

McGee could see the question on Hunter's face. He needed to tell Duncan something. Not everything. At least, not yet. "I did."

Hunter was pleased; and his face said so. "May I ask, how?"

"I said 'she was a *Jane*, that she was one of mine.' She was central to one of the deepest infiltration and undercover missions ever attempted by our place." Hunter was impressed with the cleverness of the response but was also reminded that one of the CIA's most tragic events was when an intelligence officer went deep underground and the CIA lost contact with him. Agency handlers never know if their operations officer died, or defected, or if they turned and slinked off somewhere to live in a mud hut with an Afghani girl in total obscurity. Duncan had been sent in a few times to extract them from their hellholes; it was the only part of the *Noble Savage* program that failed with regularity. When they don't show up, it can't be your fault.

Sometimes the human mind was very fragile, and sometimes the Agency put people in a place where it was beyond their capability to function as expected. When intelligence officers go missing and are never recovered their identities are never revealed, but they are memorialized with a star on the CIA Memorial Wall.

"I know we have lost others. I tried several times to extract them; SOCOM too, but no joy." For the moment, Hunter couldn't shake the inkling that men who went deep undercover could actually disappear. On their own volition. *But of course they could.* He had seen strong men "cross-deck," as the Navy would say. Friendlies who switched allegiances and went to the other side. *Sometimes they had no choice if they wanted to live.*

McGee said, "I know. DOD has their MIAs and so do we."

"Where is she now?"

"Didn't Nazy tell you, or did you have your tongue so far in her mouth that she couldn't speak?"

Hunter was almost embarrassed. He knew he would not get a straight answer on Nobley's location. He had learned long ago not to pry with members of the USIC. McGee was being coy when there was no reason for him to be coy. There had to be more to the story. McGee would tell him in his own time. Hunter asked, "But she's safe?"

"Your excellent girl is taking most excellent care of her. I have to say, you're turning the CIA into your own Peyton Place or something. Your life is like a soap opera with a serrated edge. Wives, daughters, girlfriends. Unique hideaways. The only thing you're missing is a shirt-lifting gay lover, a rotating bed, and a disco ball. Then you would have it all."

Hunter couldn't think of anything else to say on the women in his life. He dropped the Nobley discussion like dirty laundry into a hamper and picked up the conversation regarding the mission with two *Yo-Yos,* as if there had been no break in the action. He glanced at Max sleeping on the jet's floor and remembered his other question. "What about Chernovich?"

"We're still looking for him. We'll know something soon."

The answer was sufficient for the moment. Hunter returned to the mission and asked, "The institute looks as if it complemented the natural declivity. This would make it difficult to level by *Tomahawks*. But maybe not impossible. Why wasn't it considered?"

"Several things have coalesced into us racing to react to a threat. Our in-house defector may have been neutralized. An al-Qaeda affiliate, an ultra-violent gang is in Ashgabat ready to roll in on the compound. We think they've ripped a page from your paper and plan to steal a deadly bug and spread a highly contagious coronavirus through airports in China, Europe...."

"And here." Hunter hated being right, and he hated bugs.

McGee nodded and continued, "And your girl Saoirse gave us a key piece of intel. She said Haqqani boasted about the lab using infidels, American and British tourists, and whoever else they could get their hands on to be...."

"You mean *lab rats*?" Hunter's eyes were wide from the information, and then he closed them in pain and sorrow. The once statuesque Saoirse Nobley was working for them, and he was proud of her. *How is that even possible?* Yeah, tossing Tomahawks to level a facility where Americans were being held hostage wouldn't play well on the front page of *The New York Times*. That is news the Iranians would be sure to get out to the western media if the place was attacked and leveled.

"Yeah, human guinea pigs and human shields. Apparently, your Miss Nobley can speak Arabic, and Haqqani didn't know."

"What? How?" *I didn't know that either!*

"She told Kelly that she took Arabic in college; her husband's native tongue was Arabic, and she took classes to learn the language, but she never told him. He showed no interest in her classes, so he never found out. She had planned to spring her new language skills on him when they traveled to Egypt to meet his parents, but she was drugged and kidnapped. The short story is she did whatever she could to live—just as if she had the SERE (Survival, Evasion, Resistance, and Escape) course under her belt. You may not know they took her children from her in order to control her. Apparently, Haqqani would direct her in English as she served tea to him and the people she believed to be terrorists. He talked to them in Arabic. Haqqani ignored her and spoke freely in Arabic, so she picked up slivers of information. She overheard her husband's visitors' planned attacks, such as al-Qaeda-inspired plans to blow up Heathrow, St. Paul's Cathedral, and the *Concorde,* and ISIS plans to blow up hotels in Paris and London, just to 'kill as many as possible.' In Iran, they're using *infidels* to conduct biological experiments." McGee pointed to a structure on the satellite photo. "There's an incinerator—here—that we believe they use to burn victims who succumb to the viruses."

"On humans?"

"On humans. It's a cremation furnace from Europe. From France."

"Sounds like the latest model from Auschwitz or Dachau."

"Even Germany buys them from France—maybe they are prohibited from making funeral furnaces. Anyway, our in-place defector hasn't been heard from since his last contact. He believed then that they were holding as many as four dozen tourists. The guards like the Western women and abuse them before they're removed from their holding cells for live testing. New information: Most of the people missing from Pakistan, Turkmenistan, and Kurdistan—and even Iran—were women, snatched from markets and bazaars. Women off the streets of Iran; American women visiting their Iranian grandparents. Some such BS. In Iran they have their little vanity Nazis with sticks who beat female tourists if a strand of hair slips out from under a head covering. I now know why Nazy wears her hair long. Maybe it's her way of giving them the middle finger."

"She is too refined for that."

"I think I said that. Anyway, you suggested it, our defector endorsed it, and the strategic planners agreed, if these crazies are conducting tests and are using human subjects, they....well, you tell me what we're going to do. You and me." McGee took a wedge of pizza and looked at Hunter. *He's the genius. Let him figure it out.*

"So, instead of *Tomahawks*, the mission is to rescue the hostages...."

McGee nodded. *And....*

"Safeguard the viruses and blow the place up? At least set it on fire. Fire can be a disinfectant."

McGee nodded again. *Was it that easy? That transparent? I don't think so.* He said, "*Maverick,* you're a smart ass."

"I hope you brought enough stuff so we can do this. This is a '*we* mission.' I can't do this alone. You know that. I see two airplanes but only one pilot." Hunter wanted more of an explanation.

"You and me, together again." McGee ran down the list of weapons in the many boxes on the aircraft pallet. He pointed at a fiberglass shipping container and said, "You know what this is."

Hunter said, "That looks like the container of one of our quiet UAVs."

"Correct. Tell me about it."

"We, I mean Quiet Aero Systems, developed a family of capabilities—laser, camera, FLIR—for a government contract that we did not win. At home Carlos plays with them."

McGee smiled at the gentle reminder and said, "I assume Carlos and Therese are doing okay, holding down the fort."

Hunter nodded.

"Give them my best. Anyway, I thought it might be helpful to have one with us. It's quiet, and it has a FLIR."

Hunter agreed. "Absolutely! While we are on the ground, we will be sitting ducks, blind to other aircraft or vehicles approaching the institute. Once released, the AI of the *Blackguard* can monitor five square miles at a hundred feet and 100 square miles at five hundred feet. I can control it and receive data and images on my BlackBerry."

"That's your baby."

"That's my baby."

"We'll also have at our disposal four hundred pounds of C-4—I know it looks like Italian ice, but you can't eat this stuff."

"I know it burns. Does it really taste nasty? Um, you have four hundred pounds of C-4?" *Not on that pallet you don't!*

"Not here, exactly." McGee looked at Hunter a good long time to convey there was something more to having a few hundred pounds of *plastique* available. Hunter nodded and glanced over at the huge aluminum pallet, trying to see what else McGee had brought aboard the jet. McGee continued, "We have one hundred over there, and we have three hundred M112 demolition blocks, approximately two inches by one-and-a-half inches and eleven inches long, waiting for us when we land."

"Does the Air Force know this?" Hunter's eyes drifted to the cockpit.

McGee and Hunter locked eyes; the big man shook his head. It was hard for the CIA Director to lower his voice so he spoke in code. "We've been here before, you and me. *I said you're insane!*"

I remember. Yeah, it's me or the rest of the world is absolutely insane. Hunter took another gander at the boxes on the pallet. Then he saw it. It had a lock. None of the others had a lock. *Oh my, Director McGee! You're full of surprises. I'm gonna burst a blood vessel. This is why you're on this mission. Holy cannoli! A few years ago we stole suitcase nukes from some old Soviet colonels in Turkmenistan who wanted to sell them to the Agency or al-Qaeda, and now you brought one for this? I remember you telling me, "All SEALs are trained to be proficient in every rifle, assault weapon, and pistol manufactured from every country. We are trained in every man-portable shoulder-launched weapon ever made, to include the Soviet one, two, and five-kiloton 'suitcase' tactical nuclear weapons. If we couldn't carry it, we ignored it."*

That day there were ten. Bullfrog said I was insane, but I convinced him to see things from my vantage point. I programmed a YO-3A to fly unmanned with a couple of suitcase nukes in the seats and sent the Yo-Yo into one of

Iran's nuclear weapons facilities. Hunter sighed loudly. *The other eight…we drove them out of the country and into Afghanistan…until the Army came for us. God, that was a hell of a night!* Hunter raised a single finger. *Please confirm we only have one suitcase-sized tactical nuclear weapon. Soviet designed and built.*

McGee gently nodded. *That boy is pretty bright. I fought with Duncan that night until I saw that there was an element of...genius to his argument. I remember that it's a two-part process. To detonate the weapon, you need a battery control unit and a control head – a programmer that controls how it goes off: Timer, impact, booby trap.*

The sound of the wind passing over the jumbo jet was distracting yet tolerable. The men looked at each other and relived that night. McGee killed two men with his bare hands to secure the devices. Hunter flew from Afghanistan to an abandoned remote site in Turkmenistan and secured the area so they could work without interruption.

Hunter raised questioning fingers. One, two, five….

McGee raised two.

Two-kilotons. Hunter understood the seriousness of the situation. *That night from the bowels of an abandoned pit mine, McGee brought up ten aluminum cases, reminiscent of oversized, high-end, aluminum video camera shipping containers. He stacked them neatly in five columns of two.* Hunter repeated what he said that night, "God, *Bullfrog*, you're an animal with gigantic orbs. You must have a *Tyrannosaurus-Rex* for a pet. I guess if you're going to be a bear, be a Kodiak."

McGee had heard the accolades before, but when *Maverick* said it again he chuckled and continued, "Anyway, we have one of your unmanned *Blackguards* that can monitor a small town; we have C-4, chem-cord, and grenades. We have what you wanted – the guys at the S&T also called them *Firestarters* – NCS said we should've had these a long time ago. They're so light – they're essentially magnesium *spitting* flares with timers – we have a lot of them, and we may need every one of them. If the *special* doesn't go off as expected, then the C-4 will obliterate it. And we have what I wanted."

He was unfamiliar with chem-cord and asked if it was like det-cord. McGee said yes; it is a silent binary chemical weapon that when mixed, violently reacts and melts everything in sight. McGee referred to it as *Alien Blood*; the boys at S&T just called it chem-cord because it was pliable and dirty-white like det-cord and was easily distinguished from the single-strand det-cord by two strands of polyethylene-covered chemicals.

Hunter pushed the images of suitcase nuclear devices from his brain and returned to the NRO imagery. "This place isn't puny. It's like a scene from an old Nazi movie with nonsensically shaped Nazi bunkers. They look a lot like the Navy's stealth catamarans wedged into Red Rocks."

"With a runway. Their shape and critical angle would make a *Tomahawk* approach difficult. If one were to get through, it would ricochet right off." *No shaped warhead penetration. There's a reason the Iranians chose this location.*

"That's probably stolen intel." Hunter looked at McGee.

"It is, and that Navy turd is at Leavenworth banging the bars screaming he wants to wear a dress and be put into the women's ward. And we have UV bombs on wheels."

"UV bombs on wheels?"

"You asked for a remote control machine gun and we can't do that but we did the next best thing, remote controlled vehicles with a spinning red laser pointer and UV LEDs to blind anyone who looks at it. Silent and stealthy and lightweight, and better than any loud gun. And the UV-C is supposed to act as a barrier if there has been a release. That's also one of your tricks, except S&T put it on an RC car that can negotiate stairs or race across a lake. It can even jump onto a one-story roof. They'll be needed. I need you to download the controlling app to your BlackBerry. And we have your anti-jamming device. You're a wretched evil person, Duncan Hunter. You would have made a great SEAL."

CHAPTER 57

May 27, 2018

Hunter said, "I learned from the best. You and your guys get so preoccupied with capturing bad guys so you can interrogate them, I think you sometimes miss the point…."

"I brought a *reverse* jammer, something that's powerful enough to induce a signal into the firing wiring of a suicide vest to whack a *jihadi* on your terms and not his, and help him meet his 72 virgins…."

"You mean 72 *raisins*." Hunter smiled. McGee grimaced and leaned back in his seat for more info. Hunter explained, "The Communist News Network dragged a *Qur'anic* scholar into their studios, a subject matter expert who claimed that the *Qur'an* had been '*mis*-translated,' with very heavy emphasis on the '*mis*.' The 'martyrs didn't receive 72 *virgins* when they arrived in Paradise, but 72 *raisins*.'"

McGee howled!

"There's some shit you just cannot make up. Pay attention if you're going to steal someone's work and misinterpret what they say. Anyway, I'm not here to take prisoners. If they're wearing a suicide vest, yes, I would want to help them achieve *Raisin* Paradise on my terms."

"Like Indiana Jones shooting that lunatic with a sword."

"*Juramentados*. Shoot 'em if you can, or blow them the hell up before they can rush you and blow all your friends to kingdom come."

McGee was unfamiliar with the term and asked Hunter to explain.

"Religious fanatics who engage in suicide attacks under the guise of *divine killing*. In the late 1920s, General Black Jack John Pershing had to deal with some when he was in the PI." Philippine Islands.

"The Geneva Convention would have had you shot! But if we play our cards right, there will be no need for a jammer."

"I'm counting on it." Hunter was chagrined with the cryptic response. He nodded and made motions as if he were smashing a detonator button. "And, *two Yo-Yos*?"

"You're a genius. You know, I normally say you shouldn't do math in public, but you're actually pretty good at it."

"We can't carry all this shit to demolish that place, and unless you've been taking flying lessons and learning how to fly a taildragger, we still have one pilot."

"That's right."

"What's your plan?"

McGee told him.

Hunter laughed hysterically. "Now it's my turn to say, *Are you insane?*"

McGee asked, "What do the Marines say—improvise, adapt, and overcome? We can do this! Trust me. And there's more."

Hunter sensed he was experiencing the first twinges of a fake heart attack. McGee validated what he had suspected. Hunter leaned back into the nylon troop seat and looked at his boss incredulously. He needed more pizza and a diet Mountain Dew. "What's that?"

"We believe the Iranians think they have a really lethal virus. One that only kills infidels but may be an extinction event kind of virus. Can't be stopped through mechanical means like HEPA."

"Well, that's insane. Apparently, insanity is contagious." Hunter rubbed his eyes, *More candidates for the DSM and the Darwin Awards.*

"The CDC also says that's nuts."

Hunter was caustic, "What the hell do they know. They don't even know who the president is. And didn't you indicate the headmaster was some kind of crook? I bet the CDC still has pictures of 3M on their walls and not President Hernandez. You cannot trust those guys. They are all in bed with one another, and I'll bet when this is all over we'll find out they really have been sending research money to the Iranians. Somehow, someway."

"I bet you they do, too. But the Islamic Revolutionary Guard, who are actually protecting the Khomeini Institute, are smart enough to know that too, that what the scientists are working on is impossible. If any bit of the science is remotely accurate, they want no part of the distribution plan to punish Europe and the U.S., so they're satisfied in maintaining the status quo. Make extra money on the side. Go home to mama in her black bag."

"They're satisfied getting paid for the hazardous duty." Hunter downloaded the YO-3A's controlling app on his BlackBerry. He tested the program of the "UV bombs on wheels;" the RC truck with a cover over the important parts moved back and forth along the makeshift aisle on the jet with the touch of Hunter's finger. Max watched the little wheeled robot move.

Hunter looked up to join McGee's conversation.

"China has already developed a virus that kills the elderly but leaves children alone. The Chinese and the Iranians have one that attacks people with a certain blood type. Lots of possible combinations. These buffoons are getting better at creating microscopic killing machines. Confidentially, the list of manufactured viruses is growing every day. And they can engineer them to be so small that they can pass through a filter."

"So the Chinese are in the middle of this?"

McGee nodded. "They are already at war with us—*a cold war*—but so far they have not released a bioweapon; at least as far as we know. It's hard to get someone inside to work with us. We need more people who look like them than look like us. We have essentially won the war against *Dark Islam;* you've killed two hundred of their leaders—essentially, decapitating the head of the Hydra, the god of recruiting. You've broken the backs of al-Qaeda and/or ISIS, and they are running out of money and prestige and people. Before they go broke, they think they have to have one last '*spectacular;*' they need a big win to bring more dirtbags into their operation. Our analysts think you are an evil genius because of your disquisition slash terrorist handbook, and you are correct that as a last resort, they will find enough martyrs willing to be infected. They have always been good at finding the mentally deficient who can be programmed to kill themselves for Allah and the greater good."

"Our analysts and modelers believe that with a fire team-sized group they could spread the contagion to every corner of the world and kill hundreds of millions on the low side, and billions on the high side. No one is prepared for an outbreak which can be easily and quickly transmitted by the airlines and airports, regardless of their filtration systems."

"You're expecting these cannot be stopped—they might pass through HEPA filters? So our mission is that we are to stop an outbreak before they can start one." *Whoever "they" are?*

McGee frowned and nodded. "Very good."

Hunter said, "And you're going to tell me that when we stop them, they won't use the passports they have from various countries in the names of people who aren't on anyone's Do Not Fly List so it's impossible to stop them at airports. If we can't stop them, they could fly to any airport on the planet."

"Right out of your handbook, or what I now call, *The Bioterrorist's Ultimate Handbook.*"

"It should've had a better name." Hunter attacked another slice of pizza.

"It never should've been made public. It should have been classified TS."

"No one would listen. No one was interested. Having lefty professors didn't help." The men were quiet, savoring their pizza. Hunter held up a half-eaten slice and asked, "Why is pizza made round, put into a square box, and eaten in triangles?"

McGee rolled his eyes and grinned. Questions that have no real answer. Move on! "Like I was going to say, classic case of unintended consequences delayed. Anyway, it seems the great Greg Lynche, before he met you, had the Agency look at your paper, and it was given restricted access. But your school didn't do America any favors. They could have routed your paper to the FBI to see if it needed to be classified, but they chose not to. It may have been sent to the FBI where it may have been intercepted and rerouted by a sympathetic member of the Brotherhood."

"National security is not their bag, baby."

"That leads us here. The al-Qaeda affiliate, *al-Sham*, plans to use a nasty and rough group of special operations people. Real operators. They're not like our SOCOM special operators. These guys were hand-picked, and we believe they modeled themselves after *Blackwater*, Erik

Prince's old company, the NCS, and the Israeli *Shayetet* and *Mista'arvim*."

Hunter asked, "How is that possible?" He was familiar with the former but not the latter units from Israel.

"Another handful of nuggets from your Saoirse Nobley."

Hunter was intrigued.

"Nazy speculated that Toraluddin Haqqani had to have been under FBI surveillance. He was a Haqqani, and the name was affiliated with a sophisticated style of terrorism. Even as dysfunctional as the FBI is today, they hadn't been compromised to the extent they were in 1995, and they had Nobley and Haqqani under surveillance."

"Nobley verified what we suspected, Haqqani received American and British books all the time, and he translated those books into Arabic and there was a little print shop on the outskirts of Amman which turned Haqqani's spiral notebooks into hardbound handbooks. Nobley remembered some titles; she said Haqqani and his friends were fixated on the Israelis and SEALs."

"They should be fixated on them too. If their prime minister ever turned the Mossad loose on terrorist turkeys....there would be feathers flying."

McGee continued, "She gave us the titles that she remembered; one is *The Greatest Missions of the Israeli Secret Service.* She said that at the very beginning of her incarceration, when she was exposed to what Haqqani was actually doing, she saw a copy of your writings before Toraluddin Haqqani translated it."

"My paper? How could she know it was my paper?"

"Yes, your paper. Wasn't Nobley an Admin clerk and didn't you keep your computer disk on a rack on the secretary's desk? Nazy made the connection and developed the questions for the polygrapher to explore. Nobley was very open with the polygrapher and Kelly; she said she and the other Marines in the office would fire up the secretary's computer and read your work when you went on TAD. They were convinced that you were really smart. Just shows you how little they really knew you."

Hunter remembered grad school and the Marine Corps, of spending hours in the *Phantom,* and then in front of what would now be considered an ancient computer. *They read my trash!*

"She said the author's name was erased, but she distinctly remembered the title of your paper and recognized your writing. She said she could never find out how the Mossad books and your paper ended up in Haqqani's possession. She thought someone had to be buying them in the U.S. and shipping them to Jordan, because her husband always brought books back when he went to Jordan. Nobley said she wasn't allowed to read them. She said Haqqani went disguised as an academic, an English as a second language instructor."

Hunter offered, "Eastwood told a story about Arab women wearing *Shalimar* in traditional dress and woody perfumed men in thobes coming into the International Spy Museum bookstore and buying probably those same copies. I dismissed it as the activities of the Muslim Brotherhood in America. But Haqqani turned them into training manuals? That's outrageous!"

He explained what he knew of the Israeli special operations forces. "There's *Shayetet* 13, a unit of the Israeli Navy and one of the primary reconnaissance units of the Israel Defense Forces. It's like our SEAL Team Six. Both units specialize in sea-to-land incursions, counterterrorism, sabotage, maritime intelligence gathering, maritime hostage rescue, and the boarding of vessels in the middle of the night. Their unit has taken part in almost all of Israel's major wars, and other actions no one is supposed to know anything about. Like Team Six."

"But someone wanted to write a tell-all book and forgot they signed an NDA to keep their mouth shut."

McGee nodded. "And much like the National Clandestine Service, *Mista'arvim* is the undercover counterterrorism unit specifically trained to assimilate among the local Arab population. They instruct revolutionaries, perform intelligence gathering, and use disguise and surprise as their main weapons. And they do other stuff, like our guys."

"We concluded from Nobley that her al-Qaeda or ISIS husband wrote the book on training special operations units, and that he modeled their special operations units in the likeness of the SEALs and the Israelis special operators. They were sent all over the Middle East and Africa to hone their skills."

Hunter said, "I told you when *Grinch* visited me in Del Rio, I gave him Nobley's letter about getting married. Kind of a 'see something strange, report something.' I told you how I got fired for not hiring Muslims for the airport security jobs in Cleveland. On September 11th, I called Greg and told him al-Qaeda infiltrated airport security. He thought I had lost my mind, but the *Grinch* ate crow and admitted I was perfectly centered over the target."

"Yeah. That letter. Nazy found a copy in the archives. And I remember the stories. All of them. Just think, if you hadn't gotten fired that day, we wouldn't be here today."

Hunter acknowledged the observation and concluded McGee was correct.

"Oh, there's more. When I said 'she was one of mine' that was a partially true statement."

"What do you mean?"

"So what Nazy has pieced together is that you gave Greg Lynche the letter and photo you received from Nobley. Greg passed that info to some of his old contacts in the FBI before they were fully compromised. They started a surveillance plan on Haqqani, and Miss Nobley was pitched by a counterintelligence agent in the FBI, posing as an I&NS agent. The FBI agent clarified that Haqqani was like hundreds of other Muslim men who wanted U.S. citizenship, but he couldn't say Haqqani didn't love her and would discard her like yesterday's trash. The agent said Nobley believed her husband loved her, that it wasn't a marriage of convenience. She was given an ultimatum to report on her husband. From the FBI's file, she passed three messages to the agent, and then Nobley and Haqqani and her children disappeared. Haqqani and Nobley passed through Customs on their way out of the U.S. and they never returned; at least their passports were never seen again."

"Just like that?"

"Just like that. We think the FBI contact was made, and Haqqani bolted like a horse with his tail on fire. We hoped to find her and make contact again, but after years of no leads, those activities were closed."

"Just like that?" *That's incredible. I set her up. All this shit was my fault! Greg called in the dogs of intel to sniff out the husband's comings and goings. I put her in great danger without even realizing what I had done. Why did I do it? Was I trying to show off? Was I just jealous, or was I just a concerned friend? I had been investigating the I&NS and their process of determining marriages of convenience when I was with the DOJ INSPect team. Sometimes I'm too smart for my own good. Nobley couldn't have had a regular marriage because he was dirty; he wasn't the man she thought he was. Just like in the movie…Conspirator! Haqqani was dedicated to the cause; she was just a means to get U.S. citizenship and a passport and I ruined her life.*

"Just like that. I know you are thinking all kinds of inappropriate things—like blaming yourself for her life, but that needs to stop. That was a long time ago, and Haqqani in America was a terrorist in sheep's' clothing. He was one of thousands of Muslims in U.S. schools at that time. Like today, we have tens of thousands of Chinese in American schools, and they do not have American interests at heart. Remember, 3M supported the Iranian hierarchy and found ways for other terrorist groups to receive U.S. passports. There are things out of our purview and control."

"I know, Bill. I really do."

"Anyway, she had collected intelligence for years, and she shared it freely when we talked to her. So beneficial she talked to us. When she first said she would only talk to you, we didn't know what we were dealing with. Was she going to blame you for her life's woes? Stab you in the heart for ruining her life? But it was her intel that pushed us to where we are today. On our way to Ashgabat."

"With a rendezvous with al-Qaeda."

McGee made a face while gently nodding. "These guys are especially bad. It looks like al-Qaeda has units that specialized in mercenary work like the former entity known as *Blackwater*. But they also have an on-call group, super-violent. Like the *Doogies* in *A Clockwork Orange*, but they get their kicks being drenched in the blood of their victims."

Hunter wasn't impressed with murderous mental cases. He asked, *"You mean Al-Qaeda has contractors? Like Blackwater?"*

"Technically—worse. *Blackwater* was largely defensive. These guys are all offensive. Evil personified. Vicious. They leveraged plagiarism to new heights and mimicked American special operations forces as best as they could with the available literature. If Toraluddin Haqqani found gaps, it wasn't a big leap to fill in those gaps. American Special Forces stay within the confines of the law; some guys screw up and they get punished. Remember, Haqqani's guys aren't as dumb as a box of rocks like your typical Muslim outrage boys screaming in front of Al Jazeera's cameras. They are unrestrained. They can do anything, and they can get away with it."

"We believe they're college-educated, probably already vetted and trained, and with secret clearances and training from other Muslim SOCOMs. But they left their service or were disenfranchised. Maybe they were mentally defective."

McGee continued, "They're heavily funded by al-Qaeda or by Iran's Islamic Revolutionary Guard Corps. We know, but don't know exactly. It's curious that Iran has tapped them occasionally for some special ops. The Sunni-Shia paradox. Groups that can't stand each other; each thinking the other side is wrong and should be destroyed."

Hunter asked, "Like Republicans and Democrats, except the Democrats are violently, criminally insane, and I include the media among them."

McGee acknowledged the joke with a harrumph. "Gaddafi had some of these guys—same type of special-ops starter-kit guys. He sent them south to kill warlords and potentates who got on his wrong side, much the way 3M purged conservative generals and admirals and backfilled them with liberal flag officers. The Libyan dude who knocked down Flight 800 and trained Gaddafi's men is the one who shot you out of the sky."

Hunter remembered. *Flight 103, Flight 800. There are some things you never forget. The Libyans blew my parents out of the sky and no one has been held responsible. The man who shot down commercial airliners for profit held the United States hostage; he fired a shoulder-launched anti-aircraft missile at the thermal image of the YO-3A's engine, and I had to parachute from my plane. I neutralized the Muslim commandos who were trying to find me and when I finally cornered the man with the missile launcher, I placed my Python under his chin and blew his brains out. I was so incensed that I had been shot down that I dragged his carcass to where the YO-3A was burning and before I tossed him in the fire, I took his watch. Yes, sir. There are some things you never forget. I know what it is to be a little unrestrained.*

McGee was still talking. "It wasn't regular Taliban or al-Qaeda who went after the Afghan president; it was the suicide bombers they paid the poor to do. For a while Team Six protected Karsai, but we were needed elsewhere to engage the Taliban and al-Qaeda. So Karsai's next personal security team were some of the best special operators in the business, men who were drawing a government retirement check and working for the best on-call personal security company, *Blackwater*."

Hunter remembered, "What put the 'special' in special operations is having access to all the special weapons, like shoulder-launched anti-aircraft missiles and explosives." *And now bugs?*

McGee nodded. "You need specially trained dudes for the special; out of the ordinary. Guys train for years in order to execute and survive special operations. You can't trust Billy-Ray, Joe-Bob, Achmed-the-Dead-Terrorist guys for special operations; you need guys with special training, special skills. I expect their guys to be very well trained and in very high demand."

Hunter nodded. He had a few operational questions he wanted to get out. He asked if they're going to have the services of a combat meteorologist, McGee said they were getting up-to-date combat forecasting in the cockpit. All the news was good, so Hunter relaxed. "We don't need a forecast that sounds like the title of a Stephen King novel. We need CAVU."

The gentle rocking and the susurrus of the airstream passing over the giant aircraft's fuselage was making Hunter sleepy, but he fought off the sandman. He was glad to see Bill in good spirits; it was good to hear the excitement back in his voice. The additional burden of leadership positions can suck the life out of someone who has made a living in the field doing the work the regular forces were neither trained for nor capable of doing.

Hunter realized he hadn't seen McGee this calm and articulate in a long time. They were usually too busy to talk shop. McGee was not only a master of special operations forces, but was an expert in every aspect of the business; politics and contracting and the economics of when to pull the trigger and when to wait for greater rewards.

McGee went over to a behemoth ice cooler under web netting on a pallet and extracted two bottles of water and handed one to Duncan. He took a swig and looked at his friend of sixteen years. Hunter was still the same person as when they first met at the Naval War College, *Class of 2002*, the same down-to-earth character with a carefree attitude, a dump truck load of confidence, and contacts out the wazoo. Hunter was the same guy with one of the lowest rumbling voices on the planet who could've made good money as a radio announcer. He had been known as the best racquetball player in school and was the epitome of masculinity for his age—he was the oldest student in school. His suits were Saville Row; his truck Chevrolet. He was a virile, lovable rogue with a gruff façade that masked a natural charm and a knowing smile that could captivate all the single female officers in the war college. Hunter tried to pass himself off as an ordinary guy, but you would have had to be blind to see that there wasn't an ordinary bone in his body. He was a survivor of murderous Muslim men and a killer of terrorists overseas. He wasn't the local guy who delivered packages, refrigerators, or pizza.

McGee had just gotten off the jet from Afghanistan and was busy getting reacquainted with his family in Newport. While they were students, neither of them were aware of the incredible effort by the Islamic Underground and the Muslim Brotherhood to find information about him and Duncan Hunter. It was years later, after McGee had saved Nazy's life that Hunter told him the rest of her story. Hunter said he had always been intrigued by glamourous women, that everything Nazy did differed from any other woman he had ever met. In his mind she was the consummate woman. After almost being killed, he said Nazy's confidence took a hit as she recovered from her injuries, but she never gave up. And she was still the most striking woman at White House State Dinners. A ball gown could cover up the scars from the incredible damage done to her body.

McGee finished his water and said, "So, when those of us at the Agency are unable to do something that's inherently governmental, you're called in. You're not a flippin' pervert or demented, or whatever words lefties don't like using that describe them and their buddies in the DSM. You're a standout because the President knows you and has authorized you, via the *Noble Savage* SAP. You alone can take direct action on certain characters who are designated as enemy combatants that we haven't been able to or can't engage for whatever reason. We don't have other contractors hunting down and killing terrorists, and you've never been asked to target a head of state overseas. That's the job of the National Clandestine Service; they train the revolutionaries for the coup and the foreign dudes who pull the triggers. Like Che Guevara, he was hunted down, captured, and was executed by Bolivian forces that the Agency armed and trained."

Hunter nodded. It was unusual to get a lecture from McGee—it was usually he who went on and on about his areas of expertise. He was learning things that he had inferred but didn't know specifically, and it was wonderful.

"We generate a list; the President determines who's been naughty or nice. We conduct a ground op on that non-state actor, that non-governmental person and develop the intel. Because *Dark Islam* uses human shields, we can't get to them without collateral damage, so we use you to take out that one person from the air. You're very effective and efficient, and given the cost of mission failure, and the alternative—a missile from an unmanned aircraft—you're very inexpensive. Am I right?"

Hunter nodded. He had always known he was the "Hail Mary pass" in the national security spectrum. Borderline legal activities of last resort. Were the men he killed enemy combatants? Absolutely. The goal was to prevent any of them from becoming the next confident personality, the next martyr-maker like the charismatic Osama bin Laden. Yes, he and the YO-3A gave the CIA capabilities they could never consider possessing. Congress would never allow it. But in a specific context, an on-call service at the president's direction, there was no need to own the capability when they could just rent it, even if the price of the service made the CIA's CFO pull out her hair. Having a contractor provided plausible deniability on both ends and diluted the toxicity of any issue that surfaced later on. Someone could always blame a contractor for exceeding his bounds. But if you had an *official* organization with an *offensive capability* designed and dedicated to killing terrorists, Congress would find out and scream bloody murder. They would've had a CIA Director's head on a pike.

Now he understood why there was only one YO-3A pilot on the cargo jet. Over the past twenty years, he had upgraded the YO-3A to a point where it could be flown remotely or autonomously. Now a robotic *Yo-Yo* was going to get a real-world field demonstration. Hunter was needed to program the other YO-3A's autonomous landing and takeoff system, ATLS. He had a hundred nighttime missions where he had demonstrated the software's capability, and it was continually being improved by the software engineers. *Yo-Yo* number two was going to get its own mission. Takeoff to landing. Fully unmanned. All Duncan had to do was get it started, select a few commands from a Chinese menu of options, and close the canopy.

Hunter didn't think al-Qaeda or ISIS were so sophisticated to have access to enough special operators from the Middle East, and he said so.

McGee wasn't through with his best friend. "Well, we'll find out. We are in a race to see who gets there first."

CHAPTER 58

May 27, 2018

"You think…."

"One thing we got from Nobley was that Haqqani recently sought the services of one Sheikh Saleem Ali al-Qasimi."

"The Muslim Merchant of Death? He was on the *Disposition Matrix* like Haqqani; your guys could never get a bead on him."

"That's the guy. Former Jordanian Special Operations. Nobley said she remembered his name, Ali al-Qasimi. She had served him tea several times. She saw money exchanged between him and her husband. And he never stayed long. He gave her the creeps. That's a quote. Nobley said she was an invisible hostess, serving tea and pastries to a group of lecherous old men."

Like the indomitable Miss Marple in Murder, She Said. Hunter remembered the scene where the old woman served tea to a group of men who ignored her. They were so clueless that they openly discussed family secrets in her presence. *Arrogance and assumptions will bite you in the ass every time.*

McGee was finishing a whim, "Birds of a feather and all that. We are grateful she didn't get shot, and the SEAL who found her was bright enough to bring her home. I don't think most SEALs would have been able to survive what she has apparently been through. You know the most amazing women."

Hunter asked, "So you think Ali is on schedule to attack the laboratory at the Khomeini Institute? Is that what all of this is about?"

"We do. We have a positive sighting of him and likely al-Qaeda troops, *Jabhat Fatah al-Sham* assaulters in Ashgabat. That's where we are going. Our officers at the Embassy are monitoring the situation. The CDC is adamant that we can't allow Ali and his misfits to get their hands on the coronaviruses from the Fratarakas horseshoe bats…."

"Never heard of those."

"The CDC or bats?"

"Bats. The CDC can kiss my ass. These bats are so big they have horseshoes and saddles?"

McGee ignored the poor attempt at humor. "No one had heard about them outside of the discipline. They are the tiniest bats in the world."

"Sounds like concentrated death."

McGee sighed and mumbled something as he continued, "...coupled with deadly proteins from plague-borne mice. There are several government scientists at Dahlgren studying these things for the military who think the combination could spawn a radically contagious respiratory disease."

"Dahlgren?"

McGee nodded. "They have experts in the biotechnologies. Tiny bats; tiny coronaviruses. It might take a week or more before symptoms show, and then it could be fatal in hours. You know how cobra venom kills—fangs, direct injection. Think of this as aerosolized cobra venom to be spread in the ductwork of aircraft or ships or by casual contact. One thing we learned is that these manufactured viruses the CDC patented—they are engineered to be so tiny that HEPA filters cannot stop the virus."

"This is exactly why I hate bugs and exactly why my UV-C stuff is needed. Just saying." Hunter yawned. He was getting tired. Desynchronosis was setting in. *Jet lag sucks.*

McGee's nod said he concurred. "Let's just say the ubiquitous *they* considered a rare bat species from old Persia which had been observed by science only once in a hundred years and was thought to be extinct. Knowing these rare bats exist, *they*—we think a team from China and Iran—have been researching just how powerful and deadly these viruses are and the details of how to control them. *They* will help people cope with new infectious diseases."

"In theory."

"Of course. The bats were in Iran, but all the technical help came from China. I now know more about friggin' bats than I care to know. But this is important. Our people at the CDC surmised that extremely rare bats with deadly viruses could be, would be an Iranian or Chinese researchers' wet dream. Money, fame, and more money to study the big names for the little critters and what they carried. The Chinese epidemiologists located the only known Fratarakas colony in one tiny cave along one of the old Silk Roads between Iran and Turkmenistan. Some computed its distribution or range as only thirteen square kilometers."

Hunter was now wide awake and wanted to be sure he was hearing the details correctly. "So, Chinese epidemiologists with their Iranian handlers went out to find a bat or the remains of a colony?"

"Oh, they found it. A single well-hidden cave. It took them about four years, and the CDC knew the details. These guys share their work, but no one really pays attention to their findings except other epidemiologists. The CDC said that the 'team' of Iranians and Chinese epidemiologists took samples of bat droppings from the cave and swabbed a bat's anus with a cotton swab. They do this every year in the spring and fall and then take the samples back to the Khomeini Institute for testing."

"What did second place get? Putting a swab up a rabies-infested bat's butt—and you wonder why I just wanted to fly jets. I believe we have some new candidates for the DSM or the Darwin Awards. *You don't have to be crazy to work in a place like this but it helps.* Good God!"

McGee relayed the information he had received during briefs with the CDC Working Group and the Bioterrorism Task Force. "As you're probably not aware, when bats return home at sunrise, they urinate and defecate before they fly to the cave ceiling to sleep. So, during the day under the supervision of their Iranian handlers, Chinese epidemiologists crept into the cave and spread plastic film beneath the bat herd. The next day they collected bat droppings and took them back to the lab."

"I guess my impression that the viruses were *on* the bats is wrong."

"Some are, but not necessarily. I learned a lot when that double-butted maggot asshole Tim McVeigh brought down part of the Murrah Building in Oklahoma City. I was on active duty and was sent there to observe a parallel investigation. I wasn't experienced in dealing with a public emergency caused by an infectious virus. No one was."

"You were sent to respond to a release of an infectious virus when a building had just been bombed?"

"That's right. Anarchists target sensitive infrastructure. There was a group of us who took part in a *Dark Winter* exercise, a simulated release of the smallpox virus from the rubble of the Murrah Federal Building. The *Dark Winter* was spontaneous and unrehearsed. We raced to the point of the simulated release and monitored the upheaval of the recovery operations as if the building had housed a biosafety laboratory. We had scenarios for accidental releases and intentional releases from a building being bombed. We wargamed a simulated virus that ultimately spread to twenty-five other states and Central and South American countries. We also identified what equipment was really necessary for people to manage an outbreak."

"You couldn't have been the only person there."

"I wasn't." The discussion triggered a side issue.

Hunter was interested in details. "Who all was there?"

"Let's see, the Center for Disease Control, FEMA, the police department, JPEO—that's the Joint Program Executive Office for CBRN, the equipment for chemical, biological, radiological, and nuclear defense. And Y-12...."

"The National Security Complex? Oak Ridge, Tennessee?"

"Yeah, that Y-12. Department of Energy. Q-tickets. They were there on another *Dark Winter* exercise to wargame and observe an accidental or intentional release of radiation from a simulated nuke lab."

"*Hmmm.* I guess that makes sense. Our government at work. You do know the Brotherhood has been flying drones over Y-12 and nuclear power plants across the country. Eastwood told the President he had whistleblowers exposing Sandia's and Y-12's indoctrination of their employees in anti-American ideology. The Muslim Brotherhood and the Islamic Underground have infiltrated the place, and the leadership is espousing that revolutionary violence against the U.S. government and the existing social order is justified."

"All of that is true, and all of those guys got fired. There's not much I can do, not my purview, and the FBI couldn't investigate an illegal lemonade stand. I know the drones are a problem, but they're still domestic and out of our jurisdiction."

"I figured as much. We've been working on counter-drone technology for airports. Big problem."

McGee said, "Anyway, there were other government agencies who were interested in a building being demolished by a simulated non-state actor. I remember the governor played the part of the president. None of the responders knew how to play with one another. They flipped and jerked around until all the separate agencies from local, state and federal government finally began to work cooperatively. The governor was scripted to take on the leadership role, but he was too busy talking to the media."

Hunter nodded. "I'm familiar, actually. In 1998 in Del Rio, Tropical Storm *Charley* crawled up the Rio Grande and stopped over my house. We got twenty-four inches of rain in a 24-hour period. There was flooding, homes were washed off their foundations, people drowned, and the debris flowed into the San Filipe Creek and spilled into the Rio Grande. The governor declared a state emergency—he was in Austin. My building was the disaster relief control point and the site of all recovery operations. One-third of my hangar was converted into a morgue. The Salvation Army fed the rescue workers and cadaver dogs, and everyone in the rescue and recovery operation. In the beginning no one was in charge although there were a couple of Air Force colonels, the Border Patrol Chief Patrol Agent, the Chief of Police, and others. But no one wanted to be in charge; recovery efforts weren't their bag baby, if you get my drift. A lieutenant from the San Angelo Office of the Department of Public Safety was directed by the governor to become the lead, but he didn't know what he was doing either. So I pulled him to the side and talked to him. We talked two, three times a day. Privately. I got him snapped in, and he did good work. But no one is ready for those types of emergencies. Some guys are reluctant to give orders; I've never had that problem. But I can relate to what you were doing."

"So here I am again with the possibility of stopping an actual biolab breech and all the complexities and horror stories that entails."

"So you've had a simulated experience? This is why you're here."

"That's part of it. It wasn't so much that I was the guy who responded to all the bio-threats. Breeches and releases have happened before, actually multiple times. But this could be the real deal, and I'm the best trained, best qualified person in the country. We believe the Islamic Underground, via al-Qaeda and al-Sham, are trying to infiltrate a Muslim biolab and spread a weaponized virus. And that's why I brought toys and PPE that were developed for the real McCoy. I hope they will save our sorry asses so we can save the world from another set of madmen."

"What *do* you have Director McGee?"

"How about some flight suits? They were about a hundred grand apiece."

"*There's no wonder* your Miss Deng hates me! You're charging R&D to the program. Those must be the most expensive flight suits on the planet. Do space suits even cost that much?"

"Those actually cost millions. Lawrence Livermore National Laboratory scientists developed a breathable, protective 'smart fabric' designed to respond to biological agents. It's cutting-edge material which can autonomously react to microscopic dangers in a live biological environment."

"It's wearable but...."

"I know what you're going to say. Hear me out. The fabric combines breathability and protection in the same garment for safe extended use. It's nothing like the rubberized stuff on the shelves for the troops that you can only stand to wear for a few minutes. That's what you were thinking we were going to use. The new stuff are technological marvels and wear like a regular flight suit. When you touch it, you'll know it's not Nomex®. They're not fire retardant, but they confront biological threats like viruses and bacteria, and chemical agents, like sarin gas; the material neutralizes all of them. Everything. In my after action report from the *Dark Winter* exercise, I said we need robust protection from chemical and biological threats that allowed wearers a level of comfort akin to being in their own skin. What they came up with after twenty years of R&D is a multi-layered multi-functional material. The base layer comprises trillions of aligned carbon nanotube pores, graphitic cylinders with diameters 5,000 times thinner than a human hair. Very cool and a little slick."

"No shit? *Nanotubes*, like the paint on the *Yo-Yo*?"

McGee nodded. He went to the pallet and found the box of flight suits. He opened it, pulled out an aluminum-foil covered package, and tore it open.

Hunter's eyeballs went full-on Marty Feldman. *It's like the coating on the YO-3A only in a fabric! This is too cool for school!*

McGee allowed Hunter to feel the black material that played tricks on his eyes. No matter how many times you came into contact with the airplane's coating you had to turn away, for your eyes were naturally drawn to inspect it deeply. The black coating could quickly suck you in and induce vertigo. Now here was a wearable version. *And it is a little slick! McGee's been busy! I'm thinking he had this planned all along. Maybe he…maybe the CIA had been preparing for something like this for a long time.*

Hunter hoped the material wasn't so slick that he would slide out of his pilot's seat when he was wearing it. With eyes closed, it felt something like polyester fabric. McGee continued what was essentially a capabilities brief. "The nanotubes transport water molecules through their interior. This ensures a level of fabric breathability, but the real magic is that the nanotubes trap and block biological threats. The middle layer is a threat-responsive polymer that enables protection against the even tinier chemical threats that can fit through the outer layer's nanotubes' pores. The response of the material is autonomous and local. Throw it into a dryer with UV lamps and the UV kills the trapped pathogens stuck in the nanotubes. For biological and chemical environments, the material is triggered by contact of the chemical or biological threat with the polymers on the surface of the membrane. They have had the capability for years to stop a chemical and a biohazard, but it was only recently they could balance comfort and defense within the same garment, making the multi-layered material more wearable."

"So we have protective garments…."

McGee said, "Yes, they are hundreds of times more effective than a HEPA filter. And we have HALO undergarments as well."

Now Hunter was confused. *HALO? As in High Altitude Low Opening?* For no reason, he looked at Max sleeping. His eyes returned to McGee.

McGee saw the question on Hunter's face. "Yes. I brought them just in case. I'm not freezing my ass off; I thought you would appreciate the concern."

"I do. That's incredible."

"I know—I learned much from the other after action reports from the *Dark Winter* exercise. When I took SEAL Team Six into Afghanistan, we wore the first generation of this stuff. We knew al-Qaeda would do whatever was necessary to protect bin Laden. Gas us. Throw live bugs at us."

McGee continued. "So, the researchers say powerful viruses lurk in the feces and urine of bats. Mosquitoes suck the blood of bats and will also suck the blood of humans. That's one way they think these viruses can be transmitted. The primary vectors are contact and a release into the air so the virus enters a human's respiratory system. Then once infected, the micro-droplets of one's breath, sneeze, or cough spreads the virus into the breathing spaces of others."

"That requires full HAZMAT suits...." Hunter found the science interesting and paid close attention.

"The researchers who collected the samples were always heavily protected, wearing protective clothing, gloves, and N100 masks. I brought enough for both of us."

"How about UV sterilization equipment?"

"There's two boxes from Texas Ultraviolet."

"You're so smart."

"You've been doing that UV-shit forever. Kill poppies, kill coca, kill bugs after renditions. I've seen your office; what do you have, twenty patents that bring in the big bucks so you can buy old airplanes and rare cars? Tell me again why I buy your jet fuel?"

Hunter's hard smile telegraphed, *Something like that! And you know why you buy my gas. I'm just borrowing the government's jet under a drug forfeiture program. And one I just stole after Uncle Sam gave it to a terrorist. I may keep that one. Finders keepers.*

"As for bats, they don't attack people directly, but they overlap with humans living in the area. Bats come out at night to forage, drink water, eat insects where mosquitoes are more numerous. If humans are also active in the same region, there is a risk of infection."

"So mosquitoes?"

McGee said, "It's a possibility, however remote. Other viruses from bats such as SARS coronaviruses generally require intermediate hosts. Those viruses can come from bats.... I just came from a meeting that there is a worrying virus mystery in Hong Kong. Rat hepatitis is apparently jumping from rats to humans for the first time in history, and no one at the CDC seems to know how it's happening."

"Bats and now rats?"

"A microbiologist at the CDC was a little worried, yes."

"I can only assume that's really bad."

"Charles Manson bad. Computer models indicate a hybrid, a chimera coronavirus could devastate the population. But these guys, they don't know if what they saw in a single patient was just a one-off incident or if there are more. The really bad news is the Chinese epidemiologists snagged samples of the rat-to-human hepatitis E and took them to Iran. You have to wonder why they wouldn't take those samples to China to study. The CDC worries if they take the rat hep E proteins and graft them onto a coronavirus...."

Hunter said, "My guess is you could have bloody hell on your hands. Lethal combos and no treatments."

"As good as an open bullet wound festering in an African river full of parasites. These things could devastate an army...."

"But you have to be directly exposed...." Some old safety precaution crept into Hunter's mind. *Now what was that?*

"...requires an intermediate host. Mosquitoes."

"There's a reason I take my anti-malarials religiously." *Bingo! The little malaria-carrying bastards are some of the tiniest mosquitoes on Animal Planet.*

"If we get infected and survive this, we'll be in a hospital if and when symptoms occur."

"So we won't respond like *Arrhhh-nold Schwarzenegger* on Mars, with his eyes bulging as his body struggles for air. That would be bad form. You're assuming we'll be infected."

"I'm assuming the worse. We'll have the PPE, and we're already on an anti-malarial which has been universally demonstrated to be a prophylaxis for coronavirus infections. We have the UV disinfecting equipment, so we can get back on the *Yo-Yo* and this jet to go home. You know what we're dealing with. You've been to Africa; the insects are everywhere. They find the exposed skin or hitch a ride in an aircraft and get you later. We have little intel on the environment, so we have to expect the worst."

The straight-line lips on Hunter's face telegraphed he was marshaling his concerns. "Bill, one thing the commercial aircraft cabin crews do when they fly in and out of equatorial Africa, once the aircraft doors are closed the cabin crew walks through the jet spraying an insecticide to kill any hitchhiking malaria-carrying mosquitoes."

"And you think we should have some of that stuff?"

He nodded. "Yes, sir. I do. I have my guys spray the inside of the jet after a rendition flight. If there's a chance we're going to have hitchhiking mosquitoes after we finish doing whatever the hell we plan to do there...."

McGee nodded. "We'll need the protection. Something new to consider and to record for future use." He got up and walked to the front of the cargo jet and used the satellite telephone. Hunter was half asleep when McGee returned to his seat. "The Chief of Station in Amman is aware and will have some expedited to Ashgabat. I authorized him to lease a jet from the Royal Jordanian Air Academy. Miss Yassmin Deng's head is going to explode."

Hunter yawned. "I suppose the reason we're dealing with Chinese epidemiologists in an Iranian virology institute is part of a greater equation?"

"The American military has been consumed for a generation with the unrest and strife of the Middle East. Khomeini unleashed a satanic army on the Middle East, Africa, Europe, and the U.S. From the perspective of the Communist Chinese, this has been a glorious windfall, strategically. America is at war with *Dark Islam* and the left's narrative in Islamic newspapers is that we are at war with all of Islam. Propaganda, of course. Mazibuike cut Pentagon funding by a half, and U.S. forces are stretched to their limits occupying the very seat of the Islamic civilization."

McGee continued, "The Chinese throw their Muslim population into concentration camps that are worse than any gulag. They're furthering their ambitions in Southeast Asia, and you know what they're doing in Africa—trading natural resources for paved roads or cars or telephones."

"By natural resources, you mean oil. We should collapse their economy."

"Of course, and you go to the head of the class. African countries have monster fields of untapped oil reserves and China doesn't have many of those, so they trade improvement projects for natural resources while building the most massive embassies in Africa. If you are going to sink their economy…."

"Keep them from being able to fuel their economy. It's not that they have an invading force in those embassies, but now I understand those troops are there to protect oil production from being interrupted by U.S. Special Forces. I've seen the troops as I fly over the embassies sometimes. Now I better understand the oil connection."

"That's why we like your pictures of their embassies. You really do have a spyplane. Anyway, they look to shift the balance of power in the Middle East and Asia and Africa which would allow them to isolate the United States diplomatically. The Khomeini Institute is another Lego block in their collection of tools to defeat America."

"Thank you, *Bullfrog*. Now it all makes sense. We whack the worst terrorists in the Middle East to prevent terrorism's spread and to prevent another tumor like Osama bin Laden coming to power, and we monitor the Chinese. It's easier to destroy something than it is to build something."

"I'm assuming we're going to survive this. We believe that our buddies in the al-Qaeda, uh, al-Sham will voluntarily become infected. I don't know how many they will infect and put on a jet, but we're assuming they can't field a squadron-sized outfit. We think they can probably deploy a third of a troop minus snipers, if they're organized as we are. No more than ten-twelve."

"And, consistent with your paper, we believe they'll expose themselves to a virus and then it will be a race to see how many of the F-troop can contaminate the pax (passengers) on an aircraft and in an airport before they get sick or require hospitalization."

McGee pointed out details on the satellite photographs. "As you can see, there are water and trees. The Fratarakas have been feeding on insects in nearby valleys with a spring-fed water source for a millennium; it's not too far from Bājirān and the Khomeini Institute. There's some anecdotal history of travelers stopping for water and observing bats sipping the still waters of the lake. Those travelers followed the bats to their cave, scraping some *guano* for fires, but in less than a day all the humans were dead. When other bats tried to enter their caves, they would die; the cave environment is believed to be so toxic that it killed other bats. I'm told that is unheard of. These bats are so nasty, the Fratarakas *guano* is so powerful that those first epidemiologists to enter the cave wore the standard HAZMAT suits but later fell over and died like cheesy Hollywood actors on the set of *The Satan Bug*."

"Alistair MacLean."

McGee offered, "How about we call it the *Fratarakas Bug*?"

"That's a friggin' mouthful. But it's better than what I was going to say."

"Which was what?"

"*Iranian Bat Murder Machine* with *Psycho Killer*© playing in the background."

McGee grinned.

"Maybe I like the *Persian Green Death* better. None of them would play well at the *Washington Compost* or the *New York Crimes*. Can you imagine media and liberals' heads exploding if that ever got out? They would scream that the president was racist or worse. Lefties have no sense of humor."

"The goal is that they will never know. We can't allow Ali al-Qasimi and his minions to become infected and get on airliners. CDC modeling shows that with the right conditions and the right virus, we'll see 100 million deaths. That's just in the U.S. and assumes the President shuts down air travel."

"Wasn't it the CDC that whined in the halls of their place, bemoaning the election of President Hernandez? Their guy would have just let Americans turn in the wind and rot away. I don't think I would trust any of those whiny bastards...."

McGee said, "You know you want to say it...."

"...no further than my grandmother could throw a DeSoto!"

McGee contemplated what Hunter had said. "There's a lot of the *Dark State*; we have to drive a stake through their little evil hearts. But they are all we have. They claim that if they fly to the major cites of China and Hong Kong, and then to the major airports in the U.S—100 million dead, minimum. A billion, maybe two, worldwide. One mathematician at the CDC, who is the authority on modeling, even projected the extermination of humans if the bug was everything the Iranians hoped it to be and the Chinese feared. I told him he shouldn't do math in public."

Hunter said, "Are you kidding me?"

"I have to listen to these idiots; so does the President." McGee shook his head. "More *Dark State.* These people have driven science from its foundation as an objective search for truth and toward political power games." He pointed to the pallet and said, "In those boxes under the cargo netting I've brought along a bunch of *improvise* and *adapt* to help us *overcome*. Manly toys."

"I hope in one of those boxes you've brought a whole lot of luck. We're going to need it." Hunter spied two machine pistols he had only read about. *He's mad and he's serious!* "If we pull this off, we'll be heroes. Not bad for a couple of prior enlisted pogues. Do I see SP5K-PDWs?"

McGee reached for one of the weapons. He cleared it like the professional special operations warrior he was and held it up. "You do. This is a Heckler & Koch *modified* short barrel, Sport Pistol, personal defense weapon." McGee flipped the weapon around like he was on a silent drill team or teaching a weapons class, which he was; for a student of one. He pointed out the weapons' fine points and specifications. "Fourteen pound, thirteen-inch, 9mm, HK. 30-round magazine. It has the optic rail of the MP—the machine pistol—with silencer, laser sights, and the Aimpoint T-2 red dot. It's a joy to shoot, and if we play our cards right, we won't have to use it. In fact, that is the goal."

Hunter said, "Because no one is supposed to know it was us."

McGee nodded. "But if we have to, we have to."

"10-4, *Bullfrog*. What else did you bring to the party?"

"I'll show you everything, but let's defer until later. We have to get some sleep. When we land, we will be busy." McGee laid down on a group of troop seats. Max was snoring under McGee.

Hunter refused to argue with a man the size of the Statue of Liberty. He yawned and capitulated, "Aye, aye, sir. You're the boss." In minutes Hunter was sprawled across troop seats and asleep with noise-canceling headphones over his ears, a sleep mask over his eyes, and his flight jacket over his chest.

CHAPTER 59

May 27, 2018

Demetrius Eastwood prepared the sound booth for his on-line news show. He checked the lighting, the microphones, and ensured the cameras were aligned perfectly. He donned Audio-Technica Dynamic headphones, checked the audio, and with a flick of the audio master switch he began his radio show.

After acknowledging his growing list of sponsors he dove headfirst into the news of the week. "Thank you for tuning into this episode of *Unfiltered News* and welcome to the only American news broadcast where there is a difference from the communist messages out of Kremlin or Beijing or the Communist News Network. Here we have no agenda other than the truth. We see accurate and responsible information as tools with which to decide that should not be weaponized unless we are at war. But since we are at war with the criminality of the left, hold onto your hat. This could be bumpy."

"Before we comment on anniversaries, I would like to do some public service announcements. In a weekly segment I'm going to call *The Worst in Media* we'll profile where the media not only got it wrong but out-and-out lied to you. In a segment I'll call *The Dumbest Person in Congress* we'll look at the best of the Democrat Party, with an *exposé* of the top congressmen and senators who make the list through clearly meritorious malfeasant action or inaction. Who will win the prize?"

Eastwood referenced an author from "Down Under" who had researched all the known communists and socialists in the U.S. Congress, their political affiliation, and their known communist and socialist activities outside of Congress. He knew the folks "back home in Middle America" who had been voting straight-ticket Democrat Party for decades didn't know their candidates had hidden their political histories of communist and socialist activity. He promoted the Australian's book, *The Enemies of the State* and several articles he had written on former U.S. presidential candidate Senator Maxim Mazibuike and the other Democrat members of Congress with radical, Islamic, and communist connections.

Eastwood reported from sources at the Department of Defense that the wife of the ISIS intelligence minister, Toraluddin Haqqani, had died in her sleep at Guantanamo Bay, Cuba. Her body would be returned to her parents.

After he finished detailing a Democrat Texas Congressman "who didn't have sufficient brain wave activity to negotiate a salad bar, but who slavishly supported the Communist Party USA," Eastwood said, "I would like to start on the latest postings from the *dark web* and the secretive *Omega*. Cue the spooky music!"

He played the audio actuality of the most recognized bit of Bernard Herrmann's score from the horror classic, *Psycho;* the shower scene at the creepy Bates Motel complete with Janet Leigh screams as shrieking violins played in syncopation with each stroke of the stabbing knife from the cross-dressing, mother-obsessed, split-personality maniac. After turning down the music, Eastwood added, "I'm sure Norman Bates was a Democrat."

"As you know, *Omega* always begins his posts, *Do you believe in coincidences?* Last night Americans found out that there is an Iranian Institute of Virology named after the original master terrorist, the Ayatollah Khomeini of Iran. This research lab was designed and built by one of the wholly owned subsidiaries of the Trans-Atlantic Security Corporation, better known as TASCO to the traders on Wall Street. So let me repeat the charge which has the web abuzz. An American company, through its international lines of businesses, hid the construction of a biological research laboratory for Iran. For Iran. Let that sink in. For Iran. A billion euros. For Iran, which has been subjected to punishing sanctions ever since they captured our embassy in 1979. I know that was a long time ago, but America has a long memory when it comes to treachery and lawlessness."

"So in defiance of the moratorium on doing business with the Islamic Republic of Iran, a European-based subsidiary of the Trans-Atlantic Security Corporation secretly built a state-of-the-art biosafety level four, BL-4, research facility. For the education of this audience, biosafety levels are the level of biocontainment precautions required to isolate dangerous biological agents in an enclosed facility. The levels of containment range from the lowest biosafety level one to the highest at level 4."

"The Khomeini research laboratory was a BL-4 lab, but what's not known outside of the Department of State is that it was apparently built with U.S. funds, approved by the Mazibuike Administration, and certified by the Chinese. That's right, our favorite Benedict Arnold, double-crossing, traitorous president authorized TASCO to build the Iranian lab against the International Bioterrorism Proliferation Treaty and long-standing U.S. sanctions. It's so good to be a Democrat."

"So what does this all mean to me and you? Shortly after the lab received certification, an Italian news network and Al Jazeera's news network reported that Iranian scientists had found a super-pulmonary virus from bats and mice, and they were working to create a vaccine. The video, which we've posted on our webpage with subtitles for those who don't speak Italian, shows that a spokesman from the Iranian government claimed the Ayatollah Khomeini Institute of Virology was only studying viruses and conducting peaceful research."

Eastwood displayed commercial-grade poor satellite images of the Ayatollah Khomeini Institute of Virology on one of his cameras. He continued, "Few locals knew anything about the lab. One of our brilliant listeners pointed out that the prevailing winds in that area blow toward Ashgabat. That *Omega* release somehow got to the desk of the president of Turkmenistan; he was furious, and the residents of Ashgabat were understandably terrified to learn they had a secret lab essentially in their backyard, upwind of them. The Turkmenistan president conferred with President Hernandez, and the two presidents demanded Iran cease operations. They plan to take their case to the U.N. Security Council. Of course Iran rejected the United States' claims."

"Iran didn't want the BL-4 lab near any of their towns. The local Iranian bioterrorist probably isn't all that competent, but with a potential bioweapon you don't have to be competent. You just have to release the bug. When that happens will it be accidental or intentional?

It's my opinion that the Iranian scientists can't be trusted, neither can the visiting scientists from Europe and China. The people living in that part of the world are living on borrowed time."

"Our brilliant listener who provided the video of the Italian telecast about the lab indicated that it wasn't available in the United States on YouTube or any of the social media outlets. But it was posted on a billboard on the *dark web*, and we have posted it on our website."

Eastwood added, "We learned that sloppy security of a virus supposedly contained in a BL-4 laboratory in China several years ago resulted in an unintentional release. About a half-million people died. Of course we didn't hear about it then. The Communist Chinese didn't offer any warnings and didn't talk to the media. We knew there was something going on in that area because commercial satellite photos suggested the Chinese military had carved mass burial pits in the ground. Days later those pits were filled in, and the affected city was abandoned."

"As a consequence, we have reports that the Chinese labs retrofitted their facilities with the West's biological protection standard. In the event of an accidental release emergency, researchers activate a release alarm. This floods the rooms with UV-C lights. First-world countries with BL-3 and BL-4 laboratories have the UV-C lamps in the HVAC units and in all the rooms and halls—in addition to sprinkler heads for fire they have sterilization lamps."

"This morning the FBI indicted three Chinese-born U.S. citizens with twenty-four counts of stealing American trade secrets. What they didn't say is that they were *biological trade secrets.* Another researcher from Beijing on a J-1 visa, tried to leave the U.S. with dozens of vials of biological materials in her luggage. And I gave the Iranians crap for improperly handling biological samples. She told the FBI that she and some of her colleagues at Harvard had been stealing samples for years and taking them to China to sell. She said she was paid well for the vials by the Chinese military."

"Here is a sound bite I want you to hear. Pay attention Congress." An unknown voice asked, "So this *chimera*.... is what, exactly?"

An unknown voice said, "We developed a *chimera* which is an organism modified by grafting a superficial protein of a coronavirus from the Fratarakas horseshoe bat onto the virus that causes SARS, the acute pneumonia that is non-fatal to mice but lethal to humans."

On camera, Eastwood was making faces as if he were in extreme pain. "It appears the Iranians were trying to develop a coronavirus that would attack only infidels, unbelievers, and blasphemers, but not Muslims. This was their primary goal, the goal of the Khomeini lab."

Eastwood was back with a vengeance. "So this is what we now know, thanks to *Omega* and our listeners in the U.S. and Europe. With a stroke of a pen President Mazibuike dropped the sanctions on Iran. He helped fund considerably more sophisticated bioterrorism projects through contracts with TASCO International, while American scientists stopped doing all research on coronaviruses. This stopped development of possible vaccines for these coronaviruses."

"The researchers we have talked to say this research is very labor intensive, and it would take at least three years for the U.S. to regenerate the research if we had an outbreak. President Mazibuike intentionally lowered our level of understanding and response capability, essentially our 'force field,' and now the American public are easy targets."

"Before sunup I received a text message from one of my friends. He said we should ask how the national stockpile of PPE is provisioned in case of an outbreak. So I asked. Not only was the national stockpile of personal protection equipment, PPE, drawn down to critical levels during the outbreaks of the MERS and SARS, but under the direction of President Mazibuike the national stockpile was never replenished. Correspondents researching this topic interviewed some people at the National Institute of Health and discovered that they're all Mazibuike lackeys. So if there ever is an outbreak, you can bet they would load up on whatever drug they knew to be effective and deny that there are any effective drugs and vaccines, if they even reported the outbreak."

"Isn't it the job of journalists to investigate questions and offer them to the public square? That must be someone else's media. Once again, you can't trust our media. Period, full stop."

"These dudes would play power politics. I guess this is another way of saying that if America was ever targeted with a bioweapon from Iran, China, or the Kremlin, our country would be totally vulnerable to a weaponized virus, and we would be unprotected by a lack of personal protective equipment and vaccines. In short, we would be toast until the president took dramatic action."

"If this isn't some long-term plan of Maxim Mazibuike, then is it a long-term plan from the Islamic Republic of Iran? Iran is only one lab accident away from becoming the killer of the world's only hyperpower—and all without firing a shot. An outbreak on an unprepared America would be devastating."

"According to *Omega* the man behind it all is Bogdan Chernovich, the CEO of TASCO. General Chernovich, a former Commandant of the Marine Corps and a Congressional Medal of Honor recipient, seems to be at the forefront of this situation. He has undergraduate and graduate degrees in chemistry and biology, and a master's from Harvard. An investigation into the background of Bogdan Chernovich claimed the lives of two detectives. Think about that. According to the *Omega*, he has been a person of interest in the deaths of several dozens of women. Neither the severely crippled FBI nor the media will investigate him, but I know a law firm that will."

"There must be more to General Chernovich than we know. We must sort this out before the corrupt dogs of media intervene and bury the skeletons in his closet. I implore my listening audience to report what you know of Bogdan Chernovich and the Board of Directors at TASCO. I accept information. I do not accept donations. I will ask questions and demand answers. If we do not get adequate answers, we will let our legal team have a go."

"TASCO has long been suspected of aiding blacklisted Chinese surveillance firms and giving aviation secrets to the Russians and Chinese. My television network may not be willing to go along with my initiative, so I will create some reporting mechanism.... Hold on, hold on, hold on! I'm getting a message...from...*Europe*. Hold on, I can't believe what I'm reading. *Whistleblowers* has just informed me that my brilliant listeners in America may send all information on Bogdan Chernovich and TASCO to the *Whistleblowers* encrypted website. They're organized to do exactly what we are talking about.

Whistleblowers is the solution. They're listening! They are willing to play. I'm going to send them a check! Let's find out the truth!"

"This is what fighting back looks like!"

"Now, a word from our newest sponsor. Most people are familiar with the major mass-marketing publishing houses but aren't aware there are independent publishers like Black Rose Writing in Castroville, Texas. If you're tired of reading the pabulum from those big house publishers, the same stories told and retold where only the names are changed and the covers redesigned, if you are looking for something more interesting, more exciting, and more thought provoking, take a trip through the offerings by Black Rose Writing. Your mind will love you for it. Now a word from our other sponsors."

• • •

"Welcome back to *Unfiltered News*, I'm your host, Demetrius Eastwood. We have a few more things before we wrap up for the day. I would like to start on the recent White House press briefing I attended, a complementary announcement that America's military requited themselves spectacularly with the successful rescue of hostages on the continent of Africa. However, I suggest that these press briefings no longer serve any useful purpose. The gathered press showed why they have become the enemy of the people. The White House correspondents are not only rude and disrespectful, they're like child molesters running a summer camp. The American people expect Doctor Marcus Welby to report the news; the nation's Fourth Estate is actually made up of Doctor Josef Mengele clones. It's time to shitcan the program. I say tear it down and start over."

"I blame former President Mazibuike for turning the Fourth Estate into a useless, self-serving, cancerous appendage of our republic. They are so steeped in their own stupidity it's a wonder they ever made it through the birth canal. These journalists can't be relied upon to report the time of day accurately, let alone the news. They're so enthralled by the scent of their own power that they don't realize it's the stench of their own death."

CHAPTER 60

May 27, 2018

Bogdan Chernovich and the TASCO Board of Directors had been waiting for the former CEO of Lockheed Martin to join them when the emaciated man burst through the conference room doors and told the group to turn on the television. Without explanation or preamble Chernovich picked up the TV remote and selected his favorite news channel, what the rabid Right called the *Communist News Network*.

As he took his seat the man from Lockheed Martin explained, "The networks report that on his radio show Demetrius Eastwood essentially indicted TASCO for espionage."

The television was turned on as the network reported other late-breaking news. The cable news anchor exclaimed, "The President has nominated the current Executive Vice President of the American Federalist Society, Burnt Winchester, for Attorney General. Mr. Winchester was a U.S. Attorney for the Western District of Texas."

The men around the conference table were shocked. Chernovich was furious. He pounded the table with a fist. The news anchor was receiving his information directly from their White House correspondent in the Rose Garden, "Besides appointing a new Attorney General, President Hernandez made dozens of presidential appointments today, those not requiring congressional approval. He filled most of the vacant senior FBI's positions and nominated dozens of federal prosecutors and judges for those FBI positions that do require Congressional approval. Most noteworthy, for the first time in nearly twenty years there were no TASC nominees."

"What does that mean?" asked the former Director of the NSA. Chernovich shushed him.

The Atlanta-based news anchor then passed the baton to their desk in Washington, D.C. A woman behind a microphone said, "In other news reported by Demetrius Eastwood's *Unfiltered News,* the President of the United States allegedly wrote a letter to the head of the Democratic National Committee which stated in part, that the Republican Party would return to the protocols of old and be identified with the political color 'blue.' The Democrat Party may choose any color they wish, but the letter recommended they should embrace their past socialist and communist glories and be represented by the color 'red.' While we can neither confirm nor deny this apparently illegal action, the President announced the political color alternative was to be effective immediately. The Democrat minority leaders in the Senate and the House of Representatives strongly denounced the President's actions and asserted there would be a court challenge."

"Is that even real?" bemoaned the former Chief of Intelligence of the Army.

"Wait, wait, there's more." The man from Lockheed had the Eastwood presentation. "I think we should listen to it. This isn't good." He walked to the door which accessed the electronics for the conference room.

The network host continued her reporting and brought into the conversation a senior correspondent. "Wolf, dismissing the candidates from the American Bar Association for the white supremacist group, the radical American Federalist Society, has to be a slap across the face of the nation's best and most revered think tank, the Trans-Atlantic Security Council, and their Chairman of the Board, General Bogdan Chernovich."

Chernovich mashed the OFF button on the remote at the mention of his name. He turned to stony faces. "We need more intel."

The Lockheed Martin man had been Chernovich's classmate at the Naval Academy but left the Marines as a captain after being wounded during a second tour in Vietnam. He looked like a meth addict in loose-fitting Brooks Brothers. He raced from the electronics room and said he had downloaded the presentation. Chernovich, a master of the remote that controlled a million dollars of audio-visual equipment, pushed the correct sequence of buttons to transmit the contents of the video file on the three-dollar memory stick.

Mere minutes after Demetrius Eastwood's report on TASCO's involvement with the Iranian laboratory and institute of virology, the members of the board began transferring accounts from American banks to offshore accounts. The flamboyant flamingoes who made up the TASCO board of directors were leaving the building as fast as they could and heading for private jets at outlying airports, soon to fly to Europe or Dubai. The CEO admonished them not to panic but to rendezvous in Italy in forty-eight hours.

They know the location. Chernovich defiantly remained at the conference table. *Is this how it ends? The plan was nearly perfect, but with Hernandez and McGee and that asshole Hunter meddling.... They haven't heard the last of me! It's not going to be that easy to get rid of me!* Bogdan Chernovich reflected on the traps and pitfalls he had avoided for forty years in uniform.

He was within a signature of being disqualified for entry to the Naval Academy when the doctor conducting his physical suggested an alternative. He was told he wasn't qualified to be an officer candidate; he wasn't qualified to go to any of the service academies. *But he could be.*

The physician told him he was on two spectra in the DSM; Chernovich didn't understand what that meant. The doctor informed him that he had a sexual identity disorder, what was once called *inversion.* The physician probed his patient with coarse suggestive language and told him he should be automatically disqualified.

He relived the moment; the physician asked *How bad do you want this? How would you go about proving you are sincere*? Chernovich said he would do anything to go to the Naval Academy, that he would control his desires for men and suppress his hatred of women. *I think of making love to men daily. I will do things so as not to think about men.*

The physician undid his belt and unzipped his trousers while telling Chernovich he needed to avoid all sexual encounters with men. Chernovich knew what to do. The doctor continued, "You've always been different; when your friends wanted to play cops and robbers, you want to play spy. Is that right?"

Chernovich stopped what he was doing, nodded, and went back to his task.

"Your mother let you read Alistair MacLean and Ian Fleming, and you rooted for the bad guys. You always wanted to be on the other side; your whole life you wanted to infiltrate the enemy. Isn't that right? See, I know you more than you know yourself. You want to pass secrets, play the spy. Be the spy." His mouth full, Chernovich nodded.

The physician's release was dramatic and sudden. In less than three hundred seconds, Chernovich spilled his entire secret history and convinced the doctor that he could keep a secret, that he was worthy. Chernovich was introduced into a new world that pleased him but could also be his downfall. The physician affixed his signature to the document attesting that the seventeen-year-old who looked like a gangly teenage Frankenstein monster was medically qualified to attend the Naval Academy.

He remembered the old man's words. *You'll need constant counseling. The military will find out. If you cannot control your desires, you'll be discharged as undesirable. You need to be seen in the presence of women. Try to get into the intelligence field, but avoid the CIA. You will not pass their polygraph. Do not get married; when a wife finds out you like men, she will never forgive you; she will expose you and make your life a living hell, and you will contemplate suicide. Get a copy of the movie Conspirator! Learn from the mistakes of the spy. And read everything you can get your hands on; you will make a name for yourself as the best read most educated person in the military. Only contemplate suicide if you have been completely compromised. Good luck.*

The CIA's more aggressive polygraph would have exposed him and his proclivities. They know all the signs just like the doctor who conducted his examinations for the academy. He could've been subject to blackmail but negotiated an assignment to conduct training for the National Clandestine Service, "the Farm," at Camp Peary in Virginia. Chernovich rolled the dice and passed the lesser invasive counterintelligence polygraph. At all times he was sexually frustrated, surrounded by men he couldn't have. He had a few affairs in the Marine Corps with his female drivers; he had seduced, sodomized, and had them killed—all but one. The one that got away.

When he made general, enlisted women who could not resist the power of the top general in the Marine Corps lined up to be his driver.

Chernovich used the women to convince those around him that he was a straight white male. But no intercourse. It was his dirty secret that when the women complained that he didn't look at them or screw them, he eliminated them. Poisoned them. He would inject a bottle of Visine into a soda or an energy drink, which would knock them out for hours. The medical examiners rarely received permission from the families to check for rape or perform autopsies on their daughters who had been strangled.

His Tag Heuer *Autavia* with the blue-and-red GMT bezel peeked out from under his French cuffs that were fastened with gold Indian head coin cufflinks. He flipped off the remote controller and dropped it on the table. Exasperated, Bogdan Chernovich uttered, "Dory, Dory, Dory. You have just become another polyp on the ass of the Republican Party. I'm going to have to pop you myself."

The board of directors had deserted him, but they would rendezvous in Europe. He had been in tough scrapes before. The Eastwood and the *Omega* broadcasts smelled of an insider. He had kept all of them working, all of them happy. *The gay groups, the lesbian groups, the transgenders. Ah, the transgenders, with or without the surgery, they killed themselves in prodigious numbers. How did it jump the tracks? We've been exposed and this government will investigate us. She was supposed to win. The polls had her crushing Hernandez in Philadelphia and we controlled the Democracy Innovation machines. How could they have been so wrong? I did all that was humanly possible. Who's to blame? The Black Scorpion does not like failure.*

For the first time in his life he realized he was frightened and had no clear path of escape. The feeling was unknown. To be someone's target. Someone was coming after him. A partial solution came to him in a flash: *Who would know how to get in touch with Eastwood? His network boss. I could do some of that CEO-to-CEO work. Before Eastwood's broadcast I could have gotten a number or maybe the CEO could have set me up with a meeting. But now.... Now, that will never happen.*

But it's looking more and more likely that Dory found out what the CIA did to him when he was at the National Security Council. He had been my chief competitor; he orchestrated the activity that brought down the cartel boss, Pablo Escobar. That made him a star. He always seemed to be one step ahead of me, no matter how hard I tried.

Where did he get his intel? It had to be from inside. A sneak, snitch, a stool-pigeon to the movement. A defector, maybe? From TASCO? Likely. Probably some disgruntled employee who had lived the life, lived the lie. Someone who really wasn't gay but liked the lifestyle. An older man sleeping with an undisciplined stud who moved on to better things. There can't be too many like that in this place. Someone would know. But I don't have the time to find out. The corporate lawyers can't keep the feds at bay indefinitely. I have to leave.

Chernovich hit the intercom and asked his secretary to come to him. The retired Sergeant Major silently entered and stood at a modified Parade Rest at the end of the conference table. Chernovich said, "Sergeant Major, we'll need one of those special FedEx envelopes to locate Demetrius Eastwood. I want him removed from the battlefield. And we will need one of your best men for a search and destroy mission. I have the address. There are to be no survivors."

The Sergeant Major nodded. He would do anything for his General.

CHAPTER 61

May 28, 2018

An Automatic Kalashnikov model 47 with a long arcing banana-shaped magazine rested in a chair at the conference table, signifying the chair was spoken for and that its owner was nearby. Behind the eldest of the elders the green flag of the Muslim Brotherhood hung next to a black flag. The white script announced that it was the flag of al-Qaeda and depicted the *Shahada*, the profession of faith; *There is no God but Allah, and Mohammad is the Prophet of Allah.*

Since the death of Sheikh Osama bin Laden and the *Âmirikî's* incessant war to destroy them, al-Qaeda had become less visible but more quietly clandestine than the newcomer, the Islamic State of Iraq and Syria, ISIS. Terrorism's little brother, ISIS, the attention-starved group striving to be "an equal" to their big brother, al-Qaeda. ISIS knew that negative attention was still attention; egged on by Al Jazeera's cameras they got all the negative attention they desired as long as there were beheadings and burnings and bombings.

They were newly reformulated, al-Qaeda, the greatest organization sired by the Muslim Brotherhood. The Islamic Underground encompassed them all, al-Qaeda and a coalition of special interest groups led by field generals of subordinate organizations, such as Boko Haram, Jemaah Islamiyah, Hezbollah, Hamas, al-Shabab, and Ansar al-Sharia. Terrorist elders who no longer sought the rush of decapitating infidels with the sword because of injuries and other health issues, relegated themselves to strategic planning and distributing funds for large-scale operations and the smaller, but often much more important, "special activities."

Long after the sun had set, long after ceremonial tea, the al-Qaeda leaders in the room hadn't the energy to move from overstuffed chairs to the conference table. They showed signs of stress; they slumped even further into the oversized chairs; they spoke in hushed tones. They were consistently in pain; they carried bullets or fragments of grenades within their bodies. Their injuries had healed and they were still alive only by the grace of Allah. The *Âmirikîs* have been relentless.

The three represented the remaining supreme leaders, the last of a great movement, the remnants of the al-Qaeda leadership. Their field generals in al-Qaeda and ISIS and their replacements were being decimated every single day. No one wished to be in the position of having to rely on mercenary affiliates, but the situation was dire. One more defeat and the al-Qaeda would collapse.

Except for Sheikh Saleem Ali al-Qasimi of *Jabhat Fatah al-Sham*, al-Qaeda had been virtually rubbed out, and the senior members of the Islamic Revolutionary Guard Corps—those that left the protection of Iranian borders—now they were being picked off one at a time. Allah was no longer choosing when or where the martyrs would fall. Apparently that was a decision made in *Âmirikî* in a place called the *Cee âh ā*. No one wanted to admit the infidels were closing in on them. When the last of the Haqqanis was captured the intelligence spigot was shut off and al-Qaeda's ultimate demise was becoming a *fait accompli*.

After their tea had been refreshed, they agreed they had to move quickly in order to stay relevant, to stay in the game. Another leader lost to a bullet would make it necessary for the organization to take down their flag and disband. They wanted to recruit more *jihadis* for another go at the *Âmirikîs*, but Haqqani warned that they didn't have the resources, "There would be no more martyrs." Haqqani was the last to wear a martyr vest. Involuntary conscription wasn't working; the governments were hunting them down too, killing them instead of capturing them. A prisoner would have to be given provisions; a bullet was adequate to eliminate poison from the system.

Governments were paying decent wages for some new jobs, and potential conscripts weren't as political or radical. Potential *jihadis* could be found by the dozens, now they would rather play soccer, or eat pistachio *basbousa*, or play with their phones, or hang out at an open-air *hookah* bar and watch the girls without head coverings walk by. The leadership had once been fifteen men strong with cash reserves in the billions of dollars and an army of millions that dominated thousands of square miles. With the loss of Haqqani now they were three; the organization was broke, and the remaining forces were being driven out of the towns and hotels.

The Sheikh from Libya, a man renowned for bombing the *Âmirikîs* airliners, was quick to point out that there was no possible way to eliminate the captured chief intelligence officer or replace him and his network of intelligence men.

A man from Saudi Arabia, the son of a consummate Islamic warrior, asserted that trying to execute Haqqani would be just as impossible. There were questions about the wife who was also kidnapped. Why was she taken? Was she a deep spy for the *Âmirikîs*? Was she dead as reported? The *Âmirikîs* always lie.

But the *Âmirikîs* believed Colonel Eastwood. The *Âmirikîs* had bought spaces in newspapers, articles in magazines, air time on Al Jazeera, all of it pro-*Âmirikî* propaganda. Operational and propaganda funding from Saudi Arabia and Oman and Qatar had dried up. The brothers that made up the ISIS had early successes, but couldn't secure the treasuries of Syria or Iraq or Libya. Without oil, without donations, without monies, the collapse of the Islamic Underground was at hand.

There was only one option left. Release *Jabhat Fatah al-Sham*. Sheikh Saleem Ali al-Qasimi mustn't fail. Al-Qaeda's remaining funds and their future were in the hands of a man who would not wear the beard.

"Pray for Ali al-Qasimi," said the number two man in the hierarchy. "For when we succeed our troubles will be behind us. We will inspire the next group of *jihadi*." The other men agreed with the prediction if their mercenary group was successful, but they didn't believe the Saudi's cheery outlook.

They had one last chance to punish the infidel for eternity. Send in the most vicious *jihadis* in all of Islam. To do less would be an affront to Allah. "Sheikh Ali al-Qasimi *will be* successful!" They mumbled, "*Inshallah!*"

CHAPTER 62

May 28, 2018

Kelly Horne and Saoirse Nobley entered the first boutique salon they encountered, the *Silver Fox Beauty Shop*, on the outskirts of Pittsburg. The goal was to get Nobley's hair and nails done. No other customers were being serviced and a chair was offered immediately.

The pedicurist had never seen a woman's feet so damaged. The manicurist had never seen a woman's hands and nails in such terrible shape. Kelly felt sorry for Saoirse and talked with her throughout the procedures. When asked what color she preferred on her nails, Saoirse sat and cried. Just as Kelly surmised that the trip into town was probably "too much, too soon," Saoirse recovered and composed herself. She looked up to the manicurist and apologized. "I have had no polish on my nails in some time, and it's one of those things that you just stop thinking about. I don't suppose you have Mary Kay's Cherries Jubilee?"

The manicurist said she might have the color in the back room. In no time at all she returned with lipstick and matching nail polish. She had been looking at Nobley for some time and got the impression the woman might have been in prison for twenty years; she was surprised the discontinued lipstick and nail polish was still useable and said she wouldn't charge Nobley for them.

Saoirse's official Marine Corps photographs had captured thick blonde tresses. Now her hair was thin and gray and stringy. The hairdresser ran her fingers through Nobley's hair; she had never seen such lifeless hair. The strands felt like steel wool. She asked Saoirse what she wanted to do with her hair. Saoirse said to do whatever would be appropriate. As her hair was being washed, Saoirse asked Kelly if they could stop at a church and a bookstore.

Kelly pulled out a smartphone and said, "I'll find one for you."

The flat handheld device shocked Saoirse; she had seen nothing like it. During her captivity she had missed several generations of technology. She asked to look at the device and handled it with wonder. Kelly immediately figured out Saoirse hadn't been exposed to the latest in cellphone technology and promised to show her later. First Saoirse's hair needed shampooing.

The hairdresser had watched the flabbergasted woman who couldn't keep her eyes off of Kelly's smartphone and said something nosey, "Where you been, honey?" Saoirse looked at Kelly for an answer. Kelly replied for her, "She's been *abroad*. Her skin is very dry. Do you have some lotion?"

The new question demanded action. The hairdresser wanted to know more, but Kelly peppered her with questions about clothing stores and restaurants in the surrounding area. As her hair was being washed, Saoirse spied a flat panel electronic screen and thin keyboard. It wasn't anything like the big and clunky secretary's computer she remembered or the IMB Selectric that sat on her desk when she had been in the Marine Corps. As tears ran down her face, she wondered if typewriters even existed anymore.

Kelly directed the hairdresser to continue working; both women hoped Saoirse would stop crying.

After a shampoo and conditioning and a blow-dry, Nobley's looks had improved a thousand percent. When the hairdresser held a mirror for Saoirse to check her hair, Kelly panicked but was grateful that there were no additional outbursts of tears. *Maybe she has already seen herself?*

During a physical at the Walter Reed National Military Medical Center, she had been run through an MRI from head to foot; radiologists were alarmed that her arms had been broken several times and bloodwork revealed she was anemic, but the good news was she didn't have tuberculosis.

Seeing herself for the first time in over a decade, with the sunken eyes of a starved and depressed refugee, Saoirse looked through the image and ignored the reflection. She convinced herself she had to stay strong for when she saw the *Captain*.

Kelly informed the driver they would go to an outdoor mall. She gave directions. Saoirse watched Kelly flip though screens on her smartphone with a feather-like touch. Kelly selected the Ralph Lauren outlet store. Inside, they selected clothes in subdued colors and styles.

Then they found the food court. Having been deprived of food for decades, now Saoirse was always hungry. She had been condemned to death, confined to a black cloth bag for twenty years, hidden from man, the sun, the world. Every moment came with a sense of urgency and angst, because she had become a time-traveler; she had been teleported into the future and couldn't believe anything her eyes told her. Kelly held her hand as Saoirse responded to every new sight and experience like an old Soviet defector visiting America for the first time.

Kelly recalled a lecture in the CIA auditorium on communism given by one of the foremost authorities on the Soviet Union, a former eastern bloc general in the intelligence service. She left the event thinking the Communist Party had really studied the mind and learned how to control people. Another lecturer, a career intelligence officer with a PhD and former Naval War College staff member said some key things which resonated with Kelly. "I know you've heard the stories of defectors from the USSR going into a grocery store in America for the first time, and how they can't believe the shelves in every aisle were stocked full, the mounds of fresh produce and fruit, and the selection of meat. There was no waiting in line for a three-day-old loaf of bread. Bread was plentiful, there were dozens of varieties, and all of it fresh. There were stores and factories and superhighways and airports where the masses could fly on the cheap. Through their media, the Kremlin could create a false universe with which to control their people. But when defectors see the American and Western reality, many Russians refuse to believe they have been lied to." Even after living in America for her first twenty-two years, Saoirse reacted to the American world of commerce with that same shock.

After underwear, bras, socks, jeans and long-sleeved shirts to hide the scars on her arms, Nobley asked to get some cologne.

Kelly said, "Sure—was there something you had in mind?"

Saoirse remembered the sunshine in a bottle that made her smile; the cute yellow and white stripes on the box, the niche fragrance that was very difficult to forget, memorable, and long-lasting. She remembered, the first time she wore it off the air station, she was barred from entering a restaurant because of its intensity.

After acquiring a bottle of cologne, they made a trip across the street for running shoes. A couple of men from the protective staff took Nobley's new belongings to the Agency vehicle. The group ate at the only P.F. Chang's in Pittsburg, and Saoirse ordered more food than she could possibly eat. Leftovers were carted to a Suburban. Saoirse spent an hour in a Barnes & Noble before meeting Hunter's dentist.

While Nobley was at the dentist, Kelly left the protective staff at the dental office, raced to the mall, and using her father's American Express Card, bought the older woman a cell phone, laptop, and headphones. She was feeling a bit girl scouty, and her father would approve for he was exceptionally generous to his family and friends. The dental work took hours. When the vehicles left Pittsburg at two a.m., Saoirse Nobley was sedated, had a mouth full of implanted teeth to go with her new clothes, electronics, and books.

It had been seventeen days since she had been rescued from a Syrian hellhole. A few hours of liberty and food followed by seven hours of surgery may have been too much for the fragile woman. Time would tell.

The drive back to *Fallingwater* was made in silence. Kelly was exhausted.

It would take many more hours for Saoirse to sleep off the anesthesia; one beefy intelligence officer carried her like a sack of groceries from the black vehicle to her bed. Kelly followed behind with shopping bags. Every intelligence officer got something out of the deal. Good food, a shopping trip on the government's dime, and the men and women from the Tradecraft Course didn't lose anyone practicing their surveillance skills.

Chapter 63

May 28, 2018

Ali al-Qasimi wanted to see it burn. He envisioned destroying the evidence of their incursion into the realm of the invisible and lethal. His men would be martyrs, the carriers of invisible bombs designed to kill the infidels across the globe. But martyrdom was for thee, not for him; he had other work that must be done. It was very strange, leading men who wanted to die.

South of Ashgabat on the Gandan Highway, the most southerly road connecting the Iranian town of Bājirān, a caravan of three commercial delivery vehicles trundled smoothly through the Turkmenistan and Islamic Republic of Iran ports of entry without questions or complications. They were well on their way to the heavily guarded compound of the Ayatollah Khomeini Institute of Virology. The Institute was provisioned weekly from the Turkmen capitol; there was no other sufficiently populous metropolis within hundreds of miles that could continually and economically supply the needs and wants of the disparate and demanding scientists who worked at the research institute.

In the twilight, the string of three trucks arrived at the port of entry. Ali al-Qasimi, the lead truck driver, apologized profusely to the border guards who was giving the al-Sham leader grief. It was part of the show to demonstrate their power and authority. It also meant that something more than words would be required to pass.

Ali al-Qasimi had played this part a hundred times before and slipped the guard a stack of 100,000 Iranian *rial* notes. He said, "Your currency is being devalued every day by the bastard *Âmirikîs.* We are running very late. A little extra for your overtime." Even with the best legitimate passports money could buy he was accustomed to the waiting associated with visa-issuing government bureaucrats and border guards. Those bureaucrats in the decision-making process demanded a "pinch," a little extra cash over and above their salary.

The men in the lead vehicle imagined they could see the glow of the streetlights of the Institute on the horizon. Ali al-Qasimi wasn't focused on what was ahead of him but "the escape." He envisioned being back in Ashgabat getting on an aircraft bound for Amman, Jordan. His men, outbound to China and Hong Kong and Mumbai. He was grateful to have received their entry visas into Iran, but he was most excited to have finally received their exit visas from Turkmenistan.

He worked very hard to control his temper. He had lost two incredibly stupid men to the authorities; they had been inept, acting the part of amateurs. Murdering tourists was a terminal offense that didn't warrant Ali al-Qasimi's help. *I warned them. They were stupid! They chose earthy pleasures over serving Allah. Now they can rot in a Turkmen jail.* Ali al-Qasimi worried that if he lost one more man, he would have to scrub the mission. Eight was probably too few, and too few assaulters meant there was a better than even chance they wouldn't be able to control the compound unless they could eliminate all resistance.

But Ali al-Qasimi had other worries. Al-Qaeda had paid for three things: Incursion, infection, dispersion. As much as they had trained together and worked together and lived close to one another, Ali al-Qasimi knew his men were mercenaries, mentally defective radicals, not ideologues. Since two of them had killed indiscriminately for carnal pleasures, he would have to view the rest of his men in a harsher light to see if they were committed to prioritizing the mission over the potential for sex and money. There is a time and place for killing in the name of Allah.

If they could obliterate the security forces quickly, Ali would give some of his men some celebratory time; those who wished to kill and destroy needed the space to do so. Ali al-Qasimi would wait a few minutes for them to rape and pillage and celebrate their conquest over the Westerners, before he would refocus them on the mission. All extra activities would have to be after the security guards were neutralized and al-Sham controlled the compound.

Urged by the barrel of a gun, Iranian scientists would do his bidding and give up their access cards. Then he could consider entering the laboratories where the viruses were kept. But if they discovered they were under assault would they destroy or release the invisible bringers of death and infect his men, or would they yield? *Will they destroy their access cards and deny me my destiny?* Ali al-Qasimi quietly wagered the cowardly scientists would submit and surrender their electronic keys to the laboratories as if their lives depended on it, because in every way they did.

Ali al-Qasimi had been educated in the finest schools in Cairo and Amman and had read the proscribed books. Unlike Muslim women who were conditioned to be subservient, African, *Âmirikî*, Western, and Christian women needed to be captured before they could be made servants of Allah, *to be forced to submit!* Western and Christian women were conditioned to be free in mind and spirit in contravention to the *Qur'an*. It was a special situation to be celebrated when Western and Christian women were captured, for they fought like wildcats whenever they believed they would be forced to submit to the men who would willingly give their lives for Allah.

Ali al-Qasimi knew there were *Âmirikî* or Western women in the compound and that his men would become uncontrollably wild with excitement. He wouldn't be able to control them, for they would want to punish the women and to fill themselves with the spirit and the word of Allah. The vicious coupling with the unwilling showed dominance over the women before they killed them in a ritualistic orgy. Ali al-Qasimi was resigned that his men would do anything for Allah, but if they found Western women, they would take whatever they wanted regardless of his orders.

From the intelligence provided by Haqqani, he knew there were Western women in a special bunker in the compound. Ali al-Qasimi would do his best to keep his men from that very special place. The women could die. He did not care.

Ali had expected floodlights of the Khomeini Institute would reflect off the high overcast, but there was no such reflection, there was no overcast. The headlamps of the vehicles were barely adequate for traveling at night over the paved road with no streetlamps. Ali al-

Qasimi kept scanning the sky, if only for something to do until they arrived. With a lack of signage, he assumed they were within ten miles of the facility, but at the rock-crawling rate they were traveling, it could be another thirty minutes or a few hours. Ali al-Qasimi wanted to complete the mission and return home. He played the best scenario in his head over and over, as if he were willing the Iranians to drop their weapons and submit. He closed his eyes. Headlines would report, *Without firing a shot, Jabhat Fatah al-Sham, the Front for the Conquest of the Levant, captured the Iranian National Biosafety Laboratory. The deadliest virus ever created in a laboratory is now in the hands of the most powerful man in all of Islam.*

Iranian and Chinese technicians and scientists would be rounded up. All personnel would be accounted for. He would line them up against the barbed wire fence. He would not have time to be anointed in the infidel's blood. Flames would come to the compound; he wanted to see them burn.

CHAPTER 64

May 28, 2018

Under clear skies and a full moon, the Agency's intelligence officers stationed in Ashgabat turned out in force. The Ambassador also showed up to meet the U.S. Air Force jet even though it was just after dusk. The Embassy's intelligence officers and Marine Security Guards lined up to meet Director McGee and shake his hand, after all he was the most decorated individual ever to wear the uniform: the Congressional Medal of Honor, five Navy Crosses, and the Distinguished Intelligence Cross. They were mustered for an important operation. The former SEAL Team Commander thanked them for their service; he thanked them for coming out to help, and then McGee shouted, "Fight's on!" With a cutting motion of his arm he separated the men and women into two groups and told them to follow the directions of the two very old white-haired men whose names may or may not have been "Bob." When you're in the CIA, you never really know.

Hunter watched the spectacle with crossed arms. He was fully suited up with the nanotechnology flight suit, silent-soled steel toed flight boots, and lightweight spider web body armor. A Kimber Model 1911 ACP with a silencer was slung under his arm. Max the Malinois sat next to him, waiting for the direction to "Go." But there was no room for the canine, so Hunter told Max to "Stay." Hunter advanced to the cockpit of the YO-3A closest to the rear ramp. The aft seat had been removed and filled with the things Director McGee thought were necessary for the mission, such as a suitcase nuclear bomb.

Bob Jones said he would move and assemble the first aircraft. He had already removed chocks and tie down chains and hooked up the battery. He watched Hunter scurry onto the partial stub of a wing, raise the canopy, and take the front seat. Like a football coach, Bob cautioned the men and women to "not to look at the black coating because when you do you'll get dizzy. Listen to the directions, feel the airplane with your fingers—just do not look at it." Bob broke out into a full smile and then said, "You drop a wing and I will personally beat the hide off of your young ass—do you hear me?"

The intelligence officers grinned back at the old codger like they were Marine recruits at Boot Camp as they shouted in unison, "Sir, yes, sir!" The warning was legitimate as the nanotechnology would mess with the uninitiated mind and could scramble their equilibrium. When moving a wing the last thing needed was to drop it. Bob assigned two men to fill gas cans then directed the other men and women to push the airplane out of the cargo jet. "Gas can guys pump; I just need the rest of you to push." Hunter watched for unmatched effort. He maintained directional control with differential braking until the *Yo-Yo* was off the jet's rear ramp. Bob exhorted them to push the airplane about a hundred feet past the C-17's tail.

Bob Smith's group lifted and removed the YO-3A's thirty-nine-foot wings from their transportation cradles. A Marine was pumping gas. Two gas cans had been filled; two more were in line to be filled. The intel officers manhandled the wings and wordlessly stepped slowly through the cabin, then gingerly down the ramp. Bob Smith directed his group like a high school band director; the left wing was under the direction of the other Bob. Once the groups arrived at the difficult to see YO-3A fuselage, the Bobs directed, "Don't look at anything but me." One Bob gave simple commands—left, right, a little up, a little down, and "slow down…we're not in a race" until he told those with the "fuselage ends" of the wing to stop while those with the "wingtip ends" to "keep walking, keep walking, keep walking. I will tell you when to stop." The people holding the wings were told to stop, then as directed they carefully flipped the wings 90° and waited for Bob to guide the tangs of the wing spars into the clevises in the aircraft. In less than sixty seconds wing tangs were inserted into the fuselage clevises, the Bobs had hammered the pins home, and inserted the safety keys. The old men were pleased that they had hung the wings in record time.

Two men brought gas cans. Bob and Bob showed the gas can holders how to fill the wing's fuel tanks. When Bob Jones said, "There should be two more" another pair of men with "high and tight" haircuts emerged with the heavy gas containers. As fuel was dispensed into the wings, the groups coalesced around the old men to see what came next. Wrinkled experienced hands connected the QDs (quick-disconnects) for electrical wiring and fuel lines, and the flight control cables. With the wing tanks full and gas caps on, the intel officers helped the Bobs tape down the fuel panel and the edges of the fairings where the wings joined the fuselage.

Hunter waited until the wings were being taped before he turned the MASTER POWER switch on. The cockpit came alive with lights which totally fascinated the intel officers who wondered if Air Branch was back in the business of secret black airplanes that no one was supposed to know. They were interrupted by the taskmaster, Bob Jones, "Ladies and gents, *that* was fantastic. If this intel thing doesn't work out for you, I can find you a job in a NASCAR pit crew! But we have one more to do! *Back inside!*"

With electrical power on the aircraft, Hunter started the engine and programmed the mission computer from one of the YO-3A's multi-function panels. He checked that the aircraft's AI computer and his smartphone were synchronized. McGee and several intelligence officers approached the running aircraft from the rear carrying nylon bags, one the size of a human torso. The rear cockpit was already loaded to the gunnels.

Once Hunter was satisfied that the programs needed to run the unmanned operation were working, he ran through a flight control check to verify there were no obstructions and that the linkages had been hooked up correctly. Then he climbed out of the front seat, and McGee carefully handed him bags, the biggest ones first. Hunter loaded the front cockpit and secured the bags into the seat with lap and shoulder belts. Once Hunter ensured nothing would come loose or interfere with the control stick or throttle, he lowered and locked the canopy, and climbed off the YO-3A. He wondered, *How were we ever going to find room for a Malinois in there?*

The engine of the unmanned YO-3A idled, and much to the amazement of the Agency intel officers, the motor's exhaust was virtually silent.

After the other *Yo-Yo* was pushed out of the C-17 and assembled, loaded, and started the CIA Director and the pilot climbed in. From his BlackBerry Hunter gave the first YO-3A the command to execute the automatic takeoff and landing system. He lowered the ANVIS-9 Aviator's Night Vision Imaging System on his helmet and monitored the progress of the unmanned aircraft as it raced down the runway of Ashgabat's international airport.

Once airborne and on a heading to the institute, McGee said, "I knew we could do it."

Hunter said, "Getting your guys out of the rack for something they will never forget was a nice touch. They saved our bacon. You knew where to get good help. And good help is so hard to find these days." Hunter trimmed the YO-3A and set the throttle to follow the other *Yo-Yo* at a safe distance.

McGee passed the latest intelligence. "Ali and his turds are about two hours ahead of us. That's ground time. There's eight of them in a cavalcade of bread trucks. The Chief of Station said the road to the port of entry is a new freeway, so they won't have any issues getting to Iran. He said he blew his budget on getting the airport to allow our C-17 to park on the taxiway until we were off, and Turkmen customs officials delayed the al-Qaeda group until the Chief of Station gave the signal when we were a couple of hours out."

"So you purposely let Ali and his band of merry al-Qaeda into the country?"

McGee ignored the interrogatory for the moment. He looked out of the canopy's transparency, out over the expanse of nothingness. He didn't even see a nomad or his campfire. *Did I want them to go ahead? Was I moving lethal chess pieces? Yes.* He said into the microphone, "We have good weather."

When McGee avoided the question Hunter knew better than to press. *McGee will tell me in his own time.* "We do. The forecast is for good weather for a few days."

"I didn't think it was productive to kill them in Turkmenistan. Delaying them was innocuous. I look at it as shaping the battlefield. They could've suspected something was afoot, broke cover, and disappeared in the city. This way, they're in front of us, and we can manage them. They may even prove to be useful."

"Like securing the compound?"

"10-4. They don't know we're coming. I don't care if they do the dirty work. Let them be the Pitbull turned loose on a poodle. One less thing for us to worry about. I want to contain whatever virus they intend to use, and if we can find him, extract our defector. If we can get their records...."

Hunter questioned his friend but not aloud. *I don't think acquiring the Institute's records is in the realm of feasibility. There's no time for downloading information, and we're not carrying servers back. This is a Yo-Yo, not a Hercules. There might be a way for that, but I just don't see a path forward for that now.* Soon he was back to being a pilot. Hunter exhaled and was suddenly huffy, "There's another damned thing a robot airplane can't do."

Everything is going along so well. What's he talking about? McGee spoke into the microphone, "What's that?"

"It can't hurry."

CHAPTER 65

May 28, 2018

Demetrius Eastwood was floored to hear a FedEx envelope had arrived for him in the downtown network mail room. The woman in charge of Eastwood's fan mail wasn't impressed. "Colonel Eastwood, you said to call you when we get packages."

"I did. Thank you, Scarlett. So you received one. Did you open it?"

"I did. It contained a document and a stunner. There is a single sheet of corporate letterhead paper from The Corporate Council on Colombia, Office of the Chairman and Chief Executive Officer, inviting you to dinner."

Radar contact! That was fast. No such company. "And the other?"

"We think it's a transmitter. We have seen nothing like it before—you know we run all your mail through the X-ray machine, and the electronics showed up clearly. If you weren't paying attention to its weight and balance, you would never know that there was a hidden layer in that envelope. Between layers, it looks like the flattest cellphone known to man is connected to a circuit board which is connected to some metallic thing you might find in the bottom of a disposable microwave dinner tray. We knew we had to call; we think it might be from the CIA, or something."

And now they may have my cellphone number! From the bleachers of the Colosseum to the lion's den. He didn't panic and said, "I take it you ran it through the anthrax detector?"

"We did—but it was the X-ray tech who stopped it. We have seen nothing like it. What's it mean, Colonel Eastwood?"

"It means it goes into the incinerator. That it's a fake. *Look up Stingray cellphone tracker.* I think it's a device to get my cell number, and with you and me talking this minute, they might have it now. Not your fault. Not your fault at all so don't worry about it. Not all is lost.

I'll contact you from another number. But be aware that there may be more attempts to find me. Thank you so much. Please know that you may have saved my life."

Eastwood terminated the connection and dismantled his cellphone. He leaned back in his office chair and scanned his surroundings through the windows at 7 World Trade Center and pondered what his next move might be. He was like an automaton. He went through the motions of disabling his cellphone without really knowing why he would do such a thing, but he knew it was the right thing to do. After freeing the device from the rubber protective case, Eastwood pulled the cover from the back of his cellphone and removed the sim card and the battery. *I wish I had other phones. The possibilities were few. Worst case, they may have just pinpointed my location. It's time to go.* He grabbed his wallet, the truck keys, and his go-bag. He stuffed a Kimber Model 1911 ACP with laser sights into his pants. A laptop went into an expensive thick leather briefcase that the manufacturing company had advertised, *They'll fight over it when you're dead.* Eastwood didn't want to give anyone the chance.

He raced out of the office with his hands full and headed for the stairs. Passing through the fifteenth floor, he stopped for a second to toss his phone's entrails into a trash receptacle. He made it to the basement where the Hummer was parked between two electric cars. As he tossed his things in the front seat he hoped the thing would start. He instantly regretted not having used it for several weeks. Within a millisecond of stepping inside and sliding behind the steering wheel, Eastwood retraced his steps, stepped outside, cautiously looked around the parking area, dropped on all fours, then flipped onto his back to check the underside of the Hummer.

He nearly wet himself when his eyes fell on something incongruous, a thick square sheet of what looked to be undercoating material directly beneath the driver's seat. His eyes wandered quickly over the underside of the truck. It was rebuilt in Texas, and in Texas they rarely undercoat their vehicles because the roads are never salted. If he had checked the underside before and familiarized himself with the truck's capabilities he would have known. But he didn't know. Now he had a dilemma. Eastwood stared at the odd rubber coating and scooted further under the truck. Then he saw a thin line of the dull black material pressed into the right-angle junction of the frame and the ballistics metal floor of the undercarriage. Two wires emerged from the rubber material and were inserted into a steel protected wire bundle which ran from the engine compartment to the rear of the vehicle. *Wires! Wires! Wires! They hid the goddamn wires! It might be real or it might be a decoy. Back up! Back up! Back up and get out of here!*

Eastwood was more furious than afraid. He wanted to rip the wires from the truck, but an inner voice from Marine training long past told him he could not. *I recognized the danger; that something was out of place. A roadblock where there shouldn't be a roadblock. I yelled at the driver to 'Back up! Back up! Back up and get out of here!' I don't want to be captured. But being captured was part of the training. I got that T-shirt; I don't need another.* He withdrew the pistol from his pants, flipped over onto his belly, and looked for movement underneath the other vehicles. *I have to assume I've been discovered! Shit, shit, shit!* An inner voice told him to move. *Get out of the garage and the building! Don't do what's expected; do what's unexpected!* He jumped up from his position, recovered his go-bag and briefcase, and raced back to the service elevator and stairs. He mashed the fire alarm inside, called for the elevator, and then disappeared back into the stairwell.

Eastwood ran out of 7 World Trade Center and down Greenwich Street to the Oculus of the World Trade Center Transportation Hub. He hoped no one would follow him. He raced down the escalators to the bottom of the basement levels and took the first available train, track four of the RED LINE, toward Newark. The subway doors were closing as he dashed inside the subway car; he spun around to see if anyone followed him. Eastwood plastered his face to the subway car window to observe any latecomers. His lungs were heaving, and his heart was pumping out of his chest. But there was no one. He dropped his bags in a seat that didn't require a copy of the *Times* for protection. Dory Eastwood celebrated with a fist pump; no one had followed him.

In order to escape from New York City he had to survive; *survive* was the first part of fifty-year-old SERE training. For a few seconds he couldn't remember what the acronym stood for, but then he did: Survival, Evasion, Resistance, and Escape. When he sat down he looked over the other people on the subway car. No one seemed to notice; no one seemed to care. People jumped into departing subway cars all the time; some make it and some don't.

Eastwood ran his hands through a white crew cut. *I need a hat or a hoodie. Hell, I need all sorts of things. I know where to go, and thankfully, I'm going in the right direction.*

• • •

Thirty minutes in the New York City subway system changing cars and directions was enough for a lifetime when you are running from people who want to kill you. Demetrius Eastwood spilled out of the MSG (Madison Square Garden) subway station and found what he was looking for; a mob taxi. Not an Uber, not a Lyft. A taxi service "off the books." One that kept no records. Cash and carry. Eastwood got in the back seat, thrust a folded $100 bill over the front seat, and told the big burly man to drive. "There's another one of these if you can help me out."

The man snatched the Franklin and didn't even look in his rearview. As he pulled away from the curb, the 400-pound monster grunted, *"Whaddya need?"*

Eastwood told him.

The man garbled, "That'll cost ya' extra."

Eastwood felt safe enough to check his finances. $800 in big bills in his wallet and another couple of thousand in his briefcase. Credit cards and an ATM card. "I need a phone. A couple of disposables." He quietly slipped the Kimber out of his trousers and slid it inside an outer pocket of the briefcase. He didn't think the driver would rob him but he wasn't averse to jamming the pistol into the man's ear if he deduced he was being taken for a ride. He rolled the dice and asked, "Excuse me, sir. Do you know who I am?"

The driver finally looked in the rear-view mirror. It took a few seconds before he recognized *Colonel* Eastwood. The driver's haughty demeanor transformed instantly to helpful. He asked, "Colonel, I listen to your radio show all the time! Are you in a pickle, sir? I have people. I can help."

No time for explanations. "I need a phone."

"I can get you an iPhone for a C-note. Unlisted number."

"Let's do that for starters. Thank you. What's your name?"

"When I was on active duty, my friends called me, Bubba."

Of course they did. He handed two hundred-dollar bills over the seat, like before. "Bubba, nice to meet you. I need to get out of town. Can we do that; can you take me out of town after you get a couple of phones?"

"I'm on it Colonel. I used to be in the Marine Corps, sir, but they let me go. I had a few problems with my weight." Bubba laughed as he slapped a fat belly. He picked up his cellphone and was soon engaged in conversation.

"You know I got booted out too."

"You got screwed, sir."

"Shit happens."

"I'll have ya' a couple of phones near Harlem. Have ya' eaten anything, sir?"

"I'll buy pizza if you know where a good shop is."

"I know where the best New York-style pizza is. That's a deal, sir." Bubba and Eastwood exchanged glances in the rearview. "I want to tell my brothers that I had Colonel Eastwood in my car—but those assholes would never believe it."

"Bubba, I would like this to be our little secret. Maybe next time."

"*Our secret, sir!* I'll give you my number if you need me for other work, sir. I will stop what I'm doing to help you anytime, sir."

"That will be great. Thanks Bubba."

• • •

After pizza and phones, and a nice pleasant ride into New Jersey, Eastwood paid for a first class ticket on the next Acela to Union Station in Washington, D.C. He didn't have to wait long before he was flying down the rails in AMTRAK's high speed express.

The network chartered a limo for their star reporter and deposited him at the Army Navy Club where he got a room. Eastwood didn't know if he had escaped another assassination attempt. He didn't know, but he was fairly certain he hadn't been followed. He was so worked up that he could not fall asleep quickly.

But sleep eventually did come. It did not announce its presence, and he did not sleep like a baby. Eastwood dreamed of a murderous giant with different colored eyes; the guttural scream of someone trying to flee their executioner startled him to consciousness. He realized he was drenched in sweat.

Chapter 66

May 29, 2018

"This might be easier than I expected. But you never know—first contact and all."

Didn't Clausewitz say no battle plan survives first contact with the enemy? Old Carl didn't have a Yo-Yo. Duncan Hunter had set up the YO-3As to orbit the Khomeini Institute. He and McGee monitored the thermal images of the delivery men interacting with the Islamic Revolutionary Guard Corps on the ground. The FLIR scopes in the two cockpits were set for maximum gain. McGee provided a running commentary. Hunter was mesmerized with the activities on the ground; it was like an old black and white movie but with competing hoodlums. *It would be easier just shooting them, but Bill has a plan.*

The FLIR systems had improved significantly from almost sixteen years ago when McGee was a SEAL. The old hand-held devices were useful for detecting heat sources against a cold mountain, but little else. McGee wasn't used to such detailed wide-area motion imagery. Hunter had hundreds of hours using the specially configured million-dollar Star Safire system. The thermal imagers provided high-definition imagery that could be used with facial recognition systems.

McGee said, "They're inside the wire, and they are leaving the gate open. Evidently the guards believe they are who they say they are, and they will leave soon; they are even too lazy to close the gate." McGee asked Hunter to enhance the sensor on the leader. "That is Ali al-Qasimi. This imagery is almost better than our photographs. You can make out individual hairs. Astonishing granularity."

Over the interphone, Hunter said, "I usually find the guys with weapons in places where you wouldn't expect to find people, on mountain tops, in drug labs, guarding hostages. I've never witnessed an ambush. This is very interesting." Hunter told McGee he was lowering the *Weedbusters* laser system into the airstream.

"Roger. It's going to get more interesting here in a few minutes. I don't want to interrupt the enemy at work. I would like to let them eliminate the Guard Corps—that leaves just eight of them for us to deal with. We are not dealing with smart people here."

"And they are not wearing any eye protection."

"Why would they?" McGee was focused on the FLIR screen. "And you'll disable them with *Weedbusters*."

"I can get them to look up."

"They are making believe they are making deliveries. That they'll be quick—in and out. No need to close the gate. This is the point when their disguise should fail them. They'll stop work. Guns will come out. It should be soon. Very soon. We are set up very well to take control of this when the opportunity presents itself."

Hunter used the FLIR to make a 360° sweep of the surrounding area to ensure when they engaged the enemy, there would be no reinforcements for some time, if ever. McGee said the crystal-clear imagery the FLIR provided would make the business development and marketing people justifiably proud.

The institute buildings were darkened. Illumination came from dozens of LED sidewalk lamps spread throughout the research facility. The loading dock of the mess complex was also partially illuminated, more by a surfeit of the interior lighting than by external recessed floodlights. The intel brief suggested that deliveries were usually made during daylight hours, and the dining facility was a hubbub of clean-up activity when three trucks arrived. Two men with hand-trucks transported cartons of food out of the back of the trucks and inside the dining facility.

McGee said, "They're going to get tired of their charade pretty quick. The guards aren't paying much attention—which was the whole point of the charade. Now they'll want to get the show on the road."

"If those trucks are loaded…full, then they've moved maybe a third of their load."

"Yeah, they just want to get it over. If someone was paying attention inside, they might become suspicious." Inside of a minute, the two men returned with empty two-wheelers, ostensibly to load more supplies from their trucks.

Hunter listened to the master of special operations at work, managing the battlefield. Everything that Ali and his men were doing and would soon do was something that SEALs had seen and trained for countless times. Monitor the battlespace and know when to attack. This time the eye in the sky wasn't a camera on a drone, but the eyes of the master SEAL himself. Here among the combatants McGee was in his element.

After a few minutes of ground activity McGee said, "Here they go." The man identified as Ali al-Qasimi and another man approached the bunker identified on the overheads as the IRGC dormitory and the command and control center for compound security and internal and external telecommunications. One of Ali's men approached the guard tower, and another walked toward the entrance checkpoint with what looked like a pastry box. McGee said, "You may have to shoot those two who went inside. This could get ugly quick. Pistols in pastry boxes. Ali has crossed the forward edge of the battle area."

With a flick of a switch, Hunter lowered the aircraft's TS2 gun and checked that the system was locked in place and ready to fire. He said, "Roger. Just give me the word."

"I want to blind them all if we can get them all together. They are undermanned, and after the security has been neutralized, I expect them to coalesce for the next stage of mass killing. I expect the staff will soon pour from their bunkers. That will be the time to hit Ali's men."

Hunter breathed into the microphone, "Roger."

McGee asked, "How do you get them to look up?"

"I run the motor to takeoff power then idle. It sends a soundwave that is unmistakable; incongruous. They'll all look up; they always do. If we were at a much lower altitude the laser would act as a cutting tool and shred their eyeballs. White pain is the last thing they'll ever see."

"That's nasty."

"War is hell."

McGee said, "They are carrying silenced pistols. I don't know why they haven't broken out the AKs…."

Hunter said, "*There you go*! I think someone just pulled a fire alarm. People are pouring out of the buildings."

"Showtime." McGee was transfixed with the FLIR imagery. The aircraft was stable, no bouncing around in competing thermals. Hunter was glad the winds in the foothills were negligible.

The men at the gate and the guard tower were quickly taken out; the deliverymen's ruse had taken them by surprise. In the FLIR, McGee and Hunter witnessed each al-Sham assassin shoot their assigned Iranian guard. The thermal imagery traced two white-hot bullets into each terrified face. After the Iranian men in the guard tower were disposed of the al-Sham men raced back into the cafeteria complex.

• • •

The first to die would be the Iranian Shi'a. As the men and women emerged from their dormitory bunker; al-Sham men directed them toward the perimeter fence. The Iranians were herded to the fence; some were screaming and kicking, knowing they were going to face the *paredón* to be shot.

McGee suggested the last to die would be the Chinese. They would be murdered within seconds. McGee found it incredible that they were as docile as a flock of sheep bedding down for the night.

• • •

When two men emerged from the Islamic Revolutionary Guard Corps building, Hunter zoomed in on the lead man. McGee said, "Ali al-Qasimi. That is the sign they neutralized the guard. That's good for us. Now we don't have the Iranian Guard to contend with. If our luck can hold out just a little longer…."

"I have number two in a holding pattern about 500 feet above the airstrip," said Hunter.

McGee almost whispered, "Old Ali is making it easy for us. He is totally predictable at this point. Now he has to get the access cards in an orderly fashion. You don't want to take lanyards off dead people. That takes forever, and they don't have forever."

• • •

Ali al-Qasimi ran to where the compound's personnel were corralled. He told his men to, "Throw them up against the fence!" Many of the condemned froze in terror when they saw their executioners arrayed before them; others turned around to not face the murderous butchers. Some tried to scale the fence to escape, but others pulled them back.

• • •

"They're seconds away from going *Allahu Akbar* and whacking the rest of the compound, but they can't do it with handguns, and they have yet to relieve them of their key cards." McGee was astounded that there were over a hundred people outside. Maybe a hundred and fifty. He said, "Where's the AKs? Standby on *Weedbusters*."

• • •

The remaining men dashed from the mess, onto their trucks and emerged with AKs. One tossed an AK-47 to the al-Sham leader. Ali al-Qasimi racked the charging handle and motioned for the masses to line up along the edge of the fence. Two unknown men with weapons walked the length of the string of humans and removed the lanyards and access cards from each of the terrified men and women. They separated the access cards by color as they moved through the masses.

• • •

McGee said, "They managed them with pistols! That is incredible." A few hundred feet below the YO-3A the mass of people were crushed against the chain-link fence. McGee said, "They're trying to bunch up they don't want to see their executioners. And they don't want to give their killers an easy shot. Ali was brilliant: getting them out of their beds—they are in no position to organize and mount a counterattack. It's like they don't even care."

For the moment, there was protection in numbers but no one was willing to rush a man with a weapon with a 65-round magazine.

• • •

A few men again tried to scale the fence. Ali al-Qasimi was in a near trance. If he had more time, he would have beheaded them instead of shooting them. His men were not moving fast enough. He shouted commands for the institute's personnel to remove the electronic access cards from their bodies; Chinese personnel surrendered their access cards when their Iranian counterparts surrendered theirs. Armed al-Sham men ran down the line and took all the access cards. When they had them all, they raised their weapons and rushed to join Ali al-Qasimi.

• • •

McGee watched the thermal imagery as armed terrorists held people at bay while two terrorists confiscates lanyards. They raised their AK-47s to signal that they had the access cards for all the compound's rooms, offices, and laboratories. McGee counted eight al-Sham holding their positions and waiting for the signal to fire.

McGee barked, "*Throttle!*"

Hunter cross-controlled the flight controls and jammed the throttle to the *Yo-Yo's* firewall for a full second at takeoff power. The aircraft dropped out of the sky and supersonic shockwaves ripped off the propeller tips and propagated to the ground.

• • •

The institute personnel knew what was coming and were horrified the interlopers had what they came for. They turned and hung their heads; death was imminent.

Ali al-Qasimi filled his lungs to shout the preparatory command for the firing squad to kill the assembled scientists and support people….

Just as the al-Sham men racked the charging handles of their AK-47 assault weapons, they heard a *roar* immediately behind them, and jumped. They instinctively spun around to face the unexpected threat and looked across the compound and then up with eyes wide, searching the sky for the threat they could not see.

• • •

Maverick centered the flight controls and leveled off at the targeted altitude. The al-Sham men were all in the laser's field of view. He mashed the *Weedbusters* fire control button activating the ultraviolet laser. The effect was instantaneous. The heads of the al-Sham men recoiled as if they had been shot in the face with a pistol. All the men threw their hands up to their damaged eyes. FLIR imagery detailed the men's excruciating pain of having their eyeballs destroyed by the ultraviolet laser at a very low altitude. *Weedbusters* was no longer an irradiation weapon but a cutting tool with an edge finer than a scalpel.

Bullfrog was shocked at what he saw; the results of an instantaneous incapacitating weapon. He found his voice and commanded, "Now shoot them. Ali first."

Hunter put a laser-guided bullet through the sternum of the eight blinded men. Ali al-Qasimi was the first to experience the Terminator round exploding out of his chest.

The sound of the heavy spent-uranium rounds startled the people along the fence. They screamed in terror. There was sufficient lighting to see that the al-Sham men were on their knees and keening in agony. Every few seconds they heard a curious sound as if a melon had been dropped from a great height onto concrete. One by one the terrorists dropped to the ground and were silent. Blood and body debris were thrown great distances landing on some of the institute's personnel.

There were shouts and pushing as the Iranians and Chinese workers ran for their lives...out through the compound gate and into the darkness.

• • •

Less than a minute later, the eight al-Sham men all had stopped moving. McGee sat back against his parachute and said, "*Allahu Akbar, assholes.* Ali and his minions will not become infected and get on airliners, and they will not have a chance to infect world leaders. We will soon have all the access cards. How easy was that? I think God *is* great."

Hunter slewed the FLIR in the direction of over a hundred thermal images stumbling down the road to safety. He said, "I'll bet they know the area is surrounded by minefields, and that is the reason they are staying on the hardpan." Hunter fired the remaining two rounds in the gun's magazine behind the group to encourage them to move faster, to distance themselves from the horror at the institute as quickly as possible. Hunter zoomed in altitude and scanned the area again for reinforcements. He said, "The only images are of those in the group moving out. And there is no one else within about forty miles, which means we have about forty minutes if no one got off an alarm."

McGee said, "Uh, huh. No thermals in the compound. Duncan, that's what you call 'shaping the battlefield.' Now I think we can land."

• • •

They unloaded the unmanned aircraft first. McGee said it was, "...better to get everything out of the unmanned *Yo-Yo* just in case a *Firestarter* went off and set the whole damned airplane on fire."

Hunter said, "Are you saying they're more fragile than a loose Tesla battery pack on a gravel road?"

"We won't know until we use them." McGee loaded the suitcase nuke atop one of the two robotic mules. He had explained the bio-threat detection capabilities of the two mules on the C-17 a few hours before landing. The mules had helmets with automated bio-detection sensors that monitored the air and set off alarms if a bio-threat is present. They're designed to collect and detect aerosolized agents for all four classes of biological threats, spore, viral, cellular, and protein toxins. On the sides of the mule's helmets were UV-C LEDs.

As the men unloaded the two aircraft, Hunter recalled McGee's capabilities brief. "The mules are from your company, Texas Robotics. I'll blame you if anything goes wrong with them. And, yes, those are your UV-C LEDs in their helmets. We will rely on them to kill bacteria, viruses, and other bugs."

From a bag, McGee removed a black paddle-like wand that looked suspiciously like the metal-detecting hand wand the TSA used to check people who set off the magnetometer when going through an airport's security checkpoint. On one side it was covered with dozens of LEDs.

Hunter said, "That I recognize."

"You should. It's for disinfecting us when it's time to leave. Oh, and we have to pull the coverings from the mule's legs and exposed pieces. Like this." McGee removed the blue film from the exposed parts of the mules' legs and torsos, the neck and the control head. The mules' parts were coated with the same light-killing nanotechnology covering as Hunter's airplane. McGee said the mules responded to hand gestures and were programed to stay close by.

After the two aircraft were unloaded and the contents distributed across the saddlebags of two mechanical mules, McGee said, "Let's do this. I'll tackle the bugs; you find our guys. Be careful. We don't know if Ali missed anyone."

Holding their helmets between their legs, Hunter and McGee attached the self-contained breathing apparatus that special operations forces used during High-Altitude Low-Opening parachute jumps onto the modified night vision goggles helmet. After donning his helmet, Hunter could hear himself breathe in his earphones and it calmed him.

All the additional weight on his head, although counterbalanced, made him conscious of not making any quick movements with his head. No nodding. For a moment, he felt like a helpless baby bird that had fallen from its nest. Although the al-Sham men were dead, it would take some time before he was comfortable being on the ground in an offensive role. The adrenaline spikes that had made his skin tingle had disappeared. With a big exhalation Hunter focused on the moment and the mission. The four-tube NVGs were providing clear color images, and the O2 bottle was providing a stream of ABO. He steadied his nerves and said, "Radio check."

The supremely confident McGee said, "Lima Charlie." He reached down to the robot's heads and activated the UV-C LEDs and the bio-threat detectors. Then he activated the robotic mules and quickly checked their functions.

Hunter and McGee slung Heckler & Koch SP5K-PDWs with 30-round magazines and laser sights over their shoulders. Hunter's gloved hand checked the security of a Bowie knife strapped to his calf.

Out of the darkness walked two blacker-than-black robotic mules laden with overstuffed saddlebags and two blacker-than-black uniformed men, one extra-large, one average sized, both with backpacks, gloves, and self-contained helmets. The four-tube, panoramic night vision goggles with multi-mode experimental thermal and color imagery were the only ones in existence. A forearm pad controlled the different radio functions of the helmet, GPS tracking, thermal, synthetic, and night vision equipment. Hunter filled his lungs with the ABO. Pure oxygen had a way of clearing one's head and when faced with the reality that the security forces had been neutralized, his confidence increased.

They scanned their environment with the tiny FLIRs in their goggles, looking for any hostile thermal imagery. Finding none, McGee switched back to colored images from the NVGs. Hunter found the movements of the overloaded mules and their footsteps to be more precise than a Lipizzaner Stallion. Gyroscopes and sensors fed an internal computer to ensure the mules would not topple over in the event of a misstep or a collision. Their robotic steps were mechanically choppy, but their foot-placement was exact. And the robots were silent. Hunter loved that.

Hunter walked straight toward the dead al-Sham men and the pile of access cards. *That's why McGee got the colorized thermal goggles. The man is so smart.*

On the jet, McGee gave Hunter "the gouge" on the color scheme of the access cards. Months earlier the in-place defector had provided the key—solid green cards provided the owners unfettered access to the laboratories. Black cards allowed access into the security and command and control bunkers. Red cards were for Chinese scientists; they could access their dormitory, the cafeteria, and the laboratory they were assigned. Striped green and red cards for Iranian researchers. McGee explained the special access of holders of blue and gold cards for computer access and the administrative offices. Hunter and McGee separated the cards for their specific needs.

Then the men separated with a thumbs up.

McGee went toward the below-ground laboratory bunker, and the mules with their funky clunky steps followed him into the research laboratory deep in the mountain's interior.

With a silenced HK and the laser sight leading the way, Hunter walked cautiously into the IRGC bunker and stepped over or around bodies. He saw that the guard's weapons were still in their racks, signaling their deaths had been a complete and total ambush. Every man on the floor had dark bullet holes in their shirts and seemed dead. *This is how the Sunni gets along with the Shia.* Hunter wasted no time putting the HK's laser pointer on each guard's head and pulling the trigger. Each bullet created a neat round hole and ensured that no one had been playing dead. He raced through the building finding bodies of Islamic Revolutionary Guards in their beds, on the toilet, in the halls. Hunter was impressed that Ali al-Qasimi had been so effective in overpowering the security regiment and neutralizing them.

Hunter returned downstairs to see if Ali had destroyed the command switchboard for the compound; he had not. But the labels for the controls and switch positions were in a combination of Farsi and international symbology. Hunter threw all the switches forward to the international sign for OFF, then turned to a control panel with the international symbol for EMERGENCY GENERATOR. In less than a minute, some electrical power had been returned to the compound, but not to the position lights atop the water tower. He transmitted to McGee, "And, then there was light."

McGee acknowledged; he was now in a lighted tunnel, and as expected the doors were electrically controlled. Every door opened with a green color-coded card. He opened the door to the lab but he didn't bother turning on the lights. The NVGs and the IR flashlight allowed him to see, but he stood in shock. What he saw was beyond his comprehension. The intelligence had provided a certain level of granularity and confidence, but it was woefully inadequate.

Before heading toward the holding cells, Hunter stopped at the emergency generators dock. He wrapped chem-cord around the feed lines from the emergency generator's 10,000 gallon fuel tank and set a timer on a *Firestarter*.

Hunter bounded toward the bunker where he and McGee believed the hostages were being held. Dozens of different-colored access cards spun around on lengthy lanyards. He first tried a black access card, and the door opened. In a room the size of a Motel 6 suite, Hunter found four nude emaciated women; they were awake, terrified, and shackled to individual beds. *Could be holding cells or an Iranian rape room. The guards had their way with them. No doubt, no longer.* Softly Hunter asked if they spoke English, and they nodded vigorously. They knew immediately that help had arrived. The emotional strain was so intense that they began crying. Without hesitation or additional words, Hunter removed the Bowie from his calf and cut the restraints, freeing the women. When the first one was free, he gripped her hand to show he was there to help, not hurt. From a lower flight suit pocket, he removed a red laser pen and handed it to her. He showed her how to use it and cautioned her to only shine the laser on the floor. Hunter cut the other women free. He gripped their hands once in the dark to assure them. He whispered again, his deep voice sounding like a growl through the facemask. "Hold hands and follow me slowly, be as quiet as you can. Stick as close to me as tattoo marks. I will not leave you."

Hunter's HK and its red laser sight led the way as he moved to the next room, and the next. Each time he checked the hall with the thermal sensor in his helmet-mounted night vision device before proceeding. Midway down the hallway, Hunter found a linen closet. The women held hands like a daisy chain and couldn't see that he had pulled a bedsheet off a shelf. He handed it to the closest woman. He whispered into her ear for her to stay there and "use the sheets" while he checked the remaining rooms. Hunter freed more women. The final door he entered wasn't a holding cell for women, but he recognized it for what it was. He had been a prisoner once before. In a stock. He recognized the accoutrements of a dungeon, the furnishings and tools designed to inflict pain. *The final level of Purgatory is an Iranian rape room.* Hunter removed a *Firestarter* from his backpack, set the timer, and withdrew.

When he finished his search, he led the barefoot women, now wrapped in sheets, out of the concrete structure. Once outside, Hunter stopped and the women gathered around him on the concrete walkway. "You'll need clothes and shoes to get out of here." He handed them a handful of access cards and said, "These should open the rooms in the dorms." Even through his mask, Hunter's deep dark voice was soothing and confident, and they crowded him. He explained, "The people who ran the facility have left, and there should be plenty of clothes to choose from in the dormitory bunkers. I'm certain there is power on in the dorms. We have about ten-twelve minutes. Then we are leaving."

CHAPTER 67

May 29, 2018

Women wrapped in bedsheets ran or hobbled to the dorms as if their lives depended on it, and Hunter transmitted to McGee, "I have forty and we are ready to go in ten. No IPD." *No In-place defector.*

There was a hollowness to the radio transmission, likely an effect of the comm repeaters. Communications were extremely difficult and tricky in underground situations and maintaining contact among thick concrete walls, tons of dirt and rock, and heavy cave walls required the latest in tunnel warfare. As he made his way further underground to the main laboratories, McGee dropped small rubberized, shock-resistant Wi-Fi repeaters on the floor; they were also illuminated, helpful visible devices like high-tech breadcrumbs to show the way out of the underground and unfamiliar environment.

Hunter was thrown a curveball at McGee's defeatist tone and message. "Houston, we have a problem. What I see is, ah, it has *six* floors, not one. It's like I'm on the top floor of the Texas Gaylord. There are offices on every floor below me, and the bottom floor is the main lab. I thought I would take their magic bug for our scientists to study but there are literally thousands of samples. They don't have 300 hundred viruses under study; there's probably six..., maybe ten thousand. Maybe more. On six floors. I don't have time."

"10-4. But no bugs out and about?"

"No. The sniffers indicate the air is clean, and I guess the LEDs don't have any bugs to kill. I'm heading for their server room. I'll be back with you if this is also a bust." Two minutes passed before McGee transmitted, "I found the server room." McGee found the hard drives could be removed with a 90° turn of a fastener and took as many of them as he could extract from the stacks of servers. Once he was done, he would find a place to set the special weapon.

McGee took the mule with the nuclear device down a modern glass elevator to the lowest floor in the underground facility. There would be no communications here; the near line-of-sight Wi-Fi repeaters were out of sight. He unpacked the device and armed the special weapon by first installing the control head and then the battery pack. He set the timer for two hours, then he and the mule returned to the server room level.

Four minutes had passed since his last radio transmission. McGee finished stuffing the saddlebags of the robotic mules with the last of the computer hard drives, then he set about placing explosives and *Firestarters* on the floor. Hunter finally got through with a good connection, and they talked of exfiltrating the women. Hunter said, "Most of the girls cannot run the trucks across the border. Some of them are in bad shape, but they are all ambulatory. We're gonna need all three trucks. I think I should take them."

McGee didn't immediately dismiss the concept. "You can program the *Yo-Yos* to get back." His statement wasn't a question.

Hunter was convinced that McGee's portion of their activities—secure the hard drives and set the bomb—was accomplished. He didn't think it was good for McGee to be part of the rescue. There was no need for the CIA Director to further expose himself to capture, and Hunter told him so.

"I can do that, but Bullfrog, if something were to happen, we can't let you get caught in Iran. We will not violate the Eleventh Commandment."

McGee frowned in his mask. "Eleventh Commandment?"

"*Thou shall not let the boss get caught in Iran*. This isn't a suicide mission; you would never come out. You came for the bug; the bug is in the too-hard-to-find category, but you have their hard drives and big Mike is set. Therefore, that part of the mission is complete. They won't be able use the lab again, and they won't threaten anyone after we leave. You, sir, are done. Set the timers and let's get out of here."

McGee harrumphed to himself. Hunter could throw orders with the best of them. *Sometimes the ninety percent solution is close enough*. He asked, "We can be out of here in ten-twenty minutes?"

"10-4."

"Set as briefed."

"10-4." *Two hours for the big bang…twenty minutes for minor fireworks display I hope to miss.*

Hunter turned around to see clothed women pouring from buildings with a man running from them. But they weren't about to let him escape. They pushed and kicked him; they tripped and pummeled him creating a moving, hostile, murderous gauntlet.

In the ambient light of the lamps which outlined the walkways, the bloodied man made a break for the spaceman in black clothing and the odd-looking helmet from a sci-fi movie. The women sensed that he was going to kill their savior and benefactor, and moved like a swarm of bees to stop him. At Hunter's feet the man shouted out the emergency code word of the in-place defector. Hunter threw up his hands as if he was trying to stop a speeding locomotive. He shouted, "*Stop, stop, stop!* He's one of the good guys."

The nondescript man repeated the English code word again and again. "*Rosebud! Rosebud! Rosebud!*"

Hunter marveled, *Citizen Kane's ridiculous sled? Who thinks up these things?*

When *Rosebud* was no longer being attacked, he rolled over onto his back, his lungs heaving, and his face a bloody mess. He looked up at the man with the helmet; it was the strangest thing he had ever seen.

An accusatory voice from within the newly clothed mob said, "He was hiding in a clothes dryer."

A little Iranian dude with forty pissed off women beating him like a drum would be one for the books. Hunter asked, "Do you speak English?"

"Yes, yes, yes."

He lowered the HK's laser to fall on the man's forehead. From behind the night vision goggles and mask Hunter asked the man but the women heard, "Did this man abuse any of you?"

The strange helmet looked up as heads shook furiously. Hunter made eye contact with every woman for assurances. *Dude, you are sooo lucky.* The laser pointer on the HK was turned off. "Ok, let's not kill him. I understand he has been useful." As he leaned over the man to grab him by the stock and swivel the HK slid off Hunter's shoulder and the Red Bull can-sized silencer lodged under the Iranian's nose. Hunter didn't move the weapon but asked, "Can you drive a truck?" The man's eyes tried to focus on the silencer smashed into his nose, but he nodded to indicate that he could.

Without preamble, Hunter helped the man to his feet and turned to walk to where Ali al-Qasimi and his men had fallen. He picked up two of the AK-47s and said, "Ladies, we are getting out of here. We should get about a third of you into each truck. Is there a driver among you? Someone who can drive a stick? I'm certain these things have sticks." He shook the weapons and said, "And I need ladies who can operate these things if we need them."

One woman stepped forward and said, "I grew up on an Iowa farm. I can drive a stick and shoot a gun!" Several women found their voices and stepped forward to say they could drive a manual or had firearms training. Hunter took one AK-47, dropped the magazine to verify it was loaded with ammunition, slammed the magazine back into the weapon, and racked the charging handle to lock a round into the chamber. He showed one volunteer that the safety was off. He handed her the weapon and instructed her to keep an eye on the defector. "If he does anything funny, if he breathes too heavy just shoot him; got it? Keep about twenty feet away." She said, "*Yes, sir!*"

Hunter sent women to the command security bunker to get weapons. He transmitted to McGee, "How much longer?"

"I'm setting my last set of charges now. After activating the emergency disinfectant system, I'll be topside in five or six."

Hunter could hear his friend labored breathing. "10-4." He sloughed off his backpack, kneeled down, opened the top cover, and announced, "I need some help." Volunteers stepped forward with wide eyes and energy. "Gather around – this is what I need you to do." He withdrew *Firestarters* from his backpack and gave one to each of six women. He explained what he wanted, "Put one in the middle of each bunker, preferably near a wooden door. Here's how to turn them on." He set the timers on each one and handed them colored access cards. The women ran off in different directions. "Hurry, but know I'm not leaving without you."

Hunter began dragging the body of Ali al-Qasimi toward another fallen al-Sham man. Several women broke into little fire teams and dragged the other dead terrorists to Hunter's feet. Some women could do no more and sat down and put their faces in their hands. Hunter picked up each dead man and threw them in a pile like they were bales of hay. He removed Ali's watch, set the timer on a *Firestarter*, and shoved the device in the bullet hole of the dead man. Hunter had two *Firestarters* left and his neck was aching.

Duncan turned to one of the eldest of the women and asked, "I think I know the answer, but were there any men here, and if so, what happened to them?" Her whisper confirmed Hunter's suspicions. *They were separated from the women a long time ago.*

Rosebud coughed and said, "There is…a…*man*. American. In a cell. I think he is a criminal. First floor. You'll need a black card."

Hunter leaned over *Rosebud* and demanded to know where. Duncan's neck muscles were getting a workout from the heavy helmet. He told the women to, "Stay here." He ran back to the command and control center with a black access card wildly flipping around at the end of a lanyard. *I thought I checked every room. But I obviously missed one.*

McGee stopped to scrutinize a wall-mounted Organizational Chart that he had passed on his way in. It held photos, probably of administrators and scientists. He removed his smartphone and took a picture of the wall and another of the names and photographs of the facility's board of directors. McGee struck the glass over the top picture, shattering the glass. He pulled the head-shot photograph out of its frame, folded it, and slipped it into a lower pocket. He took off again and had just emerged from the main laboratory complex leading the robotic mules when a woman flew through the entrance door with an access card in one hand and a *Firestarter* in the other. He asked what she was doing.

She was surprised to find another man dressed like her benefactor. She said, "The other guy dressed like you told me to put this thing close to a door near the middle of the building." She held up a *Firestarter*. McGee wordlessly asked for it; she yielded it to the oversized man. McGee jammed the pointy-end of the *Firestarter* into the nearest door, flicked the switch, and said, "Let's get out of here." He held out his free hand, she took it, and they jogged out of the structure. The mules maintained their herky-jerk pace, the funky walk of overloaded drunken draft animals.

Hunter shouted into his radio, "I have to check the security building one more time." Three minutes later, he transmitted, "*Bullfrog*, bring a truck to the bunker. I have an American; he can't walk." A minute later, Hunter emerged with a thin disheveled man as McGee pulled a delivery truck close to the building. The men in black helped the man in rags into the back of the vehicle. Before closing the doors McGee asked, "Who are you?" The answer chilled him.

McGee and Hunter returned to the group of women and gave them a few directions. The women dutifully separated into groups of a dozen or more, climbed into the vehicles, and found a place to sit or hold on, although some remained outside and watched the two men in black approach the strangest shadow of an outline, the silhouette of an aircraft. At least that's what they thought they saw.

Hunter manhandled the tailwheels and positioned the two aircraft, one behind the other, so they would track straight down the airstrip. Once he was satisfied with the aircraft's positioning, he climbed up onto the wings and locked the tailwheels. As McGee loaded the airplanes Hunter fired off the engines, programmed the aircraft for the return trip, and then helped McGee into the rear seat of the number two aircraft. Using his BlackBerry, Hunter engaged the automatic takeoff and landing system for each *Yo-Yo*. A ten-second interval later, Bill McGee waved to Hunter as the aircraft's ATLS computer ran the throttle to takeoff power, released the brakes, and disappeared into the night.

Returning to the crowd of women with empty mules and carrying one of S&T's remote controlled "UV bombs on wheels," Hunter was grateful that he hadn't had to load the mules back onto the YO-3As, although their cargo of computer memories were in the cockpits. *The mules served their purpose, and I'll take them if there is room in the trucks. I don't want to leave any evidence. That'll be another couple hundred-grand the CFO won't give Bill crap about.*

He was afraid he was running out of time and didn't want to spend any more of it in the compound. He visited each truck and gave directions to the drivers and the women with weapons. He gave the hand gestures to command the robot mules to climb into the trucks and shut down. Hunter strained to keep his emotions under check and asked the women if they were ready. They were. He said, "We are out of here. Everyone else, keep your head down, don't look forward. And don't look at the mules. …the paint will play tricks on your eyes." In the safety of the food trucks, some of the women broke down and cried. For a few the tension was simply too intense, and they trembled uncontrollably.

As Hunter drove the first vehicle through the open chain-link gate, the first explosives McGee had set went off inside the Ayatollah Khomeini Institute of Virology. The *Firestarter* incendiary devices erupted seconds later. Hunter looked in the outside rearview mirror and saw the entrance of the institute's main laboratory burning. Ali and his men would soon be engulfed in their own pyre. *In two hours this place is going to be a smoking hole. I hope we can get far enough away first.*

• • •

It was a minor source of consternation that Hunter had seen no trace of the people who escaped from the institute on the road as the three delivery trucks drove toward the Iranian port of entry. The sally port of the Iranian checkpoint was lit up with fluorescent lamps. Vehicles were to stop at an orange cone barricade. As he approached the Iranian Border Control checkpoint, Hunter slowed the vehicle down, stopped, and explained to the people in his truck. "I need everyone to turn their faces away from the front of the truck and close your eyes tightly. If you can, put your head down and put a hand over your eyes. I don't want to blind anyone other than the guards. I'll tell you when it is safe to open your eyes. Now close them."

Hunter stepped from the truck with one of the S&T's remote controlled trucks, the "UV bomb on wheels," and placed it at his feet. He extracted his BlackBerry, touched two icons, and the wheeled device started moving. In his NVGs, Hunter steered the "UV bomb on wheels" toward the building. A tap of an icon on his screen sent the command to energize the laser; the laser beacon began flashing. He still hadn't activated the banks of UV-C LEDs. With a delicate finger on the touch screen he steered the remote control buggy through the three-barrier chicane and into the checkpoint a little faster than walking speed. A lone guard outside was suddenly aware and couldn't resist the flashing red light. He stared into the direction of the red laser wondering what it could be. One tap of the other icon from Hunter's BlackBerry and the LEDs fired off, instantly blinding the guard.

The man shrieked as his eyes burned from the flash radiation. He wailed, but didn't drop to his knees, surprising Hunter. Two other guards ran outside to find their comrade wailing and covering his eyes. When they spied the red laser beacon approaching them, they were also hit with the UV-C LEDs; they screwed their eyes shut at the first onset of pain and tried to make their eyes work again, only to receive another eyeful of retina-searing radiation. The effect on the men's eyes was immediate.

Hunter stopped the "UV bomb on wheels," shutdown the red laser, threw the truck into gear, and drove around the concrete barriers to the checkpoint. He stopped, set the brake, got out, and removed the three disabled male obstructions in his path. Hunter tossed them out of the way like rag dolls. He recovered the "UV bomb on wheels," tossed his remaining *Firestarters* into the guard shack, and returned to the truck. The three vehicles roared through the checkpoint, unmolested and out of Iran. A minute down the road, Hunter saw in the rear-view mirror that the checkpoint was in flames. *I love those things!*

• • •

As the vehicles entered the access gates at the Ashgabat airport, McGee came up on the radio and complained bitterly, "That was the worst flight of my life!" Hunter, still wearing his four-tube NVG helmet laughed as he got an earful of McGee's complaints; there wasn't anyone to talk to, the robotically piloted airplane was slower than dirt, and it took forever to get out of Iranian airspace. Although the automatic takeoff and landing system had done what it was supposed to do, McGee had been afraid to touch anything for fear he would disable the system and crash.

Hunter terminated the encrypted radio conversation and laughed all the way to a pair of parked C-17s; another U.S. Air Force cargo jet had joined the party. He didn't see any shadows of the blackened YO-3As and assumed they were already loaded aboard one of the huge cargo jets. As he removed his helmet, Hunter saw that Max the Malinois was still in the place where he had left him. Max ran to Hunter and jumped into his arms as if they were long-lost friends. Just then the ground heaved from a seismic event. Hunter's arms were full of dog and everyone around him was commenting on the earthquake. Hunter thought, *Big Mike went off early!! You sure can tell where Bullfrog has been! I think I can stop shaking now. We are safe.*

They had been waiting for him and his cargo. U.S. Embassy personnel and Air Force nurses in HAZMAT suits tried to take charge of the women gingerly stepping from the trucks, but the former hostages demanded an opportunity to show their appreciation for their rescuer. Hunter told Max to sit and directed some nurses to attend to the unknown man and *Rosebud*. Once that important business was completed, Hunter turned around to find forty women in various unmatched clothing waiting patiently.

They expressed their gratitude; the kissing and hugging took some time. They wanted to know his name. Hunter said, "You can call me, *Maverick*." He pulled off his gloves and wiggled his fingers to highlight his wedding band. For some, *Maverick* having a wife didn't matter.

There was an immediate chorus of, "I love you, *Maverick*!" With arms akimbo, Bill McGee, Bob Jones and Bob Smith and the crews of the two C-17s stood and watched the women surround Hunter waiting for a turn at the old guy. The embassy crowd had departed; McGee had filled their hands with handshakes, director's coins, and coins from the Special Activities Division.

Hunter may have been twice as old as the women, but they found him dashing, rugged, and very good looking; the quintessential savior. Each woman had some time with Duncan, holding his hand or touching his face, kissing his cheeks or lips, or telling him a simple "thank you." Some spoke languages he didn't know, which totally surprised him, but an embrace or a kiss on the cheek was a universal language for "thank you." Several of the older women broke down in his arms, they eventually succumbed to the gentle proddings from the eagerly awaiting Air Force flight nurses in personal protective equipment—face shields, N95 masks, gloves, aprons—who took control of the women and guided them aboard the other cargo jet. Their next stop, Hunter surmised, Germany and a military hospital.

After the last woman had made her peace with Duncan, McGee and the Bobs approached him. Max joined the group for pets and pats. McGee was first in the chute and pointed a big boney finger at him. "This is exactly what I knew would happen. I do all the work, prevent Wet Work of the Seventh Kind, and you get all the glory. 'I love you, *Maverick*?' You are sickening."

"Gee, Bill, 'I love you, *Bullfrog,*' just doesn't have the same cachet. Don't you know that everyone loves a *Maverick*?" McGee and Hunter and the Bobs all laughed. Duncan asked Max if he was ready to go home. The Agency crew plus the Malinois boarded the C-17 for the next leg in their journey. There was no clash of egos, ambitions, greed, or passions. Everyone had a part to play, and they celebrated as a team.

Bill McGee, America's most decorated military officer and formidable expert on military weaponry, wasn't the least bit envious of the younger man. Accolades at his level were rare; CIA directors who fail spectacularly get fired by the president, like Allen Dulles did for the botched *Bay of Pigs* invasion. McGee was simply grateful that his plan had gone off without a hitch. He had seen the possibilities in his mind's eye, he definitely needed Hunter and his airplane. He thought he might need canines, but Hunter's robotic mules had proved to be the more perfect solution. McGee settled in his seat; he was content to bask in the brilliance thrown off by Duncan Hunter and his airplanes, the CIA's most decorated duo in the CIA's most decorated special access program. Hunter deserved something special. He would discuss it with the President.

Hunter sent Max to find a place to sleep and was about to snap headphones over his ears for a little decompression music when McGee yawned and said, "I have one more thing."

Hunter parked the headphones around his neck and with an upturned chin encouraged McGee to speak.

McGee leaned in to close the gap between them and whispered, "So, you basically eliminated everyone off the *Disposition Matrix*. Are you interested in one more who should be on someone's shitlist?"

Hunter was intrigued.

McGee said, "We know where Chernovich is, at least we did a few hours ago. Your little trick worked. They all have private jets and didn't know or care if *Tailwatchers* were spying them." He provided Hunter with the details. The man from TASCO had camped out in a fortress on top of a mountain. Hunter thought any attempt to get at him was impossible. McGee very gently nodded and said, "Maybe not, G.I. Dog. There might be a way."

"Let's hear it."

Hunter nearly fell out of his seat as McGee explained. McGee yawned and asked, "Could you do it? I don't know. But I could do it. In a heartbeat. And after tonight, I think you could too." Duncan didn't have an immediate response. McGee laid out his CONOP if he were to attempt an intercept. Afterwards, he asked, "How many do you have?" The implication was the number of gold Krugerrands.

"Thirty."

"I'll give you ten more. That way you'll be able to get home. You can do it. Think about it. I think you can do it easy. You have a passport. If you're not comfortable with it, maybe there will be other chances. Ideally, you want to strike when they least expect it."

"He would never expect that." Hunter nodded, and nodded, and nodded. He had gotten a tiny taste of what the mighty McGee experienced in combat, and it was enough. *Enough of what?* His feet belonged on rudder pedals, not on the ground with an HK slung over his shoulders. He recalled a letter he had received from one of his grad students, an F-16 driver who had been deployed to Iraq. They armed him with a Beretta 9mm semi-automatic pistol and told him to stand guard when all hell broke loose. A terrorist had climbed over the wall and breached the "Green Zone" in Baghdad. He confided to Hunter that he had been terrified; that he was worthless to the men and women he was supposedly protecting. He lamented that he had been shaking so severely he could barely hold the pistol; there was no way he could have aimed it effectively. *I know what that's like now. If you stop moving and think about what you're doing, you'll shake yourself apart. Mission success is an energizer.*

With newfound energy, Hunter bounded into the cockpit, chatted with the aircrew for a few moments, and thanked them for their service. The aircrew's attitude was a little strange, as if they had a secret and could burst out laughing at any moment. Hunter was too tired for analysis and asked, "Was anyone able to get you some food?"

The pilot pointed to a Yeti cooler in the cabin and said, "The embassy folks brought several pounds of spicy kebobs and flat bread. And they are very good. Will that do?"

"Hey, that's admirable. A couple more things. A couple of requests."

"Name it, sir."

Another incongruous emotion and darting eyes from the pilots. What is their problem? Hunter was serious and asked operational questions. The aircrew became alert and fully engaged. They rarely planned for a mission change on the fly.

Hunter said, "I doubt anyone will be back this way anytime soon. I understand it is sort of a tourist attraction. A hole in the earth that's on fire but isn't a volcano. Might be worth a look if it is not out of the way. And then again, the trip might not be worth a milk bucket under a bull."

Hunter wasn't surprised that they were unfamiliar with the fiery location in the earth. The copilot said, "We'll get vectors and we should see it. Hunter thanked the aircrew with handshakes. Director McGee would see to it the aircrew received coins.

After Hunter left the cockpit, he swore the aircrew was laughing at him. *My joke wasn't that funny. I must be so tired I'm hearing things….*

After he had eaten and the C-17 had made a slow pass of Darvaza Crater, Hunter and the others viewed the scene as hypnotic, the vent in the ground resembled a bloody open wound on the rough and wrinkled skin of a massive dinosaur. He returned to his seat and reflected on the dynamics of the evening. *That was insane. Bill managed that like a master tactician, he anticipated their every move perfectly. He moved those terrorists around as if they were pieces on a chessboard, and they didn't even know it. McGee is a true Svengali. And amazing things were possible from an old aircraft you couldn't see or hear.*

Ever looking out for his subordinates, McGee asked, "Did you get something to eat?"

Hunter nodded and said, "Kebobs. Very good. I'm certain 'vegetarian' is Turkmen for 'lousy liberal hunter.'"

The Director of the Central Intelligence Agency grinned and shook his head.

After a moment of silence, Hunter asked McGee, "Do you know who *he* was?"

McGee said he thought it was someone who had gone missing from the Agency a decade ago. "He's in very bad shape." He told Hunter what was in store for the man after they nursed him back to health. Debriefings under polygraph. "We have to make sure he's not a double. That he hasn't been turned." He continued, "A double agent is someone who works for the Agency and conducts espionage activities in another country, but is also spying on the CIA for the other country's intelligence service."

"But he is out of there. I'm glad *Rosebud* said something. I missed him. He was in a corner of their holding cell. Maybe we should check him for the plague." McGee patted Hunter's leg; Hunter patted McGee's leg and chuckled. "And you are out of there, even if we scared the crap out of you."

McGee nodded in agreement. "These are the things you live for, the things that make you keep coming back for more. The best part, Ali and his turds did all the work. The world is full of bunglers, some so bad they can even mess up a one-car funeral. They never knew we were there. You cannot do what we did with a UAV. The YO-3A made it easy. That is an incredible capability. With them out of action, I really didn't have to do anything other than set some charges and take hard drives."

"...and blow the place up *early!*" Hunter explained he had placed the al-Sham terrorists in a pile with a *Firestarter*. Nothing more needed to be said about the activity other than, "It's hard to get something like that out of your system. It could've been bad, real bad." With the wall of excitement well behind him, the yawning started.

McGee nodded. "That's my last real time out of the office." *It went better than we could have planned. Found the defector, got the women, put the Iranians out of the bug business with a stolen Soviet suitcase nuke. Found one of our lost children. That's a bonus we never expected. Any evidence that a special weapon went off in Iran will be blamed on the Russians. Hell yes!*

Hunter said, "You knew what they would do."

"I did. It's the same stuff I had trained to do all of my adult life. But I have to tell you, being able to manage the battlespace while you're on scene—anticipating their every move, that was beyond words. And you got them to respond to the sound of the prop. I knew the *Yo-Yo* was effective, but it takes something like that to appreciate what quiet aircraft can really do. We saw everything in real time, not some electronic view through a straw. Aural stealth was the key, because it got us into position to use the laser to disable them. They probably shit their pants thinking Allah had smote them or something."

"I hope it was good for you. It was for me."

McGee ignored his friend. He yawned and stretched. "I'm gonna hurt for a week. It also proved something you've been trying to tell me for a long time, that fully *unmanned* black airplanes are not yet ready for prime time. That's why it takes a C-130 load of people and equipment just to fly one UAV to give us one tunnel vision view of one target. Multiple targets infinitely more complicated."

"Greg said, 'The eagle that chases two rabbits catches neither.'"

As his brain could not solve the multiple equations, McGee nodded.

"Yeah, for what we did, we proved you still need a human in the loop for the smallest attack footprint possible. Greg and I tried to get the Border Patrol some quiet aircraft, what over twenty years ago, but it's the same thing. The boss has to see what it can do for himself. And then there are the computer geeks; they can make a drone takeoff and land from an aircraft carrier. Soon, they will have AI fighting a fighter pilot. But they couldn't have handled the very complex situation we were in." Hunter yawned until tears leaked from his eyes. The jet lag had finally caught up to him.

McGee was suddenly serious. "I'm thinking it's time for a next generation aircraft. Optionally manned. I didn't like it, having to fly home without you driving, but you were right again; I had to get out of there. We were the two guys on the planet with the right skills to do that job. We will not have that situation again. We need something with more capability; something better than the Liberia op. And something that is quieter than that lousy reduction gearbox. God, when you're not distracted, you notice that thing vibrates like a paint shaker. It's so noisy! Even with the noise-canceling headset. Anyway, give it some consideration. What we did tonight—it would not have been possible without the *Yo-Yos*. I'll leave the design up to you. Work with Air Branch. We'll extend *Noble Savage* another ten years."

"Ms. Deng's head will explode." Hunter and McGee prepared their sleeping bags for the return trip. Noise cancelation headsets and sleep masks were pulled from bags.

"She'll get over it."

"Bill, I don't know what to say."

"Yeah, I know. Umm, you need to wash that face only a mother could love. Apparently, you were unaware forty women kissed you *with lipstick*." The CIA Director reached inside of his flight suit, withdrew a folded photograph, and handed it to his friend. "I found this interesting."

Hunter unfolded the 8x10 photograph. He recognized the man. He was more curious than alarmed. Hunter found people with *nom de guerres* more interesting. After several seconds of silence, Hunter looked up and said, "Rho Schwartz Scorpii.... The *Black Scorpion*. The *Puppet Master*."

McGee said, "One of the wealthiest men in the world had his picture on the wall at the Khomeini Institute. Scorpii's picture was atop an organization chart; he may be the Chairman or on the Board of Directors. I couldn't read Chinese so I couldn't tell. I find it interesting." He continued to look at Duncan and broke out into a wide smile.

"Wouldn't that make the anti-Semitic, socialist billionaire knee-deep in biologicals? Is that a new area for him? I know the bastard buys up oil companies in Europe and all the rare watches now. One of these days, that will be his downfall. Watches, that is." Hunter returned the photograph to McGee and reflected on the significance of the *Black Scorpion* being in the most secretive virology institute on the planet. "Was that item ever in the President's Daily Brief?"

"It will be now."

"You would like to find him."

"We need to find him. You have an idea?"

Hunter nodded. After listening to Hunter's plan, McGee nodded and said, "You just need his watch. So this just might work out." McGee returned the photograph to the leg pocket of his flight suit and then extracted a foot-long carbon fiber tube. It was much smaller than the diameter of a BB with threaded mounting holes near one end, top and bottom, where something could be attached. The opposite end had a larger-diameter with perforations at discrete angles. He handed it to Hunter who scrutinized it carefully. McGee said, "On the basement floor, they also had an S&T-like capability; a room where they could make delivery devices."

"That's exactly what this is. Screw a CO2 cartridge to the bottom for the handle, screw a vial of something lethal on top, and this thing at the end is a miniature silencer. I guess they could shoot viruses across the rooms with this, and you couldn't hear the release of gas. That's incredible."

The men looked at each other as Hunter returned the device.

"The media could easily hide this in their cameras and shoot a stream of lethal viruses at world leaders."

"The *Black Scorpion* strikes again." Hunter exhaled and shook his head. "Where are we headed now? Home?"

"Jordan. Crew rest. We'll leave when it gets dark." McGee snapped a sleep mask over his eyes, turned his back to Hunter, and relaxed and was asleep quickly.

Hunter wiped his face with wet wipes and was flabbergasted at the amount of lipstick that came off with every pass of his face. More wipes, more passes; decreasing traces of reds and pinks.

He found himself suddenly awake. It would take some time before he could get back to sleep. Hunter found the Glitch Mob remix edition of *Seven Nation Army*; it blared from his headset. It was one of the more interesting selections in his library. He liked it more for the sound than the lyrics. It was music you could feel to your toes. It was the perfect music to celebrate beating the hell out of your enemies, even if the enemy did all the work.

After letting the song play three times, Hunter shut down the White Stripes and traded the active headphones for the noise canceling variety. He would try to sleep again but an old thought crept into his head. An old problem, long unresolved. Something stupid and silly that kept learned men up at night: *Why does it matter?* The four words had haunted him for years. The mission to Iran shook him just enough so he could see the question in a different light. It was enough to make a palpable difference, like James Bond being able to tell if a martini had been shaken or stirred. With a smile, Hunter realized there was a part of his brain that was always working on the old questions. He withdrew his BlackBerry and typed *Why does it matter?* on the first line. For the next half hour he texted Eastwood *Why it mattered. A mission for Omega.*

He set the alarm in his BlackBerry. His brain was finally at rest as he lay on top of his sleeping bag, his old Marine Corps flight jacket pulled across his chest. Hunter changed his mind and swapped the noise-canceling variety for music earphones. He found the song he was looking for and piped in Red Rider's *Lunatic Fringe*©. It took a while to play; it had a slow start. He slipped a black sleep mask over his eyes.

Lunatic fringe
I know you're out there
You're in hiding
And you can hold your meetings
I can hear you coming

I know what you're after

After the song had finished playing, Hunter shut off the music. His last conscious decision before he fell into the deep sleep of the exhausted, *I have some unfinished work to do. I'm after a watch.*

• • •

President Hernandez had dispatched a C-32 to Amman, Jordan to retrieve the CIA Director. At the base of the stairs, Hunter told McGee, "I'll call when I get home."

McGee nodded and entered the big jet. Under the wing of the mammoth C-17, Hunter watched the white and blue aircraft taxi to a runway and take off.

There was a lot of daylight left and Hunter walked with Max to some of the rougher parts of the air base. Every place that wasn't concrete was a potential doggie toilet that required significant sniffing. Mother Nature and the desert heat would take care of Max's puddles and land mines.

• • •

After a night takeoff from the Jordanian Special Operations base, the lights in the C-17 cabin remained red for night operations. Hunter's four-tube NVGs was firmly on his helmet and working and O2 flowed into his mask.

As they got close to the drop zone, Hunter shuffled to the door with Max strapped to his chest. The dog wore his own custom-fitted O2 mask. Hunter tracked the time for him and Max to flush nitrogen from their bloodstreams and complete the required pre-breathing period on aviation breathing oxygen.

The loadmaster checked Hunter over and patted him on the back and Max on the head; she gave him thumbs up. The side door was opened. When the light flipped from red to green, Duncan Hunter wrapped his arms around Max the Malinois, stepped into the wind stream over Europe and was gone.

CHAPTER 68

May 30, 2018

Seismic sensors along the unpaved portion of the driveway entrance to the lodge sounded the alarm that a visitor had approached the gate. Carlos Yazzie was startled by the ringing and moved to the security monitor and telephone. He wasn't aware of any packages that were to be delivered to the lodge; all deliveries were made to an office at the Jackson airport. When the lodge was being refurbished by contractors, Yazzie had built a shelter outside the gate for packages to be stored until a contractor could retrieve them. Solar-powered stealth cameras monitored the lodge's entrance and the access road. Yazzie moved the computer mouse to wake up the monitor so he could see who was near the entrance to the lodge. He was agitated.

When the monitor came alive with the images from all twelve cameras, he was shocked by what he saw from one camera that was a few hundred yards from the entrance, two miles from the main residence. He touched the pressure-sensitive surface of the monitor to select that camera for full-sized viewing. Yazzie couldn't believe what he was seeing. He shouted, "*Therese!*" Yazzie picked up the telephone on the workstation and dialed 911. He told the sheriff's dispatcher that there were armed men with what looked like M-16s on his property and coming up his driveway. "They parked across the street from the lodge, removed assault rifles with scopes from carrying cases, climbed over our fence, and are now in the tree line paralleling the driveway. We're moving to a safe room."

The only time Therese would listen to Carlos was when there was an emergency with substantiation. The safe room beneath the lodge also had security monitors, and the first thing she did was to validate the alarm. What she saw terrified her. *Where is my Carlos?*

Her face was glued to the twelve channel monitor. On one camera she saw a man carrying an assault rifle and wearing night vision goggles. Therese was familiar with NVGs. Captain Hunter had several sets and had showed them to her on a moonless night and had shown her the glory of the Milky Way. On another camera she saw her Carlos leaving the garage, controlling the Captain's creepy black drone. Ninety seconds later Carlos was closing the door of the safe room behind him. He explained what he was going to do with the drone.

He hit a few keys on the computer's keyboard, and one of the cameras that had been feeding imagery to the security system was replaced by the video from the camera on the drone.

Therese was mesmerized at Carlos' expertise in handling the little black aircraft up over the trees until it located the thermal imagery of one of the men. Yazzie tapped a few keys and explained he was activating the laser. The green laser spot was as bright as a flashlight, and Carlos used a joystick controller to move the beam toward the armed man.

The sight of the bright laser spot tracing across the ground toward the man was enough to stop him in his tracks. He ran from the marauding green trace and up onto the prepared surface of the access road to gain speed. He zigged and zagged from side to side hoping to defeat a sniper's bullet. The man's partner had also come into the FLIR's field of view as the men raced back toward the entry gate. Yazzie could see in the distance the thermal imagery of a pair of vehicles with light bars on their roofs. *Deputy Sheriffs.*

Carlos killed the laser as the men mounted the fence to escape. Two sheriff SUVs arrived on scene. Carlos continued to fly the silent four-rotor drone past the men, never losing sight of them in the FLIR.

The sheriffs took cover behind the driver's doors and drew their weapons. They demanded the men stop what they were doing and drop their weapons. Carlos Yazzie waited to see if there would be an exchange of gunfire, and when the two interlopers opened fire on the sheriff's vehicles, he instinctively tried to protect the lawmen and hit the criminals with a blast of energy from the laser, blinding them. In the FLIR, when he saw the white-hot traces of bullets from the deputies weapons slam into the men, he shut down the laser and flew the drone back to the garage.

Therese watched the scene play out in the multi-camera monitors. For the first time in a very long time Therese was proud of her Carlos.

Later in the evening, the sheriff's dispatcher called Yazzie's cell number and informed him that there had been an attempt to stop and question two men, but they immediately engaged the officers in a firefight and were killed. Carlos asked if the sheriff's deputies were safe and was relieved that they were. He also asked if the sheriff's deputies needed anything from him, such as a statement.

After a full check of the lodge's security system, Carlos and Therese left the security of the safe room and repaired to the guestroom in the main house.

The incursion was a first for the residence in Jackson Hole, and the real test of the security system went well. Hunter and the Yazzies had moved several times as the people who wanted to kill Hunter always seemed to find where he lived. They had been chased out of Del Rio and Fredericksburg by the drug cartels and Islamic extremists. Carlos had thought that tonight it might have been some criminals from the local area out to case the property and steal whatever they could. But in the FLIR Yazzie thought the men appeared to be much larger and older than expected. They were big and muscular like RECON Rangers; not the puny Muslim men who had found the Captain's house.

He didn't want to believe the Muslim Brotherhood and the Islamic Underground had found them again. These men were different. Carlos sent a text message to the Captain's BlackBerry.

Sleep wouldn't come easy for the Yazzies. There had been no more bells or alarms in the night to send them back to the safe room. They were again thankful their *Captain* had used his wealth to protect them from harm.

CHAPTER 69

May 30, 2018

Greetings to the truth seekers who find today's media totally corrupted by special interests. It's Wednesday, May 30th, 2018, and Maxim Mohammad Mazibuike was the most corrupt president in U.S. history. I've said that he is the only U.S. president who can recall the opening lines of the Arabic "Call to prayer," reciting them with a first-rate accent, but he couldn't recite the Pledge of Allegiance and didn't know the words to the Star Spangled Banner. There was always something wrong with that guy, and it pained me to think there wasn't a damned thing I could do about it.

That is until now.

It is an issue of "why it matters and what to do about it." In previous posts I specifically referenced how lawyers used law reviews to claim that the U.S. Constitution is wrong; that it should have read native-born vs natural born citizen when stating the requirements for president. These same lawyers claim the Constitution is discriminatory, that naturalized citizens are not eligible to run for president and therefore they are being discriminated against. The original law review articles were written well before President Mazibuike was elected. These law review articles were a poor means to disqualify Republican presidential candidates who were born abroad of American parents, such as Barry Goldwater, et al. But the real purpose of those articles was for Democrat presidential candidates to challenge Republicans in an election on the theory that the presidential natural born citizen requirement was faulty – that instead of being specifically defined in the Naturalization Act of 1790 as – "the children of citizens of the United States, that may be born beyond the sea or out of the limits of the United States, shall be considered as natural born citizens" – the U.S. Constitution should have read "native-born citizen." In theory, that could be used against their opponent by resorting to federal court litigation. None of those stupid arguments were ever considered, and for over two-hundred and twenty-five years everyone in America knew what was meant by "natural born citizen."

Constitutional eligibility to hold office is an implicit condition to certification for receiving funds under the Federal Election Laws. If you are not eligible, receive campaign funds, and get elected you've committed a fraudulent act. Big-time, jail time.

But most interestingly, an opponent may cite election law to challenge the validity of bills signed by the candidate, while in office or after leaving office. The FEC laws look to be the path to overturn the Mazibuike legacy and render all of the laws he signed null and void. Some people will dance in the streets. Democrats and the corrupt media will be screaming at the top of their lungs.

That is why it matters. Hat tip to Maverick.

So for the new Attorney General, your serve, sir.

Now again, why does it matter? What we have seen is when the left and the media elect an ineligible candidate for president, they celebrate the greatest battlefield victory of socialism and communism and Islamism in the war for America, all without firing a shot. For America, the ultimate constitutional protection had been breached and the hordes were coming over the wall. We were on the fast-track to one-party rule to their advantage, and a few steps away from putting the United States into a George Orwell 1984-like purgatory as Mazibuike and the Democrats and the communist movement turned the criminals and the mentally deficient loose on a peaceful population. In their effort to achieve ultimate power over their enemies, to eviscerate and subjugate the U.S. Constitution, they conspired to destroy Christian values and norms, and attacked the right. Driven by anger, hate, rage, and revenge they sought ways to subdue this country and subjugate or murder law-abiding people, ransack their homes and cities, and plunder the wealth of America. The left now attacks publishers to ban books from Republicans and Conservatives. They were so very close to achieving their goals. Aided by the timely election of a man of God and action, we elected President Hernandez who is reversing the policies and the idiotic theories of the left and Mazibuike and the Democrat Party.

I will say we didn't see it at first and could never fully appreciate the importance of the disclosures in the Mazibuike file and the DNC's archives. The former president sought to destroy the very foundation of our republic by injecting anarchists into our government and controlling the outcome of our elections. An unknown patriot stopped the left and the communists and the Islamic terrorists in their tracks. Thank God for the person who released that file. Republicans and Conservatives no longer need to feel afraid. The charlatan has been exposed. Our president has energized the right again. Politics is combat by other means. Now we know we are under assault. We have patriots who are fighting back, and we may actually avoid the horrors of Orwell's 1984 and Metropolis and the book burners of Fahrenheit 451. We live for liberty and will fight the left to the ends of the world.

This is just breaking. The newly nominated Attorney General, Burnt Winchester announced the DOJ has indicted the bomb maker responsible for the 1988 destruction of PanAm 103 over Lockerbie, Scotland. About time.

This is the Omega.

CHAPTER 70

June 11, 2018

The networks cut into the prime time programming to issue Alerts and Breaking News. The President had called for a press conference. The word was that hostages being held at an indeterminate unnamed facility, probably in the Middle East, had been rescued and an unknown number of them were at the White House. They had been taken to a medical facility in Germany, and the President was going to recognize them for their bravery.

Network anchors filled dead air time with basic information from an on-line encyclopedia website. "Hostage rescues are the purview of Tier I units, most likely Army Delta Force or SEAL Team Six…."

Televisions across America turned to the networks to see what was being touted as "explosive news." People crowded televisions in airports, at the Pentagon, at Special Operations Command in Tampa, Florida, CIA Headquarters in McLean, Virginia, the Hotel Campo Imperatore in Italy, the U.S. Embassy in Ashgabat, Turkmenistan, and residences from Jackson Hole, Wyoming to southwestern Pennsylvania and New York City.

From the presidential lectern in the Rose Garden, President Hernandez, surrounded by three dozen women all dressed in summer finery and sandals, announced the federal government would assume responsibility for all data collection and reporting for the *Diagnostic and Statistics Manual for Mental Disorders*. The DSM would become the purview of the Secretary of the Health and Human Services Department. The United States would impose on the nation of Iran the most sweeping package of crippling sanctions in history. He then gave glowing praise to the U.S. Special Operations Command. He didn't claim Iran held American hostages or that SOCOM was responsible for the rescue. President Hernandez focused his remarks on the brave men and women at SOCOM, dedicated patriots and loyal, brave Americans.

Some in the audience wondered if they had heard correctly. The U.S. government would assume control of the DSM? *Would the White House also reset the effective date of the DSM to a previous version, thus reversing another of President Mazibuike's initiatives?*

• • •

The SOCOM Commander in Tampa was shocked. He interrupted the teleconference. He scanned the faces of his officers around the conference table, threw up his hands, and asked, "We rescued hostages?"

The Deputy said, "Not this time, sir. I think it must be one of theirs…."

The SOCOM Commander nodded, *Likely CIA.* "What's with this DSM bullshit?"

The Deputy offered, "It doesn't look like we'll have any more SEALs with sexual disorders demanding to be called 'girls.'"

• • •

The CIA Director asked the Deputy, "SOCOM rescued hostages? Who knew?"

The Deputy Director sat beside McGee. He had been "holding down the fort" while the Director was gone. He suspected the Director to have been "free lancing." What McGee could have been doing was discussed around the conference table. The Agency executives agreed, *Once a SEAL, always a SEAL.* He said, "Again, apparently. They claim they didn't do it." There was no way the Deputy or anyone else would ask if the Director had been involved.

Like nothing had happened in any part of the world, Director McGee asked, "And the feds are taking control of the DSM? That should benefit the federal government greatly. We shouldn't have confused men who think they are women and confused women who think they are men working on our most sensitive projects. I think the last ten individuals to be charged with the Espionage Act imagined they had cervixes when they did not. They were all on a DSM spectrum."

The Deputy said, "Yes sir. But I think that will be challenged in court."

McGee offered, "No doubt, but that means no backdoor infiltration of the IC by people with mental disorders. We should only hire people who are totally well-adjusted, without mental disorders for the most challenging positions in government. The President's announcement to roll back the DSM to the 1992 edition was not expected but will be appreciated by us and DOD."

The Deputy said, "Yes sir. New business. While you were away, we determined who bombed the PanAm 103 jet."

Director McGee rubbed his chin and said, "That is good news."

• • •

Electrical power had finally been restored at the Hotel Campo Imperatore. Investigators sifting through the rubble of a parking lot on one side of the historic ski lodge determined an electric car had spontaneously combusted. Two guests were missing from the hotel and were believed to have been in the vehicle. Noxious fumes likely had knocked them out before the vehicle burst into flames and destroyed the power transformer and several vehicles, but miraculously left the hotel untouched by flames. It would take some time to identify the bodies,

The hotel manager pointed at the television and shouted the Americans had rescued an Italian girl from a Muslim dungeon.

• • •

A few Agency personnel at the U.S. Embassy in Ashgabat, Turkmenistan held up challenge coins from their Director and the large "*Grim Reaper*" coin of the Special Activities Division. The telecast was on a slight delay.

The President turned to the women behind him and clapped his hands; the men and women in the Rose Garden stood and expressed their support.

On the other side of the world the U.S. Ambassador to Turkmenistan stood, turned to the men and women of the CIA, "As you know, rarely are one's efforts rewarded in the intelligence community. Rarely is anyone mentioned in dispatch. You are expected to do more than just your job. And when you are part of a collective effort that results in lives saved, it is a time to be mentioned 'in dispatch,' it is a moment to be savored. Well done!"

The sound of the Embassy's Agency personnel clapping for themselves and for each other was deafening and drowned out anything coming from the television.

• • •

President Hernandez was in a jubilant mood and had fielded questions, mostly on the Emergency decision from the Federal Election Commission stating former President Mazibuike was ineligible for the Office of the President. Subsequently, the Attorney General declared that the former president had committed multiple impeachable offenses of fraud. President Hernandez cited violated election laws as the basis to reject every bill signed into law by President Mazibuike. The government federalizing the *Diagnostic and Statistics Manual for Mental Disorders* was in response to a voided Mazibuike executive order. He said, "One more. Colonel Eastwood?"

Demetrius Eastwood consulted his notepad, "Mr. President, I think government control over the DSM is long overdue and the FEC's announcement is stunning and will be debated *ad infinitum*. This announcement stops the left's drive to leverage the power of violent protest as a way to legitimize pedophilia and give people with mental issues access to our national secrets. Kudos to SOCOM for yet another *boffo* rescue mission. I'm not really keeping track, but this is mission number *eleven* by my count. Your Administration has not been afraid to exercise American power to rescue American citizens held by a hostile power. The previous administration would have let Americans rot in whatever hellhole they were in. I, for one, would like to commend you, sir, on a job well done. Now sir, I think we would all like to hear something from one or two of the ladies who were rescued. Would that be possible?"

President Hernandez was used to long-winded and circuitous questions. He nodded and turned to the assembly behind him. One woman was pushed forward. The President adjusted the microphone height for her and unfolded a step so that the lectern didn't hide her. Then he introduced Christine Simbach. She was a bit wobbly and her body language telegraphed anxiety and apprehension; she was still recovering from her ordeal. She didn't want the limelight. She was a little embarrassed and reluctant to speak. Ms. Simbach didn't know what she should say. *No one will care,* she told herself. Short and sweet was all that was necessary. She filled her lungs, took the step, grabbed the edges of the lectern, and found the courage. "I think I can speak for all of us who were rescued. We are deservedly indebted to the men and women who made this all possible. Days ago we were in despair. Today, we are in a state of disbelief, celebrating liberty and freedom, and having lunch with the President of the United States." She turned and said, "Thank you, Mr. President for not abandoning us; thank you for making dreams come true! America is the greatest country!"

President Hernandez and the crowd on the lawn stood and erupted in applause.

That wasn't so bad. She scanned the crowd hoping to see if *he* was there. The crowd quieted and anticipated what she would say next. She breathed twice and nearly yelled into the microphone, "That's all I really have to say, but as a group *we* would like to give a personal thank you and say…*We love you, Maverick!"* She raised a fist to the sky, stepped from the lectern, and into the open arms of the President. The rescued women surrounded the President, much to the annoyance of the Secret Service. The assembly continued clapping as President Hernandez tried to extricate himself from the grateful women. Most of the reporters from the media sat on their hands or just turned away.

Eastwood returned to his seat. His smartphone was buzzing in his pocket; notices from the wire service, likely. As he fished the device from his suitcoat, he thought, *The more the media snips at President*

Hernandez like little Chihuahuas, the more you know that was a great moment for him and the Republicans.

Those clowns....they are the left after all, and anything they tell you, the opposite is pretty much true. They are our news media. It's sad, it's tragic, and it's a terrible thing.

His eyes fell to the smallish screen. His mouth fell open. His eyes darted between the spectacle before him and the lines in his hand-held device. The Iranian news agency *Fars* was reporting the Ayatollah Khomeini Institute of Virology had been destroyed by violent earthquakes. The facility had collapsed into a five hundred-foot deep crater and was still on fire. It was expected to remain on fire, much like the Darvaza Crater in Turkmenistan that had been burning for decades. The BBC was reporting the remains of the CEO of TASCO, Bogdan Chernovich, were found after a car fire near a famous Italian hotel. Police reported he was identified by the only remains not burned beyond recognition: a wrist and a hand with a ring and his fingerprints. The article included a headshot of a smiling Chernovich with his arm resting in front of him and wearing his Naval Academy graduation ring and a rare TAG Heuer *Autavia* GMT.

Eastwood's eyes narrowed. His eyes ping-ponged from the women surrounding President Hernandez and the subject lines in the email. His head shot up. *That cannot be an accident!*

• • •

In Jackson Hole, Wyoming Carlos and Therese Yazzie swelled with pride. Tears trailed down Therese face. *We know that is my Captain!*

• • •

With a Tilley's *Wanderer* pulled over his eyes, Dory Eastwood walked out of the White House Visitor Center and proceeded to E Street on his way to Union Station. He received more news from a digital feed to his smartphone. He avoided the latest "progressives," not the insurance kind but the other kind who were screaming at the top of their lungs and throwing things at the "Death to America March" along Pennsylvania Avenue. *I guess that's what they call progress.* Waiting for a light, he read that California was having rolling blackouts. *It used to be the envy of the world! Model for the world. But now they have blackouts like the third world state they've become. I grew up in a Democrat household, but these people are not rational anymore. The whole party is not rational – it has become a violent criminal organization. Across America they are looting and plundering, committing arson, burning things and playing the victim, naturally. These people are insane.*

He arrived at the train station with a few minutes to spare. Eastwood found his seat in first class and began outlining his next *Omega* posting.

CHAPTER 71

June 11, 2018

At the old summer residence in the woods in southwestern Pennsylvania, Kelly Horne hung up her smartphone. The gate guard announced an expected visitor. *It's going to get emotional!* She couldn't say a word, wouldn't say who had arrived.

Saoirse Nobley stared into the computer monitor and mouthed, "Yes, we love you, *Maverick*." She turned to Kelly. "That's why he hasn't been here. He's been working."

That was the moment Duncan Hunter, wearing a white Stetson *El Presidente*, burst through the door at *Fallingwater*.

Kelly knew introductions weren't in order and hugging her father was out of the question. Anything she wanted to say would be overshadowed by her father's presence with the woman he knew twenty-something years ago. Duncan took off his hat; Saoirse looked dumbfounded, and Kelly took a walk on the terrace to let them reconnect.

Kelly's emotions were disjointed. Her face registered the internal turmoil she was feeling. She missed her father and wanted to say so. Had her emotions been a ping-pong ball, it would have hit everything in the room but the lottery. She refrained from looking back at the couple and expedited her departure with an odd frown. *What about Nazy?*

Saoirse Nobley and Duncan Hunter locked eyes. He looked better than she remembered; he was older, more muscular, and more confident. Tanned. *He still has his hair, and lots of it.* She trembled and worried about how she looked. She determined that even after almost a quarter of a century the torch of your first love can never be fully extinguished.

The image of Saoirse Nobley saddened him. The girl with the prominent cheekbones, luminous skin, and the most crystalline violet eyes of her day, the girl who set pulses racing with her insane curves was gone. Her once spectacular figure was now shapeless, hidden in a billowy top. He would not let his emotions betray him. Her vivaciously bright face was now blotchy, and only when she smiled with a mouth full of teeth did Hunter truly recognize her. His undying vision of Corporal Nobley had been erased. *It was undeniable that Saoirse had suffered terribly. A person doesn't really know what men can do to women until they see something like this.*

Hunter was grateful Nazy and Kelly had cleaned her up after years of neglect and abuse. She still had just a little of that Liz Taylor thing. He assumed her legs were like sticks, that she had lost her muscle mass and would probably never be called "Legs" again.

She hesitated several times—trying to overcome years of programming of *"It is not permitted to touch a man who is not your husband."* Saoirse staggered a bit as she walked into his arms; he cradled her gently as if she were the thinnest porcelain. She sobbed; he held her close for several minutes. Fountains of tears drenched his shirt. He held on with comforting words. Duncan patted her back like a child who had been hurt on a playground.

Hunter had been in this position once before, when Kelly had found him in his classroom and announced that she was his daughter. Then and now, he was addled in thought, inadequate in response, grateful to hold her and comfort her, because it allowed him some time to think about what he should say. When he found the right words, he buried his face into her hair and said, "Saoirse, I'm so sorry. I hope you will find it in your heart to forgive me. I'm glad that you are ok now. I'm going to take you home."

• • •

The Gulfstream G-550 departed from Arnold Palmer Regional Airport. Kelly flew in the pilot seat; Duncan observed from the copilot seat and helped when he was needed.

Saoirse sat in one of the over-stuffed chairs in the cabin with an unobstructed view of the cockpit and watched every move the pilots made. During the time she had lived in squalor she could not have imagined the luxurious interior of the business jet. It was not in the realm of the possible, could not be conceived, and was not to be believed. But she had new clothes, *western clothes*; something else she had given up seeing again. And shoes. The Sauconys on her feet were so lightweight she could barely feel them.

She didn't know what they were doing in the cockpit, flipping switches, moving throttles, adjusting knobs, making radio calls; but the interaction between the two aviators was strange, nearly intimate but without contact. Their actions complimented each other. Saoirse told herself, *He trusts her more than my father did when I was sixteen going to test for my driver's license.* Then it hit her; there was a slight resemblance. *Kelly is Duncan's daughter!* She hung her head. *What happened to my children?*

Well before leveling off, Hunter squeezed out of the confined cockpit and stepped into the cabin. He took Saoirse by the hand, and they moved to a pair of opposite-facing chairs. He said, "Saoirse, I don't even know what to say other than I thank God you're alive and out of that place."

Saoirse Nobley looked from him to the view outside the window then back at him. She thought she had much to say, but she couldn't face him at the moment; it would take a little while. She stared out the window and remained quiet for a long time. *It was the 1990s, a different era. I wasn't a victim. It wasn't traumatizing. I knew what I was doing. I wasn't an innocent schoolgirl. I always acted a lot older than I was. I was a grown-up at twenty-two. I knew I had the power to pick whatever man I wanted. I was keen to have every experience I could, but I wasn't willing to settle for just anyone. I do not blame you. Once I did, but those were the thoughts of a child.*

For the short time I knew you, you were so special and so good to me, and you became a part of me. All I could think about was kissing you and sleeping with you, but you left me. I knew you had to go, but I didn't like it. And yes, I blamed you. I thought I would hurt you for leaving me. I wanted you so much! I thought I married a rich man, but he was a demon. I tried to punish you for not staying with me, for leaving me. Now you have rescued me. It feels so strange not to want to touch you, to thank you. Thank you, but I've grown to hate men, hate mens fingers. Please forgive me. I still need some time. I need some time. When she turned, Duncan could see the pain in her eyes.

He had more pain for Saoirse. He told her no one could find out what had happened to her children. She whispered that she had always hoped that they would be safe but when Haqqani stopped threatening her with her children, then she knew.

Saoirse had said little on the trip from the residence to the airport. The flight was three hours with the headwinds, so there would be plenty of opportunities to talk. When Hunter asked her if she wanted to sit up front he surprisingly got a nod. He helped Saoirse to her feet and ushered her into the cockpit and the copilot's seat.

Kelly got the hint and exchanged places with her father.

The distraction was sufficient for Saoirse to start talking. She couldn't face her benefactor, but after being locked in a box for twenty years the view from 30,000 feet could not be ignored, even for a second. She talked to the window virtually all the way to Ottumwa, Iowa. Her story was harrowing, pitiful. A beautiful girl had made the ultimate mistake. Her defenses were down, and she married the wrong man. Her mother would not have approved.

In some large part, Duncan felt responsible for Nobley's situation. *I'm sure she felt I had abandoned her. She was just a kid, and she probably thought she could punish me by getting married. If I hadn't gone through with my promise to see her, take her to Hawaii, she wouldn't have felt the need to get back at me. It was still fraternization in a weird sort of way. It was an abuse of power even after I left the Marines. I set her up for all of this.*

• • •

As Kelly flew the approach to the regional airport, Hunter looked over the buildings on the airport and said, "Ottumwa looks like…it used to be…a military airfield." Once they were inside the terminal building, photographs hung on the wall proved Hunter to be correct. Kelly secured two rental cars for her and her father. Duncan drove Saoirse to her childhood home where her mother still lived.

The Nobley family reunion created more water flow than the Bear Run waterfall after a gully washer.

Upon seeing Nobley's mother and sisters, Hunter quickly concluded, *Good God, I can see where she got her good looks and those incredible eyes.* His mission was complete. Apologies made, apologies accepted. It was time for him to go. Saoirse threw caution and old memories to the wind; she rushed him, threw her arms around him, reached up quickly, and kissed Duncan on the lips for a final time.

She disengaged her lips, put her mouth into his ear and whispered, "You have nothing to apologize for. Thank you, Duncan. For everything. You were worth the wait."

Mother Nobley and the sisters didn't want him to leave, and kissed him on the cheeks as he departed. Everyone loves a *Maverick.*

He sat in the car for a few moments. Hunter started the engine and quietly stared at the double doors of the Nobley residence. *I had never gotten over Kim. Even when I was with you in Hawaii, I thought of Kim. I thought you might make me forget her but I thought you were too young and I was too old.*

Hunter breathed a great sigh and recalled *Saoirse* meant *Liberty. She was seduced by a snake whose only goal was liberty and freedom for himself. She couldn't realize her liberty could be taken from her.* He sighed again, put the car in gear, and drove away.

On the return to the airport, he checked the rearview mirror several times for any lipstick residue. In the mirror of a Casey's General Store restroom he saw that he still had some reddish-pink lipstick on his face. He wondered for a moment if it was the old Mary Kay brand Kim and Saoirse liked. *That stuff has to be obsolete; it had to have been discontinued long ago. Like the Liquid Ebony for my cars. I'm getting so old. Everyone's wearing greens and blues and orange now, even the men.* Hunter washed his face thoroughly and returned to the car. Before entering, he scanned the surrounding area. *So, this is where Radar O'Reilly was from. You have to love Middle America. This is probably a pretty good place to hide out from murderous terrorists. If you ever needed help, the boys in these parts have guns.*

Kelly rolled into the airport at virtually the same time as her father. She carried a hot pizza box and cold sodas onto the jet. Hunter closed the door on that chapter of his life when he locked the aircraft door. In the copilot seat, he didn't perform any of the copilot's preflight duties but ate the Papa John's while it was still hot. Hunter wasn't focused on flying so Kelly took down their clearance to Elmira, New York. He was quiet and composed and remained so through takeoff and level off; she performed the pilot's duties flawlessly.

She confirmed their next stop would be the National Soaring Museum.

Hunter nodded and said, "Tomorrow."

CHAPTER 72

June 12, 2018

Several vintage but flyable aircraft were stored at the old Schweizer Aircraft Company hangars, and three others were in various stages of restoration. Of the three flyable aircraft, the most notable was Hunter's most recent acquisition, a Supermarine *Spitfire*. It was being detailed after a long ferry flight from the United Kingdom. After a rousing hotel breakfast with the former owner of the World War II fighter, Hunter finally received the checkout of the aircraft that Director McGee had interrupted with his phone call. A few hours later under the watchful eye of the former owner, Hunter started the Rolls Royce Merlin V12. Obstructed vision during taxi and a remarkably fast takeoff were normal experiences for a taildragger pilot. After an hour, he returned to the field. Hunter thanked the old man and led him to the newest aircraft on the airport, a Gulfstream G550. As agreed, Hunter started, taxied, and took off with the old man in the copilot seat. Kelly rode in the back.

The man stayed at the controls of the jet all the way to John F. Kennedy International Airport. Hunter offered to let him land the jet but he said, "I know my limitations" and demurred. At the executive terminal, Duncan Hunter handed the old gentleman his ticket to England. JFK to Heathrow. British Airways. 747. Hunter pointed out his seat was in First Class, 7A, the same number that was on the *Spitfire*. Before the old pilot boarded the shuttle to the international terminal he shook hands with Hunter one more time and said, "Thank you for allowing me to fly the Spitfire at the Normandy memorial. That was a very emotional time for me. My life is complete. Thank you again, sir." He exchanged salutes with Duncan.

Hunter knew he would have to wait, commercial traffic had the priority for takeoff. He pulled out his BlackBerry and texted McGee to ensure there wasn't another rendition to be performed; there wasn't. Hunter wasn't prepared to mess up a perfectly good business jet transporting undesirable elements from al-Qaeda or ISIS. McGee's answer included no update for Nazy's ETA.

Once he was cleared, Kelly Horne took the runway, blasted out over the ocean, and turned back toward Elmira, New York. Hunter had several more deeds to do.

• • •

With Maui Jim sunglasses over his eyes, Duncan stood arms akimbo and watched his little girl blast off from the runway at Harris Hill. A Cessna 172 tractor pulled the two-place competition sailplane down the runway which was airborne well before the end of the runway.

While Kelly was aloft Hunter again checked the ETA status of his wife. She had been in meetings in Australia and was still a few days from home. A call to Carlos Yazzie confirmed that all of Duncan's vehicles were stuffed into a new hangar at the Jackson Airport. The only vehicles at the lodge were a couple of armored Hummers and Hunter's and Yazzie's Silverado pickup trucks. Hunter asked about the incursion.

Yazzie relayed, "Captain, it was a strange incident in that it wasn't *Islamists* who had tried to gain access to the property. The armed perpetrators were *Yankees*; dead *Yankees* after their firefight with the sheriff's department. The *Yankees* had a few small drones with them like no one at the sheriff's department had ever seen before. They pushed the incident to the FBI and the feds said the drones had 'shaped charges' and were probably secret devices used by Special Forces. But the most amazing thing is that the sheriff said one of the men was a retired Marine Corps Sergeant Major. Is that crazy?"

"It's still under investigation?"

"It is Captain."

Hunter said, "Good. We're not moving." He knew the words would be music to Yazzie's ears. But those sound like *killer drones. Not good. Not good at all. But I have some ideas on how to stop them. And why would a Sergeant Major be mixed up in….* Hunter frowned. He knew. He then asked, "Carlos, how many drones do we have in the garage? Six, right?"

"Six total."

"Can you take four of them to the sheriff's office as a token of our appreciation?"

"Captain, that would be my pleasure."

He made several calls to McGee and Eastwood. Hunter told McGee what he wanted to do. McGee said he needed some time to set it up and that Nazy might be back in time. Eastwood indicated he would move a mountain to see Hunter's plan unfold.

After an hour in the brilliant sunshine, Hunter watched the spectacular ultra-long wing sailplane turn hard to port, line up for the runway, and silently shoot between the trees of the airport on top of the hill before skidding to a landing. The look on Kelly's face when she emerged from the tiny cockpit was pure jubilation. She squealed like a little schoolgirl, "*That was incredible!*"

• • •

She and her father walked hand in hand to their vehicle. The Agency pilots spent a few hours touring the museum. Hunter's mind was running apace.

Over dinner in Corning, Hunter told Kelly, "Your boss thinks I need a new airplane. You saw what that Allstar glider can do. I'm thinking they might develop a powered version that is not electric. I have some ideas."

"That would be incredible, Dad."

"Bill said he would fund it. The challenge is to design it. I can't ramrod an engineering project. I still have work to do overseas. Bill wondered if you might be the right person. Transfer to Air Branch. Program manager."

"I *might* be the right person." Kelly was excited at the prospect.

"That's what I said. You're an aero engineer and a pilot. This is right up your alley and will require more work that you can believe. Just a normal day at the office." Hunter smiled and continued. "Not Space Shuttle stuff, but I would definitely look at exotic materials. I read where someone at MIT was spinning new para-aramid mixes with Kevlar fibers at the microscopic level, turning aramids into new nanoscale building blocks, which include nanoparticles, nanowires, carbon nanotubes, and graphene—those are just the ones I've heard about. Structures that are many times lighter and stronger than aluminum. If we're going to do this, then we're going to do this right. I think we have to keep this in the family, at least for the time being."

"I would also look at the old guys who created the *Yo-Yo*—you can find them at the Quiet Aircraft Association. They created those special aircraft, and the old guys have had a long time to think about how they would improve on the basic design."

Kelly raised a glass of wine to Hunter's water glass and sealed the deal.

CHAPTER 73

June 13, 2018

Demetrius Eastwood prepared the sound booth for another episode for "The Outlaw Broadcasting Company." After a salutation "to my valued listeners," he rolled into his scripted opening. He thanked his growing number of sponsors and acknowledged his sponsors were clamoring for more episodes. Instead of an hour-long show weekly, his sponsors wanted a three-hour show five days a week.

"I'm humbled by your support, and we'll see what's in the art of the possible. Your desire for more airtime for *Unfiltered News* and for more of what I bring to you is really a klaxon call, warning us that our media are corrupt; in many ways they have become our enemy. They no longer report the facts, they try to push their twisted narrative on the American people. Their reporting is a form of brainwashing."

"Nothing demonstrates media corruption like today's announcement that Iranian scientists at the Ayatollah Khomeini Institute of Virology were conducting research on—*surprise, surprise; gollllly Sergeant Carter*—bat coronaviruses. Yes, coronaviruses and specifically, methods to protect the Muslim world while enhancing a coronavirus' lethality on non-Muslims. In other words, they were trying to develop a super-lethal virus that kills Christians and Jews and everyone else except devotees of Islam. The *Persian Green Death,* that name is mine." *So I stole it from Hunter; he will not mind.*

"The *Persian Green Death* from Persia, of course; green is the color of Islam, and death as in 'if they had been successful in mutating a bat coronavirus to kill innocents.' Of course, the Iranian mullahs claimed the research was entirely humanitarian; they were discovering cures for viruses and developing vaccinations for all Muslims. The American intelligence community has no comment. I don't know if it is related or not, but there are reports President Hernandez fired the

CDC Director for loss of confidence in his abilities to lead and dozens of CDC employees followed their boss out the door." *And the President authorized the emergency purchase of PPE to replenish the national stockpile. Not going to say anything about that....*

"Counterterrorism experts are mum tonight on why the Ayatollah Khomeini Institute is now rubble as reported by Al Jazeera. The U.S. Geological Survey recorded a seismic event in the area where the Khomeini Institute of Virology was destroyed. If there were flames, I wonder if the folks on the International Space Station could see the institute burning?"

"President Hernandez announced that approximately forty women were rescued from some unnamed location. Now I'm no Dick Tracy, but when we have Americans being rescued on one hand and an Iranian research lab leveled on the other, and the CDC Director being shitcanned, I'm inclined to believe they are related somehow. We have evidence of the outcome, just not the details of how or why these things happened. Hats off to our Special Operations Command and President Hernandez. The former president was a back-stabbing, traitorous, gutless wonder and would have never sent American Special Forces into the Middle East for anything that would have saved lives or killed criminal Islamists."

"In a related bit of news, the CIA and the Intelligence Community quietly announced they had severed ties with the Trans-Atlantic Security Corporation just as the head of TASCO, former Marine General Bogdan Chernovich, passed away in a fire at a resort in Italy. *Severed ties* is Pentagon-speak for having your contracts canceled."

"We have also recently received never-before seen footage of the September 11, 2001 attacks in New York City. I will play all, almost nine minutes, of the attack. I wish to remind my viewers what al-Qaeda, the Islamic Underground, and *Dark Islam* have done to America and the world. These people won't give up. We have to protect ourselves from them in the only way we can. And I must say, President Hernandez is the anti-Mazibuike; he is undoing every piece of legislation the former president signed into law. Under Mazibuike, we were one step away from George Orwell's dystopian vision of a government that will do whatever is necessary to control its people and the narrative."

Eastwood started the video, which was dumped into the cameras in his studio. He watched jets fly into the towers again and didn't make any comments until after it ran its course.

"The bad news is that al-Qaeda, the Islamic Underground, *Jabhat Fatah al-Sham*, Hamas, Hezbollah, Jemaah Islamiyah, al-Shabab, and literally a hundred other fractured terrorist groups, all under the rubric of *Dark Islam* will never give up their goal of world domination and the destruction of the Jewish people and Christians wherever they find them. The good news is that each of these terrorist organizations is in distress or decline or have had their leaders destroyed. America once again is making a difference."

"In what may be a turning of the worm, Iran's top nuclear scientist was assassinated in Tehran Province today. An organization no one had ever heard of, the *Persian Resistance* movement, took credit for the killing. If true, we may witness the first cracks in the ayatollah's total grip of power on the country. We'll monitor them."

"In the most populous country in Africa, Nigerian Christians have been at war with the al-Qaeda splinter group, Boko Haram. Recent intel suggests the tide has turned, and now those murderous bastards are on the run. Special Operations Forces have decimated their top leaders. The U.S. Air Force is training Nigerian pilots. Under President Hernandez we may actually see the wholesale destruction of *Dark Islam* in equatorial Africa. We are living in extremely dangerous times, reminiscent of the Chinese Communist Cultural Revolution. We have communists and leftists and a fascist media that cover for them in ways that are reprehensible. I understand the cries for liberty, for freedom of speech and truth."

"That's enough free press for the *dark media*. It's a day of celebration for this special edition of *Unfiltered News*. I would like to think Americans were involved with the destruction of the Khomeini Institute of Virology. *It's the romantic in me*, as the Prefect of Police would say in the movie classic *Casablanca*. Americans, like the warriors at SOCOM, are quietly doing the work to crush international evil."

"Americans have been at peace and prosperity for many years and I think many of our citizens cannot comprehend the evil that resides at our door. I can't believe this evil. We are a tolerant bunch. We've let many of our institutions fall because we failed to counteract the evil of the left. Their intentions are more psychopathic than intelligent, more violent than compassionate. In coming episodes, we'll be tackling these issues, like why the left attacked and killed the Boy Scouts, and we'll see if we can reverse the evil that has crept into our public policy. We should not kowtow to the mob; the mob should be governed and where necessary, incarcerated by the people."

"So I am announcing here tonight that I will be leading the effort to reconstitute the Boy Scouts of America. It is the first step to take back our country. The mob will not dictate what is right and righteous; God-fearing people who made this country great have had enough of their crap. We will fight them in the streets and in the courts; and we will not give up the fight to protect our children from the left. Stay tuned for our progress."

"That's it for tonight. We review the newsworthy events of the past week that you likely heard nothing about in the media. Here we don't have an agenda. We see information as a tool used to make decisions; information that is not weaponized."

"Today is a day to reflect on our heritage as Americans. The United States of America is the universal beacon of freedom—*freedom*, the one preoccupation that has been the focus of healthy minds of subjugated men and women for millennia. I can't comprehend why some hate America, but hate they do. They are preoccupied with stealing; stealing your stuff, stealing your liberty, stealing your life. Freedom-loving people are in direct conflict with them. Our Founders understood the mind of the subjugators, and wrote the Bill of Rights on behalf of freedom-loving people, not the mentally deficient or criminals."

"We have a president who is not afraid of deploying our military to destroy those who intend to harm us. It has taken me some time to realize America has been under assault for two centuries. Whenever the country is on the edge of falling, somehow we get a man of moxie who isn't afraid to brawl with these bandits. It's time for someone like our President Javier Hernandez. Get a copy of the U.S. Constitution. Read it. Get a weapon. Learn to use it. Educate and protect yourself."

"There is some hope. Sometimes a blind squirrel finds a nut. The brain dead liberal governor of California is now admitting that their green energy program is a colossal failure. The rolling blackouts every evening when the rich plug in their electric cars to charge them should have been the first clue. Politicians are not engineers. Politicians are professional liars. So what do we do with all the electric cars? We could set them on fire and toast marshmallows."

"That's it for today. Semper Fi to all of my Marine Corps brothers and sisters. I'm standing and saluting the men and women of the military, first responders, law enforcement, the farmers and the factory workers, and all the law-abiding citizens across the fruited plain who make this country work. Good night. Eastwood out."

CHAPTER 74

June 13, 2018

The sun was high in the blue sky and there was little wind as the elder McGee, newly promoted to Brigadier General by President Hernandez, was helped from the cockpit of the TP-51C *Mustang*. Duncan Hunter extricated himself from behind the pilot seat. The *Mustang* featured the latest in digital radios, electronics, and GPS NAVAIDs in the cockpit; all the equipment for touring on the airshow circuit. An instructor's seat and flight controls had been installed behind the pilot for training P-51 pilots. Near the row of T-hangars, a fuel truck waited for the signal to refuel the immaculately restored warbird.

The McGee family, including Nicole and Kayla in their Academy white uniforms, and Demetrius Eastwood were on hand to watch Captain Hunter give the 100-year-old retired Air Force fighter pilot his final flight in a military aircraft. The aircraft's livery was from World War II with a bright red nose cone, a red tail, and *KITTEN* freshly painted in red letters across the nose. "*KITTEN*" was the pet name of the general's late wife. The restoration and the paint of the *Mustang* duplicated the highly polished aluminum aircraft that U.S. Army Air Corps Captain McGee had flown in combat during WWII. The General's name and rank were emblazoned under the bubble canopy. Eastwood and the McGee family took pictures of one of the last living members of the Tuskegee Airmen in his brilliant blue flight suit with silver command pilot wings on his chest as he stood on the *Mustang's* wing. *Maverick* saluted the general who returned the honors.

Maverick requested that no picture be taken of him. He waved the fuel truck over to top off the tanks. The fuel truck driver provided a fuel sample; Hunter spun the sample in the glass jar and double-checked that the purple fuel was free of water. The driver manipulated the controls on the fuel truck, and *Maverick* refueled the *Mustang*. As the fuel ran in he talked to McGee's girls and asked them how they got "off the yard" for a ride in the warbird. "We just said we had an opportunity to fly in a P-51 *Mustang*. We didn't think anyone was going to believe us, but we had to tell them what we were doing. The Superintendent wants pictures."

"And Colonel Eastwood will provide, I'm sure." *Maverick* saluted the midshipmen who gave him a massive hug before they returned to their parents.

Bill McGee waited until the refueling was complete, then excused himself from his family. He stopped Hunter before he took the *Mustang* back to Elmira. McGee said, "You never cease to amaze me. Apparently you can execute a night parachute jump. Huh! Who knew?"

Hunter smiled. *Don't tell Nazy!*

McGee nodded as if he understood. He returned to the present and said, "Thank you. You don't know how thrilled he was. The girls too. You're spoiling them."

Maverick beamed and nodded, and gritted his teeth. It was an emotional time. Sometimes you just know you "did good." After a moment of reflection, he said, "As this greatest generation of liberators dwindles, it should be a time to reflect on who these heroes were and are; lives dedicated to liberty. The old become an inspiration for the young, to seek greater futures and guard against lesser evils. Your dad helped vanquish socialism."

McGee was caught up in the moment. After several breaths and nods he said, "*Maverick*, I cannot believe you let him fly. All of his friends—those that are still living—seem to fall with the frequency of a one-legged drunk on an ice rink, and you had him piloting a plane. That is incredible."

Maverick grinned. *Yes, it was a little screwy, but I checked his strength and was convinced he was strong enough to handle it.* "He's amazing. I was up on the wing and got him situated in the pilot's seat and then I told him to close his eyes and tell me where everything is in the cockpit, and damn, he could still do it. I figured that since he is still walking without a cane, that he's an incredible specimen for 100, that he might get it off the ground. And I had a set of flight controls just in case there were any problems."

McGee said, "You told me after your accident your CO said, 'It wasn't your time to die. God has plans for you.' I firmly believe Dad couldn't go until he could get behind the stick of a *Mustang* one last time. You made the impossible happen. Thank you again."

After the accolades, *Maverick* found his voice, and placed a hand on McGee's shoulder. "I was just thrilled he didn't kill both of us! You don't know, but your dad went immediately to the rudder pedals—he knew how to work the rudder for a taildragger even after all the years flying jets. You rarely touch the rudder in a jet. But the general knew exactly what he was doing; he knew where everything was. He powered it up, he didn't have to re-start it three times like I do and he countered the weather-vane effect like he hadn't ever been out of the plane."

"He was good?"

"God, *he was great! Smooth as glass.* Flying is a perishable skill, but your dad still has the touch; landing and taking off you never forget because you do them under immense pressure all the time, it becomes muscle memory. The general did nothing unexpected and he was aware of his limitations. He was just back in the cockpit of an airplane that he had spent hundreds of hours in. When he said we should start home after about ten minutes, I said, 'That's probably enough excitement for one day, sir. I'll take it from here.' Warbirds are beasts to fly, and I thought if anyone could handle it, it was him. He took off like a pro and I landed it like an instructor pilot. I'm sure if the FAA finds out about this they will kill me, so this will be our little secret. Your dad's a great American, *Bullfrog*."

Maverick wasn't getting off so easily. The general had been surrounded by McGee's petite wife and gamboling girls in their uniforms, taking pictures with the man of the hour. Eastwood followed the group with a Nikon. General McGee shook *Maverick's* hand one last time; he held on with a double-hand clasp, and said, "Thank you, *Maverick*. You're a true gentleman and a scholar, and one of the finest officers I have known." This time the general saluted the captain. McGee's daughters and wife teasingly shouted what they had heard in the Rose Garden a few days earlier, "We love you, *Maverick!*"

Maverick thanked Director McGee for taking time out his busy schedule. He helped Eastwood into the rear seat of the *Mustang*. Once he was buckled in the cockpit, Hunter waved goodbye.

The group shielded their eyes from the sun as the Red Tail departed the Easton Airport.

The Rolls Royce Merlin motor roared when he pushed the throttle to the firewall. *Maverick* lifted the *Mustang* off the runway, retracted the landing gear, and kept the nose low to gain speed. Before he was clear of the runway, the old Marine fighter pilot pulled the aircraft up and to the right and gave the McGees one last low-G airshow-type maneuver before heading to Elmira.

CHAPTER 75

June 15, 2018

Duncan Hunter returned the *Mustang* to the Elmira plant. He nearly needed a crowbar to extricate Demetrius Eastwood from the back seat. After lunching at a local pizzeria Hunter and Eastwood boarded the Gulfstream for the return trip to Manassas. Eastwood wanted to know what happened to Chernovich.

"All I know is that his bio indicated that his gender preferences were 'he' and 'him' but now they are 'was' and 'isn't.'"

"You would like me to change the subject."

Hunter answered with a grin. "Thank you, Dory. And thank you for the watch. That *Submariner* with the red letters is rare."

"For all that you've done for me. Thank you."

"I surmised you got it when you graduated from the U.S. Naval Academy."

"That's easy to surmise but wrong. Grads don't go into town to shop for out-of-the-ordinary watches. The Naval Academy bookstore got the best and newest offerings from all the expensive watchmakers. I drooled over them, like all the Mids. Owning one sort of put you in the fraternity of the accomplished. Virtually all the grads bought gold class rings with whatever precious stone they could afford, and the top grads or the guys whose parents had money got the most expensive watches as graduation presents. I knew my parents couldn't afford one then, but I finally got that steel Rolex *Submariner* out of an AFEES catalog when I was in Vietnam."

"It's worth a fortune now."

"You've spent a fortune on me; I still feel I'm in arrears."

"You are not and never will be. We are a team."

After trading the jet for a Hummer, Hunter continued their conversation on their way to downtown Washington, D.C. He told the story behind the *Daytona*. "I was at an airshow and there was an astronaut from NASA, which is so very unusual—NASA rarely allows astronauts to go to airshows. He had brought a NASA T-38. I asked, 'What did it take for him to get into the astronaut program?' He offered, 'NASA likes PhDs and test pilots. Get some of that stuff on your résumé and you might get into the program.' So that's what I did. Over time, I learned that the smartest guys on the planet help make the instruments of space exploration—Apollo capsules, Mars landers, moon rovers, Hubble Space Telescope, Space Shuttle. And let's not forget the space-based cameras. Extremely complex stuff. When America put a satellite into orbit, we didn't just launch a dog like Moscow did, we put a functioning spy satellite into a polar orbit to take pictures of the Soviet Union's launch facilities."

Eastwood knew where Hunter was going. He didn't interrupt as Hunter continued, "The smartest guys—not just the engineers and the scientists, but the most accomplished operational guys on the planet are test pilots and those working in space. I had orders to Navy Test Pilot School. I was on my way when I got hurt—now you know the rest of that story."

Eastwood nodded and waited for the storyteller to finish.

Hunter said, "So what's with the watch? Pilots need pilot's watches. Any astronaut wannabe needs an astronaut's watch. This one is differentiated by a solid rose gold case and the obsidian dial with a star-field of tiny dots of luminescent material. The dial was created by Switzerland's most renowned enameler. This watch was given to the first man to set foot on the moon."

"As for this watch, what people don't know was that immediately after his inauguration in 1968, President Nixon inquired what it would take for a special watch to be constructed for a very special event and for some very special men. Three were especially manufactured by Rolex by Presidential Order and the Republican president personally paid for the special timepieces for the Apollo 11 astronauts. There are Naval Aviator wings engraved on the back with the date Neil received his wings and the date he stepped onto the moon. Inscribed on the back: In Commemoration to Neil Armstrong, First Man on the Moon. It came with the original genuine wood box and green printed box. Hardly anyone had heard of rose gold before. When the

Shah of Iran heard of the moon watches in 1972, he had fifty of the same color made by royal order as gifts to his generals."

"I bought Neil's watch, and now you're going to give it to the Smithsonian. Maybe it can inspire another boy or girl to reach for the stars as a test pilot or a fighter pilot before they take all the pilots out of the cockpits of high-performance aircraft."

• • •

Duncan Hunter watched from a distance as Lieutenant Colonel Demetrius Eastwood presented the rose gold Rolex *Daytona* to the Administrator of the Smithsonian Air & Space Museum. Hunter had set the time when the Apollo 11 lunar lander touched the surface of the Moon, 4:17 pm, on July 20, 1969. That was the day, the moment, when hundreds of millions of people had heard, *Houston, Tranquility Base here, The Eagle has landed.* Eastwood relayed the story of how President Nixon had commissioned three special watches for the historic mission. He said, "Chevrolet had gifted the Apollo astronauts with Corvettes; on behalf of all Americans the President gifted Rolex *Daytona* Cosmographs to the Apollo 11 astronauts. These uniquely constructed timepieces were specifically designed to withstand high levels of vibrations and intense magnetic fields expected during spaceflight."

Eastwood did not convey that Neil Armstrong, the astronaut who was given the cliquish and complex cosmograph before launch, reportedly hated it; not because it was a Rolex, but because it required winding daily. Shortly after all the parades and ceremonies given for the first moon walkers, Armstrong traded the manual for a self-winding gold and stainless *Submariner*. Somehow the *Daytona* "moon watch" found its way to a Rolex shop in Okinawa where it had been ignored; no one believed it was real because there was a significant market for bogus Rolexes. However, Hunter asked the shopkeeper to remove the band; he copied the serial number, wrote Rolex, and bought the watch.

The Air & Space Museum Administrator thanked Colonel Eastwood and said they would present the watch to the public on the anniversary of the moon landing on July 20th.

• • •

The CEO of the International Spy Museum was speechless when Eastwood presented Sean Connery's big-crown "James Bond *Submarine*r" to display at the museum. Eastwood remarked, "It is probably the most famous movie watch of all time and you can see it in *Dr. No, From Russia with Love,* and *Goldfinger.*"

After returning to the Hummer, Eastwood reminded Hunter that he had promised to tell him the story about "getting a U-2 flyover." Hunter would have to be quick as the men could see Union Station several traffic lights away.

Hunter smiled and said, "Remember where we were. I was telling you about TASC, about Chernovich, but there was nothing I could do about exposing him. Like there was nothing I could do to expose Mazibuike until I had something."

"I do. You told me I could do it as I had a pen, a microphone, and an audience."

Hunter explained, "In other words, there was something you could do if you were appropriately motivated *and equipped,* because you had some basics that I did not possess. I could have a theory, but it wouldn't go anywhere until the conditions surrounding the situation changed. So this story begins with an old Air Force colonel who ran the U-2s at Laughlin Air Force Base in Texas during the 1960s. This was the time where I was officially working for the Air Force as their number two senior civilian—it made for good cover—the Deputy Director of Maintenance. So this old colonel, Ernie Worley, came up to me and reminded me that the 4080th Strategic Reconnaissance Wing was having their biennial reunion soon. These guys, those who remained in Texas, were all in their late 70s and 80s. It was probably going to be their last reunion. Ernie said they would have Gary Powers' son as the keynote speaker, and then he asked me to see about 'getting a U-2 flyover.' It was absurd to think a civilian could get the

U.S. Air Force to reprogram one of their strategic assets for a little 'flyover' for a bunch of retired officers."

"Yeah, I can see where that's impossible."

"I told the good colonel he needed to talk to the Wing Commander, to do some of that colonel-to-colonel, secret-sauce, special handshake stuff, but Ernie shook his head and said I was one of those guys who could get things done. Later that day I went to the Operations Group Commander and asked him. He was pretty emphatic that not only had Colonel Worley lost his mind, but I had also lost mine. He said it was impossible, that he was lucky the base got an airshow every year so his instructors and students could see the different aircraft in the Air Force's inventory. We called those airshows a travelling 'petting zoo.'"

At times Hunter waved his free hand wildly for emphasis. "Now, I was also on deck that night with a night school class for Embry-Riddle. It was a huge facility and relatively new, with an auditorium, classrooms, and briefing rooms. It was the biggest building on the base. So I started my lecture in one of those very classrooms and gave *my little darlings*—mostly instructor pilots—a little history lesson. I told them about the contributions of the 4080th during the Cuban Missile Crisis and especially, Major Rudolph Anderson, U-2 pilot extraordinaire, who flew from Laughlin to Cuba. Anderson was the first recipient of the Air Force Cross, the U.S. Air Force's second-highest award for heroism, and was the only fatality by enemy fire when his U-2 reconnaissance jet was shot down. I said the Air Force usually has little monuments around the base for things like that, and in fact there was only a shard of granite with a tiny brass plaque near the flag pole that honored Major Anderson. I told them they had walked by it countless times and didn't even know that it was there."

"I also said something like the Air Force dedicates buildings on the base and names them after its fallen heroes. I said I was certain there was even a military working dog that had the shitter on the golf course named after him or her. But there is nothing substantial in Del Rio named after Major Rudolph Anderson. All Rudy got was a rock."

"And I said, 'I was thinking that the building that we are in doesn't have a name; that it hasn't been dedicated for anyone. I was thinking that the day of the 4080th Strategic Reconnaissance Wing reunion would be a good time to give this building a name, something *appropriate* for a fallen airman, like *Anderson Hall.*' I said, 'You know the base was named after Jack T. Laughlin, a local B-17 pilot from the war.' Some of my students were understandably more confused than a chameleon in a bag of Skittles, so I told them, 'I'm not the *right guy* to suggest such a thing, but I am old, wise in the ways of the world, and I know how these things work. If one of you believe this is a novel idea, maybe you will float that trial balloon with your squadron commander. See if it does anything.' One of my students said he would do it."

"So what happened?"

Hunter's non-driving hand was flying again. "The next morning before eleven my hand-held radio went off. The Group Ops O wanted to see me. I marched across the street to his office, and he is in a huff. He wagged his finger at me like a pissed off cop who wanted to give me a ticket but could only admonish me for doing something stupid. He said, 'I know what you did. You got one of your students to float the idea of turning the Ops building into Anderson Hall during the 4080th's reunion. Am I right?' I nodded. It's a funny thing to get your ass chewed out by an Air Force officer, because they just don't know how to do it. Marine Gunnery Sergeants are the masters. Then he says, 'So let me tell you what happened. Your student tells his Squadron Commander who thinks it is a marvelously fantastic concept. The Squadron Commander says he's flying with the Wing Commander this morning, giving him a check ride. The Wing Commander thinks it is also an awesome and wonderful proposal. The Wing Commander calls his boss, the two-star in San Antonio, who thinks it is a tremendous and exceptional suggestion, so he calls his boss, the four-star, who said it was an unrivaled and timely tradition that he would fully support.' He called his four-star buddy at Beale—where all the U-2s are to see about getting a U-2 flyover."

Eastwood howled with laughter. Hunter joined in.

"So you can imagine what it was like when that amazing black jet with the incredibly long wings flew over the newly designated Anderson Hall. We had a boatload of colonels and generals for the ceremony. It was an optimal day for a bunch of patriots. No winds, no clouds. Just CAVU perfection. Colonel Worley sidled up to me with the remnants of tears on his face and shook my hand. 'I don't know why, but I knew that only you could have figured out a way to do that, and we got the biggest building on the base named after Rudolph Anderson. He was one of my closest friends. I thank you.'"

"Were you surprised?"

"Not that it happened. I was, however, a little taken aback at how fast it happened. Timing and how the cards are aligned makes all the difference. You have to analyze the problem and know how those things are solved. 'No' wasn't the right answer. Some things just require a well-placed, well-timed nudge. I learned a lot from a Marine colonel, a CO who wanted to be a general so bad.... His strategy was to dedicate buildings or aircraft and invite generals to the ceremonies. He didn't have a sponsor, so he tried to create one. I needed to plant the idea in the sponsor's head, but I didn't have access to the sponsor."

"You needed a general to sponsor the project."

"I didn't care who got the credit, I just wanted Colonel Worley to get his U-2 flyover. It's a lot like getting General McGee into the cockpit of a *Mustang* one last time. These patriots would give anything to experience the thrill of their pasts one last time. I believe flying a jet or a warbird is the most incredible experience one can have."

Eastwood was quiet for a while before he asked, "Do you think you can predict or manipulate human behavior?"

"If they have a normal mind; one that is not trying to figure out how to get over on someone else. But if they have a disorder, like the mass shooters, like Washington Democrats, it's like Forrest Gump's box of chocolates—predictability is uncertain. They are people who are really out of control, and you don't know what you're going to get."

As Hunter pulled into Union Station, he thanked Eastwood for all he had done. He shook his hand and gave him a salute which was returned. Eastwood thought their business was finished, but business is rarely "finished" when it comes to Duncan Hunter. He asked Eastwood for a favor.

Eastwood wanted one in return. *What really happened to Chernovich?*

Hunter said, "No can do, *G.I. Dog*. But don't you already know the answer? You know I will need you for another adventure."

Eastwood said he probably did, and Hunter's favor wasn't really anything. He bade Hunter farewell. He had a watch to deliver on Hunter's behalf, one that had been factory repaired after it had been removed from the wrist of a dead terrorist. Eastwood expected a much more somber setting when the factory-repaired steel Rolex *Daytona* returned home to Del Rio, Texas.

CHAPTER 76

June 18, 2018

The White House Press Secretary announced that President Hernandez would not engage the Democrats in any discussion over the issue they had dominated for over twenty years. The Republican National Committee Chairman announced their position on political colors. The press secretary reiterated, "The Democrats need to stop avoiding their heritage of socialism, communism, Marxism, and racism and embrace the left's natural historical political colors. The President approved of the Republican National Committee's (RNC) stated position and signed an executive order. This should not be a big deal. If ever it were true, today's Socialist Democrats are forever intertwined with the color 'red.' They are the left; the left is associated with the color 'red.' They will always be associated with red, of blood, of anarchy, and the red flags of totalitarianism everywhere. The Grand Old Party will forever be associated with the color of liberty, of freedom, national blue. If they don't like it, they can always take this issue to court."

"And while we are discussing the Democrat Party's association with red and anarchists and communists, the White House is seeking a Congressman who will bring a resolution to the floor that would ban any group or organization that have historically supported the Confederacy, slavery, Communism, or Marxism in the United States."

A lone timid White House correspondent raised her hand and asked, "Does that include the Democrat Party?"

The press secretary was confused, "Are you trying to say the Democrat Party has historically supported the Confederacy, slavery, Communism, or Marxism in the United States?"

• • •

Three zeroes in the BlackBerry screen probably meant the CIA Director was calling. By his calculations Nazy wasn't due to land in

Washington yet, and Hunter anticipated this was going to be a request for another rendition flight. Anything to keep him away from his bride of many years. Instead McGee had some news. Hunter was incredulous. All he could say was, "Seriously?"

"Seriously. You're about to get another boatload of money off of your patents. I informed the President how vulnerable we are to drone incursions at airports and to weaponized viruses. I explained close quarters on our surface ships and subs are the perfect breeding grounds for an epidemic to spread and incapacitate the crew. The U.S. Navy just awarded multiple contracts, some for Quiet Aero Systems, for anti-drone technology to be installed at military bases. Your Texas Ultraviolet will be contracted to design and install ultraviolet sterilization equipment in the HVAC units aboard naval surface vessels and submarines. The Secretaries of Agriculture, Education, Justice, and Defense have issued RFPs (request for proposal) for ultraviolet sterilization equipment to be installed in the HVAC units of meat processing plants, schools, courts, and military bases and shipyards. If a bug is ever let loose in America, we will be prepared. And if the imams try to send a drone into the intake of a jet, we'll send them to the intake of a jail or deportation court. Maybe even GITMO."

Hunter shouted, "That's *major!* We had been talking about protecting bases from suicide drones, and commercial air carriers should put UV-C in their HVAC ducts because HEPA isn't enough to stop the small viruses."

"Yeah. And the military's lab that was researching weaponized pathogens before Mazibuike shut it down has gotten new interest and increased funding to research the viruses and coronaviruses and pathogens. Anyone involved in those programs will have to be polygraphed, to include the CDC. Those traitorous bastards are now running around with their hair on fire and jumping out of windows. While the focus was on the Islamic Underground infiltrating the FBI everyone missed the communists infiltrating State and the Gambino crime family at the CDC. President Hernandez concurs we will stop the infiltration of bad actors into our most sensitive programs. If you were unaware, he fired the CDC Director and that whole den of snakes."

Only President Hernandez has the guts to fight the lefties and their idiotic PC culture. Hunter laughed into his smartphone. "About friggin' time!"

"There's more. China is in an uproar; they believe the Khomeini Institute was hacked and they lost all their files. Apparently, their epidemiologists did not forward any of *their* research. The Chinese epidemiologists weren't getting paid for their work and they kept Beijing from getting any of it."

"*Oh, no!* Say is isn't so!" Hunter wasn't sad at all.

"The Chinese are not taking the loss of what they call 'their Institute in Iran' lying down. They're blaming Russia of course. One of their surveillance aircraft detected the residue from the detonation of an old Soviet tactical device near the border in Iran. They are claiming the Russians stole their research and detonated a nuclear weapon to cover their tracks."

"That is positively *fascinating,* Director McGee."

"Apparently they had dumped billions of yuan into that place just so they could conduct the most dangerous research. It gave them plausible deniability and didn't expose their people if there was an accident. They're pissed."

Hunter offered, "It reminds me a little of when the Soviets stole the plans from France to make their own supersonic transport."

"That didn't go well, as I recall."

"I understand that facility is still on fire. That's huge, *my captain.*"

"Which reminds me, just came over the wire, the seismic event that destroyed the facility also incinerated the only colony of Fratarakas horseshoe bats...."

"Oh, that's too bad. I'm sure PETA will march in the streets. Set the place on fire. I understand they were nasty critters."

"PETA or the bats?" McGee was enjoying being impish.

"Yes, sir."

"One last thing, *Sir Duncan*. Seems some of the *birds* you freed were Brits, Italians, a German. French. The Queen has invited the President for a State Dinner and because we, but mostly you, helped to rescue British subjects, not only are *we* invited, but the Queen is apparently going to give *you* something."

"That was a team event, *Bullfrog*."

"I wasn't supposed to be there, so I officially wasn't."

"But you were handing out challenge coins like they were Halloween candy!"

"I was on an *official visit* to Turkmenistan—I needed to see my folks."

Hunter chuckled. Life is good when things go your way.

"I told the President you would downplay your efforts. Not going to work."

Hunter tried to be a wiseacre. "Ok, maybe I'll get a Bentley. I do not have a Bentley, but I don't want an electric Jag. Do we have an inbound on Nazy yet?"

"You'll take what's coming to you, and you'll be happy getting it! As for your *bird*, she's about four hours out. She indicated you know where to meet her. One last thing. The President would like you at the Oval Office immediately. I'm working on a good time; it could be in a few hours. I will pick you up. I have to go."

Probably wants to give us another medal. "Bill, I don't have a suit for a POTUS party—I'll have to go buy one."

"Then go buy one! I'll see you in a few." The speakerphone went dead.

McGee grinned at Hunter's wife across the office desk. He gave her a "thumbs up," and she reciprocated. Nazy wore another billowy dress and colorful Hermès scarf. She had crossed her legs and bounced a python Ferragamo on a foot. She debriefed McGee; McGee debriefed her. Immediately after arriving, he had said, "Nazy, I'm probably violating a hundred HR rules about comments on another's personal appearance, but your new hairstyle is...*most becoming*."

Nazy had held on to a devilish grin for much too long until she finally said, "I want it to be a surprise."

He returned to the present. "Oh, *Maverick* is in for a jolt! You look so different!"

Nazy chuckled and said, "Thank you, Bill." *For playing along and for not saying anything.*

"He's in for a treat. We might need an ambulance and a guy with paddles." He thought of what Hunter was in for at the White House. In one of his best *double entendres,* he said, "He might need one of those horse needles full of adrenaline to get his heart going again! What you and the President are going to do to him, this will be epic."

CHAPTER 77

June 18, 2018

In a city full of limousines and personal security units it wasn't unusual to see a limo and its accompanying vehicles stop at a Starbucks so a federal agent could jump out for coffees and Danishes and such. Few heads turned on the streets of downtown Washington, D.C. when the string of black Suburbans with blacked-out windows stopped in front of the Brooks Brothers store so a sharp dressed man with a 50s-style chapeau could get into the middle limo.

Hunter removed his hat once he was in the vehicle. He smiled at his boss. *Seems like I can't go very far without seeing you. And then there are weeks when I don't. Sometimes this is just quixotic work.* Hunter was a little surprised Nazy wasn't traveling with Bill; it would have made for great surprise if she had jumped out at him like a jack-in-the box. If McGee's intel could be believed, by Duncan's calculations she was still a few hours away from landing. They chatted about nothing until Hunter asked him if he had heard anything about a drug smuggling aircraft that went down over the Colombian jungle.

"In fact, I got a brief on that weeks ago. The DEA had lost track of it on radar, and it never appeared again. Obviously, you know something."

Hunter shot a finger pistol, the kind of gesture that could get a first grader in the Socialist Republic of Maryland suspended from school.

"It was briefed that he was likely flying without external lights and crashed into the jungle. DEA found the aircraft and the dope, but the pilot was nowhere to be found. So that was you? Well, obviously, since you knew about it and...."

"...had first-hand information. Yes, sir. That was me. I did not put that in an after action report." Hunter nodded his little nod then quietly handed McGee a blue Chivas Regal pouch with "Royal Salute" embroidered on it. He emptied the bag into his hand; a TAG Heuer *Autavia* GMT slipped out. McGee returned the watch to the pouch and placed it into his suitcoat pocket as if it were an afterthought. The CIA Director knew exactly what needed to be done with it. He also knew exactly how Hunter acquired it and didn't need Hunter to explain it; after all it was his plan. The U.S. Embassy in Italy relayed an article from the Italian media that what had happened to Chernovich and his lover resulted from an Islamic Revolutionary Guard Corps-style hit job. The IRGC had taken revenge on General Chernovich for the killing of General Roustaie.

Hunter searched McGee's face for clues to his admitted extracurricular activities over Colombia. Would divulging his little secret disqualify him in some way? Bill could keep a secret, but he couldn't keep a straight face. Something was up.

Entry into the White House grounds was made automatically. The CIA Director's car was always waved through. Radio coordination.

The Oval Office was full of generals and admirals, Bill McGee's girls in their Naval Academy uniforms, his wife, and father in the uniform of an Air Force general officer. President Hernandez greeted Director McGee warmly and then Hunter. The President held Hunter's hand with a two-hand grip and relayed that he understood Duncan had taken General McGee flying in an old *Mustang*. "That *had* to have been a sight!"

General McGee was encouraged to comment by a Presidential smile. He said, "Mr. President, he is either the craziest man I have met or the bravest."

President Hernandez finally released his hold on Hunter and concluded it was the latter. He patted the Texan on the back and thanked everyone for the quick meeting. He had several things he wanted to do before "...these two get back to work in the service of our country." The Chairman of the Joint Chiefs of Staff called the room to attention and barked, "Attention to Orders!"

McGee and a very confused Duncan Hunter took a position facing the President of the United States. Hunter noticed he had not been mentioned as *Maverick* and whatever else happened, not being outed was the desired outcome.

The Chairman held the parchment up to his face and read through bifocals, "The President of the United States takes extremely great pleasure in awarding the Distinguished Intelligence Cross to William Randall McGee and Drue Duncan Hunter. Under Special Access Program *Noble Savage,* you demonstrated uncommon and extraordinary acts of heroism and valor. You faced unforeseen dangers with exemplary courage and determination, you contributed significantly to the complete destruction of the murderous terrorist group *Jabhat Fatah al-Sham,* and at significant peril to your safety, you successfully rescued and recovered scores of American citizens and British subjects kidnapped and held by another terrorist organization. Your unilateral actions saved countless lives, your unwavering courage and steadfast devotion to your country reflects great credit upon yourself and upholds the highest traditions of the Central Intelligence Agency. Given under my hand this fifteenth day of June, in the year of our Lord, 2018. Signed Javier Hernandez. President." The Chairman retrieved two wooden boxes from the corner of the Resolute Desk and handed them, one at a time to the President who presented McGee and then Hunter with the medals. Hunter was in a state of shock. He had been outed by the President.

President Hernandez continued and said, "Remain at attention."

The Chief of Naval Operations shouted, "Attention to Orders," and read the promotion warrant. The President promoted Captain William Randall McGee to the rank of Rear Admiral. The Commandant of the Marine Corps stepped forward, called, "Attention to Orders," read the promotion warrant, and the President promoted Drue Duncan Hunter to the rank of Colonel in the United States Marine Corps. President Hernandez led the men in reciting the oath of office of their new rank. He asked McGee and Hunter to stand "at ease." He said, "Like all senior promotions yours were approved with the consent of the Senate, just this afternoon. The Senate Majority Leader is also here to witness history being made. Few people are aware of *Admiral* McGee's exploits, but they know of his awards. The Congressional Medal of Honor, five Navy Crosses, two Distinguished Intelligence Crosses, five Legions of Merit, a dozen Purple Hearts. *Admiral* McGee is the most decorated man to have ever served in uniform. As for Colonel Hunter, this makes five Distinguished Intelligence Crosses to go with his twelve Meritorious Service Medals."

"I can think of no finer men who understand the fundamental nature of war and the price of liberty, men who are committed to defeating every threat to our nation and who are undeterred by the high price of victory. No finer men have served, in uniform or out, in the service of liberty and to our country." The President shook McGee's and Hunter's hands and said, *sotto voce*, "Admiral McGee, Colonel Hunter, America will never know of your courage and heroism or your accomplishments contributing to our National Security and Defense. On behalf of a great and grateful Nation, please accept my deepest appreciation and gratitude. We will be forever in your debt. Thank you and congratulations."

For the next several minutes, McGee and Hunter shook hands with a dozen flag officers, the Vice President, the Senate Majority Leader, and the National Security Advisor. Up until that moment, other than the President and the McGee family, no one had a hint who Colonel Hunter was, no one knew why he had been promoted, or why he had received several Distinguished Intelligence Crosses. There was no doubt everyone in the room knew who Admiral McGee was. The President thanked everyone for coming. Admiral McGee leaned into the President and said something into his ear, which made him erupt in laughter and subdued applause. Nearly everyone was curious about the Presidential eruption. President Hernandez said into the ear of the Chairman of the Joint Chiefs of Staff, "*Admiral* McGee said we have to get *Colonel* Hunter a new headstone for Arlington." Hunter half-laughed at the inside joke but wondered what he had just witnessed. Maybe his cover hadn't been blown. There was no mention of *Maverick*, which suited him just fine.

As quickly as the ceremony came together, it broke up just as fast. Virtually everyone was ushered out. Three men remained in the Oval Office. The President was going to make an announcement if it met with Hunter's approval. Hunter was understandably confused. He looked at McGee for clarification. The *Admiral* stood still and allowed his eyes to fall on a bust of Winston Churchill. President Hernandez said, "Duncan, Director McGee and I wanted to nominate you for the Office of Strategic Services' William J. Donovan Award, but that would mean we would have to bring you out in the open."

Hunter pinched his lips and rocked his head. *Unbelievable!*

"I would also be honored if you would be my National Security Advisor. There is no rush on a decision; I know what it would mean...."

The response was immediate. "Mr. President, I am so grateful for all you have done for me, Nazy, my favorite *Admiral,* ...our country. Sir, I am deeply and humbly honored. But...I...just cannot leave what I'm doing. There is still so much work to be done. Mr. President, I regret I must humbly and respectfully decline." *Not until I find the man who killed my parents.*

The President said, "Admiral McGee said you wouldn't do it and I half-expected as much. I can always find a suitable National Security Advisor, but Bill and I are convinced we can't find another patriot like you. Just know the job and the Donovan Award are yours if you ever want them. You've been fantastic, frankly, in anything we have asked you do."

"Thank you for understanding, Mr. President."

"You're not going to get away from me that easily. Peace is breaking out across the Middle East and I'm very busy. I have another job for you, if you want it. Director McGee and I will explore the realm of the possible at another time."

Hunter nodded. "Whatever I can do for you."

The President continued, "I'm sorry Nazy couldn't have been here, but I understand she's traveling and is looking forward to seeing you soon? I miss her analysis during the PDB."

Director McGee interrupted. "Mr. President, there is an issue."

"This is free-fire zone, Admiral. What is on your mind?"

"Mr. President, you know Europe has been off limits for a number of reasons."

"You want to go after the criminals on the *Disposition* Matrix who are hiding in Europe?" The President was incredulous. *It had been briefed it was very difficult to impossible to do.*

McGee nodded.

President Hernandez crossed his arms and listened to the CIA Director's proposal. The President said, "Those are very large fish...." *Now I understand, Hunter's work really isn't over.*

McGee said, "We think we have the right bait...." He looked at Hunter, who was in a state of shock, simply nodded.

After receiving the President's approval, McGee collected the two wooden boxes with DICs inside and said, "It's time, *Colonel Hunter!*" *While Hunter is here, Nazy is on her way and should be in place shortly. In the big scheme of things, Duncan will not mind that she wasn't at the White House ceremony. He will completely forget it even happened when he sees her. Will he be surprised!*

The President again thanked McGee and Hunter for their service and dismissed his band of patriots who made the impossible possible.

CHAPTER 78

June 18, 2018

It was dark when the Agency Suburban picked Duncan Hunter up from the Arnold Palmer Regional Airport and headed toward the remote summer residence created by Frank Lloyd Wright. The sun was setting and a summer breeze spun some loose leaves into an unseen vortex as the vehicle entered the forest. In short order the heavy limo negotiated the winding route to the iconic building constructed over the waterfalls. When they stopped, Hunter bounded out of the vehicle and fast-walked to the door he had used days before. He entered and found a woman out on the terrace with her back to him. Hunter thought he recognized Nazy's legs but the woman's hair was completely wrong. He blurted out, "Excuse me....can you tell me where I might...."

Nazy recognized the deep rumbling voice and took her time turning around. She had seen enough of the old B movies to know how to turn around and when to turn her head for maximum effect. Husband and wife locked eyes; Duncan was clearly having issues processing what he was seeing.

"*You cut your hair!*" He was both shocked and pleased. "Oh my, you are so beautiful!" He ran to her and they embraced and kissed for a long time. He ran his hands through her hair as if it was some new element to be explored. *No more braids or ponytails – it has curls and body!* When they separated, it wasn't for long as Nazy wanted more. For the first time in weeks Hunter actually felt there was no work to keep them apart; he had been missed. He peppered Nazy with questions; her hair had been such a part of her being and her recovery.

He held her hands. He demanded to know how it happened.

She said, "I was in Paris at a counter-intel and aviation terrorism conference for Bill and someone stepped on my hair, twice. I realized it is too much trouble and it looks like *elflocks* no matter what I do. So I decided it was time. That was it. I love what they did, and the rest of my hair was given to some charity."

After ten minutes of talking about her hair; they moved on to their version of "How was your day?" beginning with Saoirse Nobley and the activities on the Iranian high desert. He got promoted, got a medal, was offered the National Security Advisor position. But the real highlight was still her new hair. Better than any medal.

She wasn't interested in sharing any of her conference work other than to comment, "I've been in America, away from England and the accents for so long that when I went to Canberra, Strine sounded like a foreign language." Nazy and Duncan laughed and smiled at each other spontaneously as lovers do. But Nazy was setting her husband up; she had heard about Duncan and the rescued women, again. Nazy teased him, "I hear everyone loves *Maverick*."

He turned 180° to place his butt on the terrace wall, she stepped between his legs. He placed his arms around her waist; she hung her arms over his shoulders. Every dozen words or so they would come together like magnets.

"You took her home?"

"I did; you and Kelly did a good job taking care of her. I thank you. That must have been hard."

"Kelly did all the hard work. So, did you kiss her?"

Duncan chose his words carefully. "I think it is more accurate to say she knew I was in love with you, that I was devoted to you, and that she kissed me as a thank you for all we had done for her. If I had a sister, it was like kissing my sister. Once she was home with her mother and sisters my work was done, and I left."

"She was very helpful, and her intel was crucial, timely. Duncan, who was she, really?"

"That's what I hear." Hunter supposed Nazy was past thinking Nobley could have been a threat to her. He told her, "Her story is a lot like an old movie I once saw. We haven't watched it. It's based on a book about a beautiful teenage girl who chases an older man, a military man who is actually a Soviet spy. After they marry she finds out the truth and demands he stop, that he must choose between her or his spying. He is torn between the life he wants to live as a spy and the life he has with her on his arm. She realizes she married a traitor who cannot change, and she calls the authorities. Before they can capture him, he commits suicide."

"That is eerily close."

"Maybe one of these days, we'll watch it. In those days, Nobley looked very much like a very blonde teenage Elizabeth Taylor."

"The woman I saw was no Elizabeth Taylor."

"Yeah, I know. I am just astounded she is alive. Bill said she was key to focusing Agency efforts on Iran. She had the key piece of intel." *There were other women there being used in a vile manner.*

A nod from Nazy confirmed McGee's analysis.

"She's a smart girl. A survivor."

"Isn't that something? Darling, Duncan...."

"Yes, baby?"

"Who was Bogdan Chernovich and what really happened to him? Please tell me you didn't jump out of your airplane."

He told her of his long tortuous history with the retired Marine general. He ended with, "I know I promised not to jump out of my airplane and I didn't. But when Bill thought Chernovich could be at a resort on top of a mountain in Italy, I jumped out of a C-17—with a canine."

A canine? That's incredible! Nazy was speechless.

"And, Nazy darling, I have been perfecting my parachuting skills. I know you worry about me because in the past I haven't done well at the end of a parachute. But now I can jump with the best of them. You're not mad at me?"

"I could never be mad at you. So you have new-found skills? I'm still in the dark, how did we find him?"

"You were out of town; *Tailwatchers* had tracked his jet to the airport at the base of the mountain. The intel from your guys, I presume, was good; I found him on the second floor in the Presidential Suite. I don't think I want to say anything else. It was a private matter. He was responsible for the deaths of about fifty women. But if you insist, I'll tell you. I just don't think he is worth talking about ever again."

Nazy really didn't want more; she wasn't interested in the details.

They found his remains from a car fire. They also say his watch was missing. He had help for all of his murders.

Nazy asked, "How did you get home?"

"Apparently some new Gulfstream jet had been abandoned in Italy, and we needed a ride. Max the Malinois is back home with his handler. Nice dog."

"So now you have three jets?"

Hunter smiled like a devil who had a winning lottery ticket and kissed her for a good long while. "It appears that is the case. And several new old cars." *It's a seventy-five million dollar jet and there are about fifty dead women because of him. I can't return those women to their families, but I can sell the jet and provide an honorarium of sorts.*

Nazy smiled at him devilishly. He believed she might be interested in something more than just kissing. She said, "My intel has it that you had about forty women kissing all over you. What do you say about that?" She moved into him seductively.

"Apparently, you cannot trust the CIA Director with *any* sensitive information." She smiled as he relayed how he had found the women shackled and emaciated. "They were in terrible shape. It was horrible. Their wrists and ankles were rubbed raw by the restraints. I cut them free and got them out of Iran. I think they were just expressing their gratitude."

Telling Nazy about them being naked would serve no useful purpose. She didn't need to know those details. She said, "Being their savior definitely deserves a kiss, but no French kissing from the French girls?" Nazy was teasing, but then she kissed him hard, their tongues frolicking together with an increasing sense of urgency. "Thank you for rescuing them, but your lips are only for my use and pleasure." She kissed him as if her kisses were the only ones that mattered; kisses to make him forget all the others. When she tried to pull away he gently sucked her bottom lip very sensually.... *What's your hurry?*

Duncan whispered, "There's *something* special about you Nazy Cunningham, there's a certain *je ne sais quoi* about you."

She loved it when he spoke French; she gulped and whispered, "We all love *Maverick*."

After several minutes Nazy bumped her forehead to his and cooed, "Bill said we would probably get an invitation to a State Dinner in England in honor of President Hernandez."

"When?"

"Several weeks from now. These things take time to set up. It'll give me time to find a ball gown."

"You will be the belle of the ball."

"I will worry about the Queen trying to kiss you for *services rendered*, and all that. Bill said you are a chick magnet."

The lovers laughed until Duncan drew Nazy close and kissed her again. He asked, "Do I have you for a while or do you have to go back to work?"

"This place is so wonderful and magical. I thought we would go through it. Wasn't this the inspiration for *Timber Rock*? I don't see it."

Oh, no.... She ignored my question! "It was, supposedly, according to the realtor, but I can't see it. *Fallingwater* is in a class all by itself, like you, but I've seen enough. I'm ready to go."

Duncan seemed to always know what to say, when to say it, and how to say it. As he pulled on her and encouraged her to leave, Nazy explained, "The protective staff for Saoirse has completed their mission, and everyone is just waiting for me to leave so they can wrap up the operation and go home."

Hunter said, "I sense a but...."

"Well, Bill was going to give me a week's leave. But he needs a favor. From you." She moved into him to kiss him passionately. They embraced for a very long time.

I just saw him! Bill McGee must really want a big favor and now is using my wife to get it. That coward!

They held hands as they walked out of the building and into an Agency Suburban. Duncan opened the door for his wife. The ride to the Arnold Palmer Regional Airport was made in near silence. Nazy slept along the way. *Jet lag hammers the best of us.* Hunter couldn't help but think, *Baby, you're burning the candles at both ends.*

Once safely airborne Duncan leveled off to enjoy the crystal clear night sky. Calm winds aloft; no *haboob* below. A perfect night for flying. The windscreen was full of lights; an uninterrupted view all the way from Newport, Rhode Island to Norfolk, Virginia. Hunter set the heading for Baltimore-Washington International Airport and he turned to his bride.

Nazy pointed ahead and asked, "Is this what CAVU looks like?"

"Yes, baby. That's what CAVU looks like. So what is Bill's *special* request, like I don't know?"

Nazy said, "This morning the Mozambique port of Mocimboa da Praia was captured by ISIS. It was seized following days of fighting between Mozambique military forces and a new ISIS group, *Ahlu Sunnah Wa-Jama*."

ISIS. Islamists. We-be-jammers. They metastasize like a cancer. I'm beginning to hate these guys. "What happened? Do we know?"

"Apparently Mozambique forces were overrun when the soldiers at the port ran out of ammunition and were forced to retreat."

"Mozambique is Christian?"

"Primarily. The president is trying to rid his country of a growing radical Islamic influence."

"Good luck. Is this a continuation of hostilities or was this unexpected?"

"We don't have a lot of resources on the ground. What we know is that there have been several attacks on the nearby towns, but they occur infrequently. Nothing substantial, nothing like Boko Haram. Mozambique's Muslims have always been a small fraction of the population; it was something the locals thought they could manage."

"Those guys never have enough police."

"That's the case here. But then, overnight, two dozen ISIS soldiers appeared waving a black flag, and overran the military base near the port. We believe the Islamic State captured machine guns and rocket-propelled grenades."

"Any MANPADS?"

"No." Nazy shook her head for emphasis. She didn't want the bad guys to have the capability of shooting down her husband.

"Big port?"

"One of Africa's biggest single investment projects. The port facilitates cargo deliveries to the natural gas projects near the port."

"LNG?" Liquefied natural gas.

"Yes and some oil. American petroleum workers are also on the ground; they are barricaded in their compound."

"The potential for ISIS to make a ton of money is off the chart." *And a stray bullet can start an inferno.* "Were you expecting any of this?"

"Textbook. Mazibuike denied the Christian president U.S. foreign aid. The Chinese wanted the LNG, but the U.S. said to sell it to South America. So, eventually, probably. Open invitation for ISIS mischief and makes one wonder if the Chinese aren't funding Islamic Underground activities in Africa. Al-Qaeda is essentially in hospice."

"They need African oil and gas."

"They do. Under 3M DOD was virtually prohibited from helping Mozambique, and they have no intel capability to speak of. We haven't been able to get Marines in the area to conduct training exercises for some time. Mozambique's military is underequipped to defend their strategic sites from surprise attacks, and at the encouragement of Director McGee, Tanzania launched multiple offensives against the *jihadists* on the border with Mozambique. Bill thinks they need a little help. With you, it's a one-day event."

"If it means finally being able to have some time with you, sign me up."

"Bill promised; a quick in and out. Take out ISIS."

Just take out ISIS. Always more work. Hunter chuckled. *Anything for Bill, anything for Nazy. But no time with Nazy. I guess I'm on my way to Africa! Again!*

After Hunter set the autopilot, Nazy debriefed her husband. "The U.S. Intelligence Community Inspector General is looking into the Agency's contracting practices; TASC and TASCO received an inordinate number of non-competitive sole-source contracts, much like *Blackwater* did after 9/11. Bill canceled all of TASCO's contracts with the IC. Yassmin Deng thinks he did it because they tried to flip her. Maybe he'll tell her the rest of the story if she ever gets read in."

Hunter provided details and some granularity on the mission leading up to the mad dash across the world to stop al-Qaeda's plan of infecting the planet with the *Persian Green Death.*

Nazy offered a few new data points on the war on drugs. "A submersible from Colombia reached the shores of Spain."

"That's incredible."

"They crossed thousands of miles of ocean with two tons of cocaine and probably thought that they had dodged the law and the Spanish Navy but were stopped by a fishing net. Spanish *federales* tried to board the vessel, but they wouldn't come out, so they shot some holes in the sub to get them out."

"And it was sunk. *Ole!*"

"Yes."

"Well, I haven't been able to get them all. Serves them right."

Nazy said, "Bill wants you to build some quiet airplanes for export to South American counties; mostly Colombia. Maybe Nigeria too."

"I did not see any the last time I passed through Lagos. We delivered six for Nigeria a few years ago, and their pilots are only now graduating Air Force flight school. Now, those quiet airplanes could be somewhere else, but I don't think so. Look for the U.S. to sell both countries Super Tucanos—small counterinsurgency aircraft to help eliminate the Boko Haram and drug smugglers and drug labs."

Nazy continued, "The South Americans need FLIRs, just to patrol the coastline at night and find the submersibles."

"With the FLIR they'll find a few subs. That sensor is a game changer on a quiet airplane. Drug labs, smugglers—it can find them all."

Nazy said, "It's time our allies deal with their own bad guys."

"Yeah, Bill mentioned it to me on our way home. State Department has resisted that for years because they don't want to be told what airplane they should fly, and they think the Colombians are rocks." Hunter asked, "While we are on the topic of Colombia, any word on the anomaly?"

"Bill wanted to tell you after you gave his father a ride in that airplane...."

"That *airplane,* my darling Nazy is a TP-51C *Mustang.*"

She knew what the airplane was and avoided rolling her eyes. Nazy just wanted to get a little rise out of her husband, and she did.

"And you were the first one I took for a ride in it."

"I loved the *Mustang*. That was so cool." *I did love that. It was so exciting. I know a little more why Duncan collects aircraft, even though he cannot fly them the way they could be flown.* Nazy relived the flight then said, "You have no idea what the anomaly in Colombia is, do you?"

Hunter looked at her as he spoke into the tiny boom microphone pressed against his lips. "*Hmmm.* Well, I'm hoping it's a queenly Boeing 314. A *Flying Boat*. I know that Pan-Am's 314s were removed from service in 1946, and the seven surviving and serviceable 314s were purchased by the start-up airline New World Airways. I know they sat at San Diego's Lindbergh Field for a long time before they were flown to Baltimore to be scrapped. But there was this strange rumor that the salvage company initially reported one of the 314s was missing and then changed their story. If you were to believe the initial report, someone supposedly had left another four-engine aircraft, a Douglas C-54, in the 314's place minus the batteries, which are needed to start the engines and again, supposedly, were the same type of batteries needed to start the 314. The rumor went that the salvage company removed the engines from the aircraft and put them into shipping containers. Then they cut the Douglas C-54 into tiny pieces before doing the same thing to the *Flying Boat*s. That was the rumor."

Nazy was impressed with Duncan's mastery of aviation history. She hadn't really been interested in airplanes until Duncan had taken her to dinner at the *Azteca* in Hondo, Texas after a ride in the Howard 500 taildragger. She could scarcely believe the power of the 18-cylinder, air-cooled radial engines, and after he allowed her to fly the aircraft, she found herself hooked. "Bill asked one of his friends in the SEALs to check out the location you provided. They found what you described and took a picture of the 'data plate.' Is that how you say it?"

Hunter smiled as wide as the Grand Canyon. He agreed with a click of the microphone and a nod.

Suddenly Nazy was excited as if she had a secret and couldn't wait to tell her man. "You're not going to believe this, darling. Not only is it a *Flying Boat*, but it's a historical aircraft. President Roosevelt and his staff used that aircraft, the *Dixie Clipper*, to attend the Casablanca Conference. You were right. You found a grand *Flying Boat*! What are you going to do?"

Hunter relished the moment and reached for Nazy's hand. He had long suspected but was afraid to believe the rumor could be true. Now Hunter wanted to know how it wound up in a remote Colombian river. *Could someone have wanted to use it for a smuggler's airplane? It would have been perfect with one exception – there are no spare parts and the salvage yard destroyed all the spares!* "It's not like I see it being put up on a stick like the A-12 in the Agency's backyard or the decommissioned DC-3 at a New Zealand McDonald's. Flying boats are huge and they are aviation royalty. I understand the *Philippine Mars* is on its way to the National Naval Aviation Museum in Pensacola, Florida. They all wore Navy livery in the war. Maybe I should talk to them. I know *an admiral….*" They laughed. Sometimes her husband could be amusing.

"If not the Navy, then maybe Boeing would be interested in restoring it or maybe one of the historical aircraft preservation organizations. I don't think any organization outside the manufacturer could handle such a project, but my buddy in Bridgewater has tackled monumental jobs of restoring large radial-engine airplanes. I'll talk to him. It is always an issue of money, and it would be worth Quiet Aero Systems' help in restoring it. And, I must tell *Bullfrog* thanks for the help." *And the Air & Space Museum could do it. I gave them a priceless Daytona; maybe they could restore the flying boat as a form of payback. Probably not.*

Nazy told Duncan what it cost to rehabilitate *Fallingwater*. He didn't flinch and said it would take every bit of that and probably more to make the 314 airworthy again. With old airplanes, it could be a ten-year project. Remanufacturing parts takes a lot of time. He thanked Nazy again for stepping up to fix the crumbling residence in the woods.

"Bill said we're going to build you some new airplanes?"

"He wants a new *Yo-Yo*. All that pure unmanned nonsense is gone. And someone in the National Clandestine Service might be the pilot."

"I would not count on that. That SAP is too successful to allow just anyone into such a dynamic program. Bill informed President Hernandez that you have, what I understand is probably a trade secret, *proprietary* tracking skills. You have developed them like a craftsman and an apprentice will take years to learn them. This is the President's counterterrorism initiative, and only you are trained, qualified, and allowed to conduct kinetic activities. Kelly or someone else can do the non-kinetic counterdrug flights."

"Baby, you might be right."

"I am right. We got wind that Iran is looking to retaliate against the U.S. for killing General Roustaie by assassinating an ambassador or two. Iran would not fall for the news reports that they killed Chernovich and vehemently denied the assassination. President Hernandez went on Al Jazeera and told them in no uncertain terms that any attempt on an America politician, businessman, or tourist will cause the destruction of Tehran's palaces and the ayatollahs and mullahs residences."

"Sounds like he is not playing nice to those crazies."

"The new Attorney General announced an investigation to determine any links between the 2,000 U.S. passports given to Islamic countries by Mazibuike and the Muslims recently elected to Congress. He's also looking into voting machines that can change outcomes."

Hunter looked at Nazy incredulously and was immediately interrupted by air traffic control. He made the required radio calls and returned to his thoughts. *Hmmm.... Voting machines that can change outcomes: Democracy Innovation machines. The Liberty Machines were never killed off and were in the U.S. after all. Bingo!*

Nazy continued, "And Duncan darling, promise me you won't jump out of any more airplanes unless it is absolutely necessary. You are not getting any younger."

Some words tried to bubble to the tip of his tongue. *I suppose that means that the only way to stay out of the crosshairs is to grow old by doing nothing. Nazy doesn't want to hear BS. She needs to hear a few words of comfort.* "Oh, Baby. With new airplanes and new technology, I won't need to jump out of an airplane."

"Thank you. You may or may not know the other person on your previous rendition flight, Hamsi Fareed al-Amirikiu, was a constant guest of the Mazibuike White House."

"I do. It was a not-so big secret that he was the leader of the Islamic Underground in the U.S."

"Correct. Then you also know of Mazibuike's ring?"

The one I took off of his finger after I cut off his head? Hunter nodded. He was more familiar with it than Nazy could ever imagine. "The one with the Islamic declaration of faith, the *Shahada*?" *There is no God but Allah, and Mohammad is his Messenger. I should not have kept a souvenir of killing him. I shouldn't have been that sentimental.*

How would you know that? "Er, yes, that's the one. In his personal papers confiscated by the SEALs during the raid on Haqqani's place, there was a photograph not seen by anyone in America. It's a close-up of Mazibuike's hand and ring on a *Qur'an* as he was being sworn in by the Chief Justice of the Supreme Court."

Hunter broke out into a huge grin. "The media carried the news that there had been a second 'swearing in' ceremony; no one knew why they would do that in the Chief Justice's chambers. I remember there were other presidents who had a second 'swearing in' in front of photographers in the White House, usually when January inauguration weather was rainy, crappy, or something."

"Correct. Apparently, the same photographer who took the Oval Office photos of the three leaders 'bumping fists' with their rings inscribed with the *Shahada*, also took the photograph of 3M being sworn in on a *Qur'an*. Bill's analysis is that all of those Muslim leaders in the Middle East who doubted Mazibuike's Muslim heritage and commitment to Islam were shown the photograph."

"The implication was that Mazibuike claimed suzerainty over America and the United States was now Islamic and there was a Muslim in the White House. And we may have a Supreme Court Justice who is not all he claims to be. I'll be watching him."

"Again, correct."

"Well, that was long suspected yet without proof; it was just a conspiracy theory of the Republicans."

"So darling, Director McGee knows how much you disliked 3M…."

Hunter quickly interjected, "…the usurper of the U.S. Constitution?"

Nazy didn't break stride, "...so as payment for taking his father flying in the *Mustang*, he's given me that photograph for you to give to Eastwood; I suppose if he wants he could send it to *Whistleblowers*. Bill plans to declassify and use it the next time he's in front of Congress." Nazy was proud of herself. *Others would have dismissed it as just an old immaterial photograph.* Few things delineate Democrat perfidy and Muslim Brotherhood treachery more than declassified photographic evidence of their traitorous president.

Hunter couldn't look at Nazy as he thought, *And I have that asshole's ring. I cut his head off, took his ring, and threw his head and body out of the top floor of the Burj Khalifa. I was so fired up that night I didn't think of taking the asshole's watch. I'm not sure what she or Bill would think of me if I told them what I did. They probably figured I would punish him for all of his treachery. I don't like keeping secrets from Nazy, but I think I have to keep this one. Oh, yes; there's Scorpii....*

He hadn't been brought up; there was no discussion of the old billionaire communist, so I'm not going there. Hunter said nothing for a few minutes. Nighttime air traffic control could be sparse, even on the eastern seaboard. After checking on the electronics, Duncan changed the subject. He said, "And I expect you must go with Bill, which will mean all the congresscritters and their staff will lust over you. They are going to love that hair. I think you look like one of the Bangles! *But taller!*"

CHAPTER 79

June 18, 2018

He was in love with her all over again. She didn't know if a Bangle was American for a person, place, or thing, but she gave him a disarming smile to thank him for the kind words. It was enough to break whatever surface tension was present. She wanted to go home with Duncan, but Duncan had another fast moving mission. Nazy looked south and then back at Duncan. She wanted to finish the debrief and said, "General Roustaie's daughter married the new head of the Muslim Brotherhood in Egypt."

"One goes down, another one pops up. More targets for me, maybe."

Nazy returned to an incomplete apprehension. "Duncan darling, you promised me you won't jump out of any more airplanes. Is that even possible with a new airplane?" *Jumping out of an airplane to save the President, he almost died. I don't want that to happen again.*

"I talked to an exec at Lockheed, but they are not interested in building a handful of anything for anyone. They know how to build jets in secret. If they did it, each copy would be wildly expensive. There are lower cost alternatives; my guys in Texas could probably do the airframe and the wings and build the cockpit. It will require a specialty shop to build a reduction gearbox. To keep the project a secret will be daunting."

"No electric motor?"

"I need something dependable. Give me that good old antique aviation gasoline. An electric motor means batteries and unnecessary weight. Then it's only a matter of time before one of them lights off and I'll be jumping out of an aircraft again. Only it would be on fire, and with my luck I would probably be over a Colombian rainforest and a caiman would have me for lunch."

"We don't want that happening. But you're building and refurbishing aircraft...."

"But they don't require the secrecy of a black airplane. New aircraft with reciprocating engines and restoring warbirds; that's open source and there are other players. But I like the technology behind the competition gliders. It would be nice to have a slick airplane that we don't have to put tape all over to keep the bad guys from hearing it whistle. It would be an engineering challenge to fold the wings—Bob and Bob are over seventy and are just about at their limit when it comes to removing and replacing the wings. I expect any day they will tell me they have had enough. I'll need someone new to take their place, and the sooner I do it the better off I'll be. I think the engineering challenge will be to build a new generation reduction gear box. The personnel challenge will be to find two fantastic mechanics who can work together and make plenty of money by keeping their mouths shut. I'm thinking we may get lucky with the mechanics on our LM-100J. They are cleared and hard working. And they can keep quiet."

"Well, I just know that when the new aircraft are built Bill intends to hang one of your YO-3s with the other black aircraft."

"Not outside?"

"No, inside, in the atrium."

Hunter rolled his eyes. If there was going to be a ceremony and the hanging of a YO-3A, he would have to have the mastermind of the *Noble Savage* special access program, the retired CIA executive Greg Lynche, on hand for the dedication. "Getting Greg to come back could be as difficult as me getting into West Point. I can see a Schweizer up in the rafters but not a *Yo-Yo*."

"Have you talked to him recently?"

"He won't take my calls."

Nazy turned to Duncan. She sighed, "You know I erased Greg's CIA history with the DNC and the Communist Party of the USA, and I purged his files at *Whistleblowers*. Greg always kept it a secret. The indiscretions of youth."

Hunter said, "Greg was never interested in the violent overthrow of the government. I got a hint of his past when he and Bill and I toured the CIA's House of Diaries. The DNC's archive, their documents scared the crap out of him. I knew there had to be a reason." *But it wasn't for the reason I thought.*

Nazy said, "We've all done things in our past we're not especially proud of. Like having a twenty-two-year-old girlfriend...."

Hunter play-acted like he had been fatally wounded in the chest with a Mameluke sword.

Nazy laughed at his histrionics and continued, "Sometimes it's marrying someone who isn't who you think he is. Saoirse and I fall into that category. Many people don't recover from those mistakes. I'm so fortunate you came into my life."

Oh baby, yeah; you and Saoirse married terrorists. Hunter said, "I have often scolded myself for wearing the *Daytona* the day I ejected; that's just for starters. But I'm sure, somehow, if I had not worn that watch that day I would never have chased down sexual predators. By extension, I would have never changed my field of study or written my dissertation on aviation terrorism. I would not have met Greg or attended the Naval War College, and I wouldn't have met you.... I literally cannot think of or want anyone else but you, and now my life is not only so much better....it is *complete.*" Before descending into BWI he reached across the console of the Gulfstream to kiss Nazy.

After several minutes Hunter inquired, "Nobley said the Haqqani's separated her from her children and threatened to harm them. Were you able to find out anything on them?"

Nazy looked out of the copilot window and shook her head several times. After a minute she said, "The last official record was from the State Department. They believe they went through JFK to Egypt, then nothing." *My guess is they are dead.*

After several minutes of silence she picked up the rest of her spiel. "While you were abroad Eastwood had a panic attack, I guess I can say that; I asked the boys from Fredericksburg if they could look at Eastwood's Hummer. Eastwood looked underneath his vehicle to see if it had been booby-trapped. He saw some wires and freaked out. No harm."

"Anyway, you got the in-place defector out of the Khomeini Institute and Bill got most of the hard drives from the facility's servers."

"That's right."

"What you probably don't know is the defector had over a hundred *flash drives* full of data. He was the head of their IT shop. He wanted out of Iran by any means possible."

"You know, I realized I never even searched him! So *Rosebud*—that's what I called him—was like Edward Snowden except he helped the good guys."

"Exactly. You've rescued some important men the IC wanted to extract but were been unable. The special operations guys...."

"You mean the dudes who specialize in that sort of thing?"

Nazy hummed an affirmative. "Bill has the notion you can do more of them. Maybe if we find some of our lost souls, men who went deep underground and went missing, we can bring them home. We have about twenty active files. European countries mostly."

A lot of stars on the CIA Memorial Wall are missing their heroes. Hunter looked at her for a while. "Bill said we did. I nearly left one of them behind in an Iranian cell, but the IT dude said there was an American. Bill said it was someone who had been missing for a decade."

Nazy frowned; she hadn't known. Bill did not mention it, and it wasn't like Bill to keep something like that from her. She had been away and was only given a partial debrief. Nazy knew the Director would tell her in due time and moved on. "The word on the Muslim street is our President will tolerate no one harming Americans abroad. He authorized the killing of Roustaie, and he is making political hay with the Islamic nations. Seems Roustaie terrorized them too."

"About time." Hunter nodded at the sunset.

"For a while that was the norm, when Americans were not molested as they traveled or worked abroad. Then Khomeini stormed into Tehran and put a bounty on every American head, alive or dead."

"In addition to President Hernandez holding the heads of nations accountable, he has demonstrated he has no compunction punishing them. They had become more aggressive with their dwindling number of Islamists, and the terror groups' influence are diminishing significantly. That was one reason I went in Bill's place. American and Middle East and Muslim intelligence communities will work together much more closely, and we negotiated an agreement to share intelligence on aviation threats and all other terrorist threats. The most amazing thing is that we now have Muslim nations recognizing Israel. They have agreed to grant landing and overflight rights to El Al for Saudi Arabia, the United Arab Emirates, Jordan, Bahrain, and Kuwait. At least so far. There is little doubt that President Hernandez will be nominated for a Nobel Peace prize."

"So that is what you were doing overseas? Sprinkling peace and goodwill across nations that have been at war?"

She smiled and nodded. "It was. I know you have agonized over having your dissertation being corrupted by al-Qaeda. I want to you know we used it in the manner for which it was intended. We literally took pages out of your paper to provide guidance to their secret police for enhanced airport security and to prevent criminal Islamists from infiltrating Muslim airports. Now Islamic airport employees get a polygraph and so do student pilots coming to the United States."

"Congratulations, baby! Apparently, you were wonderful again!"

"The President and Bill said that in hindsight I should have been part of the delegation all along. President Hernandez will announce the treaties we negotiated at a Rose Garden signing with all the players. And.... There will be a state dinner, and we are expected to attend."

"So I get to take my darling bride to another dance?"

"And dinner. Everything will be Kosher."

"Everyone will have an Angus fillet."

Nazy beamed like a lighthouse. She pursed her lips and agreed.

"That's just fantastic. You cannot mollycoddle terrorists. I think the President is reversing the policies of not only 3M but some of our other—what do you call them?"

"I believe the nice words you are looking for are 'weak swimmers.'"

Nazy said, "Righto—the *weak swimmers* who were elected to the White House and did nothing. You harm an American, then you and your country will be damaged. Economically. Militarily. Diplomatically. Severely. You control your Islamists, then greater trade and relations will come your way. But the United States is going to have to do something with Rho Scorpii funding terrorists. Just as we have shut off terrorist funding from Middle East nations, we think he is picking up the tab. Is that right, *the tab*?"

Hunter nodded. "You mean the *Black Scorpion*."....

"They call him the *Puppet Master*. He is now spending billions of dollars funding terrorist operations in the more democratic Muslim nations like Indonesia and Malaysia. He now contributes billions to Democratic and Muslim candidates here at home. Do you know where that is coming from? Yassmin Deng. Our CFO."

"That's very good. I guess she got the message. As for Scorpii, he was never on the Matrix."

Nazy said, "That's because he hides out in Europe, and you said long ago that flying in Europe is a very difficult. If you've changed your mind, you need to let Bill know. Scorpii has been responsible for thousands of American deaths."

And we've set into motion a plan.... Hunter said, "I'll talk to him. Westernization gets outspent from billionaire-funded communism."

They looked at each other several times. Hunter's eyes always strayed to her hair.

Nazy noticed. "What do you really think of my hair?"

Hunter extended the speed brakes and lowered the flaps to slow the jet down. He said, "I love it. You look like you belong on the arm of some handsome movie star instead of some scarred-up bum from Texas. You're lovely, you're exquisite, and you give me vertigo...." He lowered the landing gear, aligned the jet on the runway, and softly landed astride the centerline. He taxied to the executive terminal.

Nazy took his hand and finished the line from the movie, "And, I adore you, Duncan. I love you, *Maverick*."

"Life only matters if it is with you." Hunter smiled at Nazy and was getting a fun sort of vibe. Her eyes were pleading: *It's been over a month!* Hunter got the hint and radioed the executive terminal. He said he would not be shutting down and asked the nice lady at *Signature Flight Control* if there was a place he could park where he would not impact their ground operations with extended APU operations. He was given directions to a remote parking spot away from the FBO that was usually reserved for the jets of visiting international dignitaries.

Hunter set the parking brake, radioed that he would call when he was ready for a re-spot, servicing, and shutdown. He asked if someone could go out and inform the limo driver their passenger would be delayed about an hour.

With the jet stopped and Duncan on the radio, Nazy kicked her shoes off, climbed out of the copilot seat, and left the cockpit. Duncan finished his radio transmission, removed his headset, double-checked the engines were shut down and the parking brake was set, then he raced to get out of the cockpit. She pulled him along and he stumbled; he went down on all fours and tried to crawl to the cabin. It was a comical situation and Nazy laughed and giggled; she stopped him before he could reach the cabin seats by knocking him off balance. Still laughing, she pushed Duncan onto his back onto the Berber carpet, straddled his torso, and ripped off his shirt. They raced to undress each other. There was a sense of urgency between them that could not be denied.

• • •

The limo driver and security detail were waiting in the executive terminal with plenty of fresh coffee. The driver and the uniformed lady serving as *Signature Flight Control* passed the time with discussions of the different aircraft that passed through Baltimore.

• • •

An hour later Hunter called *Signature Flight Control* for permission to taxi. The limo driver turned from the counter and announced to the women of the security detail, *"Showtime!"* She turned to the lady behind the counter and whispered, "I guess if a Gulfstream is a rocking, don't go a knocking."

July 30, 2018

Towering puffy clouds against a light blue sky did not signal rain but shade below. Some wind kicked up from the cloud's outflow but nothing that approached severe; there would be no waterspouts or white caps from the lazy school of cumulous that moved across the islands.

The Caravan 208 Amphibian avoided the clouds and made a wide sweeping approach on the forty-eight foot Beneteau sailboat anchored abeam of one of the tiny islands in the Caicos, Seal Cays. The passenger confirmed through binoculars that they had found the correct yacht. *Scoundrel II.* There wasn't another boat to be seen in a thirty-mile radius.

The sound of the turboprop landing nearby interrupted the quiet and brought a man and a woman from the cabin below deck. They watched a man dive off of one of the amphibian's floats and swim toward them. Once the human cargo was free of the aircraft, the pilot of the float plane took off and headed north to the big island.

Halfway up the boarding ladder, Duncan Hunter asked permission to "Come aboard." *Grinch* and his wife, Connie, were amused—as they always were when Duncan visited unexpectedly.

Greg said, "You're like a bad penny. You never know where you'll turn up again."

"Just don't throw me back. *Grinch,* I'd like you to come to headquarters for a dedication. No YO-3A but a Schweizer. One of your brain childs will be hoisted up in the atrium where the other black airplanes of Air Branch are." With the mention of "Air Branch," *Maverick* flipped *Grinch* an Air Branch challenge coin. Lynche immediately recognized the change in the shield. "Air America" was replaced with "Air Branch." It was the rarest challenge coin in existence, at least according to the world's largest on-line auction.

Connie sat in a deck chair and listened. She was unmoved.

Maverick and *Grinch* talked old times. *Grinch* was fascinated with the coin and their conversation wandered all over the spectrum, but never got close to the intelligence community. Hunter said, "Your *Yacht Master* is now a major collectible. Anytime you want to part with it I will make you an offer you cannot refuse. Buy you a new one." Hunter checked his Rolex for the time. The amphibian would return for him in minutes.

With a sense of urgency pushing him, he said, "*Grinch*, I know what you did. Nazy told me of your youthful indiscretions; voting for the communist candidate for president before joining the CIA. Working as a double for the DNC. You knew that a communist president was a losing proposition, someone who only got less than point-one percent of the vote. But it got you to thinking about what it would take to get someone like the head of the Communist Party of the USA into the White House. You have to change the vote when your candidate was losing. Am I right?" *Macht nichts in my book; we all do stupid things when we are young. But you were too clever by several measures.*

Grinch wouldn't look at him but nodded as if it was an afterthought.

"Under the guise of ensuring terrorist organizations would not gain seats in the executive or legislative branches of local governments, you dropped this concept on the desk of the Director. Your old place contacted, my money is on your number one contractor, TASCO, to develop a voting machine, *Liberty Machines*, that would count votes and tabulate votes like regular voting machines but with a flick of a switch or a cell phone signal or an internet connection, you could flip the votes in favor of your candidate. You didn't even have to process a ballot. Am I right so far?"

Lynche spread seventy-year-old tanned legs and clasped his hands between his knees. The *Yacht Master* brilliantly reflected the sun. For the first time the career spook broke his vow to take all the Agency's secrets in his head to the grave. *Grinch* said, "You're…*right*."

Hunter thought, *Our politics were always at opposite ends; the liberal and the conservative. Maverick* and *Grinch. We had jobs to do and never let politics get in the way. When we put the gun on the Yo-Yo, that was a bridge too far for you and, my greatest best friend, you walked away from me and from the program. You were my hero, you saved me from a life I did not want, and made me your partner. But then you left me alone….*

The Grinch's hair was thinner. His skin was as dark and rough as shoe leather. Lynche looked away, out over the flat clear water. He didn't feel like a hero. Anyone's hero. He allowed the *Liberty Machines* to be imported and used domestically, for special elections. By the DNC. He felt like a traitor.

"And I know, at least I think I know what you did on election night. Right before you left…."

Lynche cocked his head so only one eye was on Hunter. *Oh, he knows! How could he?*

Suddenly Connie was confused and concerned. There was a strange sort of tension. She hadn't seen her men at odds with one another ever. What had her husband kept from her?

Hunter spoke quickly. "In the third world countries, the political parties weren't as sophisticated as the Democrat Party. Democrats had to be extremely careful how they used the newly packaged *Liberty Machines*, now called *Democracy Innovation* voting machines in the U.S. for if they used them too often in too obvious a fashion and in political races of only moderate importance the Republicans would have caught on and raised holy hell. Only big-stakes elections, such as Tussy's election, were the old *Liberty Machines* brought out of the dark. But there was a problem in the last election, even Democrat polling had the president winning by a significant margin. The only chance the Democrats had was to cheat. The Democrats had to make the state's vote count look plausible; keep it close. Control the narrative. Avoid the scrutiny."

"You knew Eleanor Tussy was going to win. She was supposed to win. Wherever there were *Liberty Machines* with new housings and badging, the Democrats would ensure their candidate would win. But on election night, in the battleground states, President Hernandez was racing away with the election and was receiving many more votes than Tussy. Like the *Liberty Machines*, the *Democracy Innovation* machines were programmed to spit out a winning tally for Tussy. In Philly, where they have a centralized tabulation office there and have had for probably a hundred years, everyone knows Democrats always win in Philly, regardless of how well a Republican does."

The *Grinch* hung his head. "We had to make sure the good guys won the elections in the Middle East. North Ireland. Africa. South America. Across the globe. No terrorists. Terrorists cheated, they threatened the people, and would retaliate; they would destroy families if the election outcome didn't go their way. Yes, we used a third party and the *Liberty* voting machines to our advantage to keep the terrorists and criminals from winning elections."

Maverick said, "And on election night in the U.S., you knew what the Democrat Party was up to because *Liberty Machine* had been one of your special access programs. Like *Noble Savage*. Another one of your babies. I got patents approved; you got special access programs approved. I still don't know how many of them you engineered."

"A lot...." Lynche nodded absentmindedly.

"You allowed the DNC to acquire and use an updated version of the *Liberty* voting machines all across America. But for whatever reason, on election night, you couldn't go through with it. My money was on President Hernandez, who is a great man, and Tussy was a shrieking, flaming, carpetbagging communist."

Maverick was on a roll. "But the Democrats couldn't cheat worth a shit. I checked the surveillance video again. In the end, it came down to Philly—notorious for stopping the count late so they could present their final result with as much drama as a B movie ending. All the Republicans with their red access cards were told the election was over; the Democrats with their little blue access cards ushered them out of the building. The Republicans protested as the Democrats went all out to remove President Hernandez. There was no chance to physically add ballots to adjust the totals so the Democrats had to electronically adjust the final count. But the new *Liberty Machines* that were so carefully placed in the Philly tabulation center would not take the signal to register bogus ballots. Right?"

Lynche mashed his lips together and nodded.

"*Democracy Innovations* and *Liberty Machines* were designed to interact, in an emergency, with the signal-killing powers from *Growlers*. Pure genius. You had an election official in Philly with a *Growler*—I'm thinking a *Growler* that looks like a regular portable radio that no one would give a thought to being in close proximity to a voting machine—to kill the bogus compiler signal of the last-in-the-process *Democracy Innovation* machine. Like he had done across the country, President Hernandez clearly won the election and while the Republicans were banging on the door to let them back in to monitor the counting, the Democrats in Philly kept trying to change the vote tally electronically, but the *Growler* shut down the machine and stopped the Democrats from stealing the election. The *Growler* stopped it. Whitaker Chambers would have been proud. Welcome back to the fight."

Lynche continued to nod. He said, "We had to have a way to kill a bad machine on our terms. How did you find out?"

"There were clues and I asked Nazy. She briefed me on *Liberty Machine*. There was an article on *Democracy Innovations* and all the hell they created. Then there was Gunner Foggel. He was in my war college class. I met his wife, she runs the S&T now. I called and asked him. I told Gunner I recognized him and his shoes from the Philly security camera video and he confirmed he had a radio *Growler*, and that the S&T made him a blue Democrat access card with all of the accesses. He was disguised to look like a Democrat election official and had unfettered access to the Philly station."

Husband and wife exchanged looks.

Connie said to Hunter, "You always find a way, don't you?"

"It's a gift and curse. But there are no hard feelings. Greg, I now have a better understanding why you did what you did and why you dropped off the grid. You knew someone would figure out you defected or got a *Growler* inside and you would be on their shit list. You knew it was only a matter of time before they found you. You had to go."

"I had enough...."

"I know you never really wanted the job but you took it on my account. For whatever it is worth, in my book you were a great CIA Director."

Lynche nodded and smiled. *Still one of the best decisions I ever made.*

Hunter saw the floatplane before it could be heard. *Fighter pilot eyes.* He said, "You know I love you guys, and that is unconditional. Your politics never mattered. In my book you saved me and the world; the right guy got elected. You sir, are a patriot's patriot. I won't tell anyone. Our secret."

The amphibian landed near the yacht and it was time for Hunter to go. Lynche hugged his protégé, slipped off the old Rolex *Yacht Master*, and handed it to Duncan. Hunter tried the three-cheek air-kiss goodbye, but Connie kissed Hunter on the cheek and held him until her tears stopped flowing.

He dove off the sailboat into the crystal clear still water and swam to the float plane. Hunter's tears mixed with the salt water, there would be no evidence of him lamenting the loss of his longtime friend.

Greg showed Connie the Air Branch challenge coin. Lynche thought trading his watch for the unique coin was more than a fair trade. He had other watches. Connie thought her husband would throw the coin as far as he could, but he grasped it tight and slipped it into the pocket of his shorts.

• • •

The bidding had been fierce during Sotheby's auction of fine rare timepieces. Several desirable watches from former heads of state, heads of intelligence services, and other fascinating men of history were being offered at auction at no reserve. At the start of the auction, the head auctioneer announced some depressing news. Watch collectors had been crushed to learn that the Apollo 11 astronaut, Neil Armstrong's Rolex *Daytona* Cosmograph that had been specially manufactured by Presidential Order and had been missing for decades had surfaced at the National Air & Space Museum in Washington, D.C.

The auctioneer recognized retired Marine Corps Lieutenant Colonel Demetrius Eastwood sitting in the auction hall, who had presented the first cosmograph on the moon on behalf of an anonymous donor who asked that the watch to be displayed for the public's enjoyment. Then the auctioneer announced that Colonel Eastwood had recently donated the timepieces of Sean Connery, now on display at the International Spy Museum, and Steve McQueen, recently gifted to the Motor Museum of the 24 Hours of LeMans. He announced that the colonel had brought another timepiece, this one was for auction.

Watch collectors from around the world were sent into a panic believing the vast majority of unique and rare watches would be given to charity and not traded at auction. The auctioneer was ready to sell the auction house's latest acquisition.

What the crowd came to see and bid on was one of the rarest watches offered by the auction house in years. The final auction offering was a "reverse panda" with three white registers on a black dial. A model 2446. The auctioneer highlighted the watch's rarity; fewer than ten of the "Jochen Rindt" chronographs were still in existence. "This is the only example that has been offered at auction for several decades." The auctioneer refrained from mentioning that virtually all the type had been worn by strong and powerful homosexual men but showcased the provenance of their owners on electronic display monitors.

"Here you see the American actor, Rock Hudson, wearing a TAG Heuer *Autavia* GMT in the American cinema, *Ice Station Zebra.* It is an excellent example of a Jochen Rindt racing timepiece. The British actor, Leonard Sachs, in the James Bond classic, *Thunderball,* owned a Jochen Rindt, a TAG Heuer *Autavia* GMT. He flashed it on screen several times across many pictures." The auctioneer showed photographs of the other known owners of the rarest type of Heuer *Autavia.* "Considered the 'Holy Grail' in the TAG Heuer watch collecting community, there is one *Autavia,* one Jochen Rindt with the blue-and-red GMT bezel unaccounted for. And that is what we have for you today, offered at no reserve. This was the personal timepiece of the Congressional Medal of Honor winning American Marine General, National Security Advisor to President Maxim Mohammad Mazibuike, and Chairman of the Board of the Trans-Atlantic Security Corporation, Bogdan Chernovich. It is engraved on the reverse with General Chernovich's name, the United States Naval Academy, and date of graduation. I would like to start the bidding at one million pounds."

In the front row, a nondescript man in a fresh Saville Row double-breasted suit, Gianni Versace tie, and Crockett & Jones handmade shoes raised his paddle exactly three times during the bidding. When the hammer pounded, signaling the auction was over and that a record for an *Autavia* Jochen Rindt had been set, he remained sitting, allowing most of the crowd to disperse. When the quiet man lifted his head, he stood and made eye contact with some associates, and then proceeded to the cashier to pay for and collect his winning bid.

The buyers ignored Demetrius Eastwood and never looked at him.

Few people gave the virtually bald man with a stringy red beard at the rear of the auction hall a second notice. He looked out of place and didn't bid. He didn't appear to be interested in the auctions or the offerings. The dark suede Merrell *Moabs* with the cheap business suit were out of place among the highly polished oxfords of the clientele at Sotheby's.

During the bidding of the final auction the scraggly red beard finally expressed a modicum of interest of the unusual watch listed in the bidder's guide. He was more interested in the unusual chronograph and the pristine accompanying packaging than the bidding process.

Under the watchful eyes of the chronograph cognoscenti, a tall thin man emerged from offstage wearing white gloves and carrying a presentation box. He removed the contents, certification documentation and a leather-wrapped inner box, and carefully placed the TAG Heuer *Autavia* GMT inside; returned the documents and closed the presentation box. It was handed to the buyer who placed it in a velvet bag and then slipped it into a dull black Halliburton case. Those remaining in the auction gallery twittered about confirming the winning bid had gone to the private attorney of one of the wealthiest and most secretive men in Europe.

Much of the auction crowd was loath to leave until the watch, the man, and his personal security detail entered a new Rolls Royce.

The unimpressive bald man with the few strands of red beard pretended to cough into one of his hands.

A Rolls Royce was about to enter the motorway. A radio crackled in the ear of a woman in the passenger seat of a Bentley. She announced, "One is on the move."

ACRONYMS/ABBREVIATIONS

AB – Afterburner
ABA – American Bar Association
ABO – Aviation Breathing Oxygen
ACP – Automatic Colt Pistol
AFS – American Federalist Society
AFSOC – Air Force Special Operations Command
AG – Attorney General
AGL – Above Ground Level
AAFES – Army & Air Force Exchange Service
AFI – Await Further Instructions
AI – Artificial Intelligence
AK – Automatic Kalashnikov
AM – Amplitude Modulation
AMTRAK – The National Railroad Passenger Corporation
ANVIS – Aviator Night Vision, night vision goggles
APU – Auxiliary Power Unit
AQ – Al-Qaeda
ASAP – As Soon As Possible
ATLS – Automatic Takeoff and Landing System
B – Boeing
BB – An air gun shot pellet 0.175 inch in diameter
BCC – Blind Carbon Copy
BIAP – Baghdad International Airport
BLM – Belligerent Leftist Mob
BMW – Bayerische Motoren Werke
BOG – Bogotá International Airport
BS – Bullshit
C – Cargo aircraft
CABAL – Computer Assisted Biologically Augmented Lifeform
Cal – Caliber
CANX – Canceled
Cat – Category
CAVU – Ceiling And Visibility Unlimited

C-band – Ultraviolet wavelength from 100 to 280 nanometers
CDC – Center for Disease Control
CG – Commanding General
CI – Counter Intelligence
CIA – Central Intelligence Agency
CEO – Chief Executive Officer
CFO – Chief Finance Officer
Chem cord – Chemical cord
CMC – Commandant of the Marine Corps
CNI – Chief of Naval Intelligence
CNO – Chief of Naval Operations
COMM – Communications
CONOP – Concept of Operations
COPD – Chronic Obstructive Pulmonary Disease
COS – Chief of Station, Chief of Staff
CT – Counter Terrorism
CTC – Counter Terrorism Center
C-4 – Composition C-4; a variety of plastic explosive
D.C. – District of Columbia
DEA – Drug Enforcement Agency
DELTA – 1st Special Forces Operational Detachment-Delta
DEVGRU – U.S. Naval Special Warfare Development Group
DD 214 – Defense Document Form 214 is a document of the U.S. Department of Defense issues upon a military service member's retirement, separation, or discharge from active duty in the Armed Forces of the United States.
Det cord – Detonation cord
DHL – A German international courier, package delivery and express mail service
DHS – Department of Homeland Security
DIA – Defense Intelligence Agency
DIC – Distinguished Intelligence Cross
DJ – Disc Jockey
DNA – Deoxyribonucleic acid
DNC – Democratic National Committee
DNIF – Duties Not Involved Flying
DO – Director of Operations

DOD — Department of Defense
DOE — Department of Energy
DOJ — Department of Justice
D-21 — A supersonic reconnaissance drone from the Lockheed Corporation
Econ — Foreign Service Economic Officer work with U.S. and foreign government officials, business leaders, international organizations, and opinion-makers to promote national security through economic security
EMT — Emergency Medical Technician
EPA — Environmental Protection Agency
ETA — Estimated Time of Arrival
EVP — Executive Vice President
F — Fighter aircraft
FAA — Federal Aviation Administration
FARC — *Fuerzas Armadas Revolucionarias de Colombia;* the Revolutionary Armed Forces of Colombia
FBI — Federal Bureau of Investigation
FBO — Fixed Base Operator
FCC — Federal Communications Commission
FDR — Franklin Delano Roosevelt
FedEx — Federal Express
FITREP — Fitness Report
Five Eyes — The anglophone intelligence alliance comprising Australia, Canada, New Zealand, the United Kingdom, and the United States
FLIR — Forward Looking Infra-Red
FM — Frequency Modulation
FMFPAC — Fleet Marine Force Pacific
FSDO — Flight Standards District Office of the FAA
F Troop — A satirical American television sitcom western about U.S. soldiers and American Indians in the Wild West
F-4S — Phantom
F-4U — Corsair
G — Gravity
G — Gulfstream aircraft
GAO — Government Accountability Office

GDSE — General Directorate for External Security
GITMO — Guantanamo Bay Naval Base, Cuba
G-1 — Military Flight Jacket, fur-lined collar
G-IV — SP Gulfstream Model 4, Special Purpose
G-550 — Gulfstream Model 550
GM — General Manager
GMT — Greenwich Mean Time
GOP — Grand Old Party
GPS — Global Positioning System
Gray Eagle Award — The Naval Aviator on continuous active duty in U.S. Navy or Marine Corps who has held that designation for the longest period of time
GS — General Schedule
HAZMAT — Hazardous Materials
HEPA — High Efficiency Particulate Air
Hep E — Hepatitis E
HK — Heckler & Koch
HQ — Headquarters
HQMC — Headquarters Marine Corps
HR — Human Resources
HVAC — Heating, Venting, And Cooling
H1N1A virus subtype of *Influenza A virus* that was the most common cause of human influenza (flu) in 2009
I&NS — Immigration & Naturalization Service
IBM — International Business Machines
IC — Intelligence Community
ID — Identify/Identity/Identification
IED — Improvised Explosive Device
IFR — Instrument Flight Rules
IG — Inspector General
IO — Intelligence Officer
IPD — In Place Defector
IRGC — Islamic Revolutionary Guard Corps
IRS — Internal Revenue Service
ISIS — Islamic State of Iraq and Syria
IT — Information Technology
IU — Islamic Underground

IV — Intravenous, the Latin number four

J — Jet Engine

J-1 — A non-immigrant visa issued by the United States to research scholars, professors and exchange visitors participating in programs that promote cultural exchange, especially to obtain medical or business training within the U.S.

J-79 — An axial-flow turbojet engine produced by General Electric Aircraft Engines

JPEO — Joint Program Executive Office

J-Tag — Department of Justice license plate

KGB — *Komitet Gosudarstvennoy Bezopasnosti;* the foreign intelligence and domestic security agency of the Soviet Union

LAX — Los Angeles Airport

LD — Laser Designator

LED — Light Emitting Diode

Level 1 — Level 1 Yankee White clearance consists of those staff members who work directly for or have direct contact with the president or the vice president

LGA — LaGuardia Airport

LIDAR — Light Detection and Ranging

LM — Lockheed Martin

MANPADS — Man-Portable Air Defense System

MBA — Masters of Business Administration

MCAS — Marine Corps Air Station

MD — McDonald Douglas, Medical Doctor

MERS — Middle East Respiratory Syndrome

MFR — Memorandum For Record

MGM — Metro-Goldwyn-Mayer

MIA — Miami International Airport

MIA — Missing In Action

MiG — Mikoyan

Mil-Air — Military Airlift

Mil-Spec — Military Specification

MIT — Massachusetts Institute of Technology

MI5 — British Military Intelligence

MI6 — British Secret Intelligence Service

MM – Millimeter
MMOA – Manpower Management Officer Assignments
MPH – Miles per Hour
MQ – Multi-mission Drone
MSG – Madison Square Garden
MSL – Mean Sea Level
MVP – Most Valuable Professional
M-4 – Carbine version of the longer barreled M16
M-16 – M16 rifle, officially designated Rifle, Caliber 5.56
NASA – National Aeronautics and Space Administration
NASCAR – National Association for Stock Car Auto Racing
NATO – North Atlantic Treaty Organization
NAVAID – Navigational Aid
NBC – Nuclear, Biological, Chemical
NCS – National Clandestine Service
NCTC – National Counter Terrorism Center
NDA – Non-Disclosure Agreement
NE – Near East Division
NGA – National Geospatial-Intelligence Agency
NM – Nanometer
No. – Number
NOB – New Office Building
NRO – National Reconnaissance Office
NSA – National Security Agency
NSC – National Security Council
N95 – The air filtration rating of the U.S. National Institute for Occupational Safety and Health, minimum efficiency level 95%
N100 – The air filtration rating of the U.S. National Institute for Occupational Safety and Health, minimum efficiency level 99.97%
O – Observation aircraft
O&M – Operations and Maintenance
O-Club – Officer's Club
ODO – Operations Duty Officer
O2 – Diatomic Oxygen, oxygen in our atmosphere
OKC – Oklahoma City

OPCOM — Operational Control
OPS — Operations
OQR — Officer Qualification Record
OSS — Office of Strategic Services
OTIS — Occult Terrorist Identification System
OXCART — The Lockheed A-12, a high-altitude, Mach 3+ reconnaissance aircraft built for the CIA
PanAm — Pan American World Airways
PAX — Passengers
PD — Police Department
PDB — President's Daily Brief
PDW — Personal Defense Weapon
PETA — People for the Ethical Treatment of Animals
PFC — Private First Class
P-4 — Personal For
PFT — Physical Fitness Test
PhD — Doctor of Philosophy
PI — Philippine Islands
P_k — Probability of Kill
PMO — Program Management Office
PNG — Persona Non Grata
POAC — Pentagon Officers Athletic Club
POTUS — President of the United States
PPE — Personal Protection Equipment
PT — Physical Training
P-51 — Mustang
Q — Quartermaster
Q — Drone
QAS — Quiet Aero Systems
QD — Quick Disconnect
QEC — Quick Engine Change
Q-ticket — Department of Energy security clearance
R — Radial engine
R&D — Research and Development
RC — Radio Control
RCA — Radio Corporation of America
RINO — Republican in Name Only

RJAF — Royal Jordanian Air Force
RNC — Republican National Committee
RPG — Rocket Propelled Grenade
RPM — Revolutions Per Minute
RTB — Return to Base
SA2-37B — Schweizer single-engine low-noise profile aircraft
SACEUR — Supreme Allied Commander Europe
SAD — Special Activities Division
SAM — Surface-to-Air Missile
SAP — Special Access Program
SAR — Synthetic-Aperture Radar
SARS — Severe Acute Respiratory Syndrome
SAT — Scholastic Assessment Test
S&T — Science and Technology Directorate
SCI — Sensitive Compartmented Information
SCIF — Sensitive Compartmented Information Facility
SEAL — Sea, Air, Land
SERE — Survival, Evasion, Resistance, and Escape
SES — Senior Executive Service
SF — Special Forces
Silver Hawk — Earliest Naval Aviation Designation Date
SIS — Senior Intelligence Service
SOCOM — Special Operations Command
SOF — Special Operations Forces
Space A — Space Available
SR — Strategic Reconnaissance aircraft; as in SR-71
SRB — Service Record Books
STRATCOM — U.S. Strategic Command
STU-III — Secure Telephone Unit
SUV — Sport Utility Vehicle
TAD — Temporary Additional Duty
TAG — Techniques d'Avant Garde
Tally Ho — A very old traditional cry made by huntsman to tell others the quarry has been sighted. Used by aviators to indicate other aircraft or targets have been seen.
TASC — Trans-Atlantic Security Council
TASS — Total Aviation Security Services

TASSER — Trans-Atlantic Support Services,
TASCO — Trans-Atlantic Security Corporation
TNFA — Take No Further Action
TS2 — Terminator Sniper System
10-4 — Message Received, from Ten Code
3M — President Maxim Mohammad Mazibuike
300 SL — Mercedes
T — Trainer
TS — Top Secret
TSA — Transportation Security Administration
TS2 — Terminator Sniper System
TS/SCI — Top Secret/Sensitive Compartmented Information
TV — Television
TWA — Trans World Airlines
U — Utility
UAE — United Arab Emirates
UAV — Unmanned Aerial Vehicle
UHF — Ultra High Frequency
U.N. — United Nations
UPS — United Parcel Service
U.S. — United States
USAF — United States Air Force
USAFA — United States Air Force Academy
USAID — United States Agency for International Development
USNA — United States Naval Academy
U.S.S. — United States Ship
UV — Ultraviolet
V — Fixed Wing
VFR — Visual Flight Rules
VHS — Video Home System
VPN — Virtual Private Network
Wilco — Will Comply
WM — Woman Marine
WMD — Weapons of Mass Destruction
WWII — World War Two
WX — Weather
Y — Prototype aircraft

Yankee White – Clearances for those staff members who work directly for or have direct contact with the president or the vice president

YO-3A – Prototype Observation aircraft, model 3, series A

Yo-Yo – Nickname for the YO-3A

Y-12 – World War II code name for National Security Complex in Oak Ridge, Tennessee

XK – A two-door 2+2 grand tourer manufactured and marketed by British automobile manufacturer Jaguar

XKE – Jaguar E-Type; the most beautiful car ever built by no less of an authority, Enzo Ferrari

ACKNOWLEDGEMENTS

I owe a special debt of gratitude to Barbara Hewitt, my editor and wife, for her careful reading and editing of my manuscripts, and her many excellent suggestions for their improvement. Her continuous good advice and encouragement has been invaluable throughout the making of my books. I am not afraid of her red pen.

I'm also deeply grateful for U.S. Air Force Colonel George "Curious" Fenimore, Retired, and the brilliant "recovering attorney" Rosemary Harris for their unfailing patience and good humor that helped turn my very rough ramblings and ruminations into something of a set of coherent thoughts and a better story. George must be something of a genius for his reviews and precise penetrating insights often leave me muttering to myself, "I am not worthy."

A hat tip to David King of Black Rose Writing for his incredible copy editing, book blocking, and cover art. I've seen other book covers and Dave's work is by far the best in the industry.

A personal thank you to Reagan Rothe, the consummate publishing professional. I will forever be in your debt, good sir.

Any errors found in this novel are my responsibility.

ABOUT THE AUTHOR

I consider myself one of the luckiest men on the planet. For half of my military career I was an enlisted avionics technician who worked on helicopters; the other decade-plus was served as a U.S. Marine Corps officer, where the highlight of my time was to be able fly the aircraft of my childhood dreams, the amazing F-4S Phantom II. I served in leadership positions with the Marines, the U.S. Border Patrol, and the U.S. Air Force before leading and managing aviation activities and aircraft operations for international corporations in the Washington, D.C. area. I also fixed a few airports along the way, like Monrovia, Liberia after 15 years of war.

Somewhere during my professional journey I became a member of the intelligence community, with a top secret security clearance with SCI and had to take a polygraph. One of my greatest thrills was the time I entered CIA headquarters and saw the models of the Agency's "black" aircraft suspended from the ceiling in the atrium. My manuscripts have been approved by the CIA Publication Review Board.

My interest in spies and spyplanes began when Francis Gary Powers, the U-2 pilot shot down over the Soviet Union, splashed onto the headlines. I was just a kid but I followed the case as closely as I could. I found out the Director of Central Intelligence declared the CIA would no longer put men in surveillance aircraft over the Soviet Union. We lived eight miles from the East German border and MiGs routinely flew over our house. While my family was stationed in West Germany, I was guilty of smudging the windows of my neighbor's 1963 Corvette Sting Ray virtually every day and became enamored of sports cars, American and European. My mother read everything in the base library and I read the Hardy Boys and everything I could sneak into my room, primarily Alistair MacLean and Ian Fleming.

My Duncan Hunter books reflect my various life experiences and my love for all things aviation. I've logged time in gliders, jets, props, C-117s, helicopters, and qualified as an aircraft carrier pilot. Take it from me, being shot off the pointy end of an aircraft carrier is the most fun you can have with your clothes on.

I wrote what I knew and saw that was unclassified, and it was a natural fit to see my protagonist as a CIA pilot flying a rare spyplane to get deep behind enemy lines to hunt down the world's worst terrorists. More than one CEO has called my novels "a case study for conducting counterterrorism missions with special purpose aircraft."

I have traveled extensively, to places that would be probably be considered dangerous (Afghanistan, Iraq, Colombia) or just hellholes (Liberia, Nigeria, Angola). When passing through US Customs with a thick passport full of visas, I was often asked, "Just what the hell do you do?"

For 12 years I served as an Assistant Adjunct Professor for Embry-Riddle Aeronautical University. I earned a Master of Arts degree in National Security and Strategic Studies from the Naval War College and I hold an MBA in Aviation from Embry-Riddle Aeronautical University.

I'm blessed to have a great bride, wonderful adult children who make me very proud, grandchildren who treat me like a king, and a great granddaughter who is a walking bundle of joy. Like I said, the luckiest guy I know.

Note From The Author

Word-of-mouth is crucial for any author to succeed. If you enjoyed *Special Activities,* please leave a review online—anywhere you are able. Even if it's just a sentence or two. It would make all the difference and would be very much appreciated.

Thanks!
Mark A. Hewitt

Thank you so much for reading one of
Mark A. Hewitt's THRILLER novels.
If you enjoyed the experience, please check out our recommended title for your next great read!

Special Access by Mark A. Hewitt

"Duncan Hunter is a great character... an excellent read."
–A Good Thriller

Made in the USA
Middletown, DE
12 May 2024

54247319R00383